Dear Gil:

I'm afraid that I simply can't hold c[...]
GAN STEW any longer, much as I'd l[...]
to Marv.

I can't tell you how much I admire the book. It seems to me superb, as a matter of fact, it is one of the most remarkably conceived and executed novels it has ever been my pleasure to read in manuscript—and I have been in this frustrating and thankless game for fourteen years now.

However, the sheer *cost* of doing your book is insurmountable for a small, still struggling house like this one. To be frank with you, I must show a profit to the parent company before I can even consider getting behind a project like yours. Don't misunderstand me: I will *not* publish schlock so as to make the money that might justify doing MULLIGAN STEW, or books like it. But I feel that the books on the Fall list are not only *good,* but have definite market appeal. Of the six books on our Fall list, three are really exciting and I am quite proud of them. One, already on the shelves, is, it seems to me, a necessary addition to "Beatle lore"—*The Compleat Beatle Wardrobe Book.* The other two— *The Films of Roy Rogers* and a zany, wonderful novel about life in California, *Screwing In Sausalito,* are risky but have received great word-of-mouth publicity.

So, Gil, if things go well and MULLIGAN STEW is still looking for a publisher in a year (although I can't believe that a larger, better-off house won't snap it up), try me again.

All best,

Harry White
Editorial Director

Dear Marv:

Thanks for sending Gil Sorrentino's MULLIGAN STEW. We've had several interested readings here but the conclusion, I'm afraid, is that the narrative doesn't rise above its own irony—although one of our readers, a Sorrentino "fan," felt that the irony hasn't the precision to cope with the strong narrative. I'm sorry about this.

Thanks again.

Yours,

Frank Bouvard
Editor-in-Chief

Dear Gilbert Sorrentino:

It's wonderful of you to think of us here at New Views Press as possible publishers for your new novel, MULLIGAN STEW. Wow! as my seven-year-old says, all too often, six hundred pages sounds like something! When you say you worked on it almost four years, I can well believe you!

I'm afraid my "batting average" at second-guessing "the Boss" is somewhat less than 1.000 right now, but I'll go "out on a limb" and risk telling you that it seems very doubtful that we can even consider taking it on, "alas"!

I'm sure you've read the newspaper "stories"—albeit many of them were predictably exaggerated—on the dolphin-training project that L was deeply involved in and that came, unfortunately, "a-cropper." L was rather upset, partly because of the money loss involved, but more importantly, because he hoped to publish an anthology of "Dolphin Poems," translated by Dr. Mullion Blasto. You can imagine what a "blow" it was to L when Blasto went with Disney. But enough of our troubles!

At the moment, as above noted, I would venture a tentative guess that L simply could not think of publishing such a work as yours. We are still "picking up the pieces" here. I take the liberty of wishing you and yours well, and of extending L's good wishes to you.

To "good letters,"

John Cates
Managing Editor

Dear Marv:

You asked me to enjoy it and I did enjoy it. Whatever Gil Sorrento does he does solidly and with panache: he makes well what he makes: always: but why in hell did he bother to make this? Ah, well.

Lookit, you are talking to a man who would have turned down "Anna Lydia Plurabelle"—and with no regrets. Not that I'm suggesting that there's a parallel between that'n and MULLIGAN STEW, save in respect of the horsing around. Which last is the point if you get my point.

Put it this way: I am off play: for the rest of my life: even in my own fictions. I however, know what Sorrento can do—and what Joyce himself could do—when he is not playing, and I will wait my time for that. My warmest regards to Gil.

All best,

Edgar Naylor
Senior Editor

Dear Marv:

After two readings and considerable discussion here, I'm returning Robert Sorrentino's novel, MULLIGAN STEW, without an offer.

It's not easy to turn down such an ambitious, literate (and literary), seriously conceived, and, in part, so entertaining a book. We were properly respectful of Sorrentino's wide reading, inventiveness, skill at parody, overall brilliance, and comic sense. What we *don't* respect as much is his sense of economy. The book is far too long and exhausts one's patience. Its various worlds seem to us to lack the breadth and depth and width as well to sustain so many pages. Comedy of this sort, i.e., the highest level of allusive comedy, should be more of a hit-and-run affair, with, if you will, a laugh on every page, much like the comedy of the Elizabethans. Sorrentino's narrative, however, seems splintered and made tentative by its own satiric emphases. I guess you get my drift.

I'm grateful to Sorrentino for the good moments—quite a few!—his manuscript gave me. But it is not the totally perfect stunner such a book must be to make even us undertake it.

I would love to see anything that Sorrentino does in the future, and please tell him that for me.

As ever,

Alan Hobson
Managing Editor

Dear Mr. Koenigburg:

I *am* sorry that I did not get around sooner to MULLIGAN STEW. As you surely know, it is an enormous book and it took time to unravel the warp and weave of the author's purpose, if purpose he has.

I wish I could say it is for our list, but alas! it isn't. It is much too long by half, and to this eye, needlessly so—the author seems obsessed with (unnecessary) insertions, (useless) repetitions, twice and thrice-told tales, and reams of incomprehensible lists. Another thing that really bothered me a lot was a cliché quality in the writing—life as a jigsaw puzzle, or the sky's "flawless blue," etc. Really! The author also seems sorely in need of a lesson or two in English grammar and the use of syntax.

So, not being in real sympathy and admiration for either form or substance, both of which seem to me to be more "shadow" than anything else, I return the manuscript to you, with my sincere apologies for the delay—delays are always cruel to young authors, particularly if they raise hopes that will be dashed.

Sincerely yours,

Yvonne Firmin
Editor-in-Chief

Dear Gil Sorrentino:

I'm sorry that Marv Koenigburg didn't tell you that I am in fact no longer with Bond and Howard—or barely so. I am about to leave to join my senior colleague Dack Verlaine in starting our own publishing house, a subsidiary, wholly owned, of Cynosure Oil. I won't therefore be able to consider your novel one way or the other for Bond and Howard, nor for our new venture—our list is pretty well set for the next year or so.

We'll be doing little fiction here anyway, for the economic reasons you so expertly outlined in your good letter. As you certainly know, I am a novelist too, my first book, BREAKING GLASSES, being touted as "best first novel" of 1964 by Dempsey Dumpster in *Bookiana*. My second novel, even more brilliant and evocative of its time, has gone begging for five years now, and everybody in America loves it! It's so dated by now that I'm thinking of calling it GARTER BELT DAYS. So you see, it is hard for all of us artists, no matter what! The situation is so bad that if they *did* publish my novel, I myself couldn't buy a copy!

Heard a lot about your IMAGINARY QUALITIES AND THINGS!! I'd *love* to read it if you have a copy lying around. Good luck!

Cordially,

Flo Dowell

Dear Marvin:

Thanks so much for thinking of us for Gilbert Sorrentino's MULLIGAN STEW, an amazing book. In some ways, I think a great book, perhaps even a masterpiece. It has the same painfulness and paranoia as—and much more bone-deep eloquence than—Galsworthy's sketch of a writer, and it is also funny as hell. Everything in the book has the touch of the virtuoso. Trouble is, I got bored, and so did another reader. The book is so long it took us the better part of two weeks to read it. It's also a book that is terribly bookish and only a very special audience will take to it at all.

I'm terribly sorry that I couldn't "respond."

Sincerely yours,

Charlotte Bayless
Senior Editor

Dear Marv Koenigburg:

Gil Sorrentino is at times a brilliant innovator and at times is quite hilariously funny. But this novel within a novel within a novel—if that *is* what it is—would find few readers, I fear. It strikes me as, above all its fantastic surface, shallow and incoherent. You know how much I loved IMAGINARY QUANTITIES OF THINGS; even though we couldn't take it on, it was wonderful. MULLIGAN STEW, on the other hand, seems to be just a lengthy combining of separate things into a whole—that *is* a whole because the author says so.

So, outside of the very rare flashes of brilliance, I couldn't respond.

Cordially yours,

Morroe Reiff
Publisher

Dear Marv:

Thanks for sending the Sorrantino novel—MULLIGAN STEW. Parts of this really tickled my *outré* sense of humor, especially the section on the porno photos and magazines, the orgy scene, the section of mock-erotic poems, and the descriptions of the girls' costumes in the nightclub scene.

But how to piece all this together and make sense of it for myself or for readers, is beyond me. Maybe Gilbert Sorrantino knows what he is doing, although I don't think he really does; but I as sure as hell can't figure it out. Thanks again, Marv, and sorry I'm out to lunch on this one.

Best,

Chad Newsome
Editor

Dear Mr. Sorrentino:

I regret to say that I can't offer to publish MULLIGAN STEW. While I have great respect for the literary intelligence behind the book, I have to say that it didn't work for me in the way that a novel must. It was neither engaging nor exhilarating, nor was it full of the simple zest of life, as novels really must be to be novels that compel the reader. Indeed, I confess that I found myself actually working to read it. The prose style seems so solemn and "dark"; surely a murder mystery must have zip and speed. Well, maybe I'm just "old fashioned."

I wish you luck in finding a publisher for it. I am returning the manuscript to Marvin Koenigburg.

Sincerely,

Claude Estee
Editorial Director

Dear Mr. Koenigburg:

Thanks for giving us a chance at MULLIGAN STEW, Gilbert Sorrentino's new "novel." Although we admired the writing just as *writing*, I am afraid that we could not respond to the book as a *book*. The major characters seem wooden and unalive, almost like cardboard figures, and the structure of the novel no more than a collection of bits and pieces, despite the latter's occasional sophomoric humor.

One of our editors thought the novel rather dismally uninformed as far as the female characters and their presentation. She thought them "fantasy figures" far removed from the reality of Woman that is all around us today. And, I must confess, I myself thought that the play that is in the book essentially gross and vulgar, and totally lacking in that moral commitment that is, and always has been, the novelist's responsibility.

But these moral and ethical questions aside, our basic feeling is that the book (I hesitate to call it a "novel") seems to be a rather slapdash collection of notes, gibes, and needlessly elaborate jokes. And as Galsworthy once said, "remarks are not literature." I'm not sure I *know* anymore what literature *is;* but I doubt that it is MULLIGAN STEW.

All best wishes,

Sheldon Corthell
Editor-in-Chief

Dear Barney:

The xerox copies of the rejection letters that I have enclosed are self-explanatory, and will inform you as to the fate of my poor but honest *Mulligan Stew* over the past three years. You will see that the manuscript apparently acts somewhat like paresis, clouding men's minds before it drives them mad. Can "Dr. Mullion Blasto" exist? He sounds like one of my characters. Or has "John Cates" (another suspect moniker) suffered the same dementia that seems to have afflicted all these other "editors"?

Anyway, would you like to read the MS with an eye to publishing it? I regret to say that it is not about a sensitive, intellectual, middle-aged university professor who falls in love with a girl young enough to be his daughter and turns into Anthony Quinn, but what can I tell you?

The book, wallowing in the mortal sin of bookishness, has virtually no chance of catching the eye of a mogul of The Communications Industry, nor will it nurture the moral sense of the young. It is a long book and thus will cost as much as a few bar Scotches and a bad movie —far, far beyond the purchasing ability of the intelligent middle class. It is, in certain parts, insanely hermetic and in others, rife with longueurs. Yet it should bring a smile to the face of anyone not of the Methodist persuasion. In other words, it is a work of the imagination and, as such, seems eminently suited to Grove.

If you'd like to consider it, let me know and I'll ask my agent, Marv Koenigburg, to stop gnashing his teeth and rending his flesh long enough to send it over.

As ever,

Gil

READER'S REPORT

MULLIGAN STEW By Gilbert Sorrentino

This is a remarkable "fiction"—one hesitates to call it a novel—one that bids fair to act as a kind of limping, bedraggled, yet noble and undefeated rear guard of the Late-Post-modern movement. Like that wondrous after-dinner cordial, or, more precisely, cluster of cordials, the Pousse Café, Sorrentino's latest fiction is a dazzling mélange of colors, flavors, textures, and tones—yet each one keeps its essential "selfness," which last is a major "tenet" of the rarefied air of Ur-fiction in which this work swims, or floats.

Basically, this novel, or "fiction," tells the "story" of an avant-garde novelist, one Antony Lamont. He is writing a novel, an intellectual detective-mystery story in the manner of Robbe-Grillet or LeBrouillard, one that he hopes will finally "make his name." We are permitted to read the chapters of Lamont's novel as they are completed, rewritten, revised, agonized over, and they reveal to us an exquisite, if rather shakily oneiric talent. They reveal also, and more importantly, a starcrossed author, for Lamont's failure is prefigured and reflected in his novel.

Lamont's major figures, two friends and business associates, are given their reality through a series of chapters that analyze their characters ruthlessly. Their names are Martin Halpin and Ned Beaumont, and as we plunge deeper into Lamont's novel (which, by the by, is no more a "novel" than is the "novel" in which it rests—if it can be said to "rest" at all), we discover that they are in love—perhaps!—with the same young woman, Daisy. Daisy is the classic Surfictionist creation—a blur of insouciance, a touch of the disingenuous, a waft of grit. But into this triangle intrude two women, fictitious characters that I feel sure will take their places alongside the unforgettable creations of Dickens and Delmar. Their names are Corrie Corriendo and Berthe Delamode, and their entrance marks the beginning of Lamont's novel's catabasis, a catabasis bordering upon the xenophobic. They are frauds, charlatans, prostitutes, businesswomen, entrepreneurs, writers in their own right, black magicians, witches. They bid fair to walk off the page, their hot blood almost bursting through their warm flesh. Their creation alone is enough to place Lamont (and of course, Sorrentino) squarely outside the concerns of self-reflexive reflective fiction, which latter is, of course, intent upon the limning of cardboard figures that exist in so far as they may be *said* to exist by those authors who say so.

It may be interesting to note that Lamont's "fiction" undergoes a title change: from *Guinea Red* to *Crocodile Tears.* One must read this work to see exactly how important that change is, but let me say here that the odd ambiguity of the first title (ethnocentricity *cum* politics *cum* focus on economics *cum* the urge toward intoxication) acts as clue to those chapters written *under* it. The change to the second title permits us to reread the earlier chapters in the light of Lamont's growing awareness of his pose, a pose not unmixed with bitterness as his fortunes decline.

His fortunes *do* decline, with the assistance of his sister, her husband, his ex-mistress, an English professor, *et al.* Remarkably, *Guinea Red/ Crocodile Tears* undergoes rapid and deeply structural changes at the same time. We are allowed to compare these changes with those in Lamont's life through the medium of letters, written by and to him, entries in his notebooks, and odds and ends preserved in his scrapbook. Sorrentino's marshaling of these data show an unerring use of the fictional "strategies" of "Monk" Lewis made new.

Beyond the various data given us in the form of chapters, letters, etc., etc., Sorrentino quite literally cracks open the world of Lamont's fiction—and, indeed, the world of all fiction—by giving Lamont's characters—particularly Halpin and Beaumont—lives *outside of the work* that Lamont is writing. That is, Halpin and Beaumont are "alive" as people other than the Halpin and Beaumont Lamont creates. And Martin Halpin keeps a journal that is every bit as detailed and replete with information having to do with his "real" "life" as are Lamont's notebooks, etc. Rather than allowing such Post-modern Ur-techniques to clutter the page as so many shards of compositional process as has been the fashion these past ten years or so, Sorrentino makes these paradigms, as it were, flesh. It is a notable coup, a kind of stylistic ventriloquism accomplished with great verve.

Not least among the various jewels that this novel displays is the remarkable masque, "Flawless Play Restored." Based squarely on the Jonsonian masque, or more exactly the "ante-masque," it resonates with all the essential themes of adversity and ultimate triumph that Lamont's career encloses; and it may well be the essential core of what seems a tale of failure and misery. One might also say that Lamont's two creations, Beaumont and Halpin, also triumph over *their* adverse fortunes. All, *all* is reflected and prefigured in the formal dance that this masque choreographs in its curiously claustrophobic space.

Finally, let me touch on the theme, or themes, of *Mulligan Stew.* It is a brilliant case-history of genius succumbing to paranoia as well as to schizophrenia (as Lamont grows more unstable his work takes on absolute aspects of many other writers, and, sadly enough, most of them his inferiors if we are to judge by his first, felicitous chapters); it is a study of sexual obsession; a detailed survey of blasted love; a series of biting observations on the literary world; an exposé of diabolism . . . one could go on and on. The "fiction" may also be read as Sorrentino's projection of himself as Lamont (or as Halpin or as Beaumont—or even as Daisy); Lamont's projection of himself as Halpin or Beaumont, Corriendo or Delamode; Halpin's "revenge" upon Lamont; Halpin's "creation" of a "real" Beaumont, etc., etc. We may amuse ourselves with the consideration that Lamont and Beaumont employ the same final syllable in their very names! I suspect that the book changes radically from reading to reading, depending upon the "glass" one chooses to see it through.

Not the least compelling aspect of this book is that it has, far beneath the tortured story told by the author (one should say, "authors"), a dry, subtle, and delicate humor, a humor so fragile and evanescent that one reads it while almost literally holding one's breath, lest too gross an apprehension of it should make it scatter to the black winds that sweep and roar through the "fiction." For some reason, I kept thinking of the question that Dickens has his old mad gentleman pose in *Nicholas Nickleby:* "The Young Prince of China. Is he reconciled to his father-in-law, the great potato salesman?" Sorrentino's gentle humor is of the same tenor as this angst-laden query.

I strongly recommend that this book be published. It is not only a profound meditation upon the creative process and its undoing, it is also (and I weigh my words most carefully) a landmark in Sur-Neo-fiction, an almost perfect example of the analytical intelligence in action.

—*Horace Rosette*

Dear Mr. Kent:

Re: MULLIGAN STEW, by Gilbert Sorrentino

The manuscript that was enclosed with your letter to me of June 20, 1978 is attached.

Hasard House does not elect to distribute this work under the agreement that we have with Grove Press.

Sincerely yours,

Arthur Gride
General Counsel

Dear Mr. Gride:

Your letter of June 21 simply states that Hasard House does not elect to distribute the novel MULLIGAN STEW.

It would be of genuine interest to us at Grove to know the reasons for this decision. We have an obligation to inform the author as to why his book has been rejected.

The author has previously published many books, including two with Acropolis, a division of Hasard House. Sections from MULLIGAN STEW have appeared in many of the most respected literary journals in the country. Mr. Sorrentino is an important writer of recognized talent and accomplishment, as well as being a hell of a swell guy.

I look forward to your response.

Sincerely,

C. Milo Kent,
Vice-President

Dear Mr. Kent:

Re: MULLIGAN STEW by Gilbert Sorrentino

With reference to your letter dated June 29, Hasard House did not elect to distribute Mr. Sorrentino's novel because it was not considered by our legal staff to be of sufficient merit to warrant the additional investment in inventory. "Merit" in this context is to be spelled "bottom line," if you follow me.

Our decision is not a *rejection* of Mr. Sorrentino's manuscript, which presumably has been *accepted* by Grove Press, heaven knows why! Be that, however, as it may, we here at Hasard House simply have exercised our option under our contract with Grove not to distribute that work for Grove, nor to have anything to *do* with that work. Grove is now free to arrange for its distribution by others and, if I may say so, lots of luck!

Sincerely,

Arthur Gride
General Counsel

MULLIGAN
STEW

BOOKS BY GILBERT SORRENTINO

Fiction

Aberration of Starlight
Blue Pastoral
Crystal Vision
Odd Number
The Sky Changes
Steelwork
Imaginative Qualitites of Actual Things
Splendide-Hôtel
Flawless Play Restored: The Masque of Fungo

Poetry

Selected Poems: 1958–1980
The Darkness Surrounds Us
Black and White
The Perfect Fiction
Corrosive Sublimate
A Dozen Oranges
Sulpiciae Elegidia: Elegiacs of Sulpicia
White Sail
The Orangery

Essays

Something Said: Essays

MULLIGAN STEW

A Novel by
GILBERT SORRENTINO

GROVE PRESS / New York

To the memory of Brian O'Nolan
—his "virtue *hilaritas*"

Acknowledgments:

Sections of this novel have appeared in: *Atlantic Monthly, Chicago Review, New Directions in Prose and Poetry, Partisan Review, Seems, TriQuarterly, Vort.*

The section entitled "Flawless Play Restored: The Masque of Fungo," was published as a book by Black Sparrow Press, Copyright © 1974 by Gilbert Sorrentino.

The author would like to thank the Ariadne Foundation, the John Simon Guggenheim Memorial Foundation, the National Endowment for the Arts, and the Creative Artists Public Service Program for financial assistance granted him during the composition of this work.

Published by Grove Press, Inc.
920 Broadway
New York, N.Y. 10010

First Evergreen Edition 1979

Library of Congress Cataloging-in-Publication Data
Sorrentino, Gilbert.
  Mulligan stew.
  I. Title.
PZ4.S717Mu [PS3569.O7]   813'.5'4   78—67419
ISBN 0-394-62361-4

Manufactured in the United States of America
10 9 8 7 6 5 4 3 2 1

"That is my personal musical instrument," said MacCruiskeen, "and I was playing my own tunes on it in order to extract private satisfaction from the sweetness of them."

"I was listening," I answered, "but I did not succeed in hearing you."

"That does not surprise me intuitively," said MacCruiskeen, "because it is an indigenous patent of my own. The vibrations of the true notes are so high in their fine frequencies that they cannot be appreciated by the human earcup. Only myself has the secret of the thing and the intimate way of it, the confidential knack of circumventing it. Now what do you think of that?"

—*Flann O'Brien*

"Ber*serk*. *Ber*serk. Ber*serk!* Ber*serk?* *Ber*serk! *Ber*serk . . . ?"

—*Philip Vogel*, in conversation

I done me best when I was let. Thinking always if I go all goes. A hundred cares, a tithe of troubles and is there one who understands me? One in a thousand of years of the nights? All me life I have been lived among them but now they are becoming lothed to me. And I am lothing their little warm tricks. And lothing their mean cosy turns. And all the greedy gushes out through their small souls. And all the lazy leaks down over their brash bodies. How small it's all! And me letting on to meself always. And lilting on all the time.

—*James Joyce*

1.

How absurd it is to find myself in this dilemma! It was I who made Ned Beaumont what he was, anyone can tell you that. Perhaps not "anyone." Why should I kill him? If I did. Why should I even want to kill him? All I ever wanted to do was keep him out of trouble. He was getting himself deep into it too, that's for certain. The way he was going, the things he was doing these past few months, portended nothing but disaster for him and Daisy, Daisy with the dark, shining hair. Of course, I *wanted* to help. They were both dear to me—dearer, perhaps, than I can bring myself to say. Well, let that go?

They were dearer to me than I can bring myself to say, I have said. Let's just say that I thought of Ned Beaumont as a brother, a wild, hotheaded, let us say "peremptory" brother, but a brother nonetheless. Daisy Buchanan? Have you ever seen moonlight on some lake? Have you ever heard mission bells ringing? That was Daisy. Oh, I know my own reputation as a hardheaded, ruthless "tycoon" of the publishing world. But Daisy—she would melt you, truth to tell, destroy you with her gentleness. Ned Beaumont was breaking her heart. Of course I was concerned. That doesn't mean that I would have *killed* him! If I could only remember what happened earlier this evening——— But I *will* remember!

The police should be here soon.

It's I who called them. Halpin's the name.

Let me take you back, and take myself back too. (What good is it if I take you back and leave myself here? Who then will tell you the dark tale?) Back to the beginning of this unbelievably tragic affair. Perhaps the truth can then be seen, emerging like the image in a jigsaw puzzle. Perhaps it will not, but lie there (the truth) in myriad pieces, waiting for a surer hand and a more perceptive eye than mine to put it all together. If people are hurt, they'll just have to be hurt.

Call me Halpin—Martin Halpin. Some of my friends call me Marty. Some few call me "Chuck."

Better not think about it.

I've used the name Halpin—Martin Halpin—for so long now that we might as well be done with it and say that it *is* my name, and that I have no other. After all, what portends in a name? 'tis mine, 'tis his.

The lake is speckled with little whitecaps flicked up by the wind

1

from the darkling Canadian forests. It's beautiful in an unearthly way. One would never think that next door, in the den, Ned Beaumont lies on the floor, his head bashed in by an andiron, or some other blunt instrument.

It's all unreal.

Let's say that I'm Martin Halpin. Who cares? For the purposes of my story that name will do as well as any. If you'd prefer to call me by another name, that's all right, but remember what it is you choose to call me so that when you hear the name "Martin" or "Halpin" or even "Marty" or "Chuck," and so on, you'll know it's I. I've done all right as Martin Halpin for years, and I'll keep on doing all right. If there *are* any more years!

The police are on their way.

I called them about two minutes ago.

Next door, in the den, Ned Beaumont is slumped in a chair, a bullet hole above his right temple.

So if Halpin is all right with you—it's certainly all right with me—then, call me Halpin. The night is dark and windy. Winter is in the air, a cold front from Canada is moving in. In the den next door lies what is left of Ned Beaumont, my friend, golf partner, business associate, the would-be fiancé of Daisy Buchanan, fresh Daisy, ah! "They" used to say, "fresh as Daisy." They'll say I killed him, perhaps I did. But why would I want to kill Ned Beaumont? "You, Martin 'Chuck' Halpin, killed Ned Beaumont, your business associate, didn't you?" That's what the police will say. And what will *I* say?

They're coming now. . . .

I'm distraught tonight. Nervous. I don't know why.

I have no motive, not really a motive. Oh, yes, I was—was?—*am* in love with Daisy Buchanan, but that's no motive. I happen to know that she didn't really love Ned Beaumont, that she would never have divorced Tom, her husband, for Ned Beaumont or for anyone else. And she would have tired of Ned Beaumont. I can never forget that party for the publication of Cecil Tyrell's new novel, *Broken Bottles,* when I overheard Daisy at the bar saying, "But surely! Ned Beaumont? You can't be serious! Why he's just an amusing young man." So you can see that I have no motive, no motive at all. If I had wanted to kill someone it would have been Tom, her wretch of a husband. The only thing to do, of course, is to start at the beginning.

The wind is beginning to howl like a damned soul.

Daisy is coming too. I called her right after I called the police.

I somehow want to go in and make Ned Beaumont comfortable. I think I'm beginning to lose my nerve. I don't want to do that. A brandy should help. I'll pour myself a brandy and start at the beginning.

2

I suppose it all really started with Ned Beaumont and that "magic" act that he took so seriously, Corriendo and Delamode. Oh, certainly it started before that, but it was when those two heartless, gold-digging, and perverse women appeared on the scene that everything started to go downhill—for all of us. Let me tell you about this act. Let me tell you how these two, these two—charlatans—administered their poisonous potions to completely destroy Ned Beaumont's personality and character.

I'll start at the beginning.

The windows are rattling as if some damned soul wants to get into this house of the damned.

Perhaps as I talk the pieces will fall into place like the pieces of a gigantic jigsaw puzzle, and the truth will be seen plain. Perhaps God, or Fate, plays with *us* as we play with the pieces of a jigsaw puzzle, toying with us, trying to make us fit where we don't belong, dropping us to the floor. When I was a boy I remember I had a jigsaw puzzle that depicted a destroyer in action on the high seas. It was a beautiful ship, a "can" of the "Horace Rosette" class. I remember playing with the pieces, toying with them idly, dropping them on the floor, trying to make them fit where they did not belong: perhaps—perhaps God, or Fate, or whatever, toys with us as I toyed with those multicolored pieces.

It was a beautiful ship. That it was a *destroyer* now seems portentous.

How long ago it all seems now!

It's getting colder now, the wind seems to be calling to me, calling to me with Ned Beaumont's voice!

It was Corrie Corriendo and Berthe Delamode, implausible names (implausible women!) if I ever heard them, who were at the root of this sinister tragedy.

Dear Professor Roche:

Thank you so much for your letter of October 16. I am grateful to you for your interest in my work, and particularly your high praise —I might even say fulsome praise—for my last novel, *Fretwork*. I am afraid that it was neither a critical nor a commercial success, but that is, sadly, something that I am used to. After the really vicious reviews the book received your delight in and understanding of the novel is heartening indeed.

You are, of course, correct when you write that "Clive Sollis is clearly a figure who exists *only* in the protagonist's mind," and you might be amazed to know that not one of the reviewers who assassinated *Fretwork* made the slightest mention of that fact, even though it is central to an understanding of the novel.

It is exciting to me that you are considering giving a course in the American experimental novel, and that you are going to use my work as a "cornerstone" (if you will forgive such a term) of the course. I am afraid that you have your work cut out for you, as I have always thought of the experimental novel, here in America, at least, as a kind of elaborate jigsaw puzzle, whose image does not appear whole until the entire history of such novels is traced meticulously.

Yes, you are correct: *Baltimore Chop* is out of print and quite unavailable, unless one is willing to pay a collector's price for it. It was published in 1961 by Crescent and Chattaway, a small, adventurous firm that also publishes the novels of Sheila Henry and Léonie Aubois. It is my great pleasure to send along to you, under separate cover, an inscribed copy. The novel has its flaws, but it is not what one would call an unaccomplished first novel; certainly, I am not ashamed of it. I trust that you have to hand copies of my other two novels, *Three Deuces* and *Rayon Violet,* since they are still in print.

I am presently just beginning a new novel, one written in the first-person singular. I have, as yet, no working title for it. All I can tell you is that its structure is that of a mystery novel . . . plus. Plus what, I don't as yet know, as I am struggling with this book and its characters with the well-known might and main.

Most sincerely,
Antony Lamont

My dear Sheila,

Just a quick note to tell you how glad I am that you and Dermot have come to some sort of understanding. I don't think he's really a louse at heart, but the nature of the hack work he's done all these years has somehow calloused his emotions. That, plus the fact that his

4

life is almost wholly sedentary, makes for a difficult man. In any event, the whole thing seems to be working out to *your* satisfaction, at least. Maybe that talk I had with him over the Labor Day weekend made him see how selfish and irresponsible he was being. God knows, nobody expected him to *marry* you, but he has some sort of responsibility to your good heart.

I'm just now starting a new novel and it's proving to be a son of a bitch to get started. And did you get the copy of *Fretwork* I sent you? You'll see that some of the scenes are taken from "real life," as they say. I haven't heard from Bart Kahane or Anton however, so perhaps they are offended, after all.

O.K. Take good care of yourself. Eat an apple every day.

Your loving brother,
Tony

Lamont's Notebook

Beaumont dead in den of lake resort house. Halpin doesn't know whether he killed him or not. Call Beaumont "Ned Beaumont" throughout book? Must be clear that Halpin really doesn't know whether he is lying or not about murder. Corrie Corriendo, Berthe Delamode: these names O.K.? Tawdry enough? They must be brought in no later than Chap. Three. In Chap. One Halpin mentions them and their nightclub magic act, his disgust with them and with Beaumont's "belief" in them (or what he has told Halpin was belief). Should Halpin say that he is in love with Daisy? Or let it be revealed slowly and organically? Check *Baltimore Chop* to see how I handled the secret love therein of Max Champagne for the waitress at Club Ding-Dong. That subtle revelation.

From *Baltimore Chop,* pp. 121–122.

Max was drinking too much, too fast. He felt as if he were about to float off on some cloud or other, somewhere into the blue. Looking surreptitiously over the rim of his glass, he saw her. He felt—he felt as if he wanted to bite the rim of the glass. The ineffable power of love! he thought. Suddenly, he realized she was looking at him, boldly, honestly, without fear or coquetry. In her hard straightforwardness, she was at once soft, yet yielding. Her hands! How he loved her delicate yet manly hands, at the moment hidden beneath the enormous tray of drinks she carried to some people at a rear table; such were the breaks. As she walked, he followed her with his eyes,

5

blurred now from the strong spirits and salty pretzels. She gazed back at him, her long legs decisively pistoning her through the revelers. She walked into a man at the jukebox, hidden partially in the dense clouds of blue cigarette smoke the bar produced as a volcano produces lava. Her order quickly fell to the floor, her eyes still on Max, he thought.

Where have I seen eyes like that before? he thought, and ordered another drink. His first impulse was to go over and help her clean up the mess, but he knew that she would take it wrongly. He laughed bitterly. His whole bitter life seemed to come out of him, seemed to wrench itself free of his cynical and too-wise soul: oh, Max had been around, God how I've been around, he thought. Fool! Fool! He looked across the room, their four eyes strung on four threads of oblique meaning.

He fought against the tenderness that welled up in him. Can love exist here? Love? Ha! Ha! He spilled his drink, and thought, bitterly, I spill my life as I spill this drink. Fool! Yet he couldn't bring himself to walk over to her.

A fat man, wearing thin white socks and a rumpled gabardine suit was whispering something to her, his mouth an obscene joke. He was helping her to pick up the broken glass and soaked napkins and, he thought, she looked at him, almost tenderly? An ice pick of remorse stabbed at Max's heart, at his vitals. So he believed sardonically. Max knew that he couldn't interfere now, for the fat man was the owner, the flabby millionaire who ran The Fly Paper as his private fief; the fat man had to be, Abe North, known to every private investigator between D.C. and Baltimore as "True" North. Shamuses had their little jokes. I grinned.

My gaze on him was, I supposed, cool and casual. But he knew, he could feel the icy heat of my jealous rage; he looked at me as if seeing me for the first time, a beautiful act. I almost admired him, his face honestly bewildered, then breaking into a huge, falsely cordial, smile. His dentures were too large for the tiny, cupid's-bow mouth that looked rouged; then he moved heavily forward, amazingly agile for so huge a man, his heavy shoulder muscles surging ominously under the too-tight coat that oddly became him.

"Champagne? Is is really Max Champagne? My God! What are you doing in town? Is your glass filled, I trust?"

I looked past him at *her,* at long legs, at narrow, somehow vulnerable back, at quaking bosom, at harshly bleached, platinum-blond, hair, and felt my guts twist!

"Hello, True," I said. "You've got a little platinum mine here."

He laughed obscenely, a hint of phlegm in it like a muffled curse. I imagined his fat, hairy hands on her loins and fought back the desire to break his wet, epicene mouth. As she stood up, our eyes caught, tangled, broke apart, and caught, *again.* The faintest wisp, of a smile, a dark and somehow warning, smile . . . "played" over her lips. I crushed my glass in my hand. I didn't feel the pain except as part of the constant pain that was my whole bitter, shabby life.

Max reached out to pat True's shoulder as he approached, expertly feeling for the shoulder holster that he knew was there. In that holster was a Smith and Wesson persuader that, Max knew, had killed Jeannette Caldecott-Box. Things seemed to be moving very fast now. Too fast, Max thought.

Dear Professor Roche:

I'm delighted that you have received—and read—*Baltimore Chop.* I despise the jacket design myself, somehow the combination of a crab, a baseball bat, and a skull makes the book look "lightweight." I flatter myself that it is deceptively simple, and not at all what it seems to be on the surface. Certainly, Champagne is an anti-hero, perhaps the anti-hero to out-anti-hero all anti-heroes. He is so much *more* than just a private eye.

I've always liked Champagne, his quick wit, his tender, almost casual cynicism, his idealism, his belief in an absolute scale of values. I've even considered using him in another book, but I don't want to get into the detective-story business; I certainly don't want to be pigeonholed—not at this stage in my career, anyway.

Yes, *Baltimore Chop* and *Deuces* have absolute affinities with each other. In the former, the burden of narration is carried by me, the author, with sudden shifts into the voice of Champagne for certain effects of immediacy; in *Deuces,* of course, the narrator is Tab Jazzetti, that lost man; but you are right when you suggest that Jazzetti's voice is not really his own, but the voice of the author *cast as* Jazzetti's: a subtle point, and how delighted I am that you ferreted it out.

I've already told you that I'm at work on a new novel, another first-person narrative, but this one with a real *persona,* a man who doesn't know what he is doing, or, for that matter, what he *has* done. I'm afraid that I am having trouble getting on with it, and am casting about for the correct "tone" to give this voice. The working title is *Guinea Red,* the vulgarity of same being rescued by the ambiguity that the structure of the book will ultimately lend to it.

I am utterly astounded that you know my sister, Sheila. She is a marvelous young woman whose quick-wittedness must have been immediately apparent to you last summer. How did you like Aspen, by the way? I've always wanted to go there, but somehow never seem to get away from the city except for brief jaunts to nearby places.

In any event, please let me know what you think of my poor, ignored *Rayon Violet*. I admit that it was a falling off in my work, but I'd like to hear what you think, anyway. Till then, I am, most sincerely,

Antony Lamont

P.S. You might be interested to know that Sheila's first published piece, an essay entitled "643: The Double Play in Malamud's 'The Natural,'" has just appeared in the *Object Review*. I think it's a *remarkable* piece of criticism!

8

1. FALLEN LUCIFERS

If it were not essentially so terrifying, it would be amusing to sit here, alone with the body of Ned Beaumont, in this dark house by the black, cold lake, the wind howling outside with the voice of a damned soul. I feel as if I am at rest in the hand of God, a fragment of the incomplete jigsaw puzzle that is my life.

You must believe me when I tell you that I honestly don't know if I killed Ned Beaumont or not. I know that he lies on the floor in the den, his face contorted in rage, that rage that had become so much a part of his life when he was among the quick. I "know" that he has been shot. I know that I still feel deeply for him, for the remarkable partnership that he and I had for so many years. But I don't know whether or not I shot him. But *was* he shot?

Imagining myself looking at myself, I seem to be relaxed. What exactly is it that I see? A man, large-boned, dressed casually in a seersucker suit (a bit too light for the sudden autumn weather that has startlingly blown in from Canada), a Scotch and soda in my right hand, in my left a cigarette. My glance is, I suppose, cool and almost distant. I am waiting to make up my mind to call the police. Ned Beaumont is dead. I must face up to that fact. I must face up to the possibility that it is I who killed him.

If I could remember the events of the evening! If I could logically, chronologically present them to myself, follow them up to that moment when the pistol harshly barked! And spat sullen flame! Perhaps it was suicide? Perhaps. But why would Ned Beaumont wish to end his own life, with so much to live for? Daisy loved him—no, let me correct myself—Daisy *adored* him. And Ned Beaumont, in his careless, flamboyant way, adored her. Now he lies, dead, in the den, his poor aching head toward the fireplace, his feet in a sickeningly tangled pile of old magazines, his face crestfallen and distorted. His shoes are cheerfully glistening in the starlight that comes in the window, reflected off the waters of the lake. Odd and ironic epiphany! If I could remember . . . but it is all a welter of unconnected things, little things.

Earlier (it *must* have been earlier), we stood together, looking out the same picture window through which the reflected luminous light of dim and distant stars now eases eerily.

"A drink, Ned Beaumont?" I said.

"That would hit the old spot," he barked.

"What would you like? I mumbled. I have everything here . . . vodka, bourbon, gin. . . ."

"Scotch would be fine," he sighed. "With a splash of branch."

"What is 'branch,' Ned Beaumont?" I inquired pleasantly.

"Branch? Branch is a kind of swell, pure water," Ned Beaumont whined. He sat heavily in a chair, distracted.

"Will plain 'tap' water do?" I asked, moving swiftly toward the little bar of which I felt strangely and inordinately proud.

"Of course," Ned Beaumont replied wearily. "The word 'branch' is a sort of affectation usually used in the affected term, 'bourbon and branch.' "

"I don't follow you." I was doing my very best to be genial, but cold fury was sweeping through me. "Bourbon?"

"That is the drink I *mentioned* in order to give you an *example* of how the word 'branch' is most often used. 'Branch' is a kind of terrific spring water, or well water, or stupendous crystalline-stream water. It actually means 'something' and water . . . I mean that I want Scotch and *water,* that's all."

"I follow you now, Ned Beaumont," I chortled. "What you need is a tall Scotch and water. Rocks?"

"What? Come again?"

"I say: Rocks?"

"What in God's name are you talking about?" Ned Beaumont sputtered.

I could feel the cold fury, that had not ceased to sweep through me, turning, to glacial ice! He was looking at me as if seeing me for the first time, always a bad sign with the great hulk I called "friend."

"I merely wanted to know if you prefer your drink on the 'rocks' or not, Ned Beaumont." My eyes were filled with the unwanted—yet oddly pleasant—pain of my incredible, my overweening anger, and I felt as if I could crush his hat, then and there.

"What is 'on the rocks,' man? For God's sake!" He was trembling visibly, with anger, fear, or was it overweening frustration?

"The rocks? The rocks? Surely, Ned Beaumont, you are joking with me. Why treat Halpin this way? The rocks, Ned Beaumont, the rocks! Think, man! Think!"

He stood up and very slowly turned toward me. I noticed, with a sudden loathing, his heavy jowl, his blue-shadowed face, his rumpled shirt, sweat stains peering out from beneath his armpits like a brace of obscene jokes.

"Marty," he whispered. "Am I losing my mind? Did I or *did I not* hear you ask me if I wanted my simple drink, my teeny Scotch and water, *on the rocks?*"

I laughed brusquely, a chill traveling the length of my spine. "You did, Ned Beaumont, you most certainly did. That's what I asked and that is what I still want to know!" I realized that I had been standing in the exact position for what seemed minutes, hours, days perhaps. I could have sworn the clock had stopped. I had no idea how long we had been discoursing. I was sweating visibly, in one hand a tumbler, in the other a quart of Scotch whisky. "Yes, Ned Beaumont. That's my question. I await your reply. "Is it . . . *so* difficult?"

Ned Beaumont strode to the window with that long, masculine lope of a stride that had first brought him to the attention of Daisy Buchanan. It had been at a publication party for Cecil Tyrell's *Broken Bottles*, and Daisy had watched him all evening long, her eyes riveted on his striding legs as he loped his way from group to group. Her husband, Tom, was off at the bar somewhere, as usual, neglecting her in the cavalier way that was his wont. I have lain awake for nights, for centuries, it sometimes seems, wishing that Daisy might have bent that admiring glance on *my* legs. Now, the possessor of those legs was at the window, looking at the wind-whipped lake stretched out before him like a dark and mysterious hand, oddly crusted with whitecaps like a kind of loathsome eczema.

"One could *probably* call that water 'branch,' Martin," he rasped. The words seemed to catch in the air, and hang suspended. I could almost descry them laboring toward my ear, lurching through the silence that had suddenly fallen.

"So it'll be rocks then," I laughed, gripping the quart bottle in a kind of maniacal fury, or, a wintry hatred.

"Rocks will do," he said, his voice exhausted. He turned toward me and I saw that his face was the face of a tired old man. "Martin . . ." he began.

"Ned Beaumont," I stated. "Ned Beaumont, 'rocks' is an expression somewhat akin to 'branch.' It means 'ice cubes.' That's all. It is a kind of slang term—or perhaps a jargon. I did not mean to bait you. I didn't know. . . ." I felt myself softening toward him, the great polar cap of my anger melting and flowing like . . . branch water. I crashed into plangent laughter.

"That is extremely interesting. That is interesting in the highest degree. Rocks," he grinned. "I can see now how that term might come to be used. It is superbly inventive, Chuck, superbly inventive!" He threw his head back and laughed his Great Laugh, the Laugh that Daisy, I knew, adored. His Laugh was like Art. I could not bear to tell him that I had not invented the term. I felt that it was

11

better, somehow, to allow him to go on believing exactly as he wished to believe. God knows, he had little enough. He seemed grateful, and almost helpless. His eyes were upon me, doglike in their gratitude. Ned Beaumont flung himself again into laughter.

"You have a remarkable laugh, Ned Beaumont," I laughed. "A laugh that can only be termed infectious. How come?"

"Laughter is the gift of God," Ned Beaumont smiled. *"In risu veritas."* He Laughed *again!*

"How true," I remarked softly.

"What?"

"How true," I cried. "So they say."

"Yes. Of course. There's no need to shout, old man," Ned Beaumont allowed.

Somehow, I made his drink, and one for myself. Our talk had exhausted us and we sat before a strangely blazing fire, drinks in hand, thoughtfully smoking. I knew that the reason for our meeting was hovering in the air, like a great sinister plastic animal that was waiting its opportunity to come between us and give us cancer. Ned Beaumont's lack of self-control, his failing memory, his unearthly Laughter—it if indeed *was* Laughter—all brought again to my mind the reason for this meeting. I searched my fevered brain to find a way to bring the two—"she-demons"—into the conversation. I knew Ned Beaumont's "feeling" for them, I knew the power that they wielded over his life, I knew his absolute inability to tolerate criticism of them.

Sipping my drink, I suggested, offhand: "Have you seen Corrie and Berthe lately, Ned Beaumont? My, what a cheery fire! I believe I can see shapes therein!"

A kind of sick and sullen semblance of silence descended on the room, a silence from which Ned Beaumont's voice issued like a rogue's curse, like the paranoiac soughing of the wind outside. But . . . was it really *outside?*

"I'll not speak of them with you or with anyone else," he bit right off. Sweat stood out on his bulging forehead in great beady pearls. His hands began to shake so much that he spilled some of his drink.

"You're spilling some of your drink, Ned Beaumont," I opined. "The merest mention of those two young women seems to inflict an unusual nervousness upon your person. At the moment these names are causing a small accident." I chose my words with the most delicate precision.

"You've no right to speak of them—here!" He flung his arm out to underline his last word and his drink now cascaded out of the glass, most of it landing on the wild flames in the fireplace. They spat and danced like trapped things, the shadows in the room leaping wildly.

12

For the first time, I was *afraid*. Afraid of what I might have to do!

"Ned Beaumont, just *why* do you think I asked to meet with you tonight? We never talk together anymore, our confidence in each other is well-nigh obsolete. Face it, man. Face it!" I was almost shrieking above his sudden Laughter, trying to ignore the fleeting images of various Old Masters it crafted.

"They are *marvelous* girls, *marvelous!*" He loped, to the bar, to make himself another drink! "I don't expect *you* to understand," he mumbled.

"What, Ned?"

He turned to me, his face a rigid mask of livid yet fervid rage. He despised me.

"I say, old chum, that you can't, or *won't*, understand—it's the same thing." He busied himself unnecessarily with his drink.

"Oh," I intoned. "But you're wrong, Ned Beaumont. You're *wrong*. I've waited for weeks, for *months*, for you to tell me about them. Granted, I have not, up to this point, understood. I see—I see *something* in them. Their charm, their grace, their 'powers,' supposing that they *are* powers. They even have a sort of wondrously achieved elegance and style."

"I'm glad that you can see *that*," Ned Beaumont spat.

"But why," I queried, "why have those puerile ladies those large, flexible, ears?"

It was as if I had struck him full force in the faded face. He blanched, he blenched, his hand shook, he came at me with a hoarse cry, like the cry of an animal in pain, his visage that of a plastic animal trapped in a lair.

I *cannot remember* what happened after that! I *cannot remember* whether we fought, or argued, I *cannot remember* whether or not I —killed him!

I sit here now, in the silence over which keens the sound of the damned wind. The stars are luminous, their light a million pure points of hope, of beauty, of promise for someone. But not for me! Soon I shall call the police, and face their crude questions, their ceaseless and unimaginative probings for, the "facts." As if the "facts" could possibly explain what has happened here tonight! As if the "facts" could possibly reveal the sinister hold that Corrie Corriendo and Berthe Delamode had on Ned Beaumont! And Daisy? How will Daisy ever believe that I honestly do not know if I murdered, here, in this desolate summer house, her adored Ned Beaumont? Beaumont the laugher, Beaumont the loper. . . .

But there is time. Time to call the police, time to call Daisy Buchanan, time for everything. Let me take an hour or two of *your* time and trace the obsidian pathways of this tragedy. Let me take you back, then, to a brilliant winter afternoon no more than a year ago. A year? It seems an *eternity,* as remote as the impassive and extravagant stars whose light shyly shivers upon us, here, in this twisted world, of error, and heartbreak. Let me tell you the story, then, as if you were sitting here with me, comfortable in this silent house, the black wind hurling itself against the windows, the taste of good whisky in our mouths. It will be easier if you let me ramble on, and not interrupt me. The whole story will be told, I promise you. It isn't pretty.

So. Picture then, a brilliant afternoon in January. The sky is a faultless blue.

2. BEST INTENTIONS

A brilliant day in January, the sort of day that I have always liked, a day when one can forget one's minor and ephemeral troubles in the sure knowledge that Nature does not care, that Nature, in the old surge and flow of itself, moves inexorably onward. The sky was a flawless blue, a faultless blue, that blue that has about it somewhere a touch of yellow, or perhaps pristine white, a subtlety that seems mixed with the pale azure that makes it, perhaps, even paler.

I was walking across town to meet Ned Beaumont for lunch in order to discuss a new manuscript that had come in the week before from B.B. Brophy, the young Anglican radical. But, of course, my mind was on the new and rather disturbing relationship that Ned Beaumont seemed to have almost, one might say, *created* for himself with the two young clairvoyants, Miss Corrie Corriendo and Mme Berthe Delamode. It was too early for me to place my ideas on clairvoyance, in general, as a wedge, or wedges, between Ned Beaumont and the two young women, seeing, as I surely did, that nothing that I could say, or even hope to say, on the subject, at least at the present time, could be of the least value, seeing as how my conception of such a discipline, or gift, was that of the amateur, or even the dilettante, but I thought that I might allow my vague uneasiness on the relationship, to rise to the surface, of the chummy rapport, that we had, so that my colleague and dear friend, might glimpse it, and perhaps look at the liaison he was involved in, with a more objective, and, perhaps, even a suspicious, eye. At the time I didn't know how far the little drama had gone! The blue sky, flawless as it was, seemed uppermost in my mind—its almost virginal clarity banished the dark thoughts from my wearily weighted head!

How curious that I should have thought of the blue sky as virginal in its clarity! It almost seemed, so I flattered myself, a brilliant idea. How I hummed! In tradition and, of course, in Art, blue is the color of the mantle worn by the Virgin Mary, in which case it symbolizes modesty. Modesty, of course, is not necessarily virginal, but the two have much in common, I mused! How then, can blue also be the color of heartbreak, of sadness, of "the blues," of a sort of grinding despair? Curiously, I recalled that Eusebius, Plato, Mnemosyne, and Maximus the Younger, as well as lesser thinkers of the Athenian Middle "Pe-

15

riod" have told us that blue is the color of the clothing of the gods, especially of Juno (Queen of the Heavens), sometimes called Hera, or Here. The blue worn by these pagan gods was, however, not of the same saturation as that of the Virgin's mantle, the latter's "cloak" being more what we might now term a royal blue; whereas the former wore garments that were not far removed from ultramarine. Of necessity, no doubt! For those ancient Hellenic deities to term their clothing a "royal" blue would have smacked of *hubris*, that mortal sin of the ancient, dark religions. How dark, indeed? I laughed, bitterly.

Yet certainly, since light blue—sky-blue—in Christian art, was a symbol of divine eternity and human mortality, so was it paralleled in Hellenic religions in like terms; and thus, came to be a mortuary color. How could I have forgotten that the coffins of the young were once covered with blue cloth, and the mortuary cloth was also of this color? Yet I *had* forgotten! Was, then, the very sky itself a kind of covering over all of us "children of the gods"? And what of the fact that brides in Eastern Rumania wore blue garters on their wedding day? Certainly the commentary of Sir Vyvyan Brier on such folk practices seems to indicate that the blue at once symbolized the sexual "life" and the orgastic "death" consummated by the youthful couple. In a paper published as an addendum to this work, which latter, I recalled, was always known as "Brier's Folk-Wedding Studies," but which has the formal title: "Magic and Ritual in Folk-Weddings in the Jijia River Valley," Sir Vyvyan notes that the practice has been discontinued because of what he delicately notes are "political considerations," as well as the introduction of garter belts. Indeed, I snorted.

Glancing again at the canopy of heaven, I remembered that the ancient emblem of heaven, a "canopy," was termed the baldachin, and it was blue beneath; and church *ceilings*—from the Latin *caelum* or "heaven"—were generally painted blue (except in the churches of the heresiarch, Fr. Gonsalvo Poniatowski—the "Orange Priest") and powdered with gold stars just cute as pie. With a sudden slashing nostalgia I recalled the church of my youth, Our Lady of the Bleeding Eyes, and *its* blue ceiling, bespattered with those same gold stars. It was meet that it was so, meet also that one received gold stars on blue cards for excellence in primary religious studies.

Of course, blue likewise signifies piety, sincerity, and contemplation! It seemed sad to me that church vestments are no longer of this redoubtable color, almost as if something has gone out of the Holy Church, as indeed, something has. What could it be? I wondered aloud. Scallope-Seviche, in a book that we ourselves published some years ago, *Midnight Sunburst*, tells the story of coming across, in the

16

remoter reaches of Ireland, an ancient priest about to celebrate mass in an electric-blue chasuble. When Scallope-Seviche asked the old man the nature of the mass which he was about to celebrate, the latter replied, with not a little dignity, "Electric blue is your only man!" Ah, the Irish have grand hearts, I muttered as I sauntered, a speck in the sunny world covered with the blue baldachin of God.

Is it for nothing that high priests (or "rabbis") of the Jewish faith wore blue about their garments as significant of divine contemplation? You've got to hand it to them! They know how to worship God, I thought. It takes years to realize that one never finds a Jewish person in a poolroom! What would the high priests, their magical blue all about them, say about such a thing? Terrible even to contemplate. Jewish angels' garments are always blue, symbolic of faith and fidelity, the very *flag* of Israel is blue and white, Christ knows why.

My spirits were lifting, the flawless blueness of the sky had borne me across town effortlessly, and I felt that my meeting with Ned Beaumont would be productive, *more* than productive, perhaps. The very color of the sky had infused into my soul and made it shimmer with fidelity to my own ideas on my partner's "trouble" as well as with faith in his ability to make the right decision as soon as I had pointed out to him his waywardness. I was delighted to discover that I had worn a blue tie to this luncheon meeting. It seemed to me to be a sign from Juno herself, and I suddenly thought that blue, worn at the celebration of certain things, is significant of humanity and expiation, as well as of unbridled lust. Fitting, I thought, fitting to be sure. The young women in question were—"redolent"—of that latter state. There, I knew, was the problem with Ned Beaumont and his uncritical adoration of their "magic." But I felt that my cravat, or tie, a heraldic blue, if it was anything, and thereby a kind of blazon of chastity, loyalty, fidelity, and good reputation, would enable me to carry the day against these two with my dear and old friend.

I spied Ned Beaumont at the corner, waiting impatiently for me. As I came up to him and shouted a greeting, he turned, looking at me as if seeing me for the first time. "Martin?" I extended my hand, and saw that his bewildered gaze had wandered away from my face and that his eyes were carefully picking their way down my person, cutting back and forth in the vicinity of my shirtfront. "Of course it's Martin. You were expecting maybe a miracle?" I laughed gruffly, reaching back for an old joke we both were inordinately fond of.

Of course, it was my tie that he was examining ever so minutely. "How fantastic that you're wearing a blue tie!" he cried. "It's a dead giveaway! A dead giveaway!" He was slapping his thighs convulsively. "What is it, Ned Beaumont?" I queried, smiling in a kind of oneiric bewilderment, a habit that I have acquired when I wish to disguise the fact that I am nonplused. For a moment I hated him. "Baby, I was just reading Brophy's manuscript and he says that blue" —and he pointed at my tie—"is the Mongolian color of authority and power. Authority and power!" He suddenly looked soberly at me, his arms and hands ceased their spastically facetious movements. "Are you going to pull some 'rank' on me? About, maybe, Corrie and Berthe?"

I looked at him, amazed, trying to disguise my perplexed frown with a smile. The sky had somehow ironically tricked me that morning. The luncheon meeting was disastrous. It was soon after that our friendship began to crack apart. I'll try and tell you about it as calmly and coolly as I can. The wind is getting stronger now. My eyes are riveted on the lake, all a-spume . . . with chancre-like stuff!

Let me place you in the restaurant with us, at the same table. Let me try and show you the beginning ugliness that would end with ugly death. How curious that it should begin on a day of dazzlingly flawless blue.

Lamont's Scrapbook

ARE YOU EMBARRASSED AND SILENT when others speak of books, politics, theatre, the cinema, philosophy, and all the other subjects that cultivated men and women delight in discussing? Now, a revolutionary new method of *thought expansion* through *free association* can help you to be the interesting, provocative, and spellbinding conversationalist that you have always wanted to be! The WRITER'S HELPER MONTHLY, a famed journal that has been consulted by *professional writers* for years, has developed a simple, pleasant, and *foolproof* method whereby *you* may use your inherent *brain power* the way that *famous writers* do!

WHAT'S THE GIMMICK? No gimmick, we assure you. It has long been known that the *imagination* can be trained, just as the body is trained. Trouble is, most of us are so weary after the day's work, so besieged by the hectic pace of contemporary living, that we let our great gift, our *brain power*, lie dormant. We think, we reason, certainly—but our imaginations are *asleep!*

TAKE A LOOK at the ten questions and answers enclosed. The questions were asked randomly of people—laborers, housewives, mechanics, carpenters, business executives, teachers—who have taken the WRITER'S HELPER MONTHLY's *thought-expansion* course. If you don't agree that the answers are astounding, delightful, and totally individualistic, then we've been mistaken in sending this offer to you. But don't write, don't send *any money*, don't apply for the course—yet! We want to send you, over the next few weeks, more representative questions and answers, for a grand total of 50. If, at the end of that time, you agree with us that these diverse questions have been answered in the most *exciting, intelligent* manner possible, we'll be delighted to accept your course application.

NOW—read and enjoy yourself!

> Sincerely,
> E. Elwood Sprenger
> *Managing Editor, WHM*

Is it true what they say about Dixie?

In time and of the essence, river of tender adolescent tears, as whispered by the ghost, long wind-grieved and not yet laid, it may become true. When old Dixie shakes, when those good ol' boys stop walking down those hot red clay roads, or when lovers make no rendezvous 'neath the magnolias. Certainly, it is false to speak of honeysuckle, tobacco, grits, slaves, Confederates of stone far gazing, deserted rocking chairs on shady verandas in the heavy heat of August afternoons, and whatever other items from Dear Old Southland that come to mind. The argument seems to be that nothing whatever known to Yankee man is true of Dixie. From other voices we may hear the harshest truths, from baking cotton fields, from other rooms, down on the levee, in the Mississippi muck, O drawling ghosts! Crackers in the sleepy town square, rawboned and still. Them mercury vapor streetlights leading to the highway!

Who is Sylvia?

Sylvia Sackett Besunder, white, female, 34, of 3025 West 2nd Street, Brooklyn, N.Y. Elementary-school teacher, beloved by all. Her construction-paper suns and pussy-cat silhouettes shine out and purr upon the streets of raw Canarsie down below.

Is that the Chattanooga Choo-Choo?

No. From its general construction and style, as well as its size, silhouette, and the insufferable noise it makes, it may be the Wabash Cannonball, the Redball Express, the Hondo Hurricane, the Laredo Limited, the Delaware Lackawanna and Western Delight, the Erie Smoke, the Santa Fe Savage, the Missouri-Pacific Blazer, the Texas-Pacific Tornado, the Union Pacific Paramount, the Missouri-Kansas-Texas Zippo, the Toonerville Trolley, the Zenith Hummingbird, the Western Pacific Wendigo, the Pennsylvania Phantom, the Long Island Stroller, or the Tuscaloosa Breeze.

What do you do in the infantry?

You die, you die, you die.

Can Jack-an-Ape be merry, when his clog is at his heel?

Marry, an' as the wise old king who plugged a dozen holes of an evening was wont to say, his encarnadined phiz covered o'er with the juice o' the sacred grape, a varlet'll come to his galliards an' his corantos late, if he come at all, for the wine goes round in his whirling eye that the faithful sun doth scorch to a desert consistency as like as to powder as m'lady's damask skin beneath her plackets when the reeling moon doth sport with her desperate suitors, the stars. An' why not then a thing so shaped in man's decided visage as the poor dumb fettered baboon? 'Tis not a clog that'll let a gay old dog, or, an't please you, the grinning fool, Jack Ape.

20

Nov schmoz ka pop?
Inter belfuscu idionie tae brezhnov da poz, pu ka poppa taemoz ka don aeroplane, peru tae kaloz; taen melozhnoz, p donzu donoz perlopki.

Is fancy sick, or turned a sot, to catch at shadows which are not?
Nay, 'tis the line that makes one puke on one's fedora or peruke.

If God be with us, who can be against us?
Strategic Air Command, New York Yankees, First Marine Division, Fuckin' A, Army of Northern Virginia, the Administration, Japanese Marines, Schutzstaffel, 82nd Airborne Division, Viet Cong, Zeros, Pittsburgh Pirates, Army of the Potomac, Adolf Hitler Division, Apaches, the times, Internal Revenue Service, Camp Pickett, diseased whores, Crazy Horse, Nelson Rockefeller, book reviewers, Stukas, 2nd Army, Peoples' Republic of China, KP pushers, the customs, bookmakers, Geheime Staatspolizei, CIA, platoon sergeants, the odds, Fort Hood, San Francisco Giants, narcotics dealers, the past, Joint Chiefs of Staff, the rich, the future, landlords, and the advertising business. Others on request.

Where are the snows of yesteryear?
Under the shadow, by the piers they waited.

Who threw the overalls in Mrs. Murphy's chowder?
Cornelius A. ("Connie") Ryan, late of Morristown, New Jersey, who dreamt drunkenly away the long and placid summer afternoons over many a tall and frosty Tom Collins in the cool, dim taproom of the Hi-Top. Blest be his lost and gentle youth.

My dear Roche:
Thanks for your long and careful letter on *Rayon Violet*. You raise a number of interesting points, which I'll try to answer and/or comment on as best I can. It's been a long time since I've read the book, so I'll do my best to check the passages you mention. Sometimes it seems to me as if someone else wrote the book. I suppose that is an occupational hazard!
1. Elena Esposito actually *does* disappear in the middle of the narrative. The girl who narrates the last half of the book seems to be Elena, but she is not. There are many clues scattered about in order that the reader may discover this fact—color of hair, penchant for low-heeled shoes, dislike of mussels, etc.—but they are subtle, and, I suppose, many people missed them. The subliminal "horror" of the

second half of the book lies in the fact that *its* "Elena" thinks she is the *true* Elena. That we never know just who she really is deepens, or so I hoped, the "sexual mystery" with which the book grapples.

2. Paul Shanahan is a cardboard figure, I agree. But his formal place in the narrative, given its loose and interwoven structure, is to act as a foil: am I being overly defensive when I say that I *meant* him to be one-dimensional?

3. The overriding symbol of *Violet* is plastic. God knows, I am not a didactic writer, and have no ax to grind in this novel, nor in any of my other novels. I am interested in what I shall, perhaps arrogantly, call aesthetic joy. Topical rubbish, or what some call a Novel of Idea, leaves me cold. Yet plastic, in this novel, seemed the perfect "control" for such a sterile and lost group of people. But it is a *literary* concept, not a social or political one.

4. You are right that Indianapolis and New York are interchangeable in this novel, and that the names of streets, parks, restaurants, etc., are identical: I thought to use this technique to get across my feeling that our world has become featureless. It works, if you want it to work. I agree that it is, perhaps, "cute."

5. I think you have missed the point of Shanahan's long soliloquy in Chapter 12. When he ends it by quoting the famous lines from Trumbull Stickney, he is suggesting a beginning, not an end, to his campaign to seduce Blanche Schwarzmann. The soliloquy is a verbalization of his rampaging desires, although I grant you that he is doing his best in it to convince himself that he has mastered his lust.

6. You remark that it would be "interesting to know where you got the title of the novel, *Rayon Violet*, since it seems to have little or nothing to do with anything at all . . ." It is from a poem of Pierre Dusort's, "L'Orgie du Coeur." The line in question runs, "Rayon Violet, rayon violet! Armée étrange!" I admit that a reader should know Dusort's poem in order to discover the aptness of the title. But I think that a writer can *occasionally* be obscure.

7. Shamefully, shamefully, I agree that Levenspiel is a wholly unrealized character, and that the Yiddish patois that I have put into his mouth is inexact burlesque. I must also confess that the only reason that I put this character into the novel was because of a mad desire I had to "cash in" (God, what a vulgar phrase!) on the "Jewish novel" that, at the time, was all the rage. It stands as the only time in my career that I succumbed to the urge for quick money. Shalom! my dear Roche, shalom!

8. Finally, let me defend myself against your "charge" that the formal structure of the novel is overly complex and self-defeating. The concept of the flashback within the flashback, this entity pre-

22

sented as something occurring in the future, is, I maintain, the only way in which I could disorient the time factor in the book, so as to match the progressive disorientation of the characters. I admit that the use of the future and past tense, occurring in some sections on the same page, often within the same paragraph or even sentence, is difficult to follow, but I accepted this dilemma and did my best with it. The work that was put into this little novel was tremendous, and I feel that its treatment at the hands of critics was ill-deserved. I grant you that it is a difficult book, one that demands the closest attention. I also think of it as a comic novel. But let that be. Nobody has seen the humor in the book, and I certainly do not want to bore you by pointing out what to me are hilarious passages. But then, how many people can discover the endless slapstick in *The Possessed?* It is all a way of looking at things.

All right. Enough. As I come to the end of this too-long letter, outside my studio window I see the moon, a white clipper, plunging through seas of streaming cloud. How I wish I could be aboard!

My new book is proving difficult, if not *quite* intractable.

With my best wishes,
Antony Lamont

From *Rayon Violet;* pp. 44–45.

The rain pelted down on Levenspiel, running down the inside of his collar, chilling him to the bone. Have mercy, have mercy, God, he thought. I have my life to realize already. I shouldn't have a little pleasure out of this rotten world? My mother with the paranoia, knocking her head against the wall—I should pay the doctors for another twenty years for her? God forbid that she should pass away, but am I made of money? My wife with the fur coats, the new dresses, the tight pants so you should see her whole body, I need this? My little girl who is not so little she hasn't got the baby pills and the lousy boy friend from Coney Island Avenue who has no respect for his own father, he should have respect for me? Better I should have stayed a presser than have these heartaches already. So who needs them, God? I sit with my wife at night, she looks at me, I look at her, this is living? Once in a while, you shouldn't think I'm a sex maniac or something, but once in a while I think maybe we might have a little fun. Am I in my grave yet? I can't do anything with her, not to mention a shtup. Am I asking to be the President? Once a month is all I ask, she looks at me like I'm crazy. Have I got a cancer she looks at me like this? My father, the bastard, God forgive me, but I'm glad

23

he's dead, he put a complex on me when I was a kid. Is money everything? Better I should be happy than live like a sick prince. You I offer prayers. You don't seem to hear me. You I offer money through the temple, with the smart rabbi. No results. What kind of a rabbi is this anyway, smart guy he is, reading the Communist magazines, his name I see against the war whenever I pick up a paper. This is a rabbi? God forgive me but he can't speak Hebrew. He sounds like a goyische, if you aren't afraid of facing the truth. Nu? I ask him about my daughter, maybe he could break his heart and have a word with her about her carrying on—she needs a social disease at seventeen? Children expect a great deal of freedom nowadays, the great rabbi says. It's the atom bomb, he says. It's the war, he says. I should believe that the Communists and the Congos or whatever are forcing my daughter to let this rat bastard she sees, with no respect for his father, take her underpants that I pay for off? Please don't make me laugh. I'm dying from the laughing already. The schwartze maid who comes in I ask maybe she could clean the den a little more, like maybe she could empty an ashtray? Would it break her arm? Would it kill her? Who is paying her forty dollars a week for nothing? The NACP maybe? Maybe it's Malcolm X or Luther Martin who picks her up at the bus stop twice a week, no questions asked? I ask her to maybe wipe a little dust off an end table, she looks at me like I'm Hitler. Am I made of stone? Give me credit for a little sensitive feeling. My wife says I should have more feeling for the Porto Rickans who push the dress racks, do you hear me? More respect already! Is a dollar ten cents an hour nothing for this work? Forgive me that I call it work please. One rack of dresses to go three blocks, the deadbeats are gone two hours. Am I a moron or an idiot that I don't know they're drinking wine and talking over how maybe they can stick a knife in me one day? Do I need this misery? Do you think I'm surprised my partner dropped dead two years ago? Believe me, he's a lucky man. With the worries over how you can show a profit and still be a human being it's a wonder all of us don't drop dead. With my wife playing mah-jongg and rummy which she loses all my money at every January in Miami, I should give the help maybe five dollars an hour? Also a bonus for not getting drunk before lunch? It's enough for me my daughter calls me a fascist reactionary, now my wife tells me I'm an exploiter. It was maybe the schwartzes and the spicks that Hitler put in the ovens? When they were turning us all into soap where were the schwartzes and spicks then? Pardon me, I couldn't hear a word from them.

Halpin's Journal

How to get away? That must stand as the overwhelmingly important question in my life as of this moment. It is quite impossible for me to go through this charade for too much longer. Were there a God I would beg Him to tell me why he allowed this *scribbler,* this unbearably pretentious *hack,* Antony Lamont, to place me in this ridiculous position. The things that I have been forced to say! The utter silliness of the "story" so far. What have I done to be plucked out of the wry, the amused footnote in which I have resided, faceless, for all these years in the work of that gentlemanly Irishman, Mr. Joyce? "An old gardener," so I have been for these thirty-odd years, an old gardener who has never gardened, never even seen, so far as I can remember, a garden—and happy *not* to have seen one, by God! What a delight to reside in that quietly monumental world all this time, a small part of it, content behind the letters that form my name. In a way, I *was* the letters, no more. Now I find myself in a cold vacation cabin of some sort, perhaps I am even a murderer, if this hack chooses to make me one. There has to be a way to free myself, and if not that, at least to discover what sort of landscape this Lamont has made for himself in other books, if he's written any.

The crowning humiliation was that absurd dialogue Beaumont and I were forced to carry on about "branch water" and "rocks." Afterward, Beaumont sat at the table and hid his face in his hands, ashamed to look at me! I tried to tell him that it might possibly get better, after all, we didn't really know anything about this Lamont, it could have been worse, etc., etc. Hollow optimism, I admit, but it was difficult to watch him in his pain. He mentioned something about "better days" that he had had years ago, when he lived in a more reasonable world. "I took a lot of punishment there," he said, "but it all came out beautifully. Here, good Jesus! Here, I'm *dead* before I start!" I looked out the window at the lake, cold and forbidding. It hadn't changed a bit.

I can hide this journal under the rug. It wouldn't do to have Lamont suspect it, and I'd prefer it if Beaumont didn't see it. I have the nagging suspicion that Beaumont, being dead, will slip away from here one night, or one weekend when Lamont is out of his study, and never be heard from again. He hints that he has a place to go, if he can get there. I don't believe him. It's I who will have the trouble, of course, telling the "story" as I am constrained to do. And Lamont may well be one of those writers who is always looking over what he has written, in which case, it will be impossible to find a moment in which to leave. That thought fills me with nausea.

25

I can't understand how Mr. Joyce allowed him to take me away! Surely, it can't have been for money! Or does Mr. Joyce even *know* that I have gone? Maybe he's dead. I have no idea of what arrangements have been made, I certainly ought to be given a decent salary, telling, as I am, the whole story. But what possessed this man to make me out such a fool? I would have been delighted to play a small role, even an anonymous role, somewhere in this vulgar work. Some superintendent who lives in a basement apartment, or even the caretaker of this lodge. The smiling roomer down the hall. He could have put me in a rowboat far out on the lake, a man seen from the window. I could troll. If I must be the star why can't I speak intelligent lines? I'm not a robot, I'm not immune to ill treatment. Mr. Joyce, knowing that I could do nothing at all, merely stated, *stated*, mind you, that I performed "odd jobs." That is what one may term nicety of expression. Nowhere was I made to perform, actually *perform* these "odd jobs" for Brophy—who, of course, this shameless man has also taken over and made into some sort of radical author. Perhaps Lamont somehow purchased the entire footnote, or even whole sections of that quiet world in which nothing ever happened—at least in my small area of it. I don't know, I just don't know.

(I am writing this following part of my journal late at night. I want to record a brief conversation with Beaumont that I had just after finishing the sentence preceding this parenthesis.)

Beaumont entered. He saw that I was writing in this notebook and was curious.

"What are you writing?"

"A letter to—my sister."

"Oh. I've never had a sister. Do you think Lamont will give me one? I'm afraid I wouldn't know how to act."

"God knows." I casually closed the notebook.

"Look, Halpin. Did you ever hear of Dashiell Hammett? I mean, over in that 'dream world' you said you come from?" (His voice was weighted with irony.)

"I'm afraid not, Ned. A character?"

"No, not a character, an author, like Lamont, only. . . ." He shrugged.

"I've led a quiet life, Ned."

"So you have, so you have. Well, I worked for Hammett. I was a very big star for him. An actor—a *Hollywood* actor—even impersonated me in a movie they made from a book I worked in."

"This junk must *really* be hard for you, Ned. I'm sorry."

"It's all right. What I mean is, I'm not used to this 'absurd' dialogue, what do they call this crap, experimental? And I'm not used to being dead and alive only in flashbacks. I don't know if I can do it for too much longer. I dread to think what that man will put me through when we get into that restaurant he left us at."

"So do I. I've never even eaten anything, I don't know if I'll even like eating."

"It's fine. I've eaten, myself. God only knows, of course, what he'll make us order."

"Do you think it will be tomorrow?"

"I don't know his work habits. But I tell you, if it's not, let's go down to the lake and take a swim, O.K.?"

"It's too cold for swimming, Ned. And it's pitch dark—except for those damn stars." (We did not yet know that it was only from inside the house that the lake was dark.)

"Of course it is." He groaned. "Of course it is."

There was a silence. I knew that Beaumont was trying to say that it was easier for *me* to be here than it was for *him*—after all, I had never been a major character. I suspected that he wanted to suggest that I might try embarking on a digression long enough to allow him to escape. I suppose I would do it if I could, but if there is one thing I learned while working for Mr. Joyce, it is that one cannot escape for long from a writer, unless he decides to completely rewrite a whole section. When that occurs, there is a moment, *just* a moment, when one may assert oneself. Occasionally, the writer will allow this assertion to stand, and one's character is thereby subtly changed. In fact, sometimes the whole world in which one is employed is changed. But Lamont struck me as being ruthless, as well as stupid.

"Ned, I know how hard it is for you, I really do. But let's get some sleep now. I have a feeling we'll need it for that restaurant tomorrow. And, Ned, if it turns out I've really murdered you—no hard feelings?"

"Of course not, Martin. Do you think I'll hold it against *you?* Hammett had me beaten to a pulp but I knew he had to do it."

That was the gist of the conversation. I'm going to hide this notebook now and get some sleep. Ned is snoring on the couch in the study. God, I can't bear this place! Why couldn't he have given us a bright, sunny day to work in?

My dear Sheila,

How delighted I am that you and Dermot have decided to get married! And to live in San Francisco! That has always been one of my very favorite cities, somehow a really cosmopolitan metropolis that has escaped the dehumanizing process that most other cities seem to become involved in. It has always reminded me of a collection of the most elegant cupcakes. I heard from someone the other day that Dermot is hard at work on a new book, some sort of "Western" that takes place in, of all places, Ireland! Can this be the fact? I don't know how he's going to swing it, because Westerns have become almost passé, and he'll have to spice it up with plenty of smut in order for a publisher to even consider doing it. Shouldn't be too hard for him.

The one thing that troubles me about your coming marriage is what I take to be the great gulf between Dermot's literary tastes and your own . . . not that I am criticizing your choice. Please don't think that for an instant. There have been many artistic marriages that, on the face of them, looked utterly hopeless, and yet which worked out beautifully for both parties. (My *own* disastrous marriage is not to be viewed as a paradigm.) But Dermot, as you well know, has for years set his sights on commercial success and his writing has suffered terribly because of it. I sometimes wonder if he will ever again achieve the startling freshness he showed in those early stories of his, "Moonface the Murderer" and "I Divorce Thee Husband." I know that you know that a writer must keep his pen, as it were, well honed. On top of this is your own penchant for critical writing, which becomes more and more trenchant and cogent as time goes on. It would seem to me that there might well be some sort of friction between you because of his ideas and yours. Let us hope not, and, in the meantime, let us keep hoping for Dermot's return to letters.

How wonderful that you are doing a book on Nabokov! There has been so little written of this wonderful writer that a really first-rate job on his work is sorely needed. It is one thing for an Antony Lamont to be neglected—granted, my work is not for everyone—but it is incomprehensible to me how an author as good as N goes virtually unnoticed. I have spoken to Chattaway about your project and he appears "interested," whatever that means. In any event, I'll keep mentioning you to him and when you have a decent chunk of the book written I'll be pleased to show it to him for you. He's not a bad sort, although in recent months he has shown a disturbing proclivity for publishing what he calls "meaningful" books. I would guess that he means things like *Right On . . . Rip Off!* by Ishmael Melanzana and *Nazism and The Nuclear Family* by Henri Kink. These are all right as far as they go, but it would seem to me that there will always be room for fiction and the study of fiction.

Speaking of fiction, my own new book, *Guinea Red,* is giving me more trouble than I bargained for. I am trying to write an "absurdist" mystery story—if you can conceive of such a thing. My narrator is a man who has lost touch with his life; so much so that he doesn't know whether or not he *is* a murderer. The trouble lies in giving him a true fictional shape through his voice—and his voice, of course, must give the reader hints of madness and alienation. There are scenes written and projected in which the dialogue is nightmarish and totally ludicrous. If you know the *nouvelle roman* you will get an idea of what I am trying to do . . . only I have my figures in an American setting. The strange thing is that Halpin (my narrator) seems to be bursting with the desire to say and do things that I don't *want* him to say and do. This has always been, of course, a novelist's problem, but in this book it seems more of a problem than ever. The feeling is extraordinary—almost as if Halpin has a life of his own, one that he lives when I am not "looking," as it were. He strains against me. I've got two chapters done so far, and am preparing to write a third. I don't know whether I like them or not, but there's no turning back now. The book will be written. In that room, facing that blank sheet of paper —well, it's the loneliest place in the world. As if you didn't know!

Ask Dermot to write me. We used to be good friends back in the days when, to take small liberties with Milton, "Fame was the spur that the clear spirit did raise." Ah God, we had good times. What Great Artists we were going to be! Well, we do what we can, as we can.

Take care of yourself, and I'll see you in the funny papers.

Love, from your brother,
Tony

Halpin's Journal

There's a great deal to set down today! Many things have happened since I last wrote, and I'll try to record them all, carefully and in, I hope, order.

The first thing to note is that Lamont has not employed us in some time, I would say at least ten days, perhaps even more. This is a great pleasure, in one sense, because Ned and I have dreaded the restaurant scene, dreaded the ridiculous dialogue that Lamont will surely put in our mouths. He's probably working up his fiendish notes. (By the way, it is an enormous pleasure to me to be able to say, simply, "Ned," instead of "Ned Beaumont," as I am constrained to say when we are working. Where Lamont ever got the idea for that particular affectation is a puzzle, but it seems to be a part of the fabric of his book, and I certainly can't protest.) On the other hand, it's much more comforting to be working for a writer who employs one every day, with, say, Sundays off. One knows where one stands. In any event, this long layoff has allowed me and Ned much time to find out about our predicament.

The most amazing discovery is that it is always nighttime only *inside* the house; that is, when one ventures outside, it is day. It is only in here that Lamont has managed to arrest time. Ned says however, that that is only because Lamont is not "looking" right now. He can do *what* he wants outside *when* he wants. We are *slaves!* The night is, somehow, artificial. And so is the day. Ned says that he once spoke to a man, an Irish newspaperman, one whose name he somehow didn't manage to find out, who told him that a neglected genius, one DaSalvi, maintained that night is simply an insanitary condition of the atmosphere due to accretions of black air. If this is so (and it certainly seems reasonable), it would seem that Lamont can manage to "set" these accretions—but only in one place, that is, directly before the windows of the house. When he wants. It is an odd thing to come in from a rosy-pink morning, go directly to the window, and gaze out at a chilly, choppy, pitch-black lake! We were both quite taken aback at first, but have now reconciled ourselves to the fact that we are, while in the house at least, virtual prisoners. But as soon as we can we'll do a little exploring down the road.

Ned and I have been speculating as to the owner of this house. It is a rather odd house, to say the least. There is the living room and the den, but we have not been able to find any other rooms. It *seems* as if there are other rooms, but when we approach them, they are —I don't quite know how to put this—they are simply *not there!* There is no kitchen, no porch, no bedrooms, no bath. At the side of the living room, a staircase leads "nowhere." Oh, I don't mean to say that it disappears into empty space, it simply leads to a kind of . . . haziness, in which one knows there is *supposed* to be a hallway and bedroom doors: but there is absolutely nothing. Neither Ned nor I dare to say what is uppermost in our minds, that is, that if we walked into this haziness, we would walk somehow into another dimension. (Ned thinks—wishful thinking!—that we might walk into another book!) For us, this house is the living room and the den. It certainly seems to belong to someone, but it certainly isn't *mine,* and Ned laughed when I tentatively suggested that it might be his. The only clue to who might own it lies in the old periodicals, papers, and books that are in the den. But they are so diverse that one cannot imagine them being the property of any one person, unless he is a "renaissance" man. Ned and I spent the better part of a morning (or part of a "night," considering that we were inside the house) going through this stuff, and, after weeding out different issues of the same periodical, etc., we came up with an inventory, of sorts, that I think it valuable to set down here. I make no claim to completeness, since there may well be other materials in those "rooms" that do not "exist." The list is as follows:

BOOKS: *The Orange Dress* by Sheila Henry; *Daredevil* by John Charleville; *Stolen Fruit* by Jymes Vulgario; *The Dry Ranges* by Gilford Sorento; *The Ouija Kiss* by Harry Bore; *Cobbler, Rend My Shoe!* by Thom McAn; *Acey-Five* by Richard Tracy; *Crab Hunting* by Joseph Bush; *The Model House* by Iolanda Puttana; *Buccal Violation* by Carmine Rod; *The Male Lesbian* by K.Y. Geli; *Stupid Bastard: The Life of Harry Purim* by Meier Meier; *American Vector* by Guy Lewis; *Lubricious Lubricants* by Reg Margarine; *Mary, Mother of God* by Xavier Amice, S.J.; *Jackoff in the Old Red Barn* by Ricky Dickey; *Girls, Grapes, and Snow* by Aristotle Rich; *Red Flanagan's Last Throw* by William Tracy; *Stick 'Em Up* by "Toni"; *The King's Son* by Hurley Lees; *Thank God for My Gonorrhea* by Joseph Viejo; *Tie Your Own Tubes* by V.A. Szechtomijh; *Put It Right There* by Vera Panting; *One Thousand Occasional Sonnets* by Gordo Kelly; *Crazy for Corsets* by Van Raalte; *The Truth About Vegetables* by Harry Krishna-Rama; *Sexual Fulfillment in the Woods* by Birch Humppor; *Men's Room Madness* by Gabriel Power; *The Boon of Unemployment* by Milhous Hoover; *Lace Me Tighter!* by Merrie Widdoe; *30 Days to a Bigger Thing* by Novena Lodge; *It's Great to be Champeen* by Gorman Sailer; *The Cry of the Serbo-Croats* by Boris Crzwcwzw; *Schultz is Dead* by Una Cazzo; *10 Days to a Hairless Body* by Alice Guné; *Yes, We Have No Bananas* by "Sister Veronica"; *Myth and Methodology in the Albanian Novel* by Julius Naranja; *The Big Lie: Myths About the Third Reich* by Sepp Schutz-Staffel; *Country Album* by Nicholas de Selby; *The Wiener in Bavarian Folk Art* by Nathan Famoso; *Repairing Your Motorcycle* by Anton Harley; *Our Friend, The Cockroach* by G. Blatta; *American Lake Poetry* by George Stardust; *How to Understand the Deaf* by James Joyce; *The Man Who Sailed Away: A Memoir* by Harold Barge; *Tomorrow I'll Get Straight* by Alex Schmecker; *The Sexual Aspects of Integral Calculus* by Manuel Joie; *Light in the Head* by Roberto Bligh; *Dust From Chickenhouse Floors* by Boris Vozneshenko; *A Whim of Grit* by Howard Dick; *Born to be Italian* by Myles na gCopaleen; *So You Want To Be Jewish?* by Saul Bernard Roth; *Runs in My Nylons: My Life As a Transvestite Editor* by Hanes Gossard; *Negroes With Buns: The Story of the Harlem Cooperative Bakery* by Rose Towne Krug; *Brekekekéx Koáx Koáx!* by Ali Garoo; *How to Hit .212* by Clinton Hondo; *What the Vice-President Eats* by "du Garbandier"; *Confession Can Be Fun!* by Vito Calzone, S.J.; *Traprock Ridge* by Lewis Watchung; *Metaphor is Real* by Clay Clayton; *Nutcracker Sunday* by Gloria Shinem; *Unicorn Crimson, Unicorn Grey* by Rupert Whytte-Blorenge; *Algebraical Puzzles, Nuts, Wrinkles, and Twisters* by Albert Einstein; *A Pint of Plain Is Your Only Man* by Jem Casey; *Sexism at the Battle of Waterloo* by "Jilly"; *Come in Your Trunks:*

Entertaining at the Shore by Buffie Whitestone; *Whores: Are They Human?* by M.C. Puerco; *Years of Grease* by Meg Barn; *A History of the Latvian Theater* by Juan Simón; *Jesus in My Glove* by Mac "Octopus" Vouty; *Cellophane Soldier* by George Pompson; *Counterrevolutionary Crimes of Fried-Egg Vendors* by Fidel Sofá; *"Death in Venice" and the Comic Spirit* by Sol Mallow; *Some Uses of Vaseline* by D.A.F. Sodd; *Fun in Newark* by Rosario Oglio; *No More Unsightly Bulges* by Maria Sangre; *Napalm and Its Role in World Peace* by Maxwell Champagne, Lt. Gen., USAF (Ret.); *Blue Ray* by Raymond Blue; *Are You Coming With Me, Jesus?* by Malvern Bird; *Having That Affair* by B. Boylan; *Vaginal Imagery in the Later Poems of Trumbull Stickney* by Lillie Bullero; *Waco! Wedge of Paradise* by Tex Mex; *Golf Your Way to Sexual Fulfillment* by Franz Godemiche; *Lad With A Dream: The Story of Herman Con* by Pablo Petard; *William Carlos Williams and the Sioux Nation* by Fred Engels; *Call Me Gay, Call Me Fey* by Biggs Richard; *Blood and Bills: My Life As A Successful Surgeon* by Kirk Benway, M.D.; *Stick It Under My Oxter* by Finn MacCool; *Fall, Denby, and Daugherty: Genius in Action* by Warren G. Harding; *Physics for Foreigners* by Nicolas Chauvin; *On A Chinese Honeymoon* by Mao Tse-Tung; *My Favorite Christmas Tales* by Reinhard Heydrich; *Gon' Git Down On Some Sweet Wine* by John "Shots" LeKing; *What It Means To Be A Coprophile* by "Raymond"; *Suck My Whip* by Regina Fury; *From Burgers to Billions: The Saga of MacDonald's* by E. Coli; *Covering Your Lawn With Sheet Metal* by Leo Kaufman; *Fire Pail* by Vladimir Papilion; *Studies in the Egg Cream* by Jem Spaa; *I Miss the Hangers* by Jonah Jonah; *Say Yes to Love* by Molly Bloom; *I Married A Socialist Worker* by Linda Lovely; *Throw Away Your Truss* by Charles Atlas; *Victor Mature: Man of Two Faces* by Jacques Auteur; *Baudelaire: Bourgeois Swine* by Jean-Paul Roi; *Things to Do in Mechanicville* by Ole Moses; *Jesus Christ!—A History of Fort Hood* by Bert Sonnertino; *Regular Guy: The Life of Nelson Rockefeller* by Barry Grovel; *My Life With the Seattle Pilots* by Joe L. Tremont; *Playboys in Heels* by I. Miller; *How Do Accidents Occur?* by B.G. Conondrom; *Sheila Sleeping* by Louis Henry; *Getting Rid of Unwanted Sweat Glands* by Mr. Tod; *I Am Jesus* by Viva Papa; *How to Eat a Lobster* by K.C. Max; *Bridges: Poets Express Their Love,* Horace Rosette, Ed.; *Reet Wilson—Jazz Genius* by Booker Fusto; *What's New?* by Richard Detective; *In My Own Bag* by Louis Vuitton; *So You Want to Sell Your Lot!* by Joseph Matines; *Imaginary Jollities on Factual Wings* by Gilberto Soterroni; *The Lady or the Tiger?: A Study of Sexist Repression in American Popular Fiction* by Medusa Queynte; *Omar Bulbul, The Persian Nightingale* by P. MacCruiskeen; *Fun With Your Foundation* by B. Jolie; *A Dish of Irish Setters* by Rock Wagram; *King Stink* by Campo Dawes; *Oblique Qualities in the A Priori Thought of Carl Jung* by Lewis Fielding; *Gay is Gut!: Homosexuality in the Sturmabteilung* by J. Wohl; *A Delirium of Garters* by Joanne Popsi; *The Smiling Medico* by Solway Garr, M.D.; *Norman Mailer's Greatest Fights* by Patsy Tanker; *Alger Hiss and the Meaning of Patriotism* by Bjorn Ayer; *Favorite Songs of the American Legion* by Horst Wessel; *So You Want to Dance, Act, and Play the Clarinet!* by Priscilla Peck; *Bitter and Vicious: A Study of the Later Writings of Gilles de Sorentain* by H. Poloie; *The Vacant Mind* by Sue Sunday; *Meet Ms. Missy Massy* by Ms. Madeline Munck; *Repairing Your Tree's Crotch* by Henry Thoreau; *Hiroshima: An Act of Christian Charity* by Rich Buckley; *Thighs and Groans* by Frank Newman; *New York is Really Swell!* by Ronald Paloma; *The Cedar Tavern Book* by Guy Wadson; *Lieder and its Influence on Mick Jagger* by Aaron Alwitz; *My Most Memorable Lunches* by E.D. Martini; *Of Course, Dear: The Married Couple's Guide to Sexual Perversion* by Davis Rube, M.D.; *The Layman's Missal* by Buck Mulligan; *Masturbate Those Pounds Away!* by Weary Reilly; *Painters and French Wines* by Orlick Trellis; *The Marxist Orientation of Nabokov's "Pale Fire"* by Richard Schiller; *Pretty To Think So* by Jacob Barnes; *Studies in Alum Theory* by Richard Blister; *Lesbianism in Western Ireland, 1886–1891* by Olive d'Oyly and Winnie Carr; *Plagiarism in Gilberto D. Ricardo's "Tinta Fabricada"* by Laszlo Syntax, Ph.D.; *A Priest Looks at Group Sex* by Pedro Nanismo, D.Th.; *Lacies in Loo Water* by Josephine Brewster; *The Delights of Pork* by Jorge Chicharrón; *Fly By Night* by Holden Talon; *Phallus Worship in Queens* by Aubrey Hawtree Creek; *The Early Films of Chico Zeek* by Baylor Freeq; *A Philosophical History of the Geography of Latvia* by Daniel Deever; *Best Cartoons from The Voelkischer Beobachter,* Kurt Bunde, Ed.; *Stars! The Story of My Orgasm* by David Bromide; *Meat is My Tongue* by Michael McCloud; *Carrots in Siberia: Soviet Literature Before The Thaw* by Igor Pantzoff; *Directing Plays for the YMCA* by Giovanni Simone; *Cocktails and Turtle Soup* by T.R. McCoy; *A Skeleton Key to "Rabbit, Run"* by O. Christ; *A Layman's Guide to the Flies of North America* by Rex Mattachine; *Those Happy, Laughing Sicilians* by Ruggiero Lupara; *A Dream of Tureens* by Ignatz Geezel; *The Velvet Trench* by Joy Cumming; *The Foundations of the Bulgarian Diplomatic Corps, 1945–1949* by Olga Warner; *Low Comedy in the American Private School* by Orson Cicere; *Kreplach in the Congo* by Reb Yellen; *The Blazon of Colours* by Montgomery Crisco; *Son in Caïna* by Court Royal; *Cold Porter* by Lisa O'Deavis; *Emergency Clergyman* by King Billy; *The Dead Chink* by Sing Wu; *Are Women the Woogies of the World?: A Symposium,* O.K. Boss, Ed.; *A Bridal Idyll* by A. Bandonado; *1001 Ways to Stuff a Watermelon* by Etta Peeche; *Under My Apron* by Annette Ancilla; *Favorite Clarity* by Asa Glass; *A Marigold Window* by Rhoda Dundrums; *Kindly Bulk* by S.Z. "Zoot" Alors; *Lifeless Hulk* by Amerigo Barraxa; *Venetian Bird* by Venezia Uccello; *Pathetic Kink* by Etta Sock; *Uppity Loins* by Randy Harvard; *Apples Make the Grade* by Christopher Joe; *Meher Baba Dropped His Body, Baba Lovers Say* by Maharishi Rigveda Obōkēn; *Keeping the Scene in Confusion* by Len Bobby Kluvingham; *Kitchen Sink* by Jilly Gibby; *Cheerful Tearful* by Maureen Saro; *French Letters* by Mlle de Beauvoisin; *James: Preserves and Jollies* by Stuart Gorman; *Being Together Again* by "Happy" Air; *Stale Lox: Impasse in the Middle East* by Abba Dabba Melliluna; *The Beans Do Speak* by Essex I. Daheau; *Blackeyed Daisy* by C. Foam; *A Scoop of Delight* by B. Robbins; *Dear Pal, Send Me A Book* by Edmund Dorme; *Approaches to Tenure in the State University System* by Robert Fischholder; *Life Is A Juice* by Harry T.C. Amherst; *The Sores of Life* by Louis Valley; *There Is No Air* by V.A. Lewis; *Life Becomes An Acid* by A. Dardinella; *A Man Out of Wax* by J.G. Fellowe; *The Memphis Ferry* by P. Tah; *White Mercury* by Davis Foster-Bethune; *The Coils They Left Behind* by Clanton Würme; *Sincere Black Bird* by Martin Giovanni; *Sleepy Gossoon* by Mayo Lagoon.

PERIODICALS: *Icelandic Fiction Studies; Gusano; Doggerel; Chicanery; The Absinthe Review; Tempus Actum; Hysteria; Sartrism Today; Falling Roof; Corset Weekly; Shove!; Slow Decay; The Modern Poetaster; Muscle; Tampon; Moose; Fist!; Miz; Heavy; Rotten Music; S & M Monthly; Mas; Woofer Weekly; Donchaknow; Off the Pigs Review; Compost; Dry Hump; Blockbusters Monthly; Sunset Park; Dildo News; Blax; Mees; Bitch; Vews; Roles in Rock; Hambone Weekly; Suck; Mus; Rubberwear Annual; Menstrual Times; Moony; Kansas City Breakdown; Lox; Moss; Wrongo; Gloria Mundi; Up Yours; The Greenpoint Guardian; Lacy Frillies; Oooff!; The National Flamethrower; Vomit; East St. Louis Toodle-oo; Bush League News; War Games Review; Queens in Blue; The Del Rio Patraña; Penis Parade; Owls Head Oracle; Hosiery Heaven; Alcibiades; The Belleville Blah; Google; Lesbology; Grasses, Legumes, and Forage Crops; Diesel Monthly; The Marching Goop; Medical Dick; O.L.B.E. Parish News; Wimpy; Girls in Garters; Filthy Joke Review; The Journal of Lyrical Abstraction; Senator Street Rag; Steel Teeth; Relevant Dentistry; Varlet; The Sade Newsletter; The Red Hook Independent; Texas League Times; Babes 'n' Boobs; Synthetic Box Weekly; Plumbing Crafts; Golden Hours; Mrzclwcz; White Blues; The Bronx Journal of Free Verse; Lewd Thoughts; The American Meatcutter; Deep Image Studies; Akimbo; Stet; Sm; Sneaker Lovelies; Infantry Frolix; Object*

Review; Jocks and Janes; Quim; Butter and Egg Monthly; Grope; Songg Festt; The Homosexual Host; Dears and Rears; The Analist; The Catholic Voyeur; Paedophilia Southwest; Sweet Cats; Terre Haute Skidoo; Hack Prose Review; Mu'fugga; Kips Bay Klaxon; The Radical Pharmacist; Gay Screen; Crud; Communist Humor; Screen Sluts; Adultery Today; The Sophomoric Joker; Nylon Nymphs; Avant-Garde Pottery; Ceramix Illustrated; Muff; Germ's Choice; Woogie; The Ornamental Sheet-Metal Worker; Glubit; Flikk; Ropes and Gags Monthly; Tin Ear; The Coney Island Head; The Lascivious Bride; Knickers and Knockers; Little Nothing; Fat Honeys; The New Fascist; Gay Day; The Imperialist Pig; Captain Lust; Addicts' Digest; New Female Chauvinist; Deshabille; The Georgia Gunlover; Fun Bars Guide; Third World Cuties; Corrupted Movements Monthly; South Brooklyn Savant; Frou-Frou Freeks; Hump!; Honky Babes; The Mediocre Teacher; Nu?; Weepers' Annual; Snooker News; The American Basket Lover; Italo-American Cafone; The Vermont Trotskyite; Knude Knights; Bleeding Jesus; The Ugly Tribade; Super-Realism Daily; Gibraniana; Yankee Toilet; Black Belles; Huh?; Stalinist Humor Gazette; Zim; Mixt Drinx News; The New York Review of Gluttony; New Simonist; The Review Review; The Hots; The Harlem Nocturne; New Mormon Lecher; Whore Views; Girdle Goddesses; The Maoist Busboy; Jelly Roll; Sumpn; The Zildjian Symbol; Delicombo; Foot In Mouth; Frilly Lacies; Fletch; Instar; Silly Ladies; Bra Monthly; Erotic Crossword Monthly; Hooker Lib; Lazy Fillies; Jungladventures; Misterioso; The Kitchen Kink; Deep Image Quarterly; Simp; The Liberated Pimp; Glamma Girlies; Gewgaw; The Kitchen Policeman; Cotton Boll Review; The Taos Saxophone; Sicilian Boffs; Bath Beach Cellar News; Neoneoneon; Zonk!; The Pipples; Chartreuse; Young Falange; Hog News; Smut 'n' Chaff; Gaga; Fub; Soviet Corn Monthly; Hip Dick; Seed; Jaysus; Whip Fun; Belle Bottoms; The Brooklyn Boogie; Breast Culture; Scaffatune; Li'l Bugger; Early American Crock Studies; Tit-O-Rama; Kapop; Inept Surgeons' Review; The Omaha Swingeroo; Twatz; Parcheesi Weekli; The Male Apostate; Poems From The Floating Mind; Best Huck Reviews; Hurry; Priests In Petticoats; Delicious Shame!; Boring Bridge; More Pricks Than Dicks; The Broken Dike; The Dumbasa Post; Ptui!; Greasy Spoon Guide; Hot Chili Extra; The Fargo Catamite; Frails in Furs; Organic Illness Weekly; The Manhattan Sink Installer; Snots and Tears; Woogie World; Rosy Blushes; The Anomic Extrovert; Bonnie Googol; Pig Slick; Hip and Thigh Gazette; Nuns in Nylons; Go Bare; Wanton Flyer; Mangomania; Kitsch 'n' Sink; Quaking Pumpkin.

Whatever one may make of such a list I don't know. Certainly Ned has no idea what it means. There doesn't seem to be any particular

35

uniformity to the materials, they leap from one subject to another, one "entertainment" to another, one discipline to another, in the most haphazard and bewildering way. In any event, it has been a long and rather boring task to sort this stuff out, particularly since I have done it all myself! Ned, although a reasonably pleasant and engaging companion, has done nothing whatsoever to assist me. I begin to suspect that he is indolent, unless, of course, his depression at being trapped in this absurd book is beginning to totally undermine his morale and *esprit*. I may be giving him the worst of it, but I think that he is careless, if not slipshod. I wonder if he is actually the wondrous fellow that he claims to be? Perhaps his past employment has been as undistinguished as mine.

Compiling this list then: Ned "helped" me by looking out the window at that damn lake. When he wasn't doing that, he sat on the floor and browsed through the materials I was trying to catalogue, occasionally laughing to himself, occasionally reading to me from one book or magazine or another.

One of the things he read to me struck me as being interesting enough to copy out in this journal: an interview/essay with the English author, Thomas Renfroux McCoy, that appeared in an issue of "Letters Lore" (the Sunday book supplement of *The Dumbasa Post*) of some years back. The interview was conducted by Richard Schiller, who is described as a man "with a special interest in modern novels and novelists." I feel that there is, somehow, something to be learned about Lamont from these comments by and about McCoy— something to be learned about *all* authors.

Note: I've let Beaumont in on my journal. Thank God, he is remarkably uncurious.

CHATS WITH THE REAL MCCOY
By Richard Schiller

Brussels, Belgium

"There is a complex *jeu d'esprit* of a novel in progress to be engaged under the usual enormous pressure," notes Thomas McCoy.

*

Rheum gathers in his weary eyes from the harsh sun and motor exhaust. He slowly, patiently wipes it away and smears it, with his curious, blunt, laborer's thumbs, onto his lavender ("Lavender? You'll find it's amethyst," he says gruffly.) sport shirt. He wipes and smears, wipes and smears, but the rheum continues to well up in the magical old eyes, his shirt is streaked.

McCoy sips his warm bourbon and ginger ale. Or Bronx. Or brandy and soda. Not Scotch. Why is he not drinking Scotch?

We are alone in the billiard room next to the bar at the Hotel Splendide. He and Hattie, his devoted wife, make their home at this splendid old baroque hotel, in the winter and summer, and in the fall and spring as well. "It is our adventure," he smiles. The Splendide is somewhat disconcertingly eerie, particularly in the off-season, when almost all the rooms seem to be occupied by nobody save the strange creatures of McCoy's celebrated imagination. In the vast dining room (which, McCoy remarks, "reminds one of those preposterous American gymnasiums where people indulge in, what is it called? baskets ball?"), on some bitter January evenings there are "three old rouged catamites and a doddering priestess of Lesbos," says McCoy.

But he adores (if one may say that McCoy "adores" anything) the attention and service. "When your eyes become rheumy and your body recalcitrant you get cranky about service," he says. McCoy is eighty this year. "The concierge is as creative and resourceful as a great *saucier*," he chuckles. "There are not many left who can read, let alone spell," he continues. "This exquisite *bijou* gets every message perfectly correct—a pleasure to read. R-e-a-d." McCoy himself loves to spell and often amuses himself after writing by doing so for hours. It is suggested that he will spell anything. "Not quite *anything*," he grins slyly.

When he travels, which is rare ("One stays at the Splendide because one does not like to be *too* far from France—but one does not actually wish to be *in* it!"), McCoy complains that the concierges often misspell messages, both from and to him. He cannot bear this because his compulsively nagging irritation with it puts him off his work.

An exception to this amateurism is the Melanzana in Rome. The service there is brilliant, as is the spelling. "They even manage to spell punctiliously in Spanish, that barbarous language," he remembers, the rheum clouding over his nostalgic gleam. Once McCoy thought he saw Rupert Whytte-Blorenge and Sheila Henry there, in the coffee shop. "I could have staked my life that it was Whytte-Blorenge and Miss Henry," he says. He seems hurt as he recalls that his wife told him no, it was not Rupert Whytte-Blorenge and Sheila Henry, merely people who looked like them. He saw them again, two days later, at the bar, drinking morning Bloody Marys, and was so disturbed that he went to the concierge. No, said the concierge, it was not Rupert Whytte-Blorenge and Sheila Henry—though these two *were* staying at the Melanzana. "Not together, the good man hastened to assure me," he twinkles.

Strange, strange indeed, he muses, his thumb in his eye.

Italy is an impossible country, he insists. He is always outraged by the wild, fruitless gesturing of the people and the continual noise. And the unbelievable food! Nobody can spell *anywhere* in Italy, he decides, except at the Hotel Melanzana. "Not even Dante—a ridiculously overrated author—could spell. I've been thinking of writing a letter about my researches into this to *The New York Review,* but one hesitates for fear of becoming embroiled in a literary feud with outraged Italians. That city is chockablock with greaseballs." He is wryly amused at his sally.

*

Q: How do you prepare each day to face the day?
A: I look at my bankbooks.

*

His wife has contracted a bad case of hives and is confined to her room. They had planned on a short trip to Kink, a seaside resort where, they have been assured, the sunsets are superb. Now they must put the trip off indefinitely. McCoy has suggested that it is the material of which the Splendide's sheets are made that has given Hattie her detestable hives, but admits that he is perplexed as to why it has never happened before. Perhaps it is a swift, subtle change in his wife's metabolism? Hattie disagrees and suspects the white wine of the area. They have been taking it with their meals of late. "Tragic and superbly fruity," says McCoy. "It could not harm an infant." He sticks to his metabolism theory grimly. The doctor is reassuring but vague and evasive. Meanwhile, McCoy grumbles. They are missing the Kink sunsets. "A rather good title, don't you think?" he barks suddenly from the depths of his rattan chair. McCoy has an unswerving devotion to rattan furniture, and it seems to fit him. *"Kink Sunsets.* Very . . . very New York. The literary clique would absolutely worship it, don't you see?"

*

Q: What literary complexities do you find most interesting? That is, what do you like most to "solve," so to speak, as a novelist?
A: One wishes to create characters who will speak directly to the minds of comparative literature professors and intelligent book reviewers.

*

Before Hattie's attack—which McCoy has magically and facetiously transformed into "Hattie's Horrible Hives"—the couple had gone to a new hotel at Asse, a small city noted for its scrupulous typists. Here, in this quiet place, he began his new novel, of which he has finished sixty pages.

He calls it *The Mounted.* "You might think of the title in relation to taxidermy," he says. "That sort of life in death—or death in life," he says. "One does not wish to convey anything of the sexual, you see. Sex is something for the cinema people."

*

Q: What do you feel have been your literary failings, if any? How would you defend these failings, if such there be?

A: My only literary "failing," as you so drolly put it, has been in my reticence to attack that greatest of literary frauds, James Joyce, or Shame's Voice, as I have somewhere justly called him. Have you ever read those letters of his? Good God! They are the letters of a man with a grocer's assistant's mind. They are concerned only with getting help, or love, or money. To defend this "failing" of mine, I would simply say that one has a responsibility to refrain from kicking at a mere drudge of the Muse.

*

The Mounted will not be quite as long as *Sublime Porter*, but, McCoy admits, it is "very difficult to write. One stares and stares at the lonely page, wishing that the connections could somehow make themselves. Fond folly!" he gently snorts. He presses on with it in his room, at the bar, in the solarium. The manuscript has on it spots of water, liquor, what not else? He is unruffled as he moves carefully through the typed pages, revising, correcting, adding notes to himself in the margin in the famed boyish scrawl. Most often he uses a Bic pen, but sometimes he uses a yellow Venus pencil, Number Two. In his room, he writes lying on the floor, so that he can nap instantly when the demands of his book become too great even for his canny old brain. "I used to write on the bed," he grins almost pleasantly, "but I found that there were—what shall I say?—sensual memories that intruded themselves upon me." He turns to Hattie and tenderly squeezes one of her hives.

*

Q: What would you say is your position in the world of letters?
A *(sings):* I'm CELL!-o-phane!

*

McCoy rises at 4:30, washes carefully in spring water shipped to him from the Alps, and begins to write. His revisions at such an hour are carefully made, and he will tune a sentence for hours in order to make it "tingle," as he puts it. Later, after lunch, he takes care of mistakes by throwing away the whole page. "I have, I suppose, lost many a short story that way," he grumbles. "But one is trapped within one's obsessions, *tant pis.*" As a young man, he wrote with a red-lacquered penholder and fine nib. Later, as he mellowed, he switched to a green penholder, then to an Eversharp fountain pen. Now he uses a Parker Jotter and makes his corrections with the Bic and the Venus. He must use black ink. "There is a purity to black,"

39

he explains. "Once, in Zurich, I could get nothing but blue ink and wrote a novel—I should say, the beginnings of a novel—that read exactly as if it had been written by Nabokov. Nabokov! Can you imagine that? It was quite disconcerting to me to discover the tropes and tricks of that old fraud set down there *in my own hand.* I wonder if he used blue ink," McCoy muses. "It's very very interesting."

*

Q: Then you do not approve of Nabokov?
A: Does one "approve" or "disapprove" of Zane Grey?

*

McCoy writes in notebooks all specially made for him by a firm in Budapest. The recto of each page is lined, the verso blank. On the right-hand page he does the actual composition; on the left jots reminders and messages to himself and exhortations to his characters to look alive. "Characters *must* look alive," he drawls, "or critics may confuse one's work with non-fiction."

He employs five notebooks. The first is for the rough draft; the second for the revise and rewrite of the first draft; the third for the second draft; the fourth for the revise and rewrite of the second draft; and the fifth for interpolations and addenda to the revisions of the first and second drafts. The final draft is typed from the fourth notebook onto green tissue ("in memory of Lorca," McCoy explains), revised and typed on blue tissue, revised again, and then typed on white bond, on which draft McCoy puts the finishing touches. This draft is then typed once again and is, in McCoy's words, "the *perfect* draft, like German beer." He chuckles at his small, exquisite joke. All the typing is done by Hattie, who will not trust anyone else to reproduce her husband's exact spelling.

The notebooks in which his first great success, *No Clue,* was written, were presented to the post library at Fort Hood, Texas. McCoy will not say why and it is unwise to press the point, as Hattie unfailingly warns visitors.

*

Q: What are the problems posed for you by the existence of other authors?
A: You are confusing me with someone else.

*

Many people insist that McCoy is richer when translated into almost any other language. He is understandably irritated by this and will not talk about it. "They know nothing of spelling," he mysteriously hints, then lapses into a silence broken only by the sound of Hattie's quiet scratching.

He cannot take seriously the rage for Soterroni's writing. An inferior "novelist," he maintains, spewing venom on the sacred word,

40

"a murderous wise guy." Yet he has ordered a copy of the latest Soterroni novel, *Fake Skrip.*

His wife has recently read the coterie novel, *At Swim-Two-Birds,* and assures him that he will find it faintly amusing, an afternoon's entertainment. But McCoy will not read it, noting that the book was praised by Shame's Voice. Dismissing it, he says "It must be a trick." Later, Hattie informs me that McCoy privately calls it a *thick* trick.

*

Q: What is your favorite book? I mean, what book do you turn to, or reread most often, for your personal pleasure?

A: *A Big Eye* by Sue Dot. It is a triumph of magic.

*

He has been invited to lecture at San Francisco State College in the fall for, he admits, "a grotesquely inflated fee." Can they spell in San Francisco? he wonders. Hattie half-smiles and says that he may leave his heart there and he stares at her blankly.

*

Q: Over the years you have waged relentless disdain for the writings of Andrew Mackenzie. Would you care to comment on this?

A: There is nothing to comment on. Mackenzie's work is mere slush. Mince pies!

*

When news came last year that Biaggio Flynn had won the prestigious Prix Ivrogne, McCoy was of two minds concerning the award. He has scorned prizes for years, yet was piqued that he had not been chosen. "A bauble, a bibelot," he calls the prize. "Yet one would like to have the opportunity to deprive Flynn of *everything.*" His eyes glower through the slowly gathering rheum.

*

Q: What do you think of death?

A: I think it is a distinguished thing. I have termed death, as a matter of fact, "the man in the bright nightgown." The image amuses and somehow comforts me.

*

Have you heard that Meg Barn has finally "come out" and declared her Lesbianism? he queries. He thinks this a huge joke. As if dear Meg could even know what a Lesbian is, he continues. "She thinks it has something to do with the sex act," Hattie adds softly and sympathetically. Silly, silly Meg, McCoy goes on. Something in the American air that drives one to these puerile admissions, he says.

McCoy is gentle in his criticism of Meg Barn, and is perfectly candid in admitting to the influence of her masterpiece, *Years of Grease,* on his own flashing and elliptical style. As for the erotic symbolism that recent critics have found in this seminal novel,

41

McCoy is silent. When pressed, he will say only, "a pride of trace in the mind."

*

Q: Do you have a favorite story that you like to tell?

A: I do indeed. Although I would not go so far as to say it is my favorite story, it is one that warms me when I think of it. Some summers ago we were invited to the Cape cottage of one of America's foremost men of letters, a man who is often dubbed the Prometheus of American criticism, although he is more the Epimetheus. It is not my intention to reveal his name, though you surely will have guessed it. I disagree with this man in almost every particular of his literary enthusiasms, although I must confess that he was instrumental in bringing my *Sublime Porter* to the attention of the intelligent reading public. I am grateful to him, despite the fact that he is a pompous ass.

In any event, my host was, during that summer, engaged in taking notes on a book that he wanted to write—something about left-wing populism in the United States during the Roosevelt administration. A beastly boring task, at any rate. The book has since been published, by the way, and it is dismal stuff. I suggested to him that there was no way that he could truly complete his research unless he consulted a volume on this subject that I knew to be available only in the Boston Public Library. My friend, highly excited, as are all pedants when an obscure tome is mentioned, left the next morning for Boston. When he returned, the following day, he asked me, quite forcibly, to leave his house, that he could countenance our friendship no longer.

You see, when he reached the library, and finally, with, I like to think, trembling fingers, opened the book, a note fell out. "Hello! *My* name is Mud! Sorry you've wasted your time." It was, of course, *my* note. It was a simple joke, intended to puncture the balloon of this man's ridiculous pretensions to scholarship. Do you not think it droll? I must say, I was quite put out by his reaction to it all. Quite lacking in nicer judgment, I would say.

*

Q: I would call it a marvelous *blague.*

A: Quite. Rather excruciatingly French, I would say. Much too subtle for the American sense of humor, or what laughingly passes for it.

*

McCoy enjoys attack rather than praise when he deigns to write critically of his fellow authors, although he admits that he would love to write a laudatory piece on the work of Jem Casey. "There are things in Casey's work that make for what one might, with justice, call *permanence,"* says McCoy. "His work will live."

He is not particularly interested in Vladimir Papilion. "Flash. Flash and fustian." He is adamant about this. "I cannot see why my own work has ever been compared to his," he sniffs. McCoy is unhappy and vexed about it, and Mrs. McCoy, with a swift birdlike glance (it suddenly occurs to me that she is quite like a small, nervous bird), warns me away from the subject.

He rather cares for Wagram, but feels that he made a grave error in his last novel by making the Irish setter the narrator of the tale. "It's all been done, and done so much more—elegantly." He rises, serene in the knowledge that it was he who did it, in the remarkable *Bunny Lewis.* Neither Hattie nor I are so gauche as to speak, but we know that the old wizard is aware that we know.

McCoy heaves himself out of his rattan chair and looks out over the balcony of his suite at Brussels, somehow magnificently comatose— uncannily like the cities in his own novels—below. He likes this polished old hotel, he likes this city. ("One does not like to be *too* far from France," after all.) A comfortable old lion, enjoying his powers.

*

Q: What do you think we can do about fixing, or at least pursuing, the elusive mercury of truth?

A: Learn to spell. S-p-e-l-l.

*

The strangely blunt, no-nonsense thumbs are at the eyes again. He explains that the rheum seems to intensify at the beginning of each new work. "As if God is giving me a kind of subtle warning to desist," he says. He does not smile.

*

Q: When is a man not a man?

A: When he is a sham.

I'm tired now. I've written enough for today. Ned, of course, is sleeping already, after having grumbled for a half-hour that Lamont could have at least given us a bedroom in this house. Well, perhaps he will.

I will set down here that I must remind myself to reread and ponder this McCoy interview. Can McCoy be anything at all like Lamont? I am particularly intrigued by his remark that "characters *must* look alive." Then why, if this is so, has Lamont made *us* out to be such imbeciles?

My dear Roche:

You have certainly taken me by surprise with your request for a *curriculum vitae*. To want such information for a descriptive brochure must mean (I certainly hope so!) that your course on the experimental novel is beginning to take shape. I am replying to your kind letter immediately, so that you will have the information before the holidays are upon us all, with their troublesome gifts, friends, relatives, and what not. I must be showing my age. I take it that you will be getting under way with the brochure immediately following the New Year.

Since I last wrote you I am ashamed to say that I have got no further with my novel. As a matter of fact, I am thinking of doing Chapter One all over again: it still does not have that exact "feel" I am searching for. But then again, I may forge ahead with Chapter Three and return to Chapter One for another go later. I'll have to see how things turn out.

My poor "life" follows. I hope that the narrative format does not put you off—I hate setting my life out in a codified "schema"—it always reminds me of a job résumé. On second thought, it might not be a bad idea to compose such. You wouldn't have any openings in your English Department for a slightly frayed, slightly weary, experimental novelist, would you? I'm joking, to be sure.

I was born in Gray Star, Washington, in 1925. It was a poor town, dependent upon the sugar-beet crop for its well-being and prosperity. My mother was a devoted churchgoer, intimately involved with the local church's choir, its Strawberry Festival, its Thanksgiving "Poor Basket" gala, and all the rest. My father, an almost illiterate farmer, patiently suffered my mother's desire for a social, outgoing life, although he himself had little to do with the village. I always see him sitting under an old chestnut tree before supper, his cracked leather cap on his knee, and in his mouth one of his beloved corncob pipes. I suppose I got from my father whatever perseverance I have exhibited in my life, and from my mother my love of books and music. My mother read to me from the Bible, *Treasure Island, Pilgrims Progress, Growing Up Straight and Sound, Scales and Feathers, Modern Business English,* and other books in our little library.

My schooling was haphazard, for, like most farm boys of the area, I was regularly taken out of school by my father at planting and harvest time. To this day, long division and fractions are beyond my powers, and I have only the haziest idea of geography: for instance, I only recently discovered that Bolivia is not part of Eastern Europe. When I was eight years old, I began to write ridiculously long and fantastic stories, the plots of which had to do with otherworldly creatures who came to our poor area to enrich the good and punish the evil. My father thought these stories impious, and even my mother was alarmed. They forbade me paper except for schoolwork, but somehow, by careful conservation, I managed to save enough paper to continue my compositions. In 1942, when I was about fifteen, I won a prize for an essay I wrote in school competition, "What I Can Do To Help The War Effort." As I recall, it had mainly to do with the importance of saving bacon grease. Shortly after, lying about my age, I joined the Army.

My military career was spent in downtown St. Louis, where I was attached to an anti-aircraft battery, whose guns were set up on towers in one of the city parks. It was in this city that I met my (now divorced) wife, a bright, vivacious girl who played the clarinet and trumpet, sketched, painted, took ballet lessons, and wrote poetry. We were married before the war was over and lived in a small, furnished apartment until the war ended. We then journeyed to Taos (I had been reading Lawrence), where I made my first tentative attempts at writing fiction. I remember that our windows looked out on the Sangre de Cristo mountains, and to see those snow-capped peaks turn blood red in the evening sun is an image that still enchants and haunts me, and that has found its way into two of my novels.

There really isn't much more to say. I published in many of the ephemeral "little magazines" of the day, along with such writers as Heather Strange, Harry Polenta, G.R. (as he was then known) Soterroni, John LeKing, Horace Rosette (at that time a playwright), Elman Beshary, John Furriskey, and others. My wife and I separated, and later obtained a divorce, and I came to New York, where I still live. My books you of course know.

Physically, I have what is unkindly called a bullet head; I am wall-eyed and snub-nosed. I suffer from indigestion, and have a bad habit of sucking my teeth when nervous or bored; I also habitually finger my tie knot. I favor two-button, single-breasted brown suits, wear a heavy woolen undershirt in the winter, and a light, sleeveless one of cotton in the summer. I prefer linen shirts. The palms of my hands and the soles of my feet are calloused, a reminder of the days when I did manual labor to support myself while writing my early work. I love the daisy (which I prefer to call the day's eye), and know nothing whatsoever of other flowers and shrubs.

As to colors, orange and yellow are my favorites, and I abhor blue and green. I like to watch baseball and play chess and, I confess, Monopoly, at which I always go bankrupt almost immediately, no doubt a symbol for my precarious life. My penchant for "the grape" has determined my hobby, mixing cocktails, although I suppose that I could say that reading McCoy is another. I am not particular about food, although I love to read recipes. They rest me with their supreme inanity. However, I despise kohlrabi and the sickeningly fruity wines of Belgium. (I might add that I also despise the sickeningly winy fruits of *all* countries, particularly Canada. There is something about a Canadian fruit that makes me think of that sort of academic verse in which the poet finds something of the "Truth of Life" in a flower—or a mussel.)

My mother and father being dead for some years, I am closest to my sister, Sheila, who is soon to be married to the popular novelist, Dermot Trellis. She has been wonderfully kind to my writing, and probably knows more about it than anyone else on earth. She is presently doing a (long overdue!) book on Nabokov.

My favorite painter is the Picasso of *Blue Proles.* My favorite author is the wit, John Phoenix, whose epistolary novel, *George Horatio Derby,* has been a constant delight. I also have a warm spot in my heart for the beautiful and moving *No Award* by Abel McLaughlin. I have little ear for music, and, I shamefully confess, can listen to almost anything, and often do, including bad advice.

Although I have never won a literary prize or award, I have been twice nominated for the Audrey Wurdemann Medal for "the poetic quality inherent in [my] fiction."

As far as noting "what my work and my life as a writer mean"— how shall I speak of that? As I compose, I think sometimes of the lovely and yet terrifying phenomena of all the world: immense waterfalls falling, gigantic gales from the four corners of the earth carrying in their gritty teeth chunks of rough-hewn farmers' tables and beloved credenzas, dust and excreta from Iowa barns, the sweet simplicity of the voices of both Cohens and Kellys, laughter from gay, come-what-may places, girls with braces (glistening with their tears) on youthful teeth . . . how to speak of these things? How to speak of what the tiny, yet handsome vase from Java, the dew-touched day's eye trembling in it, means to me? Of a half-frozen sparrow, beak worrying a Carnation condensed-milk-can wrapper? Of the masculine rhythms of Dostoevski's anger and comedy and compassion? Of the memory of the memory of first love? How . . . ? How can one explain what it means to think continually of those who were truly great? Of the rough expertise of the air-conditioner repairman? Of American cities, wrapped in local mystery—Natchez and Mobile, Memphis and St. Joe: raw towns that we believe and die in? Of The Last Supper and the wine on the table on that evening of mystery? How is it possible to articulate the surging emotions felt watching children in the playground, running, playing, gleeful on their divine seesaws? The images crowd together, mix with the emotions, judgment is suspended, one is drunk as one is drunk on wine, and laughter. One writes ceaselessly, one writes—*everything*. The notebooks fill, the black ink of the recording pen sets down the rhythms of life itself, rich nuggets of symbol, image, both clear and mysterious, deep, lie buried, waiting for the moment when they will be rescued from their temporary home. Meaning is held in an almost unbearable tension on the dizzying edge of the meaningless, and there! There lies the quicksilvery truth that makes one's life as a writer meaningful and endlessly rich. The wearisome hours of staring at the white paper, the lonely white paper, the clock ticking inexorably on—all of it is worth it as the haunting image of the emotion is wrenched free from the mulchy notebooks and transformed into sheerest beauty! But how does one explain . . . ? To recast one's chaotic life as purest art—that is the program. That is what my life and work "mean." One would like to achieve full expression of one's inchoate and sinewy self. In one's self, in the dark shed of the untameable mind, lies the truth, waiting to be released into the line, the sentence, the story or novel. I strive for it continually.

I hope that will do for you, my dear Roche. Please let me know if you wish to cut any of it, or, conversely, if you would like me to expand on any of it. Since you gave me no idea of the length of my entry in your brochure, I had no idea of when to stop. I do hope I have answered the last question satisfactorily. It is difficult, as you know, I'm sure, to set out one's ideas of one's life without getting into a dry didacticism. I chose a loose, expressionist statement—which I hope will suit your purposes.

Please let me know what you think. I am going to have a bite of lunch now and then get on with GR. My two heroes will then have *their* lunch, in what I hope will be a pivotal chapter in terms of their relationship with each other. I have what I must use in my "mulchy notebooks" already. Now to put it together!

My best wishes,
Antony Lamont

3. PAINFUL DIGESTS

*"Vol-au-vent de ris d'agneau aux truffes et champig-
nons?"—Napoleon Lajoie*

In my desire to place clearly before you the state of my mind upon
entering the restaurant with my colleague, I have neglected to mention the name of this establishment. It was, of course, the legendary
Rocher de Cancale, probably the finest restaurant in the city, and one
of the finest in the entire civilized world. It is gone now, its place
taken by a small, fast-food-delicacy café, The Surprise, a bistro fre-
quented by the "new breed" in publishing circles, where, at any
table, one may see young editors and their writers engaged in that
relaxed "shop talk" that makes the publishing business so endlessly
fascinating. The Surprise, incidentally, serves a specialty dish of kid
and garlic that is said to calm, to tranquilize, to empty the mind. It
is highly appreciated by its clientele. Although I think I understand
this "spot's" popularity, it is *not,* most assuredly, the "Canc."
But let me assure the reader, if this hymn of black despair *has*
any readers, that I am not at all interested in *haute cuisine.* I am
what Jason Fatz, the "smiling genie," calls, not without some
small sardonic amusement, a meat-and-potatoes man. Neither
Gargantua nor Manimustes am I, nor Heraclodian of the gorged-
dove pasty. But Ned Beaumont had (the tense, even now, gives
me terrifying pause!) the true gourmet palate, and it was in order
to please him that I suggested that we lunch at the storied
"Roche," now gone where all marvels go, alas! Or, as it has been
phrased: Whither? Oblivion!
Let me confess that, my mind being made up that I would force
the issue concerning the relationship between the two young ladies
and my partner, I had decided that the latter should be in the best
possible mood in order that he might receive my delicate objections
to his conduct with, shall I say, patience and good will? Therefore,
the "Canc"! His indelicate remark to me on the sidewalk had, however, struck me with bricklike force, and it was with some misgivings
that I led the way through the oaken doors of the restaurant, Ned
Beaumont's mischievous smile leading, I am afraid, him. If, indeed,
I am to be accused of "buttering" him up, it must be clear that such
an act was necessary, even unavoidable, if we were to converse on
any level other than the most superficial.
A hard row to hoe was to be my lot. We, as I have hinted, entered.

The Rocher de Cancale was recognized as being first among the supreme few when it was part of the old Hotel Splendide, that is, that Splendide that enjoyed so many years of fame as the only hostelry of excellence within the Arctic circle. There are some who go so far as to say that when M. Allumette, the original proprietor, decided to bring his establishment to the city, the old hotel immediately lost some of its accustomed luster. Be that as it may, the "Canc" retained all the grace and charm of the old ice-coated Splendide at its best, stark on the sub-zero polar cap, the breathtaking beauty of the Northern Lights feverishly vying with its own million-lamped effulgence. One did not *eat* at the "Roche"; one invariably *dined* there, no matter the simplicity of the meal. Even the tumblers of water were endowed with a dazzling bravura, a certain cheeky chic! I, normally unimpressed by all this, was, here, impressed. Ned Beaumont of course fell into a kind of ecstasy, ah, beaming, shining, unashamedly sensual. Everything—the silver, the glassware, the china and napery, the lighting and furniture, the service—everything took one back to the splendors of the charmed hotel as it was before the War. To dine here was to expect to see Whytte-Blorenge, a coarse jest on his lips, or T.R. McCoy, forever lost in his wry imagination; one looked to glimpse at any moment Bart Kahane, or the "baseball bard," Leo Kaufman. The magic of the room did not preclude the possibility of greeting even the trombone virtuoso, Thomas Azzerini, or even the mysterious publisher, "Flebseau"! In the midst of these musings, we were seated. I felt that it would not do to broach the subject of the ladies too quickly, so we began, in wayward fashion, to discuss the Brophy manuscript—pitiful mask! It is not too much to say that we fidgeted with our silver, its soft chiming punctuating, our diffident conversation. The memory of that tiny bell-like sound is almost unbearable to me now, as I sit here, the mad wind clawing at the windows of this cabin of Death!

It must stand as a testament to the mind's ability to heal that I am unable to recall what we had for lunch. All I remember is that midway through the entrée, I made some remark concerning the marvelously, if rather vulgarly well-endowed figures of both Miss Corriendo and Mme Delamode; since they appeared, often, on stage, clad in black tights and black net stockings, this observation was not, I must insist, an odd one. Ned Beaumont flashed me a look of mingled suspicion and pleasure, excitedly squeezing a small bun as he did so.

"Hô, hô!" he laughed. There was something unimaginably *evil,* something . . . *trapped* in that laugh, and I tried to conceal my shudder. Ned Beaumont looked at me evenly, his eyes narrowed, as if seeing me for the first time.

"I don't mean to be disrespectful, or crude," I said, rather lamely, to his chorus of chuckles, gasps, and gentle snorts, that faded like a busted mousse.

"Farce pour mousse de poissons . . . de *poissons,*" he pursued amiably. "Barbue aux huîtres, non? Há, há, há!" He seemed genuinely *pleased!*

"Perhaps," I countered, "but to be so profligate of one's flesh . . . beautiful, yes, but women, one thinks of *other* women, charming, delightful women with whom one may share a quiet *apéritif* . . . while they may be equally as provocative in their flesh, I mean, as delightful. . . ." I was floundering badly, things had begun cataclysmically! Ned Beaumont riveted me with his glance, and barked:

"Sagou! Sagou pèse-sirop!" His eyes blazed with anger and I was suddenly aware that my hand was lost, hopelessly lost, in the basket of breads. I might even go so far as to say that I was vulgarly "paddling" in the basket as one might "paddle" in macaroni.

"No need to be angry, old man," I minced softly. "They are remarkably attractive *and* refined young women."

"Hè, hè, hè," he finally brought out, visibly, thank God, less tense.

"My only point in all this is to talk to you, *friend to friend,* about the nature of your friendship with the young women. It is clear that you have become more, what shall I say?—insouciant? since you have met them."

"Laitues en chiffonade, Martin," he assured. "Oui, laitues en chiffonade ficaire limande-sole flan aux cerises." He looked past me, his eyes soft as custard, remembering God knows what. "Tarte de demoiselles Tatin."

Tatin! I thought, with a shudder of malaise, then protested, "Perhaps the brevity of the costumes has *something* to do with it?" It was a long chance and I kept my voice as casual as I could, buttering a piece of the sinister bread, not daring to look into Ned Beaumont's eyes. It is dangerous to trifle with a man's erotic eccentricities.

"Ahá! Ahá, há, há! Mais oui, Martin, oui. Tourte froide d'anguille . . . Rabelais? Jambon persillé, oh là!" He gaped like a pheasant.

"So I thought," I acquiesced. "Believe me, I am not unaware of their charms." I did my best to leer appreciatively, while my heart twisted in me like a boiling lobster.

The wine that Ned Beaumont had consumed had inflamed him and this conversation about the two hussies has not cooled his ardor but had, rather, inflamed him, further! He was flushed and smiling, enjoying, I thought, his sense of proprietorship of them, or what he naively *thought of* as proprietorship. The shoe, however, was on the other foot, or, more exactly, the other feet. I noticed that one of his hands had disappeared beneath the table. He smiled at me dreamily, and breathing rather rapidly, mumbled:

50

"Cabillaud . . . frit . . . pané . . . pané . . . oooohhh coquilles . . . à
. . . à . . . la bigarade . . . oooeufff!"

The waiters were trying their best not to stare at Ned Beaumont's
wacky and distorted visage. I despairingly poured more wine into his
glass. It was at this moment that I knew how far my old friend had
gone in his wild obsession. Daisy Buchanan's innate "purity" seemed
utterly powerless to affect this debauched figure whose shameful
writhings socked me speechless and embarrassed.

"Cabillaud," he groaned again, then hissed a final "ocuff!" and it
was at this moment that his crisis, *seemed* to pass. His "face" beet-red,
his eyes starting slowly from their sockets, his visible hand lying
limply on the table like a fallen artichoke, it seemed to me that I had
never seen a man so utterly possessed. Slowly the blood drained from
his face and he returned to a "kind" of normalcy. It was clear to me
now that those two trollops had exercised the most malicious powers
on the brain of my friend, turning him into a bit of flotsam, a chip
of wood, an orange peel, on the raging currents of middle-aged lust.
The image of the horrific currents, carrying him to certain destruction, brought to mind the picture of my mother's demise, of which
more anon, and her tender memory strengthened my resolve to help
my friend free himself from this malefic tyranny. Had I known then
to what an end it would all come, I would have left him to his fate;
at least he might have been still *alive!*

"Drink a little wine, Ned Beaumont," I urged as gently as I could.

"Noix sous-noix," he whispered, not daring to look at me, his glance
instead falling on his foo ruby slacks. "Crashing" on them would be
a more exact description, although it gives me great pain to say it.
When a successful man's eyes crash on his slacks. . . . It isn't pretty.
I silently handed him a napkin for his perspiring and such face, now
the delicate shade of that rose legend holds subtly blooms in San
Antone. It wasn't the moment to upbraid him, and I held my tongue
until I was sure that my urge toward harsh criticism was under
control; only then, I spoke.

"All right, Ned Beaumont, all right. I *understand*. But now, you
must get hold of yourself and tell me all there is to tell . . . the whys,
the wherefores, the whole, incredible, no doubt sordid, story. What
have they done to you? What? Is there any way of wrenching yourself
free from their unhealthy influence? You *must* confess to me—everything. Slowly at first if you prefer, but—*everything!*"

The reader will see that I plunged, holding nothing back, no longer
the discreet friend I had determined to be since this sordid affair first
became obvious. I was striding, with the boldest step, through the
dim and musty locker room that Ned Beaumont's life had become.
Grit blew, as it were, into my eyes, grit from the torn playing fields

51

of his psyche, from the splintered grandstand of his id, from the chickenhouses and cattle barns of his raging albeit still poetic libido. I "walked" on, unafraid. How I wish now that I had shown more circumspection! I was about to open a can of botulistic beans!

His eyes were pleading with mine, almost as if one could hear them speak, whisper, "I plead with you, Martin. I plead." But I was adamant.

"Martin, Martin . . . pêches rafraîchies aux framboises." He made a strange sound low in his throat, a tiny bell-like sound that, to this day, chills me, to the bone, to think of it. It was the sound of a soul doomed to torment, such a sound as Lavaliére must have made when confronted, at last, by Joseph Metternich's hired assassins.

"Dindonneau farcis," he begged, "farcis béchamel porte-conteau, turbotière, topinambours à l'anglaise." He was helpless as a child, a shaking gelatin, a blancmange!

"No need to bring the blasted English into it, old friend," I piped, laboring to be light and trying my best to mask the concern that percolated within me.

Suddenly—*"Zut alors!"*—a voice thundered, and the hardly credible bulk of Ugo Lambui, the maître d', loomed anent our table. On his usually genial face played, in ripples, compassion. He had "sensed" something wrong at our table, and true to "the Code of the 'Canc,' " had approached us in order to see if there could possibly be any service he might render us. Long a fixture at the "Canc," Ugo was world-renowned for the expertise he brought to his demanding tasks, and for his remarkably refreshing manner of speaking. His ordinary conversation was a fascinating synthesis of all Europe, all, one might say, the world.

"Zut alors!" he boomed again, a quieter boom this time, something like a mortar round hitting a mess hall. "I hear with my right and my left ear strange mouth noises, expressions of chaotic import I gather in with the eyes from this table, from your esteemed clutch of *due.* Therefore, I reckon it ain't out o' my line to ply you with verve and cheer, gent'mans! Is it the *vin* that does not entrance the palates with sparkling zip? Hath the salt lost its savor? Is, perhaps, a lively *cucaracha* disporting his loathsome frame upon the greens? Speak to me, *monsieurs,* or *sacré bleus* and puissant *carambas* must rend my spirit."

Ugo's lighthearted speech touched me, touched also Ned, who had, amazingly, composed himself with great haste, and sat, smiling up into that great bear of a face.

"So," Ugo went on, "is it an earthquake? Is it only a smock? Gentle bodies such as your own, men on the roof, the very *penthouse* of that building some label Success, but others, wiser still, call Honest Work

Well Done, should off the winter garment of repentance fling. Your meals should be ennoblated! Arhythmic gestures, expressions of *misericordia* are, for the digestion, how does one say?—effluvious and sorely lacking in vim. Take me to heart."

Kindly bulk, I thought, viciously wiping the tears from my eyes. But what were *Ned's* thoughts? Indeed. He was appraising Ugo as if he had never seen him before, and the expression on his face was not a kind one. Then, chillingly, he uttered, "Glacé à la Romaine." That was all and enough, perhaps too much. Ugo colored, blanched, then colored again and blenched.

"Of course, Monsieur Beaumont," he returned, discomfited. "One discovers one's place and joyously enters onto it. Yassuh! Yowzah! Indeedy, respected chums!" And he was gone, standing against the wall across from our unhappy table, for all the world as if we were nothing more than a couple of sweaty Jewish persons in off the street.

And what *of* this room against whose wall Ugo now stood, what *of* this restaurant, this legendary space, this beloved "Roche"? What can one do more than to quote its famous, and fading, inscription, writ in golden, now flaking letters above the hearth that glows with a hearty warmth of almost Hawthornesque flame all during the wintry months? VENITE AD ME: VOS QUI STOMACHO LABORATIS ET EGO RESTAURATO VOS. Surely a subtle, a gentle command to all men of good will who feel that the stomach's care is central to an understanding of the self. Was it not Pindar who said "ariston men hydor"?—a phrase which Ugo has succinctly rendered as "men need more than water." Was it not the subtle Count Metz, considered by many to be the creator of Tapioca Supreme, who enigmatically remarked to Louis IV, "Had God not meant the stomach to be secretly served He would have placed it on the face"? And Lester Joël, in his definitive work on baking, *The Beautiful Bun*, has said, "A man eats what a man *has* to eat," bringing, it seems to me, the entire discussion of the artistry of cuisine to a perfect if arbitrary close. Thus the "Canc"!

The "Canc" gave all its attention to those fortunate and sophisticated enough to recognize, that there is more to ingestion than craft, there is high Art. Notwithstanding the virulent and pandemic virus of "democracy" that has infected, it seems, the entire world, the restaurant catered to those who, so to speak, know the difference between a coaster and a caster, to those few who understand, to speak more obscurely, that there is an enormous difference in *style* between "parcheesi" and "pachisi." Again, so to speak. It is not the clod who draws funny ketchup faces on his children's fried eggs who appreciated the aura, the *holiness* of this shrine. As Ugo would put it, "Allow them to pilot their tinny Chryslers through the corridors

53

of divers hicksvilles, all, all in the second basement as it were, as they are!"

But what of this room? I have asked. Was there anything in the rather ordinary, albeit immaculate napery that suggested that one may have partaken, here, in this peaceful oasis, of the very finest bottle of Château-Beychevelle in the world? I doubt it. What of the murmuring waiters, forks in breast pockets, *cordes sanitaires* mutely pendulous from trouser flys (the latter one of the many uniquely minuscule touches that distinguish the restaurant)? Further, how was one to judge the influence of the then current proprietor, Duval Royale, on the *ambiance,* the *quidditas,* if I may so put it, of this room that hid so shyly among the fabled canyons of steel, an avatar of the days, long gone, of lustrous silk hats and lace-whispering corsets? It is certainly a form of sorcery—thus rán my lengthy and not unpleasant ramble. . . .

But my reverie must be interrupted, as Ned Beaumont, who, just a moment before, had seemed frostily composed, was now frostily quaking with a kind of ague that seemed to embody what I had come to think of as "Guilt." His conduct, which I had discreetly questioned, with those two Amazons of the stage, had intruded itself into his— may I call it?—conscience, that is, the memory of his conduct (certainly *not* so very discreet, I am sure) *had* done so. The physical reaction was swift and disquieting. Perhaps he was ready to confide in me. Perhaps.

I stretched my arm across the table, subtly grazing the bottles, glasses, and dishes arrayed there, as was my habit, like so many harsh and unspoken reprimands, stretching, along with it, my hand, the hand that Nature had so firmly fixed to the end of it. With this hand, I seized—oh, I will not go so far as to say "seized"; *clutched,* perhaps, grasped, no, not so much grasped, *clutched,* would more precisely describe the action of this hand—I, then, *clutched* Ned Beaumont's listlessly placed one, squeezing it with all the reassurance and friendship that my spirit could force down into the digits. As if at a signal, his hand trembled, trembled and came alive! turning then, quite slowly and marvelously on its back, so that his palm, of needs faced, mine. It had the uncanny countenance of an old scallopini. Some godlike force seemed to lift both our hands off the table, so smoothly that I could not tell if I had initiated this action or not. Solemnly, we shook these hands, our eyes deftly searching each other's for meaning. We continued our shake. I felt as if some great weight had been lifted from my heart.

"Martin," he urged. "Martin. . . ." yet he could not go on, his teeth were literally chattering like a pot of boiling soup bones with his need to tell me *all*. A wave of fear and apprehension swept its darkness over my now-light heart. But I pressed on.

"Speak English, Ned Beaumont," I reassured, "let the story come forth . . . trust me."

As a dog, when one's strong hands release themselves, through the intercession of whatever idea or vagary, from his muzzle, so that he finds himself free, begins by first opening wide his jaws, then emitting a whine or yelp of gratitude at his delight, before he decides to chew one's arm off, so did Ned Beaumont. And emotion issued; a surfeit of it.

"Letters . . . letters," he intoned, whiningly. "Make you . . . understand . . . some . . . of it. Home . . . come home . . . see letters." I signaled Ugo for the check, he arriving at the table with his accustomed celerity.

"The esteemed *caballero* M'sieu Beaumont has encaptured again, one can glaum, some of his old quilibrium, no? *Bon! Bon!*" His homely face creased into the warmest smile, I saw. Though racked clearly with pain and shame, even the subject of this observation seemed moved. A perfect, single, crystal tear formed, for an instant, at the corner of his eye, and then was—gone! How compelling life is!

Somehow, we got out onto the busy streets. The hum of life went on as if nothing had happened in the time we had been out of it. We were in a cab then, heading for Ned Beaumont's apartment, and God only knew what terrible secrets.

The sun shone on as if the world were good. The sky was, of course, the most innocent, the most impossibly innocent blue.

Dear Sheila,

Thanks for your note giving me the date of your forthcoming marriage to Dermot. It will be a good way to welcome in the new year, blessed be it! And, before I forget, my head nowadays being in the usual muddle when I am *enceinte* with a new book, let me wish both of you the very best of holidays. I hope that you have a wonderful and festive time. I always remember with great fondness those gay piñatas that you favor at this season. May they be filled with your favorite things. For myself, I'm afraid that it will be work as usual, although I have been invited to a Christmas party by one of my old flames—she is now a schoolteacher—Luba Checks. Perhaps you remember her from the last time you visited? As I remember we had a marvelous time (Famoso's, Umbrielli's, Brigid Brewster's—I don't know *where* else we went!) over a four-day weekend. In any event, Luba has sent me a card asking me to come to an afternoon-evening party on Christmas Day and I think I just might take her up on it: the change will do me good. Outside of this brief diversion, I have nothing else lined up for the holidays, and very little news. Somehow the holidays always put me in mind of a curious scene in a novel of some years ago—I forget the author—called *Quantities of Imagistic Things.* One of the characters receives a box of the most fantastic stuff from home; each item (there is a long list of them given) conjures up the most hopeless, yet agonizingly sweet memories of a simple and dead America. Have you read the book? It's probably out of print, I picked up my (now "borrowed") copy for 49¢ at a remainder sale.

Speaking of books, my own is coming along, but to be perfectly candid, not at all to my satisfaction. I sometimes feel like scrapping what I've already done and starting all over. God knows, there isn't that much of it to scrap. The trouble is that if I scrapped what I already have I honestly don't know if I could begin again anyway. I've never felt so in the dark about a book, nor so unsure of myself. The other day I wondered—I mean *seriously* wondered—if all this trouble is worth it anyway. All my years of work and—let's face it! —I've produced nothing first rate, nothing, nothing at all! Oh, there are flashes of good writing in, I suppose, all my novels, but truly, I have an aversion for the bulk of my stuff. Sad confession. Apropos of flashes, let me bore you with a page from *Three Deuces* that you might remember. It's something I can still read with pleasure.

Somewhere: say Indiana: the sinister and dragonlike clouds. An almost impenetrable darkness at the top of the very firmament, a cruel heaven lay there perhaps, crueler than any hell. Yet seemingly light, light, against the incredible darkness that fingers them or which they

56

finger: malign. Such darkness, too, fingers the exhausted and invisible landscape, corn. Before them, behind them, alien corn, indeed, they seem, eerily, to create, it, as they pass, endlessly, so it almost seems, through it. Dead, dried stalks, keening subtly in the creaking wind, the macabre clouds falling to the enervation of earth in crepuscular streamers from the indigo vault. Are they the fingers of God, a blind God, or of some crazed Satan? Of some intransigent, unearthly, yet intelligent power that holds them all in thrall? Human beings, corrupted and weak in their corrupted and weak flesh, are not meant to pass, through, this queer darkness into the saving light of, the golden West. Are they, then, to be seen, bars, of some impenetrable prison, supernatural, from which no one is ever paroled? These vapory clouds—are they fingers, dripping black blood? Dead cornfields, forbidding; sky.

And the towns, cruelly clear as paintings by a light-deranged realist. The houses, the storefronts unfriendly, barred. Anonymity of truest evil, there is no life, behind them. There is no life, on the deserted streets, they lie, exhausted, in the hateful glare of sodium that stuns them: harshest relief! Around them, the town: fields of sere corn beyond to eternity. Past the light, blinding, through which the car crawls, the clouds, the fingers, are barely visible. And now a duck, or goose, blinded, lone, lost, migratory grieving duck, or goose, waddles in the vacant street, his green neck glisters iridescently in the dazzle, shimmering against the patriotic blazon of the barber pole, likewise ashimmer: for what event of glory? The scene is fixed as in a bitter mordant photograph. The duck, or goose, moves, through the thick light, they move, as well. The town lies, still, dead and thickly silent, as these poor things move through it stunned.

You'll remember that scene, I trust. It's the beginning of the end for Jazzetti. Well, there's nothing even remotely like that in the new book. I don't want to upset you, because I know how you've always encouraged and carefully criticized my work (you've been my *only* critic!), but I often wonder lately, in these dark, wet, winter days, just why I am a writer anyway. My new book! What is it? It seems to have certain absurdist and comedic elements that might endear it to the few who are aware of the work done in that genre—but what else? My two characters so far are wooden, they don't strike me as being funny, they are certainly not pathetic. I really want to throw the whole thing away and compose a Gothic romance "by Viola Tremble"—the moors sullen under lightning, the cold and eerie house, the howling dogs, the shadows, the rain, the secret in the attic, or the cellar, or the greenhouse, or the maze. Somebody turns into a giant slug and eats the silverware. What I mean is that I want to get out

57

of this "career" that I have chosen. Or is it that I simply want financial success? I don't know.

You know the kind of press my other novels have received. This one will be the same. The old cold shoulderoo, the punch in the literary nose. The horrible thing, reading over those old reviews of my books the other day, I thought that maybe those little time-servers who "teach English" and have "a special interest in the modern novel" were right. Maybe all of my work has been silly, useless, vapid, formless, determinedly avant-garde, experimental, etc., etc. I hardly dare look at my books. I don't think I've ever felt so lost.

My darling sister, how can I put this? Dermot is Dermot—he looked for easy money and accolades and got a touch, just a touch, mind you, of both, when he abandoned the vision that gave us "Moonface" and "I Divorce." I've spoken of this before, as you know. My point is that Dermot later *deliberately* wrote in that weary, bankrupt vein so beloved by the corps of geniuses who fire their salvos of praise or damnation from the fortress of *ignorance.* God knows, they didn't make him into an overnight Great Writer, but they gave him a little bit of a shake, *The Red Swan* reviewed by Schnobb, along with novels by Venezia Uccello and Benjamin Bullett. They also took pains to run that review alongside a long essay on Miller and Borges, if you remember. And it was that review that prompted the reissue of the book as a "fad" item. You of course know all this. What I am trying to get at is that Dermot *very consciously* took apart the fabric of his inspiration and put it back together again to match his conception of what was fashionable. Disturbingly enough, my own work seems as meaningless to me sometimes as Dermot's does, and *I* have written honestly. So, wherefore, etc.? Why does my work strike me as shallow and ill-made? This very letter seems to have more to recommend it than my fiction.

This *Guinea Red:* It is like a piece of bread stuck in my throat. I can't swallow it and I can't bring it up. My narrator is a fool, perhaps mad, perhaps a liar. Because of this, I have to force him into situations that strike me as having the consistency of gruel. He has not spoken a word that is not a cliché, not performed an action that has flair or style. I had, you will remember, somewhat the same problem with Max Champagne in *Baltimore Chop,* but in that book, the interest of the narrative and the layered plotting more than made up for his character weakness. In this book, try as I may, Halpin, my narrator, burbles and bumbles—flat! Christ, how flat!—and so does his friend, Ned Beaumont, whom I despise. I'm using a kind of flashback technique in the book and *that* is boring me to death.

Sheila, what can I say? I want very much to send you the draft of my first three chapters, but I'm really ashamed to. Ashamed and afraid that you will say what I suspect: that it would be best to tear the MS up and begin again—at the *beginning*, straight narrative, with a character who can be *somewhat* interesting. But I know myself: I've committed myself to this idea, and although I may rewrite what I have, I'll stick to the concept. The last chapter, Three, which turns on the incredible stupidity of Beaumont, looks as if it might stand up, but the first chapter is still unsatisfactory. I think that I might change the location, they are in a cabin, the "murder cabin," etc., etc. I swear to God I can see those two walking around right now, bitter at the scenario I've given them to act.

This has developed into a longer letter than I planned to write. I meant only to say Merry Christmas, etc., and love, and happiness to you both. Let me know when you are settled and *write*.

Love,
Tony

P.S. Please don't show this letter to Dermot. He knows how I feel about what he has done with his talents, but I don't want to open old wounds. (I'm beginning to sound like my characters!) They are, thankfully, almost healed. Tell him I'll write him soon. What a ridiculous life!

My dear Joanne,

By the time you get this letter it will probably be the new year—although it hardly seems new to me. Forgive what seems to be my gloom at this festive time and forgive this letter that I'm sending you, as you will know, through Ellen K., since I know that you are married. Perhaps it is foolish of me, but I don't want even to *approach* the possibility of causing any difficulty between you and your husband: hence, this unnaturally clandestine act.

But this season and my beginning work on a new book. . . .

I remember that I had just begun *Three Deuces* when we first met and that it was Christmastime. We first "went out" together to a Christmas party at, I believe, the Marowitz house. It was a terribly crowded party, but for me there was only you. How proud you were when I broke that gay piñata! As in the old song—"are the stars out tonight?"

You'd bought a new black dress for the occasion, and a marvelous, floppy black hat. You were absolutely, utterly breathtaking! You were also breathtaking later that evening when we got home, *do you remember?*

Where has that loveliness gone to in my life?

Forgive me, forgive me! I know that I made your life a hell during that year, my misplaced and aberrant sense of duty to my damnable ex-wife continually coming between us. Callousness aplenty, as they say. But my guilt and remorse cannot eradicate the image of you in that black sheath, black stockings, that pearl choker, that hat . . . such sweetness has gone from my life, forever.

I don't know if you are even reading this letter, but I go on.

Let me be honest and say that I go on as much to purge myself as to speak to you. I know that you won't care but I must tell you that I have not had another "affair" (I despise that word!) since the day we separated. There have been women, certainly. But none who even came close to replacing the presence of you, a flower in my heart.

I am pleased that you are married, happily I'm sure, pleased to know that you are saved from the loneliness that has been *my* life these past few years.

When I think of you now, the recurring image is of me watching you from the apartment window the day you left. I am in the window, smoking. The sound of the door being closed in that shimmering silence that fell between us as you packed is still in my ears, at this very moment I hear it, a door closing on my life. How gently you closed that door, as if to avoid breaking my heart. . . .

I wait, in my memory, at the window, wait for you to appear on the street below, and then I see you, crossing the street, entering the park in the soft September twilight, walking toward the far end. I think that you might stop and turn back! I think that I might open the window and shout to you to come back, shout and scream, beg! I think of rushing downstairs and overtaking you . . . I stand there. I smoke. I go to the study and sit at my desk, stare at the wall until it is dark. It is not until then that I begin to cry.

Then this image dissolves and I try not to think of you anymore. I have been more and more successful at this lethean exercise lately, except for now: this season, this moment in time, these fiendish similarities of time and occupation have fleshed you out again in my memory. I have even followed women these past several days, thinking they might be you. Ridiculous! I've thought of calling Ellen to find out your number, but if I had it, what should I say to you? Suppose your husband answered? What should I say to *him?*

"Excuse me, this is Tony Lamont. I used to be deeply in love with your wife. May I speak to her?"

So I write to you . . . I don't know *what* to write to you!

Shall I remind you of that summer we spent on the beach, that tiny cottage? Do you remember the storm that came crashing across the Sound that night, booming off the tin roof while we lay warm in that rented bed in which we had learned each other's bodies? I thought it was God's benediction on us, his approval of our innocent and sparkling love!

What we had is gone, even that summer is gone. How can such things happen?

Yet, I love you. I love, anyway, the love we created so bravely.

I love your handbag, your bathing suit, your stationery. I love your sad quiet.

I loved being a writer when we were together. Now it is drudgery, I have no critics, nobody to read my first drafts, nobody to laugh at my occasional *faux pas,* nobody to point out errors and weaknesses, nobody to argue with me. Everything is lonely silence.

My new book is a mystery to me. I reread those parts I have completed and they seem as if written by someone else. To whom can I show this work? I want your lovely eyes to see it first, and that is impossible.

I want to stand in a bar with you, Christmas decorations around us. The Scotch better than it is at any other time of the year. We can do anything we want! We will live forever! We drink and laugh, friends, envious of our happiness, stop and chat. My just-begun book is my anchor to life, my earth, and *you* are my heaven.

I'm lonely, my dear one, help me!

If I could see you, my darling, be with you for just one hour, drink with you in some warm, noisy, vulgar, gloriously Christmasy bar, crowded with Christmasy people.

Perhaps it would snow.

It is all gone now, I know that. It is impertinent and unmannerly, perhaps even immoral, to ask you to reply to this chaotic letter. But, my *dearest!*

To this day, I go into our favorite bar when "our" bartender is on, so that I can hear him ask, "How's Joanne?" It is your name I want to hear, your *name!* Then I can lie to him, lie and lie and lie and repeat your name, your dear name, hold it in my mouth tenderly, as I once held the cool tips of your breasts. I see the envy in his eyes.

Fantastic elaborations, fantastic distortions, fantastic inventions.

I revivify you in the sweet syllables of your name. I play the songs we loved.

Partly drunk, I stare at the sullen face in the mirror behind the bar. I wait for you to come back from the phone booth, or the cigarette machine, or the ladies' room. I wait for you to rejoin me, I hold long conversations with you under my breath, smiling at the empty bar stool next to mine. I don't know to what lengths of fantasy—even madness!—I have gone to conjure up your self, your lovely self!

I leave the bar, solitary and drunk in the street, and see you again approaching me as you approached me on that dark and cold terrace the night we first met. Your brown dress, tan shoes, your hair in a loose, soft chignon. I lose my breath as I lost it that mild September evening, the party noise faded into a murmur to accompany the love that sang in my heart.

I want to see you! *I want to see you!*

I want to sit with you alone in our bar at a little table, the soft lamplight on our touching hands. I want to believe the waiter to be witty and suave and wise, the Martinis the finest, the coldest, the driest in the world.

Who will read my book? Who will tell me that I am, I *am,* a good writer? Who will hold me, past all error and heartbreak? Past savage despair?

This is madness. I love you. I love what is alive in my memory and its attendant images. Isn't that a sign of madness, to think the past is real?

If you want to reply . . . if you want to. . . .

Ellen will see to it that I get a reply, safely, discreetly.

Just the possibility of seeing your hand on an envelope, open, strong, blunt yet delicate, will hold me through the emptiness of the holidays that are about to engulf me.

My darling.

Your sweet, sad face.

I love each inch of you.

Unforgetting, your unforgetting

Tony

Lamont's Scrapbook

YOU HAVE READ IT IN THE PAPER

YOU HAVE SEEN IT ON TV AND RADIO

NOW YOU CAN SEE HER IN HER HOME

MRS. LOUISE ASHBY

Healer, Reader, Advisor, Seeress, Prophet

Will Make

YOUR WISH COME ABSOLUTELY TRUE

I'll Reveal The Sickness That's In You

MRS. ASHBY

The Religious Woman, God's Holy Healer and Prophetess of the dark and mysterious Future and well known ESP, garantees to remove Suffering, Bad luck and evil Spirits from out of your Body.

She will name your Enemys by name and tell you plainly Who to keep away from.

She is a Religious and Holy Woman who learned when she was just a young Girl that she was chosen for this arduous course in Life.

Are you suffering? Mrs. Ashby will touch you and with your own eyes you will learn to believe how the pains will cross out of your Body and into her Holy fingers.

Are you sick? Touch her radiant Body and her Power and Faith will flow into you. There is no problem too difficult for her to solve. She has brought Peace to even the most tormented in Mind and Body and Spirit and she can do the same for you. Through her, God will cleanse your soul and forsoe danger for you. She will also tell you of love affairs of the Heart with no ifs ands or buts about it. The proof is your belief. Mrs. Ashby has mastered the Occult and is an expert on all types of reading to ease the Mind.

DON'T LET RACE OR RELIGION STOP YOU.

Immediate Results Garanteed

Mr. B.K. says: I had failed in one business after another because of evil influences and bad friends. People were talking about me and I was drinking too much and gambled away all my earnings, and finally I went *blind.* My wife had left me and I had nowhere to turn until I heard of *Mrs. Ashby.* One visit to her and today I am a business man in the growing Art Field.

Mrs. J.L. says: I was flat on my back suffering from immoral desires and an incurable disease of the brain and I had lost all faith and hope in doctor's and my husband had become a drunkard in his despair.

63

Then I met *Mrs. Ashby*. After I saw her just once I am well and cleansed in my heart and soul. I am now in business for myself and have remarried happily to a wealthy and understanding man in Advertising. Thank God.

Mr. A.H. says: I was never happy unless I was eating and drinking. I had lost all my friends and family had deserted me because of my excesses habit. I went to see *Mrs. Ashby* and thank God for her but today all my friends and family are once again gathered around me and I stopped my drunkard and glutten problem immediately. Today I am a happy and well-off man with my own successful Lumber and hog Business in the country.

Mr. D.D. says: I had become such a gossip and busy body behind people's back that my wonderful position in the Creative Field of adult magazines was in jeopardy. Nobody liked me and I could not help myself. *Mrs. Ashby* taught me to mind my own business and got me interested in the great world of Sports and today I am happy with a wonderful raise with a good chance for lots of overtime. I thank God and this amazing Woman.

SEE HER FOR YOURSELF

My dear Roche:

I'm glad that you liked and approved of the "bones," as you phrase it, of my *vitae*, although I hope that you are not going to cut it *too* much. I sympathize completely with your need to trim it down so that it will not overwhelm the brochure, and I thank you for your generosity in suggesting that I may see what you have done for final approval.

No, no! I am not at all disappointed that you have decided to give *all* the books that will be dealt with in your course equal attention . . . I confess that I was somewhat nervous at being singled out for specific attention anyway. My only problem (and it is not your fault) is that I have been giving a great deal of thought to and taking copious notes on my novels, and stories as well, to enable me to make up a kind of "source" essay that you might draw on for assistance in teaching the course. I hate to see this work go to waste. But I'll try to whip something into shape anyway, concentrating my fire, as it were, on *Three Deuces,* since your letter implies that this is the novel that you will use for the course. I hope that you will not take it amiss that I will pay some attention in my notes to my other works, since I see all of my poor waifs as inseparable. They have equal power in my mind, though they all have their faults, as you point out in your letter. I agree with you on some points, but I think you are incorrect when you state that my short stories are, how did you phrase it, "self-indulgent." I don't know how many of my stories you have read (only eight of them have been published, and those in what are generously called "fugitive" magazines), but I think that you will find the germ of both *Baltimore Chop* and *Fretwork* in the story, "Belated Adjuster." The connections are, granted, tenuous and subtle, but they are there, waiting "breathlessly" to be elaborated in the picaresque adventures of Max Champagne. To be blunt, as blunt as I can be without being thought hostile and uncooperative (for no author has ever been more cooperative than I) let me state that a cogent critical view of *Baltimore Chop* cannot be taken without a knowledge of "Belated Adjuster." That is not to say that *Chop* cannot be read, understood, and enjoyed as a novel *sui generis,* but the *critic's* task is to unearth, reveal, point out, etc., etc. I *know* you agree. What you term "frivolity" (although, again, I don't know exactly what stories you are speaking of) is a Beckettian attempt to come to grips with the void. The "belated adjuster" in the story, the cliché private eye, is a prototype for the figure of Champagne. His cynical, yet romantic ideals are meaningless in the world of "polite" criminality and evil which he faces as his career fades. When he finally does "adjust" it is "belated" and the change cannot save him from failure and the dissolution of all his ideals.

Another story that is of critical importance in an understanding of, I would say, *all* my novels, is "O'Mara of No Fixed Abode." I think that you might get hold of this story fairly easily, since it was reprinted in *The Far-Out World of The Underground* just three or four years ago by Barnumbooks, in paper. It is a story in which my obsession with the mysterious quality of the substantive is focused clearly, and perhaps for the first time, successfully. My protagonist, O'Mara, a vagrant, embodies in his life and being all those irrational clashes and antitheses that make humankind so inexplicable. I here tried to extract the essence of those warring feelings by setting one against the other, without resort to emotion or explanation, but simply by verbalizing their quintessence in short, simple phrases, each one poetically (I trust) concrete and pure. Certainly we know that all men are masses of contradictions, but fiction has always tried to explain these contradictions in terms of emotional qualities, elaborate memories, etc. I thought: Why not simply array these jarring qualities one against the other? Why not concretize them in brief, pithy phrases that will not only reveal O'Mara's fluctuations as a *persona* but call up to the reader his own nostalgias, surges of despair, wild joyous memories, etc.? So I relied on the power of the *noun* in chaste lists, and then added "associative" comments to enrich my character's psyche, his *projection,* if you will. I flatter myself that this technique not only comes into play in all my novels, in one form or another, but that the story itself sets up a curious, haunting resonance.

It might interest you to know that "O'Mara of No Fixed Abode" was a preliminary selection by *two* of the editors of *The Literary Laboratory: Best Experimental Stories of the Sixties,* but that a third editor vetoed the story in final selection because he thought it "boring and impenetrable." I was not hurt by this, but, rather, amused at *his* opaqueness. But, my dear Roche, I hope that old O'Mara is not one of the stories you call "frivolous." I cannot believe that you could read the story and not see its value as experiment, nor understand its relation to the way I employ the "noun phrase" in the novels— detached, pure, harshly naked.

Please write me when you are freed from the holidays, on which, by the way, I wish you all joy and merriment.

My very best wishes,
Antony Lamont

P.S. On second thought, why don't I enclose the kernel, the nucleus, as it were, of "O'Mara"?

"O'Mara"

What, then, did he like, what were the things we were able to ascertain about him from a perusal of his private papers and diaries, his letters and journals, his casual remarks to acquaintances and friends, lovers and wives, over this forty-year period of his life, his "richest years," spanning almost half a century, from 1915 to 1955, the sad year of his mysterious disappearance?

He *may* have liked many other things, but we know for certain only that he liked a sweet summer breeze, stars shining softly above, memories (made of This), his mother's rosary and her posary, an old-fashioned melody, broken hearts, baby shoes, a garden of love

66

just made for two, moments passing into hours, pretty hubba-hubba babies, the roses of Picardy, the moment when the band started playing, a little home for two, gleaming candlelight, beautiful Alsace-Lorraine, heavens above, and smiles that make you happy.

He clapped his fat and sweaty hands together anent the place where the morning glories grow, beautiful Ohio, that dear little boy of his, Hindustan the Man, the end of the rainbow, a baby's prayer at twilight, getting it up in the morning, Marie, Rose of No Man's Land, that wunnaful mudder of his, an Alice blue gown, Daddy Long Legs, sweet Dardanella—the Amherst nightingale, dreams that fade and die, Indian summer, letting the rest *(sic)* of the world go by, a little gift of roses, that mammy o' his, his isle of golden dreams, Peggy, a pretty girl who was like a felony, Rose of Washington Square, first seeing "her" on the village green, that naughty f———g waltz, and the whip poor-will.

He was also partial to Avalon, bright eyes, apple-blossom time (saucy days!), the silver lining, a love nest and Mary Palesteena, when his baby smiled at him and when Buddha just simply smiled, a Wild Rose *(see* Appendix IV), April Showers and her Dapper Dan, Ka-lu-a (who-a?), a phantom kiss, Peggy O'Neill, Sally mit moonlight behind her, a sweet (?) lady, when Frances danced with him, *l'amour toujours l'amour* the "french" way, crinoline-crinkle days, hot wips, a stairway to Paradise, a kiss in the dark, his buddy, trees runnin' wild, his wonderful one by name o' Bambalina, a bbabblingg hbrook, and every road that has a turning.

He was wont to have an accident over a girl that mens forget, lingering awhile, being on the mall and swingin' down the lane, wild flowers, Charley his boy, fascinating rhythm, a June night, his best girl, his dream girl, his Katharina, a lonesome babe lost in the wood, the winks of a angel, a rhapsody in blue, a serenade post-orangeade, tea for two, a love that's true always, a cuppa coffee (jive java, Jim!), a sangwich and her, Dinah, drifting and dreaming, a Swiss miss who missed him, sitting on top of the world, and moonlight and roses.

He loved, to crosseyed distraction, the pal of his cradle days, the way to go home, a sleepy-time gal, sweet Georgia Brown, that "certain" feeling, a black bottom (tsk-tsk), blue room, breezin' (along with the) breeze, Charmaine (the girl friend), to only do the things he might, a lucky day, Mary "Blue" Lou, mountaing grinnery, his dream of the Big Parade!, one alone to be his own, someone to watch over him, a sunny disposish, the red, red robin *soi-disant,* the Delaware Lackawann', love that can come to ebberyone, blue skies, Chloe from Swamp City, dew-dew-dewy days, Diana of the Dark Roof, the girl of his dreemz, jost a memory already, a smile as his umbrella (cf. *The Grinning Bumbershoot*) on a rainy day, being lucky in love hotcha!, him and his shadow ("earmuff weakness"), old man River a.k.a. "Green," reign, Ramona the "paloma of Pomona," a Russian lullaby, the melody that lingered on, his "life so glamorous," a sweet yet moist lollapalooza, and the Carolina moon.

He was busting with a nickel's worth of ecstasy in re: the glory road, a garden in the rain, honey-diamond bracelets—Woolworth's doesn't swell, the sweetheart of all his drims, lilac time, a melody out of the sky, being independently blue, makin' whoopee with Marie, his lucky star, a (precious little!) thing called love, a morning sunrise, Sonny Boy, sweet Sue, cream *in* his coffee, not on it!, a Broadway melody, a great day comin' *mañana,* a honeysuckle rose, kissing her hand to beat the band, straying a million miles away, a feeling (woo!) he was falling (wow!), Jericho, his sweeter than sweet, Siboney from Bologna, singing in the rain, a malady (*Op.* 463) that haunted his reverie, springtime in the Rockies, when the organ played at twilight (snickers), a him to her grace, Zigeuner (pronounced "hedge"), something that simply mystified him, all the king's horses, what was beyond the blue horizon, a lucky moon and a sleepy lagoon wit waves dat wash the pontoon.

You had best believe he went ga-ga bananas when he considered the river of Gulden's Creams, when his heart grew tipsy in him, happy feet dat did dere stuff!, confessing at O.L.B.E., the Kiss Waltz, moonlight on the Colorado, his ideal, something to remember her buy, eight little letters, walking his baby back home, the waltz she saved for him BUM-bum-bum, the fundamental things of life (cf. "Rocks' Bottoms" by The Fictitious Collection), looking for the light of a new love, to dream *ad nauseam* a little dream, a million-dollar baby, Louisa (a wench out o' wax, sir!), a parade, just one more chance at the Bowl of Cherries (*vide* "A Minute to Play at Fontbonne Hall!"), the name that she signed, a noo sun in the sky, ooh that kizz!, ev'ry howre sweete as a flowre, soft lights and sweet music (or, *Mighty Mazda's Maudlin Melody*), the heaven that must have sent her his way, spending one night with her and her "little" glass of wine, moonlight saving time, taking his sugar to tea, where the blue of the night meets the gold of the day a man ain't nothin' but a smoke!, Forty-Second Street, the journey from here to Astar, sweet symbols (by Zildjian!) in the moonlight, a Louisiana hayride with Miz Iberia Pepper, the lullaby of the leaves (*see* Flagging's study: "The 'Jewish' Novel and Its Uses in Sleep Therapy"), night and day ho, rise and shine hum, shuffling off to (screech!!) Buffalo, as well as the song his heart had to sing.

He found pleasantly diverting (to say the least!) a little tenderness (was he not fletch an bludd?), an old Softee, heaven in his arms, the old ox (read: "cattle") road, flying—e'en filled with fear—down to Rio, the waterfront, good old mountinn moosick, the likes of her, a paper moon sailing over a cardboard sea (*vide* D. Philps: "New Thoughts on Lambent Solidity"), lazy bones, his little grass shack in Kealakekua, Hawaii, his moonlight madonna, the Shadow's Waltz, a sophisticated lady wit fake fingernails, the touch of her hand as well, yesterdays, a glimpse of stocking on a *bas bleu*'s gam, the beat of his heart, cocktails for two, the ripples on a stream where disappeared some hatless pipples, hands across the table (and a Buick in her eyes), his idea of nothing to do, his secret heart, June in January (*vide* "Odd Behavior Indeed" by "Boots" Stekel), love in Bloom as limned by James in his Giant Preach, any cozy little corner, moonglow, funny magic, the object of his affection, *one* nite of love *one!*, a field of teagarden white, a sweetie pie, a lovely evening, the one he wasn't worthy of, two cigarettes in the dark park, the difference a day made, the night and the music, and also cellophane.

How his heart went boom-boom-bummy 'bout a beautiful lady in bluo, Bess, dancing cheek to prancing cheek, a house a showplace, the mood for love, one of those bells that now and then rings, a castle-rising in Spain (*viva la muerte!*), red sales in the sunset (example of *furor scribendi*), summertime, top white hat, white fop tie and hot tails, his lucky stah, dancing unduh duh stahs, the chapel in the moonlight, a little old lady (*not* Maw Green??) passing by, moonlight and shadows, *No Regrets* by Curt Warner-Goode, pennies from heaven, stumpin' at the Savoy, waltzing Matilda and the touch of her lips, when his dream boat came home (and his face fell in the chowder), bloo Havaee, the dipsy doodle, harbor lights, the moon in its flight (which few remarked upon), his love to keep him warm, the free, fresh wind in his little buckaroo's hair, September in the rain, slumming on Park Avenue with sweet Leilani Sue, plus a gold mine in the sky.

He oft experienced a surge of naughty thrills when he thought on a crop of kisses, things that happened for the first time, falling in love with gloves, a pocketful of "dreams," those peepers, fine finnan haddie *or* fruity cup *or* juicy cocktail, a September song, a thwell thip of thparkling Burgundy brew, a beautiful baby, the promised breath of springtime, the oceans' white (with foam), an eighteenth-century drawing room, the old mill wheel that showed a shapely calf, down México juay, a stairway (hein?) to the stars, all or nothing at all on Blueberry Hill, a cabin (nu?) in the sky, a ferryboat serrynade, the last time he saw Paris (behind a busted chariot), the nearness of her San Antonio rose, hearing those strumpets blow again, and Capistrano and sfogliatelle.

There was a warm spot in his very bowels for the "Chattanooga Choo-Choo Cha-Cha," Dolores (wotta paira silver things!), New Jork in Yune, the Jersey bounce, a couple of jiggers (wot?) of moonlight, the Saturday dance mit shteamers und beer, the stage-door cantee-ny-weeny, the blow of the evening, an old familiar score, one dozen roses, a goilish stringa poils, a heart that's trew, a white Christmas with chestnuts to match, a wing and a prayer (or, "Salvation Army Thanksgiving"), the seam of anyone's dream, a kiss by a lazy lagoon from a cunnin' gossoon, the right thing to wear, one "More" for the road, what makes the world go round go bare, coats of navy blue candy, where the West commences (and folks jes' walk the other way), ron y Cocy-Coly, swinging on a star, an autumn serenade with Injun corn and pumpkinade, cruising down the river (*see* "Fruits of the Lower Hudson" by Tod Bruce-Tad), the simple life, a queynte (ach! Gott!) caravan, a grand a night for singing, a face in the misty light (one of the few from whom one may learn of Art), what it seemed to be, a well-developed personality that's one of Nature's sheer delights, the winds of March that made his heart and all its cockles a dancer, doing *whott!* came naturally, a doll he could carry, the sun in the mawnin', a good day for singing *el song*, a midnight masquerade, and too, a rainy night in the Rio (or comparable fleabag).

His dry old mouth would drool for shoofly pie and apple pan dowdy that could make a person nauseous, the girl he was near, anyone (anywhere) who *knows*, golden earrings with gypsy wench attached, smokey dreams (from Holman's store), buttons and bows, faraway places, hair of foo gold, eyes of troo bloo, the rainbow when there was no rain, a lovely bloody bunch of bleedin' coconuts, *mañana baña-nas*, a slow boat to China, e.g., the S.S. "Rollins," red roses for a blue lady, Bali Hai in flowerai bra, dear hots and gentle purple, a wish his heart made, the four winds and the seven sees, Hucklebuck Pie with Parker House Rolls, an old-fashioned walk with lissome poon in tow, a mule train, the old master painter sitting by a window, that lucky old sun, A. Bushel and A. Peck: Attorneys at Law, whoop-de-doo songs, the middle of a warm caress, the old piano-roll blues, Sam's song, viz., "Hello, You Pompous Bushwa Schmuck, Hello!", Belle, Belle, his Liberty Belle, a talk (uh-huh) to the trees, the cool, cool, ghoul of the evening, a lonely little robin, the loveliest night of the year, *Mixed Emotions* by O.M. Boston, the morning side of the mountain, his first and his last love, and Shanghai.

Joy unbounded almost knocked his greasy hat off concerning sweet violets, the corner beneath the berry tree, Delicado L'Inconnu, walk-ing to Missouri with Matt, the Wheels of Fortune: Prop.; some Greek, the ebb tide, the wrong face, limelight, a rock around the clock, the second star to the right, wonderful, wonderful Copenhagen to bust out yer beak, the lure of her, the belle of the ball, a girl! a girl!, his kinkdom for a girl!, green years, Hernando's Hideaway, Honey Babe (a.k.a. "the Blue Box"), the little shoemaker, Paris in the winter when it drizzles in your vin, a loving spree, the mambo Italiano wit' sweet peppers an' a liddle erl, his restless lover, Skokiaan where the lingonberry blows 'neath the midnight sun, steam heet, the barefoot Contessa, Connie Pazze-Cicc', amore, three coins in the fountain, autumn leaves while others stand and wait, cherry-pink and apple-blossom white with scarlet shower curtain and blush-rose bowl, a many-splendored thing, Pete Kelly's booze, an irresistible force, a tender trap, and *whatever* Lola wanted.

Yet, lest we too hastily assume that we may glean from the above a fairly complete picture of this complicated man and his wide-ranging tastes, his constantly changing and growing personality, let us temper this portrait with a recital of those things—and they are many—that he heartily *disliked*. They including whizzpering treezz, waking up to a rag (so he say!), every light on Broadway, honky-tonk towns, dark clouds waiting, smiling more or less through his tears, eyes that don't mean what they say, every swell Suzio and sweetie Sal, new-mown hay, Indiana ("Hog-Caller of the World"), drums rum-tumming, smiles that made him blue, the daughter of Rosie O'Grady when she pitched into the punch, chasing rainbowse, K-K-K-Katy Kkootie, paddelin' Madelon, pretty Mickey, Dixie Melodies (e.g., "My Pickup is Parked Outside Your Heart"), that tumbledown shack in Athlone, the heart of a rose, Chinese lullabies sans starch, his sister Kate, forever blowing Bubbles, Mandy, a one-horse town, how he cried about her, the all pinky-goldy Miami shore, and basement air.

His was a veritable typhoon of loathing o'er Swanee, tulip thyme, when the town went dry, waiting for the same old sunrise, Broadway Rows, the Japanese sandman, that little town in the ould County Down (q.v.), Lindy Lou, Margie the lass so liked by lost lake shore, a pale moon, Tripoli, whispering (which he *weally* wesented), young men's fancies (he thought them catamitous), to be all by himself, the flowers that bloom in May, the rose in the devil's garden (*vide* "Mephisto's Late Bloomer" by Fleur Frilly), kittens on the keys, pictures out of books, second-hand Rosé, the Sheik of Araby or, "Mr. Profilaksos," songs of love, three o'clock in the morning, the Wabash Blues (champeens of the Chili League), Carolina in the morning, Chicago, China Boys (*see Peking Robots* by Wao Ji), dancing fools, Georgia, ladies of the evening adrench in deshabille, the Limehouse Blues, lovin' Sam (who though broke yet hath his purse entire), the Sheik of Alabam' who am whut he done am, the South Sea moon, Nellie Thanwhomwhich Kelly, being on the Alamo, Rose of the Rio Grande, a chicana chick, stumbling on the road to Being 'way down yonder in Nawleens, Annabelle and Barney Google, *The Bugle-Call Rag*

("All The News From Shit to Hint"), Charleston, Dizzy Fingers, "the nose-flute king," Raggedy Ann, that old bang of his, being all alone by the telephone the day that Sally went away (cf. "Anomie in Cincinnati" by Ursur Kostelfeder), the Indian love call, someone who could make him feel glad just to be sad *(vide* Venus Furs's *Further Adventures)*, memory lane, nobody's g.d.s.o.b. sweetheart, a prisoner's song or, "Framed!," Rose Marie (the veriest spindrift o' the seaside), sugar caca, a photograph to tell his troubles to, and the Bam, Bam, Bamy shore.

He like to fainted from ennui when entertaining thoughts of Cecilia, gypsy eyes brazen, Rose with the turned-down hose (his partiality was for opera stockings), drinking songs, the hills of home, Jalousie (a.k.a. "La Ventana"), a cottage small by a waterfall where a pall of smoke did plash, when lights were low, the song of the vagabonds courtesy Texas-Pacific RR, Sunny and His Ukulele Lady, Valencia, "Baby" Face, Er.A., the mirth of the blues, hard-luck stories that "they" handed him, desert songs, horses, climbing the highest mountain with determined mien, stars peek-a-booing down, little white houses (*vide* Bukka Cairo's study, " 'Honky' Myths in Western Architecture"), when nighttime came stealing, the moonlight on the Ganges that fully floodlights flotsam foul, muddy water, his little nest of heavenly blue (the time it played a trick on him), playingk andt dancingk jeepsies, the Riff song, how when day was done day left, a broken heart among his souvenirs, Bill Crazywords and his crazy tunes, a dancing! tambourine!, a funny face looking over a four-leaf clover, Mississippi mud, his blue heaven, when his heart stood still, Paree (*vide* "Farm Desertion after 1918," U.S. Gov't Printing Office), the rangers' song, "Rio Rita," and Sam the old accordion man.

His head was a gourd chock full of dreariness in the contemplation of going along singing a song, the Varsity Drag—known as "the lewd lineman," Miss Annabelle Lee, his land and their land and kasha for two, pain in his tum-tum and fogg in his brayn, Crazy Rhythm (or, "Drunk Again"), women crazy for him, rain a windowpane and darkness too, a ding-dong daddy and his pornographic prong, a red, red rose, Jeannine the Sweetheart of Racine, the Manhattan Serenade, one kiss o' shortnin' bread, stouthearted men, sweethearts on parade (Wacy Women), a rainbow round his shoulder, the sale of his dreamboat and the yegg on his dear, those tears in his eyes, deep night, a talking picture of hers, vagabond lovers or, venereal vagrants, magic spells that were everywhere just a'-moaning low, his sin whispered in crepuscular confessional, the one rouse that was left in his heart, pagan love songs (viz., ugga-boo-clabba-donggoo, etc.), the lonely hours knee-deep in stardust, wedding bells that go yingle-yingle, that thing called love, a man who

72

ain't got a friend, a bench in the park, plus Betty Co-Ed.

How his weak and watery eyes did snap in spite when he heard tell of any Russian play, a cheerful little earful, crahn fo de Caahlahns, dancing with tears in his eyes, everything that was fine and dandy plus plum cake and sugar candy, what actually *happened* in Monterey, the part (thou small! thou meaty!) he was playing, the lazy Lou'siana moun, little white lies, the sunny side of the street, Stein songs (like "Grin With Gin"), time on his hands, two hearts in three-quarter time, the part that once was his heart, the devil and the deep blue sea (*see A History of Keels* by D.B. Boiler), a Cuban love song (i.e., "Yo Bedder Not Eat Op Dees Fried-Huevo Sangweech"), dancing in the dreck, droms in his hott, heartaches, the only time she hauled his was when they were dancing, the game of "Stay away!" or, "Presbyterian Honeymoon," a ladee of Españ, French letters in the sand, Minnie the moocher of 8th Street, a mood indigo, the chaynes that bounde him, their old rendezvous (cf. "Tristes"), why darkies were brown, a Wabash moon, sleepy time down Sout' where statues rule, when the moon came over the mountain and his hat fell into the drink, when Yuba played the rhumba on the tuba, April in Paris *(see* Stekel, *ibid.)*, a cabin in de cotton, and a shantih in old Shantihtown.

He became physically ill when he thought of a thing that ain't got swing, every little star, an echo in the valley dat yodels "Dot's right, Dieter," little streets where old friends meet Mimi, a hungry yearning burning inside of him, a shine *(semper idem)* on his shoes, too many tears, the Harlem Moon (in 2 oz. gin float an egg yolk; serve); an old smoothie name o' Lily of France, Annie who don't live here no more, the Boulevard of Broken Dreams (*vide The South Bronx: Why?* by Chas. Manhattan), a dream walking, the Easter Parade, a tropical heat wave as created by "Mr. Jesús," the valley of the moon, "Ode to A Muslin Tree" by Harry L. Amherst, the talk of the town, the last round-up—when podners chomp their chaps for chuck, the old spinning wheel, orchids in the moonlight sobbing prettily, smoking, drinking, never thinking of tomorrow's stormy weather, "Two Tickets to Georgia (Where the Pines Decay)," *The Big Bad Wolf* by D. Walt Vidal, a brue moon, a cattle call (as advtd. in Bean's), the Continental isle of Capri, a little Dutch mill, his old flame, his (?) shawl, the good ship "Lollipop," his Sóuthêrn äccent, solitude among tumbling tumbleweeds, as well as the little solitary kinks that everyone ought to do.

He chawed his lips and ground his choppers to dust when a faint memory came to him of wagon wheels stark in a winter wonderland, nights of tropickal splendour lightly touched with scent of rotting cantaloupes, Broadway Rythum in all its vain glory, how you say "revolutions" in Spain, songs coming on, plenty of nuthin' which all can somehow spare, a little geepyseepy tearoom with a sticky cot in back, the thing that you're liable to read in the Bible, little white gardenias on her corduroy slip, the lullaby of Broadway (cf. "Rhythum"), the moon over Miami's Piccolino-Hilton, a prairie moon that gleams 'pon a Latin from Manghattang, the song of the open road, the strings (how oft they broke!) of his heart, empty saddles, "Yesterday's Mashed Potatoes" by H.H. Bickford, old cowhands putting all their aigs in one basket, what they say (and *what* they say!) about Dixie, the warning voice that came in the night or, "melody from the sky," and the shoe shine-boys, Snap and Pop.

How many sick headaches were caused by stars in his eyes, not a sine of people, twilight or whatever on the trail, the Whiffenpoof Song, Bob White *(see Biographical Notes)*, a foggy day in London town—the very day that Willy Sikes faw down, the moon growing dim on the rim of a hill in faraway Tim-buc-too!, Johnny One-Note (*née* Simon), the moona of Manakoora, the ripe and ravishing Rosalie, the leaves of brown 'neath shoures sweete, that old filling, a lull in his life, a toy trumpet that hirts the ears, a little yellow basket, cathedrals in the pines bathed in that Hollywood lux, Flat Foot Floogie: NYPD, the park across the bay with the penny serenade, dizzy spells from a julep or two, a summer with a thousand Julys *(satis superque!)*, deep purple old Dutch gardens with the lilacs (ah, the lilacs) in the rain, his prayer that she'd do it the South American way (thighs apart, soles together), a sunrise serenade, half a love (cf. *The Geld Twins on Pepperidge Farm*), a dolly with a hole in her stocking, his heart above his head (he crawled on his belly like a rep-tile!), the Johnson rag which was inadequate to say the least, a make-believe island, rhumboogie or, "A Drunken Zulu," a sleepy lagoon a mirror ruffled gently by the trade winds, an anniversary plotz, a simpering, whimpering child, blues in the night *(see Cigarettes, Sawdust)*, daydreaming flamingoes (dat sudden boist of pink!), moonlight and motor trips, "Chief" Jim Bluebirds, the white cliffs of Dover, the craziest drim, Idaho (Shoshoni for "Chips"), gals in Kalamazoo, bells that jingle jangle jingle jongle, serenades in brew, old "Black Magic" and his "Warsaw Concerto Jump," some head in the clouds, the river of the roses (for it had only thorns for him), a holiday for strings, and Oklahoma (pronounced Ocjcwczw).

He utterly despised, in spades, his rose and his glove, the San Fernando Valley, a surrey with the fringe on top (*vide* S. Freud, "Genital Symbolism in the 'Pop' Song"), Mr. In-Between, bell-bottom trousers, Rainbowville and its maple-syrup crick, the loneliest night of the weak, sentimental journeys with strange music, the trolley song, "Big" Backyards, the steel-drivin' fellow, doctors, lawyers, Indian chiefs, shadowed boxes in the dark, Laura Foots, what he heard down the hall, a royale affaire, Atchison, Topeka and Santa Fe (the Barcelonas of the West), a cigarette that bares lipstick traces, Sioux City Sue (the poetess *pro forma*), the end of time while waiting for the train to come in, Chiquita Banana, a señorita of the *oddest* tastes, a fool moon and empty arms, a gal in Calico, U.S.S. "Glocca Morra," Linda O. Devilmoon (the old lamplighter), a Sunday kind of love, the old buttermilk sky that made his tummie sickie wickie, Wyoming ballerinas feuding and fighting, ivy, Stanley Steamer (late of Lundy's), trees in the meadow, strange-sounding names (e.g., Mungii, Elmowrk, Pradshitte, etc.), a fella with an umbrella, *Haunted Hearts* or, *Terror in the Finished Basement*, a most unusual day, nature boys amid the sunflowers, careless hands that messed his meerschaum, Coppers' Canyon, dreamers' holidays, happy tawk, the Hopscotch Polka which always ends in tears, hot canaries (they wuz twect), the Mona Lisa, riders in the sky, Rudolph (yet *another* Kraut who loathed the Führer!), a stranger, hand trailing in the punch, across a crowded room, Candy and Cake (the friendly Dobermans who ate old ladies in Larchmont), Christmas in Killarney, a man around a house, muzik! muzick! muzikk!, an orange-colored Skye (a ugly cur), Our Lady of Fatima who did not bring him a bike, sleigh rides, "Sunshine" Cake (*née* Wilhelmina Boutonniere), crazy hearts, Elisa, a kiss to build a dream on a marshmallow moon, Misto Cristofo Columbo (cf. O.Oglio's "Remember When Oil Ran Out?"), Mockingbird Hill with the sparrows in the treetops, the blue tangoo, high noon, and one Mr. Callaghan.

Vitriolic delirium shook his frame upon being reminded of one little candle in Pittsburgh, Pennsylvania, Thumbelina of the Foul Fingers, April in Portugal, the "doggie" in the window *(see Hamburg, Entertainment in)*, yust anodder polka, watching the night go by, Ruby Baubles, Ruby Bangles, and Ruby Beads, a blue mirage, Fanny and the finger of suspicion, Hajji Baba (the "High and the Mighty One"), being home for the holidays, a woman's world as fer as cercled is the mapemounde, the Jones boy fresh out of Beth Israel, little things that mean a lot (few could name three and whistle), Mister Sandman ("the man that got aweigh"), the naughty lady of Shady Lane who did odd things in her arbor, whoever stole the wedding bell, the typewriters and Adelaide, a sighing blue star, Mr. Banjo when he shaked his bones fo de peepul, love and marriage, the man from Laramie (the galoot who could say "yes" and "no"), strange ladies in town, an unchained melody, and, last but not least, "Yellow" Rose of Texas, who had an arrangement with a certain Capt. Copro, U.S.A.F.

4. THE TRAGIC JESTER

"An't please Heaven, a jest's your tragickal
mow bedaub'd on the phiz of that low-creeping
Machiavel yclept Fate."—*Sir Giles Demurrer*

Suspended, as if Time itself were suspended, like the hand of God, perhaps, extended over the incomplete jigsaw puzzle that men call their lives! So it seemed, as we sped, through the alabaster canyons toward Ned Beaumont's apartment, there to confront, together, the canker that had loathsomely crept into his life. We sat together in the cab, Ned Beaumont withdrawn, huddled into the corner, I, "pretending" an interest in the hurly-burly of the streets, gazing out the window. Yet what I was gazing at was my life, my, yes, *jest* of a life. It is perhaps proper for me now to set down this life, at least the bones of it, its most visible outlines, for you, dear friend. It may help to explain. . . .

I was born in Sunburn, California, in 1929, a true child of the Depression. My first whole memory is that of an old Okie swearing at his old truck, held together miraculously by spit, Juicy Fruit, and The Lord's Prayer. His vehemence mounted as each moment brought the truck closer to what struck me, even then, as complete paralysis. It was my father! After that I somehow lost consciousness.

My mother was beautiful and smelled nicer than my father, who had the odor of an old horseshoe, and she excelled as a pianist, organist, and singer. Much of her musical talents were employed in the Sunburn Pentecostal and Revivification Christian Church. My father allowed her this release from the workaday chores of domesticity, in return for her silence concerning his reputation as a fop, drunkard, tavern raconteur, rake, and the Lord knows what else. If he did not succeed in breaking my mother's heart, it was because she had placed that delicate scarlet organ in the peach-oilcloth-covered tabernacle of the P and R Church, where it often beat faintly for many niggling years.

My father was given to swearing mighty oaths, and chasing my mother up and down the stairs after he had partaken too heartily of the convivial glass. My heart was often numb at these scenes, my knuckles rawly gnawed with that fierce, burning carelessness of boyhood, alas! Many the evening he pounded on the bedroom door, a blasphemy dancing on his coarse teeth, trying to make his voice

76

heard above my mother's sweet contralto raised, as often as not, in a popular hymn of the day. I pretended to read one or another of the books in our meager library, that small collection gathered so painfully by my mother's arthritic and strangely calloused hands. There could have been no more than a dozen books, books I loved, and which I read over and over again. Among them I remember, with a twinge, *Poems For Real-igious Americans, Only God in Lonely No-Man's Land, Odd Behavior Of African Violets,* and *Business English for Some Californians.* There were other books in this meager library, gathered so slowly by the painful and oddly rough hands of my mother, but these few stand out in *my* annals of nostalgia.

These "misunderstandings" between my mother and my father, if I may so term them such, always ended in the same way. My father would come down the stairs, swollen, his knuckles bloated and reddened from his quizzical pounding on the door, and enter the small alcove in which I would be sitting, my eyes rigidly fastened on the page of some book. He would glare at me, his breath projecting an invisible yet blue cloud of alcohol over me. . . . His bruised hand. . . . The words would crowd out from between his flecked and clenched lips. "You're your *mother's* son all right! Jubal's ghost! Thunder and electric damnation! Religious maniacs! Creeping Jesus herself and her son!" He would then don his overcoat and a cigar in his lips, slam out of the house to waste his time; *and* our substance at the Third-Degree Café, where, I knew, he would disgrace himself and his family by telling off-center jokes to the wastrels with whom he rubbed elbows and touched shoulders. Later, I was to discover, with horror, that most of the jokes had to do with pastors and their female admirers. Often, after one of these scenes, I would somehow lose consciousness.

When I was seven my father was killed in a fall in his suspenders from the attic window of the "widder woman's" cottage, nestled close. In Sulfur Acres. It was impossible for my mother to hold her head up in our town after that, and so the tragic remainder of her harsh and calloused life was spent bumping into objects and people as she went about the town, her skinny arms full of washing, her more often than not fat mouth full of pins and needles. Unjust! I screamed inwardly, curiously moved. In that year, or the next, while waiting for my mother to come out of the church after an evening sing, how wonderful it was, I espied, through a stained-glass window and an accompanying blood-red dizzying haze, my mother and the pastor engaged in what I was later to discover was fornication. It was at this moment of traumatic shock, during which I must have lost consciousness, I later learned, that I decided to become a writer.

How bracingly English I felt, despite all. My chum of those days, "Lead" Burke, tried to hearten me by assuring me that the scene I had witnessed was no more than a crude attempt on the pastor's part to take my mother's temperature, but I gave not a countenance to this chestnut. The pastor was no doctor! To this I cleaved. My cheeks burned with a curious shame as my bosom heaved, it was as if I had seen my mother for the first time, and it was with a strange relief that I realized I had not.

When my mother made her wonted egress from the "house of shame," she was flushed and withal crestfallen, as are many after their ashes have been hauled. Her head, however, still inclined toward the ground, her arms, thinner than ever, still clutched a pile of wash. I strode, nonetheless, manfully toward her and announced my intentions toward the quill. I would go to San Francisco, I laughed joyously I remember, the Queen of the Bay, there to whet my pen and win fame and wondrous wheaten bread, stone-ground, as is its wont. Just as my boyish legs had almost carried me to her, a storm, one of the many that churn up the Central Valley, struck! Ripping unmercifully, it clawed! The honest shacks of the poor folk were dazed by the fury of the storm, as were the great mansions where arrogance and hauteur were no match for the clawing and ripping mercilessness of the howling maelstrom, that, beast-like, struck. I was dazed and must have lost consciousness. When I came to, "Lead" Burke was gone and about my mother's knees swirled an interesting cascade of angry water, CCC boys, and sordid Okies, their force, away! threatened to sweep her broken frame on the raging current! Away!

Forced by this "sign," the storm, I suppose, I remember, it seems that she must have raised her head, her frightened eyes meeting my calm ones, wherein she saw my determination as they sought out beyond the surrounding hills, the nearest route to the Bay Area. She saw in the blue depths of my orbs the same pluck and stubbornness (grass dared not sprout beneath me!) that had driven my poor father to hurl himself out the "widder woman's" window in the adamant belief that he was on her porch. Her mouth trembled; a smile, the first I had seen in months, began to form, pulling her lips up in a tender smile, she raised her match-stick arms, the wash cascaded into the hellish tide, her pins and needles slipped after the linens, down, down the street as an omen of disaster, that I somehow sensed with that part of the brain that cannot think, but only feel! All was— strange, all was—evil! It seemed for a moment as if the whole world was One!

No! I screamed, *Mother!* No Frisco fame! No tearing the roots up! I shouted! Sunburn I was at, Sunburn I would stay in! Too late! She did not hear me as, at that moment, a jagged crash of lightning struck beloved Ma in the pelvic area and she fell into the boiling drink, her helpless dear cinder of a body carried spuming downstream along with the laundry, the Okies, the muddy CCC boys, many still clutching their now almost useless spades, who hopefully clutched back, but it was now to no avail! Was it God's ironic will? Who can say with any certainty?

With nothing left for me in this leafless burg, I journeyed, on to San Francisco, quaint cupcake, there to take up the Life of the Pen. But somehow my age became known, despite the cool irony of my early writings, and I was sold to a Catholic orphanage, where I spent the next nine years of my jest of a life. My dreams of becoming a great writer waxed to a strange nightmare. My life seemed no more than a jumbled—puzzle—yes, a giant jigsaw puzzle swept by the Maker onto the floor of Life in a fit of unfathomable Pique.

Somehow, I survived. There is nothing to say more of. (Lester Bowls, the after-dinner speaker, has written the definitive memoir of life in a Catholic orphanage in those blasted years, in his moving and well-documented *Seek But the Bird and Thy Sole Shall Be Heeled*, and there is little, if anything, that I can add to this moving memoir.)

Released at the age of seventeen, I belatedly plunged into the life of letters, although I grant you that I knew all too well the amount of "bellows work" that would be required of me to fan the dying coal of my almost-thwarted ambition once more into glowing flame! A fierce bout with the gleet was my first cross, after which I married a young woman who, at the time, was the favorite protegée of Silas Quot-Binj, the avant-garde potter, the artist who made "throw" a household word. My initiation into connubial sexuality was devastating as those of you who have read my book of marital memoirs, *White Slip*, will know. It must have been about this time that I became interested in window boxes, a way to sublimate certain unsavory tendencies on my part, tendencies that threatened to frighten and upset my wife. Alas! They ultimately, sadly, made her into a monster, and thus destroyed the tenderness we had on occasion laughingly risen to. I wrote furiously, gardened furiously, attempting mastery over the unruly yet furious flesh, but as I spun out my unpublishable stories, I somehow knew, hidden behind crates and cartons, away in the barn safely tucked, my young mate was, even now, standing, clay-smudged, pushing back, more than likely, a stray lock of hair, with her curiously stubby fingers ("potter's fingers," she had often cruelly laughed!), glazing, throwing, firing. With a strangled cry I would fling myself upon my notebooks, there to weep silently all the morning. The tortured knowledge of my latent harelip did not help still the small voices of despair that whispered "failure" to me. At

79

such moments the incredibly difficult and lonely job of President or Mayor of a great city seemed almost preferable to my lot, and many days saw me on the edge of entering politics to run for such offices. Yet "suicide was not in my line." I hewed on the mark. My magical color, blue, saved me from total madness, and even on those evenings when my wife would enter our small library, dressed as a cardinal or archbishop, biretta in hand or perched on her tossing, russet curls, a smile of incredibly vulgar promise on her maddeningly rouged lips, I would murmur, "Blue." Who can tell why? Yet, we would fall to "it," with *monstrous* appetite, my parched need reaching out for my assigned role, that of the blushing virgin at confession. Monstrous! I grant you that it was monstrous, I could feel my moral fiber flying away from me like a shot off a shovel, as they say. Lest we forget, I whispered, my head swathed in her heavy, perfumed robes, that swirled about me like the soul's very doom. I almost always lost consciousness for minutes at a time during these forays.

This "life" went on for years, and somehow my writing, nay, my very dedication to this most difficult art (or act?) suffered terribly. I became instead, an authority, under my wife's direction, on glazes and ceramics, publishing several monographs on the subject, the most bruited being "Craze and Crackle in Moorish Majolica." My wife smiled upon my labors from her, one might say (if you will forgive the pun), Olympian heights, and always in the background loomed the figure out of the past and even, and this was the horror, the present and future, of Quot-Binj, his swarthy gypsy-like features encased in a mask of mockery as perfectly inscrutable as one of his sultry and infamous vases that surrounded me like so many grapes.

One evening, sweating and groaning under the nameless humiliations and commands of Jean Cardinal Zobop, one of my wife's favorite alter egos, I seemed to see a softly colored vista, and a vision therein: my old mother's eyes, peering from the crested flood! They "spoke" to me, as eyes will do, saying, through dreamy lids, "Marty, son, *watch out* for this man!" I knew that I had to change my life and, crawled as best I could away from the "Cardinal," her shrieks commanding my return! her aromatic garments, swirling about my body, which crawled. I *had* to get away—out of this jest, this tragic jest, of a life! She followed, shouting, coarse oaths flew from her half-parted teeth, knowing that I threatened to sever our uneasy relationship. Now imploring, now threatening, now offering up to, my good ear, lavender vistas of forbidden delight. A cauldron of her holy gloves rang about my rear. And clattered! But I got to my room and heard her garments collapse to the floor, her body surely but unwillingly following them. I had "won."

It had taken me eleven years.

The next day she was, with each pot and vase, gone. The key was in the mailbox wrapped around a sheet of paper on which were the words, in her curious blunt yet, spidery "hand," *Qotu Bxo,* a cipher of malediction. Strangely, I was not unhappy! Every trace of my traumatic trance was gone! My new life beckoned. It was not long in coming to me, for within the very month, while dining at my club, I chanced upon the resplendence of Ned Beaumont, whose name I cannot now utter without a shudder. His gruff laughter is silenced—forever!

He was a sight, old Ned Beaumont, in those days of youth and bubbling high spirits in which we more or less moved—his crass ways, yet withal hearty; his (then) toothless chuckle; his wildly eclectic wardrobe, so chosen as to make him appear to be the *artiste* that he truly became later, as time passed and he realized that *arte* of some adult and remunerative form was his fated call. How did he look? You ask? Imagine a figure in a grey tweed benny given him by his accountant brother from Yonkers; a wine-dark zelan jacket, acquired in trade from a bard of the Great Southwest, one of the "sweetest" men one could ever hope to know; frayed shirts, uni-roned, from the extensive wardrobe of his friend Bob, a known sign-painter; a navy watch cap from Hudson's with which he was wont to set the table on a roar when he pulled it over his face, and, most extraordinary, his vast collection of trousers, one pair for each week in the year, changed religiously each Sabbath for all his life (oh God!) long! They were extraordinary mostly because of their unearthly beauty of color, and were chucklingly described to me once by Ned Beaumont himself as being coward yellow, driven-snow white, magic black, Florida orange, funk blue, seeing red, rayon violet, prose purple, blush crimson, envy green, young cherry, time lilac, neon amethyst, lot-of brass, o'connell tangerine, study brown, washington square rose, water lavender, chartreuse chartreuse, lowry's ultramarine, lazuli lapis, blow peach, isle emerald, foo ruby, star sapphire, autumn russet, heaven azure, rage livid, dark pitch, panty pink, mare grey, hide tan, mother pearl, squash lemon, rickey lime, tongue silver, goose gold, old chestnut, kisses wine, bard kelly, pipe rust, woman scarlet, france burgundy, words honey, god bronze, oil olive, man straw, youth flame, blindman buff, desert-closures cobalt, brooklyn carmine, and tough copper.

He wore also unmatched socks, too small for his horny feet, and thus called himself in tragic jest, "The Emperor of Ice Cream," an obscure reference which he would never explain to me. Perhaps you know from it. No matter! On these feet were clamped cracked and filthy desert boots (the poet's pride!); his underwear came from the textile mills of Blackmontane, where he had once worked as a youth

81

and which burg he never forgot, nor would he ever let any interlocutor forget, for long.

Then picture *me*, if you will, at the loosest of ends, free at last from torment and, obsession! Meeting this fantastic figure from the world of, as I then thought of it to be so, Art and Beauty. Our friendship ignited and flamed instanter—we were made "for" each other. I was not surprised to find that Ned Beaumont was a poet *marquée*, for was not I? And who all else? Then what more natural than that we should start a publishing venture together? I ask. Had I but known of his fatal, tragic flaw . . . one among a host!

What can be said, indeed, of the fatal and rich-rich years that followed as creative business associates? Is then, publishing a business? I hear Ned Beaumont's flashy lightning wit lancing out with "go f——— yourself!" And he was right, of course. He was almost always right, except for his last, mad passion. . . . But I digress.

As *we* lived and loved it, it was a symphony, a poem, a lubricious pâté, a fresco, a black lace garter belt, a trip to the moon down Dulcimer Lane, a Nabokov *mot*, other, *gossamer* things! Can one go on? How! We surrounded ourselves with first readers who were *devotés* and *devotées* of Lanier and Malier, with copy editors who had shed the puritan shackles of orthographic nicety, with proofreaders lightly clutching just a touch of advanced myopia, with production assistants who possessed the "humorous" shakes, with designers who worshiped at Chagall's fit, to coin a synecdoche. We bought the brightest of yellow files, modern formica chairs, cutesy mushroom lamps, gas-turbine percolators, girls from Bard, Bennington, and Barnard, editors who were all just getting "that" novel under way, space salesmen with suede caps, Porsches, and lewd grins, college travelers who could no longer read, and other swiftly interchangeable items. A business? You ask! A piece of cake!

Ned Beaumont and I devised contracts that scrambled, boiled, fried, poached, roasted, sautéed, baked, broiled, and basted our faithful authors at every turn; marvels of economy, they ever wert. Our correspondence fluttered, then flagged. Our clipping service read *The Fresno Bee* each day. Perhaps our proudest achievement was a list of phrases to be used in rejection letters—still the awe and paradigm of the entire industry. If I may so bold wax as to list a round fifty of these phrases, they were:

1. at the present time
2. we just don't see our way clear
3. while we felt . . . we also thought
4. while we thought . . . we also felt
5. lack of narrative structure

6. undeveloped character of
7. not quite believable
8. although our first reader
9. book never quite engages
10. curious lack of emotion
11. curious surfeit of emotion
12. hard to get hold of
13. on occasion, it works brilliantly
14. work of someone very sure of himself . . . not getting it across
15. work of someone not quite sure of himself . . . fails to get it across
16. the prose *as prose* is very good
17. the writing *as writing* is very good
18. the style *as style* is very good
19. the plot *as plot* is very good
20. the characters *as characters* are very good
21. the main character *as a main character* is very good
22. certainly can write
23. writing is wonderful just as wonderful writing
24. although the writing is arresting in itself
25. fails to make his valuable observations interesting
26. chances of our taking on . . . very slight
27. missed the pull of continuity
28. missed a deep involvement with the characters
29. seems to be too deeply involved with the characters
30. has a strangely ambiguous attitude toward his characters
31. rather tough fiction market
32. really tough fiction market
33. impossible fiction market
34. found the characters rather wooden
35. found the characters curiously flat
36. found the characters strangely mechanical
37. found, oddly, the characters merely mouthpieces
38. found the characters somehow too elaborate
39. found the characters irritatingly simple
40. although we loved the characters
41. could not work up enough enthusiasm for the characters
42. not something for us
43. don't think we can take the plunge
44. not quite our kind of book
45. afraid we'd all take a bath
46. without everyone's solid enthusiasm . . . know you wouldn't want us
47. grateful to you for sending

48. good of you to give us a chance at
49. very interested in seeing anything . . . in the future
50. always very pleased to read anything . . . in the years to come

After some years, during which time our firm did truly prosper, despite my innate conservatism and Ned Beaumont's flamboyance (perhaps it was this conservatism on my part and equally Ned Beaumont's flamboyance on his part that caused it to prosper: who can say for sure what strange ways in which Fate works?), I noticed a change, subtle at first, then growing ever more noticeable as time winged on, in its wont, in my partner and friend. My friend! I was near to shouting, many the time. What can be the matter?! But I held my shout and continued, urbane. He became secretive, moody, racked by gusts of strange laughter, in short, he wallowed in melodramatic dumps, why knock it?

Well, of course, it was a girl, or, should I admit, a woman—a *married* woman! Out of the long years of loneliness Ned Beaumont had emerged into what he hoped was the light of a relationship that would make to flower his mellow years, he had met this lovely, lovely woman, it could of course, come to naught, yet . . . how I remember his voice rasping on and on about her.

"Fresh as a daisy Daisy! Ah, she is lovely, pretty too, tall and slender, ebon hair, cheerful, luscious, and a brilliant snob, O most subtle Bryn Mawr speech, skirts above her winsome knees, soft in nylon arch and calf, O Helen-swell of gams, rotund chuckling bottom in the cuts and folds of gay New York, blasé Paris, *haut monde* her place, *haute couture* her love, *haute cuisine* her mundane fare, laughing, all her teeth of snow so straight, nestled in among them purest, smoothest gold (envy the hairy dentist whose hands play in her mouth, O envy Dan'l Denton, D.D.S.!) to assist her in her dainty dining, small but not too small her breasts, high and proud, the variegated world her oyster, O glance upon the fragile silver fork her life is, made to pick into it and find always, never failing, the purest, roundest opalescent pearl; her health, her tennis clothes, dazzling white as Aspen winter, panties snug-stretched over flashing buttocks, Love! Love! she cries in ringy voice, debutante legs blurring 'gainst the emerald grass, her partners all bewildered, hot in heads, July forever in their virile veins, to see her, just to see her turn, to catch her smile, her fine-arched nose aglisten, beaded with her silky sweat, O naughty minds! guilty minds, rummaging beneath her garments seeking e'er her jewel, ah Daisy! Day's Eye, her swains all cry, O sweetest, brightest Daisy, whose yen two wol slee them sodenly, dove-grey eyes of winter sky in London, softly melting fixed upon them, Daisy! Elegance of mountain flower, luscious Daisy, is already wed!"

She was kind and cared in that way that women like Daisy have of being kind and caring. Do you know what I grope at? I think she grew to—*love*—Ned Beaumont. I'd somehow like to think so, even though I . . . but that is another part of my story.

How can I blame her for the lifeless bulk that lies next door? Yet.

Will she arrive with the police, who are on their way? Perhaps before them, or after them? How can I bear to look into her sweet, scatterbrained gaze?

I have more to tell, more, much more. But the taxi has arrived at Ned Beaumont's house. We will, together, descend into the maelstrom that awaits us, seething, churning, indigo, blue.

Lamont's Scrapbook

What is all this juice and all this joy?

Tomato, V–8, apple, orange, grapefruit, clamato, cranberry, grape, cranapple, pear, plum, peach, clam, and love. The joy: all the rich, long-lasting suds you could possibly want—a dermatologist's treatment for your mitts. After the dishes, you might wish to silently ope hubby's trousers with your dovesoft digits. He'll beat his feet on the Mississippi mud, guaranteed.

Will a duck swim?

Aye, an't please his lord, the gibbous moon.

How do you speak to an angel?

In thus wise: Go, my dear Angel, I beg of thee, to where my Jesus lies; say to my Divine Redeemer that I adore Him and that I love Him with all my heart. Invite the adorable Prisoner of love to come into my heart and make it His fixed abode. My heart is too small to afford a lodging for so great a King, but I purpose to enlarge it by faith and love.

Quis custodiet ipsos custodes?

Lupus in fabula, nomen et omen, rara avis.

Doth a fountain send forth at the same place sweet water and bitter?

Hardly. Yet the quality of the water often does vary widely from place to place; such variations, however, are often more apparent than real, and have to do with the drinker's emotional and psychological relationships *vis-à-vis* the locale in which the water is encountered. *Vide* J.R. Morton, who writes: "Michigan water tastes like cherry wine, Mississippi water tastes like turpentine."

If winter comes, can spring be far behind?

Spring will be a little late this year.

What cannot Gold do?

A number of things, the more prominent among which are: make the pivot, shoot the rapids, differential calculus, speak Spanish, hit in the clutch, carry a tune, get a job, say no, walk a crooked mile, swim, hold his liquor, support his children, write a poem, play tennis, pay his bills, trim his beard, shine his shoes, take a shower, use capital letters, keep his sex life private, be proud, speak to an angel, take a little walk, boil lobsters, open clams, like women, cut it out, grow up, move to Yonkers, cease and desist, jump over the candlestick, act his age, fly a kite, go two rounds, catch a fish, make a salad, write a check, wash the windows, eat crow, crack corn, fly the coop, take a powder, go anywhere alone, bunt, write a play, stop the shit, cut the comedy, know Brooklyn, mind his business, sharpen his ax, make an apple pie, honor his father and his mother, be a Jew, shoot crap, make a list, see himself as others see him, play pool, be joyful and triumphant, take off his hat, wash a glass, deck the halls, mix a Sazerac, be a clown, sing in the rain, jump with Symphony Sid, make 'em laugh, stand a ghost of a chance, button up his overcoat, love a mystery, get started, and shudder.

Where are Elmer, Herman, Bert, Tom and Charley?
Elmer: Brooklyn, New York; Herman: White Plains, New York; Bert: Anaheim, California; Tom: Tampa, Florida; Charley: Flint, Michigan.

If things did not break, or wear out, how would tradesmen live?
Why, by sticking it up and snapping it off, in time-honored custom.

Do the drummers in black hoods rumble anything out of their drums?
They do. Among their renowned compositions are the following: *Tough Davy Daybreak, I Caught That Chick in a Web of Love, Krupageneous, Big Sid From the City, Will My Buddy Love Me (Now That He's Struck it Rich?), By a Cozy Coal Fire, I Heard the Voice of J.C. in the Desert, Marable's Miracle, Wily Wilson's Nothing But a Shadow, In the Old Morello Tower, The Life of Riley, Murray Likes 'Em Sunny Side Up, Tutti-Frutti-Zutti, Waiting in the Wood Yard of Your Heart, The Prophet Moffett, Ay! Qué Chanopozo!, G.I. Jo, Perpetual Motian, A Cool Rudy Collins, Jumpin' Joe Philly, Harold Went West, Stompin' at McKinley Junior High, Lamond's Wands, Don't Fool Fatool, Higgins Ink, I'll Stabulus His Fabulus (And Spend the Rest of My Life in Bed), High-Greer Cruisin', In Dear Old County Shaughnessy, Denzil's Best Bet, Lo Mein at Li Yung's, Let My Love Be the Coalman in the Cellar of Your Heart, Tell it to Dougherty, Damn Ye!, Alvinparadiddlestollerapalachicola, Bendixonia, The Night They Sank the Barrett Deems, Clarke Street Ramble, The Ballad of Tornado Jones, Poachin' Roaches, Our Kiss on Connie Cay, Wettling Your Whistle, The Black Art of Shaky Blakey, Doin' the Harewood Glide, Cowboy Thompson Et Up All the Chuck, Shake Hands With Brother Haynes, Taylor Made, Culling Dr. Donaldson, Osie Blues, Shoepolish Jones (Gave the Birds the Willies), Mardiganapolis, Saunders Pavilion Stomp,* and *Cowans' Can o' Corn.*

Halpin's Journal

My mortification (if that is the word) at being burdened with this grossly vulgar "life" that has been invented for me is so great that even Ned's comforting does little good. But this is the way it has to be, I suppose. Did I really think that *I* was going to get away with anything? Ned played the clown in the restaurant—so it was my turn to be equally ridiculous in the "tale of my life." It is quite clear now that not only is Lamont a very bad writer, he has no clear idea of what he is doing in this book. Ned, of course, is nervous about the next chapter, which will deal with his involvement with the two ladies whom he has not yet met.

I mentioned in an earlier entry the possibility that Lamont might neglect us to the point at which we might be able to secure a little freedom and explore a bit. Well, that has happened, not in exactly the way I thought it might (actually, I had *no* thought of how it would occur, if it did), but in a more satisfying way. In brief, Lamont has made a great mistake, inadvertently to be sure, but a mistake nonetheless. Apparently, by his use of what I understand is called the "flashback" the esteemed author has rent the time-space continuum, thereby allowing us a modicum of freedom. To be macabre for a moment, he has, as it were, brought Ned back from the dead, and set him walking about and talking, *in the past,* which, somehow, has become the novel's *present.* I don't understand how all this works, but the fact is that it is now possible to walk away from this summer cottage and its immediate environs! That is, while Lamont is in the "past" we are free—for a time. Ned, yesterday, walked for about two miles down a road leading away from the lake. He encountered no one, but said that he felt that he was well on his way toward a neighboring town, or village. If this is so, and why shouldn't it be? there is no reason why we cannot go to this town and try to find out something about Lamont's life and his earlier writings. Perhaps we can find somebody who was employed in the past by this grind. There are many possibilities, not the least of which is that we both might simply walk *away* from this ludicrous world and not turn back. But that is something to be thought of in the future, after we've found out more about this "open door" that Lamont has given us.

There are questions, of course.

If there *is* a town, did Lamont make it? Is it waiting there, for *us?* I mean, does he *intend* for us to walk into it, and find ourselves there, awaiting, so to speak, his pleasure?

If *he* did not make this town, who did?

Is this town the creation of some other writer? Is this *cottage* the creation of some other writer?

If we should desert this novel, will we ever find employment again? Or will the desertion be construed as proof of our unreliability? Authors can be strange.

These questions, disturbing as they may be, cannot preclude my excitement at the possibility of our freedom. He's fiddled with time, let him pay the piper. Had he told the story straightforwardly, we would have had no possibility of leaving him. Ned would *end up* dead, I benumbed with fear and guilt. The old "grip of steel" would have been real. But he's torn the physical laws open and we may take advantage of the space he's made. While he has complete control over us while we are working, he now has no control over our leisure. We do *not* have to sit here in this room, waiting to be whisked through time and space at his whim. We may walk out into the world, whatever kind of world it may be.

But we must be careful. As yet, I am not completely sure of Lamont's work habits, but it seems fairly clear that he does no work at night, i.e., *his* night, "real" night. So it would seem that we are free to do what we will for a certain eight-or nine-hour period out of every twenty-four. It also seems as if he does no work on Sundays, but we'll have to wait and be sure of this. It would not do for us at all if Lamont were to require us and find the cottage empty, devoid of us, his star clowns. In the meantime, small explorations of brief duration are definitely in order.

Two days later: Ned has found, tucked into the pages of *Light in the Head* a clutch of typed sheets containing excerpts from reviews of Lamont's *four* published novels! Four! My God! My suspicions concerning him are remarkably strengthened, considering the attitude of the reviewers toward his books. I incorporate this material *in toto* into the pages of this journal, including the almost totally incomprehensible marginal jottings present on these sheets. The excerpts seem to be in chronological order.

Baltimore Chop

Murderers to make their marks, pliz! "Sometimes awkward, always banal, Antony Lamont's first novel, *Baltimore Chop*, deals with what the author is pleased to call, in a dust-jacket quote, 'reality, of course.' The trouble is that we've heard most of this before, and it is always difficult to make out Lamont's own voice in this welter and confusion of 'tough guy' talk and stock characters. I'm afraid that al- *Caldecott-Box a stox?*

*Sow's Ear!
Pig's Ass!
Pearls and
Swine!*

though Mr. Lamont has tried to give us the detective novel to out-detective all . . . etc., etc., he has failed rather flagrantly . . . a book that is neither fish, flesh, nor fowl. In short, he does not hold his audience. . . ."

—*Purse*

*Your true
morphodite,
as my sainted
mother, etc.*

"I picked up Antony Lamont's first novel, *Baltimore Chop,* prepared for an exciting, even demanding read, remembering the shock of pleasure I received some two years back when I heard Mr. Lamont, as a member of a symposium on the modern detective story as a vehicle for the serious novelist, address that subject brilliantly. Instead, the novel is a real letdown . . . invites comparison with two famous writers against whom this disaster of a novel can only appear juvenile. . . . Conceivably, the generous critic might be able to claim the book is rebuttal rather than imitation, but in the face of such dullness I, for one, am not inclined to such generosity. On the dust jacket, Lamont claims that his book is a search for what he is smugly pleased to call 'reality, of course.' Unfortunately . . . *Baltimore Chop* is no more a search for reality than pottering about in a junk shop filled with ugly furniture is a search for antiques."

*Mark the Mark
and Luke the
spook?*

*Fuckin' A,
mouche
éclatante!*

*Only Clemente
could field this.*

—Gerard Rubé, *Dixie Review*

*Cracker
faggot.*

"Makes Mickey Spillane's 'noisiest trash' read like Thomas Mann . . . a disaster on all counts."

—Hilary Tampon, *Flint & Steel*

*Another diesel
churning down
the long high-
way of Life.*

Three Deuces

"In this, his second novel, Antony Lamont, whose first book, *Baltimore Chop,* was an interesting, if failed experiment in the writing of a 'detective' story, gives us a portrait of a preposterously insensitive American in decline. . . . The story of one Tab Jazzetti's (yes, that *is* his name!) trip to Miami Beach through the exotic flora and fauna of such 'engaging' places as Illi-

*And a credit
to his race!*

nois, Arkansas and Louisiana . . . a terrible bore . . . and yet another third-rate novel sure to be remaindered for forty-nine cents in a few months."

As Gide said of the outhouse, "It's America!"

—Paul Schmueker, *Daily Pharaoh*

". . . a blur of geography in which Tab Jazzetti (!) is followed by the wearily repetitive eye of Mr. Lamont's novelistic camera . . . few realistic names or places, no scruples, moral or otherwise, and no continuity . . . make this a tiresome prolongation of a clinical case study. . . ."

He who steals my nurse, steals gash!

—Jon Carrot, *Library Studies Annual*

(!)

". . . the attempt to create a 'poetic' novel is pathetic, although Mr. Lamont has learned all the superficial tricks of the modernistic poetry canon. . . . Tiring story of the age-old search for meaning in life . . . alas, such meaning escapes Mr. Lamont's trite, one-dimensional characters as it escapes the author himself. This is, amazingly enough, a second novel. This reviewer would have thought it one of the more pompous failures in a college creative-writing course."

The Bathetic Heretic of the Pathetic Poetic Novel.

Is it himself now, begob?

Oft, to the lesions of sweet amaze . . .

—Saul Bianco, *Fresno Firefly*

The Duke of Muscatel.

Rayon Violet

". . . Antony Lamont, one of the unfortunately (for us) indefatigable journeymen of what used to be known as the *avant-garde*, has here written, in *Rayon Violet* (the title is never explained), his most incomprehensible, most viscous work to date . . . only the most dedicated masochists . . . will find their way to the end of this travesty on the art of fiction, replete as it is with . . . cardboard characters, others who disappear (or change) halfway through the book, shifting locales which 'seem' to be the same in many particulars, and a particularly offensive caricature of a Jewish businessman, done without . . . taste or sensitivity. A total failure.

Yessir! that's my Baby!

It's a honky-tonk parade!

Hast'ou heard tell of the Dubowitz Curse?

—Moise Abraham Dubowitz, *Kings Think*

A gritty wit, a witty grin.

"Another sad example of the *grosseteste* branch of the *avant-garde* school of fiction, *Rayon Violet* oozes along without meaning, message, or muscle. . . . The overly elaborate fracturing of syntax, voice, and tense only serve to irritate and, finally, bore the reader. . . . We cannot care about the *poseurs* created by Mr. Lamont, who seems to me to be no more than a *poseur* himself. . . ."

"Grosse-garde teste poseur, avant violet, rayon?"

—Ward Hijl, *Creative Review*

". . . ultra-hip *angst* about which, finally, one does not care at all . . . one-dimensional and plastic (in its pejorative, not artistic sense) . . . nothing to recommend it to any but the most tasteless reader, who will get what he deserves."

—Barton Lofts, *Los Dulces Weekly*

Lofts of hypo-boardwalk fame?

"Even if Mr. Lamont had any talent, *Rayon Violet* would be an abysmal failure. . . . Helter-skelter chronology, meaningless and amoral characters, and lack of discernible form make this novel . . . utterly lacking in literary worth."

—*Near Ear*

Bitterly smacking of funerary mirth.

Fretwork

VOUT POUTS AIMS KNOUTS AT SNOUT.

". . . a dreadful novel which seems, at times, a parody of Anderson Forrest, Selby DeCubb, and Dermot Trellis."

—André Vout, *Yellow Review*

"Antony Lamont has, with *Fretwork,* proven correct my suspicions concerning the death of the *avant-garde.* It is not only dead, but it has decayed. . . . at this late date, pseudo-Proustian silliness is not *only* silly, but insulting as well. There is a kind of horrible mindlessness at work in this book, a disorganized consciousness in which anything goes . . . a book that makes no

92

Either this plan has fled or my Scotch has slopped!
sense, achieves no beauty, creates no form, even on a third or fourth reading. . . . A gimmick that fails more decisively than most."

At the YMCA, there you feel free . . .

—John Simony, *Bella Bella*

"Somewhere in *Fretwork*, Clive Sollis, a character who co-exists with the nameless protagonist as friend and enemy alike, says 'I can't stand it! I *won't* stand it! It's too disgusting!' Those, gentle reader, were my words as I, as calmly as possible, placed this product in what the army fondly calls File 13. . . ."

This doughty queen was drummed out of the corps for cleaning half the pipes in Baltimore.

—Paolo Dux, *Tux*

Paolo, Son of Arubba.

Oft in the gloaming, he toyed with his thing.

"Satire is Lamont's thing, and he is *almost* good at it, although his subject, the Indianapolis 500, may not have universal appeal. He adores and prostrates himself at the ripped sneakers of the Beatniks. His style shows it, long, excessive, turgid, five-page paragraphs—the flow of conscience type writing which was fashionable when Thomas Wolfe was living in a cold-water loft. Lamont is very crude. He also reads a lot of the more gamy parts of James Joyce. . . . Clive Sollis is the central figure. Maybe he's married, maybe not. He seems to be a poet.

Read: "Vera cruz."

The Spick as Hick: A study in Charlotte.

—Ramón Chicago, *Laredo Lasso*

As I have noted, the marginal jottings are incomprehensible to me, as they are to Ned. They seem to have been written in by someone friendly to the author. It is also possible that Lamont himself may have written them.

Dear Sheila,

Please to forgive your errant brother for not replying to your note. Congratulations to you and Dermot! I hope that you are both as happy as I am for you, and that this will be the beginning of a creative, fruitful, and fulfilling life for both of you. I would very much like to see you again for a long talk, as in the old days. (Not so old at that, are they?) Anyway, my book comes along, a little better now I think, that is, I think it's gathering a little steam and beginning to find its shape. Apropos of this, I'm sending on to you, under separate cover, an envelope containing my just completed Chapter 5, "Burst Loveletters." I know you'll be able to see what I'm getting at in this chapter, without knowing "what has gone before." I am *very* anxious to hear your comments and criticism. Do not spare me—I know you won't. But have some charity, please, for your scribbling brother. You may also, if you wish, and if *he* wishes, show this chapter to Dermot, whose comments would also be welcome. By now I'm sure that you will be able to determine that I'm quite proud of this chapter: it's epistolary in form, the letters cutting back and forth to, I hope, illuminate and comment upon each other. There may be some few flaws of expression, but on the whole I think they work quite well, for what they are. You'll guess, I'd guess, that they are all "drawn from the life" with changes, additions, etc., to enable me to fit them into the novel's pattern. I think I've broken through with this chapter and I begin to feel pretty good about the book.

In the same envelope I am sending you a copy—a faithful copy—of a prize-winning essay I wrote in elementary school, when I was about fourteen. It was in a copy of an old grammar that I've kept all these years, and I had forgotten all about it. You can blame this essay for my choice of a career, for had I not won the prize, I doubt very much if I would have gone on to become a writer. The title is "What I Can Do To Help The War Effort," and it is really not too bad—anyway, it's good for a chuckle or two. I send it to you with love, and my greetings to Dermot. How is *his* writing coming along? And how is your essay on the similarity of imagery in Bob Dylan and George Herbert progressing? I'd very much like to see that.

With love to you both,
Tony

WHAT I CAN DO TO HELP THE WAR EFFORT
Antony Lamont
8B–1

There are many things I can do to help the War Effort as a boy. True, because of my age, I cannot take arms against a sea of troubles, actually. But there are other arms besides chattering machine guns, cracking rifles and automatics, booming bombs, and frighteningly flashing flame throwers. Others indeed! Others, not as glamorous, not as effective against our tyrannical enemies; others, that might seem laughable to a smirking Nazi; others, that might make a yellow ape

94

of a Nip set the table on a roar! But—*others!* Those laughs, those smirks, those roaring tables will soon be silenced if I, and hundreds, nay, thousands of other boys and girls do our daily part!

Bacon Grease! The very word makes one think of warm kitchens, odorous breakfasts, steaming platters of delicious viands. Yet a moment's thought will reveal to the most careless the lurking terror that is potentially contained in the seemingly harmless term. For bacon grease, carefully stored in glass containers and jars, and taken to a conveniently located collection site, can be turned, by the skill of dedicated scientists into prime ingredients for bombs and cannon-shells that can help to lay waste, flatten and raze to the bare scorched earth the bastions of fanatical Dictatorship! So I can, when next I ingest with wonted enjoyment my crisp breakfast bacon enjoy it even more, in the thought that when I complete my repast, I can pour the drippings into a jar that will eventually be dropped in vengeful devastation, like a bolt from the blue, upon the Madmen who have plunged the World into War!

Next, *Tin Cans!* Common items are they, that we see and handle almost every day of our lives, that we aloofly cast into the garbage. How many of us think, as we open a can of "Green Beans" or "Vegetable Soup" that this humble container is made of the same metals used to manufacture those engines of war that our GIs, our Gobs, our Leathernecks, our Aces of the skies and our Guardians of the coasts employ in their never-ending assault upon the Capitals of Corruption? Few, I fear. But how can these modest cans, you inquire, assist our brave Fighting Men? Are we to send them the cans, unwashed, replete with their colorful labels? Are we to fill paper bags with the cans still in their familiar cylinder shapes? No! is the answer. The steps are simple ones, and the mothers of all boys and girls, even the smallest tyke, will surely assist them and even be gladsome in seeing their kitchens spick and span and free of messy garbage, cluttered debris, and rotting flotsam. So as we help our gallant boys at the front, all over the globe, we also help our gentle mothers.

First, we wash them out with hot water. Then we pull off or soak off the identifying labels, that say like "Lima Beans," "Carrots and Peas," "Sauerkraut," etc. Next we make sure that we cut out with our can openers not only the top of the cans so that we, naturally, can get the food out, but also the bottom. Next we place the cans on the kitchen floor on their side, on a piece of newspaper so that we may refrain from marring our mother's linoleum and causing her more work, and step or jump up and down on them until they are quite flat. Then we take the flattened cans and their *tops and bottoms* too, for these items are also made of the same precious metals as the cans themselves, and can be turned too, into Freedom's Weapons, and place everything in a stout bag. When the bag is full, we may take them to a Collecting Point, where the second line of Defense, those who serve also who only stand around, our Defense Workers, can pick them up and turn them into tanks and planes and rifles and cannons. Often, as I open a can of common food, I seem to see in my hand, not a can of homely "Succotash" but a hand grenade ready to be shoved down a filthy Nazi's throat! I sleep better that night, with Victory for all Mankind a reality in my Dreams.

Thirdly, the *Daily Newspapers!* The daily newspaper is something that even the humblest of citizens in our great land bumps into every day. Either a person purchases a morning or evening paper, or he picks it out of a trash basket, or he gets it off the dumbwaiter, thrown away the day before by a neighbor. It seems that even the poorest laborer, the sunburned farmer, the carefree tramp or hobo or bum, with a song in his heart, yea, the least and littlest of us all, somehow peruses a daily newspaper even if he reads it a day or two late. But shamefully, although Boy and Girl Scouts and other organizations have for a while now been conducting newspaper drives through heat of summer and bitter cold snows of winter, rain of spring and wind of autumn, still! Still people throw these papers out as though they are only mere garbage.

How simple it is to save these papers in neat piles!

How simple to tie these piles into foot-thick bundles with puissant twine!

How simple to take them to Defense Collecting Points or wait for the helpful Boy Scouts or Girl Scouts, with a laugh and a jest, to come for these piles, to hear them ring the bell, crying out cheerfully, "Collecting Newspapers for the War Effort!"

I am sorry to note that I have not quite discovered what role the newspapers play in our concerted War Effort, but they are necessary and important to the success of our indomitable front-line boys. I believe they are somehow turned into a pulp or mash by the genius of our scientists and used to pack bullets or something like that. But whatever! No less personages than famed politicians have asked us all to pitch in with our piles and bundles to assist. It is certain that they are up there with Bacon Grease and Tin Cans as important items to insure us that we may forever have Freedom of Speech, Religion, Assembly, and Want!

So, when I agonize over a headline of an accident or a military setback, when I ponder the measured words of an editorial's considered opinion, when I try to puzzle out the wisdom in the President's latest speech, when I improve my mind and expand my vocabulary by doing a crossword puzzle, when I follow the exploits of my favorite Nine or Eleven, when I chuckle softly to myself at Ching Chow's

Oriental wisdom, when I learn pertinent medical facts from the Doctor's column, when I pass a lightsome and delightful moment with Dick Tracy, Orphan Annie, Harold Teen, and the rest—my pleasure and profit in the daily newspaper is expanded, since, in the back of my mind, I know that this very paper may stuff or pack the bomb or bullet or shell that will blow Herr Hitler's horrible head off and put an end to the hellish Horrors of War!

Now, after doing my utmost to *collect* vital materials for Uncle Sam, I can turn to more vital and *active* ways of helping in the War Effort.

The first and perhaps most important of these is to volunteer as an *Air Raid Messenger!* When the siren emits its warning wail, the Air Raid Wardens, men who in everyday life are your grocer, your garbageman, your butcher, your police officer, your candy store proprietor—don their distinguishing armbands and white helmets and take to the streets of their own neighborhoods, with nothing more than whistles and flashlights to defend their sacred homes and the equally, to them, sacred homes, of their friends and neighbors against the possibility of a sneaky Axis attack, more than likely one launched from the heartland of the Third Reich, except for those Americans who happen to live in California, etc., who must scan the skies, ever alert for a repetition of that cowardly attack that propelled us into War, by the stinky monkeys of the Rising Sun!

In backyards, down alleyways, vaulting fences, making their way down streets illumined only by the moon, they come, these Wardens, nobodies by day, Defenders of Freedom by night. They check constantly for those seemingly harmless points of light peeping out from a carelessly adjusted window shade or curtain—*seemingly*, I say! For one smallest glow may be enough for a cruising Heinkel Bomber to use as a target location point to devastate the city! The pilot may think he is over the wastes of the bucolic glens until the "harmless" gleam assures him he is above the spires of a Metropolis. And then —Good Bye! That is "all she wrote!" Yet what if one of these men need to get word of some urgent occurrence to another, or even perhaps, to Headquarters? His post cannot be deserted, his appointed rounds must be exactly made until the heartwarming sound of the "All Clear" sends the city back again to its wonted bustle. Yet he must get word out!

This is where I, as an Air Raid Messenger, can be of invaluable assistance. Running swiftly between one Warden and another, or between Warden and Headquarters, I can carry messages that may prove vital to the security of my block, my neighborhood, my City —maybe my very Nation! At the same time that I perform these duties I can narrowly observe the Wardens as they carry out *their*

97

tasks, preparing myself for the day when I can take my place as a full-blown Warden myself! And, along with the riveters and welders, etc., the Air Raid Wardens and their eager assistants, the Air Raid Messengers, form a sturdy Home Front ready at all times to take up the domestic cudgels to back up the sacrifices being made on all the far-flung battlefields of the world.

The second active thing I might do is save money to purchase *War Bonds and Stamps!* Although boys and girls find it difficult to realize, a dime or a quarter spent for a War Stamp will help end this war sooner. If you sacrifice a movie, think, someone has sacrificed a leg! If you go without a Baby Ruth or a handful of root beer barrels, think, someone has gone without bread! If you pass up that 3 cent chocolate or icy Pepsi, think, someone has passed up his supper to feed a starving infant in China!

And, of course, each penny, each nickel, each dime adds up to Bonds—and Bonds are Bullets! All of the things that our Government buys so that our Fighting Men may have them as they need them must be bought just the way your mother buys a quart of milk or a loaf of bread. Does the Army need a tank? Why then, it shall have a tank! But the tank must be bought! Does the Navy need a "tin can"? (Destroyer) Why, and so it shall have one! But the "tin can" (Destroyer) must be bought! It is the same old refrain for a warplane, a truck, a rifle, a doughnut, a shirt, etc. And to buy these things so that our Armed Forces can remain the best fed, best clothed and best equipped in the entire world, our Government must have plenty of money. That money can come from us, from boys and girls, who sternly forsake pleasures and fun so that their small coins can buy these things.

Who knows, those Necco wafers you did not buy, those Walnettos you bravely spurned, that Dixie Shake that you refused to quaff, but instead quenched your thirst with cool water—who knows, they may be the very things that the money you might have spent on them was used, if you bought War Stamps instead, to buy the bullet that may wipe the smile off "velly solly" Tojo's sneer.

Lastly, but importantly, remember that "A Slip of the Lip Can Sink a Ship." Remember *War Secrets!* Innocent as it may seem, don't go blabbing in the ice-cream parlor about an Army truck you may have seen purring down Main Street! Don't talk to your chums in the schoolyard about a lone plane you may have seen winging its way toward—Destination Unknown! If a ship leaves your harbor, weighted down with what is probably all sorts of military equipment to help sink the Axis—don't go running up to the boys in the street playing stickball or hide and seek, and boast of your knowledge! Innocent as these pastimes may seem, these childish words may be caught by an Ear, an everpresent and always listening Ear—in the service of Dictatorship! That young man, sitting alone in the ice-cream parlor, toying with his lemon Coke and listening to the Andrews Sisters, may be in the employ of Schickelgruber. The woman outside the schoolyard fence, pretending to fix her stocking, may be a hired hand of Mussolini. The furtive-looking stranger who has just asked directions of some street urchin may draw his salary from the Bank of Nippon.

So: if you *see* anything, *hear* anything, or *suspect* anything of a military nature going on, *button your lip!* Do not tell strangers of these things. Do not even whisper these things to friends in the presence of strangers. As a matter of fact, it is best not to ever tell anyone of the truck, the plane, the ship, etc., as that "someone" might let the information slip out the next day over his lunch pail or beauty parlor, or in a store or saloon. Keep these things to yourself and you will help keep Democracy alive!

Finally, after doing all these things, what is left for me to enact? What is left is unspeakable. It exists more as a fleeting thought, a mood, than anything that can be put into so many words. It is the feeling of the mountains, the prairies, the oceans' white with foam; the mental vision of purple mountains majesty; the overpowering effluvias of the fruited plain; it is the sure knowledge that these beautiful things that we call America are to always be—*or not to be!* In a word it is that painful ache in the chest, that thudding of the heart, that swimming of the brain that brings a shining tear to the eye, and that can be summarized in one small word—Patriotism! I must, I know I must, to truly help the War Effort, this holy cause, feel, think, speak, and *be* Patriotism! All the Bacon Grease, Tin Cans, Newspapers, all the service as an Air Raid Messenger, all the War Stamps and Bonds scrimped and sacrificed for, all the carefully kept War Secrets—none are worth a fig without Patriotism.

But with Patriotism as the flame I can, out of these little things, forge a weapon, one among *millions,* that will bring the Axis to its respective knees, begging for the Mercy that it will be ours, as Victors, to grant or not. With the Stars and Stripes in front of our eye, and Old Glory planted in our heart, we shall with God's help, bring this terrible War to a swift and wonderfully victorious end.

And may the sapient Maker grant that it be soon! Amen.

5. BURST
LOVELETTERS

Maelstrom, indeed! A maelstrom, in comparison with which the seething fury of my emotions would have seemed a peaceful pond, a bucolic rill, the summer sea.

Ned sat huddled in the corner, his dull face in his meaty hands.

I sat across from him, in the other corner, with a huge bundle of letters that he had placed into my hands, wordlessly. How somehow numb my hands felt! I read, and read, deeper into the madness that his life had become in such a short time! My hands then trembled from time to time, and I bit and bit at them, *savagely,* to steady them. For a long time after that afternoon and evening I turned over in my mind the question as to whether I had the right to reveal these letters, this dark record of a man's decay. But the Truth must be honored. What else is life and Art for?

I read, as I say, dozens, perhaps a hundred letters, or even *more.* From them, I took those that will give you, my auditor, my sympathetic friend, the gist, or, the *thrust,* of this progressive collapse. God knows, I don't want to try your patience, and, further (a small voice whispers), I don't want to shock you into a state of staring imbecility, as I into same was almost shocked. I select for you those letters necessary for an understanding of this sad story. Most I leave out as being too horrible! Let me present them chronologically—I leave off dates as being superfluous. They have a sinister movement of their own, an insidious and tragic structure that no dates could possibly enhance. You have a drink, then? You are seated in a comfortable chair? Good! Begin.

Dear Ned,

How sweet and wonderful you were to poor silly silly me the other night at that *very* important party where I was *sure* I would disgrace Tom and you, and Mr. Halpin who was very understanding too! Not as understanding as you, my *very nice* man! Anyway, I wanted to write and give you a super duper big strong handshake from me and Tom who would also write but he thinks it's a wife's Duty and all. He is strong and silent.

Oh! It was *such* a nice party with all those Famous literary people, writers and editors and just everybody! Thanks again for a real "all reet" time! Wow! Terrific!

> Your friend,
> Daisy Buchanan

Dear Mrs. Buchanan,

I'm delighted that I was of some small help in making you feel comfortable at the party last week. They *can* be stuffy and boring but the presence of such glittering and interesting people such as you and your husband always saves such stifling affairs.

I will thank Mr. Halpin for you.

If you are ever in our neighborhood, shopping or browsing, please drop in. Mr. Halpin and I would be delighted to take you to lunch.

> Cordially,
> Ned Beaumont

Dear Ned,

Oh! What a wonderful lunch! I'm still tasting it *and* the conversation you provided! I *loved* that little French restaurant, so warm and real. And the wine! Yummy!

Thanks for the memory. Isn't that an old Jack Benny song? I'll drop in again—if I may, sir!

I'm sorry that Mr. Halpin couldn't come to lunch—poor dearie, with all that *horrible* work! You poor men *frighten* me sometimes with your work and money and serious talk. Oh dear!

> Soon, I promise,
> Daisy

Dear Daisy,

Yes. Saturday night would be wonderful! I know the most charming inn in Connecticut, near Middletown, where the steaks are thick and rare and the Martinis icy and dryest. I am thinking of you all the time. I have so much to say to you that simply can't be said in a letter.

> Your Ned

Dear Ned,

Is it true that it's been only two teeny-tiny weeks since I was in your arms? I don't know how much longer I can stand this, but I don't think it would be very smarty to fly in the face of Tom's wishes. Oh, the old football star definitely suspects *something* of his sweet little Daisy. I don't care! Can you understand that I—don't—care? I dream of your arms, your legs, your barrel chest with the matty hair on it. Am I being wicked and horrid? I suppose that we *have* been wicked —I know that *I* was a bad dirl to go with you to that swell inn in Conn. What terrible fakes we were! To pretend that we were driving all that way just to have some din-din! Even though the din-din was dee-licious, and the Martinis! They must be the "food of love" is it?

Yesterday, one of the girls I lunch with told me that her husband has just bought the cutest little castle in Scotland! I immediately began planning some way to get you, my darling Pooh, to buy a castle in which we could live and love forever. Like a king and queen in Grim, is it? I could order the most fascinating robes from a little dressmaker I know in the 60's. It would be too very perfect.

And you in your breechers do they call them? And doublets and gauntlets with falcons on your head. Oh, Ned. Am I being a crass silly? Don't pay any attention to me.

It must be this forced social whorl that Tom insists we partake of. But very soon I am going to trip up to your office on my little glass slippers and just *force* you to take me to lunch again. I don't care what Mr. Halpin thinks *or* your secretary! I'm so lonely. Not even the cream I put on my facey wacey can get the puffiness out of my eyes from crying and Tom glares and snaps at me over the Wall Street Times every morning.

My love!

> Con una abranza,
> Daisy

Dearest dearest Daisy,

Will you ever forgive me for what happened in the office yesterday? I don't know if it was your perfume or your dress or your shoes (your glass slippers!) but I simply lost control of myself. When I think of what might have happened had my secretary or Martin come in —with the two of us on the desk—it still gives me a "terr'ble chill." But I know it was truly beautiful and fine and that you love me, Daisy darling. You could never have allowed me to assert myself so bestially did you not.

I'm so sorry about your stockings. I'll buy you a hundred, a thousand new pairs. Love, love, love, and kisses.

> Your mad lover,
> Ned

Darling adored Ned,

Would you think me a terrible horrid and "dirty" old lady if I came to see you twice a week for "lunch"? I mean, would it be safe as houses or would tongues start to wiggy waggy?

102

Soon the nights will be ours. Tom goes away on a business trip in a month and he'll be gone two weeks or more! Your arms. Oh dear. I remember your super strength.

I won't ever say anything to you, you silly thing, about what "happened" in your office. Don't you think I wished, I *prayed* for you to lose control of yourself? Why do you think I wore my shortest skirt? Do you think now that I'm "really" dirty?

It was fun with our clothes on anyway, fess up, you bad thing. Tell your naughty mistress. I won't tell anybody except my pillow. And don't worry about my nylons for *goodness* sake!

I kiss your tongue,
Daisy

Dear Mr. Beaumont:

This is a rather difficult letter for a man like me to write, sir, appreciating, as I'm sure you do, being a man of wide experience in the dog eat dog world of business, that I'm more comfortable in the world of action than in a letter, being at one time as you may have heard a rather well-thought of player on the Princeton football squad. Be that as it may be, I feel that as two men of the world we ought to be able to discuss what is on my mind with a certain calmness, although I assure you, Mr. Beaumont, that the calm tone of this letter is a damn sight far from what I encounter in my heart or head. Sometimes I feel as if I have no head left but be that as it may be. Let me come to the point, difficult as it might be for both of us, although as I say we are both men of the business world, although publishing is a business which, I assure you, I don't understand. Possibly because I'm not much of a reader, except of profit and loss statements and broker's reports. Ha ha. That probably amuses you? Mr. Beaumont? But I assure you that I have real feelings too, you may be assured, especially concerning *Mrs.* Buchanan, that is, *my wife,* Daisy.

Far be it for me to actually come out and lay an accusation at your feet of not behaving in what we used to call at Princeton, a gentlemanly manner, that is, in re: my wife. The fact remains that my wife, Daisy, has all she can do to keep from mentioning your name to me morning, noon and night, be assured. And, sir, I am damn well sick of it! I will be blunt with you, Mr. Beaumont, concerning the pass to which our marriage has come. It is not what you can call a happy marriage, and has not been so for more than a little years, indeed! Your arrival on the "scene" has not made it any happier or easier, I assure you. I have spoken to my attorneys about the possibility of a divorce and I think that my wife has assuredly spoken to hers. These conferences, if you will, took place before we had the pleasure of encountering your friendship, by which I mean to say that Daisy, my wife, and I were not getting along connubially before your intrusion on the scene.

Now, be assured that I speak as diplomatically as possible sir, as one hardheaded business executive to another as equally hardheaded. More hardheaded perhaps, though there are few more hardheaded than I, a point of pride with me, I assure you. My wife's interest in you is "kopasetic" with me, and yours in her is equally O.K. But I would beg you, Mr. Beaumont, to take into consideration my role and that of Daisy's in the social world in which we move! I mean that it will not do for Daisy to put herself in the path of malicious and dirty gossip, gossip not only a detriment to her chaste image but gossip highly bad to my position businesswise and socialwise as well, sir. To be blunt further, Mr. Beaumont, I do not want to be a cuckool! I was not a cuckool as a Princeton man, as a junior executive, nor as a rather important leader of the business community which, I assure you, I am still at the present writing.

So, Mr. Beaumont. While I do not thunder *j'accusee!* at either you or my wife, though I am sure that she suspects that I suspect her, I suggest, suggest mind you, sir, I repeat, that you may have been tempted occasionally concerning my wife's charms, of which, and I know that I don't have to assure you of this, she has plenty and has no wish to keep them under a bushel, and never has.

But sir, with your name always on my wife's lips, with that faraway look in her eyes whenever she happens to think of you, and I know when she is thinking of you by the strange faraway look in her eyes, her odd neglect of shopping and luncheons and benefit galas, etc., etc., what else can I think, I ask you sir? What?

A last word, sir, and I will lay pen to rest. The other afternoon Daisy came home from an auction of antiques, so she said. It must have been in the gorilla cage at the Zoo, or perhaps it was—*something else!* Her stockings were full of runs, her hair dishevelled, her skirt wrinkled, and she had one of her intimate garments stuffed in her handbag! If you know what I mean. Her underpants, sir! You may laugh at this tortured, I assure you, confession, if you will, from me, or think me a base scoundrel to speak of such things to you concerning my wife, a more or less perfect stranger. But, sir, I feel assured that you *know what I am talking about!*

In short, sir. If Daisy loves you and vice versa, I beg you to show some restraint, or failing that, to exercise some discreetness in your doings with her. I cannot keep her chained up and I understand that you might be attracted to her. But have thought, sir, on my career, my standing society-wise and on *Daisy's* reputation as my wife and devoted companion. Tongues may be soon wagging and the three of us made laughing stocks.

Soon, I assure you, Daisy will be free. Until then, sir, I trust that you will conduct yourself in a businesslike manner in re my wife's passions.

Very truly yours,
Thomas Buchanan

Dear Mr. Buchanan,

Thank you for your good letter. Without being longwinded about it, let me say simply that I know exactly what you are getting at, and that the "interest" and attraction you speak of so delicately *is* a reality.

I am sorry to hear that you and Mrs. Buchanan are experiencing marital difficulties, but they happen to the most blissful couples. I am also gratified that you are aware that I am not the cause (more the result?) of said difficulties.

Rest assured, Tom—may I call you Tom?—that from this moment on, I will be the very soul of discretion as the saying goes. Again, thank you. I am, cordially,

Ned Beaumont

Dear shining sweet darling Daisy,

Your husband, I'm afraid, knows everything! We must be more discreet until you are legally separated, at least. Please do not come to the office anymore. We will see each other, my love, only when we can do so without compromising your reputation and honor. I know this sounds old fashioned, but like it or not, you have a position in society to uphold.

Daisy, my dearest, I told you to put your panties back on "that" afternoon! But how can I be angry with such a sweet scatterbrain?

I adore your little nose—
Neddy

Dear Sir,

We have decide to offer direct to a selected numbers of perspective customers, our exceptional, UNUSUAL, and extensive stocks, of really truly HE-MANS' HOT PHOTOS.—They are available only, from us—and exclusive! SATISFACTON GARANTEED. We offer, only hard-to-get sizzling items inobtaineable in any other parts at whatever price you can pay.

To prove to your satisfacton that we have the SPECIAL ITEMS

you want, please send us $3 dlls. for our RED HOT sample ass'mt #1, or $5 dlls., for our HE-MANS' sample set, together with our FREE price list, information, etc. etc. etc.—

If you have a doubts about our sincereity, honesty, and reliableity, then send RUSH only mere $1.25 dlls. for a FREE price list, broshure, and exciteinge SAMPLE. You can send the money in the shape of a money order, or if, you prefer a dollar bill shape pluss 0.25¢ in forms of U.S. mint postal stamps.—We respectably sugest that to save time, to order our HE-MANS' sample set, In all cases, however, place a piece of black or dark, paper inside, your correspondents in order to avoid transparence, seeing the contents, detection and, possible, loss of $ money by theft. WE SELL ONELY to ADULTS, and NEVER to MINERS!—

If you decide to contact with us, please to keep our name and address in your files because, our price list will not bare our name and address, on it, and all merchandise and literature, will be sent in plain envelops without our name and address on it too.

We do not include our price list because we have no asurance that you may be definately interested in our items, and, because we are insure that we are writting to your correct name, and address.

We can gess for sure that in the past you may have been cheated by "unusual" offers from other firms, but, we can ASURE you that we have what you desire to have and, that we are know to be honest, and reliable WORLD-WIDE.

If you are a lover, and admirer of lovely, pretty, and really good builded and beautiful YOUNG GIRLS in really HOT poses, please, to not overlook this UNUSUAL OPORTUNITY never before presented and never since again.

We know as we say, and have gessed, that you have been defrauded in the past by dealers and firms of unusual offers of hot material, etc., But we know we have the sort of HE-MANS' photos you look for often, in vane. As we say SATISFACTON GARANTEED.

We begg to inform you that these are the "Real" Macoy. Specialty items with gorgeus, YOUNG GIRLS, in such things HE-MEN have interests in as, NYLON STOCKINGS, HIGH HEELS, BOOTS, WHIPS, RUBBER, CORSETS, GARTERBELT, LACE AND SATINE, etc. etc. All expertly worn and posed to bring out the really beautiful forms and bodies of these pretty models who are ALL in poses that are SIZZLING!!!

If you have still, scepticalism, send then just a $1.25 dlls. for an exciteinge sample, price list and broshure. But, we advice you to send for the $5 dlls., to start, HE-MANS' sample set, that encloses ONE OF

EACH of the specaltys listed above. We are of confidence that you will order more, and more of them.

If not interested, sir, please to DESTROY this letter. Thank you.—

C. Corriendo
P.O. Box No. 54113
Mexico 12, D.F. Mexico

Dear C. Corriendo:

Please send me your HE-MAN'S sample set, together with your free price list, information, and other materials as advertised in your circular letter to me.

I enclose a U.S. Postal Money Order in the amount of five dollars ($5.00).

Very truly yours,
Ned Beaumont

Dearest Pooh,

I know this sounds too good to be true, but my impossible husband is sending me off to Aspen next week, with two girlfriends as chaperones (ha ha!) for *a week*. Isn't that cute? He thinks it will do me some good. I don't *want* to be good. I want to be bad and naked and do dirty things with you!

I know it's an awful lot to ask, but a flight to Denver and then the teeny-weeny hop over the mountains on Aspen Airways takes 5 hours or so, in all . . . do you get my suggestion? My "chaperones" are looking forward to their own week of hanky-panky sexy-wexy, and won't care what *I'm* doing! Why are we girls so *terrible?* Oh Ned, please come . . . I want my mouth . . . Oh, I won't say it, I'm beginning to blush *all over*. Come! I'll meet the plane if you say yes. *Say yes!!*

Don't you have some *terribly* important business in Los Angeles next week? A note will make me so happy.

Neddy! A whole *week!* Oh God.

I love you,
Daisy

My darling Daisy,

Yes. I'll land in Aspen one way or another on the afternoon of the 21st unless the Rockies may tumble. My dearest!

You'd be ashamed of me if you knew the things I've been thinking about. Soon we'll be doing them.

My love, I adore you,
Ned

Darlingest Ned,

Don't be cross with me for writing you so soon after that heavenly week. I've just now got into the apartment and it seems as if we've been separated forever! And it's only been an hour and 58 minutes. Oh Ned, I don't know whether you're good or bad for me but I know how I feel. (I'm also sore in a couple of places. Guess where?)

The strangest naughty feeling has come over me about Tom. I mean, I don't care if he knows or not that we were in Aspen together. I feel like sitting him down and taking him by the ears and telling him *everything* that we did together. I don't care. Isn't that horrible? I'm getting excited. Is that really *too* gross of me?

But don't worry. I won't be such a goose. I'll be silent as the mouse no matter what inuendos is it? he makes. Just thinking of you makes me go all weaky in the knees. Soon I'll probably fall down when I just see you! Somehow you're like that Spanish fly to me. Is there such a thing? I'd just wear you to a frizzle if I ever took any I'm sure! Can you get some?

Write me in the usual way, I don't care about old Tom!

And I cross my heart and hope to die that he won't get into my bedroom any more. Not now, not ever ever ever. Or into anything else!

I'm going to take a bath now and daydream about you. Then I'm going to go out and buy some really "spicy" undies. You're making me into a terrible young woman, Mr. Ned Beaumont! And don't I love it?

> Your "Cherry Tart"
> Daisy

Dear Mr. Beaumont, Esq.,

Thanking you profusely for your order of the HE-MANS' sample set, which, I here enclose I hope to your complete satisfacton, May I take liberties with your honor, by writting to you personally, asertaining, as I have through my volumous fileeing system, that you are a customer that we hold in high regards as a LEADER OF BUSINESS. To wit, I enclose a SPECIAL insert of the kind of picture books from our RESERVE STOCK, that we offer to such discrimminateing buyers as yourself. They feature our most LUCIOUS models!! Which a moment's perusal will convince you of, of that we are sure.

Of course, along with this SPECIAL INSERT comes your set of pictures of LOVELY YOUNG GIRLS, as you can see and, which I hope proves to be highly satisfactory. Our price list gives, for your ease in ordering, for future delights, all you must know for such ordering.

Also inserted are further informations about other packets and sets of pictures in 3 DIFFERENT SIZES, both, in black-and white and FULL NATUREAL COLOUR.

The SPECIAL INSERT gives you the informations you need to order, sets of books that have been discrimminateingly considered by connosseurs to be the BEST and HOTTEST of all such items on the market, You will soon, I am sure, see why. A hasty glance will I'm sure, convince you that this is so.

Please to note the prices for these RESERVE STOCK sets of photo books, given at the end of the broshure.

We thank you in advance for your attention to our products. And we are looking forwards with eagerlyness, to your order.

JUST RELEASED!! THE ULTIMATE IN BIZARRE BEAUTY!!
NUDES
IN
LEATHER * HIGH HEELS * CORSETS * ETC.

Yes mens! Fantastically proportioned Blonds, Brunets and Redheads in exotique costumes of shineing Leather, gleeming Satine, formfitting Rubber, vice-constricting Corsets, spikeheeled Shoes and high Boots, and MORE!!

These poses arc DIFFERENT!! The Rare Garments posed in by these TOP MODELS were colected in England, Germany, Denmark, Holland and, from SECRET PLACES on the globe! The girls too, were carefully selected for those who UNDERSTOOD onely were chosen. NOW! The sophissticated connosseurs of the UNUSUAL can be own photos never before available!

AND MENS! These are not the simple pacquets of photos that can get lost or drop into UNWANTED HANDS!! These photos are printed in BOOKS WELL-BOUND, and, on high quality glossey paper in FULL COLOUR! Order all 6 NOW!!

Nudes in Leather *SUSAN . . . Tall, Blond & Fair . . . Susan has learnt her lessons well! See her eagerly disrobe in her black patent leather, hip-length boots, corset and accessories . . . JEANETTE . . . Strong Willed Brunet casualy brandish her bull whip as she undresses to her shinning black leather pantys . . . LINDA . . . from red leather gloves to cruely tight corset she is a gasping Vision of the Bizarre. Watch her sip her cocktail removeing her red leather bra with a Luger, to protect her from intrusion. Be Ware!*

Nudes in Rubber *NANCY . . . Dark and Deliceious . . . Her blue rubber boots and airline stewardess jacket clings to her every delectible curve as she mixes a "apertif" for her lucky customers in the clouds . . . CORRIE . . . A Master of Strictest Dicipline, her strong body buldges against her black rubber corset and stockings as she twiches her 9 Foot catta nine tails . . . TERRI . . . A vivaceous Redhead in her Business Executive outfit of tailored rubber suit with high heels. She relaxes in her Office by peeling down to her black rubber garterbelt and nylons.*

Nudes in Corsets *MARIE . . . Blond, Big & Buxom . . . See her doo her morning exercise in her shiny, tight patent leather, corset with the waspwaist . . . GIGI . . . Scowling, Sultry & Brunet, she menaces the unlucky window washer with an Automatic who happens to gaze in and see her in constricting corsets of snow white lace . . . BERTHE . . . A raven haired Lady who loses her dress in a fitting room! . . . See her tremble with shame and blush as the Manager discovers her that night in her red satine corset and black nylons, and Nothing Else!*

Nudes in High Heel Boots *MICHELLE . . . A Platinum Blond Mistress who likes to cook in her silver knee-high boots and black net stockings . . . Maybe she'll cook something up for you! . . . ROXANNE . . . Fair, Young & Nubil . . . She looks innocent in her gingham dress and pigtails but her Hip High patent leather boots and transparent black pantys are all she has on underneath . . . as you soon discovers! . . . JANE . . . Tall, and Tough . . . She doesn't wear those spike heeled boots over her muscular calfs for nothing . . . Wow!*

Nudes in Ultra High Heels *BARBARA . . . Lucious, Tall & Eager to Please . . . In her 5 inch heels she will submit to Your every Desire . . . LOLA . . . A Female Police Officer who captures attempted rapeists with her suave patent leather heels and teriffic gams! . . . SANDI . . . A Nurse who proves that Black is Beautiful in her pure white corsets, nylons and 4 inch heels. Oh Nurse!*

Nudes in Satine *MARLENE . . . a Satine Doll with Undies to match . . . See her divest her street clothes and get ready for action! . . . PAT . . . Neat and Petite, this dark haired lady believes in the Best in Bras, Corsets, and Pantys . . . Watch her disrobe them off as she prepares a bath . . . PHYLLIS . . . This Dusky Beauty is sensational in brown satine and lace corsets and swirling cape to match . . . See her French maid ANNETTE, lace her cruely up garbed in her own outfit of black satine undergarments and black mesh hose.*

110

ORDER NOW! $10 dlls. per book! All SIX for only $50 dlls! THESE ARE THE REAL THING!! Not the usual cheesecake items advertised by other firms and wich your SICK of! But, really NUDE lovelys, in the most thrilling undergarments and acesories. SATISFACTON GARANTEED! Please to send money in the form of a money order for QUICK SERVICE!!

Dear C. Corriendo,

Please send me all six (6) of the BIZARRE BEAUTY books as advertised in your SPECIAL INSERT. I enclose a money order in the amount of fifty dollars ($50.00).

Very truly yours,
Ned Beaumont

Dearest darling Ned,

Are you trying to drive your Daisy crazy? Crazy Daisy! That's good. I mean, Pooh, why haven't you scribbled one little line to poor me? I've been waiting and waiting for a teeny note from you and can believe only that for some reason you're angry with me? What did I do? I thought that maybe you tried calling me but I know how set against that you are but why don't you get in touch? When can we meet?

I've even thought of going up to your office but I don't want you to get nasty-angry with me. Do I? I couldn't bear that. I know that we must be discrete.

Tom has been dragging me to party after party and dinner and the theatre and I keep looking all over the city for you, even out the car window like some silly sophomore or something. But, Ned, my lover love, when I think of you I get goose-bumps all over from my head to my toes even including my you-know-what!

Oh God Ned. What's the matter? Please acknowledge this *dumb* note?

Your love slave,
Daisy

Dearest Daisy,

Don't be cross with me, my dreamboat—I've been swamped with boring publishing matters and even more boring authors ever since Heaven (Aspen), but I think of you all the time and do things *for myself* that I wish you could do *for me*. Do you understand, my lovely butterfly?

I think that you ought to come and see me this week at my apartment. Certainly you can get out of the house for one evening—if you

111

love me. I can't wait to see you in those "unmentionables" you bought. Are they really naughty? I mean—"bizarre"?

Please come soon, Darling,
I love you forever,
Your Neddy Pooh

P.S. The doorman is blind, deaf and dumb, his faculties having been deftly removed by a fifty-dollar bill.

Darling! Darling!

I never knew that anything could be so wonderful! As if a veil had been dropped from my eyes! All these years and now at last it seems as if I am seeing myself and Tom as if for the first time! It's so warm, the feeling, and at the same time so squeeky and clean like my hair, after a shampoo.

I'm going to talk to my lawyer again next week and really get this divorce thing going—Tom is willing as long as there is no *scandal!* He's such a borey-snorey old square. But what can you expect from a football player?

Yum! I love you. I kiss you a 1,000,000 times.

Crazy Daisy

Dear Mr. Ned Beaumont, Esq.,

It is of great pleasure to me to send here-with your six BIZARRE BEAUTY books as per your kindly order. We are of a sincere trust that you will enjoy them as has many HE-MEN who orders them do. You may be surprise to learn that from many satisfied custommers we recieve letters stating happily that these SIZZLING books have help them to adjust their lives more satisfactory with wives and girlfriends. Strange but—True!

You are I am, surely wondering just what can the reason be that I write to you in person, a strange act, is it not you may enquire for a person, who knows you only as a respectable custommer and of course, a LEADER OF BUSINESS? Allow me then to hasten to inform you that I, Mme Corrie Corriendo and my business partner and long time friend and confidante, Mme Berthe Delamode, latter of Paris France, are of the consideration that we desire to "shake the feet" of the dust of Mexico and journey to the United States, singularly New York City, New York.

Besides the business of supplying to respectable HE-MEN the kind of pictures they like and that are of a certainly proved highest quality of the REAL THING, Mme Delamode and I some years ago in various European capitals, seats of culture, wealth and elegance, had a

112

marvellous and famous niteclub show, based on Mme Delamode's unrivalled *clairvoyance*. You may of course perhaps have glimpsed occasionally such entertainments often, called by the name so we are led to understand of, "Mind Reading Acts." Is it not so? In any events.

You, sir, are no doubtedly forming the question in your mind, "Why should this lady be unburdening herself to me, a total stranger whom to her can be nothing more than a respectable HE-MAN custommer and business LEADER?" And so, in shorts, permit me to answer what I am sure your question must be. To wit.

Mme Delamode and myself are of the hopeful feeling that yourself sir, established as a business LEADER in the Communications Industry, may well have certain friendlyness with other gentlemens in the Field, some of whom may we dare, hope might of possibility be involved in the Entertainment Branch of the Field. To wit. Agents, Public Relations, Club Owners, Managers, Film Scouts, et al. Such we dare hope in our wildest dreams.

Sir. What I ask in all candidness is that, can it be at all possible for you to smoothe our way in New York allowing, then, for us to perform our Art before someone who might "book" us somewhere into a club, or bistro?

I know that this letter may, possibly be thought by yourself to be presumptious but Mme Delamode and I feel that our multi talents are seeding to waste here in Mexico where certain Legal and Police constraints restrain us from following our chosen Arts.

Please, Mr. Beaumont, to consider this carefully before you say— "NO" and throw this letter into, I fear the trash can! We would be grateful for the leastest assistance from your eminent generousness, believe me.

In passing, by the way, permit me to point out to you that CORRIE in black rubber corset and stockings is I and BERTHE, in the fitting room photos is, Mme Delamode. We often assist the other models in makeing up the books. I've hope that you will find us not to UGLY in contrastment with the other girls!

Finally we, would both be honored to meet you in persons and, to become really *close and intimate* friends.

With much hopes for your helpfulness, and with kindest sincere regards from Mme Delamode, I am, with the greatest of respectfulness,

(Mme) Corrie Corriendo

Dearest Daisy,

Just a quick note amid the press of getting the fall list in *some* kind of shape. What an insane business!

Of course I love you, my garter, as I told you on the phone (and always tell you). But is there really such a rush to get your divorce? Think of poor Tom. Oh, I know that he will get over it, and that he wants a divorce too, but can't you go about it in a more leisurely way, as befits Mrs. Buchanan? These Reno things are often so tawdry and tabloid-like in their feeling. Much too much so for my sweet patootie.

I hate to wait any longer than I have to to find you in my arms a free woman—a *single* woman. But you really must be very careful at this stage as you are a woman who moves in a world always fair game for gossip columnists and society writers. And Tom *has* been fair, gentlemanly, and I may say magnanimous about everything.

So, slow down a little, my little doll. I can't wait for the weekend!

Your adoring Tom

P.S. I bought you something *special* to wear for only me.

Dear Mr. Beaumont,

Be assured, sir, that I do not write you this letter to, as they used to say at Princeton, cavil, or find fault with your conduct which has been exemplary to a fault. But sir, as one tough-minded businessman to another, what is going on? My wife, Daisy, tells me in tears that she wants to delay the trip to Reno even though her attorney, my attorney, and myself are ready for this divorce. As Daisy, my wife, is, as well. She says that she must think of me, "poor Tom," she calls me. Sir, I assure you, that I am anything but "poor."

I have taken all precautions that this divorce will be seemly and sophisticated and without a whisper of rumor or a breath of scandal. Now, Daisy, my wife, says she wants to wait a while, while just a week ago she was climbing the walls in her eagerness and telling me plans of her honeymoon trip with you, with intimate details, I am embarrassed to say.

Now sir, I assure you that you have been discreet in all matters touching on your friendship with my wife and I further wish to assure you that I appreciate it. Daisy, my wife, has blossomed and, but for the fact that her bedroom looks like a lingerie shop, she has been "tops" since she met you.

But sir! I implore you to assure my wife, Daisy, that the quickest route to divorce at this point will be the best for all concerned. She wants to marry you, you, I am sure, want to marry her, you are certainly honorable sir, I am assured, I assure you, and I want my freedom as well. Also, our attorneys have come to an amicable agreement concerning settlement, alimony, property, etc.

So, my dear Mr. Beaumont, assure my wife, when next you happen to bump into her, that she should act with speed. After all, divorce should be approached like any business problem, I don't have to assure you.

Very truly yours,
Tom Buchanan

Dearest Neddy Teddy Bear,

I'm so mixed up I could just *die!* We all want the divorce, I mean just everybody that matters, but you, dear, tell me I should still wait. But wait for what?

God darling. You remember the things we did last weekend in that lovely hotel, just like the one in the Cole Porter song, was it? All alone, who needs a steeple? And the mirror, and the undies? Where did you *get* them? I've never seen anything like that at Bonwit's or Bergdorf's or anywhere! Anyway, my Tiger, you can't but remember you naughty smutty dirty boy—the things you asked me to do! And I *did* them! I'm getting all hot in the face just remembering it all. Anyway Dearest . . . We could do those things *every night* in our own home! Haven't you *thought* of that?

Anyhoo, please don't tell me to WAIT any longer. I can't stand it any more, do you want me to just faint, my Willie Winky?

Where did you learn all those things? When I think of Tom . . . Oh well, live and learn as Shakespeare said, was it?

I have *got* to have you.

Right now I'm all naked in my bedroom, writing this letter and looking at your picture and doing *something else*, too! I wish you were here to *watch* me, you nasty-nice Tiger Pooh!

I *will* get a divorce—right away. And you'll be stuck with me forever. Daisy Beaumont—Oh, I like that.

Here I come!
Dazy Crazy (about You!)

My Dear and Esteemed Ned Beaumont, Esq.,

How can it be possible for Mme Delamode and I to assure you in totality of the immense gratitudes we both feel for your kindly acts? To wit. Speaking to on the long distance phone myself and she to inform our truely thankful persons that you have called Mr. Abe North, the owner of the new Manhattan supper club, "El Jitters."

I will instantaneously upon terminating this—"Thank You"—note, to you, write to Mr. North at your wise suggestion, to in a manner of speaking introduce Berthe and I to him. If as, you suggest, Mr. North shows the interests in us and our Artistry you so truely opine he will, then Mme Delamode and me can be on our way to New York City within two days after listening to his opinion that is, if it is favorable to us and, if he desires to see us "running through" our "act."

Again, so many thanks to your true generousness to us poor ladies. Both of us are quite of impatients to meet you and make your aquaintence. I have the deeper feeling that the three of us could become *dear dear friends.*

I sieze the liberty of enclosing some PRIVATE photos, of myself and Mme Delamode in personal acts that you may, I trust discover enjoyable?

With greatest respects and also, from Mme Berthe, I am,

Corrie Corriendo

Dearest Honey Pooh,

Oh darlingest! I knew you were really spitting mad from your voice on the phone this morning, but I just *had* to call you—waiting for your dear dear letter that never never came. I cross my heart and hope to die that I will never never call you again at the office! There! Are you a little less angry with your silly girl now? If you won't forgive me I'll curl over and die.

I'm going ahead with the divorce. I know that sweety pie that you are, not a man to hurt a fly, you still think that I'll hurt Tom or myself but darling! Our lawyers who are very wise and rich and important wouldn't let us be *silly* about this and they grump and harumph and say that we should go ahead with it all, that it is the best time to get divorced because of some boring portfolios or taxes or something that, thank goodness, girls like me don't understand.

Don't be angry with me or I'll whither up and blow away like an old tumbling weed is it? Please? I'm sad enough allready that I can't kiss you to pieces this weekend or next either, with your work and that dull trip to Baltimore that you have to make. Why does one of your warehouses or whatever they call them, have to be in Baltimore? I'd like your warehouse to be in the Plaza if you know what I mean?

I'm sending you some Polaroid pictures of me that I had my maid Opal take of me last night. I told her some crazy story about color coordinated underfashions that I had to be able to see myself in objectively (see how intelligent I sound?) to do my Fall shopping. I *think* she believed me but she is a colored girl and what does it matter if she believes me or not? Who can she tell on me, Amos and Andy or Ray Wilkins or something?

Anyway, I hope you like them. And the silly girl inside them too?

With my broken heart on my sleeve,
Daisy

116

My dear Daisy:

Please forgive me, sweet, for this really not unexpected crush of business that has ruined and, it looks like, will continue to ruin our holidays indefinitely. I am more or less living out of a suitcase lately, never quite knowing where I will be from one day to the next. Martin Halpin is also on the go, so I can't expect him to carry my burden of work too, as you suggested that day on the phone. Apropos that day, dear, I was annoyed, but certainly not "angry." I mean, you are getting very close to your freedom now, your reputation and Tom's are unsmirched, and it's best to "play it cool."

I must also say, risking your displeasure, my love, that no matter what your lawyers say, a quick divorce will enable certain people in town to put two and two (or one and one, in this case) together, and connect you with me, to everyone's embarrassment. Please mention this to Tom. Not everyone has his generous heart.

Thank you for those extraordinary pictures! I do hope your maid has a close mouth. Some of them are *quite* provocative—as if you didn't know, you little musky minx! I kiss you everywhere!

Your lover,
Ned

P.S. I'll write and let you know when I'm off this business merry go round.

Dear and Esteemed Ned Beaumont:

Berthe and I, Corrie, cannot thank you so much for your instrumenting our first step on the ladder of entertainment success in New York City. Mr. Abe North was of a complete delight when he met us and in an instant, wisked us both, to his apartment where we were made urgently by him to perform various acts upon terminateing of which them, he sumonned his lawyer and a good contract was drawn up by this Worthy gentleman for working us as the Prime "act" in El Jitters, all this wondrous activity to commense, in two weeks so that, in this intervaling period Berthe and I can shine our artistry up and buy costumes and so forth and so on etc.

We also with greatest pleasures in our hearts and of course our bodies too, want to tell you of the shear fun!! that we both had on that first night in your apartment suit. You are thogh, I think Berthe will insist too, a very bad boy! And, next time we three have a tete a tete you will have to be chastised I fear a sterner way or two! You *understand* what we mean I am feel certain!

We thank you sincerestly also too, for the Cash that can allow us to purchase quickly the kinds of garments that Mme Delamode and I have the knowledge that you truely adore. Believe us when we asert that we are of possession of exact knowledge of your tastes in these hard to get and *expensive* items.

You from this letter head, will gather what Hotel we are staying in for some brief time until you search out an apartment suit suitable to *artistes* for living and receiving guests. Berthe and I like it too much, I trust you will know, but there is nothing comparative of *privacey* of the own home where one can do what she likes whatever it is!

We would like to see you this Saturday evening if you can free yourself for dinner that, we are sure, you know where to buy the most excellent in all of New York City. After our repaste we will think of a quiet night in our Hotel rooms or perhaps, in your apartment?

Until that occurrents, dear gentleman, cogitate upon some of the things we might be able, to arrange to perform for our mutual entertainments.

I greet you fondly "Hello" and Berthe too says it.

Corrie Corriendo

Dear Corrie and Berthe,

My goddesses! How is it possible for one man to be so happy! What strange lucky fate is mine that we came to know one another? Your sensual arts, your devotion to the dark mysteries of Eros make me almost swoon with pleasure when I think of the things we have been exploring together! I cannot wait for the glorious weekends we share so deliriously. At least, *I* am delirious and I have a suspicion that you may be too—just a little?

I knew you would like the apartment! The rugs, the fireplaces, the huge beds, the mirrors! Believe me, my darlings, all of these things were selected by me with pleasure and comfort in mind. I've thought of "something" by the way, that is new and wildly exciting for us to try this weekend. I don't even know if you will want to *do* it! Oh, God!

Now, please. Buy these following things for the weekend. They will be necessary for our little play. Charge them all, of course—and if there is anything else that you want to add, go ahead. Surprise me!

Two pairs evening-(full) length white kid gloves. Two white girdles with garters attached. Two pairs of white nylons. Two pairs of white tennis shoes (sneakers). Two white (nurses') uniforms. Two maids' uniforms with lace caps and aprons. Two pairs of white ribbed knee socks. Two pairs of white "Mary Jane" shoes (the shoe-store clerk will know what you want). One pair of handcuffs. One Polaroid color camera. One jar of cold cream. 1 bottle of mineral oil.

My adored ones! If I think of any other small items that might contribute to our happiness I'll bring them along.

Perhaps you will even guess what my idea is! My delights! My sisters of mercy! My Florence Nightingales!

Tremblingly, forever,
Ned

My most darling Ned,

I'm beginning to think that you find it fun to break your Daisy's heart. You don't write or call. It's been three weeks since I've seen you. Ned Pooh, it has been *torture!*

But what is worse, what is really rotten and lousy for me to live with is that a friend of mine—some friend!—told me yesterday at a lunch for the East New York Art Center, that she's seen you with two very attractive, very sophisticated European women—not once, but twice. And as she put it, having a "hell of a goddam good time." And on the weekends—on one weekend anyway.

Pooh, I know that being a famous publisher means seeing all kinds of people, having dinner, wining and dining them, etc. But I'm *green* with the jealousy monster, until I know who these ladies can be. If they were older or homelier or looked like lady authors look I wouldn't care but my friend said they were pretty. Actually, she said they were *beautiful.*

I just *know* that they're writers or illustrators or editors or something smart and bright like that, ladies who play the piano and speak French and own little exclusive boutiques and went to Sarah Lawrence and so on—but I want you to *tell* me who they are, my dearest! I love you! I have a right to know? *don't* I. After all, I'm going to be Mrs. Beaumont and do everything you want me to do or at least the things I can learn to do.

Think of me, darling! Last weekend I wept all through some late movie, some silly romantic English movie with Trevor Coward, and then I discover that you are out with two gorgeous girls, not a mile away! Oh dear. I know that you are working Ned, but darling, it hurt me so uchmay!

Please write and let me know about this. I know I'm a goose but I want you so much, so much, and now. I'm in bed.

Silly, adoring,
Mrs. Beaumont soon to be

My dear Daisy,

I'm rather shocked and a little disappointed by your letter, Daisy. Do you think it fair of you to interrogate me as to the identities of two women that I have had the honor to escort to dinner, the theater, etc., a number of times? Your "friend" (and I am glad to see that you hold her in no great esteem) is clearly a troublemaker—exactly the sort of person you should stay clear of now that your divorce is becoming a reality.

If you must know, and I tell you only because of the intimacy we have enjoyed in the past and may, again, enjoy in the future, that the two young women in whose company I have "been seen" are European *artistes,* whose pioneering experiments in clairvoyance have earned them enormous renown in Paris, London, Rome, Milan, Berlin, etc. They entreated me to help them to find employment in New York suitable to their skills, and I have done so. We have also been speaking of a possible book on their experiences. They will open this week in El Jitters, a new supper club owned by Abe North, a friend of mine of long standing. My "being seen" with them is evidence merely of a desire to be courteous and helpful to two very refined young women who are strangers to our city.

Dear Daisy, had my intentions *not* been honorable, do you really think I would have been so candid in my actions? And where, my dear, did you ever get the strange idea that I am ready to marry you? Surely, we have had a certain emotional *rapprochement,* of course, but marriage, at this point, seems out of the question. Is *this* why you have been unwisely rushing this divorce of yours? Dear, sweet Daisy, whom I thought was so innocent, who convinced me that she wanted to be free? In love, and sex? Is it just *marriage* that you want?

My dear child, I really think that we should declare a moratorium on our affair so that we can both see where we stand.

I wanted a lover, a mistress, a companion, a fabulous whore, not, I assure you, a "little homemaker."

God, Daisy, I hate to feel compromised. I think this entire episode has been unworthy of you. For now, let's both of us think the whole business over for a month or six weeks. I have a crush of business that simply won't allow me time for all these elaborate emotional and "moral" complications.

Perhaps we will be able to talk all of this over very carefully, calmly, and rationally over a drink, very soon. Until then, know that I deeply care for you, and think kindly of you. My regards to Tom,

> Yours,
> Ned

Dear Ned Beaumont,

Rather than awaiting for the opportunity to have conversations with you, Berthe, and I have arrived together at the conclucion that a short letter in detail of which we spoke to you of quickly last week would be in the order.

120

Not for a shortest moment should you think that we are not of a mutual delight at our performances at the El Jitters Club. Contrarily speaking in the fact, our work is of an ease, Mr. Abe North is a kindly and understanding chief, and our salaries are of the higher brackets. All is "peaches and milk"! Yet, as we had hinted to you last week Berthe, and I have long longed for to "set up" in our own establishment as owner-performers, in the later capaciousness to do, as we wish whenever it suits us so. But also, more important, to be able, to hire and fire and be in shorts, our own Boss.

Now, sweet Ned Beaumont, you naughty boy! We have been makeing the friendship of a gentleman who is proprietor of a small and unassumed saloon on the East side of New York City up town, as you say. The Club Zap. For purposes of his nervous health, his doctor advices him presently, to go away from New York City for an extensive rest, viz., to give away his entirprise. As I have been adviceing you Berthe, and I have come to the knowledge of this man who, likes us as his kind of "kid" sister. He is willing: to sell us his place for a summ that is quite too lofty in the view of same that we have, viz., for Berthe, and I it is very high and such a figure that we have smallest hopes of raseing even a payment to "put down."

Yet. Berthe and I have been discussing with fervore this idea that could, one, allow us to support our selfs nicely in a business we know a more than little thing about and two, let us practise our arts as the inspirations approach and not, as now and before to earn, our daily bread. Three, Be assured that we can reside for the Future in New York City that has grown upon us so sturdily. And of course to be here, means that we can continue to see *Mr. Ned Beaumont* as a freind and pleasure sharer. Is this not true?

To be frankly brutal, Ned we wish, for you to enter into discussion with our up town man to discover how best to assist us if you would consider this, so kindly? Clearly, we are on bent legs to you to loan us the money for the initial fee to make purchase of this saloon and of course, your attorneys would be of major use to percieve the details of the sale, etc. etc.

Unfortunately true is also, this fact. The saloon owner, our up town man in the question herein, have begged us to consider not, *buying* his saloon but, going with him to his new location and being his Stars and Manageress of a new place of business that, he assumes he would open so long, as he will be of a convincement that some body with niteclub experiences can do the hard work of makeing such a place "go." So Ned Beaumont.

If for many economical reasons or others you cannot see clear to doing this great favour for Berthe, and I we will soon be saying to you a sad good bye which, would sadden us both or all three I dared say a lot. We are just it seems, beginning to find out *how far* we can all go. No?

Let us know your thought on this. So that Berthe, and I can adjust our planning for the future about what your decision may be?

We will see you Saturday night after the final show. Of course? We prey that it will not be our final "party" but that, as they declare is "up on you."

Your Sex Mistresses,
Corrie and Berthe

My adored Mistresses,

I beg you, on my knees, in total abasement—anything!—to forgive me my delay in this matter of your buying the Club Zap. I don't wish to anger you further by pleading innocence, but believe me, my Darlings, my Queens of Passion! that this delay is the fault of my attorneys, who are continually plaguing me with questions as to my reasons for wishing to take funds out of the business to invest in (for that is what I have told them, for now) what they consider a frivolous and risky enterprise. You must also realize, my Empresses of Desire, that Martin Halpin, my partner, must be considered too—he doesn't like the idea at all, but he is slowly coming around to my pleas. You realize that I must be circumspect in all this, I mean that I cannot very well tell Halpin or my attorneys that I will do *anything* to keep you here, close to me. You have worked a magic spell on me and the thought of either of you leaving the city fills me with dread and despair! I lick your garters!

If I only had enough of my own money! But alas, I have not, you *must* believe me! To go through another weekend like the last, when you were both too tired for us to have our usual party, our little, lovely party—oh God! I don't think I could do it again! I must see you this weekend without fail . . . I beg you. I kiss your sneakers!

I think that the papers for the transaction will be drawn up by the end of the week, but please, please, cruel rulers, believe me when I say that I cannot hurry my attorneys without allowing them to glimpse my devotion to you both—and that is something that must be *our* secret! There are company funds that must be spent, and legal details to work out, a cover corporation, etc., etc. Believe me! I nuzzle your stockings!

Will I see you both this weekend? I implore you to call, to snarl that thrilling "yes" that I always dream of, I beg you to allow me to crawl to you across the room as you await me in your wondrous costumes, your faces cold and cruel. I die of desire. You shall have your club, your money, anything, *everything* . . . I must have your chillingly brutal love! I stroke your corsets!

> Your Serf, in dizzy happiness,
> Ned

My dear Beaumont,

Mme Delamode and I tender to yourself, "Thanks" for the completing of our business dealing, *finally!*

We are agreeing together, Mme Delamode and I, that to indulge in weekly activities with yourself is to be certainly a detrimental ocassion for us in the weeks to come, that is, with considering the amount of work to be done in making the Club Zap "go." So.

Therefore. Mme Delamode and I decide that it would be of the best for us three old freinds who so understand each other is it not true? to indulge our selfs in our brand of sex thrills one night of the month say, the first Saturday, of each month unless we are undisposed.

We are in trust that this will meet your approving Okay. If not we, are very sorry but I suppose that all relations come upon a closing, yes? Yet. We both feel surely that you dear Beaumont, would like to continue our gay tete a tetes since you are still a very naughty boy and need much more firm *Dicipline*.

So we will be looking ahead to seeing you in a time of three weeks. In the meantime please drop into our club for a complementary drink, and a short chat.

> Your understanding companions,
> Corrie and Berthe

Dearest Ned,

You are breaking your dearie Daisy's heart! I know that something *horrid* has happened. Martin Halpin won't say anything to me about it but it is quite transparent that he is *Very Upset!* Why are you acting in this way, Ned, my Pooh, my Heart? I adore you, Ned, confide in me, is it something I've done, is it that I'm a dull pupil in the things you like? Is it money? Oh Ned, I've got *so* much money!

I can't speak to Tom about any of this—he knows that something is wrong and speaks your name with viscous contempt. I mentioned your name to a friend at a cocktail party last week and she *blushed!* Ned, dearie Neddy! What *is* it?

I leave for Reno tomorrow. When I return, you must tell me what is eating away at our love, our precious and holy love.

> Your brokenhearted and blue
> Daisy

I was done. The pile of letters lay before me on the table like the gravestones in Verlaine's famous "cemetery by the sea"; somewhere in there lay the life of what had once been a man! Ned Beaumont! At the moment, the room growing crepuscularly shadowy in the dusk that sifted down outside, Beaumont huddled in the corner, his face in his hands, ashamed, and—was he weeping soundlessly? The silence was mysteriously heavy, tense between us—there seemed nothing to say, but I leaned forward, and softly murmured, "I'll help, Ned, I'll help."

His shoulders shook and I glanced out the window at the soaring towers of the iron city, touched now, as was my heart, with lengthening shadows of slate-blue.

Lamont's Notebook

"Letters" really good, methinks!! Do I see the old bottle of Ginzo Red coming to life with sparkle, etc.? A couple things, but . . .

1. Why would Ned B keep copies of personal letters? Business letters O.K., and so on, but why copies of all his love letters to Daisy? A wrong note? Error of technique that critics will seize on, by Jesus, you bet! And: 2. Why don't these people ever *telephone* each other to relate some small thing, etc.? O.K. when far away, but when in same city, how come? Again, the cruel bastards will have at me hammer and tongs. But! It stays . . . the book is mysterious anyway, vague around the edges, and strange. (They are strange characters!) —so why not these letters, their presence somewhat inexplicable, etc.

I like this chapter!

(You can say that again.)

I like this chapter!!!

Now, I'm wondering what people will say about these letters. *Who* will find *whom* in them, and so on. And my own sex life will be open to them all, so they'll *think*. Who can care?

Yes—the letters add a piquancy, a mystery to the book. Vague reminders of a past that should have stayed in Beaumont's head— now Halpin knows, and we are *forced* to know. They stay!! What will the ex-wife think? She must know that the true writer, the artist, must use everything! Everything grist . . .

What does it matter if the ambiguity is intentional or not?

My dear Sheila,

Certainly you are correct that there are objective correlatives *galore* in "Burst L's." But I cannot agree with you that this is an instance of my "emotions being held in reserve" as you seem to think is the case. Certainly, I know the dangers of being *too* remote, *too* icy in such a densely developed piece of writing, but I think you will agree with me—I hope!—that one of my constant problems as a novelist, and there are many, is that I have often become *too* involved with my characters, using them as mouthpieces, or extensions of myself. In this chapter I have tried desperately to remove myself from these people and allow them to "work things out" for themselves, guiding them as little as possible, if that makes sense to you. As a matter of fact, as I may have told you in an earlier letter, these people tend to get away from me, and I often find myself writing something, a phrase, a snatch of conversation, as if it is being *dictated* to me, as if all my people are laughing at me behind my back as they go through their paces to humor me. Now I know what Wilde meant when he said "I'm called away by peculiar business. But I leave my characters behind me." Leave them behind me indeed! And in front as well!

Be that as it may, in this chapter, which takes the book to about its onethird mark, I feel that I have for the first time in my "checkered" career used my emotions to the fullest, *but* I have wielded them surgically.

Rather than "reserved emotions" perhaps a better phrase would be "aesthetic distance." I'll buy that, as the man said. However, don't for a moment think that I am ungrateful to you for your obviously close reading of this chapter. And many of your points are brilliant. Certainly, "twisted" and "broken" sexuality symbolizes the twisted and broken thing that Beaumont becomes as he finds himself ensnared by these two lewd harpies. I thought for a long time about the propriety, the correctness of giving Corrie broken English as a language, and finally realized what should have been obvious—the mood of the chapter (and the book as a whole) not only would profit from such language, it cried out for it! It was then I saw the woods, as it were. Everything devolves on this corrupted language, it is the core of Beaumont's own distortion as a man.

I'm glad that you did not find the brochure descriptions of the "girls" distasteful, and that you saw that they too fit the pattern of corruption and decay that runs through the book like a fine seam. They, if you will, serve as objective correlatives to Lamont's growing and uncontrollable lust, and Daisy, adulteress though she may be, does not deserve to be robbed of *all* her innocence, as it is clear she *is* being robbed—plundered, in fact. In any event, I hope that there is a residue of ominous anticipation in the chapter, i.e., the suffocating sense that Beaumont may attempt to include *her* in his horrific orgies with the two bitches from Mexico —and that she might accept! Another fine point is that the lusts of C and D are for money and power and position—and they use the lust of Ned to gratify their own. Even here, we find corruption: for their lusts are not even fleshly—they are remote from their bodies; they are true pornographers of the spirit. Even their corruption is corrupt.

Alliteration in the brochure descriptions? Perhaps. Some of your suggestions are quite good and I will give them serious thought. I want to make sure, in my mind, that they ring true, that is, that they are the sort of thing that the writer of the brochure might truly say. (Do you think that Corriendo wrote the brochure copy? Let me know.) But I really *do* like the ring of "gossamer garters that girdle

126

her gorgeous gams" and "her bulging breasts almost bursting the bonds of her black brassière." But let me think on them for a while —they may be a bit much. After all, this style is a tried-and-true one, in the tradition of cheesecake captions, etc., and anything even a bit off center might destroy my intended effect.

It's difficult for me to see how the chapter can be juggled or recast so as to make C and D "symbols" for the decay of the country, as you suggest. I can see that they are indeed corrupt in terms of the pernicious American influence on what you term "honest craft" but surely the idea of getting rich quick or "making it" is not exclusively *American,* is it? And you must admit that nowhere in the letters do I say that they they were *actually* good performers, "craftswomen" if you will, in Europe. *They* say so, but they are liable to say anything. If they are symbolic of anything it is of the dark and shattering power of Eros unchained.

Finally, how pleased I am that you see that these two are based on two young ladies we both once knew. (To my regret.) But you will agree with me, I'm sure, that the pidgin English that Mme C uses quite effectively disguises our "friend." So much so that I dare say she wouldn't even recognize herself. Being my sister, I don't have to tell you how I tortured myself before deciding to go ahead and write out, however objectified, one of the sorrier and more shameful aspects of my life. Now I seem to have laid the ghost, or both of them, for that matter.

Your last point is well taken. But I decided that it doesn't matter if it seems ridiculous for people to write letters when they might more easily phone, and that it doesn't matter if it seems odd for Beaumont to keep copies of personal letters as well as business letters. I am going to risk letting all of this show, the oily machinery, and furthermore, letting the machinery be as wild and absurd as a Rube Goldberg contraption. That's what I had in mind when I decided to let these letters lie as they are. It's the reader's problem, sez I, in my best Rube Goldberg voice.

All right. Thanks for your interest and your shrewd comments. I'm glad that you like this chapter—your opinion gives me great strength and hope for the book.

I'm sure that you know that Dermot has also written me, praising the work, and has also sent me a first draft of a chapter of his Western. I will write him tomorrow. In the meantime, all happiness to both of you, and I'm delighted to hear of the progress of your essay.

Love,
Tony

Dear Dermot,

Thank you so much for your wonderfully encouraging comments on my "Burst Loveletters." I *would* like you to see more of the novel, now that I know your opinions on this chapter, but there is some revision to be done before I get anything really ready—you'll understand of course.

And thanks too for the opening chapter of your Western. It's a terrific stroke of brilliance to give the cowboys Irish speech—your contention that most of our American pioneers and cowpokes were first-generation descendants of Irish immigrants who couldn't make it in Eastern industrial cities, and ex-soldiers in the Union Army— drafted immigrants—sounds perfectly plausible, and, more than that, right! Why indeed should a boy from St. Louis, whose family had been here less than twenty years, speak with a Western drawl? That would be like expecting Richard III to speak like Noël Coward.

I'm afraid that I can't help you locate the "real McCoy" girly brochure—I'm afraid that I didn't use a specific piece of literature as a model, but put together, from memory, all the junk I've seen over the years in order to make up a kind of prototypical cheesecake-porno ad. Don't tell me that sex will raise its ugly head in the Golden West as well as in the corrupt world of New York publishing? (Although I forget that delicately understated scene of autoeroticism in your chapter, don't I?)

In any event, I'm sorry that I can't help you. And I'm delighted to have your opening. It has a swift, crackling life and "fun" to it that one has ceased to expect from Westerns, which have all gone "serious" and psychological in recent years. I can't wait to find out what happens. You are writing with a subtle combination of humor and bitterness that was always your forte when at the top of your form. How I wish my poor book had the drive that yours shows—but then, I was always damned by my nagging introspection.

Best of luck to you and your "dust eaters."

Tony Lamont

One: *Red Dawn and Blue Denim*
Dermot Trellis

Phlegm rattled and churned sandily in Deuces Noonan's throat as he casually worked it up into his gob, then salvoed it into the street with the same rattlesnake accuracy with which he was wont to fling his gleaming Bowie knife on its deadly and more than occasional errands. His spurs jingled as he stepped backward through the swinging, bullet-splintered doors of the Blue Bird Saloon into its cool darkness, cool and silent as the Pecos dawn itself. Yet, though silent, the interior of the saloon was not empty. Huddled wordlessly about the tables in the rear were the toughest, durndest trio of cutthroats, thieves, and outlaws in the Territory. When they were quiet, it was mighty unhealthy, being as it was the quiet of the diamondback before he sends forth his deadly warning of fatal attack upon the pretty, golden-curled maiden innocently gathering attractive rocks for display on her credenza, chifferobe, or chest of drawers.

A voice as harsh as a starved Sioux's cracked the stillness. "I tell ye, by God, Noonan, ye're a desperate man for spittin' a quid inter the dust o' the street."

Noonan turned scowling to face Sundog O'Haggerty, his eyes fair leaping across the room at him like two Apaches crazed with firewater and hatred for the paleface.

"You don't say so?" he fired.

O'Haggerty's voice softened to a surprisingly childlike rasp.

"I do. Ye're a lovely spitter altogether begob."

"Mebbe so," Deuces reflected, his thoughts, as often, far away. Then he turned once again to take up his post by the doors, his eyes deceptively lazy on the street and beyond—beyond, to the mountains now blushing rosy in the dawn, from whose fastnesses Big Cal O'Nolan would be coming this morning, bitter vengeance like black bile in his heart and leaden death in his pearl-handled Colts.

Suddenly, startling yellow teeth burst flashingly through the gloom of the saloon, as a mirthless smile whispered across the black-bearded face of Black Danny McGlade, the grudgingly acknowledged leader of the Midnight Gang, the hunnish riders of destruction in this Territory, of whom these three slouching killers formed a kind of council. As the smile ran away like water into desert sand, so did the face uncannily melt back into the protecting gloom, like a ravening timber wolf surprised at his gruesome feast of young dogie disappears into the bresh.

"It won't be spit ye'll be needin' to bring down a darling item like Big Cal, me boyo! It'll take all our irons and more, be-Jazus, to lay to his grave that long hard drink o' water!" The yellow teeth gleamed again in accompaniment to the swarthy leader's rill-cold laughter.

"It's quiet," Sundog muttered, "too quiet. I don't care for it." His cough was like distant thunder away beyond the Pecos.

"That's a bloody lovely cough you have there, O'Haggerty," McGlade lashed. "I think we'll have to be sendin' to Dodge for a priest."

"Is that a fact?" Sundog barked unkindly and fell again into a spasm of hearty coughing that rent the air like whizzing tomahawks.

"I recall an uncle back in St. Louis that had a father of a cough like that one," Noonan mused. "I reckon that his dang throat turned into an item like a lump of raw mutton, it did. The sight of it would make a man puke."

"Have some of the craytur," McGlade opined. "That's the man to break the cough's back."

"Is it now?" O'Haggerty gasped, putting the redeye down his throat bedamn for all the world like a mustang guzzling water with his bloody face up to the eyes in a creek.

"Indeed it is," chuckled McGlade of the tough grasslands clan. "By the Sacred Heart of Jesus, the pizen will tear the cough directly out of yer craw."

"Tis all that's needed to purify rotten flesh," Noonan winged.

"You may lay to that!" McGlade added, as their chum took another draw on the jug.

The three men then lapsed into another silence as profound as midnight when it falls over the desert surrounding Cincos Blancos. For a moment, peace seemed to hold the same sure promise of beauty that the steadily rising orb of lambent fire in the East held. But it was not to be. Big Cal O'Nolan even now was riding, riding toward the dust-choked town, his soul as bitter as raw *mescal*, his thoughts sour as the lemon that the *vaqueros* used to ease the burning of that fiery brew in their greasy, foul mouths.

For these three had killed Huge Cal, the boy's father, one of the straightest *hombres* and stoutest hearts that this vast range, from Cincos Blancos to the foothills of the Pecos and the spuming waters of Rio Cobarde, had ever known.

Black Danny McGlade, ex-chief wrangler on Huge Cal's *rancho,* the Orange O, had loved the latter much as a younger brother might. Together they'd ridden trail, fought the lousy and treacherous Mescalero, frozen in the bitter winter, and sweltered in the breathless summer of the plains under a sun that might have served as the lantern of Hell itself! Black Danny! How could he have fallen supine under the hoofs of this outlaw life, how could those granite, yet yielding lips, that had once smiled in jest, now be the gateways for such gnarled commands as Steal! Kill! Reach! Rob! Rape! Pillage! Draw! and Sack!? Yet, it was so. He led the life of the most savage predator, roaming the wilderness for victims, even as a vicious puma glares balefully at the unsuspecting doe. Black Danny! His rock-sculpture of a visage, his beard luxurious as a saloon girl's dress, his chained laughter that had flamingly ignited many a supper in the bunkhouse—had it all, all now been placed in the murderous service of the gun? So it seemed.

130

Certainly, there was nothing to be surprised about concerning Sundog O'Haggerty's place in the leadership of the Midnight Gang. This social outcast, this "breed" from the stews and cribs of languid Old Méjico, had long been hated and feared by every citizen both north and south of the border. It was rumored that he had mercilessly shot up every town in Kansas, shaming even his vandal leader, Quantrill. A snarling, pimpled killer, a social disease lodged in his throat, from which often bubbled obscene jests, his eyes were the color of dried-up waterholes and his conscience that of the Durango scorpion. Killing was like a blood transfusion to him, and he was never so dangerous as when his pimples stood blood red against his spectral pallor.

The third, Deuces Noonan, the youngest desperado, formed the perfect companion to these two. Handsome, and with an undefined and curious softness about his lips and loins that had made him a favorite around the campfire when he was a trailhand, his eyes glittered with the same malice that a pinto's displays when he has been chewing on loco weed in July. Jests continually burst from his soft lips so that it was whispered of him that when his gob wasn't lobbing globs it was spraying japes. And his razory Bowie knife enforced his every dark mood.

These three, then, waited for Big Cal to enter the sleeping town. They had killed his father when the latter had refused to string his wire to stop the advancing railroad, shot him down like a dog in the streets, while honest folk fearfully squinted and trembled in homely buckskin and gingham. That great heart was no more. They had reasoned, like the buzzards they were, that young Cal would come for them, but they had thought that his youthful impetuousness would drive him, in a shower of pebbles and manure, wildly into their waiting gunsights. They figured dead wrong, wrong as the clock in the Blue Bird, that had stopped one night in '78 when Lash La-Scarre, in a frenzy of despair over Ruth Chest, who had gone "back East" to attend secretarial school and have her nagging touch of syphilis looked after, beat it to a pulp with his bull whip. But that is another story, and a mighty good one.

For Big Cal had inherited, along with his father's taste for fine wine, mellow Habanas, and crisp Mozart, his plodding, often unnerving patience. Some had even dubbed Huge Cal "the Clod," yet one bucko with the temerity to so call him to his leathery face had clawed sky and eaten dust, his middle entirely blown away by the old man's hard shotgun. It was this blood patience that was now performing its task in unnerving the three desperate gunmen.

Each day brought the leering Vandals closer to panic, closer to that nerve-shattering fear a cowpoke feels when his horse totters and falls on him, closer to that total horror that ultimately whispers *"Run, you galoots! Git out and run, you dust-eatin' saddle bums!"* For somewhere, coming toward them in a cloud of mist and horse lather, somewhere, coming toward them as inexorably as the blind vermilion eye of Old Sol, somewhere, was young Big Cal, a dozen messengers of doom dozing impatiently at his waist, waiting for their macabre flight of freedom.

A gentle sunrise breeze carried the ravishing scent of magnolia and tumbleweed to Big Cal O'Nolan's strongly fluted nose and caressed as gently as a señorita's voice the golden locks that crowned the six feet four of lean, hard muscle that proclaimed his body. He stretched by the fire and swiftly uncoiled his springlike legs, still a little stiff from the chilly fingers of the mountain night. For a moment, he smiled at the rough effluvia that rushed helter-skelter up his deerlike nostrils, but then a dark shadow crossed his almost pretty face as his brain murmured awake, mumbling dark words of duty and revenge.

Again, the soft breathings of the mountain morning enveloped him and he was transported back to the town of Dry Bend, back to the storeroom of the little settlement's dry-goods store, where he stood —was it just yesterday?—close to the lissome frame and tossing curls of Patience Reilly—the gentle Patience, his betrothed, whose voice carried clearly as a duck's to him now on the silken puffs of morning ozone.

Must you go, Cal? Must you? Once you strap on those horrible guns your life will never change—you will have taken an irrevocable step that will—that must *haunt you until the last despairing ding-dong of dreadful doom . . . arunnin' and arunnin' like some sorta . . .* animal! *No place to hide, no chanct for a decent life, no evenin' fires an' pipes after your chuck an' grog an' the like. An' what about the Orange O? An' what about————?*

Wolfe Reno'll take charge o' the rancho, I reckon . . . honeysuckle gal! He's a darling wrangler with the great heart of a bald eagle! This is somethin' that I just—I just—gotta do, *cuz a man* does *what he's gotta do. . . .*

But what about————?

These are my father's guns, darlin'. Lovely items altogether, don't you say so?

I hate them. *Oh Cal! What about————?*

When I strap 'em on, as I'm now doin', as ye can see, I somehow feel me old da's hands on me shoulders, squeezin' an' squeezin' so as to make the tears start to me eyes. . . .

But what I want to know, you big gazabo, is, what about————?

... an' his great bloody orbs starin' into mine, the courage flashin' from 'em to make you bust yer heart cryin'. Sometimes ... sometimes, mind ye, my sweet shamrock of a blushin' colleen, when I touch the gun butts just right ... I can sorta see a kind o' transparent figure of the da kinda stridin' through the sky, the snowy peaks o' the harsh yet beautiful Pecos entirely showin' through his whole head. An' body too. It's ... it's ...

But what about——But what about me, Cal! Me! I tell you straight, Cal O' Nolan, I'll not be the wife of a hunted man! If you ride to Cincos Blancos today, I'm at home tomorrow to "Shoe" Beamish, the only man in the territory who's never shot nor maligned unjustly an Injun!

"Shoe" Beamish, the Craven Blacksmith? Shaky "Shoe"? "Chicken" Beamish?

The same! I'm not to have my heart broken by the likes of you, you strappin' big lump! Better a coward's wife ... than a lump's widow.

"Shoe" Beamish ... ptui! What class of lump just would that be?

Go—go, Cal, an' ye'll return to a town that'll not have me in it to welcome ye ... if you come back atall, atall! Marry yer darlin' irons!

C-come back, darlin' heather girl ... come ... back! My tumbleweed. ...

Big Cal shook his coiled and muscled leanness and angrily swept the tiny tears from his eyes. Mustn't let Big Jake sense my fears and regrets, he said to a lazy pine, glancing over at the superb buckskin, who was making a good breakfast on some nearby sequoia and mesquite. The magnificent beast looked up, neighed for a moment, and went on with his chawing.

Flinging then from his ice-blue eyes the tell-tale moisture, Big Cal next flung from his brain the form and voice of Patience, blushing at the bewildering sensations her memory evoked in his loins. Then he leaped from his blankets with the celerity of a maverick whose rump has just been branded by the cruel, yet kind, iron. Eager now to be on his way, his lynx eyes darted about through the clearing mists that swirled about the boulders among which he had made camp. In his mounting impatience, it was all the puerile bucko could do to rustle up a quick breakfast of jerky, sourdough, red beans, and jamoke. He ate deliberately, knowing that he would need all his strength—Cincos Blancos was less than two hours away! He shuddered, suddenly ashamed.

Even now, he knew, the trio of asps awaited his coming, joking coarsely, among the odors of whiskey and gun oil, about Huge Cal's murder. Huge Cal—the Clod!—the youth thought he heard someone say, and he whirled about so swiftly, slapping leather, that he knocked over his coffee pot and put out the fire.

He shut his eyes and ground his teeth so tightly that something deep inside him seemed to snap. Laugh, you mangy coyotes, he coughed, gulping the last of his savory java, as he waved his sweaty old Stetson at the billows of smoke that made as if to engulf his hard leanness. Laugh, laugh while you can, for soon I'll be lettin' some daylight into ye! He caressed the cold beauty of his six-guns as a man might the pure but intoxicating body of his bride and again felt the puzzling agitation that seemed to come from somewhere within his Levis. Then he broke camp, fidgeting and fussing with the area until it was exactly as he had found it. It was not for nothing that the boy had Apache blood, though few in the territory knew this. Lucky for them, he grunted.

Spurring the big buckskin down the slope in a cascade of dust and rocks, the sun flamed brightly into Big Cal's eyes and his heart swelled as he knew that today would bring him into the estate of manhood. Yet the thought of Patience, sweet, chaste Patience, brought another crystal of tear to his eye, and Big Jake, catching, as always, the scent of fear, pain, and terror, whinnied wild-eyed, making as if to throw his youthful rider into a deep ravine. But Big Cal, who had been around broncos since he was born, stroked the big fellow's muzzle, patted his head, rubbed his ears, and dug his spurs into the silken flanks savagely, until the noble beast responded to his hoarse commands. Then he laughed!

And they were off down the slope again, galloping swiftly through the foothills now, the two as one, brave horse, brave rider, toward Cincos Blancos and their appointment with justice, a justice that had as judge and jury lead and gunpowder.

Locked into the dark WC at the back of her father's dry-goods store, Patience Reilly gave vent to the long-smoldering and passionate desire that she had never let the "big galoot," Cal O'Nolan, even glimpse. She writhed and twisted in the dark privacy of the retreat, her golden, silk-encased, yet lonely legs flinging themselves about as if they had a mind or two of their own. There was no one to see but God, and Patience felt that He was peering at these shameful carryings-on . . . yet, she could not help herself. "God forgive me!" she gasped—and the prayer was followed by that soughing moan like the wind through the lonely yuccas, that moan, age-old, that moan of passion and desire that is not only mortal sin but that is also—Woman! She clawed at the gingham and crinoline garments that held her body like a prison, these clothes that had come all the way from the East—from Boston! How she hated and yet was drawn to that word! Boston! she panted, the latch on the flimsy wooden door rattling as

134

her tiny booted feet, now completely out of control, struck an erratic yet enthralling tattoo that brought sympathetic smiles to the faces of the customers in the front of the store. Boston! she sobbed into her knuckles, driving her heels smartly through the door paneling.

Deputy U.S. Marshal "Arizona" Jubal Coole shuddered like a spooky palomino in the dawn wind off the mountains. His face, which bore an uncanny similarity to his saddle, cracked and tanned by years of sun and weather as they both were, broke into a toothless grin as the huddled buildings of Cincos Blancos appeared faintly against the lightening horizon. The lawless burg looked as good to his faded eyes as a painted floozy does to a trail hand after taking a herd of long-horns through Cheyenne country.

"Ain't the man I wuz onct," he whispered to his black gelding, Francis. "Time wuz I woulda taken a mornin' dip in the icy Cobarde an' let the *wind* dry me taut an' leathery body." He sighed and with difficulty pried off the famous hat, blocked and shaped by years of sun, wind, rain, and Indian weapons, the beloved lid that was as much a feature of this harsh land as its mesas. "Ah, Francis, me man, it's a hard bloody thing to feel the years creepin' up yer legs an' stiffenin' the meat on ye all the way up to the bloody oxters." Francis neighed delightedly as he heard his old friend's gentle croaks.

He squinted again through the winy haze of the valley toward the sordid town, his glance still bright and straight as the polished Winchester that nestled snugly in its saddle holster, gleaming like a silver dollar in the morning's effulgence.

"Well, me buckos," he addressed the dusty clumps of buildings, "ye won't be *overly* delighted to see an old lawman, seein' as how I have a bone to pick with Black Danny." He chuckled, the phlegm rattling in his old throat like dice. "But ye might say that I'm desperate hopeful that Mr. McGlade and I can come to some sort o'— *onderstandin'*—about the *dee*-mise of Huge Cal O'Nolan."

He whipped out the gleaming blue death that was his long-barreled and rightly feared forty-four, and performed a series of complicated maneuvers with it, ending with a brilliant version of the border shift that culminated in a single quick shot that sliced off a menacing Gila Monster's head at fifty yards. Francis neighed his approbation.

"I just hope that I'm in time to head off that young hotheaded idjit, Big Cal, afore he gits hisself into a lovely class o' scrape. Begob, that crew of desperate bastards would claw the face off ye an' tell ye they were givin' ye a shave." He spat high into the wind then, and another swiftly thrown slug caught the wad of sputum in midair, sending a shower of moisture rainbowing about the old lawman. "The boy has

Texas Fever," he mused. "Begob, I'll break his legs if I must to keep him away from those rattlers. . . . Huge Cal woulda wanted it. . . ." He spurred his darling Francis toward the town in which the only thing awake, awake and waiting, was Evil.

Black Danny's hand crawled across the table toward his dull iron like a louse on an Arikara's scalp.

Sundog O'Haggerty spun the cylinder on his brutal six-gun and spat quietly into his filthy sombrero.

Deuces Noonan stepped, hips swinging, into the sunlight of the Blue Bird's porch to cut off the wings of a fly in mid-career with his fierce blade.

Off in the haze of breakfast-fire smoke from the O'Brien ranch that marked the beginning of Cincos Blancos, a cloud of dust that bespoke a fast-moving horse and rider came ever closer. The silence lay as thick as chili. The sun brought the promise of a scorching day—and sudden death!

In the town, only the three slaves of Satan moved. Time had come to a stop as abruptly as a cayuse throws a dude.

Noonan's sludgy eyes descried the moving cloud and he turned to face the gloomy interior of the barroom. "Hog-killin' time," he tittered, his Bowie knife glittering. Chairs scraped in counterpoint to vulgar laughter.

Lamont's Notebook

"Would you have any recollection of the name of the company that put out the 'girly brochure' which, I assume, you used as a model for your remarkable chapter? It would be very useful to me." says my transparently lascivious brother-in-law.

"Her bra bulging . . . gossamer garters . . ." etc., etc., says my winsome sister Sheila.

And now I wonder for the first time about the *quality* of that marriage. Somehow their private, their most secret acts reveal themselves to me almost as if I had caught them at it.

Sheila Lamont?

Mrs. Dermot Trellis? (Sheila Trellis.)

Up to this lubricity with that clod of a hack? Whose praise is fulsome and, I suspect, false. Polaroid Pete.

Brochure indeed!! Why not a request for photographs?

I see now: Dermot *believes* this fiction. (Applause.) He lusts for these two tramps as sharply as Beaumont. I see the book begin to glow with that uncanny green light that radiates from the pages of

136

the most meticulously crafted novels—absolute falsehood of artifice turning by magic into truth.

Of course it would get to him. The same vicious rubbish from him —his uncanny potboiling knack clear in his "Western"—"although I am a doggedly experimental writer"—"in this book I have eschewed such efforts in order to make a swift, clean tale of dramatic and virile action." Oh yeah?

And Sheila duped?

In the cabin, now, poor Martin, brought back to the reality of the situation. Must keep the forward movement as best I can.

6. SPILT INK

How real it seemed! I half-expected to hear Ned Beaumont's sob, racking, pitching, agonized, and, for a moment! . . . but it was only the wind, still frothing and keening about the cabin, O maniac wind, and my friend's voice was stilled, as I only too well knew it was. The past plays strange tricks on us, pushing its way into our present, taking up room . . . how could the police ever understand what I had meant to do for Ned Beaumont? How could they understand the terror into which I myself plunged when I decided to interpose myself between him and those two? "Laying it on the line." I speak of my body.

But what *of* the police? It seems that they should have been here long ago. Are they, too, to be swept up, by the madness and improbability, of this harsh affair? Did they believe me when I called to report this death? What *do* they believe? What goes through your ordinary detective mind when called on a case like this? Ned Beaumont would know. Why have they taken so long to get here? Or, I should say, why *are* they taking so long to get here? Odd to think of them as discrete pieces in the ominous and mysterious jigsaw puzzle that this case looms as. Yet—they are!

Is it a case?

Where are the police? I find myself getting nervous, thinking of them, of what they will say, their gruff politenesses. I want them here! I want them here before dawn . . . the night seems endless. Wind-whipped waters, banshee winds. . . .

So many things might have happened. The police car might have broken down. The driver, a rookie, may have taken the old mountain road, and run into a "Falling Rocks" area. Perhaps some Rocks fell on the car itself, or on the driver, incapacitating him, in which case a Senior Detective may have been loath to take over the driving because of union regulations, or a feeling of false pride.

Perhaps the Chief himself was hit by a Falling Rock and there is no one else in the car qualified to conduct the investigation, in which case the car is probably, at this moment, heading back to the metropolis, glittering its thousand jewels of light on the shimmering streets?

What if a Falling Rock was large enough to block the road completely, so that the police are now taking the old river road, which, like all old river roads, is in a state of disrepair? The narrow bridges, slats missing, are considered by the natives hereabouts to be dangerous, fit only for carefree boys to fish off. They rarely catch any fish, according to Old Cash at the general store. What crackers he has! If, on the river road, they should pass the Blue Bird, they may go in for a Mölte or two, crisp and with a creamy head. *That* would delay them.

What if they are drunk when they take that old mountain road, deciding against the old river road because of its horrible condition? There is a distinct chance that the Rock that ominously waits for them will be unseen until the last moment, and that the eager rookie driver may plow into it, smashing the differential or the rings or ball bearings of the vehicle—certainly an old one, since the police have not received the help they should get from City Hall. Crushed by this unforeseen delay, they may walk back down to the old river road for another crackling Mölte, and a gruff word and jest with the barmaid, who, though dazed in appearance, is a night-school physics student at the Community College. There is no phone there, so it will be impossible for the detectives to get help for their injured comrades; they will certainly not think first of *this* case when caring for their own. Would that be reasonable to expect? Policemen are human beings like everyone else, with hopes and joys, fears and dreams.

Surely, they will walk down toward the old Mathers place, and be nonplused when they find no one at home, nothing, in fact, to betoken life there save for a rusty bicycle leaning against the dilapidated fence. I often wonder who left it there! Perhaps, at that moment, they will commandeer a car, one of the few that take the old river road, now that it is shunned by all the residents, or almost all, except for a rare lover and his sunny girl, who will brave its dangers to get to the dark glade that nestles close by the falls. Yet the chances that the driver that they flag down with their police flashlights, blinking and glimmering the red of danger and caution, will be a native of the area, are slight, so slight that indeed my heart sinks when I think of it. There are few natives who take the old river road now, since its state of disrepair, its narrow bridges, with their missing slats, is known in the neighborhood, even by the children, to be extremely dangerous. Only carefree boys, so they say, fish off it. So they will probably, if they are "lucky" enough to flag down anyone, find that the driver is unfamiliar with the neighborhood, and when they order him to take them to the lake here, along the old mountain road, it is a probability that he will answer their demands with a careless shrug and a maddening request for directions.

In the back of my mind, I can see him running out of gas, in a fantastic rainstorm, the kind that often floods the highways in quaint

Arkansas, just outside Memphis. What then will be the detectives' opinion of him? Their young companion injured, the rain driving down in icy sheets, and before them, in the glare of the brights, a road cluttered with boulders! There will be nothing for them to do then but walk again, in the downpour, to the Blue Bird, where a bowl of the famous corn chowder made there may put some life back into them. The young man who picked them up will not be with them —where will he be? I would imagine that the police, in their disappointment at his stupidity, may have pitched him off the old mountain road where it bends in toward the woods and the Mathers place.

Are *these* the police I have called? What compassion will they bring to this case, their hands soiled, as it were, with violence done to the person of some innocent man, probably from out of state, who stopped for their flashing red lights, thinking that he was being a Samaritan? Their questioning will be cruel, cruel, and relentless, they will be dripping with rain water, angered by the critical condition of their young rookie driver, or their Chief, a huge knot on his head, delirious in the back of the car that they will have pushed up the old mountain road to get here, yes, pushed, and then run madly to catch as it reached the crest of the hill at Sadie's Glen, and sickeningly plunged down the other side, the Chief still in the back seat, oblivious to this new danger.

What can one fairly expect from these men, who have spent their adult lives confronting the seamiest segments of society, what can one expect when they enter this cabin and find me sitting here, Ned Beaumont a hulk huddled by the stairs, almost as if drunk? The warm fire, my expensive clothes, the bar with the finest whiskies—will these accouterments, etc., of the good life endear me to them? On the contrary, I should think that their rage would be snarlingly directed toward me as the proprietor of this elegance, if proprietor is the correct word—but you know what I mean, my patient friend, do you not? You are still listening, I hope, still following this tale of destruction and woe? Good, can I get you another imaginary drink for your imaginary mouth? No? Well, let me know when you want one!

Now, let me think what might have happened had the police taken the thruway, which has only just been opened to the public. A twenty-minute dash from the city takes one to Bigleyville, a remarkable journey in that such a trip, by the old river road, even when it was in good repair, took an hour, and by the old mountain road, *sans* Falling Rocks, an hour and a quarter. The problem is that if they had taken the thruway (which indeed, I now feel they might well have done—are not the police as intelligent as the other clods that drive this highway day and night?) they would have been compelled to exit

140

at Bigleyville, which is eighteen miles south of this sad cabin, or at Smudge, eleven miles north of it, where the wind keens like a madwoman who has lost her lover . . . the only way to this dark lake from either Bigleyville or Smudge is via the old river road or the old mountain road, the pair of them totally inadequate for motor travel (see above). I can see them heading into the old river road from the Mr. HamburGiant at Route 6, the disappointed scowls on their faces as they reach the first slatless bridge; I can see them turn their old car back into the roaring traffic at the Abe Lincoln Log Motel and drive up the rainswept mountain road, the old mountain road, curiously rainswept even when the rest of the countryside is baking in sunshine, summer or winter.

Then—the Rock strikes the Chief! Or the young rookie, smiling at a story barked at him by one of the old veteran homicide cops—the elite of the force—takes his eyes off the road for a moment, since his smile crinkles the skin around his eyes and he has trouble seeing when he flashes the grin that his wife loves, takes his eyes, I say, off the road for a moment and piles into some fallen boulders that are lurking, huddled almost malignantly, around a curve. The others, the two others, for there are probably four in the car, take him and the Chief in their arms, sweating and cursing in the deluge, and stagger down toward the place in the road where it forks off toward the old river road and the Blue Bird's Mölte.

When I think of this Mölte my heart careens in despair, a phrase I have always liked, reminding me, as it does, of the careening police car, the dazed Chief in the back seat, zooming down the road, driverless and hence, rudderless. The Mölte is strong, too strong perhaps, even for the powerful constitutions of these burly police officers, excepting, of course, the young rookie driver, who is slender and towheaded.

When I envision these officers, full of Mölte, staggering out of the Blue Bird, their Chief in their arms, or in the arms of one of them, the strongest, and then getting into their car, which is now running badly because of the grievous damage done it by its impact upon the boulder on the old mountain road, my heart sickens, and, yes, it careens.

Soused! They will be soused and arrive at the Mathers place filled with rage at the fates for having forced them out on a night like this —the rain will probably almost totally obscure their vision and the rookie may be wondering if it was a wise decision that propelled him, for that is a reasonable word, a little gauche but reasonable, propelled him onto the force. Certainly, there is also the distinct possibility that the car will not start once they have left the Blue Bird, or that they will have left it, a heap of smashed metal and glass back up on the road, dismal in the slanting rain that sweeps the old mountain road. Or the rainy river road, did they leave the thruway at Smudge.

Perhaps they have simply run out of gas, in the event of which their wrath will be a terrible thing to see. One will be made the scapegoat, the young rookie, most likely, who will be struck by the huge hamlike fists of the older dicks in their cruel passion. The Chief's body will repose in a puddle, helpless to stop this assault, fueled by rage and impotence, upon the young fellow—who, it seems likely, was not responsible in the first place for checking on the fullness or emptiness, etc., of the gas tank.

Yet there is also the possibility that the car full of police officers drove up in sunshine, joking and laughing the while, and drove right by this small cabin—that is more than a possibility! It is probable. Why not? What then? Should I make another call to the police, and run the risk of summoning more officers than I can handle? They will mill about, their muddy boots, or shoes, tracking up the floor, their hands all over everything, including Daisy. For if the weather is good, Daisy will arrive long before the police and they may feel that Daisy has been here the while, that Daisy and I—but I cannot allow myself to imagine anything like that, my friend. You understand why, don't you? It is impossible for me, even now, to think of myself and Daisy as anything but . . . friends.

I can hear, in my mind's ear, the clump of regulation boots, or shoes, on the porch steps, the crunch of footsteps in the driveway . . . but where are they? I am "banged" with terror, you understand. Words twist mysteriously in my head. Better to write something down to keep my mind off speculation. Write—what?

But first, to build a fire. (I have had some experience with detectives and know what they think of fires in mountain cabins, or cabins by mountain lakes, to be more precise.) There! The fire is laid and going . . . somehow, it brings one peace. My pen. My paper. Write, write. The wind passes the house again, hollering gently with the voice of Ned Beaumont. Where are the police? Daisy?

Where are the police? Daisy? (I write, feverishly, illegibly.) Where are the police? Daisy? A fire is good.

The fire moves like something alive, and I look at it as if I had never seen a fire before. Do I deserve the right to be so happy? Am I happy? What a poor word to describe this conflict of emotions. I, who loved Ned Beaumont, am I happy that he is dead? I think of Daisy, as I have always thought of Daisy. A rabbit, a bunny. The fire moves, upward, upward, writhing and flickering like a magic-lantern show that throws the shimmering truth upon the walls. What *is* truth? The smoke, of course, moves also, moving upward, upward to the sky, out the chimney and to the sky, where it twists upward, probing that

142

clarity like a grimy and insulting finger. Thus always smoke.

I am lost here. Where did I come from? Where did we all come from? I have listened to this dear dead friend's history, the words battered at me, filling me with guilt, full as the flue is filled with foul and fetid fumes. Well, the wine is good. The words continue, in memory, continue, they beg me to nod my head, to turn—suddenly! and trap them. Monsters of the past are here! Monsters of the past!

Yes. A sudden turn—and I *will* have trapped them. "What a time that was," I hear, I can almost swear I hear, it is Ned Beaumont's voice crooning to me. "What a time. . . ." The words settle heavily around my neck like a noose! If I *should* turn? If I should turn and, God help me, if I should turn and they should have *that* face . . . this face . . . what face? What *if* they should have that face? How bitter that I have forgotten the face!

At this point, in my extreme nervousness, the spectral wind howling about the cabin, I spilled the bottle of ink all over the paper on which I had tried, unsuccessfully, to objectify my horror, my guilt, my unrequited love, my wretched botch and stain of a life. Or on which I am trying to do same. Do tenses *matter?*

Grinning up at me from the shining and slowly spreading pool of ink that moved syrupy over the paper I had been battling, were words, still legible. I stared at them. I could not, for the life of me, *remember writing them,* they seemed to be curious hieroglyphics in some alien, some terrible and frightful hand.

Monsters of the past.

I shuddered. They were, surely, a portent of disaster. They took me back to an earlier evening, an evening when I had thought that by the careful intrusion of my strength and my honor I might rescue the people I loved. I could not, I tell you this as honestly and as dispassionately as I can—I could not countenance the meaning of those words: they were too horrible. Feverishly, I began to mop up the stain with my handkerchief, somehow less terrified by the macabre red stains upon *it* than I was by the fact that the color of the ink I had spilled was washable *blue.*

Lamont's Scrapbook

What has four wheels and flies?
A gay caballero carrying two bicycles. (Some say he floats.)

Are the stars out tonight?
They are. But before dawn some of them will have found places in various eyes, some settle on flags and banners, still others will take up residence in Hollywood and other film capitals of the world, many will be wished upon, one will be born, a handful will shimmer, gleam, shiver, glitter, twinkle, or shine, a few will either shoot or fall, dozens will cluster together, dozens more give off dust, one will be steadfast and constant, another lucky, some few have a stairway built to them, one serve as a cocktail ingredient, many will wander, one have a wagon hitched to it, another team with a garter, some form a crowd, scores remain chaste, most look down, and a group fall on Alabama.

Who needs people?
The Daredevils of the Red Circle.

What's black and white and red all over?
My Sunday Missal, Rev. Joseph F. Stedman, Director of the Confraternity of the Precious Blood, 5300 Fort Hamilton Parkway, Brooklyn, New York. *Nihil obstat.* James H. Griffiths, S.T.D., Censor Librorum. Imprimatur. ✠ Thomas E. Molloy, S.T.D., Bishop of Brooklyn. January 6, 1938. Scriptural Quotations from Revised Text of New Testament as copyrighted 1941 by Confraternity of Christian Doctrine. Copyright, 1938–1942 by Confraternity of the Precious Blood. Printed and Bound in the U.S.A.

How's every little thing in Dixie?
Cherry pink and apple blossom white.

Why are these pipples taking their hets off?
They are entering a church. It's very warm for June. Joe Namath is speaking in Ozone Park. The Phillies have won the pennant. God is just. Itchy foreheads. The flag is passing by. Pope Paul has arrived at second base. The daughter of Rosie O' Grady has appeared on Ovington Avenue. A rough beast has slouched toward Bethlehem to be born. The sudden summer shower has ended as quickly as it began. To fill them with yellow pencils. It's raining violets. They don't know no better. Ask a silly question. The winner has paid $93.40. Love's magic spell is everywhere. They've decided to stay a

while, after all. They got no respect. There'll be pennies from heaven. They have realized that Chicago is a big city. They don't want any trouble. To carry (lacking jars) moonbeams home in. To throw into Mrs. Murphy's chowder. They're crazy with the heat. Eventually, why not now? In preparation for eating them. It's a damn fool thing to do. To feel the autumn breeze. To pay homage to our rugged leathernecks. For the Sodality of the Blessed Virgin Mary. To look alive. They're a bunch of goddam idiots. Sunstroke is their delight. Sure, an' they be wantin' to show off their foine new haircuts. They're only human. Here comes a sailor. They've flipped their wigs. They've blown their tops. Should they then be ashamed of their pates? You never can tell, you never can tell. Exaggerated bows and much toadying to follow. Frank Capra made them do it. The golden final spike's been driven, hooray! The tycoon with great warm heart beneath has bailed the *Clarion* out, hoorah! Bart Kahane has regained his sight. They love loony beams. They never cared much for moonlit skies. The strains of the immortal anthem are heard far down the glittering boulevard. The new schoolmarm is alighting from the stage, silken ankle the cynosure of every eye. They should care. There'll be a hot time in the old town tonight. The sky is not falling. They have seen the light at the end of the tunnel and are glad. As preliminary to foot scuffling and toe digging. They've left their worries on the doorstep. Prince Stanislaus Poniatowski is bidding his family farewell. The "Potemkin" has dropped anchor in the harbor, rah! To throw them into the ring. They're gonna wash some man right outta their hair. Men as well as women have been liberated from the stultifying sexual roles that have for so long deprived them of the ability to function in a truly human way. Bird lives.

Did we lie down, because 'twas night?

We did not. We lay down on the orders of Inspector Hearthstone of the Death Squad.

Now what do you think of little Jack Jingle?

He's an Eskimo Pie and a Mexican Hat, a Skippy Sundae and a three-cent chocolate. All heart and a mile wide, vicarious warrior and victor at the battle of White Oaks, where his grandfather fell, he gives not his friendship easily, is a storehouse of arcane lore and amusing anecdote, and has trouble fielding the short hop. Yet and yet, there was once a twinkle in those wise old eyes and a sentence in that rusty pen. Where, oh where have they gone? Lost somewhere in the harsh midtown air? Swept off a Riker's counter with the stains of an early breakfast with crisp *Mirror?* Disappeared in the grime of Yiddish walls and Neapolitan linoleum? Drowned in the boozy camaraderie of the Lion League where they cannot hit the curve? Facing into the glare of constant incandescent lights, with a stoop and a tremble, a shuffle and cough, the magic letters of his azure cap have lost all power. Old and sad and cold.

What made fatuous sunbeams toil to break earth's sleep at all?
Twelve dollars a week in wage increases each year of a three-year contract, plus nine dollars in pension and welfare benefits for the first year and seven dollars for the second year.

How much wood could a woodchuck chuck if a woodchuck could chuck wood?

$$\sqrt[3]{-\tfrac{1}{2}q + \sqrt{Q}} = \sqrt[3]{r \cos \theta + ir \sin \theta}$$

$$= \sqrt[3]{r} \left\{ \cos \tfrac{1}{3}(\theta + 2k\pi) + i \sin \tfrac{1}{3}(\theta + 2k\pi) \right\}$$

$$and \quad \sqrt[3]{-\tfrac{1}{2}q + \sqrt{Q}}$$

$$= \sqrt[3]{r} \{ \cos \tfrac{1}{3}(\theta + 2k\pi) - i \sin \tfrac{1}{3}(\theta + 2k\pi), k \} = 0, \tfrac{1}{2}, \text{ or } 1(\text{cord}).$$

My dear Roche:
I suppose that there really is no sense in my defending "O'Mara." Your comments on it are nothing if not perceptive and clear, but I think that they are needlessly cruel and glaringly lacking in that *special* understanding that one always hopes a critic and writer will bring to a work of literature that is "outside the pale." I say one thing (and feel that the story represents this thing quite adequately, perhaps even profoundly) and you say another. You are correct when you state that my strongest work is not to be found in the short story —it's true that I need some room in which to "let my people go." But enough. This letter is not intended to be a defense of that old story but is concerned with things more important, more, to me, alarming, if I may use so strong a word.
I speak of your remarks concerning the course brochure. I had not, my dear fellow, intended to "force" my notes upon you, nor did I wish to place you in a position of "embarrassment." Surely, we are nothing if not mature men! As I noted in my last letter to you, I had, even at that time, decided from your comments to me that you had little use for an essay dealing with all my work. Well and good. But I wish that you had let me know your feelings on the little paper (notes, really) I have been writing on *Three Deuces* earlier than a

146

week ago. You *must* be aware of my preoccupation with my new book. This *Three Deuces* business has been an extra burden I could well have done without. My point is that I would not have pursued it, at all, had I but known that you felt it to be an instance of "puffery" for me to compose background material for the very book that you will use in the course.

I cannot for the life of me see why this should be considered "unethical" by anyone. Particularly by the academic community and your English Dept. My only motive for composing these notes was to help you in teaching the book intelligently; I was certainly not banging my own drum. It is a small drum, surely, and hardly *worth* banging. I did not mean to "encroach" (terrible word!) on your territory. I have not yet finished putting these notes together, luckily, and your letter, however belated, will save me useless work.

Now, let me come to what I take to be the most disturbing aspect of your letter. I cannot quite determine what you mean when you say that while *"Three Deuces* is an extraordinary work, it would not be fair to the novels of younger and less known writers to include it in the course as it is now taking shape in my mind—although I hasten to add that I have not yet come to a final decision as to what will constitute the essential matter of this course." I am lost here. Are you implying that *Deuces* will *not* be one of the novels dealt with in the course? If not, what novel of mine do you prefer to include? I had thought it was *Deuces* because of certain things that you said in your letters, which I have before me at this moment. Now, I don't quite know what to think. Please enlighten me so that I may get on with the work to hand.

I'm glad (though puzzled) that you've been corresponding with my brother-in-law, Trellis. I haven't read more than the first chapter of his new novel, so I cannot fairly tell you what I think of it. Yes, he's written other things, some of them interesting, in a curious way. I can't think of their titles at the moment. But I'm sure that Dermot will be delighted to tell you all about himself and his work—you have only to ask. It's odd, but I've never thought of Dermot as a possible inclusion in your course, or else I should certainly have mentioned him to you. His work, as you will discover, has a kind of "competence" to it that rather sets it off from that of—how shall I phrase it? —less *glib* writers. But you, of course, are the doctor.

Please clear up this business for me. Perhaps you'd like to see parts of the book I'm now working on? Let me know. I still think that *Deuces* is your best bet.

Best wishes,
Antony Lamont

Lamont's Scrapbook

Mr. Anthony LaMonte—Sir!

I am seeking an author, who would "In Cold Blood"—desire to write a book, upon the "Psychic Ability." And be one of the first, to factually in black-and-white, prove the existence; of this "agility for mind in tomorring"!

To use me as a subject for research is easy, for the skill I have in talent, is one gained obsession wise over twenty years, of my fifty-three. Out of attendance at Aqueduct, Belmont ovals, to use "form charts" in makeing selections; as a self-taught handicapper!

The investment required of $2000 dollars, is a sum necessary—to on Aqueducts opening its meet March 8th, be motivated by wagering strength to back my selections, as well as the pressures this imposes upon me, to in a twenty four day achieve answers that must be financially able to multiply profits!

The attendance at Aqueduct might only be required—up until the end of March, when I will once again be able to maintain a "telephone account" with my bookmaker and to call in my selections. From the sanctuary of a studio, where "Morning Telegraph Charts" and other printed statistics, would be had to guarantee the best results, as well as research material, as to how I score.

As to my "Psychic Ability." In simple outline, the endless nightly study of form charts, to see before intuitively—the inbetween the lines facts, that become so obvious after a race is won, the facts before hidden; now standing out—like a sore thumb!

Eventually one morning the psychic breakthru, in precognitively gaining a horses name—who won the same day and returned a $54.00 bill!

With time I gained greater controll to up through the years—at intervals, have known to me weeks ahead of time, the name of some winning horse. In a "dry run" interest in attempting selecting stocks, I scored well and precognitively gained a name of a stock.

The familiarity by now, of that mental calm into which any "acute awareness" the mind had about tomorrows outcome—could surface, I gained the name of a stock and then some thing more, I held the moment and flipped mentally the numbers of a calendar—until I had a seelling date! At which it rose to its height.

Most important!, was that this occurence gave me the clue—as to how I can impose a mental demand and setup the basic facts from which this developed mental ability can secure the outcome—in what we call in time, tomorrow.

In recent years, in several crime cases, I gained the names of

148

suspects, correctly, the blunder!, to not have gone on the record, in the correctness as predictions. Would have opened many doors—to aid me, in useing this ability in research, to see just how far beyond this threshold greater practice might allow me to go!

It is through *you* perhaps, giving me the economic ease—to function, and ego wise to soar by writing me "On Stage" that I can only but extend myself to some greater effort!

Since the potential returns are known to me—that can come out of raceing when answers are sufficiently guaranteed, to have winners, at payoff positions, in all of nine races and on each day of raceing. I know in time I can average $5000 dollars a *race*—or $45,-000, $50,000 dollars a day!

Business wise, I have a "processing method" needing a factory—already researched. In "sea salvage" an idea cleverly useing a well established technology—that can in two, to three, weeks time raise the 30,000 ton "Andrea Doria" into seeing daylight. Her value of $3,000,000 dollars, or more, this augmented by the value of a book, documentary, television rights, news media returns can only raise her value! The name fame and history makeing status—is opportunity like no other?

So what can I further say in writeing, that is best proven by sober use of "Psychic Ability," in use—so much bunk is mouthed, upon this subject, that there is much need in book form. That might serve as guidance and incentive, to younger minds, to develope the extremes in range possible of mental faculties—not as a freak of genius, but deliberate demand from the minds capacity?

If what I have is of use to you, our meeting can enlarge at length upon any subject, until such a time. I thank you for your patience in reading this I know, quite "dry matter."

Sincerely,
Joseph Beshary

Lamont's Notebook

It's not *I* who approached the academic caterpillar about my work! Soft, soft, get a leg up using any ladder. Is that what I've come to? And I've "forgotten" Dermot's works—transparent, and he'll know it immediately.

I can feel it. This is the slow shuffle off the stage. He's talked to people about *Deuces* and they've told him, blah, blah.

It's all getting away from me. This book.

I'll go on, because there's nothing else to do. Having some fun anyway, putting words in Halpin's mouth. He's a decent man. Alone in that cabin, I've made him a fool. A corpse, equally a fool.

I'll write Sheila! What good?

Maybe I should write back to the psychic handicapper (Beshary? Can it be . . . ?)—I'm getting old. *She* never wrote back to me, I thought just a jogging of memory, how she once loved me. I'll write her again.

Give the book and them both a rest from my weary inventions, for the weekend anyway.

Weary and ludicrous. Am I a hack, just hacking a different forest? No, not really. There are good things, and I can always revise, tighten it up when it's done. Give them some "life." (They have enough, I can swear it.)

A gay weekend! With television and gin.

I wish that *I* were in that cabin.

Halpin's Journal

A lot to put in this time. First, Ned has had a remembrance of what he seems to think is a theory of Da Salvi's. If (says Da Salvi) someone is forced to occupy space in *past* time, that someone cannot occupy space in *present* time, that is, speaking in terms of thought or memory. Something like that. Ned says that in an old book, *Country Hours* (?), Da Salvi develops the theory completely. He goes so far as to say that if one thinks of a person as that person was *in the past,* that person *is* in the past. If the person so thought of exists in the present and is apparent to the thinker, Da Salvi maintains that the person so "seen" is not seen at all, but is a phantom, or ghost, of the future. It's too complicated for me to understand thoroughly, but it certainly seems to work as far as this ridiculous novel goes, I mean to say that Ned has convinced me that when Lamont places us in the flashbacks of which he is so fond, we are *in* the flashbacks, absolutely. Ned is "alive" in the past. In other words, this damned cabin doesn't then "exist" and we may do as we like, including leaving it. We *are* phantoms. Lamont loses control over our "present" substances, re-creating us, as he does, in the past.

I mention all this because, having been thoroughly convinced by Ned of this idea, the other day I almost upset the apple cart. I had decided to go for a short stroll, and was about to set out, when I thought it best to let Ned know where I was going. Thank God that I took this extra minute, for, a moment later, Lamont had leaped from the past and its sordid letters of lust and greed, directly to the present, and I spent a ridiculous and humiliating hour or two lighting

150

fires and inventing nonexistent policemen and doing God knows what else—musing, scribbling, thinking what passes for thoughts with the Halpin I play—I don't really remember, and I don't want to. In any event, I was here as required.

One night Ned and I talked at length about Da Salvi's theory and how it bears upon our case. We mutually struck upon a remarkable and daring idea which *works,* and works more perfectly than we could possibly have hoped. It is frightfully simple, so simple in fact, that Ned and I worried for the better part of two hours trying to find a flaw in it—a flaw, that is, beyond the simple dangers inherent in any plan so daring. In any event, the idea is this:

Ned suggested that there is really no reason for both of us to have to be required to stay in this cabin—that is, one or the other of us may have his freedom whenever he wishes; we may alternate our "free" days, as it were, and simply. This is how it works. Ned is (at "present") dead, i.e., his presence, role, what have you, in this cabin, is that of a corpse. He neither speaks nor moves, but lies ("somewhere," as Ned laughs, since Lamont seems to forget where he put him from chapter to chapter) silent. I, as Halpin, am alive in this cabin, and I speak, walk about, etc., etc. It seems that I've been doing little more than waiting for the police, actually, and Ned points out that Lamont has not yet directed me to call them. God knows what he is up to!

The important point in all this is that right now, in this story's "present," there is only one "live" person in this cabin. Ned is "alive" only when Lamont places him in the past, and here and now is truly nonexistent, etc., etc. The one person alive in this cabin is Martin Halpin, myself. I carry the entire burden of the story. So: Ned suggested that he, being a corpse, may leave the house at any time, as long as I am here in my chair, or gazing out at the lake, or doing any of the other foolish things that I do here. Ned is "dead" and not necessary to the *present* of the tale. My references to him do not require that he even be really seen. Further, Ned says that he can play my role with Lamont none the wiser whenever *I* desire to leave the cabin. He shall then play *my part* and the corpse will not exist for that hour or day or whatever. Since Lamont has no use for this corpse there is really no reason for it to be present. Ned says that this will be simple to bring off since Lamont has no idea what we look like, nor what clothes we are wearing, since he never bothered to describe us. (Ned says that this is a modern novelist's prerogative.)

The one thing that we must be careful about is the arrival of Lamont's police or the arrival of the beautiful Daisy (who hasn't appeared at all yet except in the puerile letters Lamont wrote in her name). It wouldn't do for them to arrive and not find the body—nor would it do for them to arrive and find that the man who called them

151

had disappeared and the corpse is very much alive!

But it *would* be marvelously funny! Ned thinks that we owe La-mont a prank like that and while I tend to agree with him I feel that we ought to give him a little more time, even though Ned insists that a revision of this book will make things even harder for us. However, he *does* say that it is not a good thing to desert a job, since other authors will rarely use a deserter and one finishes one's career in "men's adventure" or "true confessions" stories, badly paid and treated with enormous contempt. You can even end up in boys' books, as an old man who comes out of a secret door or a gypsy on a mountain. Ned knows one man who wound up playing trained *bears!* But we'll see how things turn out for us in the middle chapters —they can't be any worse, certainly.

Now for my adventure, or the bones of it anyway, for the journal. I suppose that for some it would be commonplace enough, but to my quiet life it was fantastic! Ned was also excited about it when I return-ed, since I had the remarkably good luck to meet a man who once worked ("slaved" he said) in one of Lamont's earlier books. He also told me that he worked in the same book by Mr. Joyce that I worked in, but I don't remember him nor he me. But I am getting ahead of myself.

To begin at the beginning. (*I* must be turning into a novelist.) One morning, Ned well settled in the chair in which I usually sat, "trying to look like the sober Halpin," as he put it, I left the cabin and began walking down the road that runs roughly parallel to the lake. It was straight and totally anonymous, and the trees along it, for all I know of them, were all the same as far as I could tell—same shape, height, color, etc. They were trees in a kind of generic way, "typical" trees. They looked amazingly like drawings. The sun was above and behind me and did not, throughout my walk, move. I cast no shadow. All this was somewhat disturbing, but I pressed on. After all, I am not real. After about a quarter of a mile, I turned and looked back toward the cabin. There it sat, certainly recognizable, but curiously odd-angled, strangely lopsided in effect, as if lacking first one dimension, then another. At one point, as I shifted position, the cabin actually seemed to have no depth at all. Even more curious (I might even say chilling) was that the upper story, viewed now from the *outside,* was no more substantial than the same story *inside.* The house simply fades away into a vague indeterminate blueness that I suddenly realized was the sky. It was as if the upper story of the house was there, but made of a seamless glass, so that one could "sense" it, but not actually see it. I turned away and continued down the road, past hundreds more of the disheartening trees.

Coming to the top of a gradual rise, I saw before me a town! Or let me record that it was not *quite* a town. By this I mean that it was rather bizarrely and unnervingly unfinished, with buildings here and there composed of front walls and doors only, others having (like our cabin) vague and unfinished stories, and streets that stopped short and beyond which were vast expanses of mist and sky. It was a kind of ghost town, if I am using that term correctly. It seemed in excellent repair but haphazardly constructed. There were people walking about in the most amazingly diverse dress, none of whom seemed at home. They paid no attention to me at all.

Entering the main thoroughfare, I saw that the town had simply not been finished. Whatever seemed necessary to the builders or inhabitants had been built, and the rest forgotten or ignored. One street was lined with houses, all complete, and another, shady and well-paved, had on it nothing but a barbershop. On one small lane there was nothing but a front porch, a lawn before it, and a shade tree over all. The rest of the house was nowhere in evidence, yet the porch was complete with wicker furniture, lamps, a glider, even strips of fly paper hung from the rafters. A yellow insect light burned dully in the brilliant sunshine.

But let me be brief. I met a young man, an Englishman, I think, but I'm not sure, named Clive Sollis, a very decent and kind man, although he seemed to be quite drunk. He took me on a tour of the town, what there was of it, and gave me some information on the other inhabitants, although, as I suspected, none of them were true inhabitants, including Sollis. But rather than attempt a narrative, let me, for the sake of brevity, set down what I discovered during my daylong visit. (Incidentally, I stayed there until 11:00 P.M., and the sun never stopped shining, nor did it ever move in the sky!)

1. Clive Sollis worked in one of Lamont's early novels, although he could not remember the title and didn't want to. His anger and contempt toward Lamont are almost fanatic. He admitted that he was a drunkard and insisted that Lamont had made him so, since he was cast as a heavy drinker in the novel in which he had worked for almost two years. After this, he was fit only for the parts of English rotters in novels set in Africa or India, where he would sit on verandas all day long, drinking whisky in khakis. Occasionally he would perform a base or cowardly act. Once he deflowered a deaf-and-dumb servant girl. He blamed Lamont for ruining his career, which, he said, had started out brilliantly in an obscure Irish novel about a country priest. This nameless town, in which he drifted aimlessly about, was his only home. The town, by the way, was begun by an American novelist who abandoned it to become a journalist.

2. Sollis knew, before I told him, that I was in town to get away from the job for a short time so as to keep my "sanity," as he put it.

There were tears in his eyes as he said this. When he discovered that I was working for Lamont, he became extremely agitated, blanched, and insisted that I stay with him and abandon the role. He assured me that Lamont would never find me here since the poor place existed in a typescript locked away in a trunk in a Poughkeepsie attic. But I gave him the circumstances of the job, told him about Ned, etc. At this, Sollis brightened, and wondered whether he knew Ned from an early job. The name, he said, sounded familiar, although the amount of name-changing in the profession is unbelievably high. Of the people presently sojourning in the town, some were "vacationing," like myself, others were between jobs, and a few, like himself, had no other place to go, ruined as they were by earlier jobs. They had quite effectively taken themselves out of the labor market. There were three like this that Sollis knew of, one, a tall, gangling reporter whose name nobody seemed to know, and who had been mercilessly used in a book about airplane races and stunts in New Orleans; another, a simple and uneducated working man named Black, whose employer had almost destroyed him in a Brooklyn vacant lot; and the third, a hairy, deep-voiced man whose disgust at being made to play a failed and opportunistic poet in a novel about literati had spoiled him for any other role. Incidentally, it was at this point that Sollis and I discovered that we had worked in Mr. Joyce's vast construction, although we had never met. Sollis was not at all surprised at this, since (he said) nobody ever could find anybody else in that cosmos, nor could people remember what words they had said or what actions they had performed. He seemed annoyed at Mr. Joyce, but I refused to assent to his feelings, since I maintain that the man used me fairly and with kindness.

3. *Nota bene:* Sollis said that many characters who came to spend a day or weekend here often stayed longer. He was delighted that their absence often produced enormous changes in the books in which they were employed. That is, authors returning to work and not finding an important character are often forced to digress in an insane or ludicrous way. Sollis is convinced that boring and philosophical asides, ruminatory interludes, and endless descriptions of nature, buildings, interiors, and the like, all occur in novels because the author has returned to "work" and is unable to find his character where he left him. Hence, the descriptive or philosophical tripe is brought in desperately in order to push the creaking narrative along. He is also convinced that background material of a psychological nature, brought in to make a character's actions understandable, is all trash as well. He laughed over what he called a "hack reviewer's cliché" that goes "the author seems to lose touch with his characters." The author, according to Sollis, doesn't simply lose touch, he

154

loses the *character himself.* He concluded by telling me that some of the people now in town were responsible for their ex-employers' drunkenness, dissipation, poverty, etc., etc. He didn't seem at all shocked or sorry about any of this. (I conclude, by the way, that Sollis has no care at all for any author anywhere in the world, even the best and most skillful of them; as a matter of fact, he seems to think that the better the author, the more difficult he is toward his workers. He pointed out that he had yet to meet a malcontent from the pages of a "commercial" novel or slick-magazine short story. "They live in a world of kisses, nice clothes, and happy divorces, with plenty of polite sex thrown in," he said.)

4. Sollis took me to a baseball game! Extraordinary! Although he doesn't understand the game, he gave me a score card that a spectator left behind. I'll include it in my next entry and perhaps Ned will be able to interpret its incomprehensible code for me.

5. I left at about 11:00 P.M., the sun still shining, the road, the trees, etc., all exactly the same as they had been. The cabin still had that eerie, lopsided, unfinished look. Ned was waiting, eager to hear of my visit, and I told him, in detail, what I've jotted down here rather superficially. Nothing, by the way, was required of him today.

My dear Sheila:

I will keep this letter to you as brief as possible, and beg you to forgive its tone of bleakness, if the latter is not too overcharged a word for my present state of mind. You are the one person in the world who knows that I have dedicated my life to the art of literature, and if I cannot write to *you* of my innermost feelings, then to whom can I write? In any case, to be brief:

A day or two ago I received a letter from Pomeroy Roche, whom you of course are familiar with. It seems that he is hedging, or more than hedging, on using *Deuces* in the course that I have told you he is preparing to teach. His letter seems quite clear to me—I am aware of the "subtle tone" of rejection by now! He began by telling me that he thought it improper for me to prepare notes on the novel for classroom use, implying that this would be too much like beating my own drum, etc. I, who have never indulged in publicity for myself! As you well know, my work has always stood or fallen on its own merits! That the latter has occurred most consistently does not alter my intentions, to be sure! As you well know. Then, he had the temerity, the ivory-tower temerity, if I may be so bold, as to suggest that there are younger, and *less well-known* writers than I who should be given precedence in the course. I have no objection to this—I have told him that it was never my intention that I "star" in the course:

my poor *Deuces* will be perfectly happy as a member of the chorus line, as it were. But then! Then, he went on to tell me that he was not certain that he would use *Deuces* at all! Oh, not in so many words, but it was clear.

Can this academic caterpillar actually believe that I have suffered from so much exposure and acclaim that I need no more? I, who have given my entire life to the avant-garde novel, have enjoyed so little fame that I still receive letters in which my name is misspelled! Last year I got one that asked me if my novel, *Three Dunces,* was still in print! I cannot think of another novelist of my age, and with my publishing credits (if "credits" they be!) so abysmally and universally ignored. One might think that I were a poet! Is this oaf's ivory tower so high that he is unaware that I enjoy *no* position whatsoever in the literary world? I would not mind if, like Dermot, I had taken writing lightly. But I have eaten and drunk the life of letters and I have been treated shamefully—and now this!

My books have brought me nothing but a ruined marriage, a wrecked love affair with the only woman who ever truly cared for me, indigestion, and the disgusting habit of sucking my teeth. Revolting, indeed! I sometimes think that Joanne left me because—well, no matter. How I subsist, I don't know. A review here, a reading there. It's a small miracle that I never question—suffice it to say that I am always in debt. And now Roche is gently, ah, insidiously, pushing me and *Deuces* offstage! He should have been an editor! Yet Roche approached *me!* He *asked* for my cooperation! He praised my works without my urging him to! What has happened is a mystery to me— I sense the hand of an enemy here, a subtle enemy, but an enemy to be sure, as vicious as Claudius on Hamlet's father's porch! What has happened to me?

My last question, I fear, is not altogether rhetorical. Roche informs me in this same chilling letter that he has been corresponding with Dermot, with an eye, so I gather, to including some of his writings in the course. Certainly, there are works of Dermot's—I would be the first to say so, and am, usually—that date from some years back that would qualify him for inclusion in a course like this, at least on the basis of curiosity, or exoticism. But you and I (and Dermot, too) know that he has produced nothing of—how shall I phrase it?—serious consideration for years and years. Harsh but true.

I don't want to open old wounds, dear Sheila, or rake over dead coals, since I am sure that you and Dermot are marvelously happy together (I often think of you as I sit here in *total solitude*), but it is no secret that Dermot and I were never the "best of friends" in the old days. I don't quite know how to put this . . . but it strikes me that it is possible—just *possible,* mind you, not probable—that Dermot has said a "few things" to Roche designed to advance his fortunes to the *possible* detriment of mine. Would it be possible for you, as my beloved sister and colleague and a lover of good letters to discover just what Dermot has been saying to our sage Professor Roche? I don't imply that Dermot has been *denigrating* my work, but a careless phrase, an offhand opinion, etc., might be enough to set this fickle academic to thinking about a change in plans. I know that Dermot, despite our differences of opinion in the past, would never just come out and say that he thinks my work is "rotten," although he as much as told me that himself some years ago—no matter. I don't want to rummage in the attic of the past. But a small joke, a good-natured rib, a humorous crack about my lack of success, etc., etc. . . . these things can make a difference with a fool like Roche, who advances his career by climbing up on the backs of writers.

I know that I am risking your displeasure by even breathing this to you, but my state of mind is such that I *must* take that risk. It cannot be ignored that Dermot was always competitive when it came to me and my work—I fear that he was always envious at my refusal to go for the "easy buck." Not that that has damaged him in any significant way as a writer, I am not saying that, not at all. It is just that when Dermot looked at me he saw, always, an artist at work.

I wander. I whirl. I spin. And finally I falter. What troubles me most is the rejection of *Deuces*. How well, dear Sheila, do I remember your initial reaction to it. Is it my best— or is it not? A seminal work, if I may be so bold as to say so. Glance again, I beg you, at pages 13–15, 21–26, 101–107, 109–111, 131–139, etc., etc. Be, I implore you, candid. Has Dermot ever written anything with such evocative power? With such a blend of tragedy and bitter humor? Who *has*, among my avant-garde peers, written anything as trenchantly concise?

Why would Roche decide (if decide he has, and I fear he has) to omit this novel from his consideration unless outside pressure has been brought to bear? And who would bring this pressure? For what reason? I wallow in horrible suspicions!

Forgive, my darling sister, the impertinence and bad manners of this letter. But you will understand the pressure under which I am now living and working, I'm sure. Please try and help me! And, of course, there is *no need* to mention this letter to dear Dermot!

> With much love, your devoted brother,
> Tony

Lamont's Notebook

Looking through *Deuces* again. More convinced than ever that "somebody"—who else?—has been talking to Roche. No reason that he should suddenly be disillusioned about it. An excellent book! Maybe slightly naive, but with great energy, movement. A tragic hilarity. Biff Page: "Laughed and cried together . . ." Something like that at that party, long ago, long ago.

Not only the sections I mentioned to Sheila are good—almost any part taken at random can hold its own against anything of the kind written in the last few years. Stalling of the car on the Golden Gate Bridge? Scene where Jazzetti smashes all the crockery at the arts and crafts shoppe in Sausalito—what about that? North Beach drunk scene where he falls into the urinal . . . anything, almost.

That Roche could have seen and then *not* seen? Dermot always despised this book—"What? Writing *another* fucking novel?"

Or the finale of the Vegas scene, where the book takes it great plunge downward. A pearl!

From *Three Deuces;* pp. 150–153.

We went then to the Golden Nugget, God knows why, the image of her thighs slightly open on the bed in my whirling brain, Tab and Billy, "good old Billy," my "buddy," each of us locked carefully within our crawling skins. My misery and sense of irremediable loss churning with the undigested pastrami in my gut—which one would make me sick, make me throw up my terror and remorse? I thought of her thighs again, and laughed, curtly. We were at the bar and Billy looked over at me, strangely, I thought. He knew, I knew. Knew everything. In his eyes I saw the image of her thighs in *his* thoughts that he could not keep from those two beacons of lust and betrayal, like a lighthouse whose keeper has run amok.

He ordered a bourbon and soda. My gut heaved! I a Bloody Mary, to soothe my digestive processes, but I knew that nothing would help —what was happening in my deeps was more than bad digestion. I laughed again as I took the first sip of the putative elixir: it startled my palate like a dead and monstrous fish icy within a madman's creel!

Hum of the gamblers' voices. Fuck you all, I whispered.

What? Billy inquired pleasantly, his eyes strangely hooded. He was *always* so pleasant; his eyes were, more often than not, hooded. God, how severely I despised him!

Luck to them, I said, grinning, holding back the nausea that flooded me as his eyes shed their hoods for a moment and I saw therein again the image of my wife's spread thighs, open to *his* amok gaze! His vapid smile flickered and he looked intently at me, staring as if seeing me for the first time. Then he turned and busied himself with his drink.

I'll try my luck, he said apologetically, holding out his girl-soft hand to me for the twenty I pressed into it almost automatically, my eyes downcast to hide my shame. Why did I constantly give him money that he had no intention of repaying? *Why?* Why did I treat him to hot pastrami just this evening? My soul seemed to shrivel and I walked out into the harsh and artificial "daylight." Billy, smiling, changed the bill for chips. I saw this from the doorway.

Soon, I don't know how long it was, it might have been a minute, it might have been a lifetime, he joined me in the nightmare street where I stood in the ghostly red neon light, fighting my nausea. He looked at me furtively and chortled.

You———? I began, exhausted now.

Lost, he said in a whisper.

What? I gritted.

Lost! he said, louder now, louder, it seemed, than anything in the world!

Lost . . . again? I managed.

Lost   . again, he rejoined. It's *your* money. He snapped his fingers as easily as he had snapped my soul and spirit. Easy come . . . he began.

. . . easy go, I terminated his phrase, and threw up on my shoes.

He stared at me uncomprehendingly, almost malignantly, struggling to hold back his laughter. Want to go somewhere else? he suggested pleasantly.

Somewhere else? I gagged. Sure, why not? That Bloody Mary settled my stomach real good, I lied.

But you hardly drank it, Billy pursued relentlessly as a lighthouse.

Sure I did, I retched, my life falling away from me in futile shards.

No you didn't, he shot cruelly. You took a little sip and your "face" after it looked as if you'd stuck a dead—*fish* in your mouth.

Ha! Ha! I guffawed. Dead fish! That's rich! My mind was not on what I was saying, I was reeling under the realization that this shiftless man was probably my wife's lover! Rich, I repeated weakly.

I think you ought to go home, Billy smiled.

Home, I thought bitterly. Where was home? The endless road? The creaking motels? One-night cheap hotels? Restaurants with oyster shells? Home? I blurted, and threw up again, this time on Billy's shoes.

That'll cost you a shine, he drawled calmly.

I've got to split, Billy! I whined, I'm sick! I'm going home! Home!

159

Home? Billy inquired. Where's . . . home? That cheap and creaking motel?

The blood pounded in my ears urgently as I ran to the car, the tears streaming down my face, in my mouth the taste of dead fish, an oily fish, like bluefish. I yanked wildly at the door handle but it wouldn't open! I lurched wildly about, suddenly realizing that the key—the key!—was in Billy's possession!

He stood in the eerie neon light, surrounded by the walking dead, lurching as I was lurching, all of them listening to the music of a distant drummer in a black hood, rumbling madness out of his drum.

The tears furiously cascaded from my eyes as I saw Billy's figure loping toward a shoeshine parlor that had suddenly appeared as if by magic across the street. I sat on the cold asphalt and moaned my despair, despair as cold and hopeless as the surrounding desert. Maybe it was something we ate, on the endless road. Thus did I lie shamelessly to myself. Then I began to laugh quietly, but hysterically, to myself. Groping for a cigarette, I threw up all over the fender. How do you like that, Billy? I screeched to the desert winds, how do you like . . . that . . . ? Laughing and laughing, until I realized suddenly that it was my car, not Billy's, that I had defiled.

That'll cost me a carwash, I said perfectly to the fender. The black winds howled their demonic laughter, a somehow feminine laughter, off the sterile desert surrounding. . . .

7. THE WOODS SO WILD

So then I went to the club, set my heels to the sidewalk, down through the crowded streets. And I thought up repartee on that short walk, bright words to fight them, and help Beaumont also (safe in my keeping). And grit from the gutters struck my eyeballs in dirtying eddies. Corrie's the bitch, the lace-trimmed goddess! Then I walked a bit faster, through throngs jamming the corners, and with sore legs I hurried the streets, until twilight.

The day turned to night. Shadows etching the city. And I came to the edge of high-rise country, to the fash'nable place, and to phony people dressed in the latest styles, never moved by the meaning of love, nor by far stars, nor by a thought of heaven. Darkest night infected these wretched natives, their eyes rolling grimly. I came then to the place I'd scrawled down: The Zap Club.

Here then I stopped, with knocking knees and dyspepsia. But drawing strength from resolve, I fought against my despair. There would be no celebrations of *this* deed, for lust and its sweet wine, and kisses mixed with sweet flowers, are said by many a man to be brilliant perfections.

I, Martin Halpin, a stodgy man in a vest—a spoiler? a peeping Tom sullen in mood? a creep to the "Mexican" ladies? dull, and an old creep . . . what mad mood moved me to meddle?

I saw then come from The Club Zap the multinational dead, the girls, the men, and the rich who had made much; girls crying drunken tears, girls tender, men many, bored, with bronze-tanned heads, nasty, spoiled, flaunting thin, bleary charms.

These revelers crowded about me, all jeering. A pallor had cloaked me and I pushed through the throng to the doors, shouldering girls, sweating with fear, begged pardon, evaded them. To Corrie, the Strong, and Dark Delamode I made my anxious way. I found myself then in the crepuscular, cavernous den. Here would I meet my lovely foes? But first, the headwaiter came, Jacques the headwaiter, unimpressed, emperor of spotless linen, flashing a thin supercilious smile, unmoved, distant in arrogance: his glance a question. Frightening lackey! And I croaked, in terrible haste:

"Headwaiter, where can I find your employers? Are they in back, trying on costumes?"

He said, in grudging speech:

"I no spikka de English."

I reached into my wallet.

Turning down the strait passage unlighted, me he led to the office, knocked at the door there. His hand sought my sawbuck.

"Now hear, my friend," he said. "An accident, unplanned, just pure luck, brought you this far. *Nobody* saw you."

And I smiled:

"A man of discretion . . . and of good common sense."

Then Jacques had vanished, and my sawbuck also.

Then Miss Delamode came, tall, in a silk slip—and then Madame Corriendo!

Holding her highball glass, she *knew* me, and spoke:

"Jou at las' come? Chure. Man of no joy! Gaze on my matchless chape in dees darkened nightclub, come in de room, sit by my luscious body, for pleasure!"

And I stepped in. And she, heady from Scotch, said then:

"Ned Beaumont chall retorn to lovely Corrie, troo dark streets, lust *flaming* troo heem!"

And then Miss Delamode sat, next her companion. I thought: *they are evilly lovely*. I understood Ned Beaumont's doom, grasped it completely. Out of his mind, he'd succumbed—foul sirens!—to their rich, provocative, wonderful bodies! Son of a gun!

Madame Delamode, with her slip off now, in bikini, her breasts monumental, my mouth was dry, Corrie Corriendo in jet-black corset and nylons, and with no panties, wearing black glossy heels of panting desire. So that—so that I prayed for help from God in the faraway blue. . . .

Halpin's Journal

Working again, as I thought. Ned has gone into town to see it and talk to Sollis himself. Now I'm jabbering some garbled, unnatural "English." Will this man *not* leave it all be?

Just a moment to insert the scorecard of the baseball game Sollis took me to. Whatever it means! It has a certain arcane beauty to it, though. A conversation piece if I work at a decent job soon? I showed it to Ned just before he left and he glanced at it and laughed long and loud.

Charleville CRYSTALS

VISITING TEAM	1	2	3	4	5	6	7	8	9	10	AB	R	1B	SH	P.O.	A	E
SMIRNOFF 2b											2	3	0	0	0	0	1
GORDON ss											1	3	0	0	0	0	1
GILBEY rf											1	2	0	0	0	0	0
WOLFSCHMIDT cf											2	0	0	0	0	0	1
TANQUERAY 1b											2	0	0	0	0	0	1
BOOTH c											1	0	0	0	0	0	0
MAJORSKA lf											2	0	0	0	0	0	1
BOMBAY 3b											2	0	0	0	0	0	0
BELLE p											2	0	0	0	0	0	0
TOTALS											15	8	0	0	0	0	5

Tanqueray's drive in 1st hit Forester on back
Dant's WPs in 2nd hit ground 30 feet before plate
3 ground balls in 3rd went through Begg's legs
Forester dropped Wolfschmidt's Fly in 3rd and rolled ball into infield
Dant K'd side all 3 innings

No As!
No P.O. s!

AMBERS

HOME TEAM	1	2	3	4	5	6	7	8	9	10	AB	R	1B	SH	P.O.	A	E
SARK ss											3	1	0	0	0	0	0
HARPER lf											1	1	0	0	0	0	0
FORESTER cf											3	0	0	0	0	0	2
FITZGERALD 1b											1	1	0	0	0	0	0
DANIEL c											1	1	0	0	0	0	0
OVERHOLT rf											2	1	0	0	0	0	0
BEGG 3b											1	1	0	0	0	0	3
DEWAR 2b											1	1	0	0	0	0	1
DANT p											1	1	0	0	0	0	0
TOTALS											14	8	0	0	0	0	6

— GAME CALLED AFTER 3rd BECAUSE OF DRUNKEN CONDITION OF BOTH TEAMS —

Overholt's Fly in 1st fell 40 feet behind Majorska.
Forester's 3 Ks on account of dozing at bat.
Dant's bouncer in 3rd fielded cleanly by Tanqueray who stared at ball.
Belle K'd side all 3 innings

No As!
No P.O.s!

My dear Miss Flambeaux:

Thank you so much for your small book of verse. I have read it through once, swiftly, and plan to read it again this weekend when I have some time. I must say that I think it charming, with just that exact, modern combination of candor and craft that has long been missing from our poetry. As for the subject matter, no, I don't find it "shocking" or "immodest"—it is time that these deep feelings were brought into the light of day and held before the eyes of a terrified and cowardly populace. I find your treatment of these subjects courageous, to say the least.

Certainly, there are a few rough edges to your work but that is to be expected in a poet who has only, by her own admission, been writing just eight months.

I will write you again, at length, about your book—if I have anything to say that seems worthwhile. Perhaps we might even meet for a drink? It's much simpler to discuss these things informally, I think. Let me know what you think.

No, I don't consider it forward of you to publish this booklet at your own expense—many important poets began their publishing careers that way. I would advise you, however, not to worry about *selling* the book, but urge you to put copies in the hands of critics, editors, reviewers, etc., etc. Word of mouth is the thing with small first books like yours.

My best wishes,
Antony Lamont

164

THE SWEAT OF LOVE

By

Lorna Flambeaux

Hot Bodies

Hot bodies entwined together
stuck with sweat, the gorgeous guck of love.
We fuck . . .
             —all unashamed!
                         Proud of our . . .

Hot bodies!
             In my laughing flesh lies hidden
that dark inferno, Life's secret Word.

             It yearns to reach out and whisper
to your smold'ring core. It CANNOT! It CANNOT!
So you, belovèd, in my widespread loins must find
the entrance to this deep and tender Word.

             YES!!! YES!!!
                         Only the dead
say "No" to love. Our hot bodies—are aflame
with Life! And now your Life plunges
to my thrilling deeps . . . OH!!!

. . . I swiftly swoon . . .

Panting God

My bursting female flesh a field
Where thou mayst trod,
O panting God!

My pride will learn to yield
To all desires odd,
O panting God!

My wild frustrations fin'lly healed
By your huge rod,
O panting God!

My love for you is closely sealed
To you I dedicate my bod,
O panting God!

No longer do I wish my thighs to shield
My twad,
O panting God!

166

Sucking Your Lips

Sucking your lips . . .

I suck!

        pomegranates of wondrous Greece
        oranges of sultry Florida
        peaches of sleepy Georgia

I suck!

        plums, apricotts, the juices running,
        apples, happy with New England frost
        mangoes aburst with erotic jungle-lands

I suck!

        orange melons, chartreuse honeydews
        dripping nectarines of dawn
        grapefruits tart with Paris laughter

I suck!

        ambrosia of Olympus when

I suck . . .

        your lips!

I Swoon

I yearn to fuck.
To feel my body incandescent
glowing like a Xmastree
'neath yours. You turn
me on . . . I SWOON.

At the thought of your stiff poker
tempered by the fires of love, I SWOON.
At sight of its bright garnet knob, ah!
O why? I wish to be so wholly conscious,
yet . . . I SWOON.

Deliver me belovèd from
this soft sweet faint. Electrify
my body even as the ramrod of your manhood
pierces me, so that I may cry to you
. . . "I SWOON!"

Open to Your Pridehood: A Prayer

O Eros, sweet boy, and boon companion to that glorious She who, born of foam of wave demurely floating on a lustrous conk, I open my poor body to your pridehood.

O you, with the soft sweet down so feathery beginning on your dawnpink cheeks, consort of all those who are most beautiful, who drove good Pasiphaë to madness in the statue of a brazen cow, her thirsting loins stretched to incredible proportions by the rampant bullprong, accept my mundane flesh and let me open to your pridehood.

O stern man with lightning in your orbs, your blond curls flying in the zephyr, your simple linen tunic barely hiding the proud stiff with which you drive poor maids, aye! to crazed abandon, let me, allow me, O! I beg you, permit my sizzling corse to open, open to your pridehood. Amen.

Teeth

I want no twisted laurel wreath
For my poor head to celebrate my verses.
Nor the praise of critics or academies:
I call out, darling, for your teeth
To BITE ME!

If, wand'ring 'pon some lonely heath
I chance to spy a shy, retiring flow'r
Its beauty serves to call to mind your mouth
Which has in it those sparkling white teeth
That BITE ME!

When my dalirious naked body is beneath
Your energetically pumping one, and we are in
The luscious act of love, I stroke your flanks,
I suck your tongue, I lick your teeth—
"O, BITE ME!"

Homage

These things I offer to the great God Eros:

    —My wet and greeny gash and its attendant furze . . .
    —My pruny anus, hidden, yet all unashamed . . .
    —My ears that long to hear Him whisper, "Hump me!" . . .
    —My nose that I may sniff His rutty flesh . . .
    —My eyes that He may spew His seed on them . . .
    —My mouth that aches to gorge upon His prong . . .

—All, ALL my apertures are His . . .

Adorable Legs

When I observe your adorable legs, hard-muscled, straight,
And thick-entwined with manly hair, I weep
That I am not your feet.

When I envision those puissant limbs athrashing
Through the quiet glade or pistoning the pavements, then
I long to be your socks.

When in between my own two trembling nether limbs
Your masculine ones do haul your eager frame, why then
Can't I be your knees?

But it is when my eager orbs do spy upon you
Sleeping, and travel from your toes up to your groin
That I wish that I might be—your cock!

The Sweat of Love

The sweat of Love is oh! so far removèd
From that ordinary sweat that assails our nose
from noxious armpits!

                        Aye! It has its own pure blessèd odor

like unto the floral magic
of a formal garden wherein fairies play.

     Pansies and petunias and phlox
     Gaily smelling 'mong the rocks.

The luscious film of perspiration
That o'ercomes lovers' bodies
And their faces too

                 is like perfume
drenching our distended nostrils
perfume waffted from a shadowed country nook.

     Pansies and petunias and phlox
     Gaily smelling 'mong the rocks.

The great beads of the am'rous liquor
That fall from your face onto mine
Or mine on yours, if I am atop o' you!

                       Enchant us both

With its aroma of those paradises hid
In a sweet wood where sprites make attar.

     Pansies and petunias and phlox
     Do gaily smell among the rocks.

The Slippery Flesh

How slick and juicy is your body, dearest,
When all covered with your juices male;
When I inhale the sweat from off your torso
My lips do shake and all my face grows pale.

My frail hand then does slip upon your shoulder,
It slides so gaily from your chest to belly;
Oh! Did you but know that at that moment
My heart is thumping, and my knees are jelly.

And when that same small hand does reach your groin
It occupies itself to make me whole;
I pinch and prod and shake and agitate
Your monumental, proud and greasèd pole!

Envoi

Oh! Let your sex stand tall like gallant sail!
I'll act as if I'm in a deli!
To feast upon your hot pastrami is my goal!

Jungle Love

to e.e. cummings

has.ten,,,to me th(rough
the m o o n washed heat
of junglenights. tAIL and GLISTENing
with sweat; your leop
                              ard loin
                                        cloth

BULGING with yourman hood. (OH)! I (wait)
        hands clench(ED) with the wildesire
to !CLUTCH!!! (and stroke
        that swelling cro(t)ch that you—osoon!
SHall proffer me within my lone(ly)
                              tent,

        for you are my junglelove
        and tho we f(uck in sweet a(BAND) on

        in MOtels, hoTELS, backalleys andon
        seats of chevrolets

        it is the madd'ning IMAG(e) of your body!

racingthrough the rankest jungle growths
that seizes al(ways
                              my ImAgInAtIoN.

                the mother your sex quivers deep in mine
                that is even HOTter (for i am a woMAN!)))

                in my secret fan
                              tasy,

,i. hear.you.
                roar

Summerfuck: A Dramatic Eclogue

EROS: What ho! I seem to see or e'en faint descry
The shining naked body of a mortal being
There among the gorse. *(Halloos.)* Halloo! Halloo!

WOMAN: A man's deep voice! And yet . . .
It had in it a timber not quite like
A man's! Yet he is approaching whate'er
He might be. And I stark naked! *(Covers her body with gorse leaves.)*

EROS: *(Aside.)* My prayer goes up to Zeus
And down to Hades and out beyond the roaring flood
To tridented Poseidon that this naked form
Be that of a woman. I grow weary unto Death
Of wand'ring catamites of whom the bush of late
Seems overfull. *(Joyously.)* By the Oracle
At brooding Delphi! 'Tis a luscious lady—and see!
How modestly endeavors she to shield her private
 parts!
(Removing his trousers.) We'll find remedy for that
Eftsoones!

WOMAN: How like is he unto a man! And still . . .
The music sweet and wild of his deep-pitchèd voice
As there he stands amumbling to himself and
Taking off his pants makes me abandon
All my natural female shyness *(removes gorse leaves)*
And my cherished modesty! And soft! Look! Ah!
'S'blood! Where he throws his nether garments
In the creepers!

EROS: Freed at last of these encumb'ring clothes
My sex hops forth and quivers glorious
In the sugary air that softly fills this glen
And of which glistering Apollo he himself
Would find much to commend. Aha!
The maiden has espied my rampant staff, all
 brighteyèd!
Her long and well-formed lower limbs, her legs,
Do carry her delightful torso toward me e'en as I,
As deeply moved, now hasten to her side. *(He runs wildly through the trees.)*

173

WOMAN: The bell-like clanging of his tongue but does convince
me
That I stand, my charms all plain revealèd, 'fore a god!
See how he stumbles through the gorse and thicket!
His manhood hugely swollen just for me! I pray he not
decide
To godlike turn himself into a bull or frog or some
disgusting
Bird! Now look! He trips and falls! He's up again!
And not a jot the less enflamèd 'spite the bruise upon
His vig'rous head! *(She falls on her back.)*

EROS: The nut-brown wench has disappearèd! What? Oh blast
The day my mother gave me suck! No! Ah!
I see her there, entangelèd among the native
vegetation
of this hallowed place! How delightful is the contrast
Of her snowy bottom and her jetty maiden's down to
the
Almost Kelly green of th' abounding creepers and the
Omnipresent gorse! See! Now she opes to me! Ope!
Ope! fair lady! *(Shouts.)* I am he that men call
Eros!

WOMAN: Come! Come! Sweet Eros! Oh! The melodic tinkling of
his
Voice urges me toward acts of which I previously was
ashamed
Even to think or to let trek across my tongue. But now!
His darkling presence overwhelms me! And now———
oouuff!
*(She grunts in rapture as the god hurls himself
through the air and falls upon her supine frame.)*

EROS: How wondrous sweet and fair to make with this sweet
Lady—who, by the by, I now see is not exactly
Quite so young and fresh as I opined from fifty yards
away
A moment past but who will still do nicely for my
goatish
Appetites—to make, I say, the perfect image of
delightful love
—the summerfuck! Unnhh! Unnhh! Unnhhnnnhhh . . .

174

WOMAN: Fill me with your lambent stars and azure oceans, O
adored and dang'rous god!

*(Bees and wasps hum drunkenly above the softly
blowing foliage as Old Sol sets.)*

Halpin's Journal

Ned returned from town, depressed and disconsolate. His hopes were, I fear, well nigh dashed by his visit. He saw for himself and heard from Sollis that the town is a dead end, that it is filled with lost souls who have no intention of ever working again, or who stay for a time and then either wander disconsolately back into the novels they have left, or move into that nether world of magazine and children's fiction. But during his stay he *did* hear of two or three other towns, or settlements, to which beleagured characters might repair, and from which they depart into reputable novels, there to play reasonable roles and receive a decent salary. Sollis did not know where these towns are, but swore that they existed—he said, according to Ned, that they are hard to get to and that only characters who are determined to make a go of it find their way there.

Ned is determined to leave, almost at once—that is, as soon as he finds out where these settlements are. I cautioned him to wait a little longer, that it hasn't been *so* bad since the infamous restaurant scene, and that I had a feeling that Lamont, despite his stupidity, was trying desperately to write a book that would make his name, my point being that he might use us in a sequel much more sane and respectable than this one.

(Didn't tell Ned about the circumstances of meeting the two young ladies playing the vixenish vamps. Just that I had a rather innocuous "confrontation scene" with the two women who are supposed to have misled him. I'll tell him in time, but I think that it would be too much for him right now. They *are* attractive, and maybe, just maybe, Lamont will direct us to. . . . There's no sense in counting your chickens, though.)

Sollis is indeed a hopeless drunk. Ned went, with him as guide, to I don't know how many bars, cabarets, saloons, etc., of which the town seems to be largely composed. I wonder what kind of book its author was writing? But he returned with enough napkins, coasters, matchbooks, stirring rods, and the like, to fill a dresser drawer—if this weird house *had* a dresser. When I asked him why he brought them back, he had no satisfactory answer, but I think that they remind him of better days. I wondered, momentarily to be sure, just how it was possible for him to go to all these places in the time he had been gone, but then remembered the unmoving sun.

I include a play (a "masque," Ned called it) that Ned brought back with him. I haven't read it, nor has he, but he said that Sollis had given it to him, since we "had a house" to "live in." Some house! I have a suspicion that this work (that is, just the mere presence of it) was instrumental in depressing Ned so greatly. He told me that Sollis informed him that it was written by a baseball player who aspired to a kind of stardom in intellectual novels about the literary world—bright, brash, terribly witty, etc., etc. He thought that he might perform in them as an artist of some kind: perhaps a writer. In any event, he withered and "died" in town and was an object of the most cruel jokes and comment by the rest of the shiftless and transient population. Sollis told Ned that he read a few pages of the book but could make neither head nor tail of it—it seemed like a music-hall or vaudeville script. In any event, this poor man, who tried to enhance his chances for employment, left this "masque" (I wish I knew just what that word meant!) in one of the barrooms in the town and took a mean job as a rookie minor-league catcher in a series of base-ball books for boys. In other words, oblivion! He left the manuscript, in neat longhand, symbolically cutting himself off from his aspirations. Sollis knew him quite well and vouches for his seriousness of intent. Unfortunately, he doesn't remember his name, but did tell Ned that he is working under the name of Zeke Zook in the boys' books. That name makes me think that Lamont, for all his madness, is not half-bad. How could an author———? But I'll depress *myself* in a minute. Anyway, I insert the "masque" into these pages *in toto*.

FLAWLESS PLAY RESTORED
The Masque of Fungo

CHARACTERS

SUSAN B. ANTHONY, *a Massachusetts belle of some balls*

JACK ARMSTRONG, *one-time religious maniac, now an ROTC ensign from a good home*

BARNACLE BILL, *a sailor*

EDDY BESHARY, *an Arabian etymologist*

ALICE BLUEGOWN, *a small-town virgin, her cheeks suffused with crimson*

ROBERTO BLIGH, *a bard of the Vast Heartland*

PETER BOFFO, *iconoclastic editor of* Lamplighter Views

BROTHER OF SAL RONGO, *Sal Rongo's brother*

DUCHESS, *an erotically unhinged noblewoman*

LANCE DELRIO, *a man about small Southwestern towns*

FOOTS FUNGO, *a star shortstop who's lost a step*

FAIR YOUNG MAIDEN, *an innocent lass in cotton underwear*

FUCKING WHORE, *a girl with a past*

ODILE GASHE, *a tribade in sensible shoes*

HARRY THE CRAB, *a hairy wonder*

"POP" HEART, *wily editor of the* Belleville Vetch

HURLEY LEES, *a bogeyman of obscure Celtic origins*

JIM JAM, *a romantic loser, suitably accoutered*

JAMES JOYCE, *a grocer's assistant*

"SHOTGUN" JAREMA, *manager of the Amarillo Centipedes*

PADDY DOWN KILLARNEY, *a thick Irish cop*

MICHAEL "MILKY" KIDWELL, *a retired General, "the Hero of Pusan"*

SEAN ALEXANDER KURKJIAN, *a concrete poet*

KID SISTER, *a kid sister*

BILLY MCCOY, *a musical boy*

FATHER DANNY MAVOURNEEN, *a disgraced priest who lives among the People*

MINUSCULE FIGURE OF TY COBB, *a small miracle*

ABRAHAM NESBIT, D.D.S., *a fake dentist*

MONSIGNOR BERNARD O'HARA, *a North of Ireland convert with eccentric leanings*

OLD JOE, *a disease*

VINNIE PACHISI, *a loudmouthed thug*

RITA RIGHT, *a sensitive poetess from Omaha*

SIGNORINA RIGATONI, *a blazing-eyed gypsy lass*
SAL RONGO, *a remarkably stupid delicatessen customer*
CLARK SITZ, *a mysterious bather*
SENATOR STREET, *a depraved legislator*
BETSY JEAN DAISY SMITH, *one-time Miss Algebra and now the Senator's secretary*
AIRMAN SMITH, *Betsy Jean's husband*
ELEAZAR SOD, PH.D., *a Guggenheim Fellow*
MARQUIS DE SADE, *a disturbed nobleman who cannot relate*
SPIRIT OF LESTER LAVALLARO, *a ghost of a chance*
TINKER, *a loathsome fellow from Australia*
WANTON NYMPH, *a Continental vamp*
WUN EM EN, *a brilliant young book editor of Oriental birth*
CHARLES DEXTER WARD, *a dupe of the Communists*
"CRACKER" YALOBUSHA, *manager of the Biloxi Crips*
Plus Ant'ny, Audience, Bands, Blackstone, Certain Frenchmen, Chair, Discarded Wiener, Effort, God, Hope of the Future, Italo-American Toughs, Rumor, Sin of Onan, Small Group of Wealthy Texans, Thousands of American Boys, Unbelievable Pressures, USO, Villistas, Voice of Satan, White-Robed Choir, Masquers, and others.

The scene is a major-league ball park, the home of a team of disconcerting ineptitude. It is so devised as to seem to be floating uncomfortably in a surrounding sea of parking lots, subway tracks and trestles, highways, and vast areas of bogland. There is a strong possibility that the landscape represents New Jersey. At each position on the field stands a MASQUER, *dressed in garments of dull flame color, surrounded by massy clouds out of which each seems to be unsuccessfully peering. They fidget with their ill-fitting sunglasses. On the backs of their darkly fiery costumes, above their numbers, are their names, those of the nine elements of Ugliness. They are the pitcher,* DULLNESS, *the catcher,* MURKINESS, *The first baseman,* DETERIORATION, *the second baseman,* UNHAPPINESS, *the third baseman,* IMMODERATION, *the shortstop,* HOMELINESS, *the left fielder,* WORTHLESSNESS, *the center fielder,* IMPERFECTION, *and the right fielder,* DISHARMONY. *Standing off to the right of the first-base foul line is a figure dressed like all the others. He is completely enveloped in clouds which occasionally break to reveal his name, dimly discernible through the swirling mists. It is clear that he is made up of all the other elements, being* HOPELESSNESS. *The* MASQUERS *suddenly move from their positions and enter, in a straggling fashion, the dugout, where they sing this song:*

179

On the brave field of playe,
    Tu-whit, tu-whoo, jug-jug
    And ding-a-ding,
The player *Fungo* did his errors make
    Thirty-eighte by May.

What in the name of *Jesu*
    Is he doing?
Jug! Shouted each lustie fan.
Not onlie are his fingres wooden
But he's hitting .002.

But folke, observe our presentacioun
    Of brave heroicks
    And of faith and workes
Fungo shall engage his fate
To your delectacioun.

During this musical presentation, the stage has slowly revolved away from the audience so that by the song's termination, the MASQUERS *are completely hidden, and the stage seems to be bare. The lights intensify to reveal it cluttered with various characters.*

SUSAN B. ANTHONY: I long for a multiple clitoral orgasm without the intercession of the usual bore of a male organ! I long! I long! *(She is carried off, her pelvis convulsing in time to the old Feltman's favorite, "I'd Press My Thighs Together Ere I'd Kiss Your Greedy Lips.")*

BILLY MCCOY: If thy rod offend thee, pluck it! *(He commits the Sin of Onan.)*

THE SIN OF ONAN *(being dragged to a mental hospital):* I'm as sane as you are!

SUSAN B. ANTHONY *(her homely hands lost 'neath the severe folds of her chaste tweed skirt):* I feel like the dark-haired beauty in that "certain" French daguerrotype! A wanton nymph! Wheee!

WANTON NYMPH: Oh là! *(She rushes across the room, trips, and flies through the air.)* Ze hell weez your theeng! Weel zom wan pleez get me off ze doorknob? *(Blushes.)*

JAMES JOYCE: Look to the lady.

FOOTS FUNGO: It took a bad hop! It took a real bad hop! *(He kicks at the keystone sack and breaks a toe.)*

OFFICER KILLARNEY *(chewing a homemade cross of blessèd palm):* Is it the traffic ye think ye'll be blockin' wit yer dirthy commie bodies? *(Begins beating nuns, Methodist clergymen, babies, crip-*

180

ples, old Jews, tricycles, artists manqué, homosexual gentlemen, well-bred ladies, Fellows of Reconciliation, liberal schoolteachers, and many others.)

GENERAL KIDWELL: There is indeed a glimmer, a faint ray, of light at the end of the long tunnel of permissive American softness. Such men as this belovèd Irish patrolman will see to it. *(He soils his officer's pinks.)*

SUSAN B. ANTHONY *(gently placing a satchel charge into Kidwell's beribboned blouse):* You do go on, General! *(Aside.)* I hate to say it, but that's what I call a *man.*

JAMES JOYCE: I call that a scumhead.

CLARK SITZ *(bathing resignedly):* Now for a brisk towel-down.

CHARLES DEXTER WARD: The carrots are growing up through the snows of Siberia! The great submarine flotilla of the People's Navy is about to sail for Odessa! Have none of you the sanity to understand what this means for mankind? Kidwell, your blouse is oddly lumpy.

GENERAL KIDWELL *(blowing up):* Pass in review! You're to report to your C.O., Miss Anthony, for company punishment. I think you've broken a medal.

SUSAN B. ANTHONY *(turning into Lydia Pinkham, a crazed pharmacist):* At last! Now I won't have to miss all the fun! Freedom from cramps and odor on those "certain" days. *(She plunges through some nearby ice and swims about underwater in a carefree manner.)* I can swim again! No more playing at the gauche game of "beach wallflower" for me.

DUCHESS *(dressing for a ball):* I know I should be frightfully ashamed of myself but I cawn't help spying on that tinker's remarkable kidney wiper. *(A bejeweled hand disappears 'neath the lacy folds of her rich petticoat.)*

TINKER *(pissing up against a wall):* Gor blimey! This 'ere bloody Duchess is spyin' on me flamin' kidney wiper, she is, an' 'at's no bloody lie!

DR. ELEAZAR SOD: The tensile strength of these Belgian blown-glass decanters of the period 1863–1866 may well be . . .

RITA RIGHT: Hello, you Fellow!

TINKER *(shamelessly polluting himself):* Bloody sod!

HARRY THE CRAB: When suddenly confronted by a pigeon crushed to the pavement—YOU MUST EAT IT! Arrgghhh, God! My pimples, my boils! *(He scratches all over and ends by clawing feverishly at his grey fedora, which item too is covered by a repulsive growth.)* What dog will bite me today? Woe! Woe! *(His nose begins to bleed onto his fedora.)*

181

ALL *sing:*

> Who has heard tell of Crab, the corrupt
> Also yclept "the Hairy"?
> How on a morning his skin did erupt
> The sight did make men wary.
> His hirsute frame, his swinish odor
> Enough to make all flee,
> All heightened by his weird fedora
> Such none did ever see.
>
>> Here's to Harry, the Hairy Wonder!
>> God bless him, hat and all.
>> Bless his pimples, bless his boils
>> And bless his ruptured ball!
>
> Within his slouched and wondrous hat
> There drums a constant headache,
> His mouth felt oft like a welcome mat
> Beneath his painful nosebreak.
> What availed high thoughts of art or craft?—
> His ass did hideously quake!
> He might as well be dumb or daft
> His life is not too jake.
>
>> Yet! Here's to Harry, the Hairy Wonder! *etc.*

SUSAN B. ANTHONY *(gazing at a drawing of Dixie Dugan in her frillies):* Is it true what they say about Dixie? *(She unsuccessfully attempts to ravish the newspaper.)*

RITA RIGHT:

> Oh come to me not
> As chestnut blossoms ope
> Upon my carmine lips, sobbing
> Heart in thrall, Oh come not. . . .

JAMES JOYCE: A washable floatable lovable doll.

AUDIENCE: Sing "Sorrento"!
Sing "Mama"!
Sing "I Met Maria in the Pasticceria"!

They begin to toy with their gold earrings and to twirl their mustaches.

Do the fuckin' Harlem Glide!

BILLY MCCOY *(playing that old pianna on the steamship "Alabama"):* Note well how each fish and worm begins to twist and squirm!

A White-Robed Choir, including Dan Lop, Roche Mongan, Peter Cloran, Tom Treacle, Christopher Leming-Hoptt, L.M. Churl, John O. Nose, J.H. Rome, Clete Banjo, Joe H. Snart, Maj. Rumford Rug, Charles E. Chin, Pinafore Jaizus, Mary N. Joseph, Pablo Tortuga, Paulo Turrone-Tortilla, Carmela Vanella, Gibson Martini, Count Monte Crisco, Harrison Carter, et al., enters and, accompanied by MCCOY, *sings a medley of old favorites. They are: I Won't Steal Your Wafers; That Dear Old Jar of Vaseline; Skunk Cabbage, Starlight, and You; Gas, We Gave No Énémas; Your Expensive Spread Bewitches Me; Sixty-nine in Old Caroline; My Bowling Ball Has Fallen To The Floor; I'm P-Polish and P-Proud Of It; Your Sweet Soiled Nightgown in the Moonlight; My Cazz' Has Got the Hots For Only You; Marmalade and Mary in the Mornin'; The Quaint Old Catamite; We're Gonna Blow the Dikes Tonight; Gee, I Miss Those Arizona Sandstorms; Lost in Lou'siana With Lewd Lou; You're My Migraine Headache, You; Jeeter Put Saltpetre in My Greens; In the Waiting-Room of Your Desire; That Dear Old Credenza of Mine; Don't Sella! Your Swella! Umbrella!; Silver Hairs Upon the Chifferobe; In Hackettstown They Let Their Plackets Down For Me; The Glass Streets of Tarrytown; Candlelight Upon Your Stye; The Night the Flowered Sofa Fell on Dad; I'm Climbing Through the Window of Your Heart; There's a Small Focacceria in Your Eyes; A Onion and You; In the Confessional With Bill; Hail, Holy Queen; My Puella Loves Her Fella; Down in Sunny Dade We Call a Spade a Spade; My Love is Trembling on the Sheer Edge of the Meaningless; Let Me Share My Chocolate Chip With You; I Love Ya, Bibelot Belle; A Mets Cap, Rose Hips, and You; Eat My Chowder; and A Jig in a Wig.*

SENATOR STREET: I say that nuking the Reds would be a courageous act of Christian charity, belovèd by every cracker of whatever race, creed, or color in this Great Nation! Think of the Thousands of American Boys who'd be saved! To fight another day! Even spicks on welfare might make it!

THOUSANDS OF AMERICAN BOYS: Get the troops outta the fuckin sun!

MONSIGNOR O'HARA: Our prayers go out to those Thousands of American Boys. Clapped up or not, they are God's own. *(He prays.)*

JAMES JOYCE: There's nothing like a new cure for an old clap.

BARNACLE BILL: Open the door and lay on the floor!

FAIR YOUNG MAIDEN: Do I detect a bestial bulge in Sailor Bill's blue bells?

ODILE GASHE *(absently fingering her crewcut):* If you'd worn sensible shoes this brutish mariner might have ignored you . . .

BARNACLE BILL: I'll brutish you, by thunderation! I'll keelhaul yer
mizzen! *(He does so to Sapphic protest.)*

OFFICER KILLARNEY *(arresting an Ejaculation):* Come wi' me now,
ye little spalpeen. Shure, an' it's dirthying the public streets ye'd
be up to, eh? *(He scratches his head and steals an apple from a
laughing Italian fruitstand that appears as if by magic.)*

CLARK SITZ *(endeavoring to avert his gaze from the sylphlike image
of Dixie Dugan, still in her unmentionables):* When all else fails
a cool hip bath may assist the young man in tempering the flames
of desire that threaten to boin him all up! *(He begins bathing
again.)*

JAMES JOYCE: Divine views from back to the front.

HARRY THE CRAB: Would it help my varied pimples, carbuncles, and
boils? *(A large dog begins savaging one of his suppurating ankles.)*
Why is it that when I waken I am invariably covered with hair? I'll
write to Henry Miller! Wise Hank knows much of the unruly fletch!
*(He sings "The Lament of Harry the Crab," or "The Parvenu of
Second Avenue.")*

> I am Harry, the Wandering Jew.
> With piles and psoriasis,
> Eczema too.
> Whatever affliction may be about
> Ruptured anuses, measles, gout,
> Chicken pox, mumps, or the Asian flu:
> I got it—plus dogshit on my shoe!
>
> Harry they call me: dirty guy!
> With an itching crotch and a
> Wide-open fly.
> Whenever a lunger coughs and spits
> Whenever a mongrel pisses and shits
> I get some in the throat or eye!
> It's the poet's cross, I sigh.
>
> Nom de plume of Harry the Crab
> I can't, in blizzard or flood,
> Get a cab.
> The hackies chortle and pass me up
> Splash me with mud like a mangy pup
> Gas pains in my colon lance and stab—
> I'm God's gift to the pharmaceutical lab.

184

I'm Hairy Harry, the wondrously sick!
Eating pigeons in the park,
I misplaced my dick.
Searching for it in the grass
I found I'd also lost my ass!
Stung to what is left of my quick
I cursed God: who hit me with a brick!

Thus Harry the Crab, the Sick, the Hairy,
Sans pee-pee and of ass devoid;
Has nothing left for Sue or Mary,
And homeless is his hemorrhoid.

EDDY BESHARY: Must I forever stand in the laundry room of life endeavoring to refresh my somewhat exhausted spirits with a glass of Hires root beer and a Camel cigarette?

SIGNORINA RIGATONI: Zom'body do me, no? Oo wan's do me? *(Her limbs casually fly akimbo.)*

JACK ARMSTRONG *(trying bravely to peer from beneath his glist'ring visor):* I'll take a chance, ma'm. Back in Belleville, Illinois, I was known as Jack the Joint, a religious fan!

"POP" HEART *(misty-eyed):* Jack was destined for a certain fame. The only man in Southern Illinois who was born without an ass! *(He sets type.)*

FUCKING WHORE: If I had only kept up my ballet and clarinet lessons I wouldn't be this fucking whore who now stands shamefully before you. *(She sobs as someone shows her a still from* The Red Shoes.*)* Oh, Jesus! Art, beautiful art! *(She does a split.)*

SENATOR STREET *(discovered raising his secretary's skirt):* I have said it before and I say it again—there is nothing wrong with giving a talented young woman a little assistance in the jungle that is Washington. *(He massages, as if by accident, his pelvic area with the hem of the young woman's skirt.)*

BETSY JEAN DAISY SMITH: Why, Senator Street! What would my husband, a far-flung Airman Second-Class, think of this? *(She emits a modest groan as her skirt trembles.)*

Here a bluish cloud appears, high above the am'rous scene. It sparkles with a myriad lights, which on closer inspection are revealed to be various military medals, medallions, insignia, and ornaments, each dazzling, winking, and blinking patriotically as the cloud, being constructed on the order of machina versatilis, *turns about to reveal, seated in its fluffy azure center, his blue uniform this color's perfect complement,* AIRMAN SMITH, *who seems somewhat bemused, albeit comfy, as befits a military man.*

AIRMAN SMITH: I can thank the Red Cross for this visit home or wherever I am. Hello! Was that Betsy Jean's groan I saw? *(Searches frantically through his cloud.)*
SENATOR STREET: Sweet—Jesus—H.—Christ!! *(He more or less comes.)*
BETSY JEAN DAISY SMITH: Do that thing, hoss! *(She helps him along in her efficient secretarial way.)*
JAMES JOYCE: All the world loves a big gleaming jelly.
AIRMAN SMITH: That *is* Betsy Jean! Now I know why I was flung so far! *(He turns into a Jew Communist.)*

A band of Orientals of indeterminate origin enters. They play upon a thousand twangling instruments.

JAMES JOYCE *(musing):* Where could Shakespeare have heard a German band?
PETER BOFFO *(seated once again resignedly before his lonely sheet of white paper):* We do not like to hear inferior work by superior people. . . .
SEAN ALEXANDER KURKJIAN:

bark	crab
crab	bark
bark	bark
crab	crab

yayay!

sisisisis

JIM JAM *(eating his trench coat):* The man has reified the concept of the crabbèd bark! Of the rousing cheer! Of the kid sister!
KID SISTER: You wouldn't send a sight like me up on a skid like that on a date like this?
WUN EM EN: It's easy to see that he's interested in the possibilities of the language, folks! A marvelous addition to our prestige list.
CHARLES DEXTER WARD: Is there no pity left anywhere in the world for Alger Hiss? For his hidden back issues of *The Nation*? For his eyes of blue, his kisses too? There is a possibility, so rumor has it, that he now reads nothing but signs.
RUMOR: I HAVE IT!

186

FOOTS FUNGO: If I could play every day I'd break outta this slump. I have a lotta trouble with the breaking ball . . . and have to play every day to . . .

WUN EM EN: We cannot, unfortunately, see our way clear to allowing you to play every day at the present time. However, we'd very much like to see more of your work.

SUSAN B. ANTHONY: Your sexism is the more reprehensible because it is unconscious. I cannot believe that you were unaware that Fungo is a morphodite.

ALICE BLUEGOWN: De sweed sdrains of de drumpet flood drough de sygamores like gleamink candlelighd. Ah, I feel faind! *(She is suddenly felled by an acute seizure of parthenogenesis.)*

JAMES JOYCE: It was I egged her on to the Stork Exchange and lent my dutiful face to her customs.

SEAN ALEXANDER KURKJIAN: My head is red.

WANTON NYMPH: I fear 'twas ze door, how you say, knob, zat creeped in m'lady's plackets, as she creep eento mine, no?

JAMES JOYCE: You can tell by their extraordinary clothes.

FATHER MAVOURNEEN: Miss Bluegown is my good friend and nothing more. I have nothing more to say.

Clanking chains are heard.

What dark magic has conjured up the demon, Hurley Lees? *(Sings:)*

> Hurley Lees, come blow your horn,
> The king's son is in your garden.
> Hurley Lees, September morn,
> Each Baptist begs your pardon.
>
> Kindly take your chains away
> Let each roller shout and pray
> E'en rain can come another day
> So why break hump?
>
> Hurley Lees, please shove your horn
> And have a Bushmills whisky.
> In the meadows rich with corn
> Ravish Barbara Friskie.
>
> Do not burden honest folk
> With cold steel and heavy yoke
> We praise each lousy Celtic joke
> So why break hump?

187

HURLEY LEES *(clanking, etc.):* The king's son is in my garden! Ravish Barbara Friskie, eh? *(Blows his horn.)* To hell with the Protestants! *(He defiles a Methodist church.)*

EDDY BESHARY *(vocally imitating a snappy banjo break):* How excellent to witness Mr. Lees sedulously and assiduously playing upon his primitive instrument! Clearly, he is diligent in his intent to move up to the penthouse whose fabled visage is turned toward the myriads of planets, comets, nebulars, galaxies, and shivering starries.

FOOTS FUNGO: Anyone can make three errors in a row. These things all even out over the season. *(He begins to cry and protest as the team bus of the Amarillo Centipedes pulls up.)*

JAMES JOYCE: You is feeling like you was lost in the bush, boy?

LANCE DELRIO: A few weeks o' that good ol', hot ol' chili an' you'll be goin' into the hole an' makin' that good throw. *(He turns into Anthony Quinn and begins to consume his sweaty, calloused fingers.)*

OFFICER KILLARNEY: The fawkin greaser kin talk good American, by Christ!

JACK ARMSTRONG: His dark secret Latin blood stands him in good stead, the old artificial. *(He goes down with his ship.)*

CLARK SITZ *(running another tub):* That's cooling the old ardor!

FUCKING WHORE: And yet . . . DelRio was so essentially innocent, so natural in his perverse sexuality. We might have met, once. *(Her heart turns into gold.)*

SUSAN B. ANTHONY: At home, she launders and dusts. In the office, she is a patronized slave to the typewriter, the filing cabinet, and the coarse jokes of her leering bosses. At play, she must lose gracefully. In bed, she must pretend an ecstasy she neither feels nor comprehends. In her intellectual life, she must display a charming stupidity. In all the aspects of her benighted existence, she is a very nigger, a jigaboo, a boot and a woogie. One might go so far as to call her a nonpromotable. Is it any wonder that Fate has destined her to be this fucking whore?

AUDIENCE: Sing "Oh, Marie," you fuckin' puttan'!

They eat large caponato sandwiches and exude giant waves of ethnic warmth.

> Hey, wotta pair o' tits on that broad!
> Hey baby, trow some up here!

They continue to act disgracefully. As their behavior becomes more horrifying, the entire scene opens to reveal the old Fabian Fox thea-

ter, *newly decorated in trappings and hangings of Teaneck Red and Bath Beach Gold. Thousands of French-toed alligator shoes tap out the nostalgic rhythms of "Angelina" to brimming eyes and sodden cheeks. Suddenly, on the gleaming stage, the champion fox-trot team of Yo and Patsy appears, dancing nimbly and joyously through the intricate steps that triumphantly took them to the Harvest Moon Ball finals. Just as the old tune reaches a crescendo, the scene disappears even more suddenly than it came into view, and in the ensuing silence, there is only the voice of:*

FUCKING WHORE: I too could have been a great dancer had Fate not given me an overwhelming curiosity concerning the ways of Eros. To me, each erection, like the rosy dawn, is new! There is something marvelous about them. They are like—like the sea off Riis Park!

AUDIENCE: 'Ey! Trow the fuckin' whore out!
Wot kinda fuckin' language is dat?
I got my mudder's pitcher in my wallet!

From the midst of the gay crowd comes a shower of peppers, escarole, zucchini, eggplant, and other lusty foodstuffs.

WUN EM EN: Perhaps the reading public is ready for an in-depth yet popular study of the ways of these quaint and irrepressible folk.

SENATOR STREET: I abhor and condemn this violence! *(Mother Cabrini hits him with a store-front Social Club.)*

BETSY JEAN DAISY SMITH: It was an old eyetalian lady who attacked you, sugar!

CLARK SITZ *(peering at Betsy Jean's limbs):* Bath . . . bath . . . cool . . . ooohhh . . .

MONSIGNOR O'HARA: Call upon the Name of the Holy Family when temptation accosts you, my son. The Church knows that even Protestants, despite their ice-cream parades, can be tempted. Miss Smith is clearly Satan in short skirts. *(Aside:)* Quite lovely skirts, too. Hmmm. I wonder if she bought that little number off the rack?

CLARK SITZ: JESUS, MARY, AND JOSEPH! *(He eats the soap.)*

HARRY THE CRAB: Ordinarily, Satan sprinkles my skin with loathsome carbuncles when I have been impure. Woe, woe! *(His fedora decays.)*

DR. ELEAZAR SOD: In Latvia, *circa* 1889, there was a sudden outbreak of decaying fedoras. I have of late written a monograph on the phenomenon.

LANCE DELRIO: Would I steal money from a friend's overcoat? Would I rape his wife on Christmas Eve while he's away at the funny farm? Would I sit around his house all day while he works at a punch press, eating his food, drinking his beer, and porking his devoted mate? Would I starve his cat and smash his bathroom door, read his letters and write in the margins of his books? Would I steal his pen? What do you take me for? Am I a no-count greaser from the border? I am a greengo in my heart, man!

CHARLES DEXTER WARD: This unfortunate young man is clearly the product of a diet of comic books, refried beans, cold coffee, and sheepshearing. In short, an unfortunate greaseball. Are not our Mexican brothers to be allowed the sweets of the fruits of the riches of the earth?

A ragged mariachi band enters. They sing and play.

> Oh in mi cafetal
> Mi hat ees on de wall
> Mi corazón ees small
> So are mi beans!
>
> Seek out mi gleaming head
> 'Neath habichuelas red
> Jou'll find mi brain is fled
> Eat op mi beans!
>
> That ees why I sing, O!
> Mi cafetal ees blue,
> Hear the church bell ring, O!
> It's ting-a-ling for jou,
> Underneath the bush, O!
> A Mexicali Rose
> She love cornmeal mush, O!
> I kiss her op her nose.
>
> In mi machismo pride
> Lies mi arthritic side
> But passion long denied
> *(bis)* Burns op mi beans!

SMALL GROUP OF WEALTHY TEXANS: Good ol' boys! They good ol' boys! *(They shuffle around, pretending to eat some cold tortillas, and say "muchachos.")*

JACK ARMSTRONG *(surfacing)*: Lance is all heart in my book. Who can forget him as an NCO? Who cannot remember the day he threw the kitten out the barracks window. A soldier! Is not a man subject to all those temptations and so on?

190

LANCE DELRIO: Despite all, my heart is a rhapsody in blue, as is my swarthy flesh.

HARRY THE CRAB: That's *fletch!* *(He is momentarily resplendent in wispy moustache.)*

SUSAN B. ANTHONY *(seized by a nameless remorse):* Comrade consciousness-raising feminist group leader, here are my monthly dues. *(She has a wet dream.)*

ODILE CASHE: Those homespun tweeds take forever to dry, Miz Anthony. Care to slip into something more comfortable? *(She discreetly straps on a large pink latex dildo.)*

SIGNORINA RIGATONI: Blefu tozd kapozh kapozhchn Estonie! *(She hastily turns away but not before the tiny golden cross at her throat begins to disintegrate.)*

DR. NESBIT: Even I'd like a taste of that! *(He drills and extracts indiscriminately.)*

ALICE BLUEGOWN: De nodes of de drumpet sdill gome sweedly to my ears. How gan you be so blint to beaudy? *(She gives off an exquisite odor of patchouli.)*

FOOTS FUNGO: I think I've been droppin' my hands on the pitch.

WUN EM EN: We've followed you up many a blind alley, Fungo. *(Fungo is bundled into the Centipedes' bus.)* I'm afraid it's cheeseburgers, Cokes, and country music from now on for you. (FUNGO is handed a 5 × 7 *glossy photo of Bobby Richardson at prayer.)*

"SHOTGUN" JAREMA: Y'all run out every grounder on this club, boy! *(The bus leaves for Wichita Falls and a five-game series with the red-hot Sunstrokes.)*

TINKER *(performing atop the panting* DUCHESS): A bloody fookin' game for girls!

DUCHESS: Oh, you sweaty, smelly, wonderful beast! *(Runs pop in the thrilling black silk stockings that encase her lovely limbs like a smooth second skin.)*

SEAN ALEXANDER KURKJIAN: His head is red.

WANTON NYMPH: Ect had bettair come out wiz ze nombair on eet or ze Duke weel be piqued. *(She dies laughing at the memory of this chestnut.)*

FUCKING WHORE: Such repressed sexual attitudes are eroding the very fiber of the nation! My first love preferred his handkerchief to my uh-uh and now he is little more than a Chinese laundryman! *(She stands straight and proud in her proud free nakedness.)* There must be no restrictions on complete sexual expression. I stand before you as a horrible example of pre-adolescent misinformation.

MARQUIS DE SADE: The lady has the right idea. *(His cold crystal-blue eyes glitter as he fashions a little noose.)* Freedom from all oppression!

By means of the swift and expert maneuvering of a scena ductilis, we are instantly in the presence of a large and enthusiastic political meeting of a persuasion. The MASQUERS, *still clad in their resplendent costumes, are paired, two by two, with ten of the most lissome, winsome, and appetizing of maids, both male and female, their youthful bodies fetchingly adorned with scraps and patches of star-spangled bunting. The entire group of twenty, shifting beautifully and in a quiet yet pronounced rhythm forms, in rapid succession, the following motifs: a large cherry bomb; an oil portrait of Henry Ford by Diego Rivera; Ho Chi Minh's last Salem cigarette; a menu autographed by an intelligent book reviewer; a pitcher of lemonade; the Liberty Bell; Kansas; a front porch; a runaway slave; a Jewish noncom; an open fire hydrant; an all-right guy; a groovy cat and a great chick; a thoughtful Hollywood star; a gay fascist; and the Polo Grounds. As suddenly as these tableaux have appeared, the entire scene vanishes, so swiftly that one might think it was never there at all. In its place, a giant picture of Justine is seen, dominating the stage; she is partially undressed and is chewing on a gold-knobbed cane with some discretion. Great crystal tears, magically lighted from the inside by means of torches held by Terrific Young People, course down her cheeks. Pinned to her tattered chemise is a button on which is inscribed a motto attributed to D.A.F. de Sade:* "IF IT FEELS GOOD DO IT TO OTHERS." *The scene disappears into a blue Miami evening, one of many.*

GENERAL KIDWELL: I have it on good authority that it was Miss Whore who clapped up the sleepy little burg of Blackstone, Virginia, during the late glorious police action in Korea, wherein I scored as a genuine hero. It was I who saved the company clipboard.

BLACKSTONE, VIRGINIA *enters, technicolor chancres and pustules scattered over its otherwise pastoral panorama of saloons, diners, tattoo parlors, and Army-Navy stores.*

JIM JAM *(staring moodily into his drink):* In Blackstone, Virginia, I thought about you. *(A lonely streetlamp in the fog falls on him.)*
JAMES JOYCE: And still a light moves long the river, 'deed it do.
SUSAN B. ANTHONY *(involved in indescribable pleasures with* MISS GASHE): I blush! I enflame! And yet! D-d-d-d-don't s-stop! *(Her eyes roll calmly about in her head.)*

MARQUIS DE SADE: *That's* entertainment! *(He hones his dirk, visibly moved.)*

DR. ELEAZAR SOD *(in the final stages of an experiment that will differentiate shit from Shinola):* Hmm. This substance has the exact molecular structure of a decayed fedora. What can it mean?

HARRY THE CRAB: Sod is one of the few critics from whom I have learned. *(He learns.)*

BILLY MCCOY *(tickling the ivories):* Guess I'll tickle the ivories.

AUDIENCE: Tickle those ivories, kid!
    He's O.K. for an Irish!
    He looks like a fuckin' priest to me!
    Sing "My Mamma's Cannoli Was Holy To Me"!

SAL RONGO: American cheese and cole slaw on a roll is my delight! That's Friday food!

SENATOR STREET *(rising from his bed of pain):* Another ignorant ginzola heard from.

Mother Cabrini drops a large float in honor of Santa Rosalia upon him.

EDDY BESHARY: The good Senator is clearly a member of the bovine group with nationalist tendencies toward the order of orthoptera. *(He discovers a large cardboard box in which there is a map of Brooklyn.)* A map with the seemingly endless streets of the County of Kings meticulously in details and scaled to boots! With such a paradigm of the cartographer's art I may supplement my already exhausting knowledge of this remarkable environ, about which, I may addend, there is nothing funny.

FAIR YOUNG MAIDEN *(with a heavenly sigh):* I like the cut of his jib and the glint in his eye, the arrow of his song and the beg of his question. In short, a man!

EDDY BESHARY: It is of the utmost misfortune that this maiden is not a Frenchwoman. She is pulchritudinous, but what can she know of cafés, haute cuisine, and apéritifs in the mellow sunlight of a Paris afternoon, hah? She is a bumpkin, alas.

ALL *sing:*

> Him give the girl of the even
> And of the boulevards
> Although this fair young maiden
> May break the heart in shards
>   The heart in shards.
>
> The lass is alas! a bumpkin
> In cotton underwear

193

Her pickles pies and jellies
Will not his heart ensnare
        His heart ensnare.

For O! He is an Arabian knight
A debonair son of a gun!
And her idea of a wonderful sight
Is a burger on toasted bun
        On a mayonnaised toasted bub-bun!

HARRY THE CRAB: I have been reduced to selling my literary archive to Max's Kansas City. *(He weeps blood and has a beatific vision.)*

ODILE GASHE: That was indeed a shared moment of emotional release, Susan . . . may I call you Susan?

SUSAN B. ANTHONY *(her body racked with the effects of her one hundred and tenth orgasm):* Call me—anything—but don't call me—late for supper. *(She affects a girlish smile.)*

MARQUIS DE SADE: A taste of the cat would cure the whore's levity.

FOOTS FUNGO *(offstage):* Strike *two?!* Jesus Christ, it looked high and outside to me!

CHARLES DEXTER WARD: Fungo is clearly being punished by the umpires for his outspoken stand on the intentional walk in order to get to—an unfortunate phrase—.002 hitters like himself. It is arbitrary punitive action. *(He is metamorphosed into the American Civil Liberties Union.)*

SAL RONGO: Have a cheese sangwich, Charlie? It's Friday yet again. *(Aside:)* It's always Friday when you're a wop.

BROTHER OF SAL RONGO: Baloney on rye with relish, please.

SAL RONGO *(lashing him with a scapular):* You'll eat cheese!

JAMES JOYCE *(sighing):* Who brought us into the yellow world?

JACK ARMSTRONG *(surfacing):* Take all you want—eat all you take! *(With powerful strokes he makes for shore.)*

DR. ELEAZAR SOD: I must face the fact that I can't tell shit from Shinola. *(His entire laboratory decays.)*

EDDY BESHARY *(consuming two jiggers of Old Grand-Dad bourbon whisky and one glass of Ballantine lager beer):* Rest assured that it was not loafing on the corner with varied ragamuffins and hooligans of the streets that bore Dr. Sod to his present apogee of pedagogical and didactical success. Rather, the nightly burning of the midnight oil and the diligent application to countless learned tomes gave him a glimpse of the summit, the Everest, which he has now scaled up. *(He plays parcheesi, parchesi, parchisi, and pachisi.)* In short, for the scientific brain there surceases efforts in no wise, ever. Questing forever for delusive truth is his wont!

194

JAMES JOYCE: Sheew gweatness was his twadgedy.

VINNIE PACHISI *(directing a car which a friend of his is driving):* Go fuckin' back, Ant'ny! (ANT'NY *backs up and strikes a lonely vehicle which is discovered to be the team bus of the Amarillo Centipedes, on its way to Texas.)*

"SHOTGUN" JAREMA *(alighting from the bus):* What do you goddam ginzos think yer doin'?

SENATOR STREET *(crawling out from beneath the float):* Tell them, son! Tell them! They don't even look like Americans despite their infectiously warm smiles. *(Elizabeth Street hurts him.)*

BETSY JEAN DAISY SMITH: It was an eyetalian street that did it, honey! *(She is surrounded by four Italo-American toughs who force her to attend a Jewish wedding at the Society for Ethical Culture.)*

MARQUIS DE SADE *(disguised from the waist down as the groom):* Bella, bella ragazza! *(He strikes himself with his gold-knobbed cane.)* Yet another effort, Frenchmen! *(Certain Frenchman deftly make an* EFFORT.)

EFFORT: I am yet another effort, doomed for a certain time to walk the night.

JAMES JOYCE: He caught his death of fusiliers.

SEAN ALEXANDER KURKJIAN: His bed is dead.

FOOTS FUNGO *(from the window of the bus):* I haven't been gettin' around on the fast ball, that's all. Soon as it gets warm . . .

AUDIENCE: 'Trow the goddam bum out!
What kinda name is Fungo?

They begin wrapping a fig tree in burlap and linoleum.

A goddam busher!
Fuckin' hot dog!

ALICE BLUEGOWN: Will nod one among you blay the aggordion? The beaudy of its sounts rivals those of the drumpet.

JAMES JOYCE: They just spirits a body away.

VINNIE PACHISI: I'll play it honey—if you'll play the old skin flute! *(He laughs raucously and opens clams.)*

The scene swiftly changes to show a calm lagoon or inlet of the sea, rising from which, light flashing from their pearly, polished interiors in such wise as to rival the effects of the very moonshine itself, are ten clam shells in which are seen reclining the noble MASQUERS *of our entertainment. They are costumed to represent rich businessmen, rock stars, political reformers, high-priced whores, evangelists, talk-show hosts, great contemporary authors, radical activists, boring financial advisors, and celebrities of the media: in short, the*

195

cream of civilization. A babel-like din issues forth from the shells, which is understood to be interesting conversation. As if at a given signal, they all begin weeping angrily for The Poor, as a photograph of a Poor is passed from hand to hand. Intensely brilliant lights of variegated colors pass over their faces, which prove to be racked with pain. Yet, as swiftly as they wept, they cease to weep, and take on sternly courageous attitudes, listening intently to the Premier Clam, a hermaphroditic figure gorgeously arrayed in a silver jump suit on the chest of which, in flashing gems, is described the flag of the Heroic International Terrorist Brigade. He begins to sing the intense "I'll Give You Anything But Money" and the shells and their succulent occupants sink beneath the calm surface of the waters.

MARQUIS DE SADE *(beaming):* Little nippers!

SUSAN B. ANTHONY *(toying with* MISS GASHE'S *crewcut):* In a certain light you resemble Emily Dickinson, Odile.

ODILE GASHE: I always thought of myself as being more the Miz Kipling type. *(She turns into Tommy Atkins.)*

SUSAN B. ANTHONY: On second thought you *do* look like our brave Ruthie!

DR. NESBIT: Kip Atkins was never equipped like *that!* I knew it well when I served as regimental dental officer in the Punjab. There the beastly sun destroyed its molars. Lived on pap for a year before being demobbed and shipped back to Blighty.

CHARLES DEXTER WARD: Thus the fate of all imperialists! *Sic transit gloria limey.*

AUDIENCE: This guy sounds like a fuckin' kike jig to me!
Where's Patsy an' Carmine?
Send the basted an eel!
I know what he is—he's a fag, that's what he is!
A goddam Protestant fag!

OFFICER KILLARNEY *(crossing himself):* God bless the mark! *(He subdues* MR. WARD *for his own good.)*

SENATOR STREET *(emerging painfully from the rubble of Elizabeth Street):* Only an animal could stand that garlic. *(A red tenor pushcart runs him down.)*

DUCHESS *(to* TINKER*):* I've runs in my stockings, sir. Oh! You must think me ugly! *(She attempts to cross her legs but is prevented from accomplishing this feat by the extraordinary position of the* TINKER'S *body.)* Don't—look—at—me! *(Her eyes seek refuge in the heartless clouds.)*

TINKER: Unnhh, unnnhh, hunnnhh, ooofff . . .

JIM JAM *(absently crushing his glass):* The sound of whisp'ring lovers under a summer silv'ry moon makes me think about "her." I've got to forget. *(A jukebox suddenly begins to play "Our Song Will Forever Linger So I'll Never Dare Forget.")*

CLARK SITZ: A brisk run around the block can supplement the therapeutic effects of a cold bath, as any Tenderfoot can tell you. *(He ties a perfect sheepshank in his washcloth.)*

"SHOTGUN" JAREMA *(boarding the bus):* We been hittin' em, but right *at* people!

GENERAL KIDWELL: It was the thought of the peanuts and Cracker Jack at the old ball game that stood us in good stead while we fled in wild disorder in old Frozen Chosen. *(He worships a Statue of Jesus Christ that glows in the dark.)*

LANCE DELRIO: An honest job at last, selling the yokels these famous statues that actually glow in the dark. The Mex makes good with Jesus.

VINNIE PACHISI: If that greaser took the name of the Lord thy God in vain I'll break his fuckin' teeth for him!

EDDY BESHARY: Can this be the same youth which at one time daily practiced "Lady of Spain" on the accordion? It impossible appears, yet—alas!—it is so. He has become nothing more than a pitiful crustacean on the floor of the ocean of life. *(He reads* The Green Sheet *and selects a good loser.)*

VINNIE PACHISI: Watch your fuckin' mout', you joo basted!

HARRY THE CRAB: Perhaps you'd like to strike *me,* Mr. Pachisi? I am Harry, the Wandering Jew, just a sweaty kike off the streets, born to suffer, grovel, and die each dawn.

FUCKING WHORE *(refastening her garters):* *I'm* just a girl that men forget.

FOOTS FUNGO: When I *try* to hit home runs, my average drops.

There is general and prolonged hysterical laughter.

CHARLES DEXTER WARD *(flushed with anger):* These fans do not represent the People!

CLARK SITZ *(mortifying the very flesh of himself with his knotted washcloth as he gazes on* MISS WHORE'S *splendid thighs):* It's just my luck to be in love in vain.

TINKER *(rolling off the entranced* DUCHESS): Who's bloody next?

DUCHESS: It was my Playtex Cross-Your-Heart bra that caught the lecherous rogue's eye. There's something about a filthy, unwashed laboring man that attracts repressed noblewomen like me, as Lorenzo has noted oft. *(She begins to levitate, her nether garments in tatters.)* Blessèd be the unenlightened.

VINNIE PACHISI *(striking* HARRY THE CRAB): I gotta hand it to you mockie basteds! You really take advantage of an education.

EDDY BESHARY: This equine cockaroach wishes to bask in the re-flected glow of true scholarship as exemplificated by the Job-like figure cut by Mr. Crab. It is unworthy of a Son of Italy.

AUDIENCE: What's that son of a bitch talkin' the Sons of Italy?
What is he, crazy?
He looks like a melanzan' to me!
He don't have no goddam respect!

They disappear into semi-detached brick houses.

JIM JAM *(gazing down a deserted, misty street):* Crab is real people.

CHARLES DEXTER WARD: These people have every Constitutional right to do as they please within the sacred confines of their own homes. Who dares deny them their Al Martino records? I will fight with every fiber of my being for the inalienable rights of these ignorant, fascist dagos!

CLARK SITZ: They make excellent plumbers, as any impartial survey will show. *(He is suddenly trapped in a stall shower.)*

"SHOTGUN" JAREMA: If Fungo works out like we expect . . . no reason why . . . down to the wire.

MONSIGNOR O'HARA: God forgive him his little white lie. We all have our faults. *(He slips into a black evening gown.)*

JAMES JOYCE: A vagrant need is a flagrant weed.

HURLEY LEES: That dress would fit Finn MacCool. *(He rattles his chains and four boys from Our Lady of Perpetual Help elementary school tell lies in the confessional.)*

FATHER MAVOURNEEN: It's good to dig on these dudes getting out of that uptight religious bag. The church must change—or die! *(He grows a beard and reads Gary Snyder.)*

ALL *sing:*

> The Church must change—or die!
> Give me that stern yet gentle sidewalk priest
> With beard and madras coat,
> Roaming the ghetto streets like Je-Jesus Christ
> Himself.
> He sees no mote in his brother's eye!
> He loves the towns and the cities by God,
> With some female companionship on the side
> Who's to censure him?
> Who? Not I!
>
> The Church must not be U.S. Steel!
> Where are those terrific guys, their shoes streaked

With garbage and dust?
Although meditation is a pleasure, what
    Of the living God, by Christ?
Is the young Father's life not his own?
What if his close friend's name is Joan?
    Should his nerves forever quake?
    Give him a break!

Get the R.C. Church into the swim!
Let's see these cheery Padres with lovely lovers
    And winsome wives.
After a roll in the hay, by Christ, Divine Office
    Is not such a boring chore.
Should only the Protestants get their h——p?
The celebrant's only flesh and blood.
    A lissome lady in narrow bed
    Will aerate his head.

FOOTS FUNGO: I can't get those ribbies if there ain't nobody on base in front o' me. *(He shags flies.)*

SUSAN B. ANTHONY *(mounting MISS GASHE):* Will somebody tell Mr. Fungo that his worth as a man does not depend on how many "ribbies" he has? *(She begins the dark act con brio.)* What on earth is a ribby?

"SHOTGUN" JAREMA: He'll work out fine as a late-inning defensive replacement, sister! And do me a favor and mind your damn business, all right? Goddam broads don't know shit from Shinola about baseball . . .

DR. ELEAZAR SOD: Neither do our finest minds, simple friend.

DUCHESS *(crawling across the diamond):* Perhaps Mr. Fungo would prefer to shag me? *(She rolls over wantonly.)* Or would he rather I shagged *his* fly?

TINKER: It's noothin' but bloody fookin' rounders. *(He bends about a venereal gaze.)*

LANCE DELRIO *(bitterly):* These rich Anglo broads never even consider that I'm flesh and blood too, right down to my worn huaraches from Sears. Can I help it if D.H. Lawrence thought I was a goddam snake or sumpn? Where now the brilliant *luces* of nighttime San Antone? Where the unbridled joy of Lawton, Oke? When do *I* get to drink the cocktails? *(He affects the behavior of a shifty pimp.)* Eef you spec' me to be peemp I be eet, señor. All sociologists know this is so, verdad? *(He sells a tourist a naughty post card starring a nun and a Spitz.)*

JAMES JOYCE: He ought to blush for himself.

199

FUCKING WHORE: It was a naughty post card that started *me* on the road to shame. That, and an indecent proposal made me by an elderly gent, with car, whom I happened to encounter in the orchestra of the Carroll movie theater in sleepy, dreamy Brooklyn. When I placed my hand inside the popcorn container he held in his lap——

JAMES JOYCE: His lowness creeped out first via foodstuffs.

CHARLES DEXTER WARD: The replacement, within a popcorn container, of its legitimate contents by a more or less erect male organ, all cloaked in the darkness of a movie theater, may be construed as being an attempt to deceive the innocent young woman who has been led to believe that her searching hand will encounter popcorn, *just* popcorn, and nothing *but* popcorn, so help me God.

FUCKING WHORE: My hand and rights were grossly violated! If my hand happened to move in a gently stroking vertical motion when it encountered the contents of the container—blame it on my youth and my aborted artistic efforts. *(She sobs as a huge poster of Pete Fountain is held up.)* My lost king! *(Shrieks.)*

VINNIE PACHISI *(with a bulge in both slacks and throat):* Even when ya humped her she used t' sing an' all. She was sorta like—like yuh kid sister. *(He becomes Pat O'Brien.)*

JAMES JOYCE: Commit no miracles. *(He prays aloud from* The Blue Book of Eccles.)*

HARRY THE CRAB: My boils are drying up! *(He throws away his ichthammol ointment to a crescendo of sorts.) I'll* fight for the kid! Who knows better than me what heartaches are?

KID SISTER: You wouldn't doom a mate like me to a plight like that with a yid like this?

GENERAL KIDWELL: Yids can't fight. They hang around the day room and go on sick call.

HARRY THE CRAB: That's *plight,* you warmonger.

JACK ARMSTRONG: Who recalls the whispered term of opprobrium for the United States Coast Guard? Let's hear it, gang!

AUDIENCE: THE JEWISH NAVY! *(They walk off, carrying stone lions, iron flamingoes and Negro jockeys, and divers rolls of gaily flowered linoleum; they then descend into basements and play Hearts.)*

SENATOR STREET: Unbelievably poor taste. Ignorant meatballs! *(He has a heart attack on Mulberry Street and is roundly ignored.)* A nice place to visit but . . . *(He dies and becomes Calvin Coolidge.)*

JAMES JOYCE: The good go and the wicked is left over.

BETSY JEAN DAISY SMITH *(weeping prettily into her Bonwit scarf):* Oh sugar, sugar! Only I understood you, only I knew the unbelievable pressures of your office.

200

UNBELIEVABLE PRESSURES: It is true. Only this devoted sec'y knew us.

CHAIR: How will I ever be able to forget the pressure of her girlish thighs and warm heinie? *(The* CHAIR *is carried off to the Salvation Army warehouse where it is sold to a mocking Socialist.)*

AIRMAN SMITH: I'll take her back. I'll forgive her every error, far-flung though I may be. Don't I have the Good Conduct medal for eating up all my chow?

USO: Remember him, America. Remember him. If you don't, who will? *(The* USO *gazes off toward the sea.)*

JAMES JOYCE: Respect the uniform. *(He disappears into the archive at Dalkey.)*

HARRY THE CRAB: Senator Street knew the aspirations of the little man. Who can forget or long deny the hours he spent as Chairman of the American United National and Transworld Boil and Carbuncle Foundation? The telethons on which he pretended to be Jerry Lewis or some other thing? How he gravely stood in pelting rain to promise youth things?

FUCKING WHORE *(bravely):* It was through his efforts that the Old Joe was virtually stamped out in the immaculate barracks of Camp Pickett.

JAMES JOYCE: Stamp out bad eggs.

OLD JOE *(rattling a tambourine):* Just because my teeth are pearly, my head is bending low.

FOOTS FUNGO *(playing pepper and ignoring the* DUCHESS*):* He could figure slugging averages! *(He is breathless with awe and a slow-hit grounder goes between his legs.)*

VINNIE PACHISI: But the basted wouldn't except the aspirations of the Italo-American community.

AUDIENCE *(worshiping a bas-relief frieze depicting Mario Lanza, Julius LaRosa, Al Martino, Dean Martin, Lou Monte, Jimmy Roselli, Steve Rossi, Jerry Vale, Frank Sinatra, Enzo Stuarti, Tony Bennett, and Sergio Franchi as the twelve disciples, strong teeth flashing, caught for posterity's delight in an eternally joyous tarantella):*
How come he never talked up guys like Enrico Fermi?
Jimmy Durante?
Cesare Cazzabianco?
Yeah! Yeah!
Always somebody like Vincent Coll! How come?
That basted was a fuckin' harp anyway!

They leave for a reception on New Utrecht Avenue.

OFFICER KILLARNEY *(awakening from a refreshing nap in his patrol car parked beneath the Brooklyn Bridge):* Watch yer dirthy ignorant mouths or I'll make a collar! *(The Emerald Society elects him Chief Gem.)*

SEAN ALEXANDER KURKJIAN: His bean is green.

DR. ELEAZAR SOD *(emerging, dazed, from his razed laboratory):* Sod's occupation's gone! *(He is given a large grant to study The Decay of Laboratories.)*

EDDY BESHARY: Lucidly, it is clear that years of dedication and discipline have enabled the good doctor to plunge into fecal matter and emerge emitting the effluvia of a rose, if one may so to speak. In some ways he brings to mind the beetle, *Gymnopleurus pilularius,* although hastening, I attest that I speak not out of pejorativeness or obloquy, that is, I am not labeling the learned doc a repulsive coleoptera. *(He cuts down corner lampposts with fervid zeal.)*

JAMES JOYCE: Thud.

FAIR YOUNG MAIDEN *(revealing, for the first time in her life, her knees):* I'm sorely tempted to give up my precious jewel to this flower of the U.A.R.

EDDY BESHARY: ⏝Jͼ ͼ𝔯 *(He manfully undoes his trousers.)*

FAIR YOUNG MAIDEN *(a picture of health):* I hope I can please you, sir. *(She puts out her tongue.)*

FOOTS FUNGO *(sliding into second but failing to break up the double play):* I missed the hit-and-run sign.

HURLEY LEES *(staring at the point where the trembling flesh of the FAIR YOUNG MAIDEN meets that of EDDY BESHARY):* Nothing like this ever happened in the ould sod atall, atall.

DR. ELEAZAR SOD *(drawing himself up haughtily):* I am not old, sir, but, rather, mature.

FATHER MAVOURNEEN: Some unreconstructed Catholics still think such an act an instance of bestiality, rather than the thing of beauty it can be between two loving and mutually consenting adults. *(He chants the Kyrie, accompanying himself on a genuine San Francisco autoharp.)*

BILLY MCCOY *(improvising harmony to the priest's lively tune):* That's a catchy little melody, Padre, but I don't feature those lyrics. *(He is afflicted with boils on his fingers.)*

HARRY THE CRAB: A word with Miss Whore may cure your disgusting malady. Take a chance!

FUCKING WHORE: Just touch my heart of gold. *(Aside:)* I was always a sucker for piano players.

BILLY MCCOY *(collapsing before he can reach her):* I know now that life is a mysterious nothing. *(He dies a good Catholic death and goes to hell as THE SPIRIT OF LESTER LAVALLARO.)*

202

JAMES JOYCE: He is quieter now.

THE SPIRIT OF LESTER LAVALLARO *(at the gate of hell):* I chure like to ainter eento deez plaze. Look like a lodda fone!

VOICE OF SATAN: Deliveries in the rear, spick!

FOOTS FUNGO *(anally violating the* DUCHESS *as the old shadows gather in old center field):* You're my can o' corn, baby!

DUCHESS: And you're my bad hop. Whooooo!

TINKER *(still searching for fresh prey):* I'll fook the bloody umpires in a bloody minute!

MONSIGNOR O'HARA *(straightening the seams of his black mesh stockings):* Oh, Tinker! Oh, Mr. Tinker! May *I* have a word with you?

SEAN ALEXANDER KURKJIAN: His ass is glass. His anus is heinous.

AIRMAN SMITH *(arriving at the ball park):* I've been invited to kiss and fondle Old Glory during the big pre-game ceremonies . . . am I late?

JAMES JOYCE: What a picture primitive! *(He chuckles as if seeing him for the first time.)*

"SHOTGUN" JAREMA: The game's in the bottom of the ninth, kid. But God bless you! You're a credit to those Thousands of American Boys glued to tiny radios in those far-flung outposts all over the world.

AIRMAN SMITH: I wanted to offer up my kiss and fondle for the repose of the soul of Senator Street, my wife's late friend and compassionate employer.

FATHER MAVOURNEEN: I hate that goddam kinda talk. *(God turns him into a Presbyterian.)*

THE SPIRIT OF LESTER LAVALLARO *(ripping into a medley of best-loved songs of the American people):* I 'ave bin coll "the Proust of the Piano." *(Frederic Chopin strikes him with a grand piano.)*

SUSAN B. ANTHONY: It's clear that they share a strong, enlightened interest in music.

JAMES JOYCE: I'm blest if I can see.

FUCKING WHORE: The same sort of short-lived interest Mr. McCoy and I once shared—how long ago it all seems. *(She breaks down and is carried off to a modern-dance class.)*

Here the scene wherein she stands, being the warmly cluttered studio of a second-rate dance teacher, mediocre musician, and all-around sweet guy with a lot of terrifically interesting opinions, changes, and in place of it appears a desolate expanse of open country cunningly constructed to resemble Fort Hood, Texas. Spread out in battalion formation across the field, at parade rest, their boyish hands furtively clutching ragged and well-read copies of Mussel Melodies, *are*

THOUSANDS OF AMERICAN BOYS, *lost in secret thought. Their stern yet homely faces twitch as they manfully struggle to hold back the hot tears that are summoned to their eyes as, faintly, and in largo tempo, a chorus of* MCCOY's *famous "Wurlitzer Woogie" is heard, moving gently, almost diffidently, through the aromatic dust of Central Texas. They think of home and high art as the scene slowly changes back to the strangely empty, yet—not empty—studio.* MCCOY's *piece is heartbreakingly punctuated by the fading sobs of the* WHORE.

FUCKING WHORE: There's no point in trying to return to the past! *(She has a vision of a Chinese laundryman holding tenderly a handkerchief in his hand.)*

THE SPIRIT OF LESTER LAVALLARO *(faintly, from beneath the ruins of the piano):* Now *that's* what I call the reepling of the reethum! Sunumabeetch!

EDDY BESHARY: In the empty penthouse erstwhile vacated by the suddenness and tragical demisement of "Ivories" McCoy, the Rolls-Royce impeccability of piano artistry, there shall be installed in genteel domesticity, if God is just, as oft he proves, the Prowst of the piano, Carmine Caballo, the connoisseur's Liszt!

THE SPIRIT OF LESTER LAVALLARO: Thees ees *not* my llama, Arab maldito! *(The sound of enraged Latin-American nationalists is heard off stage.)*

FOOTS FUNGO: Gladys Gooding was always *my* meat! When she tore into "Tico-Tico" I got a chill just *all* up my spine! *(He drifts lazily out under a towering pop-up and falls over second base.)*

ALICE BLUEGOWN: Is dat whad you call bazeball? Id's zo beaudiful id remints me of ard. Id is lige life idself. Fraughd wid trama!

"SHOTGUN" JAREMA: All the world's a ball park, and in it we poor players are the Blue Jays. *(He thinks, and as he does so is slowly transformed into Otto Kruger, after which he ascends to a cloud or two.)*

MARQUIS DE SADE *(applauding):* Way to go!

ODILE GASHE: For one of such prosaic vision, it is a magnificent secession.

CLARK SITZ *(hopefully studying the clouds):* Perhaps there will be a rain delay?

JIM JAM: The smell of the dugout . . . the warmth of the beer . . . the sweating, shouting crowds . . . *(He wanders into a fog bank.)*

BETSY JEAN DAISY SMITH: It was the unbelievable pressures of the job that caused the wily pilot's metamorphosis, God love him.

UNBELIEVABLE PRESSURES: We *caused* nothing, young woman. We merely, ah, suggested . . . a change might be to the mutual benefit

204

of the players and Mr. Jarema, as well as being indicative of the belief that our fans deserve a team that can place itself in contention. We can't get rid of the players, so . . .

FOOTS FUNGO *(going deep into the hole and throwing wild past first base):* He told me to shorten up on the old lumber. I'll never let the skipper down!

SEAN ALEXANDER KURKJIAN: His advice was nice.

CHARLES DEXTER WARD: It is the act of an elitist, nothing more or less. As the young people, who are of course the hope of the future as well as of liberated art might say, Jarema copped out. Right on! Heavy! Rip off! Dynamite! Hip! Hep!

DR. NESBIT: You can't tell a boy from a girl anymore, thank God. *(He proceeds to fill a patient's ear.)* This will only be temporary until this strange opening in your head closes up.

FOOTS FUNGO: I'm not pullin' the ball to left as much as I did when I played in the bigs. *(With the tying run in scoring position he fouls out to the catcher.)*

ALICE BLUEGOWN: Is thad a goot hid? *(She sits on a DISCARDED WIENER.)* Who's thad? Don'd I know you?

DISCARDED WIENER: I think you are confusing me with your old voice teacher, Professor Salsiccia.

JACK ARMSTRONG *(emerging from the briny):* Which way is Ebbets Field? I want to see those Beloved Buns! Not too surprising for a military man, eh? *And* a one-time altar boy! *(He admires his shoulder boards and writes a letter to his folks.)*

OLD JOE: Just because my hair is curly, I hear those gentle voices calling. *(He dances a happy jig.)*

SEAN ALEXANDER KURKJIAN: His feet are neat. The jig is trig.

JIM JAM: I remember the smell of the Old Man rolling, rolling along. His dread and muddy might. *(He orders a nightcap in a small, deserted bar at the end of a pier.)* You'd never know it, but buddy, I'm a kinda poet.

ROBERTO BLIGH: Poems are made by fools like me. *(He makes a tree.)*

JAMES JOYCE: It gives furiously to think.

MARQUIS DE SADE: Sacré bleu! I'd like to fill the dabbler up with a goodly portion of that rascally *Treponema pallidum.*

DUCHESS: Is that you in the on-deck circle, Foots? *(She is escorted none too gently off the field and arrested for indecent exposure.)* Haven't any of you gentlemen ever seen a lady's foundation garments before? Don't you read *The New York Times?*

SUSAN B. ANTHONY: The cruel corset was invented by the barons of the whaling industry and other capitalist swine.

ODILE GASHE: Bone and lacing freaks!

JAMES JOYCE: I led the life.

BETSY JEAN DAISY SMITH: That cruel oppression has been lifted. My girlish lower torso is now concealed only by the most feminine of gossamer panties, the sheerest of weightless panty hose without seams to cut and bind, the lightest of scrumptious bodyshirt with delightfully convenient snap crotch, and the briefest of provocative shorts. Freedom at last! I guess you might say I'm that cosmopolitan girl.

JACK ARMSTRONG: Some of the fellows in the fleet call her something else!

VINNIE PACHISI: To plug the broad you gotta be Jimmy Valentine!

FUCKING WHORE: Just to make tinkle is an act of faith. God bless her courage!

CHARLES DEXTER WARD: Down with Captain Ahab! It is with such young women that the hope of the future lies!

HOPE OF THE FUTURE: Unfortunately, by the time she disrobed, it was too late to lie with her.

MARQUIS DE SADE: Give me the old-time religion.

OLD JOE: Because I like to dress a babe up in the latest style, I'm a comin'. *(He shoots crap and drinks gin.)*

SMALL GROUP OF WEALTHY TEXANS: That is why they call him Shine!

EDDY BESHARY: Miss Smith possesses little of the *éclat* of the women of Paris or Cairo, nor is her belonging the mysterious muliebrity of the babes of glowing cities of the ilk of Copenhagen or Amsterdam—yet, her beauty to wit declares itself of inordinate puissance. Frankly speaking, had I a brief moment or two with her in crepuscular hallway or on the shadowy and comfy, or even not so comfy back seat of a Chevrolette or Ford, I would instantly haul her ashes. *(He admires her from afar, hand in pocket.)*

ALL *sing:*

> When as in scanties Betsy goes,
> Then, Arab Eddy's member grows,
> And, he manipulates his hose!

> Next, do his dark eyes brilliantly
> Down to her undies try to see;
> O how he groaneth shamelessly.

FAIR YOUNG MAIDEN: Unrequited love's a bore.

THE SPIRIT OF LESTER LAVALLARO: 'Ow 'bout a liddle glass of coquito, baby? A short cerveza? You like maybe to esmoke a reefer? *(The lights dim as the Proust of the piano plays a selection of Mort Ancul favorites. Central Park hovers menacingly in the background for the briefest of moments.)*

FAIR YOUNG MAIDEN: I fear that drugs or liquor may *completely* undo me. They may well lead to a permanent lowering of that moral guard that has long saved me from the sins of the flesh.

HARRY THE CRAB: That's *fletch!*

FATHER MAVOURNEEN: The lies of frustrated priests and repressed nuns. Live, girl, live! Move to the polyglot streets of the Lower East Side and mix with the restless lives of the steamy People! Take to the rooftops and cellars! Drunk on cheap wine and bloated with greasy food let your sweet youthful passions hold sway at last. *(He takes her hand.)* Care to crash in my groovy pad, baby? It's very heavy. Day-glo walls and wondrously boring old rock posters from San Francisco? Coupla big sterling silver dynamite crucifixes to hang around your neck? Lots of other artifacts from the Age of Vinyl?

MONSIGNOR O'HARA *(disguised as a wanton high school girl):* Got room for three, handsome?

GOD: That *does* it for those two. I'm afraid that this has become just a bit too much of an embarrassment for all concerned. *(He sentences them both to Purgatory for thirty million years.)*

JAMES JOYCE: Now have thy children entered into their habitations.

FOOTS FUNGO: I don't see that much difference in playin' third. *(A line drive tears his glove off and the winning run comes home. He is removed from the game and sold outright for forty-five dollars to the Biloxi Crips.)* I'm sure I'll be able to help the team. They're a great buncha guys.

JAMES JOYCE: One must sell it to someone, the sacred name of love.

"CRACKER" YALOBUSHA *(eating a chili dog):* Ah know this ol' boy kin he'p the team. Ah plan to bring him in in the late quarters when we ten, twelve points behin'. *(Someone hands him a baseball and he looks at it with unconcealed suspicion.)* What y'all handin' me heah, boy? Some kinda kiddie toy?

ROBERTO BLIGH: He has a nest of robins in his hair.

LANCE DELRIO *(going back to his roots on the West side of San Antonio):* The maricón has even expropriated our native food. *(He joins a ragged band of Villistas and shoots his big toe off in an excess of Latin joy.)*

JIM JAM: I want to get a few bucks together and get my things out of the cleaners before I hit that lonesome old road to nowhere.

ROBERTO BLIGH: His hungry mouth was pressed.

THE SPIRIT OF LESTER LAVALLARO: Thees Joyz Keelmer was some terreefic broad, hah?

EDDY BESHARY: Oft have I bended my sloe-eyed glance of Araby

207

upon her verses. Culture is more than a GGG suit with extra pants for those casual weekends with the sporty coats.

"CRACKER" YALOBUSHA: This ol' boy talks like one o' them New Yoke spo'ts writers. *(He looks at a Louisville Slugger incredulously.)*

FOOTS FUNGO *(on the bench):* Y' gotta be in the right frame of mind to come off the bench cold as a pinch hitter and watch that third strike go by.

JAMES JOYCE: You are pure. You are pure.

"CRACKER" YALOBUSHA: A goo-ood ol' *boy! (Gesturing toward the bat he has been examining:)* What in the *hell* is this god-daym stick?

DUCHESS: Like every rotten man who has ever walked the earth, the little dear has gone out of my life.

JIM JAM: Inconstant and fleeting as the scent of magnolia over the dark'ning countryside. *(He boards a lonesome train in pelting rain. To the* DUCHESS:*)* I'll peek through the crack and look at the track.

SUSAN B. ANTHONY: Take off your skirts and lie down, darling. In a certain light you bear an uncanny resemblance to Sappho, a dynamite babe!

DUCHESS: That man, inconstant though he may be, is peer of the gods. *(She lies down, suddenly deshabille.)* Is it his fault that he can't hit the high hard one? Or the sneaky fast one? Or the big curve? Or the dinky slider? And nobody can hit the unpredictable knuckler! *(She is made an honorary Yankee fan and given the* Book of Banalities.*)* Others have overcome shortcomings as grievous. One thinks of Choo-Choo Coleman, Elio Chacón, Charley Neal. And what of the legend of Clint Hartung?

HURLEY LEES: Bullshit and broken glass! *(He frightens the City of Philadelphia by there appearing in a Cincinnati uniform.)*

SUSAN B. ANTHONY *(brandishing her foxed copy of* A Right-On Guide To Lesbian Joy*):* Who is this loutish Celt? The Board of Health should have him arrested for carrying his ass too near the ground. *(She smiles, as if remembering something.)*

MARQUIS DE SADE: Ass? Where? Who? *(He enters a comfort station precipitately.)*

LANCE DELRIO *(limping and bemedaled):* An old war wound I got fighting for my People's right to be astronauts. I don't want to talk about it just now. *(Tears form in his depthless eyes as an orchestra strikes up the lively "La Luna Caramba Azúl, Corazón!")*

ALICE BLUEGOWN: Dhere's someding aboud a soltier . . . *(She turns into Lupe Velez.)*

FUCKING WHORE: Actually, it was I who was responsible for Señor DelRio's wound—I drove him to a sense of his duty to the People by giving him a subtle taste of the Old Joe. Not even the debonair are immune to persuasion.

OLD JOE: Just because I always wear a smile, I always wear a smile. *(He shuffles into Queens and the entire population flees to Suffolk County.)*

ROBERTO BLIGH: In his joyous primal innocence, he looks at God all day.

VINNIE PACHISI: Watch your faggot mout' about God!

DR. ELEAZAR SOD: My early findings seem to point to a similarity in the process of decay in fedoras and laboratories alike. Although it is too soon to be absolutely sure, they both appear to possess the identical molecular structure of Shinola. *(His stern head is bathed in an unearthly golden light.)*

JAMES JOYCE: Note his sleek hair, so elegant, *tableau vivant.*

JIM JAM *(alighting from the 12:02 in a lonesome old town):* Time to sling the old raincoat over the shoulder, or shoulders. *(He slings.)* I'm just a stranger in town. *(His raincoat falls into a sad puddle.)* My old raincoat has slipped from my shoulders and fallen into a sad, a sad and grey puddle.

Once again, by means of the judiciously expert and perfectly executed movement of scena ductilis, *we are returned to the ball park seen at the beginning of our entertainment. The* MASQUERS *have been transformed from players of the game into a softly humming group of clean-cut youths, which worshiping body forms a perfect circle around second base, toward which "sack" their eyes are fervently bent. At first glance, it would seem that they are rapt in adoration of the inanimate object but a closer look reveals the* MINUS-CULE FIGURE OF TY COBB, *dressed in his at-home whites, sandwich boards hanging nonchalantly from his shoulders. On both front and rear of these boards is displayed the mystical number, 367. As the tiny figure prepares to speak, his mouth slowly opening, the* MAS-QUERS *softly sing a medley of the following songs of the diamond: He Strides to the Mound With the Latest Disease; I Want to Get Some Wood On It So Bad; The Sneaky Slider Made A Rattler Rider Outta Me; The Ballad of the 15.00 ERA; I've Got Splinters in My Ring-Dang-Doo; I've Come To Love My Pine-Tar Rag; They Weren't Falling In For Us (That Sunny Day); I Lost It in The Glare; He Hit .200 ('Cause They Played Him Every Day); His Smoke Got in Their Eyes; In Deep Center, There You Feel Free; and Let His Bunt Roll Foul! Then the tiny player speaks, with a voice of thunder.*

MINUSCULE FIGURE OF TY COBB: Fungo, you have been taking your eye off the ball halfway through your swing. I have noticed this in Baseball Heaven, and so I have returned to earth to caution you about it; let's say a little bird told me. Keep your eye everlastingly on the ball, Fungo, and the game will be good to you as it was good to me, despite the incursions of the latinos and nigras who have almost ruined it. Spikes high! Stick it in his ear! Put it in his teeth! No quarter! Hit 'em where they ain't! Run it out! Wait for your pitch! Break up the double play! No defense against the homer! *(He begins to fade away as fog and drizzle close in on the ball park.)* Farewell, Fungo, farewell, it is time to take the eternal field . . . farewell . . . eye on the old pill . . . *(He disappears. The* MASQUERS *buy programs.)*

FOOTS FUNGO *(staring about, bewildered, as if awakening from a heroic dream):* I heard the voice of . . . the old Georgia Peach . . . he told me . . . to keep my eye on the ball! It is the secret! How simple it all seems now. Everything true and beautiful must converge.

JAMES JOYCE: A dream of favours, a favourable dream.

AUDIENCE: Maybe now we'll see some *ball!*
    I don't believe the phony basted!
    They don't make ballplayers like they useta!
    Why don't the bitch at the organ play some Italian songs?

Sniffling, they gaze at photos of Joe DiMaggio. Mothers and aunts in black carry in Bath Beach and hoist it to the ceiling where it becomes a giant tomato plant.

DUCHESS *(swiftly rising from her supine position and as swiftly adjusting her garments and sprucing up):* What—what am I doing here? Have I grossly misjudged the moral code of the young athlete?

JAMES JOYCE: Simply killing, how she tidies her hair.

FOOTS FUNGO: I'm gonna lay back for the fast ball and——— *(He swings and crashes a homer into the fifteenth row of the upper mezzanine, 410 feet away. The ball strikes a bearded homosexual and the crowd goes wild.)*

"CRACKER" YALOBUSHA: Ah doan know whut they all cheerin' for, but they must be somethin' good about losin' the goddaym ball. *(He begins whittling at the bat in his hands.)*

SUSAN B. ANTHONY: Have I gone mad that I should stand, flushed and uncorseted, before these all-American lads, fans all? *(She retires to the ladies' room, foundation garments in hand.)*

AUDIENCE: Hit another faggot creep, Foots!
Woffuckin' power!
Since when do queers get allowed in the ballpark?
Hit one for the Dook!

JAMES JOYCE *(to* FOOTS*):* Will you carry my can and fight the fairies?

"CRACKER" YALOBUSHA: That's what ah call a *touchdown*, Foots. You play ball better than a damn nigra.

LANCE DELRIO: One of the finest examples of sportsmanship and sheer grit it has ever been my pleasure to witness. *(His war wound heals and he becomes an iconoclastic yet intelligent sportscaster.)*

SMALL GROUP OF WEALTHY TEXANS: See how y'all can be deceived? We thought that ol' boy was a Mex. Instead, he turns out to be a smart Jewboy.

ROBERTO BLIGH: Foots bends his beefy arms today.

JIM JAM: In every single window I see her face. *(He sets fire to a Lucky and disappears into the rich, flavorful smoke.)*

BETSY JEAN DAISY SMITH: That sweet budding superstar has shown me, by his example, that it is wicked of me to desire the freedom of my body. *(She begins to peel off her layers of free, modern clothing but her good intentions are stymied by a recalcitrant snap crotch.)*

VINNIE PACHISI: I'll help ya, honey. *(The gods of the Swamp Leage cripple his cluthcing fingers. At the same moment, the snap crotch of her fun bodyshirt disintegrates.)*

BETSY JEAN DAISY SMITH: It is a sign! A sign! *(She weeps.)*

DR. ELEAZAR SOD *(shaking with excitement):* This unexpected decay factor sheds new light on my "fedora theory." Can it be that snap crotches were in use in late nineteenth-century Latvia? It might explain the preponderance of impotence in that ill-fated land beyond the sea. I wonder . . . ? *(He goes on wondering, assuming the visage of Walter Pidgeon.)*

FOOTS FUNGO *(lining a double off the left-field wall):* He meant to get a curve down and in but he hung it on me. My eyes, of course, followed it all the way, and . . .

HARRY THE CRAB: The feeling has returned to my ankles! My blackheads are saying bye-bye! I feel new power and confidence as my body odor diminishes markedly! *(He gambols with five rabid Dobermans.)*

ODILE GASHE: For the first time in my life, I'd like to perform the act of shame with a *man. (She is obscured by a puff of smoke and emerges from it dressed as Pola Negri.)* By heavens, I don't look half-bad.

211

JAMES JOYCE: I rose up one maypole morning and saw in my glass how nobody loves me but you.

"SHOTGUN" JAREMA *(from the clouds):* I always knew that the boy had all the tools. He could do it all, I knew. Thank God he has listened to that ultimate voice, I mean the one that is inside every man and a woman or two.

THE SPIRIT OF LESTER LAVALLARO: For thees player of beisbol, I dedicate some of the All-Time Mageek Museec of Hollywood. *(He dozes off as his rippling fingers perform.)*

SUSAN B. ANTHONY *(reappearing from out of the ladies' room):* There! Suitably bound once more by those cruel unmentionables that make us true women, I stand modestly among those who honor Mister Fungo and his incredible triumph over adversity and plain old rotten ballplaying. A woman's place is in her stays.

SEAN ALEXANDER KURKJIAN: Her waist is chaste.

JIM JAM *(in an alley from which the sunshine has drifted):* Is her figure less than sleek? Is her chest a trifle meek? *Stays,* Susan Anthony, *stays!*

HARRY THE CRAB: My ankles! They are actually supporting my entire weight as I gambol with the Katzenjammer Kids here! *(He eats a crushed pigeon.)*

DUCHESS *(striking the* TINKER *as he attempts to force her into an unnatural act):* How dare you even think of such venery, you pig, in the presence of a long-ball hitter and never-say-die hustler?

TINKER: The fookin' rounders player's turned her into a bloody nun. *(Grumbling, he returns to Australia.)*

OLD JOE *(striding toward the Queens-Brooklyn border, straight and proud in his new-found manhood):* If dat fuckin' honky, Fungo, can git it on, so can I! *(He turns into a People and puts the torch to De Camptown Racetrack.)*

FUCKING WHORE: The Old Joe has gone militant. Woe to the innocent pudenda of unwary revolutionary lovers . . . science has shown that even radicals get the galloping whoopsie. I stand before you all as a girl who might have married even Fungo had I stuck to the old clarinet, the old dance, the old magic of art. *(She breaks down as a stranger across a crowded room plays "Limelight.")*

FOOTS FUNGO *(starting a triple play with the stab of a screaming liner to third):* I got no time for women. Occasional self-abuse to keep the eye clear and the hand steady—that's my speed. May God forgive me.

GOD: I forgive all .320 hitters and flashy infielders.

212

SEAN ALEXANDER KURKJIAN: All love his glove.

EDDY BESHARY: While I too am ensnared in the infectuous spirit of Fungo's feats and his admirable reversal of execrational forms as an athlete of the diamond, may I point my digit at the fact that though the teeny-tiny figure of Mister Cobb, the plum of Georgia, had a salubrious effect on the beloved Fungo, all may not be attributed to miraculous fortune when it comes to his startling amelioration? In other words, it was sedulous application to the divers skills one needs to master that was of no small minute in his sudden ascent to stardom's precincts. I have seen often the same thing occur in the streets of Istanbul with rotten players of their national pastime, the name of which contest slips away from my cerebrum. Once again, it is the tale of the express elevator to the roof. *(He whistles "Lola," happy as a Bedouin.)*

JAMES JOYCE: I believe in Dublin and the Sultan of Turkey.

FOOTS FUNGO *(trotting out to his position):* Don't throw bouquets at me. Just let me pose in my glove.

JACK ARMSTRONG: I suddenly feel as if I've grown something approaching a real ass! *(His well-cut trousers are burst asunder by his burgeoning nates.)*

"POP" HEART: So faith and beauty *again* triumph over fleeting fame! Go, young Jack, to drab obscurity   it's better that way. *(Printer's ink courses proudly through his old veins.)*

JAMES JOYCE *(aside):* He was grey at three.

MARQUIS DE SADE: The young officer's callipygian charms pale next Fungo's flawless play. I fear that I may be forever cured. *(He slaps his leg and emits what may well turn out to be his last joyous howl of pain.)*

ROBERTO BLIGH: Lonely Sade can break a knee.

SAL RONGO: I'm still fuckin' stoopid, but happy as a bitch that the Crips got a chance to win it all this year.

BROTHER OF SAL RONGO: Sal's a real stoopid, but a million warm laughs. *(He sneaks some forbidden liverwurst into the source of his own warm laugh.)*

JIM JAM *(over a lonely meal in an empty waterfront café):* They call him frivolous Sal.

WUN EM EN: We'd be very interested in a book on the rebirth, as it were, of Fungo, done by a romantic loser and top writer who frequents waterfront cafés and can hardly believe that last year he was nobody. Fog-walkers preferred. It'd be nice to sit down over a beer with someone like that and talk advances—someone real and warm, someone who's been around, someone with a fresh point of view, someone with a lousy agent. *(He shuffles through his credit cards and appears briefly at several college symposia on the modern novel.)*

CLARK SITZ: How about a humorous treatment of the history of soap and water? I can *tell* it to somebody! Pick me up quick, top acquisitions man, for I may never wash again! This diamond dust on my epidermis feels like silk. I have seen the sign!

"SHOTGUN" JAREMA *(booming from a cloud over left field):* He's pickin' up the signs?

ROBERTO BLIGH: He wonders lonely in a cloud.

HARRY THE CRAB: Isn't that *crowd?*

FAIR YOUNG MAIDEN *(aside):* Sans boils, carbuncles, and other pustules, I am strangely attracted to this hairy Hebe.

SEAN ALEXANDER KURKJIAN: Her cunny feels funny.

AIRMAN SMITH *(from the same cloud):* Glad to have you aboard, sir!

"SHOTGUN" JAREMA: Hi there, yardbird! Ain't you the young feller who wanted to kiss and fondle Old Glory? Friend o' baseball's a friend o' mine!

RITA RIGHT *(alighting from the crack Omaha Speedball):* Even 'way out on the forever brooding plains, we know of Foots Fungo's feats through the magic of television. *(Sings:)*

> O Fungo Foots, your doubles and your triples
> Make hearts to race, and stiffen girlish nipples,
> And when o'er far-flung fence you crack the ball
> Each lady in the stands doth come withal.

She suits action to words and a festive crowd gathers around her joy-racked flesh.

HURLEY LEES: Everyone's so happy, begob, I can't even scare a bleeding Lutheran. *(He returns to the ould sod, chains muffled.)*

ALICE BLUEGOWN *(as Lupe Velez):* I tango weeth any damn body I feel so sonomagum good! *(To* EDDY BESHARY:*)* 'Ey, beeg boy—'ow 'bout jou? Jou like to dance weeth Loop, hah? *(She reveals her lower torso which is strangely suffused with a maidenly crimson.)*

JAMES JOYCE: I rise, O fair assemblage!

EDDY BESHARY: Although somewhat of the rube still clings to you, Madam, and although there is little with which you may self-commend to a cosmopolite like myself, your lower limbs and so forth fill me with erotic bents. Let us retire to the darkened balcony of the Electra moving-picture theater, where our bodies may perspire and blend.

214

ALICE BLUEGOWN: Your leeps spik bad Eengleesh, but there's jes, jes in jour pants!

KID SISTER: You wouldn't send a spick like her up in the dark like that with a dud like this?

BETSY JEAN DAISY SMITH (*resplendently svelte in her new long-leg four-way power-net double-diamond panty girdle with nylon-lace-appliqué magic-oval tummy flattener and concealed detachable garters*): Let the child know the joys of sex before she takes the irreversible step toward responsible womanhood. (*Since she cannot sit down, she stands up straight and tall.*)

DR. NESBIT: I had a passing filthy thought, but let it go. (*He closes his office and goes to the ball game.*)

CHARLES DEXTER WARD: This is the true American way, when young people of varying minority groups can submerge their differences in the satisfaction of their raging lusts. I believe Engels had a paragraph or two about it . . . no matter.

JAMES JOYCE: Here let a few artifacts fend in their own favour.

OFFICER KILLARNEY: I'll run the Red in tomorra. I feel too good today, what with Fungo about to score the tie-breaking run.

FOOTS FUNGO (*scoring the tie-breaking run all the way from first on a single*): I got a good jump on the hit-and-run sign and just kept goin'.

SEAN ALEXANDER KURKJIAN: His feet are fleet.

GENERAL KIDWELL: Miss Riaganoti and I will be married tomorrow in a simple military ceremony at second base between games of the doubleheader. I—I (*he blushes*)—just like to *do* her!

SIGNORINA RIGATONI: Oh, Milk-ee! Do me *now!* Een front everybody, I no care. My eyes are blazink, no? No, no? NO?!

BARNACLE BILL: Don't get so sore and lay on the floor.

SIGNORINA RIGATONI (*lying on the floor*): You like thees pose, Milk-ee? You like? Aha! I see your medals begin glowink! With how you say the heat, no?

GENERAL KIDWELL: This is highly irregular, Miss Ragotiono, but— (*He does her.*)

PETER BOFFO: Somehow, in its own crazed, dark, peculiar way, this is—*literature!*

VINNIE PACHISI: That fuckin' settles it! I'm gonna make my Easter Duty right fuckin' now!

FOOTS FUNGO (*hitting a grand slam*): I just tried to meet the ball and stay out of a double play.

SEAN ALEXANDER KURKJIAN: That shot was hot.

ALL: Was hot!

The MASQUERS *now descend upon the stage to mingle with the other players and the* AUDIENCE. *The clouds and mist that enveloped them at the beginning of our entertainment are no more; there is now surrounding each glittering sunshine, and their snowy-clad figures are clear against a blue sky on which backdrop pennants snap in a cool breeze. Their uniforms, purest white, proclaim their changed names in letters of richly burnished gold. They are now, the pitcher,* SPLENDOR, *catcher,* CLARITY, *first baseman,* GERMINATION, *second baseman,* JOY, *third baseman,* TEMPERANCE, *shortstop,* LOVELINESS, *left fielder,* MERIT, *center fielder,* PERFECTION, *and right fielder,* HARMONY. *Their leader,* HOPE, *leads them in joyous galliards and corantos, which* ALL *then follow.*

FATHER MAVOURNEEN *and* MONSIGNOR O'HARA *(from Purgatory):*
Frail, jolly scene, bother of Jersey, our strife, our sleekness, and our trope! For thee do we try, dour vanished children, naive, to thee do we render our thighs, scorning and creeping in this alley of beers. Learn then, pugnacious celibates, kind sighs of calm seas, bear us; fond laughter dress our sex while dough comes to us; caressèd loot of shy bloom, seize us. No torment, no shoving, no cheating. Unwary.

JAMES JOYCE: Ere we hit the hay, brothers, let's have that response to prayer.

ALL: No cheating. Unwary.

JAMES JOYCE: Loud, heap miseries upon us yet entwine our arts with laughters low!

ALL: With laughters low!

Lamont's Scrapbook

Where have all the flowers gone?

Pressed carefully yet luxuriantly represented in their dazzling numbers and diversity, among the vital leaves of the late Lorenzo, lady-lover and body-booster, not only lovingly and whimsically described with an almost overpowering intensity (not as they are but as the poet's piercing eye descries them), but set as complements to other natural wonders, i.e., trees, clouds, mountains, lakes, beaches, mossy banks and shady glens. Their subtle perfume appeals to women, proud as peacocks though they may be, in love.

What are patterns for?

Essay-type questions will not bo aooepted at this time by Christ!

Ah, did you once see Shelley plain?

Yes. Lieutenant Colonel Edmund K. Shelley, Infantry, Commanding, at a full field inspection held on a hot Saturday morning in August, 1951. The officer (not a West Pointer but possessing the same curiously determined yet vacuous mien of one) was approaching the pinnacle of hysterical military fury moments after discovering, on a hapless private's bunk, a bar of toilet soap, which, while in its proper position, was of a white color. The colonel's rage can be understood only if it is known that his orders to company commanders, orders that were dutifully passed along the chain of command, specified that only green toilet soap would be permitted to be displayed during the inspection, in this case the soap to be Palmolive. Colonel Shelley's face was red and the sweat on it gleamed, a perfect complement to the gleam of his silver oak leaves. There is something about a soldier. One suspects that his beginning phrase, "What's this?" was clearly gratuitous, since it is clear that he knew what "this" was. The question was asked of the barracks at large, but elicited no reply.

Who the devil will change a rabbit for a rat?

Dr. M. Cranston-Lane, the renowned biochemist and prestidigitator.

Why should a rich man steal?

To butter his bread, clip his coupons, sail his yacht, race his horses, gild his lily, sing his song, ball his jack, flip his wig, dream

217

his little dream, jam his blues, eat his fill, wish upon his star, drink his bitter cup, make his face, smile his smile, crack his whip, roll his hoop, dim his brights, blow his cool, shoot his load, tote his barge, carry his burden, arch his eyebrows, paint his wagon, button his lip, open his heart, fry his fish, cast his stone, steal his kiss, have his cake, kill his bottle, end his day, ink his roller, spill his gravy, abdicate his throne, move his bowels, lay his ghost, shovel his walk, speak his piece, put in his two cents, hang his hat, crush his ice, tune his radio, take his part, do his share, capture his imagination, defend his honor, bat his brains out, wet his whistle, cancel his order, pick his brains, swell his chest, keep his head, dunk his doughnut, show his flag, grate his cheese, twirl his cane, tie his tie, back his winner, draw to his straight, accent his good points, groove his pitch, bust his balls, rock his cradle, enjoy his leisure, let his hair down, defeat his opponent, lose his touch, whip his cream, hit his point, damn his eyes, walk his narrow line, feel his oats, haul his ass, evade his responsibility, slap his leather, grit his teeth, bend his admiring glance, hold his water, burn his bridges, fly his kite, reap his harvest, entertain his thought, smash his idol, hold his line, crush his desires, check his swing, rack his brains, search his soul, waste his time, laugh his head off, take his advantage, shoot his moon, pack his bags, drive his nail, cut his rug, run his tight ship, curse his blue streak, close his account, cudgel his brains, burn his midnight oil, beat his meat, pull his daisy, slam his door, drown his sorrows, honor his flag, keep holy his sabbath day, covet his neighbor's wife, crash his party, make his mark, emit his groan, have his heart, jump his gun, seize his opportunity, rue his day, roll his eyes, throw his left, push his jab, waste his substance, sink his basket, take his base, crack his books, bare his soul, eat his crow, smack his lips, pay his piper, swing his deal, pop his fingers, sink his putt, wipe his slate clean, ride his hobby horse, live his life.

Who is the third who walks always beside you?
   The night of the first snow a polar bear lumbered between us! The snow was white against his whiteness! And your eyes were dark, ah! Winter wonderland, this stringent city!

Whither shall the ox go where he shall not labor?
   Down in the dale, up in the glade, to the soft sylvan music of zephyrs through cool and shadowy leaves, where a kiss is still a kiss and coronals of bosky flowers, tender greens and great pearls await him; where all the sprites and satyrs, nymphs and fairies dance in

218

dappled sunlight to the syrinx, pipe, and lute, thrum-thrum, where birds do sing, and lovers and their nut-brown lasses lie among the green corn fields, with a heigh! nonny-nonny-no, and over all the laughter wafts of the idle and besotted boy to whom the grape is sacred, jug!

Oh say, can you see by the dawn's early light, what so proudly we hailed at the twilight's last gleaming?
I can see a steeple surrounded by people.

What is this thing we call a kiss?
French, tongue, soul, chaste, motherly, fatherly, brotherly, sisterly, ass, genital, Judas, trembling, rough, hesitant, sweet, soft, wet, dying, fevered, good-night, farewell, burning, and chocolate.

Who killed Cock Robin?
The Brothers Torroncino, Sal, Rocco, and Gennaro, three gents of Italo-American heritage, dubbed by the press "the Mad Dog Killers." They sizzled in Sing-Sing.

My delightful and talented Miss Flambeaux:
My dear! How wondrous our brief—all *too* brief!—meeting was for *you*, I make no guess at knowing, but for me it was a small, fleeting, yet most brilliant ray of sunshine in an otherwise grey and workaday existence, the existence of the novelistic drudge, a life that your penchant and talent for poetry fortunately precludes. How handsome you are! As I told you you were that fabled evening that now seems so long ago. I trust and implore you to believe that it was not the vodka that spoke, but my own very sober mind that controlled those words that I was *almost* too shy to mouth. I meant —*everything*.
It was difficult of me to think of you as the sensual, *and* sensitive architect of *The Sweat of Love*, since your conduct with me was "above reproach" as they used to say in those well-lost and benighted days when stultifying bourgeois morality *seemed to matter*. How far we've come into the true state of manhood and womanhood!—mostly through the courageous efforts of a few writers like yourself. Not that I would have dreamed of conducting myself in an undignified and grossly leering manner, my dear lady, but often, when artists who happen to be of the opposite sex share the same enlightened views of the world and of adult behavior meet, there is a swift discarding of that stifling veil that

they are wont to present to the world of Philistia and an immediate meeting of the soul and mind. I'm sure that you have found
this to be so.

I know that you took it as a good joke—my attempt to "force" you
into a cab and thence to my studio. Writers often like to parody, in
their rough way, the absurd manners of the bourgeois world "they
never made." I know that your laughter was genuine and warm.
Actually, the incident was not an attempt on my part to play the role
of parodist. I was indulging in a subtler and more satisfying role—that
of the forward and crude Bohemian—I'm sure that you saw through
my *persona* in seconds. Of course you did! It is a face that I often
present to women, particularly women artists, to test their maturity
and individualism. You passed the test, and, may I say, passed it with
flying colors! How delicious it was when you struck me with your
umbrella and then your handbag! Exquisite perception was shown by
those prompt and decisive actions of yours, actions which clearly told
me that you had seen through my game in all its ramifications and
decided to play your part in it. When you knocked me into the gutter
and rode off in the cab alone I almost cried out my delight in your
perceptions. Marvelous!

I would, of course, "me buxom lass," be less than honest if I were
to tell you that I did not miss your presence and bubbling conversation the rest of the evening. Believe me, I had second, and even
third thoughts anent the "test" I now see I was rather foolish in
giving you. But how was I to know that you, my glittering bard, are
one in a million? My greatest regret is that I did not have the great
pleasure of hearing you read *The Sweat of Love* in the friendly
confines of my own poor studio. In any event, perhaps this loss is
not permanent. By which I mean to say that I here plead with you
to do me the honor of taking dinner with me at my studio. If you
accept my most humble invitation, please, I implore you, bring
with you all the poems that you feel that you would like to read. I
will be flattered to hear them and talk them over with you. If they
have the naked power of *The Sweat of Love* perhaps I can arrange
with my editor for a serious reading of them with, of course, a view
toward *publication*. I will also be pleased to read to you from the
novel on which I have been at work for the last few months. It is
not a run-of-the-mill narrative and I would be extremely interested
in getting the opinion of a poet, who is also a woman, about it. I
feel, somehow, that only a woman poet can truly appreciate its
rather veiled allusions and evocations.

So, dear lady, if you feel that you would enjoy a good literary
evening of talk and food and drink, please come! Let me know when

220

it would be most convenient for you—all right? I entertain very informally, so you might wish to bring along something comfortable into which you can change after dinner.

Your friend and admirer,
Antony

Lamont's Notebook

Bitch. $7.50 for a new tie. *I'm* the published writer! My luck if she by some fluke knows Dermot or Sheila! Reduced to the drunken fifth-rate poet at the party who puts his arm around all the women, the "wise father." She *better* come. Sweat of love! Bitch!

My dear Sheila,

I have started this letter three times already and each time tore it up as hopeless. Why? Because the tone seemed surly as well as hurt, not to mention defensive and hostile, and I don't want you to think that your reply to my last "walking-on-eggs" letter in any way awakened these states in me. I must say, however, that your reply neither enlightened nor comforted me, and if I may be so bold as to speak with the candor that has always obtained between us, it was hard for me to believe that *you*—Sheila Lamont (I *still* cannot think of you as Sheila Trellis)—actually *wrote* that letter, the letter I now hold in my hand. There is a sticky softness to it, an evasiveness, a scattered jigsaw-puzzle quality, that is totally unlike your usual epistolary style. One could almost imagine it being dictated to you, although I know that that is patently absurd, is it not? Of course it is. You would never allow such puerility, I am sure. But forgive this digression.

My sweet sister, I *nowhere* in my letter to you specifically *asked* you to "pry" into Dermot's literary affairs, as you so uncharitably put it. I recall I rather circumspectly—for a *brother,* that is—wondered aloud, as it were, if there might be a means whereby you might discover what, if anything, and that is a big if, since I am not accusing anybody of anything and never have, what, I say, Dermot has been suggesting to Professor Roche anent my works. Considering that you are no doubt interested in your husband's career, that does not seem too strange—it is certainly a far cry from asking you to "pry." I never even used that word. That is *your* word. Reread my letter—that is, if you still bother to save my letters. You did, at one time, do you remember? But that is neither here nor there. Such inquiry, as a matter of fact, might well come at dinner, or after dinner, or over cocktails when the tongue is loosened and the niceties relaxed. Did that ever occur to you? Such a question might arise very naturally between husband and wife, no? I don't think your sharpness of tone is called for nor do I appreciate phrases like "I will not be your spy, brother or no brother." As if I cared—actually cared!—what Dermot is doing to advance his nondescript literary career. You know better than that. God knows, dear Sheila, as do *you* and I, that Dermot has done well-nigh everything to further his fortunes in the world—anything that he might do now would come as no surprise to me. My curiosity was (and is) what one might call "professional" and concerns me in a peripheral and noncreative way. Cannot a man be curious as to his brother-in-law's doings? Apparently not, you seem to say, and in no uncertain terms, terms which shocked and saddened me a bit.

As for the rest of your letter: I was disheartened, so much so that I wonder about your budding career as a critic and reviewer, i.e., there seems to be a certain serious lack of objectivity in your current view of contemporary letters and, even more seriously, a tendency to "rewrite" *fact* in your opinions—at least as far as this letter goes. Am I far wrong? Believe me that although I speak boldly it is with a heavy heart. "I must be cruel solely to seem kind," as Othello said. First of all, your comments on my own work have become scarcer and scarcer and thinner and thinner until at times I feel that I am reading a review by Demuth Kano or Sarah Schwartzgelt. (Do you still laugh heartily at their reviews as once you did?) Your opinions of my writing are of the sketchiest nature, almost nonexistent. Surely, your Old Tony doesn't expect a full-length essay from you concerning his work, but your comments have been less meaty than jacket copy. To say, finally, that my *Deuces* is "amusing" is really unworthy of you. *Deuces* may or may not be anything else, but it is certainly not what anybody would call "amusing." Even my bitter enemy, Jon Carrot, was acute enough to call it "a blur of geography," although he did not understand the book at all. What has happened to that finedrawn mind of yours, once subtle as a plot of Nabokov's or McCoy's? (I don't like either, but credit where credit is due.)

More importantly, what am I to make of your really dumbfounding assaults on statements and opinions that I took to be commonly shared by both of us? I did indeed "mean it" (and how!) when I wrote that Dermot has produced nothing of serious consideration for years and years. This is a point that both of us often made to each other in letters and face to face. I think you once spoke of Dermot as a man who had "squandered his talents as a child squanders energy." Such talents as they were, of course. We were not talking of Fitzgerald, mind you. And now, with an alarming brusqueness and a thinly veiled contempt for me you hit me in the face with the statement that that lasciviously and crudely penned potboiler of his, *The Red Swan*, is "a small but unimpeachable amelioration in the art of narrative." Sheila, Sheila! What myopia is this? *The Red Swan* is not ameliorative, it is not, certainly, art, and one may question whether or not it is narrative. It *is*, as you and I truly know, and have laughed about many times, a third-rate (at best) novel that flirts with the porno-

223

graphic in a thoroughly dishonest way. You once called it—and I remember the words verbatim—the product of "a brain steeped in milk." Surely you remember?

The idea of a novel about a writer writing a novel is truly *old hat.* Nothing further can be done with the genre, a genre that was exhausted at its moment of conception. Nobody cares about that "idea" any more, and Dermot knew it. To rescue his shambles of a book he added scenes of gratuitous sexuality, so crassly done as to cause all but the most debased reader to throw the book down in dismay and disgust. And yet now it is suddenly become an "amelioration" in the "art" of "narrative"? Of what kind? It is hardly a book at all but a grim exercise in the soiled terrain of the marketplace, a playing to the grandstand for the transitory rewards of quick money and notoriety, neither of which the author received in the quantities desired.

I certainly don't want to say anything that might come between the happiness of a woman (particularly my sister) and her spouse— but ask Dermot yourself if he did not consistently refer to *Swan* as his "cash trash." Ask him. I clearly remember my sadness when I read the manuscript of *Swan.* You will recall that it was written almost immediately following Dermot's story, "I Divorce Thee Husband," which both you and I thought presaged the beginning of a modest but distinguished career. What aberration was this? we wondered. What madness? It was almost as if *Swan* had been written by some sinister "other" who had taken over Dermot's brain and talents for his own base ends. For a time, I struggled—surely you remember —to see in the book some subtle and hidden meaning, some hint of the profound, tried and tried to read between the lines for evidences of parody or satire, etc. And it was *you,* in a letter that I am certain that I have still, who said that I should stop trying to justify a "squalid labor." Yes, my sister, you!

So what am I now to think of this sudden change of heart? Has *Swan* changed? Is its quality of the meretricious somehow different, simply because time has passed? Or what? Why this sudden surge of praise for a piece of utter trash? (*Dermot's* word, not mine!) Why do you now call my finest novel "amusing"? Why do you write anent that section from my new novel that it is "momentarily arresting"? Why do you refuse to acknowledge that your husband may be involved in getting a leg up by pulling your brother down? A man who could write *The Red Swan* is capable of *anything.*

If Dermot wants to hoodwink Roche with *Swan* or with anything else—this "Western" he is now writing, for instance—that is fine with me. But does he have to do it at my expense? My dear Sheila, this small chance may be my last to acquire a readership among students. It could possibly mean readings, lectures, writer-in-residence jobs,

224

paperback reprints of my books, etc., etc. Wherefore Dermot's vindictiveness? Why must he advance himself at my expense? You must admit that the circumstantial evidence is great: Roche's abrupt coolness toward my work occurred at the same time his correspondence with and interest in Dermot commenced. Curious? *Chilling!*

I still fondly believe, my dear, that in you I have a champion, a critic, an editor, and a delightful reader. I know that you love Dermot in some way and you, of course, should. He is your husband and can be, on occasion, fairly interesting—and, of course, one must always remember that he once, long ago, showed a spark of promise. We must not forget that, must we? Of course not. But if you are honest with yourself you will also see that as far as literary merit goes, Dermot is a cipher—witness *The Red Swan,* that dull exercise in commercialism that its author himself called "cash trash."

You might also think on how Dermot spent his considerable *Swan* royalties. I know it will be painful for you to remember that he said that he was going away to write his "real book." "Going away" was nothing more than three years of drunkenness in saloons in Manhattan. He supposedly wrote *Swan* to allow him to write his true work —which never materialized. How he laughed at me as I labored over my obscure non-selling novels; he even said that I should emulate him as his cash poured in (not enough to suit him, but that's no matter). These things are *all true.* Now, this man has become a "serious writer," and *Swan* a book to ponder. In the meantime, Tony Lamont fades and his sister chastises and scolds him for his artistic dedication, his desire for some small measure of success, and his *very clear memory.*

My dear, my darling sister, wake up, I implore you! Dermot may be your beloved husband but he is a *bad writer* and an opportunist.

Do not be angry with me, I beg you.

All my love,
Tony

P.S. You of course understand that I have nothing against Dermot personally.

8. SHE IS THE QUEENLY PEARL

But it was not God who brought help from the faraway blue or from anywhere else, how well I remember, sitting here now, the wind—always the moronic wind!—screeching across the lake, clawing hag-like at the windows, Ned Beaumont tragically dead, crumpled in the fireplace, like an old fish, tragic, a victim, but not moreso one than I. It was not God, I say! But—a goddess! A queen! For it was Daisy, dear patient listener, Daisy Buchanan, my posy, heart's bouquet, who came in out of the moonlight on a subtle waft of cologne, brushing womanfully by the outraged but strangely submissive maître d', bursting through the door to this debased inner sanctum, lair corrupt.

In a trice, her regally cool stare took in the situation—the twisted faces of hatred the two vampires wore, the flurry of dressing gowns and negligées, my own distended trousers, the flash of silken thigh and turn of slender ankle, the hastily covered-o'er provocation of provocative garments! So all saw she, she glanced, thinking swiftly, and . . . she knew, instanter, and I was then out, somehow, safe, the gnashing of European, hellish teeth my fading memory. Escaped whole, and leaning on her frail yet purposeful arm, or perhaps both her arms. I—cannot—remember, cannot remember aught till the first fresh blast of air from the street. . . .

Later, walking peacefully on that same street, or perhaps another, for who knows truly the face of the streets? I marveled that it had been only moments before, or perhaps hours—perhaps an eternity!—that I had walked this same street, or perhaps another, for the face of the street is unknowable, we walked together, arms linked, to the world another happy couple (would it were so!), for what casual stare could have picked out the terror and depravity that we both knew, now, that we had to face? I mean picked it out of our faces. She looked sideways at me, quizzically, almost as if she had never seen me before, and I laughed, embarrassed, and automatically glanced down toward the area of my manhood. But there was no tell-tale sign there of the passion that had almost engulfed me in its black satanic power. The impersonal city, the great, dark, thrilling city, that no one can ever know the heart of, bustled and hummed about us.

Later, over coffee, she told me, haltingly, sketchily, with sobs and in anguish, bits and pieces of her life, her sad, brave little life. I did not want to hear it. I fought against my feelings but to little or no avail; the words enchanted me, wove a glittering web, like the web that Circe wove to discourage her swinish suitors, magical, enthralling. It was a remarkable story, a remarkable life, almost unbelievable, cluttered and jumbled facts and time heaped together—yet from it a strange Truth rose like a mysterious attar. And as she talked on and on, I knew that our bond had become that of steel, I knew that the sickening magic of "the Two" would not, *not* prevail over our mutually beloved Ned Beaumont. If there was Justice on this earth! Was there Justice on this earth? Ah, but who can know the face of true Justice? As Hymen of Rhodes said, bitter and broken at the end of his long life: "Who knows the face of Justice? Can a man understand his *own* face?" But somehow, I believed, believed in this flower of a girl, this queenly gem, this pearl. Her small, gentle voice went on and on 'gainst encroaching night . . .

. . . just a simple little frip of a girl with vast pretensions, thought that I'd be happy with a man of marvelous intellect, a man who had read *Paterson*, say, anyone from anywhere, a hairy beast from Ocean Parkway even. Phony little me. Well, I had the silliness knocked out of me. How I remember like yesterday, my thick little head in the oven—that was in California and I meant to scare, oh blackmail is the better word, poor Tom, working there in one of his father's platinum mines. He was happy but I missed the city. I can remember cheese Danish all over the floor and dear Tom's strickened face, that frozen visage he often affected. Then, soon, soon, I guess, but perhaps it was years, sometimes it seems like centuries, like the flight of a poem, we were heading back to New York on a 707. Tom's face in the sunlight pouring lavishly through the window looked familiar and then I realized that he looked like Steve McQueen! I shuddered and asked for a blanket, you know how you can ask for a blanket? Well, I asked for one. Then we were over New York, which I immediately recognized by the way the Atlantic heaved and shuddered. Well, Martin . . . well . . . that was the turning place in the crossroads of my life . . . that false attempt at suicide. Tom had but contempt and the like for me from then on although he always treated me well, but I could see the faraway look in his eyes whenever we had cheese Danish. There are certain things that kind Time will not erase. Oh, what a year was that! For a time I thought to return to Mechanicville where I was born and grew up. It is a leafy and peaceful village, the townspeople are kind, they laugh readily and sweat a lot, I had been happy there once for, oh, for such a fleeting moment in the scheme of things of my life. . . .

For a time she could not go on and silence reigned, silence broken

227

only by the buzzing of an insane fly somewhere, *somewhere*. How lucky he was! I felt my heart swell almost to bursting. Perhaps it did burst. Who can tell when the heart bursts? Often we think we know the truth. We know nothing! I thought of Cystis of Thebes, thought by all to be the savant of his age, who, dying, said "I have lived the life of a lentil." Daisy blew her nose daintily in a large linen handkerchief with the initials NB embroidered in the corner. My heart almost cracked with the absurdity of jealousy, an unimpeachable pain that torments the lost. But who are the lost? Why, I asked, my face a carefully frozen mask, should I feel jealousy? Absurd! Ha! Ha! Ha!

. . . and of course you are right to laugh, Martin, Daisy opined, for she had begun talking again, when she had started, I didn't know. I had lost track of time and found myself staring at her heaving nipples, those young and strangely delicate attributes of this girl's flushed beauty. And I felt again jealousy—and something else! Something . . .

. . . perhaps a shred of *pity*. But you are right, there is no sense in raking over dead leaves. Let them lie and crepitate. Anyway, our return to the city was the beginning of the end, the real beginning of the end. Oh, Tom knew it—knew it as surely as he would have known that a ball had come to his hands on the end yard or something. How often he told me of those days! His eyes would twinkle and shine. Silly me! He sensed it and a coldness began to grow up between us like a wall. He stopped . . . caring. I had my freedom, he had his business, and I became one of those gadabout women, with my first affair in the wings, odd phrase. Tom knew that too—for a big, and rather stupid man, he has extraordinary powers of perception. It must be his intrigue. I sometimes think that Tom even knew the man with whom I went to bed. Ah, it was a joyless bed, but I had to have my scatterbrained fling! You'll note that I'm really not crying. I seem to have something in my eye. My lover was a poet, tall, sloppy, with a deep voice and a head of wild hair. He lived in a hovel of an apartment on the lower East Side, crammed with huge bags of garbage and trash, which he often told me had blown in the window. Ah, he was a witty man! He knew a thing or two about love and had an endearing way of wearing a watch cap down over his ears that made him look like somebody's old grandma. How old he seemed, old and wise. Perhaps he really was, in some other life, somebody's old grandma. Oh, I hardly remember anything about him! He liked taxis, I recall. He knew a lot of people named Bob so that I never knew who he was talking about. He allowed his teeth to rot because it was natural and also he liked to pay dentists. He had been married to a woman who went to Idaho and lived in a chicken coop, I think. There she felt free. We broke up rather swiftly for some reason having to do with oral something. Tom was cruel about it, cruel. The night after we stopped seeing each other, for good, hubby came into my bedroom wearing a watch cap pulled down over his ears and began to emote the words of his school song. I wept, I suppose, but it's all so obscure . . . strange that Nature does not allow us to remember pain. But what is pain? For a long time after that I lived in bed. I would walk about once in a while in order to do things that nobody else could do for me if you understand what I mean? Swathed in the sheets, all white, like a robe . . . a robe. I've never told you about my girlhood as a singer in the White-Robed Choir of my little Mechanicville church? Of course not. I remember it as if it were yesterday. Strange how Time allows us to remember itself, or something. I stood in the back row of the choir and sang my little heart out. Often I'd find a hand, not my own, beneath my robe. The Devil also stalks the Baptists, you see. How strong the pastor was, strong and duress. His favorite sermon was a denunciation of bare legs and low-heeled shoes. "Woe to those maidens and spouses who desecrate God's House with flat heels and naked limbs!" I can still hear his burly voice and seem to see, but I may be wrong, his flushèd face. Thus did I learn first about the false face of the world. Like Hamlet. But I was happy. I seem to see from those palmy days also a cordé handbag. Odd. I seem to remember eating frozen custard of various flavors. The handbag was always stuffed with cash. I recollect a face, perhaps my own, perhaps my brother's—I don't know, for who can know his brother's face, or *her* brother's face, for that matter?—too heavily made up. Those were balmy days. Who would have thought that I would come to this—this diner?

It is a cafeteria, Daisy, I offered, my heart plummeting as I stared into the dregs of my cup, the dregs of my life. My life! I bitterly mused. My heart raged in my throat like a demented chicken as I fought the despair that threatened to overwhelm me. My harsh and chilled adolescence! *I* had had no white robe! *I* had had no cordé bag! Her soft voice was droning again . . .

. . . and though Ned, dear foolish Ned, was suffering from dementia praecox or something like that, I loved him, loved him passionately, beyond rationale, loved his little dimple, his toothy chuckle, his soiled hat. And I wrote him foolish letters that, I'm sure now, must have enflamed him . . . I acceded to his wishes as far as I was able, but—a quartet, his suggestion that we—I'm sorry, I can't tell you my shame. His request for an old boot was one thing, but . . . not that I am a prune, not at all, I've had my moiety of thrills and such. Tom can tell you of the man, a famed translator of Lorca and college instructor of note, also a poet in his own right, who liked to dress up in my undies. He bought me an orange dress once

229

that he called my Florida dress it was soft buttersoft and fit my body to a t marvelous it was actually it was called my Florida frock he had the most extraordinary habit of painting a moustache on his face whenever he felt blue do you like the way I'm talking on and on without any pauses or punctuation it's my consciousness just simply *streaming.* But enough! I'll be studgy, is that the word? studgy Daisy again and let my consciousness stumble along as usual. This poet in his own right first alerted me to the little things, turned me, in his own perverted way, into a whole woman, if woman it wert! There were so many—*little* things that I became open to. I loved the way he put ketchup on his pork chops, his baggy pants, his dislike of cats, how cute he was when lost on the IND, the manly way he sipped his tea. But it was not to be. He too wanted only the gross female, cared more for my girdles bras and nylons than he did for me. How Tom laughed when I found my underwear drawer—empty! As empty as the blind heart . . .

My mouth had flown, some time before, open in horror, so that I must have seemed the fool. But I could not "shake" that phrase, "request for an old boot." The unutterable reality of it was devastating! I was shocked far more than I was shocked that day the access to those letters shocked me—why? I cannot even now tell, even now, gazing at the poor body of Ned Beaumont atop the bookcase, the cruel knife in his back. Why? I must have muttered this imprecation aloud for Daisy flashed a look of such tender affection on me that I blanched. She stupidly twisted a paper napkin to shards before my eyes—fond girl! The full horror of it struck me as a kidney strikes a clown between the eyes at the circus. How many years it had been since I had laughed at the circus! The glitter, the tinsel, the lights— and underneath the broken heart! Often more than one! It was like life itself, or a football game. A football game! And then the kindly, vapid, yet stern visage of Tom came to my mind—that he, a captain of finance, should have collaborated in his wife's decadence. And dear Ned—to lust for a boot? And what was that about his painted moustache? I reeled.

. . . all too much like, my life that is, became all too much like a wild trip I once took cross-country with a man who had no buttocks and his friends, a platitude couple who were on the way to Mexico. There to read Lawrence and become free! Ah, *that* was a clinical case history of a trip, I allow. Such my poor life became. The grimy towns, the rains, the chili made in one place with Heinz's ketchup, over all the grim sky brooding and also changing. The dusty streets of my wretched womanhood—if I had known when I was a girl . . . and now I seem to vaguely remember sitting in my father's sinister car outside Nathan's Famous in Coney Island. Rhythmically squeezing together

230

and relaxing my nervous thighs, I stealthily ate a hot dog the while. I remember that I was wearing a red satin garter belt trimmed with white lace and that we had come from the Bronx Zoo where we had gone earlier in the day to see the bears. How grown-up I felt! God, that's a long drive. Lucky my father had a powerful blue Buick convertible! I see in my mind's eye now, yes, now I remember, a strange man at the Zoo—he was in a corduroy cap, a seedy raincoat, drinking muscatel, I should think, from a bottle. Three-day beard. How sad he seemed! How sad and shabby! I had the oddest impression that he was once a famous lawyer or nuclear physicist—perhaps a scholar of comparative literature with svelte wife and pillared mansion from whose shady veranda you can jump in the picturesque lake. Or perhaps he was a poet of local fame whose best friend had maligned him in a Roman cleft. But—forgive me, Martin—may I call you Martin? Nathan's. Perhaps it was at that moment, my dad getting lobster rolls and clam broth, and I secretively engaged in the act of girlish whimsy, that my life changed, as the poet says about the yellow woods where the wrong turn will lead you into a lot of crap, forgive my demotics. Perhaps there, there was the turn that led me to Tom and Ned and ultimately here with you, dear, good Martin, here in this lonely and almost deserted diner . . .

Cafeteria, Daisy, I sobbed. I was sobbing uncontrollably now. My trapped throat raged somewhere inside the lost despair that was me with the furor of a typhoon of emotions gone mad, head over heels, all ends up, blood pounding and the lost heart black with its secrets that no one can ever know—who can decipher the dark heart's fathomless theories and suppositions? Not to mention its illogical things? Who indeed?

. . . so many things, she trilled. How variegated it's all been, now that I have this quiet moment with someone who *understands*, to think it all over. Ah, see how my eyes dance! See my lips flutter as I lick them with my tongue to make them shine in this harsh fluorescent glare the better to see your food and read your paper by! See how I, for a moment, forget to stupidly twist my napkin into grievous orts. So many things . . . Mark Cross dresses, D'Agostino pants, Trunz handbags, one of which reminded me of my lost cordé; Merkel shoes, Packard lingerie—and the endless swirl of openings, parties, theater suppers with theater people than whom there is nobody like. Their closeness, their camaraderie, their need for adulation and applause, their basic shyness. And some other tributaries I forget just now but you know what I mean. Strange, how Tom was no slouch even though his brain had been injured on a six and four field punt or something. No slouch at all. Often drunk, yet he had his mind entire. Excuse me, my eyes—my eyes are brimming with tears and you'll notice that my voice, which up to now has been fairly strong, is faltering. He had some cute ideas too. Bought me French maid's costumes, nurse's uniforms, nun's habits. We had our good times and our bad, our ups and downs. Another American marriage of the beautiful affluent. Among whom we circulated all the time. Did you know that many affluent matrons wear support hose and drink a lot of instant coffee? Then, too, they favor tuna glop for buffet suppers. These things keep their husbands on the golf course, so Tom told me anyway. Oh we had a lot of little talks. And my father, he of the clam-broth and lobster-roll purchase, he liked Tom, so there must have been something good and fine in him, for my poppa could always smell bankruptcy afar off, e'en o'er the briny deep, a nice turn of phrase, no? Yes, Poppa liked the big sweet tackle backer, and I knew he did because at their second meeting he, Poppa, allowed him, Tom, to break one of his, Poppa's, most treasured piñatas. I remember . . . I remember . . . the little gifts falling on Tom's head, his big silly grin . . .

I kicked my heart into blinder obedience and stifled the cry that, mole-like, tried to get out of my throat. My poor Daisy! Daisy! If there is a God in heaven, I began, but a counterman's sullen stare silenced me. How I would like to shake his hand now, this humble slob, this dumbbell with the inarticulate wisdom of Estonia in his bowel. Somehow, he knew. With a swift motion I was up and out of my chair to get more coffee and cheese Danish. For some strange reason, a reason that seemed just outside my understanding, Daisy broke into sobs as she looked at the cheese Danish. At that moment her face took on the unmistakable frown that one gets on a face when one smells gas. Was that a jet plane whining overhead? Thus does memory serve us all. Did not Simon of Mesopotamia note that "I remember, therefore I was. Yet what was I?" A moment later and it was over and the dear girl gorged up her Danish happily, washing it down with coffee. Time in its kindness heals our memories of its grievous wounds inflicted without regard to race or creed or status. Does not a rich man as well as a poor yell a lot when he is punched in the mouth? Marx forgot these basic truths. Suddenly, I adjudged that Daisy had flown swiftly to the ladies' room. Had I been wrong, after all, about her? Fool! Fool! Blind stupid fool. How I had hurried on, a frail canoe with the current, rushing from the past! And now it was all too clear what a mistake I had made. I bit my knuckles until they hurt me like coals of fire. I mean like if coals of fire had been applied to them. Thus were the sharpness of my teeth. Then she was back, eyeing me narrowly and with a curious stare as if realizing that it was I that she had earlier looked at as if seeing for the first time and not someone that she had indeed seen for the first time. So does the mind trick us despite our

232

most careful ideas about things to do. I suddenly understood Kant's description of the mind as a "whatnot." Then, somehow, she was back, her trim, lithe form across the table staring at mine, words tumbling from her mouth . . .

. . . dances, balls, how he tried to fill my life with laughter and joy! Vast annual benefits for dread diseases, how we ladies posed for the newspaper photographers, trying to expose just enough of our thighs to arouse the silent and unknown audience out there—somewhere! Who knows who will ultimately see a photograph? And isn't it compelling that photographs are not . . . *real?* We did our best, the parties to stamp out crab lice, which even some of our most attractive young matrons harbored in their curlies, odd word, that. Yes, don't look aghast, it's true, even our most affluenced ladies get them now and again, from subway toilets more often than not. Think then, of the sympathy we had for those unfortunates who lived with them day and night! Like unto old "buddies." Somehow, at this time I remember sleeping a great deal—to escape from the reality of what Tom thought were my days of happy hours. He often called me his dozing Daisy—stranger to say, he could turn a phrase after business hours. In my waking moments I espy him, always in the middle of a group of the most exciting celebrities, the kind you see in the newspapers, in the back pages somewhere, all smiles and dopey tuxedos, those bony wives and their svelte husbands. Yet who can see the anguish beneath? Most of them would probably rather be eating a wiener or whatever they call it . . . Tom! Tom, always, always in the very center, the smile he bent on the Governor's wife as he listened to her speak of her work with Albanian superintendents in the area of Tompkins Square Park, sixteen blessed acres in the teeming streets. She had brought over thousands of them, freed them from Communist oppression. Their musty babushkas and dusty berets gave the little park but yet another touch of color. They were hope-stuffed days if you follow my suggestion. But then . . .

Later, under the blind stars, we found ourselves in some park, which park I don't know, that is oft the beauty of a crowded city! Out of the wonted bustle of the streets we strolled hand in hand, Daisy's face oddly peaceful in the glow from the sodium vapor lights that rustled above. *Our* park! Somehow I seemed to say this, if aloud, I don't know, but she looked at me with such a glance of fear—fear, and at the same time, a loathing yearning. The dead grass, the broken benches, the sea of glass shards that reflected the moonlight like a million rare jewels—all joined in to make this a night to remember and to mutter strange things meant only for the ears of somebody who normally might seem startled at such spoken oddities. Such was Daisy, I dared hope? Who can know the heart of a woman? Wasn't it Emerson at Walden Lake who uttered, "A good woman is a-smoke"? Though we have been forced to believe that they are strong, self-reliant, stern and singleminded, yet we do not greatly err if we consider them as cupcakes—luscious arrangements of tender flesh that live and breathe perfect affirmation. Of course, some of them are ugly but God loves them. Though they rightly demand equal pay for equal work, who can know the true desires of a dame? So these questions raced through my splintered feelings and I shot a glance into her shining eyes, eyes whose glow rivaled that of the diamond-showered park through which we aimlessly walked. "Aimlessly I wander through the park, my heart a toad." The line came to me suddenly. It was the power of poetry that had struck at me, blindly, as it often does in an atmosphere redolent of Venus. Her shining eyes! And then my throat closed up, I hoped not permanently, as I felt her odd little hand seek out mine in the healing dark. Somewhere, far off, an Albanian shrieked . . .

. . . I see—*don't* deny it, dear, dear Martin—I see that you are glancing at my oddly shaped little hand. Allow a sigh as I am brought back to the time when I baked endless loaves of black bread, guised as a peasant girl, hair in a thick braid down my back, my full, flowered skirts and simple blouses something to see. Don't turn away! It's all true . . . I lived with a poet, another one, they have always been my weakness. We found each other, blindly, like two moths who seek out the flame that they don't know is of great hotness! He came to a kind of small fame in his click and then one day went down the alley in Brooklyn—a remarkable place, so elegant in its regular whatchamacallit—down the alley with the garbage and threw himself away. When he returned he was—Someone else! Now I understand that he has become a model for characters in vicious, ugly, and slanderous novels that are written by a friend of his—some friend! Once a dedicated fake alcoholic, he now supports the apple-juice factories or orchards or something. Silly me! But then! He was tinder and music! How I baked for him! He became angry when I gave a good friend of his, another poet, a little poon while he was away at work. Odd. Now he walks the lonely streets, an odor of rose hips emanating from his beard. How he would have laughed had he seen me a scant few years later in my Muzzis and Cazzos, my tresses done by Mr. John, the sculptor turned coiffeurer or what do you call it? barber? Whatever, my hair, my clothes, my tattooed garter done by Crazy Clyde in black and crimson. See it? Don't be ashamed, *silly* Martin! How memory recalls life at the oddest times, how it is relentless in its works, so that we all are serfs to its gross custom, like the configurations of its works or not! How long it has taken me to learn this simple rule if

you choose to call it a rule. I do—but then, life is not negotiable
. . . is it, Martin?

My heart seemed to claw at my spleen with fangs of burning fire
and I felt my legs giving way. But Fate was not to be! I steadied and
we walked on and on and on . . .

. . . certainly I was on the brimstone path by now, how do *I* know?
I flung myself on its rocks and other sharp things it has there on it,
thorns and things. All around it—how one can get hurt there! Often
I would cry out in my helplessness these very words. And the answer
would come, always the same: Bajji's dark lines—"The pinching shoe
gives pain until it is removed." But I was not yet ready to believe it.
I found myself, with Tom's blessing, in Taos, where I had gone to find
"place." It is only there and in other spots like it that this phenomenon occurs. Artists know this. Instead I found an ex-war hero whom
I whipped with his belt. He was all heart and a little bit of a disappointment. I told Tom about it and he bought me a pair of boots. To
such passes had our union become! Yes, he paid and paid and paid
again—now, I comprehend, it was to surfeit me with the hot flagons
of freedom . . .

My tears burned my cheeks, if such they were. How, I reasoned,
could the man be such a brute? To buy this slip of a girl, this waif,
a pair of boats! What else was he saying but "Sail away! Leave! Begone!" Who could blame her peccadilloes? My spine cringed and
tongues of flame burned my very throat.

. . . whirled me through and through his meaningless social life,
his sterile and impotent and utterly blague social life as such it
often purports to be . . . purports? Ha! Is the paradigm of such! How
I raced back in my mind through the fields of the past! Yet I often
wonder, was it *I* who raced? I mused on a sweet boy, sweet Ralph,
who, under the stands at the high-school football field, got uckh all
over my skirt. It *was,* after all perhaps, I who raced! These bitter-
sweet memories helped to ease the strains of this abhorring life that
I had coming to me after all was said and done. It was my shoe and
if it didn't fit, then wear it! I knew the Truth but would not face it!
Once I thought of myself, as someone else, in the dim twilight of an
Ohio town, sobbing on an Indian mound, my skirt up to my waist,
lusts exposed to the stars. How do you like that? Sic semper ad
astra. How curious that now rings in my ears—but then it meant
. . . everything! There is a red Chevvy pickup lost somewhere in
the mists of time back then too, but who knows what it means? It
might as well be the park across the bay, the children's carrousel
and the likes. How these soft images would torture me amid the
endless forced gaiety of my life with Tom . . .

She sank slowly behind a broken bench into the sparse grass, and

I followed, sinking too. Chilly, I placed my coat over her legs, her poor legs, and her strange little hands. I mean *she* was chilly, although after removing my coat, I too felt the strange chill across my back. Or was it *only* my back that was chilled? I dared not think of it. In any event, we were close, I could smell the faint odor of some exquisite perfume rising from her warm body and thought how good it was that she was no longer chilly. Your hands are so warm . . . and strong, she murmured from beneath the coat, and then she grasped them tightly, so tight that I thought I would cry out with the pain that coursed through my hands, particularly my fingers, it was but a foretaste of the pain to come but in my madness I ignored it, ignored —*everything*, even the queer twittering of my conscience, that, like some obscene rodent of night, twittered. Suddenly, she placed my hands on a spot I dare not name. Grass stains appeared on my trousers, somewhere a flashbulb popped, I seemed to gaze out a window at waves that broke on an undiscovered shore, a phonograph record scratched over and over, its lonely song ended, we would have let the phone ring had we but a phone. Blind stupid fool! I thought, and just then a Roman candle burst far above the bay. I could only imagine its glorious effulgence plangent on the wintry sky off there to the sleeping suburbs to the north. Hours passed, or perhaps it was only moments—sometimes I think it was an eternity. Would that it were it! She was speaking now, her voice soft and fulfilled, muffled because her mouth was somehow lost, lost in one of the pockets of my coat which latter I now gently lifted off her. Dear, girlish voice! But I found that I was not listening, instead, my ears seemed to hear the erotical rasp of Madame Corriendo, the insouciant creaking of her stays as she rattled the ice in her highball and her voice rose to ever a higher pitch of hysterical fury. Her warning flared in my brain . . . what *was* that warning again? No matter, it was! That was enough for me. And over all, like the guffaw of a demented warlock, howled the bitter wind that chilled me to the very soul, the wind that could only have been coming down from Canada! The very word seemed freight with horror even then. How strange. And now, I glance over, the same wind tip-tapping at the windows, Ned Beaumont's two feet glaring at me like two dead crabs . . .

. . . and in the tiara-like glitter of madcap nights how often I thought of Berkeley and of my *faux pas* there, a stupid act that destroyed what happiness we had wrested from the bowels of the California air. But were we really happy? Such a question often haunts me yet and troubles the night's repast. Who can interrogate the face of happiness, and who can tell when it passes from our clutching hands? What mysteries holds this cruel and mortal coil, is it not? All I did know was that we had reached the nadir of connubial

236

relationship long before. What else but that shabby oven trick—yes, trick! For I did not want to extinguish this little light, and yet . . . I wished that I might be a pair of ragged Moors battling to tear the drawers from nubile knees. It was in a book, I think, that I read of a girl who got her husband back to New York by putting her head in an oven. It was as if the book had been written for me! It had waited for me, its true reader . . . don't you often find that a book will do that? Wait? My emotions swirled and churned, beat and blended, until I was taken in memory to a windy afternoon on some dunes somewhere. I can see him now, a film critic, painter, short-story writer, novelist, and all-around sport, deshabille behind the shifting sands while I attempted to perform an unspeakable and unnatural act upon his supine frame. Yet his manhood was recalcitrant. God! My shame was such that I felt like sinking right through the dune. Think, then, of my position. Of course, the oven beckoned like an old friend. And, in a way, though I lived, I did not live. Can life, true life, be honestly thought of as just a bunch of things put together daily that you do or not? How foolish these quick are . . .

Great storms of conflicting emotions ripped and punched their way through me, my hat, that I had somehow forgotten to remove, flew from my head, my trousers seemed strangely torn, my head pounded and ached. It was true, so! Of course it was true. I knew, with a knowledge surer than death, closer than whatever you might care to espouse, knew that I had betrayed Tom Buchanan, Ned Beaumont, and even the pure and simple love that I had had for Daisy. The cruel lust that oft will prove not to be denied had triumphed and I had sullied something fine and good. In her innocence she had opened like a clam to me and I had witlessly plucked her naive gift with no more care than a beast.

. . . oh, so many things I did to save it. Often I walked around in a fog. I even tried Mrs. Ashby, the famed seeress, but she got sick when she looked at my soul in her ball. "Bring me a hopeless alcoholic!" I remember her keening. And all this time, Tom malingered on the edge of total despair, rich and handsome though he was and, by the by, still is, as a cursory examination will prove. My dream in those days was to work in a garden somewhere, say in New England, Vermont was my dream. I would bend gracefully among the flowers, all in shapely black, plucking or cutting or whatever you do, pruning, I love gardens. And Tom would be sitting nearby, working on a novel about the platinum business—what really goes on behind the scenes —the joy and heartbreak, the greed and jealousy, and the terrible, constant *fear!* But it was not so ordained to be thus, as I came to comprehend acutely and to my great chagrin, annoyance, and black despair. And now, Martin, my poor, dear Martin, although I can't blame you as can no full-souled woman blame any man who loses the fight to the lusts that cascade through his frame—how well I remember my Ned ogling my bras—I feel that it is only right, as we near the end of our really good talk, only right to tell you—although I cannot blame you, dear man, knowing intuitively that you were horribly aroused by those two witches back there—how long ago it all seems!—I feel, anyway, that it is only the right thing to do that I inform you that I have been pregnant for fifteen minutes! Yes, Martin —I carry your unborn child!

It was as like to a thunderclap as one could fair approach. The winds howled. I laughed aloud into the tooth of them. Stupid mankind that shall never be plumbed as to its dumb acts and so forth! So I shouted. I must have seemed the maniac to Daisy, whose hands went to her womb to protect the life that grew there. Leaping up from the grass, I pulled her up and we started off across the deserted park that now seemed like a landscape of the moon. Don't . . . hate me . . . Martin . . . Martin? I laughed at the hidden moon.

Later, leaving the Abortionist's Office, we embraced. There was something real, something lost yet very personal in the way that she kissed me. I felt a kind of liquid sunshine in her mouth, a taste of the purest honey. Had I but known her years ago! I stifled a sob and cleared my throat in which a scream of despair, despair and loss hung there. And now, her voice, somehow happier now—who can plummet a woman's many moods that change like the light on the clouds as they sail, stately galleons, over the face of the unknowable sea?— went on, almost happy now. What is it that women want? I asked the ignorant wind . . .

. . . I led cheers, hung around the pavilion at Lake Hiawatha, hay rides and French fries, trips to the city, fun was all was my gauche motto, my *cri de coeur.* Harvest moons, dirty songs, the Friday night dance. My girlish heart was bursting with witless joy! A foolish girl who wished to marry a mechanic, I can see his black fingernails now. Later he became a gay fairy and did artistic interesting things in New York or something. It is all gone . . . now. But Tom had made my memories cheap and for that I can never forgive him, no, not if he crawled to me on heels and toes, never! And then I met Ned Beaumont and—you know the rest, dear Martin. We'll never tell of this night's warmth, shall we? They'll never understand and it's best we bury it in the midst of time.

In my lover's misery I nodded affirmation to her query. I whistled merrily, or so I made it seem, at the approaching mantle of dawn that chucked itself across the blushing sky. She must not ever know the secrets of my heart! Yet I had known her, known her as man has known woman till the end of time. They can't take *that* away from me, I laughed, and Daisy echoed my laughter, thinking it was because she was tickling me, in girlish frivolity, through my hat. In a sudden doorway we embraced more hotly and I took her again, passionately, roughly, my teeth scarring the mailboxes behind her glossy head. My dear, she crooned, her loins surrendering. I . . . I'm . . . pregnant . . . again . . .

How odd, I thought, as my manhood exploded deliriously for the second and then the third time. My tears mixed with hers as she fell off the milk box on which she had been standing. Did we know each other's hearts? And did it matter? All I knew was that her life was rougher than steel wool, darker than midnight, blacker than blue.

Lamont's Scrapbook

Author Sleeps, Wakes, "Finds" Novel

BELLE AIRE, IND., *Feb. 25* (UPI) George "Bingo" Pompson, a noted novelist and writer on the "ecology of athletics," as he puts it, had a strange story to tell yesterday. Pompson says that he woke Tuesday after his usual mid-afternoon "nap" to find the manuscript of a novel waiting for him on his study desk.

"It's all there," Mr. Pompson marveled, "I mean it's complete in every detail." Mr. Pompson, who won the Clint Hartung Prize in 1961 for *Jock Yocks,* his study of athlete humor, insisted that no one could have got into his study during his nap. "The door is always locked," he grinned, "and there's no window." The celebrated author assured a curious visitor that the novel is a fine job of writing. "It's meticulously plotted, interesting, suspenseful—and even rather poetically written." The slender scribe, who admitted that he has been thinking about a novel along the same lines, cannot explain how the novel came to be written on his own typewriter. "Even the revisions are in my hand," he mused, but insisted that he "did not write a word of it."

What is even more puzzling to the writer is that several of the characters in the "found" novel are characters who appeared in *Cellophane Soldier,* a novel that appeared to mixed reviews six years ago. "I can't explain the darn thing," Pompson chuckled.

The author concluded by saying that he would give the manuscript a title, have it retyped, and mail it off to his agent in New York. "I figure it's mine," he said. "I'm not even going to revise it."

Mr. Pompson declined to reveal what the novel was about except to say that it had to do with "lust and murder."

Halpin's Journal

Our gifted creator must be turning this thing into a comic novel, or else he's losing his mind. This reminiscence of the evening with Daisy is beyond comment. Whatever he has against this girl, it's hard to say. Not that *I* did not act the imbecile. *Where* did he get that language? —but to have her say those things . . . it wasn't even burlesque. And Ned was right—he *hasn't* had me call the police. I begin to feel *sorry* for him. Ned has no mercy, at one point went out of the house when he was supposed to be on the bookcase———

Two things to note: Ned found a door that, for some reason, neither of us had ever noticed before, and it was *not locked*. It opens into another section of this cabin, with a kitchen, a bathroom, and a bedroom. The question is whether Lamont built it or whether he has simply appropriated another man's cabin. It seems in perfect order and Ned urged me to jot down a description of these rooms in order to strengthen our case if we abandon this book, that is, Ned is convinced that Lamont stole this whole cabin from somebody else because of his ineptness and he feels that with evidence of this (a description that would be recognizable to other writers) we might not be blacklisted by them in the future, that is, if we seek work in some reasonable book. Ned says that it's hard to tell if this is Lamont's cabin or not—it seemed vaguely familiar to him but then, he says, all these summer cabins in mystery stories are basically alike. For some reason, Ned insists on calling this book a "mystery," but God only knows why. Perhaps because "I" don't know if I killed "him."

The rooms:

Kitchen: a woodbox piled with split wood; clean sink, no dirty dishes; clean stove, no foul smelling pots; open shelves above and beside the sink thick with cans and household staples; confectioner's sugar in a square brown box with a torn corner; near the sugar there is salt, borax, baking soda, corn starch, brown sugar and so on; inside the box of confectioner's sugar a tiny gold heart no larger than a woman's little fingernail, with an engraving on it just large enough to be read by the naked eye; in script, it says: *Al to Mildred. June 28 1938. With all my love.* Ned was triumphant with this discovery. "The goddam thief!" he shouted. But it's possible that Lamont might use this heart in the book—one never knows. Ned is not convinced.

Bathroom: nothing of note here; the usual plumbing, but it is evident that the bathroom has been built quite recently as shown by the clean celotex lining. Ned couldn't get around *that!*

Bedroom: double bed; pinewood dresser with round mirror on the wall above it; a bureau; two straight chairs; tin waste basket (more about this later); two oval rag rugs on the floor, one on each side of the bed; on the walls a set of war maps (What war? Ned didn't know.) from *National Geographic;* a silly-looking red-and-white flounce on the dressing table; in a bureau drawer an imitation-leather trinket box with an assortment of gaudy costume jewelry (Corrie and Berthe's? Ned scoffed.); the usual stuff that women use on their faces and fingernails and eyebrows—there seemed to be too much of it; in the bureau man's and woman's clothes (!!), not a lot—a noisy check shirt with starched matching collar; under a sheet of blue tissue paper in one corner of a drawer a seemingly brand new peach-colored silk slip trimmed with lace.

That was about it. We left everything as we found it and went back to the living room and argued about the possibility that Lamont appropriated the whole cabin. I confess that I could not explain why we have never seen the upstairs. And I couldn't explain the inscription on the heart. Perhaps, I said, in a chapter that Lamont is now thinking of he will have "Al and Mildred" suddenly enter this cabin. Ned admitted that authors forget the furniture when they don't need it and that they will often make a twenty-five-room house and set their scenes in but one or two rooms of it—the rest vaguely defined, almost nonexistent. But he maintains that Lamont is a cheap and shoddy writer who would steal another writer's props if he could. "Don't forget," he said, "he didn't *mean* for us to find those rooms . . . he doesn't know that *we* are as real as he is! He may have appropriated the whole cabin and forgotten those rooms—if he needs them he'll use them as is, or change them as he goes along."

A *real* mystery, one that I can't explain, nor can Ned, although I admit that it makes it look as if somebody *has* been here in the past: In the waste basket in the bedroom, we found a manuscript, torn once across—it was typed neatly. We put it together easily with some cellophane tape and I include it in the journal.

A Garland of Impresions & Beliefs Culled from a Lifetime by E.B.,
A Disappointed Author

In Jellos we uncover one of the Great Yankee Dishes. Try them with tuna and noodles in casserole. Dalicious!

Chicago is a big city altho it impresses one as being two Newarks ajoined.

If you make a better book the world will build a mousetrap at your door.

Young men named Anthony enjoy moving backwards in their vehickles as proven by observation.

A dream of a mouse means good luck. Upside-down mice means money coming without fail.

Tis best to harken when the fountain plashes for it plashes for thou.

A man's character and a woman's pride are shown in their hat; from this we get the expression "talking through your hat."

Where there is smoke there is always broken eggs.

What do women want? Spinoza queried. A lifetime of observation has shown that the answer is a sailboat in the moonlight.

When an editor says they are not interested in your work at the present time they mean forget about it.

One is enraptured by drops of water that hold the secrets of the universe inside its prosaicness.

242

The best peeza is in Ombrielli's clam house with fresh egg tomatos from the garden.

Losing 79 lbs. may win a maiden the firehouse Casanova.

The man who plays acey-five with his hat on is more often than not a fish.

Show me a homosexual and I'll write you a soap opera.

I believe wholly that on his deathbed Rilke sang "Hello! Ma Baby."

D.H. Lawrence's obsession with sex can be traced to his queer love for marmalade and flowers.

Potemkin is a vulgar movie that exploits violence for cheap laughs.

Alain Robbe-Grillet's novels can be read as reworkings of Charlie Chan plots.

Novelists distort facts to make you believe what they don't say.

They should have casted Bela Lugosi as Captain Ahab.

Philippe Roth's *The Magic Barrel* brings to its highest pitch of refinement the literary movement begun by Gerard de Nerval.

People who like Ring Lardner think they like baseball.

Often boys who hang around on street corners become bus drivers in mature years later.

Had Napoleon known enough to come in out of the rain no one would have been the wiser.

Every little breeze seems to whisper "Louis."

Alice the Goon commended itself by schlepping around.

You can always tell a good poem if your hair stands up while you cut yourself shaving.

Attila the Hun invented the accordion.

What if Proust had remembered the taste of a Yankee Doodle?

Pitchers are bad hitters because they think of the ball as their friend.

Lesbianism can be traced back many centuries as is shown by the hoary saying, "When Adam delved and Eve span, who was then the gentleman?"

One can presume that bubble gum was invented by a dentist.

A lady's love for a gentleman is incontestingly proved if she sends him a kiss by wire.

Hitler could not waltz so he decided he would be a dictator instead.

I arrive conclusively that Anthony Quinn is a symbol of decay in the arts.

"Back home again in Indiana" is a phrase that proclaims feelings of disgust.

If a whale had a thumb I believe he could dial a telephone.

Jerry Lewis is the Jules Olitski of films.

If you dream of finding a major quantity of money it means that you shall soon see an upside-down mouse. Be carefull!

Those who clang the brass bell at the Carnival of Life do not always live in the penthouse of same.

The hot barbecue sandwich for 10¢ in the Surprise Café was a revelation for many a beardless strippling.

W.B. Yeats's favorite song was "McNamara's Band."

The lowly cockaroach has survived lo! these millions of years because they do not smoke.

The lindy hop was named after "the Swedish nightingale," Jenny Lind, who invented it one gay night in a Paris boîte.

In the famous photograph of Adolph Hitler accepting a bouquet from a little girl it is clear that the Chancellor is singing "Rosy, You Are My Posy."

Bellow's *An American Planet* may well have placed his fiction in the rarified air along with those of Frank Kafka.

Often when reading the novels of Robert Frost we seem to hear the crashing of trees through our windows such is his power of making New England walk off the pages.

The Assyrians say: "Why talk of weddings with a dying man?"—a wise proverb that seems to fit the majority of cases.

In the novels of Anthony Trollope we learn that good drivers make poor poets—a just observation.

Often we are embarrassed by the words of little children who speak so innocently that we don't know what they are talking about.

If you come across a person singing "Yes, We Have No Bananas" it is meet to introduce yourself for here is a human being with a heart as big as all outdoors.

Canned soup played a major but ignored role in the opening of the West.

Lydia E. Pinkham's remedys were the books and paintings and symphonys Society forbad her to create.

The course of Western history would have been changed if Paris had Mr. Softee trucks in 1789.

It has often been said that a wise man is a fool whose lightest word is considered by some.

A historian of Old Dixie has it that Nat Turner went mad with ultimate hatred and revenge when a passing aristocratic planter told him to "rattle that tambourine, Sambo!" "Sambo" Dupree had taken the credit and become famous for a song—"Hello! Ma Baby"—stolen from Turner. The mention of the hated name apparently drove the brooding darky round the bend. Thus do trivias make History.

If Lester Lanin is Destiny's Tot, what thus was Blue Barron?

People who care about what visitors think of their City are not New Yorkers.

It is probable that Carl Jung came to his theory of the Collective Unconscious while observing people dance to the "Clarinet Polka."

Mayonnaise and mustard added are not too bad in a pinch.

Norman Mailer's story, "Naked Fires on the Moon" is not about the United States Army as *I* knew it.

Experience shows that the overwhelming sandwich favorite among shanty Irish is ham and potato salad on a seeded roll with mayo.

You got the best Mexican Hat in Arnold's Ice Cream Parlor.

Better for Mankind had there *been* "singing in the air" rather than skyrockets and Roman Candles the night the great French balloon, "La Chose," was sent aloft.

Abisante will do nicely in a Sazzerac Collins.

From the internal evidence in his letters to his wife, it may be inferred that D.A.F. deSade had a weakness for marshmellow sundaes, which he called, with his usual wit, frappés blancs. To the end, the Marquis was a boy at heart.

There is great speculation as to what Lenin was thinking about as he approached the Finland Station since persistent reports have it that he was singing "Hello, Hawaii, How Are You?"

On cloudy, hot, humid days all the crazy people come out on the street.

It may well be true that Sigmund Freud had a torrid love affair with Susan B. Anthony on one of his many secret trips to Indianapolis.

One of the highwater marks of the American Cinema is Victor Mature's sensitive portrait of Doc Holliday.

The lightest "mot" will often throw some people into a limpid rage.

Various items of decay are found in rooms in seedy hotels.

Sex fantasies mean that a person has lots of sex or not enough or none at all.

It is incontestable that sophisticated ladies smoke, drink, and never think about tomorrow.

The wafer cone expressively made to hold a Mell-O-Roll was a symbol of the Depression's frivolous inventiveness.

A hotel bartender is so kind as to inform me that W.C. Fields invented the Gin Thrill, the recipe for which is lost in misty Time.

Keats and Shelley never had any of the conversations that the slanderous Miles O'Nolan attributes to them.

In the haze of Autumn one finds many a tear-wracked visage wreathed in smiles; however, in weak attempts.

Pluck not the Rose of Desire that nods next to the gazebo; for the sun will shine hotly though dark clouds menacingly gather.

Anne Boleyn's last meal was probably Yankee pot roast with gravy, string beans and mash.

Surely Society must bear the blame for Reinhard Heydrich.

There is a certain bird in the Rockies that in the first clear light of dawn seems to twitter "Louis."

Little Orphan Annie was the spiritual daughter of Herbert Hoover out of Tillie the Toiler.

In the valleys wild of Northern Jersey the loon speaks more wisdom than man can rightly understand.

What to think of the man who buttons his coat the wrong way like a woman to hide the fraying?

The moral fiber of America began coming apart when they ceased to cook Washington pie.

You can't make soft-boiled eggs if you break them first.

You can wager that poems that are described as witty, wise and warm are not worth their salt to blow them to hell.

Melted cheese sandwiches and vanella milk shakes combined is a taste sensation for many.

When faced with grave decisions one thinks of Corporal Trim's words.

On the sheer and trembling edge of meaningless phenomenons you find Art.

With tenachious watchdogs like John Simon about it is a surety that Serbo-Croat letters will not fall into decay.

No one has ever satisfactorily proven that Guernsey cows do not give chocolate milk, no matter what is believed.

The difference between an extra-dry Martini and a Gibson is Olives and Onions that don't add up.

Poems where the poet addresses things like potatoes and snails and things tend to make the reader get nauseated.

The best white clam sauce was at Mama Gatto's on Surf Avenue, now gone under the wrecker's cruel balls.

Break in a pipe bowl carefully and get years of fun out of doing it.

The generous heart is often full to bursting with rare effulgence.

When Irish eyes are smiling the whole world laughs at them.

Lamont's Notebook

She is the queenly pearl. ??? I don't even know where the *title* came from. Let alone anything else! There is no way for me to judge this. Purple "elegant" language, although silly, ludicrous. NOT Halpin! (Then who?) How is that "speech" to be reconciled with the Halpin

I've *presented* so far? (But who is Halpin in "The Woods So Wild"? How does *that* speech come about?)

I don't think I am in *control* here. I didn't want *this* to be Daisy. Is this the Daisy of the letters? No. *She* is silly, but "refined." What is this past of Daisy's? All right, the story must take a turn on its own, live its own life. But THIS????

Halpin should here have simply had a reverie of Daisy. Unrequited love, etc. Praise, longing, discreet desire, reined-in confession of temptation. But from Club Zap to this? It doesn't work. Does it?

Is this what comes when the prose has its head? Is it from that sordid and lecherous dream of a few nights ago, Lorna Flambeaux in the park? But the book is moving in a new way, a new direction. Stick *this* in Roche's ear!

I'll let it stand for now. But try an "alternative" chapter, a reverie, soft and romantic?

"How does it come to pass—such absolute perfection? Gardenia Daisy . . ."

Shut Sheila up and *The Red Swan* chatter with it—with "Quoonly" too, if truth be told—she'd never admit it.

O.K. Two hours later. Three Scotches later. The T R U T H. If I leave "Pearl" in book as it now stands *I must revise all my earlier chapters* (or great chunks of them).

Must I?

Has Halpin *really* changed? A new aspect to his character. Why not? Revelation. After all, *he* is telling the story. He has lied before? The hell with it? What if I just let it go and see what happens, let the book become a splintered poem, clashing chunks of "metaphor." No connections, but reverberations, correspondences, is it?

In a sense, Daisy *is* the Daisy of the letters, the same one who has trouble with the language. This much trouble? But I'm not writing a goddam realistic novel.

What a fucking bore this notebook is.

I am simply trying to talk myself out of the labor of beginning the book again, right? I wish I were that guy in the marvelous news story who woke up to find his book completed. "Just send it off to my agent."

The vapid and pompous sophomoric chestnut seizes me; that as *I* have created Halpin—such as he, my God, is—*somebody* has created me. I don't *feel* like a writer at all. A fake. Whatever Trellis is he *is* a writer, rotten and ambitious, but you know he *feels* like a writer when he sits down. Nothing makes me feel that way, not even this stupid "notebook" I keep—like a schoolgirl's diary. "Yesterday

247

we went to the ice-cream parlor after school and I had a lemon coke and Martha had a vanilla coke and she told me about the movie she saw with Harold Friday night."

Write.

Maybe Beaumont will come alive.

Maybe that *cabin* they're in is the mistake. So many lonely cabins. All a result of reading *Buddy and His Boys on Mystery Mountain*.

I like the "Pearl." And I confide to you, O notebook, that I'm even a little *proud* of it!

The inevitable bad news from Roche. Expected. Gutless, pompous bastard! My shabby dream of shabby "fame" dies. Ashamed that I even had this dream, that's the terrible part. I read the new chapter again and I even laughed. I see a comic aspect to the novel now that I had no idea was there. Even "The Woods So Wild" appears to have "humor."

Send it to Roche, "Pearl," and open his eyes! But I doubt the use of it. Dermot has him convinced of *his* genius. The rumbling of drums, ever louder, in celebration of *The Red Swan*. That Roche should tell me that he has "rediscovered" it! I will lay the odds that he never even read it or heard of it before!

Who is *behind* the "rediscovery" of this piece of trash? What Midwestern Associate Professor? "A remarkable novel, sadly neglected at the time of its first publication, and blah blah." Them fryin' fishies, crackle-crackle.

I must reply.

Dignified. Take it easy. Aloof. No anger. Don't vent the rage I feel, particularly about Swan and Dermot. Nothing so sour as sour grapes.

Obscurity. Not to be even a "coterie" writer.

Write Roche!

New title. *Crocodile Tears*.

My dear Roche:

Thank you for your pithy and brief (brevity is the soul, or is it the sole, of wit) letter in reply to my letter. I must confess to you that your message confirms my worst suspicions, suspicions that I conveyed quite specifically to you in the letter noted above. I confess that I am deeply disappointed by your decision; as much by your present coolness toward *Three Deuces* (which a few short months ago you praised *very highly*), as by your remark that you don't think that anything else of mine would be "suitable" for your course, that is, in terms of a complete novel. I am puzzled also by the lack of any substantial reason for your change of heart concerning my work.

I am curious, more than curious really, to know just what book or books you are substituting for *Deuces*. Surely, I am not so naive as to think that *Deuces* has been "flunked out" without being replaced. My problem is that I cannot think of an experimental novel published in the last fifteen years that would fill the role that I flattered myself my poor opus would play in your course. Again, let me make it clear that I at no time expected my work to occupy center stage in your course. But there is a certain *élan* that my book has—if I may speak candidly—that the novels of my peers lack. A certain roughness, an adventurousness that they do not possess, despite their qualities of excellence and daring—and "good writing"; ah, let us never forget that wondrous "good writing." Would it be too much (as an "almost ran") to ask you to give me a list, however tentative, of the books you *do* plan to use? Perhaps I might make a comment or two on them that would be of some assistance to your understanding of them—not in terms of their "meaning" but insofar as they are *historical* products, etc. You are of course aware that I am not *wholly* unfamiliar with the avant-garde and its standard-bearers. Perhaps even an anecdote or two about each author would serve to illuminate the texts for you?

But enough of this. Let me go on to confess my bewilderment anent some of your remarks. You say that you have definitely decided against *Deuces* on the grounds that it is "a bit too obscure, a bit too difficult, too *special* for an introductory course." I grant you that in a way you tender me and my creation heady praise, but I think that you will find, upon reflection, that my novel works in the clearest way in terms of its internal manipulation of language, symbol, and overall architecture. It is really only the "shell" of the novel that seems difficult, and I think that the novel can be taught so that this "shell" is downplayed or even ignored. *Deuces* is in the tradition of the avant-garde novel, so much so, in fact, that it would seem a natural point from which a student might move either forward or backward in time, i.e., the "time" during which this tradition has been extant. In other words, I am saying that *Deuces* might easily serve as a key for a student's understanding of the entire corpus of the "new novel." There are two or three other novels that might serve the same function, of course. But to say this, leads me to my refrain: Why select one of them to the exclusion of *Deuces*? I don't want to nag you, but your reasoning is not clear to me.

Now, a rather delicate point: you say that my brother-in-law has suggested to you that even though *Deuces* is to be dropped from consideration, he feels that there are many passages—from *Deuces* as well as from other novels, and early stories—that might serve as "important minor considerations" in a course such as yours; and that he would be "happy to select what he feels to be appropriate sections" to act as glosses and "footnotes" to "more ambitious and profound works" of the past twenty years. How thoughtful of him! How wonderfully generous! At the risk of seeming churlish, my dear Roche, let me here say that I *forbid* you to use any selections from my works that may be proposed to you by Mr. Trellis. It seems to me that the person most suitable for selecting passages from a body of work is the *author* of that work. In addition, and confidentially, Mr. Trellis has never had the slightest idea of what my work has been about.

I don't *like* the idea of chopping sections out of my books—they are, for better or worse, conceived as wholes, with internal reverberations and connections that excerpting destroys. On the other hand, because of your initial interest in my work, and the fairly perceptive comments you made on it, I am willing to forgo this objection of mine and allow you to use as many excerpts as you would like. I would be very interested in helping to give your course the fullness and shape that you surely desire, knowing how important it is to you that you make a success of it. However, I must insist that *I* do the selecting —with the proviso, of course, that if there is a particular section that *you personally* favor you may use it. But I must remain adamant in refusing Mr. Trellis's "assistance."

I am also chagrined, I admit, by Mr. Trellis's glib references to those fabled "more ambitious works" of the recent past. What works could he possibly have in mind? A "little bird" tells me that one of them is a book by one Dermot Trellis, called *The Red Swan* (or *Peculiar Person,* as it was known in its grimy days). I may be (unfairly) reading between the lines of your letter, but you seem to be implying that your interest in this shabby tome will lead to its inclusion in your course as a kind of keystone. God forbid!

My dear fellow, I must say to you—though it start a critical debate between us—that *The Red Swan* is, in the parlance of the vulgar streets, a piece of pure *shit.* It has nothing to recommend it except its shameful reputation as a kind of "cult" book of the perverse. Surely you know that it sold in every seamy pornography store for years as a shabby paperback, published by a fly-by-night L.A. press as the aforementioned *Peculiar Person.* Or perhaps Mr. Trellis didn't bother to remember that (not that one would blame him). I don't like to gossip, but he told me, years ago, when he was writing this egregious rubbish, that he thought of it as a piece of pure hackwork that he was penning in order to make enough money to write a "serious" book. (That "serious" book has never seen the light of day—as you of course know.)

I don't doubt for a moment that your enthusiasm for this stinking garbage can of a book is genuine. To this I must say: more's the pity! To *use* such a book in your course is bad enough, but to employ it as the *pièce de résistance* is a grievous error in judgment. You will not find, I assure you, a single reputable critic or reviewer who had a good word to say about *Swan.* It plunged into a merciful limbo almost as soon as it was published and surfaced again as the putrid and infamous *Peculiar Person*—a *deviate's handbook* as far removed from literature as I am from the nearest star. I cannot, simply *cannot* understand your curious comment as to the "misfortune" of *Swan's* initial reception. It seems to me that the reviewers and critics (who have treated *me* harshly enough) did themselves proud on that one! Its subsequent shady "success" as pornography certainly does not redound to its credit. As I recall, it was running neck and neck in the porno market with a little item called *Sweating Thighs.* Even Mr. Trellis himself, a man who is not what one would call "thin-skinned," will tell you that the shuffling zombie that was *Peculiar Person* so embarrassed him that he—unsuccessfully—tried to get the "publisher" to put the book out under a pseudonym. That does not bespeak authorial pride.

But I fear that I am taxing your patience. If you will tell me what selections you require, I mean, what general trends you would be interested in, I will get to work and see if I can come up with a cogent "package."

Perhaps, after all, you are right in deciding against *Deuces:* it is strong stuff for the classroom. But I urge you, my dear fellow, to heap praise upon *The Red Swan—in private.* Do not inflict this sleazy potboiler on impressionable undergraduates.

As ever,
Lamont

P.S. I take the liberty of enclosing a chapter from my novel in progress, the title of which, by the way, I have changed to *Crocodile Tears.* You will see, I'm sure, that the handling of the space-time factor and the elliptical narrative have their roots in *Three Deuces,* that poor old tired horse. It might be a little more difficult to see that *The Red Swan* tries to use these devices but succeeds only in unintentionally parodying them. IDEA: Why not use sections of *Deuces* and *Swan* in tandem in order to demonstrate the dilution and pollution of one author's work by another? You surely know that *Deuces* was published two years *before Swan* was even conceived. But of course you would know this. It is your business to be aware of such things. Isn't it?

If you will be writing to Mr. Trellis in the near future, please convey to him my congratulations on the absolute miracle that has occurred apropos the astonishing apparent resurrection of his foul bird.

Lamont's Notebook

That one's own sister should become so unconscionably gross—so vindictive. Sheila, crowing! Worse, trying to disguise it behind a front of "reasoned critical response." (Good evening friends!) To send me galleys of this pig, Vance Whitestone's, Introduction to the NEW EDITION (!!) of this trash.

When Roche as much as told me he was going to use that trash in his course—I should have known! I was a fool not to realize that he would have been aware of a new edition ready for the fall, in time for his course.

Vance Whitestone! The editor turned "critic." Turned down *Three Deuces* so many years ago. I have the letter here.

I can see the cynical machinery at work in this "rediscovery." Whitestone's first move toward establishing himself as a "critic of importance." Picks up this obscure crap and works to make it the center of a small storm of elite adulation; he is the guru, the explorer.

The embarrassing fulsomeness and tortured comment on the skinny wretched thing that *Swan* is must put even Trellis off. I cannot imagine what book this Whitestone bastard read. It cannot be that instant coffee, that Reddi-Wip that I remember, can it?

Following hard after, the yokel Roche, who will become King of the Yokels among the Yokel Professors in the Yokel Colleges. Up-To-The-Minute Charlie! "A man who sees the wisdom of the distinguished critic, Vance Whitestone's, rediscovery of the unjustly neglected work." Maybe he'll get to review first novels for *The Times* on page 52. He will say bush-league things like "as Gertrude Stein said, 'remarks are not literature,'" and knock their hats off in Indianapolis.

I will not even acknowledge *receipt* of the galleys. To say that I might consider reviewing the book! Knowing that a good review would be impossible for me and that a bad one would be construed as sour grapes. Besides, would a bad one even be printed *anywhere* that it would matter to the book's fortunes? When the publisher-retailer-critical-academic machinery gets started . . . a steamroller!

Acknowledge receipt and say I haven't got around to reading?

Too transparent. Sheila would see my anger and misery right to its core. I can hear her and Dermot laughing themselves sick.

Doesn't she remember Whitestone and his letter? She *cried.* Such was her faith in the book.

Now: "As you must know, Tony, Whitestone is fast developing into one of the more astute and exciting critics of contemporary fiction. . . ." Webs. Mazes.

Being dreamed.

Finish my book—the only hold on reality. *Their* reality, at any rate.

Dear Mr. Lamont:

I'm sorry—and I mean *really* sorry—to have the unpleasant task of telling you that your novel, *Three Deuces*, is a project that we can't see our way clear to publishing—at least at the present time.

The second reader, another editor, and I were deeply impressed by the way you handle shifting locales and your characters came achingly alive in many scenes. Unfortunately, we could not communicate our enthusiasm for *Three Deuces* to the other editors—all of whom liked the book in varying degrees, but could not seem to get behind it one hundred per cent.

In the really tough fiction market of today (and I'm sure that you've been reading about the depressed state of publishing) it would be unfair to you as well as to us to do a book about which there was not a unanimously affirmative view. I know you'll agree.

Although it is surely small comfort to you, I'd like to tell you that you certainly can write! We'd consider it a great pleasure to consider anything you might be willing to show us in the future.

Thanks so much for allowing us the privilege of considering *Three Deuces*. I suspect that you'll have little trouble in placing it with another house.

My best wishes,
Vance Whitestone
Editor

Solid, man! Ugh, White Stone speak with Forked Tongue. And now an example of that same tongue caressing an ass! Remember—you saw it here first!

INTRODUCTION

Some dozen or so years ago I remember coming across a volume of prose fiction by Dermot Trellis, a writer whose name at that time was totally unfamiliar to me. The book, or "novel," for want of a better word, was described on the jacket by a singularly uninspired copy writer as "an excursion into the realms of the mind's dark fastnesses" —surely one of the great understatements of recent vintage. *The Red*

Swan has haunted me ever since. Although I attempted to resist the author's rather curiously machined syntax—a syntax that was at once both invention and butchery—I was soon caught up, enthralled by the novel's compelling oblivion of cacophony and relentlessly empty gesture: Mr. Trellis had flung down his literary gauntlet, as it were, and, as I discovered later, as was his wont, and was daring the reader to pick it up. I recall as clearly as if it were just yesterday the book's Chaplinesque insight and powerfully robotlike movement as it attempted to infuse the mind with its own eerie puissance. No thin gruel here. Rather, a savory, not to say gamy goulash.

It was, however, published at a most dangerous juncture in the meandering trek of the contemporary novel and so fell, like so much corn on alien ground, to its demise. Small was its notoriety and fame among the so-called *literati,* all of whom were busily discovering what they (and *Newsweek*) were pleased to call, in those amusingly naive days, "new masters of tone." I wrote Mr. Trellis soon after publication of *Swan,* but got no reply. I can't say that I much blamed him, for the book had been taken to the rather suspect bosom of that reader obsessed with the sexually exotic and was on its way to becoming a kind of handbook of the perverse, a fate that I suspect considerably depressed its author. It was not long after, that critical silence and the volume's reputation for *bizarrerie* combined, and *The Red Swan* appeared in a cheap paper edition as *Peculiar Person.* As such, it "enjoyed" a brisk sale as pornography for a time; unfortunately, and predictably, this occurrence precluded any chance that the book may have had for serious critical appraisal, and it is only in the last year or so that discerning readers have come to realize *Swan's* excellences. This new edition, in sober cloth and under its original title, should help to correct the eclipse into which both Trellis and his astounding first novel were ironically pushed.

I cheerfully admit that I am a devotee of *The Red Swan,* and have found in its mere hundred or so pages the same richness and inexhaustible delights that others find in *All Being the Being of Being* or even in *Heinz's Times.* The small tome includes the curiously gentle claustrophobic fascination of Sade, the tearful hilarity of Kafka, the dark optimism of Milne, and the jocular fidget of Proust—all in a prose so far removed from that of the *soi-disant* "tone masters" as to seem almost barbaric. In this "barbarity" lies all its strength and artistry.

Just what is *The Red Swan?*—primer of intangible loss, encyclopedia of regrets, dictionary of stupidities, blazon of decay—surely these. But it is also a depthless thesaurus of pleasures, a shopping list for the seeker of subtle and exquisite jests, an imaginative quantity of things actual yet forever unknown, a roster of oneiric possibilities. The style ranges from the frenzied and manic crackling of an unearthly static to the halting and imbecile stutter of a prophet of some barely glimpsed yet certain and jocose doom. The characters (or their varied *personae*) shift faces, costumes, and personalities as do clouds change their shapes. Yet withal, the root sadness that the narrative conveys is rescued everywhere by what can only be termed a "whim of grit," as our most *raffiné* critic of poetry has pronounced to be the tempering factor in what would otherwise be the unrelieved gloom and sleet of contemporary "crushed-simile" verse.

I see that I have used the word "narrative," yet the idolizers of *Swan* have long known and delighted in the fact that the narrative is nonexistent except in so far as it details the route of sexual catabasis —if it can be so called—which shimmers, only partially revealed, in the fiction's superstructure, as a vague moonlit path shows itself in the heart of a bog. It is a kind of narrative in reverse, i.e., it does not so much unfold *specifics* as suggest alternatives to *nonspecifics*. I think I can safely say that *Swan* would have delighted both Marx *and* Wittgenstein. There is in it that "play of the essential indigenous," that "broken-backed metaphorical emblem" that betokens the flashing mind of a master at work—or, perhaps, at play. It does not matter.

The grossly crass sexual acrobatics sketched out as meticulous chiaroscuro in the alternating cannily doddering and wildly glinting language of its pages are negated at every turn—either in the "story's" past or future—by the evanescence (at once real and manufactured) of the divers protagonists' "mind games," which are, as close textual study will reveal, breathtakingly myriad. Such a jigsaw-puzzle-like technique conjures up visions of a book that *might have been* written, another *Swan* actually, as a kind of gloss on the one we are delighting in. This unwritten *Swan* is, by some strange and wondrous legerdemain, always in the reader's mind as he reads the *Swan* that we are lucky enough to have.

T.R. McCoy, in his justly celebrated essay, "Transparency in Fictional Time," holds that ". . . it is not the book we are engaged with that holds our attention so much as that book our sensibilities suspect lies beyond the page that seems (but of course does not) to hold all the answers sought. This unwritten book is the one we truly admire: this is the *book of questions.*" (Italics mine.) Remarkably enough, *The Red Swan* both subscribes to and gleefully destroys McCoy's concept, for *Swan* is, itself, the "book of questions": it is the *book of answers* that does not exist in our grapple with Trellis's creation, and that phantasmally floats just above the pages he has wrought. Our fascination grows as we realize that the varied arcana of *The Red Swan* are all interlocked with that book the words, the shape, the

255

very form of which the novel before us *continually fails to create!* The persistent and dedicated explorer of *Swan* finds these ambiguities deepening and mellowing as his knowledge of the book grows with each rereading. Surely, Kafka's whimsical Gregor Samsa would feel at home in the adamant yet rollicking sentences of this work.

It was the poet, Elbert Harrigan, in his ur-epic, *No Body Gains Time,* who wrote: "In a pizza we find/the goddess of the world disguised/as sausage: sweet/or hot no/matter." So are things mundanely disguised in the "pizza" that is *Swan.* The green-eyed blonde of Part 1 who throws the mysterious sheet music from the sculptor's window is, perhaps, the genius-homosexual clarinetist's wife of Part 3—or is she his sister? The oddly erudite newsdealer who appears in the opening scene appears to be a dull and unimaginative sadist—but there is internal evidence, insubstantial and shifting, to be sure—that suggests that he may be the clarinetist himself, or even his wife or sister. Is the fabulously dilapidated Red Swan Hotel really isolated in its otherwise vacant lot of rubble and broken glass—or is it one of the many flophouses of a proto-Skid Row teasingly hinted at but never revealed? Is its name, for that matter, The Red Swan? Why does the murderous Zügge, in the phantasmagoric and climactic subway scene, take such pains to conceal the title of the book he is reading, so that Menafroyd can make out only the word "Birds"? In Zügge's words, it is a book about "a strange inn for perverts and misfits," but we find it hard to trust Zügge, who has earlier told his dumb and humpbacked mistress that he is going to Battery Park to visit the Aquarium—which latter has not been located there since 1941! And in the *Walpurgisnacht* section, the participants change identities literally from moment to moment, until all is chaos, babble, and darkness.

In a monograph that I have recently published on this unique work, "Corporal Trim's Flourish: Narrative as Ruy Lopez in *The Red Swan,*" I note that "what seems, on cursory reading, to be uncontrolled chaos atop chaos in this brilliant sur-fiction is revealed upon closer examination to be the continual stitching and unstitching of almost instantaneous metamorphoses. Things are not only not what they seem to be, *they never were.*" This seems to me to be the key to this remarkable creation: what seems roughness is really fluid and quicksilver movement; language once characterized as "vulgar and sick" is the vector of magical incantation and all its grunts, shouts, and whispers; what was once termed this "ill-formed and plotless monster" makes for itself, we now recognize, both "plot" and "story" out of those very elements that defeat most novels—the differing kinds of insubstantialities in the Void. In short, *The Red Swan* is a work of enormous seminal power, one that now seems not only necessary but inevitable.

In conclusion, let me assure the reader—the new one who will encounter a world hardly dreamed of, and the old one who will find again a frenetic, stubborn, somewhat crazed, but always fascinating old friend—that this new edition of *The Red Swan* is the same, in all particulars, as the original, copies of which now fetch alarmingly high prices in the collectors' market. Nothing has been changed or "refined"; nothing has been "polished"; nothing has been omitted. Although Mr. Trellis has told me that he was sorely tempted to excise some of the more obscure episodes, he felt it wrong to do so.

A final word: Those readers who know Trellis only as the author of the crabbedly difficult yet brilliant short stories, "Moonface the Murderer" and "I Divorce Thee Husband," which first brought his name to the attention of serious readers, will be delighted to know that *The Red Swan* exploits the experimental techniques first attempted in those two stories. For those of you who enter Trellis's world for the first time, it is this writer's fondest hope that *Swan* will send you in search of its dark (yet contradictorily blazing) matrix.

> —*Vance Whitestone*
> *Wellfleet*

My dear Joanne,

Once again I send you a letter through the kind (and *discreet*) offices of our mutual friend of bygone days, Ellen, hoping and praying against hope and prayer that you will reply to me in kind or even not. The shortest sentence in your fragile and wavering hand would give me the strength to face the terrible misery that seems to be engulfing me, swallowing me as Job was swallowed by Leviathan.

It is improper if not self-pitying of me to tell you of the misfortune that seems to be dogging me since I last wrote you at Christmastime (ah, what dim and wretched holidays they were for me!). It is as if the engines of malediction have been harnessed to direct their powerful bolts of ill fortune at me—and my career, such as it is, *suffers, suffers, suffers.*

Withal, my new book becomes harder to write. A word from you might send me forging ahead on it. As it is now it takes days to write a page or two and my characters are becoming intangible and without motivation. It is, you will agree, difficult to handle a novel whose characters shift and blur. Oddly enough, I have begun to feel like a character myself.

I know that you are deliriously happy with your husband. How I wish I were he or he I! Hate me if you must but I should have proposed to you! Now I see it clearly. I was stupid and naive to think . . . well, you know what I thought.

Dearest! A discreet word, perhaps a snapshot for me to place on my desk from which to draw strength in the dark days of the soul approaching . . . is that too much to ask? "Yes!" I hear you shout. "Leave me alone!" But I love you!

I love you!

I am stupid!

Do not, I implore you, hold this love cheap. I do not wish to relive the *past*. But take pity on your Tony of the *present*. You were always kind.

Yes, you were always kind.

I remember . . .

Ellen will deliver anything to me you might wish to send. It doesn't have to be a letter or photo . . . an article of apparel . . . ?

To have the illusion of touching you. I know this is madness.

Don't reject me, my life is splintering, falling apart. I have but the memory of you to sustain me, even Sheila—but I will not burden you.

Endless betrayals from those I thought were closest. Do not join those Judas ranks!

A sentence. A snapshot. An old shoe.

Break your silence and take pity on me. I shed on this paper a purest crystal tear, wrenched from my heart.

Tell me I am a writer, after all.

> Your sad and (you will never know how) loving,
> Tony

Lamont's Notebook

Knowing my state, that Trellis should be so needlessly cruel. My star wanes and his waxes. I hear the vicious laughter of him and my sister as they read over my letters together and then fall to *it*, like dogs in heat. My misery is their aphrodisiac.

"An old mutual friend sends this portrait of 'a writer.' I wonder who he can be? Anyway, I thought it would amuse you—it's *quite* well done."

Without even the courage to admit the authorship of this sneaking and tittering trash! As if anybody but Sheila could know all these things about me!

I cannot understand this violence against me. My work *cannot* be such a threat to him, it cannot!

The very fact of my being? Are they trying to drive me to alcohol or suicide? Sheila, Trellis, Roche—all their malice directed against me.

Yet even in the face of this I am strangely elated. The alternative to "Queenly Pearl" is odd, exotic, rich, rhetorical—and a mystery! I have never never never written like this—*pouring* from my pen.

No "mutual friend's" petty mockery can change this curious delight I feel in the tropes and graces of this piece of writing. Stunning!

Roche will be sorry he insulted me.

Of course it was Dermot himself—only Sheila could know about fires and trains and dark fudge; only she know about that tyro piece with Ella Cinders as a *demi-mondaine.* This is true betrayal.

I set myself now square against them.

The vitriol that would make him quote fragments of bad reviews!

An Anonymous Sketch

A maker of maddening lists, a lister of maddening names, a namer of glistering fakes, an acre of pains, a wicker of aches, a flatulent bore, a sucker for whores, an arthritic lout; a doubter of mythical lore, a chap who once knew semaphore; gastritis is his sorry lot, it's hairy and furry and hot in the belly; devourer of jelly and jam; the fingers oft crippled with pain of the pen; a yen for good legs in black hose, a shaker of fists; a lover of barter, art is his god, a garter adorer, a clod.

As a child he feared Hurley Lees, he bruised bashed and scraped up his knees; a fool for the prop aeroplane yet reasonably sane. What popular songs did he like? Peace. He liked many.

Each of his novels stood out a sore thumb (a bad penny). He ravaged the psyches of friends, rended and plundered their means and their ends as he bound them in fetters in frostbitten letters. What did they do to be fixed on the wall with the tinny nail of his prose? That was their wail. He knew their travail yet he froze them in language for good and for all. He was humorless, bitter and sour, they claimed. Yet in his island retreat he laughed to himself at the pictures his pen so carefully built up and framed. Some were mere anecdotes, lacking a head or a tale; others morose. Some murderous, flip, or crudely obscene. Most were tritely routine, yet many were clever. "He certainly knows how to write!" Why then did he never indite a reader's delight? A tome that would strike the public as funny (and make him some money)?

He looked out the window and counted his change, dreamed of a peach of a mouth that would kiss him, conjured a tongue sweet as honey. He groaned alone and saw the ladies he had known stroll in his imagination through his rooms in thyn arraye, after a pleasaunt gyse. When their loose gowns from their shoulders fell he'd cast his spell and they'd enact some shameless tricks. In such wise did the oaf amuse his days.

If he did not daily write his trash, or read, or weep his dwindling cash, or create his girls in undies heels and hose to adorn his gloomy room, he'd loaf. Where like a pillow on the bed, his eyes would dreamy close; into his stinking sewer (his dour sink) of a mind would intrude a zany name. Soon it would find its place in a line of the newest bore of a book that his busted brain spun out each day in the stupid delusion that it was fine. He can write all right, reviewers would say. Yet nor gleam nor ray of Yankee success lanced the dreary mess this writer made of his life.

Still, he lived, liked bugs, and (one himself) talked to boobs; wrote reviews for various journals (just once) till they got wise to his sordid views. He knew some Jews, drank booze when he could and loved wood; lay and squatted, sat and stood. In his books a chef, a baker of saddening mists, yet each foggy page had a turning of laughter, a churning of laughter, hilarious rages of bittersweet fun.

He put in his belly (his tummy!) along with his jam and his (yum yummy!) jelly, bourbon and beer, strong coffee, beans and bacon and eggs, some meat, an occasional candy or cookie or bun. In solitude, single, we know he lacked—pardon my crudity—nookie, and so took himself firmly in hand. (The feeling was lonely but grand.)

He rambled the past so surely ensconced in his brain, loved fires and trains. When asked by reporters the reasons arcane for his singular lack of financial success, he gently complained. The "time" was out "of" joint if not moreover, sprained, "if" not completely broken. So he subtly whined. A stitch in the middle saves nine for the fiddle, he sang as he wept 'neath the moon. Fooled himself into a stupor of bliss as his unfinished "masterpiece" hovered in front of his kisser, this lazy baboon, this drudge of an ape. Did I say that he loved seedless grapes and dark fudge without nuts?

He ogled both ladies and sluts as he gathered his rawest of sludge; which he dabbled in, babbled of, shaped into sculptures arsenically gay in the image of them those and they whom protested they done he no harm. He was firm in his crazy vocation, i.e., insulting the family of woman and man. So the rumors and gossip they rumbled and steamed, they spilled, they oozed, and they ran. (He gave not a shet nor a fack nor a domn.) Hoot! What a mon! His ex-wife (ha!ha!) had driven him mad and (haw!haw!) he her. She later appeared in his books in the flimsiest masques, a basely depraved stupid whore. 'Twas another disgustingly unfair assault by this scribbling hack of a word-grubbing scribe, this disgrace to the tribe.

What did he, this faker of gladdening twists, collecter of grist and of swill, do, that he set himself up as a god in the sky, belaboring man with endless jokes, burleycue japes, mirthless pokes, and chauvinist rapes? Did misogyny reign in his head?

Rumor whispered that an old friend had found it grossly unfunny that this pal of the pen had sketched his golden blossom frau as a jar of natural honey. Who did he fock think he wuz? Again, what did he do to turn noble thought 'gainst him black, tint great souls bluer than blue?

A lit'ry essay that fired the rancor of many sweet cats was "Leo the K: Is He Now Gone Away?"—a scurrilous, vicious, and violent slam at a man who'd o'ergiven his face to his beard. (This piece from the putrid pen of our hack hugely hinted that Kaufman, the Village Bard, had, one dark and dismal day, thrown into the trash himself away.) Another vignette, dripping venom, was called "Richard Detective: Each Inch a Dick"—in which the calloused scribbling blob suggested that one of our mauditest of poets had his brains in his (God forgive me!) lob. Too many to mention are other assaults on the innardest country of art. Yet it behooves to jot down a few: The lurid, depraved and horribly blue double entendres he suggested were true in "Sheila Henry: Yearning to Screw"; the gleeful *ad hominem* slaughter of Harley in the infamous "Anton the Ax: A Bike for a Brain"; the bitter and poisonous paper on Lewis (that wizard of translucent style), "While We're Jung." So the corrosive language flowed from that noisomest crook our burrowing, borrowing worm called a mind.

Borrowing? Aye! From the base, the sublime, from the low to the high this thief took his ore. Reading a read of a novel he'd pull out a phrase or a line; he ransacked the news; squeezed out the juice from advertisements; was pleased when a song had a word he could use; in the blues he perversely found humor, from Natchez to Mobile he ranged, from the shining mind of heaven to the primordial ooze. A persistent and underground rumor ran thus: that with unparalleled insolence he stole his very characters—all of whom (but of course) were invented by better than he. The most casual glance at his books will reveal this to be. "I know what I'm doing," he'd sneer. In an early story we find King Lear as a salesman; Ella Cinders appears in an obscene novella; in novels and plays he would tinker with Crusoe as gunman, Joseph Andrews would shit in his hat; his sister, the virginal Pam, would wantonly pose in corsets and boots and grey silken hose. The ne'er-do-well Shem, lord of the pen, would shuffle, a bum on the streets. This inky thief, jigsaw in hand, would even slice out whole sentences, phrases, grand fragments of style to give to his opera brilliant veneer, a scope and a scan his pedestrian talents alone could never come near. Was it the gnaw of the needle of failure that made him so queer? So it appears. He was weary of shabby suits straight from the doddering fifties, his torn wallet empty of cash. He wanted Brie on the beach! He wanted to sip sour mash! He rolled like a stone, blithering loss, whingeing and whining, complaining and bitching, aching and writhing and twitching and reeking of misery, penury, lost among wealthy portrayers of popular lore. *Their* shiny tomes did not bore the intelligent public! *Their* heroes and heroines caused not one snore among newspaper pundits! *Their* styles were not sinister products of arrogant wile masked as art!

He knew as his eversharp tool built his monstrous machines he was doomed, he was just about through. "Immoral, unstructured, unfinished, clever but fey"; "murderous, bitter, cluttered with meaningless litter"; "obscurantist mutter"; "a quitter"; "a sitter of fences"; "no work and all play"; "sheer kindness to shut him away"; "a gutter mentality"; "hostile to everything gay"; "one *hoped* that Studs Lonigan had had his day"; "mad overkill"; "are these second-rate characters worth all this pother?"; "a cross between Selby DeCubb and Weary O'Farrell"; "a stinking kettle of fish"; "the novelist's swan song"; "the novelist's death wish"; "no laughs in *this* barrel"; "more than just a bit petty and 'in' "; "at times he commits every professional sin"; "for a 'comic' writer, needlessly cruel"; "grating and tedious"; "he winks at the reader"; "rather thin gruel"; "self-righteous preaching and prating"; "the writer's own cleverness sinks him"; "at best, a mordant letter"; "relies mostly on rancor"; "maligns all his betters"; "vacuity is the milieu"; "he here goes too far"; "wildly destructive"; "supposedly aimed at the *au courant* few"; "very crude"; "worships and crawls at the feet of the Beat"; "just another honkie dude"; "a wise guy"; "a cynic"; "no prude"; "isn't fully a novel"; "isn't really a book"; "shows genuine loathing"; "the clinical plotting's a bore"; "his people are merely stick figures"; "a quickly tiring trick."

Yet did he not ofttimes contemplate rising or sailing or climbing into the sky, eternally azure, a snowy white cloud etched on the glorious blue?

He did.

And didn't he dream of glamorous friends who would love him forever, of crystal decanters, wonderful wines, all the concomitant items, lustrous and glowing, designed to make life worth the living?

Surely he did.

Did he not sometimes wonder why it was given to him to write these millions of words? to comb over his life for a phrase?

But of course.

What of watching the sea?

His rarely enjoyèd delight.

Did he envy the wonderful people in bistros and taverns and bars?

Ha!

Did he envy the creamy mysterious stars?

More than many.

Why did he grimly endure the holes in his sweaters? Was he a bum?

The answer is no.

Wasn't he smart?

In his out-of-date fashion.

Why then wasn't he rich? Could one fairly call him a stupid galoot, a dull-witted son of a bitch?

It wouldn't be fair.

Did he at times compose a line wrought of moonlight and silver?

He did.

Shall then we forgive him his blunders, his arrogance, whining self-pity and maddening lies?

Emphatically yes.

Dear Miss Flambeaux:

It is early evening now and I have had all day to think about your bizarre and shall I say aberrant behavior at dinner last evening. I have wrestled with my conscience (both masculine and artistic) for hours concerning the wisdom of writing this letter, and I have finally arrived at the opinion that a few words from me might serve to ameliorate what I perceive to be a very rocky and difficult future for you—both as woman *and* poet.

First of all, I think that you must admit that your actions and words last night did not "square" with the sensual and exciting woman whose voice is heard in *The Sweat of Love* As a matter of plain fact, it has even crossed my mind that you are not the author of those lusty and throbbing poems. Surely, your unnaturally frigid, overly demure, and even insulting behavior last night belies the thrilling desires and free spirit revealed in your lines. If you are *Sweat*'s author (and sadly, sadly, I know, despite my momentary doubt, that you are), then I must plainly say that you are rather a fraud. Somewhat like the "nature poet" who drives into a field in his car and from the rolled-down window "contemplates" the natural wonders surrounding, then fills up a page in his notebook. Do I make myself clear?

Allow me, my dear young woman, to inform you that I have decided *against* bringing your poems to the attention of my editor. In all candor, I feel that commercial publication at this time would be detrimental, even fatal to your poetic development. It would be cruel and misleading for me to praise your work knowing, as I now do, that Miss Lorna Flambeaux, in her flesh, has nothing whatever to do with the passionate and gloriously wanton voice heard in *Sweat*. I hope that you appreciate the difficulty of my decision. Last night's experience was a revelation, an epiphany, if you will, in the Proustian sense, and I feel that I must obey what it made clear to me.

Now to more specific matters, unpleasant as the recollection of them may be. (A writer must be willing to dredge, dredge up *everything*.) I feel it ungenerous in the extreme of you to have accused me of trying to get you drunk so that I could get "into your pants" (your phrase, my dear). A Bloody Mary, young lady, is an *alcoholic* drink; had you *preferred* a tomato-juice cocktail, I would have been more than happy to oblige. I assure you that I am not in the habit of trying to get my dinner companions, male *or* female, drunk! I have many lady friends who need no persuasion of any kind in order to feel completely relaxed with me. Pouring your Bloody Mary into the ash tray was, I must insist, a rather gross act, to say the least.

To continue: as a writer (as you *should* be aware!) I am interested in *everything*. The world is my oyster, so to speak. (I once wrote an essay on the modern novel called "Oyster World.") Everything— including such mundane items as the texture of various fabrics. When I discreetly touched the hem of your skirt—this was, you will recall, just before you charged me with trying to get you drunk—I was not, young lady, trying to "feel you up" (another of your unfortunate phrases). Certainly, such an innocent act was not an occasion for you to fling a bowl of mixed nuts in my face! Also, Miss Flambeaux, you must admit that the length of your skirt left very little to the imagination. A lady of chaste bent does not so completely expose her thighs. Or am I simply a "dirty old boob," as you put it?

Furthermore, I find it insulting that you continually spoke of our abortive attempt at dancing as a "wrestling match." I was also embarrassed and speechless when you accused me of trying to caress your breasts as I seated you at table. It was unmannerly of you to drive your elbow into my stomach, and although I laughed at the time, I may now tell you that the experience was quite painful. And what was I supposed to make of it when, just moments after our *contretemps,* you confided to me that you were not wearing underclothes? You *laughed* about it! You also said, if I remember rightly, "Give you a cheap thrill?" My dear young woman, there is a vile term for women who disport themselves in that fashion—I'm sure, as the author of *The Sweat of Love,* that you know it.

Again—the erotic drawings and photographs that I asked you to look at are not, by any means, "fuck pictures," as you indelicately put it. They are honest and often beautifully realized images of men and women allowing themselves the total freedom of healthy sexual activity! I did not intend to "get you hot." As a matter of cold fact had you not interrupted me by stamping on my foot with your heel, I would have told you that I thought there might be a very strong possibility of illustrating a deluxe, limited edition of *The Sweat of Love* with a group of the pictures you shunned; a group selected, of course, *by you*. Of course, it is now *too late* for that. Your mocking laughter and crass remark anent the pictures and my relationship with "Mary Fist" were saddening to me.

Finally, "Burst Loveletters" is, I admit, humorous in spots, but overall it is an investigation into the degradation of a warm, decent, intelligent human being. It is not meant to call forth gales of laughter. I must conclude that you are insensitive to the nuances of prose style. Sadly, I further conclude that *Sweat* is not what I thought it, but is, rather, the expression of a furtively twisted mind, a mind dead to the joys of open sexual exploration. How wrong I was about it! I see now that it is a gross, crude, amateurish, unintelligent, unmelodic, and opportunistic work. Miss Flambeaux, you are not only not a poet, you are not even a poetaster!

I will not hold my torn shirt nor the scratches on my face against you, but prefer to chalk them up to experience.

To conclude, young woman, I advise you to discontinue all your attempts at writing and to find a husband who will appreciate your games. Someone who is as coyly plebeian as you are—or pretend to be. I enclose your book, and urge you to study it for the insincerity and hollowness of its lines.

Sincerely,
Antony Lamont

P.S. I must add that your cardinal sin, in my eyes, was in your mistaking my interest in you as a poet with a sexual interest. My dear lady—sex is easy to come by, art is not. Your error bred arrogance and contempt for a man who was prepared to *advance your career*. I am not exactly unknown in literary and publishing circles. Perhaps this experience will teach you wisdom.

Halpin's Journal

Quite a lot has happened since Ned and I discovered the other rooms in the house. Not the least significant has been Lamont's neglect of us—we've been doing more or less as we please.

In the rooms discovered, we've found a few more things, some of them of interest. The important thing is: *how did they get here?* I cannot believe that we didn't see them the first time. If they are "new," then who put them here? They don't seem to have anything to do with *our* lives, but Ned half believes that they do. There is a strong possibility, Ned contends, that Lamont has started *another* book, or—and this is really discouraging—he has decided to revise! In the latter case, it means, of course, that we will have to go through another series of misadventures. If that is the case, Ned will not have to persuade me to leave with him. Even camping out somewhere would be preferable to the tortures of a revision. I've tried to argue that Lamont may be starting a new book "better" than this one, but Ned laughs and says simply "like the one Sollis was in?"

In any event, here are the "new" things that we found. First, some books. (some *more* books!) *Poetical Works* by Dennis Florence McCarthy; *The Useful Ready Reckoner; The Secret History of the Court of Charles II; When We Were Boys* by William O'Brien; *The Story of the Heavens* by Sir Robert Ball; *The Stark-Munro Letters* by A. Conan Doyle; *Voyages in China* by "Viator"; *Life of Napoleon* by Lockart; and *Physical Strength and How to Obtain It* by Eugene Sandow. The last book was inscribed "To Jeff from Shad." There was also a small publisher's catalogue listing new books. The covers had been torn off, so it was impossible to ascertain what house had issued it or when. But Ned swore that it was a list for Beaumont & Halpin, Inc. The books announced seemed singularly uninteresting, even rather dull. But, depressingly, I must agree with Ned that they seem to be the sort of books that Lamont would have "us" publish. I enclose the catalogue:

LICK UP A JUNE BEET
Derace Kingsley

More supreme adventures in organic-food explorations by one of the world's leading authorities on vegetables and the author of the best-selling *I Got A Raw Deal!* In his new book, Mr. Kingsley investigates the many ways in which the most common and essentially unappetizing foods may be prepared so that they take on new and different tastes, odors, and textures. Among the many recipes the health-oriented cook will find are those for Kohlrabi Flambé, Sorghum Goulash, Swiss Chard and Pimiento Surprise Casserole, Squash Chiffon Pie, and Crème de Sauerkraut *à la* Pickett. Profusely illustrated with cheerful drawings by ZuZu Jefferson, author of the popular children's book, *A Bookman's Letters.*

"Quirky recipes to 'turn on' the rebellious palate." *James Gotee*
SEPTEMBER $8.95

266

CHILLER ON THE CHAIN
Mildred Haviland

A taut, tingling, and topical thriller about a crazed killer who obsessively selects his helpless victims from among the shoppers who patronize the various stores of a Southern California supermarket chain. Mrs. Haviland, creator of the "Mealy Dick" murder mysteries and the author of more than 215 books under various pseudonyms, has, in *Chiller on the Chain*, fashioned a compact, "now" novel of twisted passions and smoldering hatreds that reveal the sick soul of California society. More than just "another mystery," the novel is a compelling study of pathological consumer mentality. Illustrated with maps by Albert Almore.
SEPTEMBER $5.95

THE PIG LEAP
Christopher Lavery

Montana's Boar Forest Preserve is the setting for this sensitive rumination on one of the world's great natural wonders, Fat Butte, known to the Park's Rangers as "Pig Leap." Long the secret locale for the Jet Set's eerie midnight revels and its carefully planned panoramas of unbridled license, the Pig Leap has, Mr. Lavery contends, "become the modern-day Stonehenge." The author, who spent three years disguised as a stupid homosexual policeman in order to gather his unsettling data, is the man who wrote *Secrets of Owl's Head Park*, of which Mullins Gump commented: "I laughed, I cried, I let my mouth fall open in admiration as the book refused to be put down . . . a small masterpiece."

Drawing on legend and history, fact and malicious gossip, Mr. Lavery has reconstructed the strange and glamorous ambience that has made Fat Butte a gathering place for the world's most depraved "beautiful people." With 25 infra-red photographs by Roy Buckus
SEPTEMBER $8.95

HAREWELL M. DOVELY
James Patton

Historians have traced the crossword puzzle back to the time of the Pharaohs, but never has this most fascinating time-passer been examined so lovingly as in this exhaustive critical biography of the world's great puzzle champion and analyst, Harewell M. Dovely. Mr. Patton, who describes himself as "a great fan but only a duffer," has, in this mesmerizing life of the nonpareil word genius, deftly incorporated irresistible historical anecdote into the story of Dovely's career. You will read:

- how Marie Antoinette worked a crossword puzzle in the tumbril that carried her to her death
- how Pablo Picasso hit upon the idea for Cubism while doing a crossword puzzle in the *Revue des Deux Mondes*
- why *The New York Times* was responsible for cutting short the brilliant career of Clint Hartung
- what role the crossword puzzle played at Gettysburgh

And there are literally hundreds of other unknown anecdotes, many of them unearthed from Dovely's journals and notebooks, to which Mr. Patton had complete access.

Included is an appendix which reproduces the dozen greatest puzzles of all time (with their solutions): from the diagramless "killer" that Socrates worried in his prison cell to the little stumper from *Boys' Life* that soothed President Hoover just after the Great Crash of '29.

OCTOBER $8.95

THE DRY MINNOW
Floyd Greer

Have you ever envied the fisherman who can, in a trice, fashion a lure that looks, for all the world, like a fat and lively cockroach? Or a fly that could fool a locust into thinking he'd found a mate? Or a surface-action plug that can mimic a frog squirming in agony on the hook? Floyd Greer, "the 20th-Century Walton," describes, in easy-to-follow instructions, how to do all these things—and more. You will learn how to make lures that *work* out of orange peels, eggshells, broken glass, coffee pots, socks, condoms, and fragments of rotting tent canvas.

"A must for the serious sportsman as well as the weekend angler to whom fish simply smell bad." *William McCoy*
SEPTEMBER $5.95

THE DADDY AND THE DRAKE
Louis Condy

Harry Black and his dad are forced to leave Harry's pet ants behind when they move into a spanking-new housing project from which all animals are banned. For a while, things seem to go well, but then Harry's grades in his new school plummet and he develops athlete's foot. His father, depressed by his son's strange behavior, gives up his job at the "Big Teflon" plant where he is employed as a gasket washer

268

and soon after loses interest in Nat Hentoff's writing. Suddenly, into their lives comes Hoagie, a talking duck from Canada. What happens when Harry, his Dad, and Hoagie decide to write an article on garbage-strewn nature trails makes for exciting reading. Charmingly illustrated with watercolors by "Georgette." For youngsters 8 to 12.
OCTOBER $5.95

THE KETTLE LISTER
Adrienne Fromsett

One of the greatest of all culinary frustrations is working in an ill-equipped kitchen. The beginning cook is often frustrated in the achievement of "the perfect dish" because of the lack of utensils proper to the job at hand. Much of the time, this is the result of honest ignorance, that is, the tyro has no knowledge of what the ideal kitchen *should* contain. Adrienne Fromsett, for 12 years the hostess on KPOP's popular show, "Lunch Sitting On the Stove," has prepared an invaluable guide for the hesitant cook: a manual listing every utensil that the kitchen might possibly need, their uses, and where to buy them. Among them are such specialized but indispensable items as the king *spatule,* the graduated collander, the skillet *manqué,* the Ethiopian oven, the half-spondee, the double-bottomed vesper, and the sinister poacher.

The Kettle Lister is, according to James Gotee, "A quirky book to 'turn on' the most rebellious palate," and is a joy simply to browse in as well as employ as a unique tool. With hundreds of charmingly insouciant line drawings by Ellen Kaufman.
OCTOBER $12.50

THE WRONG FOOD BUY
Eustace Grayson

In this iconoclastic and courageous book, Eustace Grayson, who five years ago caused a furor in the nutrition world with her shocking *Vitamins? Poison!,* continues her assault on the "foodmongers" who have subtly turned us into a nation of nutritional sleepwalkers. In *The Wrong Food Buy,* Miss Grayson takes centuries of wrong thinking and old wives' tales about food and exposes them to the merciless glare of truth. "Rather than amply and beneficially providing for her family," she says, "the American housewife has inadvertently been poisoning it because of her slavish devotion to the propaganda of the giant food cartels and the rabble of fly-by-night 'nutritionists' that are, like the plague, upon us."

Mrs. Grayson demonstrates that such foods as fowl, red meat, fish,

eggs, milk, green and yellow vegetables, honey, rice, whole grains, and beans and potatoes are not only unnecessary for good health but are actually detrimental to it. Focusing on basic essentials, she shows how a diet built on the "indispensables"—newsprint ash and algae— can change the body's secret rhythms and bring us glowing health and boundless energy.
NOVEMBER $7.50

BUBBLE IN MY FIZZINESS
Charles Cooney

Would you like to read the memoirs of a man who———
—Drank a quart of cola while hurtling into the Grand Canyon?
—Helped a Grand Duke seduce a famous international beauty with a simple mixture of cola and spinach water?
—Almost started a war between neighboring African tribes because of a brand name?
—Escaped a firing squad by the judicious use of Pepsi-Cola syrup?
—Rehabilitated five rapist-murderers with "Coke" egg creams?
—Passed up a million dollars because of a love for carbonation?
If you would, then *Bubbles in My Fizziness*, the story of 25 years in the life of America's most sought-after cola taster is your glass of pop. Along with dozens of deliciously effervescent anecdotes about the great and the near-great, Mr. Cooney also gives the shocking, heretofore secret formulae for Coca-Cola and Pepsi-Cola, "accidents both."
NOVEMBER $7.95

THE AMPLE HEART OF WERTHER
George Talley

A warm, wise, and altogether wonderful novel about a "little man," Joachim Werther, a sausage maker in Hundë, who travels to America's Pennsylvania Dutch country to make his fortune with the recipe that has made him famous in his homeland. Gross, inarticulate, bordering on the stupid, Werther nevertheless refuses the blandishments of the Trans-Amalgamated Meat Company to sell them his recipe, and immediately becomes a target for the most vicious attacks.

Driven almost to the edge of insanity by the catcalls of the local Spam-consuming right-wingers, insulted by the militant faction of the Rochester Brigade, who see in his sausages a threat to their native cuisine, stung by allegations of phallus worship by the Sisters of Colette, he is forced to make a stand when the minions of Dr. Piscardi, the hair-oil millionaire, begin a vicious campaign of slander in the sensationalist tabloid, *Hats Off!*

When a national emergency threatens, the President himself calls on the hearty Joachim and begs him to release his recipe to the Pentagon. What happens when he decides to honor the President's request and is besieged by an army of welfare clients who are the pawns in the war between the White House and Piscardi will keep the reader turning pages far into the night.
DECEMBER $6.95

So much for the catalogue. The rest of the day was spent in leafing through the new books we'd found (a singularly tiresome batch).

The next "day" Ned and I, now completely reckless as to Lamont's plans for us, decided to take a walk, perhaps into town. The sun shone down and down as usual, once we left the cabin. Did I mention that the cabin has no phone? An endless source of wry amusement to Ned. In any event, on our way to town we passed a small clearing in the woods and saw, at their ease, three men in what we took to be cowboy regalia. They introduced themselves as Deuces Noonan, Sundog O'Haggerty, and Black Danny McGlade. They spoke excellent, rather clipped, English. They were relaxing, they said, from their jobs in a "deplorable" novel in which they are supposed to play *Irish* cowboys. In the words of Mr. O'Haggerty, it is "a stupefying performance." Yet they seemed in good spirits and they are clearly veterans of this profession.

However, when we told them we were on our way to the little, aborted town, Mr. McGlade informed us that the town was gone and in its place was a suburban shopping center, all parking lot, pedestrian mall, and supermarket—also a "gourmet shopping hub" that stocked seventy-four kinds of cheddar and some artichoke hearts. It is the focus of a novel all about the depravity, hatred, and corruption that seethes beneath the surface of an otherwise calm and moneyed community. "Out of *Kings Row,*" said Mr. Noonan. I miss the reference. The title is *A Renegade Pulse,* or so we were led to understand. Ned asked if they had met a Mr. Clive Sollis there, but they had not. "All chrome and secret abortions," they said. "Plenty of neo-Georgian architecture." "The smell of charring steaks and warm Martinis," Mr. McGlade chuckled. "We met good old, kind old, wise old Pop Heart in the package store," he continued. "He is playing the warmly peevish yet morally upright owner of the filling station in this dog." To give us an idea of what he called the "totally degenerate ambience of the locale," Mr. O'Haggerty produced a flavor list for

271

the month from KreemWorks, the center's ice-cream "shoppe." It reads:

1. Blushing Cherry
2. Hot Nuts
3. Georgia Peach
4. Quick Lime
5. Pear Goriot
6. Washington Mint
7. Honey Moon
8. Strawberry Mark
9. Coconut Grove
10. Watermelon Sugar
11. Huckleberry Finn
12. Jack Lemon
13. Plum Loco
14. Grapefruit League
15. Java Jive
16. Top Banana
17. Big Apple
18. Blueberry Hill
19. Almond Eyes
20. Ginger Rogers
21. Clove Hitch
22. Kid Chocolate
23. Cranberry Bog
24. Grape Shot
25. Peppermint Twist
26. Rum Go
27. Orange County
28. Old Fruit
29. Oh Fudge
30. Raisin Hell

31. Go Mango

They were served up by a counterman who was working very hard at his thin, stooped posture and had almost perfected his vacant stare. His eyes were tried-and-true "watery blue." He was, they agreed, quite good. They then began to talk of the jobs they'd had over the years and I found it so intensely interesting (in a depressing way) that I've here tried to reconstruct the gist of their conversation. I'm afraid I can't remember who said what, but they all contributed their remembrances.

What about the fellow who winced no matter what he said?
Or the one who sighed all the time.
I once worked a job where a young woman had to masturbate me —she neglected to open my trousers! A frightful mess. She laughed and laughed until *she* began having to go to bed every night with her shoes on.
I knew a poor wench who was always forced to remove her stockings without first removing her shoes. She got an ulcer, I believe.
The revolver with fifty bullets . . .
Of course! But what of the pen that in the middle of the letter becomes a pencil?
The steamship that is becalmed?
Personally, I've *shaken* so many Martinis that I can't even look at one anymore. Absolutely barbarous!

I've wearied of jumping out of bed and putting on my shoes, but no socks!

Don't you find brushing your teeth without toothpaste a crashing bore?

My pet peeve is the constant heaving of myself out of chairs.

That's overstuffed chairs, of course.

Doesn't hold a candle to looking at people I've known for months as if seeing them———

———for the first time!

I feel a twinge of nausea when hearing voices that sound distant. Or strained.

How about the great feat of speaking in a voice that is not your own?

I don't enjoy getting the Truth to shine in my eyes, I'll tell you!

It's no fun to be swept by a storm of emotion every fifty pages either!

Or crippled by it . . .

There's a spot of bother when one's face suddenly darkens with rage as well.

I worked for one hack whose villains always wore clothes that seemed too large for them.

What about the poor girls who have to make love without removing their underpants?

What about the poor blokes who have to make love *to* them?

I once had to do it through slacks, a girdle, and panty hose. I was out of work for a month!

I must confess that I've become a bit of an expert at biting off my words. Or a whole phrase, for that matter.

I'm fairly expert at clipping my words short.

One tires of curving one's lips in a thin smile.

Particularly if it's a mirthless smile.

That's not as bad as forcing a mirthless laugh. Try that one a dozen times.

What about thundering an oath? Or hurling a curse?

Or an imprecation?

In one job I threw my clothes on at least twenty times.

My interest slackens when I'm forced to watch the smoke from my cigarette curl lazily in the air.

Especially when it's blue smoke . . . and it's *always* blue smoke!

But how often have you thoughtfully knocked out your pipe? Or filled it?

If I stretch luxuriously one more time . . .

Right! But how do you feel about your eyes scanning the horizon?

That's as bad as not liking *it* because *it's* too quiet.

How many times, I pray you, have you emerged into the sunlight blinking?

Not as many times as I've grabbed for the phone.

I once had a position where I wheedled every third page.

I was once dazzlingly insouciant to the point of nausea.

I'm damn sick of getting home and going straight to bed without washing.

I'm just as tired of the sun in my eyes always waking me up.

How do you like the wet streets that shimmer in the fog? I'm up to *here* with them.

I don't mind the women whose bosoms heave—unless they crack their gum. Or chew it furiously. Or simper.

I was in a scene once with a woman who primped *and* simpered. As a matter of fact, I think she also whimpered.

As long as she didn't whine . . .

Mostly it's the small chaps with pasty faces who whine.

I don't think this woman *could* whine—she was expected to spend most of her time muffling sobs.

Did she dab at her eyes?

Of course. With *my* handkerchief.

And her hands were cold?

Yes. And they trembled.

Surely her lips trembled as well. That is, when she wasn't reflectively pursing them.

Right-o! And how regularly her lipstick caked and cracked. Occasionally, she lowered her eyes and a tear slid slowly down her cheek. A crystal tear, often furtive. Which she viciously brushed at . . .

Enough! You haven't lived until you've steeled yourself.

That's preferable to listening to the trees whisper. Or roar. No, it's the wind that usually roars. Or the sea.

What of the fire that crackles merrily? Or the flames that dance wildly? Or the wind that claws at the windows?

And, don't forget, also buffets the house!

Is that the house that's so full of strange noises?

The same . . . the one that has something sinister about it. Often, it squats malevolently. In the mist.

Inside said house, is there a damp chill that not even the cheeriest fire can dispel?

Yes indeed. And the portraits on the wall seem to be staring at you. And the far end of the great hall is lost in shadows.

Those shadows, you will remember, seem to shift and change.

But it's only the fire that makes them do this, someone always says. Nervously. Usually a woman.

274

The lady who too nonchalantly lights a cigarette and wonders aloud about dinner.

This dinner you mention. Is it not often served by a sinister and unfriendly old couple who come and go silently?

It is. And they live in town.

Of course. And as dusk begins to fall they hurry nervously toward their car or cart or buggy and take themselves off.

Yet I'll take a dozen of them to one girl who hugs her knees. Or smoothes her skirt.

I don't mind that as much as the one who brushes imaginary specks of lint from hers.

I always meet the woman who tugs at her hem. Or her girdle.

I worked with a woman like that once. She tugged all the way through the story. I did a lot of reflecting in that one. As I reflected, she tugged.

I'll give you odds that she was the one who cracked her gum.

No. But you're close. She wore too much make-up.

Ah. Could you see her hair's dark roots?

Of course. And her slip showed.

Withal, yet there was something—odd—about her. Am I right?

Odd, yes. But curiously vulnerable. As if she had once known a great hurt.

A kind of emptiness in her gaze?

Exactly. A lackluster eye.

What's more depressing is walking down the red clay roads of the South.

Oh, the South! The pickup trucks, the courthouse squares.

The little towns that time forgot.

You must admit that time forgets a lot of things.

It also hangs heavy. Or seems to stop. The latter often happens at the same time that the heart misses a beat.

You speak, of course, of relentless time?

Correct. Often merciless as well.

Yet often that same time has been kind to people.

I once knew a man to whom time had lent a kind of nobility and grace. It had mellowed him.

And softened his features?

But surely. And dulled his anger.

Did this man happen to possess a gruff, kindly voice?

How did you know? His eyes were wont to light up at the sight of something or other.

Probably not too fastidious in his dress?

Correct. Some unidentified stains on his lapels and ashes on his vest. Yet an inner goodness seemed to radiate from him. His eyes crinkled a good deal.

Did he live in a small town?—something like the one you might have grown up in?

What else? A town where one heard, night and day, the banging of screen doors.

I was stuck in a town like that once. A spinster owned the tobacco shop. Or maybe it was the widow woman.

Whose hair was pulled back severely into a tight bun?

Right! She wore a black nondescript dress and was rather remote from the community. Yet one got the feeling that she knew all the town's secrets.

In the same town did the Judge live in a white house on top of the Hill?

He did. He was the one with the daughter who got in trouble with the farm-machinery salesman. Of course she ran off to Chicago.

"Good Old Doc" tried to persuade her to stay and assert herself with her father, but he didn't have the time since he spent most of the day in peering over his spectacles and most of the night delivering babies over in the poor section—am I close?

You are. And the Judge's wife, after their daughter ran off, became something of a recluse.

Never left the big white house again, as a matter of fact.

In which, the Judge took to rocking on the veranda all day.

Did he rock determinedly?

He did. Sometimes hypnotically.

Did his staring eyes look at nothing?

They did. A fixed stare, it was.

And a blank one. Yet perhaps he was seeing the wreckage of his life.

They went on in this way for another hour or two, and were still at it when Ned and I took our leave of them and started back to the cabin. Their flippant cynicism truly depressed me, yet I mentioned to Ned that despite their contempt for the work that they'd done all their lives, they had *no intention* of deserting their current job—as he was thinking of doing and urging me to do. But Ned told me that it was to prevent us from falling into the cynicism exhibited by the "cowboys" that he *wanted* us to leave. There was, he said, nothing laudable about being that kind of hack. One paid dearly for that kind of toughness. It was better to remain sensitive and open to decent, intelligent jobs than to get a reputation as a drudge who would work *anywhere* as *anything*. While authors distrust characters who run out on novels in progress, they respect them if the novels are garbage. The character who stays, to the bitter end, in a rotten book, dooms himself to a career of working in the same kind of book over and over again.

He went on and on, telling me of a Mr. Shandy and an Emma Bovary—people who had never worked again after their initial jobs. They were legendary and everyone respected them. By the same token, the poor clucks who first went to work for hack writers worked for them all the time, and became, in fact, incapable of working for anyone else. Wealthy but depraved "stars"—that's what they became, and good authors would never think of employing them at all. *We* had reputations, Ned insisted. Small but real. They would be damaged if we stayed on in Lamont's debacle.

I think he must be right. The last thing I'd want is to become a sardonic mocker like the "cowboys." Rather than that, Ned said, one would be better off working in feature roles in first novels by students in creative-writing workshops, "the bottom of the barrel." I think I'm convinced, but Ned says we must choose our time carefully, especially since the town is now gone.

9. A BAG OF THE BLUES

How does such perfection come to pass? How is it so nurtured, so brought to clear and dazzling fruition? Other females by the thousands enter into this the teary world yet do not blossom into orange butterflies like Daisy, glorious flowers amarillo nodding gently, beautifully in the mellow sun of long and luscious summer afternoons, the fields awaiting splendid autumn, the rusty red and orange yellow hues and tints that do enchant the eye. But greater than the flittering butterfly and sweeter still than any flower stands she, all in her splendor. More than splendor, whisper many men who've moved for years in circles all agleam with lissome women, winsome wives and mistresses of famous muliebriety. Delightful damsels haughty, laughing ladies hidden ineffectually behind their burning blushes. Yet none so proud as Daisy fair, none crimson so enticingly. There is a claret in her face. She is a credit to her race.

Over what rooftops of what mammoth city did the sun come beaming the day that she was born? On what sea-laved coast of this great continent did moon cast her loony beams the quiet night that saw her here arrived? None can say or dare to even hint since all think silently yet strongly that her gracious form, so pure and radiant, appeared like Aphrodite, to whom she might be a sister, suddenly, fullblown and grown, modest hands concealing partially her charms, upon the trackless vast and heaving sea, spawned in fairy foam, breakers thundering her praise. So they think! But know that she is mortal, more's the wonder then that she should be so pretty.

I place her in venusian fantasies upon a stage, an honor scroll so lightly grasped in her delovely hand, the parchment stating Daisy fair to be the most remarkable and wondrous pupil in her school, blue-ribbon girl! I can see the judges' eyes. She must have made the cutest bow. O fair streets of what bowery Flatbush that she danced upon, delirious they sweated sycamores and salvia, butternuts and phlox. Her black hair and ebon eyes the perfect complement to her chaste uniform of navy blue, her modest jumper with starched white blouse the screen for her young virgin's body, pure and alabaster, a beauteous fountain of exquisite planes and curves immaculate. Fontbonne! Fontbonne Daisy. Head bent, soft nape opalescent 'neath her coalblack tresses, thus she studied Latin, algebra, science, trigonometry, and mental health. Nursing. And there she now appears in white, a walking dream, a dreamy walker, Atalanta, Flossie Nightingale, the brave broads of cruel Corregidor brought to you courtesy of silver screens, behind her, crisp blue skies of afternoon October, crisp white wind. Below, a team plays football. They offer up their bruises and their sweat and blood to Daisy.

Beside me, in a bar. O college! In dark apartment in an orange dress. I am stricken by thick Berlioz, fat tones first heard with her, those soft hands washing coffee cups, later dark nights upon cold sands, the sea close pounding, her graceful Roman lips, her fine Hebraic nose, luminous the face beneath me, freezing winds. In yellow skirt and blue print blouse she walks with me down roads all milky in the moonlight. We can hear the crickets singing. Cars vague on other roads and we sit entombed in youth, her black sweater and her slacks melting into melting blackness of the willow plunging. Will she remember me? Does she remember? Who will have now a quiet thought for all I lost so silently? The fall rains? Moonlight on the lake? In a tavern in the misty Bronx we made promises both of us broke ruthlessly. That orange dress, cashmere coat. A bit of silk about her throat. Smiling while behind her tolled the bells of Brooklyn. La-Guardia the lofty looked gigantically down.

I hear her leading cheers. Rah! I see her calming fears. Ah! The one bright spot against the brown pain of the hospital, she lightens agonies with perfect French, oh là! Eyes across a crowded party goes the old cliché and yet. Across the noise she came to me and spoke her name. Daisy. Darling D, your brown-and-tan checked dress and beige high heels glitter in my dreams. Your vodka crackling as your lovely laughter, love me do. Love me always and forgive me for the Christmas Eve I left, for everything, Halloween, Labor Day, Independence Day, Thanksgiving and all the numbed and nasty New Year's Eves. For leaving, for staying, cruelty, praying, all my fault. I see you walk away across the smoky park into the gloaming. Fare well! Sad girl I cry on the phone for your return. That thou shouldst enter under my roof. Beneath me move the trees beneath which reel the drunks. Lees. Speak but the word and my soul shall be healed. Silence save for pigeons on the roof. And bitter tears.

She is lovely. She's the maid makes men moan childishly their fond desires. Walks out of the night. Entrancing. Walks into the light. Enchanting. Hearts on fire with romancing. Under thick suburban leaves she says O yes. Under the copper beech on a bench past which the glassy bay flows syrup toward the open sea, O yes. Moans and groans in the dark, the starlight mirrored in her hair, her odor fair, O yes. Her hair coiffed in my reverie in smooth chignon, her black-gold earrings, sweet Latin filmy in her eyes. I fall, we fall. You like

279

it? You keep it! A cabin, once a small garage, with flagstone patio. There we sat. Golden deities, immortal. Peach rose beneath her tan, rose peach, my tan on hers and rain on the roof, we stood in the torrent and kissed, my body shaking with a fever. Years later her kidsmooth hands slipped into mine while carols rang while skaters waltzed. Shoppers bought and sellers raved. Grey grim evening swiftly fell on old Manhattan. Then the starless night and snow.

Gown the color of a pumpkin, homage to the fall, in spacious living room with harvest lights, gleaming grand piano. There did I make my way through the lost leaves, russet, crunching, smoke spiced the air. Hello. How the lamp gleamed on her hair, so carefree and cosmopolitan. Silvery dream of youth rewarded with silvery dream. Famous snake that chews its luscious tail. I'll permit her not to bite her nails but instead to grow them long and pearly. Color of morning. Which she may hold against her suit, her fingers spread. Color of moon.

I found her sweet, in linen suit, night black. I found her greeneyed. Found her browneyed. Her slow smile came across the dark air of the porch. The willow weeping bitterly into the river, rock away. Place me there in silver beams! Chase me through my sunset dreams. The rainbow arched to Europe and we walked beneath it. We moved upon the beach. The screams of gulls. In an orange dress. Sitting in my chair I watched her smooth her stocking, frozen smile as suddenly she turned to face me, carmine. The empty wire hangers in the closet set up music when we entered it. Mr. and Mrs. Bravado. Was it true that I punched the green fence that enclosed the field upon which young men smashed their limbs for her most careless glance? I desire nothing but the bluest Buick ever made with whipped cream top and spanking whitewalls. To match the color of her father's hair. Silky Jewess, it must have been that finedrawn Catholic forehead and the rosary beads that hung between her breasts. How she healed the hurts of doomed and dying desperadoes. When she changed the sheets her skirt slipped up and my stars, Daisy! Firm thighs, her tarblack hair and violet smile. So that the sick would rise and whistling gambol to their graves.

What fascinating world did she escape to before this sudden reappearance? Erect wife of ex-football star, now a huge success in the financial world, novel in the works? Skull and Bones, Porcellian, old Eli Nassau? Vast windows that command Madison or Vanderbilt. Or did she stride the cobalt shores of Florida, down in sunny Dade? Through rosy glasses how the chalky beach turned pink. And here is handsome hubby, lo! A CCNY grad, his auburn curls aglisten with intelligence and rose oil, his workout body wet with handball sweat. Rum and maple and a full moustache. Golden Daiquiris and rosy-dawn Bacardis. Then the night all licorice and spearmint.

In the eye of the mind at the end of the bar. I send a drink to her, my heart in miniature afloat in it, a Valentine Fizz, concocted of blood and desire. Her eyes were dark, ah! Thick hair, full lips. A smile of old San Juan, still streets in deepest purple shade. Outside, winter wonderland. Will she adore me? She waited in the rain. Over coffee her slender fingers spread against the table top, a golden chain around the first one and on that chain a car key. That fantastic carriage waited, skyblue magic carpet. Beyond the city all the roads were choked with snow and suddenly the warm sun brought forth palm trees! But I walked back into my life. Later on she wed an artist, a painter of paintings? A writer of books. A man for whom too often just the page was real, persistent strain of dread pen fever that thinned out his blood. A sad case, a desperate Dan, arrogant and bitterly satirical, a dreamy vacancy about the eyes, he was on Sun days sullen, Mondays moody, Tuesdays tough; wavering on Wednesdays, thick on Thursdays, Fridays fatheaded, Saturdays silly. Out of such what he liked to call steadiness and perseverance came the endless pages few read and fewer praised. The man who braved the beach at Coney Island! I can't drive I muttered I think and we bade fond adieu. In the rain.

So the years, as well they might, they passed. Erratically I hear of her, the gentle nightingale, samaritan in white. She has been observed amotoring through bosky Jacksontown; there she stands in sterile Santa Fe, communing with lorenzo scrub; in the Rue Royale her precious frame is cooled by an antique ceiling fan, a Bogie Breezeking; one gent spotted her in downtown San Francisco de la Cupcake where poems die at thirty two degrees; a fool on a hill. Much of her time was spent gazing lazily into the sea all bottlegreen and creamy —that was in old Gotham town. To variegated Vegas—there you feel free!—she fled. Total liberation with lg rms, swmg pl, tv, air cond, and baby stg. In vasty desert where the one-armed bandits prey, where the dimsouled losers play, where all say together: It's healthy! It's sunny! It's a dry dry heat! Against the flickering mirage her swanny uniform, shiny as a silver buck. She was also glimpsed in rainy San Antone nibbling neatly on cabrito, munching while the mariachis played their bright vermilion tunes. An eye descried her as she et a Necco on the deck o' the Staten Island ferry. Everyone back on the bus and hurrah for St. George! Can that be she before the roaring piñon blaze in the Christsblood Range? Sold! It's healthy! It's sunny! It's a dry dry cold! And now in smartly tailored Harris tweed, trim in soft brown walking shoes with modish cloche she strolls the steelblue black and golden canyons of fabled Manahatta, which yet she will beat, on her crisp way to view the latest in the way of modern art—all made for her, zany painters cluttering the canvas in her name! Telegrams arrived placing her in Sausalito, cozy 'mid the cups and pottery, the margarine sun has made a halo round her hair. Now she's seen wining and dining with J. Armstrong, A.A.B., the naval hero of the fierce fight on the broad Potomac. A farflung correspondent aims to tell me that she's in the arms of Hosie Martin, the sheepshearing king, within the sound of mission bells down—olé!—Méjico way. He's the millionaire turned gourmet cook who shakes up God's own Ramos Fizz; in a pinch he puts out Royal Punch. But then who's the knockout dreaming on the banks of the mighty Mississippi in lazy Memphis town? My informant wired that if it warn't Daisy then he's crazy. She appears. She disappears. She steals your heart away! On a picture postcard of a sunset all spumoni a tourist scrawls the news of the full figure of a female proud against the Western sky, musing on a mesa in Coconino County—who else but Daisy? Flash! A tomato slicer name of Garry Bee has placed her, sweet arms holding eleven —count 'em—British writers in a large sedan heading for the lots. In sum, intelligence has come fixing her: you name it—she's been there. Often anonymous, alias who? darkly incognito, in banging city and snoozing town, communiqués poured in of a wonder woman who got what she wanted when knowing what it was she wanted to want. After the leventy-seventh report these seemed to be her preferred personae: Alice Awkward in Abilene; Baltimore's own beautiful Belle; Clarissa Cuddles, the cynosure of Cincinnati; Dora Darling of Denver; Eleanor Envy of Erie, Pa.; faithless Frances from Flint; Green Bay's good Grace Gulp; Hannah Hots, the Hartford hoyden; the Indianapolis imp, Inez Impure; Jane Joint, Jackson's joy; Kora Kalm of Kalamazoo; Lima's lewd Lena Lust; musical Mary Moan, lush Miami's maiden melodious; Newark's new Negro, Nina Nonsense; Omaha's oddball, Olivia Ogle; in Peoria, Patricia Perfidia; Queenie Queynte from Quincy; ravenous Rose Room, the rage of Reno; Sheila Sham, the shame of Shreveport; temperate Tess Trueheart, Tulsa's true treasure; Una Unique in Utica; Violeta Virago, the virgin vile of Venice; Wanda Wiles, Watchung's whiz; Xina Xanthodont, the xantippe of Xenia; yummy Yolande Yes, the yen of Yellow Springs; and Zenobia Zealot of Zook. Yet underneath these visages so different lay, of course, the unpolluted heart of sunny Daisy. She'd look sweet on any street.

She came in dreams to me as well as waking, scrubbed and silv'ry, in filmy deshabille, knowing full well how to please a he man! Blushing with modesty, flushing with shame, attar of innocence. Sometimes at even when old God threw his mantle cool all about the earth and sizzling Sol did lower weary bones into his tub pacific, she'd materialize for me, a dark shy girl among her tittering schoolmates, blinding beauty in her First Communion dress, white veil, white stockings, and white patent leather shoes, all in a state of grace by Christ. In her white hand her missal white a cross of gold upon its cover. Empty from her holy fast she eyes the good grey priest, old Father McPenance, agleam as well in his own white and gold. Hallelujah! O Lord, I am not worthy whispers she. I woke to emptiness and gloom, world without end, vague rustling in the air. I rushed back wildly then to Nodland, forgetting hope, forgetting supper, forgetting all that good get up and go for her honey face, her willow frame, her milky breasts, her splendid thighs, her calf so firm and ankle slim, her smile muy tropical. Once upon a twilight dreamy she brought me cakes and cookies, wine and cheese, electric bulbs and laughter, freshly laundered clothes, her body glimmering in sand-white flannel suit; on a thick and humid August midnight she arrived in bloody red, a blazing torch in hand, the flames reflected in her ember eyes, her face as if she'd seen a ghost; hopefully stammering of sweet amour she came on a rainy April eve, her thighs whispering in nylon smooth beneath the slick of her green sheath; in the middle of a night of violent storm she touched me in my bed in violet gown (to match her suffering smile!) to beg my pardon for her lack of care; in watered silk the blush of rose at just that moment when the sunset is dissolving, she entered, all in a swoon of joy for love of me; one bitter night, the thunder vying with the blizzard fell, she came when only evil spirits are about, in black dress, stockings, shoes, her pearls all black and lips obsidian—I woke and mourned the death of our desire. The thought must perish and be banished too.

Name me your heavenly harlots and virginal dames! Daisy will put them to shame. Her derrière would make a Sunday face for them. I am reminded of a hefty wench by name of Bubs LaBoca, spawned in large heartland where the corn roams free and no word e'er discourages. By many thought to be the sheer epitome of female splendor, the Planters Punch, the caviar, the squeeze play and the banana split with walnuts and an extra dollop of whipped cream, this upstart turned into a rutabaga when held against our Daisy. Another babe, Luba Checks, the younger sister of the wolfgirl, Loba de Crochet Rouge, while well versed in the minor poets of the fin de siècle, was also quite a dish. Enter D: whish! the broad but disappeared in the storm of adulation that broke upon our darling's shining sconce. Meanwhile, the latter reddened fetchingly. Sis Loba, clicking and gnashing her lupine teeth horrifically, did a dozen former swains of her kid sister eat that night, yet nothing helped restore Miss Checks the Younger to her former reputation. Daisy laughed low in her porcelain throat, her pearls all moony in the starlight. Then there was dark Sydelle, Our Lady of the Staghorn Sumac, who spent her youth stiffnippled and adaze, kissing puberty-stricken boys until their groins turned blue and ached. Her coffee-colored eyes boiled as her tongue supreme sought out their yearning tonsils. Then to the lakeland of New Jersey Daisy came one soft June night and the goddess of the groves removed to Oklahoma. I could go on and on, weaving old yarns of languorous lovelies with new needles—of Pat the Pink of freckles in the porchlight, lanky Lona Labios, the Coke sucker, Margy Van Cortlandt, Miss Labor Day of 1948, Diana Roofe, a sweetheart if there ever was one, Mary Philomena Marshall, with lavender spring coat and cross of palm, Rose Bexar on the Alamo, chewing on a Coney Island, and many more who exuded waves of womanhood. But each male fantasy, O shame! played out in bluelit boudoirs of the mind starred always Daisy as it ingenue. In silks and lace, in casual duds, mixing cocktails, laying plates, in taffeta and nylon, mashing spuds, hanging curtains, laughing gaily, spraying Windex, cranking ice cream, shelling peas, carrying the sprightly conversation, smooth in spandex, long of leg, wide of mouth, bright of teeth and deep of bosom, wrapping gifts and waxing floors, trimming bright the Christmas tree! and each small act had as its coda: Love. In bed. On floor. Behind the sofa. Against the wall. In basket, bath, or bloom. In the foyer. On the kitchen table, nookie in the breakfast nook, on easy chairs and carpets and a bet. Love laughing, panting, tears and smiles and yelps and moans and those musky odors dizzying, the kind that make a fellow leave the town. Ask Young Goodman Brown. Ask Pastor Christian Baptist who laid his Bible down. All for the love of Miss D. Dream, sweet upon her seat, her lustrous gams at forty-five degrees gesturing toward heaven. All the while she's reading a good book and listening to everything with warm smile and her patient understanding. What is life without a wife? Peaches and cream with Daisy!

I tortured and enthralled myself a thousand times imagining her as my gay companion on merry madcap tours of the incandescent city and its most exclusive spots. Would it be beer in Flynn's, with pretzels and the hoi polloi, dropping coins in the jukebox, nimbly hopping the honest vomit of the working man? She shone a blinding light through all the smoke—it was her teeth the whiteness of a cloud that turned that trick. Another fashionable spot dubbed The Lion's Den by the jovial and drunken lamb who owned it might serve as the scene wherein this gorgeous girl and I could quaff a nightcap of that good Green River, guaranteed to clean old leather and unclog your drains. At Pat's, the Pabst is passing lovely in the afternoon and fine old Gallagher's, the Subway Inn, might show us to our elbows in the free lunch, while Martin, King of the Ducks, soothes our ears with imported Oirish Oil. In immaculate Anel's my snowy shirtfront and her shoulders chaste make that flower never to be found in a bouquet; their Mallarmé cocktails (white crème de menthe and ocean spray) are world renowned. I ache when I think of the ecstasy of D and I, fresh returned from our Chinese honeymoon, sharing Presbyterians in quiet Carroll's or gulping glög in stout Leif Eriksson's, pie-eyed sailors reeling to the floor. And who of those who make up the legion of the absolute select has not heard of Henry's and its stained glass windows that bathe the mellow room in rainbows of a Sunday afternoon? How I've dreamed of Daisy there, her midnight hair a thousand points of color! In the intimate Pink Poodle Room in back, where it is always twilight, there you feel knees. We swill the nutty brew in Fritz's and in Lento's, while the angels sing, we order pizza pie du jour beneath the plaque commemorating Monte Count's brave contribution to romance. I've even thought (a shame!) of jazzing her in Papa Joe's, a hump for joy! That topers' retreat, the Melody Room, has often been my dreamy spot in which I got the lass so boiled. Cheap thrill to come. Just a few blocks down, in the quiet hush of elegance that spells White Shutter, I see the envy in a score or more of bluestraw eyes, the wash and wears standing to attention as I enter with my dilly Daisy. Oh how sweet! Surprise. They mumble with their whorish pink ladies and their salty Margarets malcontent. Did I mention dancing with that delicacy beneath the orange lights of clammy Imbriale's? Another pipedream. Lastly a thought I hardly dare acknowledge. Black with sin, blue with desire, red with embarrassment and green with envy is the lulu played out in The Keg, so dark by day as well as night that the waiters grope their way with flashlights and the customers are seen in fitful beams occasional to be dumb with lust, their bodies on the floor so many thrashing limbs. Were I to tell of my desires anent my one alone and this cabaret— but let it lie. A sigh. Many a cherry was plucked in that gloom. May saints preserve them! Let us pray.

Forgetting for a moment, forgetting—as if I could forget!—to set down here for my delight and the envy of posterity that they did never know her, I hasten to amend this oversight, I mean, the magic that her voice worked upon my poor, my yearning soul. Have you ever heard mission bells ringing? What music doth the bard's thousand twangling instruments convey to the imagination? Or the yingle yingle of a pair of fine-wrought Swedish campanellas? None of them at best could ever match the thrilling tenor of this lady's sweet vibrato, the trim sophistication of her yells. O husky huffs and puffs! In gardens soft and dark as midnight-blue velour, I place her avocado tones, her tonsils tremulous. Those decibels I fleshed in desirous tossing on my lonely cot set my brain to singing and all my skin to ache. To hear the trombone of her sighs, the oboe of her muttering!

I wished that I might be a pair of ears. Her coughs were violin sonatas and love words drifting on her breath the song of Solomon Viola. When she laughed my mind was filled with images of silken legs and thighs close-hugged by lace-edged garters. And her singing was a brace of shining heels. Thus did I vex myself, her voice so protean, invading my imagination. Her creamy sighs chinchilla, her chats raw silk—in her mouth the dullest argot turned pistachio and peach and French vanilla. A gelati, a spumoni, a cannoli, a tortoni! In my dreams I sucked the sweetness off her tongue. I woke to the all alone blues, that empty bed, big eight-wheeler rollin' down the track, far hoot of whistle, vague sounds or memories of sounds, softly slipping out the window. A moment of self-abuse and I could face my coffee, hoping that the percolator's pops would not throw up to me the maddening delight of hearing Daisy belching quietly. There was no noise that she could make, real or imagined, too crude for sly old List'nin' Tom. Brp! Frt! Hlp! Znp! Sht! Wrf! Bch! Onf! Upf! I reveled in them all! Tell me then, I whisper to the walls, why this pus-bitter gall of solitude? I want her close to me forever, one enormous never-ending female noise. O joys! Toys for the lonely eardrum. So I mumbled to intolerable privacy.

Waiting in the rain for me, recurrent dream desire, her soft coat swirling as she turns, soft calves, chocolate knitted dress with touches here and there of orange. Or snow. Or did it merely look like snow? I envision neon lights burning through the New York gloom. Fog falling silently, churning down Bronx streets. A sloe gin fizz a maiden pure's delight. A whiskey sweet for sour me. Tinsel, blinking Xmas lights, dark streets outside, a thin snow drifting down to welcome in the new year. Blank eyes of a dripping, sodden crèche, the flaking infant Jesus, her sloe eyes in mine, damp black kid gloves, a key glinting on the leather. An orange radiance suffused the living room, her long legs glowing in the firelight, snow silent, thick against the windows, faint voices raucous far away. She picked up the pillow. Bower of bliss. I am dazed by my ceaseless obsessions. We might as well be comfortable, so I have her say. Always. I hear the milk tones of her voice, a virgin, a whore, a woman totally aware of every dark perversion, an innocent. Naked in knee socks and Mary Janes, a golden fuzz upon her belly, soft between her legs. Tall in sepia corset and shining patent leather boots, uccello tightly leashed around her loins, eyes flashing fire mysterious and catlike in a brocade domino. The bells of midnight mass hover over, hang between our groans, abandoned, our venery. I want her waiting in the rain for me. The trees are lashed by autumn winds, everyone has gone, the lake is grey and kicks up cream afar. In the shelter of the lake pavilion we embrace. She will be mine forever, not grow old, I will not grow cold, our pleasures various yet stable. As the sea. Her sighs. The skies black, swiftly moving toward Parsippany. The youthful bodies of July and August home now, cabins closed, the cottages all locked and shuttered, browning lawns and the numbed birds on the boughs. She kisses me, a nun. Sun in her mouth. Then coffee in the only open restaurant. On the tablecloth a blue car key. Orange mums in heavy water glasses, brown glass ash trays. I want a lovers' meeting with her in December, waiting in the rain for me. All the Christmas Eves she's ever had with lovers, friends, her husbands and her relatives—I want them mixed and brought together in the perfect antidote to cure my gnawing misery of desire. She is under the tree, crackling night, clear and frozen stiff, on her hands and knees, her dress around her waist, cool buttocks in a frame of lace and hose. Come all ye faithful! I am the worshipful maladroit who enters her, carols booming, only I. Santa Claus in lights above the rimy lawns. She hands me a Scotch and water and we trim the tree, blue lights and shining platinum. In white unmentionables, flushed with lust, she waits for me to enter from the bathroom. We perform gloriously in the mirror, drunk with wonder at this couple's lewdness. Soft jazz, small night light. That it will perish or that it has not been makes it no less sweet. The memory makes me twist with bitterness. I take her from the party and we head for home. In a black dress, picture hat, and pearls. I touch her in the cab. Rain pearling on the windshield. We go to it with soft oaths and vile obscenities there on the couch. Thick fog and silent night, O darling Daisy! Bells ringing far, we hiss erotically through our teeth. The sun limps up. The dream dies out.

My heart is cracked for none of it has ever been nor will it ever come to be, my darling, delicate and tall. Cracked heart, childhood image from the comic strips, oho, a funny valentine. But in the chest the pieces float apart and are thought to be invaders to be ravaged and assaulted by the blood, alarmed. Dearest girl. I have lived with her for so many countless years, I have been to her all the things she wanted, all she did not want. On the sunny street, a ring, the Virgin Mary under celluloid. She stands against the background of October Lake, cigarette smoke white and stilled, it is September always in the photograph. She brings her television set and clothes to the apartment, a broken kite flutters in the tree below. Her small hand reaches toward a blue hydrangea, there are apple blossoms on a tree. She is in a gingham dress, checked brown and orange. And now the wind screams across the sound and we are close, the rain battering the roof. On the smooth old flagstones in the dying sun we face each other golden from the afternoon, in her white shorts she adores me. Pure lady, forgive me everything, even in my fantasies. Shattered heart, the splinters neutralized and swept off in the blood. Until there

287

is no heart at all. Black hair and blacker eye, scintillating Daisy, your violet smile, white teeth. Gentle twilight, gloomy, always gentle twilight as the day gives up. How does such perfection come to pass? And pass. I enter the dream again, terrified and happy. Old song. Deep night. Blue.

Lamont's Scrapbook

How many miles to Babylon?

Approximately as many as from Yonkers to Ebbets Field. (Figure in light years.)

Hast thou named all the birds without a gun?

Jove, yass! Haw-haw-haw! Quite extraordinary! Ripping, I say, bloody super! Great Scott! Zonk! Ka-chow! Bonkers, wot? Cheer-o! A rum go but perishingly clever, eh wot? Deucedly fiendish! Krash! Oh, dear! Bam! Quite! Yass, guv'nor, a large pink gin, easy on the pink, eh wot? Haw-haw! Boom! Ka-chang! Elementary! Bit of all right for the little buggers, eh old chap? By Jove, the whole thing is simply smashing! Zzzip! Quite right, a splash of soda! Eh wot? Neat? Kippers? Pow! Not quite cricket, old man? Quite! Krrrunch! Oh, jolly good, jolly jolly good, haw! Blub! Shall we bugger off? Frightfully decent of the chap to suggest it. Rather! Slam!

What will become of the mice and the rats?

Along with all the pussycats, they'll all be ground to sausage meat in Dunderbeck's machine.

Can anyone explain the wonder of love?

On a beautiful spring evening in 1932, Aphrodite appeared suddenly to three poor and simple fishermen who had just finished a long, disheartening, and luckless day in their small boat some three miles out from Sheepshead Bay. Subtly deshabille in black silk stockings, grey patent leather heels, and a pearl choker, she settled herself comfortably in the stern of the humble craft, and spoke. "Boys," she said, "if any one of you can explain the wonder of love I will give him the pleasure of my company in a swell hotel room for an entire night, box seats for each game of the World Series—in which a Mr. Ruth will perform a fantastic and hardly credible feat—and two tickets to next week's production of something, I forget what just now. Now, shoot!" The first fisherman, a hardy soul whose eyes were bigger than his birdie, spoke right up. "The wonder of love is being apprehended, naked and in an aroused state, in the shower stall of one's enamorata by her suddenly returning husband and replying to his query 'What are *you* doing here?' with the snappy 'Everybody's gotta be someplace.'" "Eighty-six," said the voluptuous goddess, whisperingly crossing her silk-encased gams. The second honest angler hesitantly opined "When the moon makes you feel like you just et scungill'?" "No, no, my good fellow," the glorious immortal gently laughed, for she was the soul of kindness and a good sport into the bargain. The third fisherman, a broth of a lad whose roots plunged deep into the soil of old County Mayo, said, with much embarrassment and furious blushes, for his eyes were fixed on Aphrodite's unbelievable built and were like to bust out his head, "The wonder of love is"—and here he broke wind—"catchin' that and puttin' it in a bottle." At this, the glorious lady gently grasped him by his crotch and together they flew, through the gathering Brooklyn blueness, in the general direction of the Hotel St. George.

Where's the peck of pickled peppers Peter Piper picked?
Waiting on the levee, waiting for the "Robert E. Lee."

Whose heart is aching for breaking each vow?
The heart of First Lieutenant Evelyn Leonard, Women's Army Corps, HQ Co., Fort Lee, Virginia. Lt. Leonard, happily married for four years to Captain Kurt Leonard, Infantry, presently on active duty in Germany, was surprised and embarrassed some two weeks ago when she was discovered early one morning in the shrubbery behind the WAC Officers' Quarters by a routine patrol of two Military Policemen. According to the MP report, Lt. Leonard's blouse was open and the rest of her uniform was "disheveled." She was also in a "compromising position" with a companion, described as a WAC corporal. Lt. Leonard appeared to be inebriated and replied to the MPs' initial questions with "laughter and filthy language." She is presently confined to quarters, and disciplinary action is pending.

Why should we rise, because 'tis light?
A place for everything, and everything in its place.

How are things in Glocca Morra?
Soft, soft, Jayzus, and it's the rain coming down as it does, general all over Ireland, the Emerald Isle, that fell from out of heaven at God's merest whisper, for God is an Irishman, ah, the land of Saint Patrick and the little green snakes and many a foine policeman's ancestors, all, all of them Irish kings, don't you know, and the memory of the mists and dews and bogs and meandering rivers brings a tear to the eye in the New World, even now, of those who cannot possibly know anything of the magic of it except through the blarney of such as Uncle Mark and Cousin Pat and Aunt Mattie, it's indeed a soft day, accent on the "f" if you follow my meaning, and begod and bedad if you don't like the weather you can take your great bone of a frame and use it for what the Good Lord intended, and disgusting it is, that is, to haul yer arse to hell and gone away from this

chosen Eden, now so luxuriant, as when is it not? with various vegetation and low-lying mists and spotted here and there, as a matter of fact, wherever you look, with foine big strapping lads and their blushing colleens and here and there the sweet-smelling Irish cows, begod, with the milk out of them enough to make yer eyes fall out with the joy of the taste of it, and what these young people do be up to in the bushes and holly and gorse and weeds or whatever the Christ (may He forgive me) it all is is nobody's business except that you can be sure that they'll be speaking up on a Saturday and telling of it if it be what is called a mortal sin or even a venial one, to that good shepherd who is in charge of this poor flock of fleshly sinners, I mean, of course, Father Danny O'Driscoll, by God and I remember him when he was the most punishing footballer hereabouts, oh yes indeed, many a back he broke on a Sunday afternoon, faith, he's a remarkable man, the type we call here a black Irishman, may God forgive me if I lie, and He is my judge, he is certainly the strongest man in the county, and handsome and strapping as well, with always a jest and a smile, though he's got a tooth knocked out in the front where a cow kicked him one day when he crept up behind her because she didn't recognize him in his Dublin clothes, all plaids and flowers and the like, and a man he is, whatever they may say of him, the old women hereabouts who have nothing but vile stories for the stranger's ear, full of understanding he is concerning the weaknesses of the flesh, a prince, a king, and if he takes a bit of the malt now and then it's to help him relax and take the damned chill off his bones, by God, only a busybody would begrudge him his taste of the craytur, am I not right? Anyway, things here are wonderful. Right as rain.

What is this thing called love?

Who dares to speak of love or even question its hidden essences when we are surrounded by what many call, if you will pardon the vulgarism, "harsh reality" and its ugly and sordid concomitants? Love alters not at all when it is confronted by other alterations, nor does it bend or vacillate with benders or vacillators. Some think of it as the Northern Star, constant and faithful, totally unlike those excitable orbs of flame that decide, now and again, to rush, pell mell, to the earth, falling, for some reason, on Alabama, more often than not. It cannot be fathomed even though it is a simple thing: a golden ring on a delicate hand, a glittering dime (thin) held gracefully by two fingers in lustrous black kid, it's funny. It's sad. But, unfailingly, it is thought to be beautiful. One may ask the Lord in heaven above about it but He will not deign to answer the question. Except— except through the agency of certain texts, the purport of which seems to be that God Himself is love. Some, however, must think of it as a baseball game on television, glaring lights surrounding, a glass of organic apple juice by the elbow, or on the elbow (or the elbow in the glass). There are misguided souls who find its quintessence in the sight of a large bowl of limp lettuce leaves, floating in seas of olive oil, in which has been crumbled blue cheese; perhaps the gallant fight of the lettuce to assert some of its native flavor symbolizes, for them, the gallantry, the "never-say-die" attitude of sweet Eros. This is what some call a roobric. It is not that the lettuce wins or loses, but that it plays the game, is it not so? Grandma Rice has said this in a lost text entitled, *De Animae Saladae.* And why not? Is it Leo? Libra? Moneyloving Taurus? Sneaky Capricorn? Gentlefolk have found its *quidditas* in the blue crackling of teeny orgones heading merrily and unerringly through the atmosphere toward the (may we be so bold?) genital region. Shall we then laugh at these box-sitters? Is it not possible that they have the secret Word? Why must we snicker and titter, in the "modern" way that we have, at these seekers after truth? Did not the great H.D. Thoreau himself say, "I think that I shall never squeeze a girl as lovely as these trees"? Was he fooling us? There are grave doubts. If its magic spell is everywhere, why do we not then (or do we?) see it, *or* its magic spell? Answer that question and you have given the whale his thumb. Or the monkey? A dog knows of love: observe him. Is it, can it be then, like God Himself (Itself)? I speak, of course, of that inscrutable God who sees in the tidal wave or tornado that destroys the sleeping Okie town the same Beauty that resides in a mother's smile. What of Frau Himmler? There was love in that smile she bent on little Heinrich, "Google Eyes" as he was called in Unschleinchstraasei. Is it a hoodoo that follows one about? Dunno. A pounding in the heart, the small coronary occlusion that gently warns one of the old "dust to dust" routine? Perhaps. It may be the image of a simple and rawboned rube beneath an apple tree in bloom. Call it, then, love in bloom. Some hotblooded rogues maintain that it is nothing more than the sight of a well-endowed young woman in nothing but tiny lace bikinis. Yet what of homosexual gents? They must be served. There are gardens in their faces, too. And if God is love is God then the lass in lacy undies? Or what? Is love, then, the luscious lass? What would Thoreau really have done if into the silence of Walden Pond a willowy gentlewoman had intruded, clad only in these same scanties? Kicked his favorite elm? Rushed toward her, muskrats all forgotten? Perhaps the sun would shine down, as is his want as well as his wont, and smile his sunny smile, for some say that the sun itself is love. There are certain ribald ethnics who maintain that when the moon hits the eye like a big pizza pie—that is love. But can the moon be justly compared with a pizza pie? Lao-Tzu has said: "Quietness is Master of the

Weed." What then? In any event, one may go so far as to say that it is, like Caesar's wife, sweeping the country.

Must business thee from hence remove?
Affirmative. (High time.)

Lamont's Notebook

If "Pearl" was curious and unlike other chapters, what to make of this "Bag of the Blues"? Better as an alternative? The unrequited lover, fits nicely with plot to date.
The chapter wrote itself. A stagy Halpin with bravura rhetoric.

It strikes me that I need *not* substitute "Blues" for "Pearl." I can have this "Blues" come earlier and have the love consummated in "Pearl."
In any event, a tentative rewrite of Chapter One, allowing Halpin to reveal 1.) that he *did* murder Beaumont, and 2.) that he is madly in love with Daisy although she doesn't know it, and 3.) that he murdered Beaumont partly because of this hidden love.
Give it a try?

No word from Roche.

Keep "Fallen Lucifers" as chapter title?

Perhaps "Blues" after Chapter Two? Or make *it* Chapter One! Immediate setting of mood. Better yet, use as Prologue!

The absolutely honest truth about "Blues" is that it frightens me. Only a man losing his grip would talk or write this way . . . but the problem, doctor, is: Is it Halpin or yours truly, A. Lamont, who is falling apart?
It must be preserved if the rest of the MS has to be torn down and built up again.

Same cabin, etc. The two men alone there. Opens with Halpin speaking, Beaumont dead, police on the way, and so on.
Only allude to "rocks" and "branch," etc. Too much yattering.
What catalyst, tiny thing, to set off Halpin's anger and cause the assault?
Business disagreement?
Definitely "Fallen Lucifers."

1. FALLEN LUCIFERS

It is I who have killed my best friend and associate, Ned Beaumont, I and no other, no matter what is said later, by me or anyone else. So I tell myself, so I shall tell the police when they arrive, which should be any moment now, of course.

It depends on the roads.

And—the weather!

The latter has a great deal to do with the condition of the roads hereabouts, up in the woods by the border of Canada. We are not by . . . the sea.

How strange it all seems! How lonely!

I could almost laugh at it all, the craziness of it, the curiously "fey" quality. Almost something from a bad novel or play. Except that Ned Beaumont's *face* is whitely staring up at the ceiling, or almost at the ceiling, more at a point some foot or so beneath the ceiling from where he lies, his rather portly body half slumped over a bookcase where it fell after I put two bullets into him. An awkward pose and one that could lead one to think almost, that he is joshing.

Yet, looking again at the curiously vulnerable body of my old friend, I see now that he is not really portly. *He is not really portly at all!*

I had not planned this murder—you must believe me, whoever you are, patient friend. Yet I can almost see that quizzical look in your eye as you observe me, a rather large, rawboned sort of chap, a Scotch and soda in one hand, a cigarette in one hand, my bulk casually covered by a seersucker suit which is much too light for the chill in the air. Autumn has blown rather suddenly in from Canada, if "blown" is the word.

I confess that I thought of pretending amnesia or feigning on a sudden an attack of dementia praecox to bewilder the police so that I might have time to think! Think! But when I spied Ned Beaumont's sprawled body (in Death as it was in Life) I knew that my breast had to make a clean sweep.

The police are on their way now, over the fear-inducing back roads, many of them mountainous, clearly, that are known to be nerve-shattering even to the strongest nerves. Time's cold chariot clatters along very fast.

Ha!

Yet . . . the harsh bark of my sudden laughter cannot dispel the quick pity I feel for those men rushing, even now, to arrest—a common murderer! I! Martin Halpin!

I am not really a murderer. Surely you will understand the impossible situation into which Fate had wrestled me like a crazed Sumo. Love was its vortex and matrix. Love formed also its cortex. There was some lust involved.

Lust! Mad fleshy desires the spice, that dizzying intoxicating spice that so metamorphosed kindly, dull, Ned Beaumont into a ravening *beast.* With pants to match, I might append jocularly, but the snappy humor dies in my neck.

In a way, I may have pleased him. He had become——

But I see you straining and fidgeting for facts. As if facts could assuage and homogenize your neurasthenic needs, no offense. I can at least tell you some of the things that—happened—this very night. Odd things. "Cute" things. What pawns we are in this absurd jigsaw puzzle that passes for life! What wag said that life is a passed ball?

It is God Himself—no, not the Almighty *He* was it who said that life is a passed ball as I just uttered—who is attempting to complete the puzzle, this curious puzzle. . . . In one corner of which, almost hidden by fens, brakes, copses, glens, bushes, brush, gorse, and furze —one might descry (if one were at, as it were, "God's elbow") a small cabin, curiously like this very one. Beyond the cabin is a lake *torn* maniacally into whitecaps by the wind that shrieks like a banshee or a lost soul from the wastes of Canada as well, of course, as from its more densely populated areas, mostly urban in nature. They are raw cities that people must believe in or die! Thus does Canadian life go. Within, by the light of the flickering flames of a fireplace, fiery framed against a far wall, two men speak, intently, albeit quietly.

So it would appear!

One can almost hear mad laughter, but not quite. Or can it be the wind from the frozen provinces (if such they be) of the Northern savannahs and steppes? Certainly, the men are not laughing but appear as if they have been sucking a lemon, if you can conjure up the image.

Perhaps it is God who laughs! He pauses, hand poised carefully with another piece of the puzzle which He now places exactly. It is an unsettlingly rehearsed gesture, I vow.

And now—now He does laugh! It is rich yet unyielding. It is a chilling gout of laughter!

I seem to see or hear a gun harshly hawking. Also spitting sullen flame, which is where the seeing part comes in. I have committed murder! In the dense thickness, so to speak, and fetching colors of the puzzle, perhaps, there is a clue to my rather unpleasant and quite uncharacteristic attitude. Perhaps . . . and perhaps not!

And perhaps not. I will do my best. Draw your "chair" closer to the fire, trusting friend, while I build it up into a cheerful (odd word so to allow it to rush from my lip!) blaze or so. So! There, so! Try to ignore the dead feet of Ned Beaumont that seem to stare through the strangely shifting shadows like two more or less sinister crustaceans. At the same time be careful not to singe or in any other way injure your *own* feet. So, there, so, good!

The puzzle is becoming clearer. The pieces seem to fit. . . .

Lurid flashes intrude themselves and then fade as I attempt to remember the events of the evening. Ned Beaumont and I had come to this cabin as to a secluded rendezvous. I wanted to chastise him and bring him to his few remaining senses concerning Daisy, the woman who adored him as best she could. I had planned, also, to tell him of my own smoldering love for Daisy, but felt, foolishly, that it would bore him. Yet I intended to expatiate upon it skillfully.

How wretched the twilight was! I remember it with a kind of sad effluvium.

His neglect of Daisy, whose glove he wasn't really good enough to carry! his neglect—please pardon the concussion of odium that burst from me—of her was a cumulative thing, becoming more intense over the past few months, that is . . . since the time the two evil spirits incarnate, Corrie Corriendo and Berthe Delamode, strange and mysterious sluts, placed themselves in positions whereby Ned Beaumont found it meet to "befriend" them. I had planned also to query him closely as to his relationship with these vixenish janes—a relationship that coincided, as you are on the point of guessing, with his congealing love for the nice Mrs. Buchanan. Who, by the by, at this very moment, is in the painful throes of legal divorce from her husband, Tom, an unregenerate tycoon and one of, if I may so impute explicitly, the school of cruder tycoons, that is, a fucking asshole all the way down the line.

How abominable Ned Beaumont's behavior had become may best be illustrated.

I recall . . . I recall . . . a somewhat ludicrous conversation about "rocks" and "branch" having to do with whisky. How tactfully we fenced, falling as rapidly as possible into that morass from whose dread bourne no traveler wends out. It was indeed a veritable swamp. It was, as you are inferring from my tic, semantic difficulties that it was. Yes! I don't deny it. Ned Beaumont purported to be ignorant of the terms "rocks" and "branch" and whatever else we gibbered.

I recall that there were potato chips! How strange. Ned Beaumont and I despised them—yet *Daisy* loved them!

Ned Beaumont absolutely sweated with malice and I attempted to puncture this swollen feeling of pride he had unlikely mantled in with well-barbed shots of reasonable derision, all, I utter now, to no avail. I can remember few details of the conversation, couched as it was in a fetor of vocabulary. All I can recall clearly is the doleful period that was the saturnine KA-CHANGGG!! of the small automatic that I found in my hand. The picture fades. . . .

If it was murder, which I'm telling you it was, it was so thus to save Ned Beaumont from the unremitting evil of the two prurient madames and, to wit also, to save the scatterbrained Daisy from that same evil that had begun to more or less festeringly pullulate in Ned Beaumont's now-scarred soul. . . .

That had begun to . . . putrefact!

And rot also!

How the wind keens! Almost macabre and somewhat . . . chilling. It was keening like this at the moment when the late Ned Beaumont opined, almost uncontrolled in a kind of yeasty rage, "Aha! It's the broads, eh? I might have known. God, Martin, how thoroughly translucent you are! Now I gather why you asked me to the cabin for the weekend. And doesn't it strike you as curious that you should have asked *me?* By God—this is *my* cabin!"

He was right, of course. At that moment it came across my brain that he was not to be permitted to go on living. I moved as if in a trance, in the fierce grippe of some outer power!

I recall a kind of laughter . . . Ned Beaumont reading . . . something. . . .

A flood of light! A waterfall! I was staring at him and suddenly, suddenly it came to me that I was seeing him as if for *the very first time*.

I imagine God scattering the pieces of this hackneyed puzzle to the floor. Who has a better right? No need to answer, good auditor.

Soon—the police will be here.

Ned Beaumont was right. I had invited him to his own cabin, this cabin overlooking a rather cheesy little lake, the demented wind from Canada now chopping it into cream puffs, or creamy puffs. I knew that "things"—if you will pardon the euphonism—that shall be nameless for the nonce, had gone too far between him and his two temptresses, the two goddesses from Méjico and various other fabled European capitals of the world—names, by God, that you know as well as I! At the moment, they were the two toasts of New York—and their fame had arrived as a result of Ned Beaumont's sale of his soul. In a not quite admirable way, his activities (as well as his actions, never fear) had allusions about it that were almost Jamesian. But I diverge. . . .

I had to talk with him, my old and dear friend, the man who had once been dubbed the "Bernard Baruch" of the publishing industry, sometimes known as a "World." How he had scoffed! One last attempt, I thought, over drinks, chess, screeching wind, and the sort, wind that, even now claws at the windows and buffets the house, as must be abundantly clear to you, my patient fellow. Allow me to place this ottoman . . . ? There, so, nice, perfect, are you quite . . . ? Ah. One last attempt, as I declaimed, to make him see reason and to abjure a bit, to return to the arms of Daisy.

You glance askance? Yet, it is *not true* that I planned his slaughter all along, despite. . . .

Yes! I do love Daisy, yet. I did not "plan" his murder. It came about naturally, the police will understand.

What? You are wondering why he came at all? Of course I shall tell you, my friend . . . there, so, your feet on the hob—kick that blasted ottoman out of your way! A cherry brandy, perhaps? No? As you wish. He would, as you will have guessed, not come had he surmised that I was going to, ah, "bust his hump" about the twin tarts who had created out of him their crazed love slave. No—I pretended an interest toward giving him my views anent a translation of *Gypsy Midnight*, Jorge Cabrón's poetic novel about a panoramic canvas of South American family life under a dictator. I had always despised Cabrón, yet I had made this appointment with Ned Beaumont in order to discuss the work. Ned Beaumont was, as always, obsessed with Cabrón's writing and felt it our duty to release it upon a world grown fat with this and that—you know of what I imply, yes?

I remember . . . remember . . . him reading from it and then the hoarse coughing of my automatic, KA-CHANGG! CHOUGHH! Once, twice, three times!

The look on his face, the scattered pages of the manuscript. . . .

And now it suddenly occurs to me like a light bulb suddenly illuminating something that he probably believed, as he breathed his
last, jerking spasmodically on the bookcase over which he slumped
that I had shot him because of the agony that had been mine as I
listened to him roll that Cabrónian treacle off his tongue in dollops
and gobbets.

In a curious way, I see that I have closed the door in the swarthy
face of Cabrón—*Gypsy Midnight* will not be done by us, I mean by
me, now. . . .

In Ned Beaumont's fall (or should I say in the blind staggers that
proved to be a death throe) he knocked a box of matches from the
fireplace mantel to the floor. As you see, they are still there. What a
curious pattern they make! They seem to form a landscape of a dark
and mysterious forest, uncannily like the one Cabrón has lain *Gypsy
Midnight* in. Staring now at that picture (and how odd that it has
certain jigsaw-puzzle-like qualities as I sit here, perhaps myself even
now a part of that jigsaw puzzle that God is working at, one in which
I realize that I have been checkmated, or more exactly, stalemated)
I hear Ned Beaumont's voice reading his beloved Cabrón. I shall hear
it no more. . . .

*. . . the sloe clouds framing her face seen shimmering almost as a
platinum coin in the water dimpled by the trailing green tears of the
lugubrious willow. Why this feeling of the tragic? Is not this that
beloved face in which the fierce rouges of the roses of Valencia vie
for hegemony with the blinding blanks of sere and austere Castile?
Yet those zircons of despair welled in my orbs and dropped their
transparent salts into the jet fluid that unaccountably formed her
image, oh, beaming through slow time as it had once gazed at the last
swollen illuminings of Diana's lamp. Am I not weeping, una-
shamed? Tears falling thick and bitter as the oranges of the passionate South!*

*Yet . . . through my love burns the ravening inferno (withal frigid
as ice and snow) of a lust that shakes my lost soul to its deeps. What
orison will temper its incessant raging heat of a precise conflagration? I say "precise" for it is, so to speak, that exactly, my moods—
wild gauchos!—stampede colorfully through the vast and silent
pampas of my prostrate and debased delights. Can the visage of this
sweet señorita make me once more whole? And still the willow falls
ceaselessly toward the sobbing sheet of ink, that* tinta negra *made in
Nature's factory where beauty alone is the only manufacture, despite
its ofttimes crude and frightening attitude. Such is often the acrid
hilarity of what men call "living"!*

And now that soft exhalation from the mouth of God as he relaxes in the Western sky, warming his great gnarled hands by the russet and vermilion ignition of old Helios' lamp—maker of heat, furnace of heaven, he who comes to joy the tough grasses and move fidgeting digits through the trees' foliage—the willow among them, the willow among them. . . . What futility it all now seems to listen to the barbarous and carnal grunts and fleshly sighs of those two phantom succubi who have purloined my broken organ that pumps, now, only bitter acids! Where have all its tender feelings fled? Yet whence did they come? Yet—futile or no, I hear in the crepuscular chattering of the nocturnal life that stirs in the undergrowth all about me the hiss and simmer of a cauldron of passions—indigo as hell itself!—that bubble and churn their wonted temptations to me. A veritable stew of lust, a soup of pleasures various—unholy goulash! The two of wistful perfidy are dragging me from the glittering face of my inno-cent maiden (God, that it were her true face in the flood and not merely the reflection of my own hellish madness!), dragging, drag-ging me toward their ivory limbs and moist labials encarnadine, their gossamer apparel draped on the arms of various underbrush that seems almost to turn away, ablush.

Dare I go? Yet how unworthy I am to stay. Soft zephyrs from the South whisper to me of the licentious periods of the gods and goddesses in the immortal boudoirs and bordellos of most high Olympus. I cannot—I cannot allow these unbridled thoughts to pollute the grey matter skulking in my sconce, else my adored virgin may somehow catch, through my maniac gaze, a horrendous glimpse, through some dark holy magic, of my filthy ruminations, and know that the two ghostly figures who await me in the prurient forest of mighty cypresses as dark as folly have encaptured me. I am lost!

So from the glassy surface of her face in the slow syrup of the river into which I drop now, without let, great quantities of sodium chlo-ride, that foolish chemical that signals bleak despair, so from it do I wrench my———

I remember then a loud STOP! And then the cruel guffaw of the pistol—KA-BOWW! KRA-BINGG! It had—you must believe me!—appeared in my hand as if by Fate. Or should I say that I suddenly *found* it in my hand?

How the demented wind howls tonight! The fire seems to have lost all its warmth, obviously, since you, gentle listener, have your feet in the flames! I shudder, somehow, shudder and shy away from

300

the shifting and sinister shadows that shake and shimmy on the ceiling. . . .

But will Daisy understand?

I must be brave enough, mad enough, perhaps, to admit that I shot Ned Beaumont for love of her. To the police, I will say nothing. To them, I will read a portion of the Cabrón manuscript.

I see, patient companion, that you stare adroitly through the dancing shadows, a bewilderment playing tricks with your "face." Of course, you will have—*must* have—an explanation. We have plenty of time before the police arrive.

I will tell you everything. Let me start at the beginning and take you back to a brilliant winter afternoon no more than a year ago. How obsidian the pathways of this tragedy!

Picture then, this brilliant winter afternoon. It is January. The sky is a faultless blue. . . .

Lamont's Notebook

An enormous improvement in this "Lucifers." Needs some more work to smooth it out. A verve the earlier version lacks: and it is clear that—

1. Halpin's language attains the strange rhythms and grotesque inconsistencies of the guilty mind.
2. Can *keep* "Blues" since H. makes his secret love for Daisy clear.
3. Now—"Blues" as Chapter One? Or a Prologue?
4. Matches on floor good—the pattern they make; also the way the image works with the chapter title.

Is Halpin insane? What kind of man uses such language? If H. is insane *and* the narrator, then does he here tell the truth? Did he kill Beaumont?

Sheila at it again. Merciless.

Sheila:

I am returning to you the clipping you so thoughtfully sent me of the *Bookwatchers PreViews* review of *The Red Swan,* sure that you will find some clod of the arts whom it will impress. I am thoroughly aware of your motives in sending it to *me;* shabby motives, indeed.

You know, backward and forward, my opinion of Dermot's foul trashy book; it has not changed for years. No slick, chatty review by one of the whores of *BP* will change that opinion! And you are aware that *BP* considers only those books that have commercial possibilities or that have a "freak" value, i.e., to have one's book reviewed in *BP*'s pages is more or less an insult to a serious writer—of course, it will not be insulting to your spouse.

If you had some idea that Dermot's "good luck" (what a ridiculous phrase!) with his trash can would fill me with envy, you are wrong. I am only ashamed and embarrassed that my sister has so lost her critical honesty that the prospect of large sales and notoriety for such a ratty performance should fill *her* with unabashed delight!

Can this be the same girl who used to weep over Melville's life? How sad!

Your brother,
Tony

302

THE RED SWAN *by Dermot Trellis. Introduction by Vance Whitestone*. Three Ring Books. $8.95

A decade ago, *The Red Swan* was the object of intense coterie adulation in the genteelly flushed *sub rosa* world of "literate" pornography. Ignored by most readers under its original title, it began to pick
up a knowledgeable and fanatically loyal audience under the new
title chosen for it by its paperback publisher, *Peculiar Person*. As the
latter, it reigned supreme, the Mt. Everest of the naughty novel, and
was snapped up by the weirdo set, who, rumor has it, used it as a
bedroom Baedecker. Although just two years ago copies of the out-of-
print hard-cover heavyweight were reportedly selling for as high as
$50 each, it received little or no critical attention. However, a few
critics saw in it more than just the usual "grunt and sigh" routines
ad nauseam—one of them, Wiley Boote, remarking that it was "the
first modern novel to describe the sexual act as a kind of physiological
anomie."

Anomie or no, the past year has been kind to *The Red Swan* and
its rather whimsically shy author, Dermot Trellis. Discerning pundits
of the *literati* have taken it to their bosoms with a peculiar avidity,
and profess to see in the steamy opus a profound investigation of the
purplish twilight world that the deviate is delightedly forced to
writhe and wallow in. Now, Three Ring Press, the publisher of such
other landmarks in erotica as *Prudence's Poon* and *Beat My Pumpkin*
has brought out a handsome new edition of the blazing trailblazer
with a cogent and persuasive introduction by Vance Whitestone, in
which the veteran bookman unashamedly pleads for the book's considerable artistic merits.

His candidly partisan remarks prove to be persuasive. While there
are scenes of sexual intrigue and depthless abandon unmatched since
those penned by the Divine Marquis, there are also strange, almost
hallucinatory after-images of ringing depth and translucent beauty
almost moral in their tone. One reads as if through a film of black
nylon and lavender lace and the bluntly provocative descriptions are
bizarrely tempered by a real *feeling* for humankind.

Unlike anything published for many a season, Trellis's libido-
caresser should certainly command a wide readership this time
around, and deservedly so. Sluiced through with mystery, fingered
by ineluctable evil, and hovering queerly on the edge of the deliciously unspeakable, *The Red Swan* proves—at least to this reader
—that pornography can be as delicately and finely made as the
most exquisite Parisian lingerie and still possess the ability to make

the juices flow and the breath come quicker. *Highly Recommended.*

—Z.J.

Halpin's Journal

Ned has never been closer to absolute despair. I haven't a leg to stand on when it comes to arguments about his staying.

More when this depression allows.

"You, gentle listener, have your feet in the flames!" My God Almighty!

My dear Baroness D'Lenox:

It was no small shock and surprise to hear from you after all these years! It's been such a long time and your letter sent terrifying memories literally *stumbling* through my head, now rather a grey one I'm afraid. Of course I remember those "gay and glorious" days when you reigned supreme as the undisputed Queen of the Literary World with its cohorts of free-loaders and swarming dilettantes. Can I ever forget the creamed tuna and minute rice that graced your buffet table?—absolutely a culinary dream! And the wonderful noodles! And the exciting olives! And what sort of squalid caitiff would I be had I forgotten the long talks I had with your father-in-law about the bedspread business? You must think me a churl to suggest, even gently, that these things have not been paramount in my mind this past—decade, is it? Your patronage of young artists and similarities living or dead was (and still is, if that "little bird" is not telling a fib) a blazing testament to the salutary ways in which money earned in the most vulgar and degrading vocations can be put to use. It is no small thing to heap high the plate of a young bard with tuna glop! You ask—as surely you would!—about the "old bunch." You always had a way with a phrase! I don't see much of them anymore, but I would imagine that it is safe to say that they are no longer in communication with the Muses. That is not to say (from what I hear) that they are not presently leading rich, warm, exciting, and thoroughly fulfilling creative lives! Oh no! Lou Henry, who caused a minor sensation with that shitheel poem of his that you had a hand in publishing, "Sheila Sleeping," his paean to his wife, the celebrated whore, is, if rumor is correct, off somewhere in Canada, where he purportedly teaches an honors seminar on Canadian influences in the novels of Ronald Firbank— surely hard and useful work, God knows. Ironically enough, the famous Sheila, as far as I can determine, has undergone a sex-change operation at the new Sexual Medicine Center in Salt Lake City, and now calls herself Drowsie. She was always droll! This brave and fearless "man" who confronted the fact that she wanted nothing so much as a wee-wee has wed Bart Kahane, the painter lately turned gay ecologist. Did you see the recent article about him in *Fruit's Salad?* He is in Southern California crusading for public support for a shelter to house homosexual dogs, who apparently have their share of troubles too. Who else? The mists obscure so many. Ah, yes! Leo Kaufman! Leo writes a column for an underground newspaper under the monicker "Leon Lion." I don't read it regularly, but I've been told it has to do mostly with down-to-earth wisdom and includes an affectionate survey of "what's new" in the marital arts. I have it on good authority that he no longer speaks to Davis Richards since the publication of Davy's last novel, *Pictures On The Screen.* It seems that Leo took offense at what he thought to be Davy's malign portrait of him as a down-at-heels garbage buff turned apple fancier. Ah, we grow old, we grow old.

Who the goddam fuck else? Guy Lewis has apparently disappeared but one school of thought has it that he's simply changed his name again. His ex-wife, Bunny—you might have known her as Joanne— has a rotten marriage going with a young multimillionaire, the man, in fact, who invented vodka. She has recently bought seven or eight blocks of the Lower East Side and is shipping them to Taos where they will be permanently installed as an "Environment." And who else? Have I forgotten any of the old warm persons? Oh yes! Dick Detective has devoted himself to writing unintelligible post cards and Anton Harley is somewhere in New England attempting to breed half-ton pigs for personal consumption. You may have heard of his recent operation in which a team of surgeons worked seven hours to remove nineteen Sicilian pizzas and a galvanized iron sink from his stomach. I would imagine that that's about it for the "old bunch."

Now, as to the "gist" of your letter, the "nugget" as you phrase it —again so aptly! Do you remember Leo Kaufman telling you that you would have made a great writer? How you laughed and blushed as you locked up the whisky! Your information about my being an editor is wholly incorrect. I have always thought that editors are on a par with sink installers, pig raisers, and bedspread manufacturers —noble callings all, yet and yet, *I* am not an editor. Nor did I "always want to be" an editor. You speak, if you will forgive my fleeting crassness, like a baroness with a paper asshole, i.e., you are full of shit.

I don't know what "photograph" you saw in what "trade journal" but it was most assuredly not of me! I do not have a "beard" nor do I "look like a weirdo." Speaking of weirdos, does your husband still wear his ass at knee level or has modern medicine corrected this minor flaw of his otherwise Apollonian physique? I remember him as a warm, witty, and stupidly opinionated man, not the sort one would expect to be the hard-driving president of Rent-a-Hat, and I was deeply chagrined to learn of the massive dose of "bull clap" that he contracted from the commode in the Café Blague. It is true that the rich have a cross to bear that we lesser souls can never know! I hasten to add, however, that I was delighted to hear of your impish conduct before a window display of French ticklers in Moscow! *That's* breaking down the old barriers between East and West!

But I am avoiding the "nugget" of your letter. I am afraid that I have neither the skill nor the time to "go through and smooth out" the paper on mathematics by your brother-in-law, Morton. By the way, isn't Morton the one who used to gnaw on the maid's shoes at your monthly *soirées?* I must say that your offer of $50 for my "trouble" is breathtakingly generous, but I simply must refuse. Even had I the essential expertise to perform such a task, the subject matter is far beyond my poor understanding, that is, I don't even comprehend the motherfucking piece of shit! But I thank you from the bottom of my heart for your offered largesse. I understand why you would want to throw such a sum my way—it is an old *mot* but one nevertheless true that women who wear steel girdles are generous to a fault.

I notice that you have sent me a xerox copy of this wondrous bullshit *sans* a stamped, self-addressed envelope enclosed, so I assume that you want me to keep the fucker for a souvenir. Your heart grows as large as your ass used to be! The world, my dear Baroness, needs more like you, and you can bet that vast keester of yours on it!

How wonderful that you will soon be journeying to Albania to bring back some superintendents! Perhaps you may find one who can learn to mix a reasonable fucking drink!

In the meantime, my warmest wishes to you and to your "hubby." Tell him, for God's sake, to stay out of the men's rooms of French restaurants! While they certainly know how to cook, all the world is aware that they invented the Old Joe and all his friends.

It certainly was warm and intelligent hearing from you!

Your old friend,
"The Editor"
Tony Lamont

P.S. You are correct in guessing that I have given up "fictioneering." It seems thoroughly irrelevant in today's world. I spend much of my time shouting at California table grapes and flogging the old meateroo. If your little legs can still carry you up six flights, why don't you come to see me? We'll have a glass of muscatel together and spit from the windows on the warm and irrepressible minorities and ethnics on the street below as they go about their daily tasks of filling the neighborhood with joyous shouts, spicy odors, and felonies. Make sure you wear your cute support hose and the natives will think you are a Welfare investigator or a mailman and allow you to pass unmolested.

RECENT STUDIES IN CONTRAVARIANT BEHAVIOR PROCESSES IN COMPLEX RESOLUTIONS
by Morton D'Ovington, Ph.D.

In recent years, researchers in the field of pure or abstract mathematics have become increasingly interested in complex resolutions[1] in terms of map and homotope functions in many disparate equations. This paper is intended to serve as a modest demonstration[2] of the possibilities of these functions as methodologies possibly useful to the disciplines necessary in the fields of both mathematics and projectile physics. While these methodologies are not herein presented as absolute, they point a way toward certain definitions that can be proved in so far as they are expedient. That is, a tentative attempt will here be made to clarify the recent epistemologies suggested by divagation and contravariant processes.[3]

First of all, we must accept as a working premise the idea that A is a complex, i.e., we must let A be a complex. Then, A left double complex x over A consists of a double complex x such that $x^9 = 0$ for $9 > 0$, and of an augmentation map: $x \rightarrow A$.[4] It seems clear then that the augmentation is actually given by the map $x^{*,0} \rightarrow A$ such that the composition $x^{*-1} \rightarrow x^{*,0} \rightarrow A$ is zero.[5] On a more practical and perhaps more simply demonstrable level, we may let A (as a map), B, and C represent three[6] men seated around a table.[7] On the precarious assumption that another integral function, D, may be able to assume a "collaborative control"[8] over their *absolute* functions, we may call D another man, but one who exerts a commanding presence[9] over the other men (A, B, C). D blindfolds the men and places a hat on the head of each $(D \frac{h}{A}, \frac{h}{B}, \frac{h}{C})$.[10] He then informs each man that his hat is either red[11] or blue.[12] We will say that x is a projective resolution of the complex D if for all $h, (1)$-(6) are projective resolutions.[13] If they are not, we will not say so. D informs A, B, C that he

---

1 The very name evokes strange and wonderful visions. But maybe your dreams are of Marrakech.
2 Occasionally you have to hone it on the back of a china plate.
3 Prismatic reflections double, but reverse, each image.
4 A dab is enough to support a two-ton car.
5 This is not a religious doctrine.
6 Why stop at just one?
7 The result is beautiful in any light.
8 Like the vibrator in a favorite motel.
9 Unspoiled. Unhurried. Uncommon.
10 Proving the shortest distance between extraordinary comfort and aesthetic excellence is not bridged by a straight line.
11 Pink has lost its innocence.
12 A "must" for today's contemporary look.
13 Most provocative!

will remove the blindfolds[14] simultaneously and that each man who sees a *red* hat on either or both of the others is to raise a hand $(h\frac{h}{(a)})$. However, as soon as he can determine the color of his *own* hat, he is to lower his hand and explain the logic behind his determination $(h\text{-}\frac{h}{a})$. Assuming that A,B,C comply, each performs according to the various rules of homotopy[15] and raises his hand. Soon one of them *(C)*, who had seen red hats on both A and B, drops his hand.[16] D assumes that C knows the color of his own hat but is chagrined to discover that the hat has seemingly disappeared from his head $(CH\rightarrow)$ and is now lodged firmly on his own $(\frac{h}{D})$.[17] At this, both A and B begin to act erratically, trading hats back and forth and spasmodically jerking. D finds it hard to "control" the activities of the men[18] and the meeting degenerates[19] into a tactless shambles. We may see in this mundane example how exactly $A\rightarrow$ zero.[20]

Our small scenario may be performed in various ways, the most often employed being the one furnished in 1924 by Dr. Beppo Durk[21] of the Institute for Hydraulic Physics. The reader may recall that Dr. Durk employed A in his example as a deranged woman[22] who spent her life sawing logs at various speeds, so that no matter how fast B or C sawed, she would always saw faster.[23] The classic example is found in Durk's "Irresolution Complexes in Map Studies" (1924); in it, the woman *(A)* saws logs with such proficiency and mindless devotion[24] that her sawing speed surpasses the speed of light, after which, as Dr. Durk says, "$A\rightarrow$ zero, no matter its homo topic pretensions toward isomorphic naturalness," a conclusion[25] that heralded a breakthrough in the abstract study of projective resolutions and isomorphic projectiles.

There is, of course, a very strong possibility that Dr. Durk would have altered or improved his famous woman[26] had he realized at the time that a particulate isomorph, such as A has recently proven to be, cannot saw logs at such speeds and remain in the same location, i.e., as the speed of light is approached by greater than half $(\frac{1}{2}(s/)A)$,

---

14 And the sensuous feeling is flagrantly feminine.
15 A handy helper during tax time.
16 An example of his sheer genius.
17 Ultra chic? Yes!
18 They have seats of genuine cane.
19 With a devilish smile and a pitchfork.
20 See the brighter middle trim?
21 He suffered from painful elimination.
22 A pleated vamp.
23 An ebullience throughout.
24 New Jersey's reception made all these special efforts worthwhile.
25 Just wipe it clean with a sponge.
26 Kept in perpetual pleasure by the new sliding sky dome.

the isomorph becomes, in effect, a *contravariant* and has forced upon it two alternatives;[27] it must reduce sawing speed if it wishes to remain in the same place, thereby permitting B and C to equal its efficiency, or it must swiftly disappear, logs and all, into the electron field that such great velocity enjoys. The latter occurrence enables B and C to surpass A's speeds and efficiency, since A, in this case, no longer exists, having been absorbed into an electron field rich in what we now think to be quasar detritus.[28] We may formulate this as:

$$[B+C+(-sl) < \rightarrow (A \cdot O) = O]$$

It cannot be insisted upon too strongly at this point that a second differentiation may be extrapolated from the lost energy vector of the unfortunate A, that is, that A maintains the fantastic and bewildering speed that ultimately eliminates it. The energy vector, as formulated by Dr. Reuben Pavolites[29] in his work on doubly graded modules[30] does not perform characteristically when the speed of light (while sawing logs) is exceeded. Instead, although A vanishes, its energy vector does not, and, as a matter of fact, insists on its own hegemony as a process[31] of individuation. In this role it is known as $A\pi$.[32] This factor $(A\pi)$, while merely the factor that is sloughed off in the enormous heat generated during the disappearance of A, becomes, when left to its own devices, a material that acts exactly as does the vanished A. In shape, color, size, weight, and motor qualities, $A\pi$ cannot be told apart from A. What is even more important in so far as the isolation of homotopic maps is concerned, it can, while sawing logs, not only exceed the speed of light at will, but it can engender a particular plus-minus[33] electron field about it, so that B and C may also exceed the speed of light; however, B and C may never "catch up" to $A\pi$.

Dr. Durk found, however, in his explorations on the behavior of $A\pi$ in situations unlike that of sawing logs, that it behaves erratically,[34] not to say poorly, so poorly that it often breaks down into those components that Durk has called "environmental failure shards." In a simple but lucid example we see what happens to $A\pi$ (as well as to B and C) when it is confronted with activities far

---

27 The crescent print. The spade design.
28 To you it's fruit!
29. A vengeful Greek tycoon.
30 Spray them all through the house.
31 Insertion, withdrawal and disposal are comfortable, easy and discreet.
32 A real treat for lemon lovers.
33 This perky little two-piecer never peters out.
34 The charm of the Italian crew.

310

removed from its wonted log-sawing. In this scenario[35] $A\pi$ is considered to be a turtle that starts off from a point in space toward another point in space;[36] one integer behind it B is started a moment later and an integer behind B, C is started—again, a moment later. (B and C are usually considered, in this example, as rabbits, but mules, wolves, or horses[37] may also be used.) According to the Achillean Law[38] first propounded by Cystitis, the turtle, no matter how slowly it travels, cannot be overtaken by the pursuing fleeter animals. He is always ahead of them no matter their speed. Why this should be so is a sublime mathematical mystery.[39] However, when the turtle is thought of as $A\pi$, and the rabbits as B and C, the turtle simply stops and begins to disintegrate[40] after a very few moments. B and C thereafter become motionless and a force field that gives off a strong odor of hydrochloric acid is created, much as galaxies[41] tend to behave upon the advent of a "dead star" eclipse.

Dr. Durk has never been able to explain exactly what happens in this particular scenario, but he has written that it seems that $A\pi$ has metamorphosed itself into an acyclic left complex, after which it disintegrates. Oddly enough, it is often resynthesized by natural means, after which it has all the properties of A again. At this, it usually begins sawing logs at the speed of light and then vanishes for good. During the moment or two when it $(A\pi)$ is an acyclic left complex, it acts in an oddly resolute[42] manner, which Dr. Durk has formulated

$$S^{n-1}T(A\pi) \rightarrow S^nT(A\pi) \rightarrow S^nT(A\pi) \rightarrow etc.$$

It is, of course, acting in a commutable way, except that it refuses to "trade" atomic structures with B or C. There is a possibility that $A\pi$, during the flash[43] of time in which it hovers between its forward motion and its initial steps toward disintegration, "thinks" of itself as a turtle and refuses to react in those ways natural to an energy vector. The possibility can tentatively be formulated thus: $\rightarrow S^nT(A\pi) \rightarrow (A\pi)$ TS^n. This theory, if such it be, becomes viable when it is discovered that the hydraulic kinesis formula[44] for the forward movement of a

---

35 Dream comes in color.
36 Heading for warmer climes?
37 But what about your dog?
38 An ingenious cover-up for yellow pad and portable papers.
39 Because love is beautiful?
40 A hint of smouldering enticement.
41 Authentic replicas of millionaire row homes made into a planter.
42 All clean crisp crackle!
43 Light where you need it most.
44 Balloons+lollipops+burgers.

turtle is expressed as $Ts \to Ts \to Ts \to Ts$. It may be objected that this formula applies only to the kinetic energy expended by the turtle's legs and not its entire body, but for our present purposes the formula will do nicely. (However, we must acknowledge that if we choose to compare turtle motion with energy vector in an *absolute* environment,[45] this formula must be superseded by the one propounded by Dr. Sanders Kupferberg[46] in his studies on the behavior of lost energy particles in an electronically deprived vacuum, to wit: $Ts(1) \to Ts(1) \to Ts(1)$.

Unfortunately, none of these theories and discoveries are of significant moment when one is confronted by the knotty problems posed by the behavior of A left double complex x over A when $x^9 = 0$ for $9 < 0$. It has been argued that if the projective resolution $(A + A'[f:A \to A'])$ is a homomorphism[47] then a map does indeed exist (at that moment.) But does A left double complex x over A then exist tangentially, and, more importantly, is it a viable formula in its own terms?[48] Interesting experimental work has been performed in order to demonstrate the possibilities suggested here, perhaps the best known being that of Professor Alexander Brandi[49] of the C.C. Coleman Institute for Studies in Velocity Mathematics. In his paper "Toward a Theory of Left Double Complex Behavior" (1959),[50] Prof. Brandi poses a fascinating hypothetical problem. For the maps he imagines three[51] cannibals and for their companions (the homotopes) three missionaries. They are traveling together through a jungle and reach a stream which can only be crossed by means of a boat[52] (the contravariant). However, the boat can only hold two men. Each of the missionaries knows how to row but two of the cannibals do not. Moreover, at no time would the missionaries permit a situation to occur in which some of them would be alone[53] with a greater number of cannibals. Prof. Brandi then states the problem: How did all manage to get across? He states the expression

$$3(x-o)+3(h+o)+B \to [3(x-o)+3(h+o)]+B[\beta^3]=?$$

---

45 A moonlit night on the Crillon.
46 A devastating aura of flirtation matches his infinite generosity of spirit.
47 This funny-looking hose thing waters plants.
48 Certainly it provides a unique fine-textured surface.
49 A star in a family of fine hams.
50 An era when all the girls were pretty and all the men were strong.
51 Three's not a crowd when they're interchangeable parts.
52 Dan River runs deep.
53 Rectal itching makes you *feel* so alone.

312

This expression has been rightly praised for its breathtaking elegance and simplicity, but Brandi's solution is even more sublime.[54] With an eye to the work done in the field of fusion transferral by E. Coli, Brandi ruthlessly and with great brilliance cuts through the myriad steps needed to make both maps and homotopes viable in terms of the "busy" contravariant that seemingly must remain constant throughout whatever permutations occur in the expression, and gives us this solution, one which has yet to be excelled and which has come to be considered by all specialists[55] in the field of complex resolutions as the foundation of all future explorations. The formula (of which only the final steps are here given) is pristine.[56]

$$3(\tfrac{rh}{x-o}) + 3(\tfrac{bh}{h+o}) \cdot \sqrt[\nu]{B[\beta]} \to [\sqrt[\nu]{B[\beta]}] - rh(bh) = 3(x-o)3(h+o)$$

In other words, in terms of the pungent scenario that Brandi has invented, the missionaries don red hats, the cannibals don blue hats,[57] and all simultaneously plunge into the stream, the boat towed behind them. In midstream the boat sinks and the missionaries and cannibals emerge from the water, *minus* their hats![58] In pure mathematical terms, Brandi has propounded a startling and pioneering theory concerning the behavior of maps and homotopes. In his realization that the contravariant in such formulae acts not as a support but a deterrent to resolution and solution,[59] Brandi substitutes (for its long-supposed supportive qualities) three isomorphic gradients and three acyclic gradients, intuitively grasping[60] that their historically "ornamental"[61] function in most resolution formulae was considered such only because their ability to sustain the mathematical life of both maps and homotopes was not appreciated. In effect, isomorphic and acyclic gradients, according to Brandi, are integral to the life of both maps and homotopes in terms of their successful transposition into viable elements of an A left double complex x over A! Brandi has reduced this theory to a formula as well-known to abstract vector mathematics as the one for the isolation of lumbagorithms in secant force fields $(L\pi r^4)$; to wit:

---

54 Any way you look at it, it's bountiful.
55 Chairs that just sit there looking great.
56 You'd think it came from a French bakery.
57 Look what they found in the swimwear department!
58 The glamour! The wit! The outrageous charm!
59 Something to be sipped and savored.
60 Wherever he puts his hand it picks up dirt, lint, and crumbs.
61 Just look at those lovely chinas with curio glass sides.

313

$$\frac{rh+bh}{(x-o+h+o)}=(x-o+h+o)$$

It will be noted that in the transposition that successfully occurs within the formula whereby the maps and homotopes are enabled to cross over and retain their integrity,[62] both isomorphic and acyclic gradients are lost, but *not until* the contravariant has been negated. With this formula, Brandi laid[63] the groundwork for all subsequent work done in the area of complex resolutions; indeed, Brandi has been not unjustly called "the father of gradients"[64] because of his faith in their mathematical efficiency in certain transpositional problems.

In the years since Brandi developed his breakthrough theory, many researchers have attempted to employ it as a key to understanding the mixed problems[65] posed by the negation of the contravariant in such transpositions. Brandi posited its "disappearance" thus:$[\sqrt[v]{B[\beta]}\,]$. While this assumption is tactically and experimentally sound in terms of the movement of both map and homotope, it has become clear[66] that it disappears only in so far as the transposition itself is concerned. It continues to exist, however, if we attempt to employ the formula in reverse, i.e., if we desire to cross the maps and homotopes back again with or without the factor *rh(bh)*. The most recent findings seem to point to the contravariant's curious mutation[67] (within the formulae posited) into a phenomenon which has long been familiar, that is $(\frac{1}{2}(sl)A)$. Clearly, the contravariant in the reversal mechanism of transposition has become a source and vector of the energy expended in kinetic activities greater than half the speed of light. As Dr. Marcus Casey[68] has rather impishly but accurately put it in the *Journal of Mechanistic Solutions* (January 1969, Vol. III, No. 11), "the famous Brandian 'boat' has been mysteriously changed—in midstream[69] as it were—into Durk's fiendishly industrious log-sawing woman." Although Casey has yet to demonstrate a satisfactorily cogent formula whereby the woman *(A)* may be extrapolated from the clearly perceived energy expended by what was initially a negated contravariant $(\frac{1}{2}(sl)A)$, he argues rather convincingly that the only factor known to the field of complex resolutions

---

62 To combat today's skin discouragers.
63 A definite urge to make women (and the gentlemen they run with) as happy as larks!
64 If you're getting married, write for illustrated booklet.
65 A mélange of pink bouquets.
66 With pale shades of sparkling excitement.
67 Tango dancers reminiscent of a past era.
68 An English muffin-breaker.
69 Why does the once-powerful Colorado River now disappear?

capable of attaining speeds even approaching this is the woman *(A)* in the act of sawing logs. (Dr. Casey admits that other factors *(B,C,D,E, et al.)*[70] employed in certain equations dealing with actual expenditure[71] and creation of energy by A also attain to these speeds, *but only* when A does, and they can never equal or surpass A's speed. He writes "thus, we may fairly state that the efficiency of all other factors in terms of attained speed is determined by the kinetic, not the potential presence of A.")

Some of Brandi's contemporaries, while agreeing with the efficiency of his Principle of Map and Homotope Crossover, found it difficult to accept[72] his insistence on the negated contravariant. Instead, they chose to express the crossover thus

$$3\frac{rh}{(x-o)} + 3\frac{bh}{(h+o)}\sqrt[v]{R[\beta]} \rightarrow -rh(bh) = 3(x-o)3(h+o) + \sqrt[v]{B[\beta]}$$

seeing in the negated contravariant only a momentary isotropism that is rectified upon the completion of the successful crossover.

However, Brandi's view was vindicated by the independent studies of Lafoch,[73] who, in 1962, while engaged in a study of the flow of heat and electricity within three-dimensional conductors, satisfied the demands of his problems by discovering what has come to be known as the "flow of incomprehensible fluid." Simply stated, Lafoch considered the flow of an incomprehensible fluid as being constrained to move between two parallel planes,[74] the particles[75] which lie in any line perpendicular to the planes at any moment always remaining in that line. His theory was that "every analytic function of a complex resolution defines a steady flow of energy, electricity, or incomprehensible fluid; the converse also holds true." His condition, that $Pdx + Qdy$ be an exact differential, namely, $\frac{\Delta P}{\Delta y} = \frac{\Delta Q}{\Delta x}$ allowed him to reach an equation (Lafoch's Equation) as follows

$$P\Delta x + Q\Delta y \rightarrow \frac{3(x-o)3(h+o)}{\sqrt[v]{B[\beta]}} = 3(x-o)3(h+o)$$

In effect, Lafoch proves that the contravariant in his equation, when taken over the complete boundary[76] of said equation, not only vanishes, but vanishes so that the map and homotope exist integrally and wholly as harmonic functions.

---

70 This chain of red candle balls strung together like a string of pearls.
71 *Making* money is still mighty important!
72 The critics sneered: Window-dressing! Smokescreen! Pipe-dream!
73 He watched the Place de la Concorde at dawn while sipping Dom Perignon.
74 Eliminates embarrassing stains on clothing.
75 With the edges all bitten away like the tenderest leaf lettuce.
76 A deeply cut, boldly edged monogram.

The ramifications of this discovery have been of enormous importance in the entire field[77] of complex resolution studies. Not only was Brandi's work shown to be absolutely correct[78] in its steps concerning map and homotope transpositions, Lafoch unwittingly directed future researchers toward an understanding of contravariant negation (or vanishing) not only in the crossover itself, but *in the reverse crossover.*[79] That is, the reappearance[80] of the contravariant as the A traveling at just over half the speed of light was seen to be an analogue to its disappearance[81] as an integral part of the flow of incomprehensible fluid. It was only a short step to the *integral transcendental series* function of *A,* at which point Dr. William Bailey[82] of the Feintuthe-Combë Institute developed Bailey's Series Theorem, which attempted to give a proof of the existence of the elliptic modular and the automorphic functions *within* the homotope-map transposition, thereby conjoining the speed and direction of this crossover (and subsequent disappearance of the contravariant) with the speed of the woman[83] sawing logs.

In a paper that is the very model of scholarly perspicuity and dry[84] levity, "Investigations of Integral Transcendence of Elliptic Modular and Automorphic Functions in Map and Homotope Transitions" (1963), Dr. Bailey sets forth his theorem.[85] In part, he writes, ". . . the contravariant may be considered as the turtle of the classic Achillean Law, that is, no matter how fast the maps and homotopes travel[86] they cannot ever equal the position of the rapidly vanishing contravariant and, as a matter of fact, defeat themselves the faster they move, since the greater their speed, the more swiftly does the contravariant disappear." He continues, ". . . so that at the moment of reverse transposition, what was a simple contravariant has become, for the purposes of complex resolutions within the boundaries of integral transference, not only an automorphic acyclic left complex $(\frac{T\Delta}{A\pi})$ but also the energy vortex that produces speeds approaching (and capable of exceeding) that of light itself, that is, it has become A. The reappearance of this contravariant in the process of reverse transposition as a gradient homotope capable of developing energies from its 'memory' of turtle life—a pure example of potential into

---

77 The *yellow* field: with lollipop trees and sunshine print.
78 Women proved it in a taste test.
79 Everything came up roses and crystal and gilt!
80 A vintage face.
81 One look at the lock and you know it's so.
82 A renowned statesman, decorated war hero and great American.
83 She conked out, but her hair held up.
84 For richness without a greasy feel.
85 His starkly simple face made a dramatic foil for a very personal message.
86 From wedding veils to bull whips.

kinetic energy force 'bursts' (*vide* Lafoch's Equation)—is explicable only if we consider it as a manifestation[87] of A as an acyclic left complex. More simply, and perhaps facetiously,[88] the 'boat' becomes a woman sawing logs at blinding speed. But we must remember that the 'boat' was *always* the Achillean turtle."

The implications of these various studies are particularly compelling in the light of contemporary opinion as to the validity of the summing of infinite series. Since there is general agreement that an infinite series can be summed,[89] we must admit the possibility of contravariant crossover in such summation. In the well-known puzzle concerning the two cyclists[90] who race toward each other at identical speeds while a fly[91] moves between them from handlebar to handlebar,[92] we have presented to us a classic problem in infinite series equations. Plainly

$$V = L\Sigma f(x,y)\Delta R = \int f(x,y)dR$$

However, the equation is valid only if we assign no extremes to R and conceive of it as a mechanical kinesis lacking the ability or desire to mutate, i.e., become a contravariant. In adhering to this concept of planar mass,[93] the fly acts as a velocity expenditure, nothing more. On this point, Dr. Luba Checks[94] of the Oyster Bay Institute, speaks directly in her "Possibilities of Invisible Contravariants in Infinite Series" (1963). Dr. Checks writes: "While the terms ΔR and dR seem clear in their suggestions, i.e., that it is a fly and only a fly that appears and reappears over and again on the cyclists' handlebars, the equation does not take into account the very definite possibility that the fly (f) at midpoint in space and time mutates into a complex limiting ratio of and by itself. I suggest

$$V = L\Sigma f(x,y)\Delta R(\sqrt{y}\,\overline{B[\beta]}) = \int f(x,y)dR$$

which expression functions almost like a Jacobian and which seems to point clearly to the probability of f at its invisible (to the cyclists) map ratio point or *region*[95] becoming a wholly inte-

---

87 Now it's that touch of lace!
88 Fun is a weapon against tooth decay.
89 Miraculous machines help minimize the problems.
90 They'll possibly rent their antique-filled villa during the summer months.
91 Green enamel with yellow smily face.
92 And finally to an evening at the ballet in Moscow.
93 Sculpture is masculine burly glass.
94 She tried her hand at bartending.
95 Germany, which has a long history of petroleum difficulties.

grated contravariant—in this case, a boat."

The publication of Dr. Checks's paper caused a controversy[96] that to this day shows no signs of abating. If her remarkable expression is correct (that is, if the introduction of the splendid $\sqrt{B[\beta]}$ is a legitimate application of Brandi's Formula), the entire problem of summing an infinite series must be re-examined in so far as complex resolutions are concerned. Surely, the theory of contravariant emanation can be seen as a contribution to the perplexing behavior[97] of left double complexes, although Revolutes, Complanations, and Eulerians[98] are omitted from her researches. The reasons for this are clear;[99] however, we must ask in default of Geometry,[100] when does Σ approach the *same* limit independently of the function-value chosen for each ΔR and the way in which each $\Delta R = o$, as their number $= \infty$? Answer: When $\Sigma Dk \Delta Rk = o$ as each $\Delta Rk = o, Dk$ being the greatest fluctuation in function-value. When is this the case? Answer: (1) When $f(x,y)$ is continuous throughout R: (2) When f at single points or on single lines becomes finitely discontinuous or indeterminate or oscillatory: (3) When f becomes a contravariant along an ∞ of lines *if only* the sum of the elements is itself infinitesimal. In other words, these changes occur when f (while invisible)[101] undergoes the transformation (during its planar mass fluctuation) into a boat, *no matter how briefly* it may "enjoy" this state. The introduction of Revolutes, Complanations, and Eulerians into these formulae would be gratuitous and irrelevant unless a boat were the energy vector in the first place, in which case its impingement as a homotopic mass upon the handlebars of both bicycles would effectuate a situation more open to explanation by the application of the equations and processes of Weierstrasse.[102]

We begin now to see the almost mysterious power that the contravariant exerts when used in those equations and expressions thought, not so many years ago, to be, as it were, sealed into themselves.[103] The transposition of the contravariant factor, both primal and reverse, offers possibilities in the studies of complex resolutions that are endless; certainly, the contravariant metamorphosis in the basic study of left double complex augmentations is, even now, a very

---

96 All across the nation men were ready to do battle against the elements.
97 They "shake it up" to the beat of the band!
98 So fastidiously French, they're named instead of numbered.
99 Their fine watches, their lust for fine food, and their famous finesse with money.
100 Famous business tycoon J.P. Morgan used astrology to achieve *his* wealth.
101 Loose-fitting trousers lean against a roadster while waiting for the 4:19.
102 Who posited: "Memorize two short sentences and flash your credit card."
103 Now we understand that they glide across softest crepe.

highly developed analysis (*vide* Luba Checks). Such an analysis or methodology is applicable to almost every area of logical thought and often asserts itself in startling fashion, as in the *Theories of Hammocks*[104] (Champagne) and the mordant *Frozen Ducks*[105] (Henderson), to which it might seem completely foreign, suddenly unlocking passages long thought absolutely secret. Complex resolution studies are, essentially, in their infancy, even though Bordagaray's Great Equation[106] $(\frac{\pi Q+A}{\pi n+A+e} = fA$, was first expressed in 1643. Who[107] could have foretold, even a scant ten years ago, that the studies in this field would lead to a new view[108] of contravariant transposition and its role in map and homotope behavior? As Dr. Ralph Van Raalte[109] puts it, summing up his paper "Certain Tensile Predispositions in Elastic Limitations"[110] (1963): "We are, therefore, on the threshold of an entirely new and I may go so far as to say *revolutionary* approach to the contravariant and its startling transpositions. Thanks to the work of Durk, Brandi, Checks, *et al.*, we have come to view such phenomena as log-sawing women, red (and blue) hats, rowboats, turtles, cyclists, and obsessed flies with more than casual attention. They are in themselves not only *those things which they are*, they are also the mundane expressions[111] of laws that we are just beginning to comprehend. Certainly, as far as our understanding of the Differential Triangle in equicrescent velocities[112] goes, contravariant transposition mutation points the way to an entirely surprising series of expressions having to do with alternately vanishing magnitudes. The problems inherent in map and homotope behavior may finally yield to this remarkably versatile key; in any event the mathematics of complex resolutions has, as they say, its foot in the door or, more to the point, its boat in the stream."

It now seems clear that the field of complex resolutions shows itself to be endlessly fertile in the generation of new ideas.[113] If, as seems likely, this subtle and harmonious branch[114] of abstract thought finally yields its complex and infinitely layered mysteries, there are no lengths to which the refinement of its processes may not go.

---

104 Silk chiffon, its special magic.
105 The food never touches the water.
106 More flirt and flutter than a column of pale, pale apricot.
107 That lady of Cordon Bleu cooking-school fame.
108 Designed for rugged men.
109 Who belongs on the cover of *Time*.
110 Everything a rubber-sole enthusiast could ever need.
111 "Stripes of summer," "Big brights," etc.
112 The great gleaming beauty makers.
113 We criss-cross stretchy fingers of elastic!
114 A mauvy lilac, a sandy beige, a Wedgwood green.

Surely, we may "say" of it that it is, in Salvatore Maglie's perfectly balanced expression on instantaneous momentum,

$$\frac{Er(9)}{i\pi} = ErA$$

My dear Professor Roche:

How nice to hear from you after all this time! I was almost certain that you were busy on a grant—or should I say *another* grant?—to study Chaucerian influences on Swahili epic poetry, or conduct another investigation fraught with interest to all. But now I see from your letter that you have been rapt in meditation *soi-disant* concerning your pioneering course and my relationship to it. Your decision is a brave one! And so boringly predictable! Your letters to me over the past few months have been—beneath, I hasten to add, the amusingly lusterless prose style that, surely, you affect for some arcane academic reason—pointedly cold and unbecomingly arrogant, to say the least. I have often wondered just what it is that you have to be arrogant about, out there with ruth in the alien corn, but no matter. My sainted mother often told me that I would do better to put my faith in a pimp than in a professor (an old Irish proverb) and her Celtic wisdom has certainly been borne out in our ennui-laden correspondence. Not that I blame you for wanting to get a leg up; I am only distressed that your stinking feet should pretend to use me for a stile!

Despite the unaccustomed cynicism that your letter has awakened in me, it contains elements of humor that, in a way, almost rescue it from your wonted drabness. Almost as if paresis had forced a third-rate comic into the surreal. A sort of depraved logic, a triumph of sophistry, pervades almost every well-nigh unreadable sentence. Although your syntax feverishly militates against them, certain "ideas" do manage to wrench themselves free, despite all, despite all. If I do not misread you, one of your basic newsy items is that *The Red Swan* is to be used in your course as the centerpiece around which all the lesser works will cluster, both giving to and receiving light from this neglected "masterwork." You do have a certain charm with a phrase —or is it a word? Further, you feel that Mr. Trellis's "hard-wrought gem" of a novel is the most important American work of fiction to have appeared in lo! the past generation! A pure posy of an opinion! What particularly moves me, however, is your prattle to me (the good doctor to the plodding student) about what you so boyishly term my "ill-considered" remarks anent this *magnum opus,* this *Marjorie Morningstar* of the avant-garde. You feel that my comments are "hostile"; you suggest that they are "snide"; behold! you go so far as to say that you find them "disconcertingly" envious. And all these years I have labored under the delusion that the only thing that truly "disconcerted" professors was the advancement of their peers. How faulty my judgment of those Great Hearts!

I will not deign to engage you, once again, in a quarrel over the offal that is *The Red Swan*. Your own fashionable stupidity will make of you a laughing stock among those eleven persons who can still read. In the crude parlance of the streets—surely you have heard of "the streets" there amid the falling apples and twangy rye?—and, I may whisper, in the vocabulary of the beloved *Red Swan*, you will be known as "the dumb motherfucker, Roche." It is a hard appellation for a Professor of Comparative Literature to carry! On the other hand, you may be loved by the "young." They have a weakness for "dumb motherfuckers," as past performance shows. You may well be a Culture Hero among these sober youths. However, I may be wrong —I'm certainly wrong about Trellis, am I not?

Not to painfully mince words, your truly and quintessentially shit-head decision not to use any selections from any of my works is not surprising, now that I check back through your last few letters. The scrawl was, even then, on the wall. But how can you, a man who, by your own admission, thought of *The Centaur* as a "breakthrough" in the American novel (surely you meant a "breakdown") say that my work, while displaying many of the "gestes" of the avant-garde, is not "truly" avant-garde, and lacks a consistent "engagement" with those subjects most germane to "the contemporary." My dear old bumbling Roche, I suspect that you would not know an avant-garde work were it to grasp you by your academic tool! Unless, of course, someone were to tell you what was grasping you, someone like a grubby editor turned critic (you will forgive the euphemism), someone with the initials *Vance Whitestone*. Although I'm sure that you pay no attention to mass-circulation critics, do you, you cowardly scumbag? That latter word, by the way, is a truly avant-garde word, found in *The Red Swan*.

And *Three Deuces* has suddenly become "rather too minor to take up the students' time with." You, sir, are an asshole, fit only to teach writing courses in the prison system, where the pupils would just as soon make wallets and bookmarks. I have never even suggested that *Deuces* is a major work, only that it is *genuine*. It is honest even in its youthful pretensions. It will not degrade the minds of those who read it, as that carbuncle of a book, *The Red Swan*, will.

After all your cretinous and self-serving remarks in regard to Trellis's "work" and my own, it was hardly a surprise to read your peachy sentences declining my offer of assistance to you regarding the books to be used in your course. Your sterile contention that my comments would be instances of undisguised hostility toward my peers' work is

321

the remark of a man lost in the muck of what we have hilariously come to call "the world of letters." Don't you know, you swinish clown, that I am aware that my comments, if used in your course, might be thought of as having your imprimatur? What would Trellis think? And Whitestone? How would you ever get those opportunities to slaughter books by the unfavored on page nineteen of the *Times Book Review?* Who would love you and tell you what was said at the last NBA cocktail party by publishers' infantry? Your courage, sir, is that of a spirochete, and I fear that I denigrate this poor creature of God who carries the Old Joe as his destiny. "Undisguised hostility" my ass! You are simply a puke.

The end of your apelike letter takes, as you might say, and probably have, the cake. I should cultivate "charity and understanding." For what? For whom? For these heat-and-serve droppings that are sold as novels? For the grinning knaves who will kill and maim for five minutes of the most obscene prostitution on the "Tonight" show? I should "appreciate the work of my betters." But you, my sun-dappled hick from the Great Enriched Breadbasket of America—you don't know who my betters are! You don't even know who my inferiors are! Have I "ever given a thought" as to why my work has been consistently ignored or attacked?" Questions like these should be sent on to David Susskind for the "routine agonizing" treatment. You "deplore," O Mr. Styrofoam, my "bitterness and frustration" while, in your best simian manner, you hump your xerox mind along after the mediocrities that other mediocrities have called "Great Writers." You would do better to spend your leisure hours in creative mastur-bation, my dear old poke; at least then you would have *earned* the title of jerkoff.

Finally, your comment on my "Queenly Pearl" should qualify you for an honorary Litt.D. almost anywhere. The smell of the academic outhouse hovers over "vaguely tantalizing, but in a way that is totally removed from true, not to say high art—without compassion, love, or a sense of tragic justice, and with a kind of bourgeois humor that depends on the debasement of womankind for its vulgar effects . . . surely, we have passed beyond that. . . ." As your atrophied brain and truly abscessed prose honor Trellis and his ooze may you advance far in your benighted "discipline." And may the next co-ed you feel up in your fatherly way kick you where your balls are meant to be.

Antony Lamont

P.S. Please return my MS post-haste. The thought of it on your desk fills me with horror—almost as if I had turned a child over to Gilles de Raiz.

10. NAMELESS SHAMELESSNESS

But it was not God who answered my fervent orisons, but the lovely Daisy, who had somehow arrived at the club zap just after me, and, eluding the sinister and oily maître d', had crept to the door of the unholy sanctum in time to hear my brief talk with the arrogant *filles de joie* whom I had confronted. At the very moment at which I felt my head swim and my loins tremble at the sight of the two wantons' lavish and immodest display of their musky charms, Daisy burst in the door, her lovely eyes flashing disdain and disgust at the two, who, smiling, pretended to drape themselves in the flimsiest negligées corrupt designer ever imagined. Glancing at me with melting gratitude (for she had guessed on what a selfless mission I had hither come), Daisy, a dream of civilized beauty in her modest tailored suit, gestured for me to sit down and then faced the two demons who had made her sweet life a hell of misery and doubt—who had, somehow, with charms and magic wiles, turned Ned Beaumont into a sexual ghoul (yes, ghoul!) whose chief pleasures lay in the disinterment of the most noisome ecstasies!

Swiftly sitting, she began to address her unwilling hostesses, who, for a brief moment, seemed softened by her reasoned pleas to allow Ned Beaumont his freedom. But their faces, as always, were false, and at the exact moment at which she had begun to redden in exasperation at their false and hypocritical protestations of innocence, Madame Corriendo rose (and I shamefully confess that my bulging eyes greedily devoured the lush figure that pushed its contours against the diaphanous gown that barely shielded it) and went to the small bar in the corner of the room, arguing that we would be able to discuss the matter in a less heated and more truly reasoned way did we but imbibe a small liqueur.

We agreed and accepted each a tiny cut-glass pony of pale-yellow liquid with the mysterious odor of the exotic rain-sodden East about it, a distillation of jasmine, patchouli, bitter oranges, and calambulaliam. As we settled back, more relaxed, more confident of our victory, Daisy continued her pleas, albeit in a less impassioned, more friendly tone. I admired her fervently as I sipped rather eagerly, I thought, at my liqueur. What a remarkable flavor it possessed! As if all the burning suns of the universe had been distilled into one heady elixir! Somehow, almost immediately, my feelings toward Daisy imperceptibly changed from open admiration to an ill-defined yet quite real passion, and I noted, in the next few minutes, that her voice had deepened and taken on a warm and burnished huskiness. Madame Corriendo had subtly allowed her gown to fall open, and with her monumentally divine thighs set rather too well apart, seemed to be daring Daisy to chastise her for immodesty. Madame Delamode had, without any hesitation, completely divested herself of *her* robe, and, half-clothed in a whisper of undies, sprawled back against her chaise, leering quite brazenly at the lissome Daisy.

How long a time then passed, I do not know. All I do know is that I heard myself chuckle from far, far away, from out of a gauzy orange mist. My legs stretched out before me, I contemplated, in a humming daze, the wanton poses of the blossoming doxies before me and the throbbing bulge that had arisen magically in the front of my trousers. Daisy's voice went on, her eyelids fluttering, her cheeks a deep cerise, and it was then that I noticed that although she sat in the same chair, in the same posture, she had miraculously divested herself of her outer garments, which lay in a heap on the floor. She sat before her smiling judges intimately clad in underraiment dazzling white as a silent snowfall, the lights, somehow softer now, shimmering off her gorgeously slender body.

As in a dream, I saw Madame Corriendo lie back on her couch, entreating Daisy to forbidden pleasures with a look so flamy that I quaked with lust. And Daisy, who still talked haltingly on of our moral obligations toward dear Ned Beaumont, suddenly ceased, and gently lowered herself to the floor; on hands and knees, cooing softly and deeply in her ivory throat, she crawled toward the lush rose that Madame Corriendo, panting, proffered her, while I helplessly began to undo my curiously constricting trousers . . .

. . . Madame Corriendo's tender mouth was sculpted by her mercilessly unleashed passion into a perfect O which her scarlet lips framed beautifully; and from this warm grotto came forth a low and surging river of tropical groans and naughty words fashioned into licentious urgings of such fantastical invention as to set the mind ablaze! Her pleadings went not unheeded by Daisy, who, softly entangled in the older woman's wantonly positioned nether limbs that gleamed in stockings glossy as black laquer, was studiously addressing with her pouting lips, with nips and twitters now here! now there!, the plump throne, pink as watermelon, of trembling Corrie's most deeply female dark desires.

Dearest Daisy's snowy luscious seat, full-rounded and bisected softly by the shaded furrow that served to only partially conceal the narrow paradiso sacred to such acolytes of venery as Alcibiades and that weary Tannhäuser of the *fin de siècle,* protruded like an invitation to delicious sin as she primly knelt before the steamy cavern offered her by Corriendo, whose voice now had dropped to a hoarse note of wheedling command. The swoony scene ignited the masculine blood that thumped within me and it rushed, swift as Pegasus, to that manly locus known so well to all fabulists of Venusian bent. What a sudden addition of stern rigidity there was! And my orbs, that up to now had been rolling like twin marbles in my head, presently fixed themselves on the long and perfect pins of Daisy and the ferny treasure nestled in between them.

In the meantime, Madame Delamode, like I a popeyed, crimsoned voyeur of the abandoned charade that sweltered before her, had flung off her transparent frillies and now reclined on a velvet couch in naught but a wisp of ice-blue satin that discreetly held her flashing sea-blue hose. Her finely molded hand had strayed to strum to a crescendo the sugary knob that now peeped from her soft pit of enchantment. And, I confess, my own mitt had seized my burning engine and was belaboring it diligently, while many a half-repressed and burning sigh issued from my parchèd mouth.

White-hot Daisy, feverishly massaging Madame Corriendo's vast alabaster spheres that were suspended roguishly in a suave apricot garment hardly more substantial than a spider web, had almost succeeded in fully burying her coral visage in the mossy garden that now lay fully opened before her, and the twitching owner of that nook, her lithely muscled frame called upon by the rigors of sweet Love to perform feats hardly credible, had bent forward and permitted her strong hands to exacerbate her busy partner's Callipygian charms, made exquisitely and unbearably more toothsome by the evanescent glaze of plum-blush satin that pretended to protect them, but which revealed the shadow and the substance of that warm divide that tends to drive all mankind to mutest adoration. Then . . .

. . . the blushing globe that crowned my lollipop had reached proportions quite magnificent as my manual attentions grew in speed and vigor. I plead the exigencies of the situation for this rude behavior, since no saint in heaven could have long fought off the excitement growing from the observation of the dreamy scene that was being played in homage to the fabled isle of Lesbos. Delamode softly had intruded on the games of the other two enraptured ladies, and, I may say, was beside herself with heat. Bejeweled with a fine mist of Sapphic perspiration, the momentary tribade, gams twinkling in a furtive mocha sheen of silken hose nipped at mid-thigh by deep pearl-encrusted bands of jet velour, loins draped in fuchsia scanties into which her Mound of Venus was so tightly packed that a few naughty strands of hair popped through the lacework of the straining V, had crept, in an attitude of homage, to the rapt Daisy, there to nestle soft against her steaming flesh. Daisy! whose maple syrup tongue now darted nervously and gaily as a hummingbird into the aromatic depths of Corrie's cantaloupe! Such a hurricane of groans, typhoons of grunts! Such creaks and whisperings of ravishing and silken stays! Just the sounds that filled the dim boudoir were enough to make the thick honey of Amour flow copiously from the pounding beam I sedulously larrupped!

While fascinated Daisy interested herself in the nectarine that Corriendo made a gift of to her, Madame Delamode had not been idle in her duty. Panting rather fetchingly, her marble thighs pressed 'gainst those of Daisy, the excited dame had insinuated the cute geranium that protruded from her golden mat between agued Daisy's coolish nates and was now determinedly performing on her like a rakish husband. What a tearing then there was of silk and satin! What a snapping of tight-stretched elastic! Madame Corriendo, her willowy lower limbs ashimmer in a haze of palest lilac, let fly a crowd of bluest words to urge on both Daisy and the plunging Berthe! My shillelagh had lost none of its wonted vim and my eyes quaffed the heady scene while my hands fiddled with my old friend and the heavy pouch that fueled him. Suddenly, almost as if . . .

. . . and now the leggy Madame Delamode, whose strength had been brought to fever pitch by the canapés of Amore, singled out the swooning Daisy for her complete attention. Their limbs, their heaving bosoms, their plumpy bottoms—now churning in a veritable sea of frothy lace all in confusion, formed a lewd kaleidoscope of Paphian gymnastics. Now this, now that, would quiver into view as they generously gave, yet also took so greedily. To my bedazzled lamps came now a delectable gap, now a yawning nether chink, dainty slippers flashed in jerky movements in midair! Silkies and frou-frous lush as lobster mayonnaise, austere as the dull glint of metallic blue! All this so enflamed my deedle that the lang'rous Madame Corriendo, who had been reclining on a rug of yellow ermine, espying it, lurched famished next to me and crushed her body, intoxicating with the scents of musk and mint and marshmallow, resplendent in burnt-cinnamon nicey-naughties that served to increase the splendor of her smoking charms, 'gainst mine. And as Daisy, flushing in a brief suggestion of rich chocolate sateen that made her white flesh radiant, took into her creamy hands the bursting globes that jutted

326

from the scandalous garment that strained to hold the opulence of Berthe's corse and crooned a song of hysterical Bacchante desire to her brighteyed love, that latter firmly sank a finger into the delight of Sade that peeped from out the richly spuming lace that skirted Daisy's petticoats, and Madame Corriendo, scorching, bent to her womanly task and engulphed my smoldering herm in her peppery mouth, while I, scrabbling furiously to thrust my hands beneath her privy garb, did soon encounter the warm Valhalla that holds all ecstasy for men. Then did I feel my manhood, now buried to its very base in Corrie's laboring face, explode! and with abandon gush its pearly liquors forth to be absorbed by my compliant profligate, whose eyes, as dark as midnights in Calcutta, rolled up to heaven. And so we . . .

. . . now the gusts, the tornadoes of brute passion that wracked the two experienced maidservants of that shifty youth the debasèd Romans dubbed the riotous Cupid, seemed to give off waves of staggering and hypnotic perfumes from their sweating bodies, all a vague streaming of taut metallic hose and bulging meat, all a constant rustling and swish of wispy edgings of whipped-cream lace, all a lawless daydream of sheer lustre! Madame Corriendo and her long-time confidante, Berthe, now idiotically blubbering in their license, their encarnadine countenances fixed in trancèd grins, were well-nigh buried to their sparkling ears in each other's lavish sundaes; locked, twisted pretzel-like, they writhed, they groaned, they swore sizzling oaths of deathless lust to all the greatest lovers of the past in language that simmered hot enough to set great Dionysos on a rolling boil. Their peachy lips adored, their posied tongues and beaming teeth gave praise, their dawnsoft tummies rolled, O! their nervous thighs ashine in scintillant pastels yawned delightedly as their arms, made strong with bold desire, rigidly encircled each other's substantial hemispheres. Slickly, silently, their urgent buccal parts paid homage then to the gateway worshiped by the Greeks. The shy apertures, now round as silver dollars in their need, took in the hungry tongues that prodded them, and sucked them into fiery interiors!

My rampant horsey, still proud as the staff on which Old Glory flew that fateful dawn on which our Nation's stirring anthem was indited, was held and lovingly performed on by the shining Daisy as she lay before me, straining like a thoroughbred, her pouting mango framed in sunny down, her superbly crafted thighs tattooed with dainty lengths of insubstantially delicious straps that gently pinched the glossy tops of the navy sheerness that caressed her legs. 'Twas a picture that filled my dandelion with bubbling ichor till it bloomed even more profligately! Then, guided by her helpful digits I plunged to the hilt of my towering charlotte russe into her waiting honeydew. The black-haired lass squeezed me with a force powerful enough to sate the mighty Herakles, and then her calves, all fidgets, locked themselves in a glistering arch above my back to hold me a veritable Prisoner of Love! And as Corrie Corriendo and gibbering Berthe shouted in their mutual delight, I also yelled as the liquor so admired by Queen Guinevere wed me to Daisy's stillest depths; then she too joined us in our mindless clamor that filled the crepuscular salon that the four of us had metamorphosed into an arena that would have found favor with crazed Pasiphaë. In a few moments . . .

. . . and Madame Corriendo's entire glowing frame was now a fantasy of blushes in her gossamer fifis the color of lips behind which her body strained to burst forth as she extended both her lazy arms to encircle Daisy's drunken loins. Delamode, ensconced beneath the spitfire Daisy, feasted juicily on the chubby mound held sacred to the corybants of yore, while both her busy hands employed themselves in attendant rituals; one rather diffidently plucked at her own dewy peony, now desperately full-blown, the other slid rapidly along the whole length of my swollen lance, whose furiously rotund head glowed rubicund as a danger flag. Then Corrie, a phantom of depravity and yet a delirium of pulchritude in shining grey and softest beige little nothings rich as custard, joined Madame Delamode's ministrations and accompanied her febrile exercises on the iron sentinel that stood out in front of me, her other hand softly tickling the engorgèd pom-pom that it sported handsomely! Daisy, weeping tears of joy, had cupped the ponderous bag in which my heavy pellets hung suspended, and was assisting her two companions in depravity to bring me to what must have been my fifteenth huge barrage. So I knelt, the very cult of their enamored hands, all which urged my boiler of unfettered pep to release, once more, the gouts of nectar that by now covered all of us. Then Daisy settled on my bucking steed with a heavy groan such as Helen must have made when first Paris placed his noble thyrsus into her picturesque and wine-dark straits, those straits known to have driven hapless Menalaos to uxorious dementia and puerile drools. Rocking her hips delectably, her milky thighs did yawn to accept, all afever, the trembling artificial shaft that Madame Corriendo had securely strapped about her eager, thrusting throne of insatiety. Now, bucking strongly as a stallion, and with grunty slaverings, the paramour buried the cunningly molded prong in Daisy's sizzling back door, even unto its entire eight-inch length. It was then, gazing into Daisy's sparkling eyes that were absolutely crossed in the overpowering grip of the acme of lasciviousness as she experienced the greatest of all fleshy rapturousness—

packed full both fore and aft—that I gave way again, and, heaving heedlessly about, now into Daisy, now onto her, now onto the other two madames, now upon myself, the floor, the sofa, chaise, the bookshelves, lamps, yea! even eight feet into the air onto the chandelier that glowed romantically down upon our revels, I let fly with profligacy my salvo of Aphrodite's unmixed wine! Madame Delamode, fixed manically upon the spouting hydrant that anew drenched all of us, had crawled from beneath Daisy's streaming carton, and in a welter of peachblow glitter, her bottom breathlessly framed in scanties of lace a startling grenadine in hue, now thrust that hungry sector of her anatomy toward my still-ready slugger, that had remained as hard as an ingot of new steel, and I courteously steered it, right up to my churning duffel bag, into her precious back yard. At this, she softly screeched and fell to nuzzling Corrie Corriendo's shuddering and globy cushions, her deft tongue finding its eager target with no small assistance from its possessor, which sweating voluptuary, who had not for a moment ceased her plumbing job upon the half-conscious and incoherent Daisy, settled with a sigh upon happy Berthe's straining phiz.

So now, Delamode seemed to act upon the streaming Corrie as a kindly goad, her love-distorted face hidden in the bouquet that Madame Corriendo offered her, her laboring tongue and lips driving the fortunate recipient of their lubricity to thrusts and gyrations that took Daisy's breath quite away—while I, feeling yet another salvo in the arsenal that fed my blistering cannon, drove now that weapon deep into Madame Delamode's scorching shangri-la.

I cannot tell how long a time of the most unheard of shouts and oaths and screams of almost unbelievable intensity there passed, while we lost ourselves in our elysian tasks, but of a sudden, all of us, within the briefest second of each other, reached our common goal, and then! What an incredible conflagration of throes and heavings was there! What a furnace of imprecations and praise! What a ripping and popping of gossamer cloth! Yet still our drugged bodies . . .

. . . surely, furtively is not the word that will explain the manner in which I now glanced at Daisy, and she at me, as slowly clarity and reason and sanity returned to us. We stood, exhausted, the fires of unlawful passion all extinguished, Daisy shamefully encrimsoned at the painful memory of our debauch. We had put on our garments and stood fully clothed, ankle-deep in an ocean of torn and tattered intimate apparel—God knows where it had all come from! Corriendo and Delamode were sprawled in sated enervation on the couch across the room, their bodies, which, just a moment (or so it seemed) before had been twisted and racked by the heights of unbridled lust, were now fully covered in voluminous and opaque peignoirs. Shivering shyly, Daisy turned to go, and I followed suit, hoping 'gainst vain hope that we would be allowed to leave without a word of triumph from our hostesses. My wish was granted, but in a way that made me cringe and cower, for, as we made our way toward the door, away from that scene of carnal imbecility, a scene, I knew, that neither Daisy nor I would forget, and that would haunt us in the bleak midnights of the future, a low laugh of victory burst from the throats of both the libertines, a horrifying chuckle.

The laughter said many things, but more clearly than anything else, it said that we had failed in our attempt to free Ned Beaumont from these trollops' chains—for had we not fallen prey ourselves to their aphrodisiac wiles? How could we pretend to free our friend from the very temptations to which we had succumbed? Further, the laughter told us that Ned Beaumont would be apprised of our adventure and that all of Daisy's contributions toward the various *tableaux* we had taken eager part in would be described in the most minute and candid detail. A final shock came just as we were leaving this room of still-warm embers! From the corner came a cough, at once satanic and apologetic, and I turned to see the oleaginous maître d', wan with onanistic exhaustion, grinning at me—a movie camera in his hand! He held it up to me with a terrible leer.

The door closed on the harrowing giggles and we found ourselves on the street. How ashen-pale dearest Daisy was! She held my hand yet dared not look at me, and we set off, faint with exhaustion, away, away from the evil mountebanks and their criminal potions. Lost in our thoughts, which suffused both our cheeks with swifty blushes, we walked, and we walked, with nothing solved, rather, with the entire problem made more horribly complex. Sighing profoundly, our hands locked together, we pushed ahead, speechless in the cascades of shame that broke over us, terribly alone under the late-night sky of brooding blue.

Lamont's Notebook

I may or may not use—it would certainly entail a revision of the situation described in "Queenly Pearl." But—use it or not, it will show them that I can write erotica, with more panache than a *dozen* Trellises. There must be *poetry!* The vulgar can be heightened no end, no end. Yet is there not an essential vulgarity to it all? Is this not the obligatory sex scene that has become a necessity in all modern novels?

Whether it is or not, it is a success!

Halpin now must feel such guilt that he is moved to superhuman efforts to free his friend from their clutches, despite his love for Daisy, whose carnal weakness at the Club Zap imbroglio endears her the more to him.

It is time to stop worrying about motivations.

How could I not have realized that the Baroness must know Roche, or even Trellis? Surely, that smug offer of "work" to me must have been designed to humiliate me. For what other reason . . . ?

There is pornography *and* pornography. Is it too much to say that this chapter is the most exquisitely defined since the throbbingly erotic poems of Emily What's-her-name? In a sense, I am not surprised, except by the subtlety of language and progression herein. Certainly, there have been sensual instances in some of my other books Jazzetti's eposode with the nun in the phone booth is, in a way, a model of the bawdy. And my liaison between Elena Esposito and Levenspiel, while skirting the edge of the humorous, retains a pathos that makes it hauntingly erotic. Certainly, I can think of no other "May–December" romantic interlude that manages to treat its protagonists with dignity and yet—with such fire!

From *Rayon Violet;* pp. 109–112

. . . and so, the game seemed to be going on, but how serious it appeared to be getting! Levenspiel, vaguely deshabille, was reclining in an easy chair, staring sightlessly at a magazine held upside down, rather flustered and perspiring, so Elena thought. Her brain turned over like a smooth turbine. She knew, knew profoundly in her singing heart of hearts, how fetching she must have looked in her tiny skirt and tight sweater molded to her smoldering form, to her body!

that body that now thrilled like a harp upon which she wished this wonderful, kindly, wise old man would play his song of love! How powerful his hands were even though crippled by arthritis! How good he was, how strong and sure, and she knew that she was not mistaken in thinking that his attentions toward her in the office the past month were more than—*ordinary*. How often he had spilled water over himself at the drinking fountain as she walked by, her eyes blushingly lowered. Once he had ruined a silk shirt, once extinguished his aromatic Habana! Once—she inadvertently flushed as she remembered her immoderate titter—he had almost given himself a concussion by walking into a wall while pretending not to notice her crossed legs! She couldn't help but smile as she leaned over now and so gently crushed her nose into his silvery sideburns.

How warm toward her he had been this very evening! She had invited him home to her little apartment for dinner—with how many stammerings and apologies! He had smiled his slow, sad smile and then smashed his knees against a radiator as he swung, grandly and imperially swung himself around in his swivel chair to render her a gruff affirmation. She'd colored as he devoured her thighs with his glittering old eyes! Sighing now, she gently tore his shirt open and watched fascinated as his buttons, real mother-of-pearl buttons, each with his family crest etched deeply therein, popped off and fell, one here, one there—how gaily they described their faint parabolas!— into the soup tureen. Lucky there was nothing in it, she gasped.

Yes, yes! He *had* accepted her halting invitation. He had not said much but his shining tears, those diamonds that welled up behind his gold rimless glasses told her that his heart had burst with gratitude! His wife had been in Miami for almost a month and she knew, somehow, somewhere in the most dark fibre of her being, how sick and tired he was of restaurant food. How he had ranted and raved and praised the odor of her ragout that permeated fetchingly every nook and cranny of her apartment. The simple, hearty dish now simmered on the stove.

Then, mysteriously and quietly as does Eros tread this hollow world on his fairy feet, she was on the couch, surprised to find herself furiously thrusting her full hips forward, always forward, to meet the manly thrusts of his own rather full hips! She had worried, at first, with a becoming little-girl worry, about the wheeze and catarrh-like rumblings that issued from his chest, but nothing, not even Death itself, could have prevented her from accepting, with her wonted grace and humor, the love, complete and freely given, of this wonderful and immaculate old man. How the sweat gleamed in the thousands of myriads of lines and seams of his sagacious face! His golden spectacles fogged over with his superhuman efforts as he drove deeper into the very source of her thrill! Yes, *yes*, YES! She was thrumming now, trembling all over, she had indeed metamorphosed into something like a giant harp, a great harp made of flesh and blood and sighs of delight! And now Levenspiel's old eyes, though watering, hid a youthful burning that she detected even behind the fine mist that shielded the lenses of his glasses, a youthful *burning* that belied his labored breathing and the fluttering of his kind and weary heart. His warm tongue was caught, flapping, like a bird with a broken wing, between his dentures, and there it fluttered, helplessly. How Elena's heart cried out—and flew to it!

She knew, and was glad, that her skirt was up around her thighs, her womanhood exposed to his smoking gaze. At some point she had shyly, almost discreetly, slipped out of her innocent underpants. That was one *less* thing she had to worry about! Meanwhile, she felt, more than smelled, her burning ragout. Lying there, almost as if she were bodiless—yet how could that be? she mused faintly—she allowed her dark and secret pounding blood to control her actions. She felt no shame! No false modesty interfered with her all-embracing love! No! Levenspiel goggled as she sensed her belly slam up against his with the force of an express train! His tongue almost freed itself from the dentures that held it prisoner and he gasped at the air. Although he was not, by her limited experience, too big "down there" (she crimsoned), she could tell that there was experience in each millimeter of that hoary organ. Her pleasure was intense, yet dull, dull as the steady force of a forest fire, almost as if it had always been there— and always *would* be there! She sobbed in ecstasy! Suddenly she crossed her willowy legs over Levenspiel's back and just squeezed and squeezed until his glasses *popped* off and landed right on her *own* glasses! She sobbed with gratitude that he had found her attractive even though her eyes were so poor that she had worn glasses for many years! How good, how truly fine he was she had never really known until now. In her delight, she reached down and caressed his heavy pouch. Such power lay in its depths! Such manliness and compassion informed it! She groaned discreetly and moved faster and faster to meet him, her flesh in total hegemony over her numbed brain, as she eyed his cheeks, swollen now with, she guessed, it was air?

And then—in a yellow-and-red burst and blaze of splendor they attained together that plateau of fabled feeling than which there is nothing so thrilling. Somewhere a bell pealed, or was it—more than *one* bell? Perhaps, perhaps, she thrilled. The seas roared over her and crashed in her ears, moving her to a song that she had never heard. Was that her own soft voice that gently screamed? She enfolded his sob-wracked body in her womanly arms, slowly unlocked her calves from around the small of his quaking back. Her body sagged beneath his and softly lay like an old and rich Persian rug beneath his own Persian rug of a body, which also lay still. Was he dead?

No! she realized with a start, as she heard him sniff the air. She slowly came to understand that her ragout was ruined! Dried out completely by now, probably hopelessly scorched. A sadness swept through her but was instantly dispelled as she felt his heart beating rapidly against her swelling breast. With a great shout of happy laughter, she gaily screamed into his ear: We can have a *salad!*

Lamont's Scrapbook

Esteemed Anthony LaMonti;

Realizing, in full and complete understanding that, an author of your certain busy-ness and dedication cannot always find time—to reply even to letters proclaiming my obsessions with "Psychic Ability"; however, in all patience and humbleness I take pen again in hand to write, a second opportunity for you to be "in on" the ground floor as far as my employing my over twenty years of skillful talents in my Precognitive demands!

In case of, your reluctanse to "join me" in the plan concerning wagering on the sport of Kings that is, the Art of handicapping the events transpiring on the turfs of the ovals at Belmont and Aqueduct at their raceing meets, there is a more glowing—"gilt edged" opportunity for you if, you wish to "throw in with me" and take advantage of—what we think of as "the Future" has to hold in the way of earning us both the plauddits and riches almost beyond comprehension; Yes! Beyond the "wildest dreams"—and what better can one pretende to offer than such an invitation? Surely an incentive not to be spurned?

Some few months ago, and—some time before I posted to you my first "missive" on horse raceing—one morning I gained a picture of vision; it came out of the "blue"! But I knew from my immersement, in "Psychic Ability" and all modes of precognition that, it was no pipe dream! What was, you ask this vision? I confess that I almost lost it because; if one cannot attend steadily the picture so to speak, fades before one is knowing exactly—what it actually portrays!

Fortunately I saw; and saw, for some time; I would say—almost five minutes, for a mind trained in gaineing the meaning of sudden visions this, might as well be "a lifetime." It came slowly to me—clearly and bit by bit that, I glimpsed the interior of the large sewer system of an enormous metropolis which, I cannot say—yet that is for this moment not important.

Certain hours spent subsequent, on sewer research has proven so satisfactory in maintaining that all great sewer systems in American are the same in their essence, the initial question therefore; can be very lightly taken.

Therefore, I simply assumed, as I do when I gain the name of a horse at one of the ovals—to trust my vision! What stands here in functional importance—of the "Psychic" vision is, that in this picture that flashed on my mind I saw—or rather, for—it is difficult to explain the mystery of such vision, there was in the sewer vast troves of wealth, almost—unimaginable!

Research wise, asking about of expert opinion and conducting certain studies in the Library, I acertained what I had suspected from, the strange vision I had possessed that morning—and that was, that the every day sewer systems in every large city has in it, the most fantastic acumulations of gold, jewelrie, diamonds, and gems of other types, watches, bracelets, coins, and—even cash! In such vast quantities that, even to have one hundredth of such a sum would enable one to average, from the salvage of such lost items perhaps— as much as $50,000 dollars a day! That figure of course is, from one large sewer, to work on more—the figures are dizzying I am sure, you will agree.

So with pen in hand once again I come you to! Anthony LaMonti, although a famous author already, surely such a master plan as this, is quite fascinating or, so I take it? The initial small investment required of, $1500 dollars, is a necessity—to purchase the primary "rock bottom" essentials such as, tools, special clothing, and other garb and some maps, of the system. Considering expert opinion—of which, I can get at no cost—or; a trip to the Library to verify researches.

As to my "Vision." In a basic sketch of same, I saw, not a "dreamy" kind of thing as to rings and jewels and so forth; but my "Psychic Ability" developed over almost 20 years does not function, in that way—who says so speaks just so much bunk! I gain spesifics! You may be pleasingly shocked to learn that I saw five separate items to which, it would be boring to numberate them herein. Suffice it—that one of them!—was a Diamond and Rubey necklace which to my impractised eye as concerns appraisal I, would still guess to be worth a cool $25,000 dollars—all by itself!

Therefore you will apprehend, that a $1500 dollar investment in this venture is as, they say "peanuts." While not able to guarantee a "life of leisure" to you for, certainly some time, a little exertion at— the start! And of course with my assistance in labors as we two could work as comrades in arms, would bring to you vast wealth long lost

—and forgotten by the original owners. Wealth not dreamed of by Kings.

Studies I have researched over the years proves that this, is no "fancy" of mine, no. Certain rumors for years have been persistent concerning a gentleman in San Francisco who—some time ago, took from the local sewers therein that City—at least, $25,000 dollars in lost jewelrie, and so forth and so on. And he had not—may I humbly add? My gift of "Psychic Ability."

In case the labor and thinking, of working; for hours and hours in such dismal surroundings should discourage you from this plan, allow me to suggest; that after say, just a week or so—since that time would enhance our coffers to the tune of about a quarter of a million dollars! We could with great ease hire laboring gangs at a salary; to do the harsh and "dirty" work of bringing the treasure to the "light of day."

Furthermore; as a penman with an avid following of readers, what opportunity like this comes to an author—it is that "once in a life-time" chance that cannot be sneezed at with impunitous scoffing! Imagine a book! That could be written concerning our adventures in —the Treasure Business! But, not in the exotic deeps of which books, I suspect the market is full enough. No, this—a book about finding a "Kings Ransom" under—Times Square! Surely, although I am a "babe in arms" when it comes to concern Best Sellers—this I can wager will be a supreme Best Seller!

I can also visualize a "How To Book"—that would perhaps capture many a reader who would like to think to follow suit; and too be, a millionaire. Media coverage you can bet too, would be "Titanic."

Perhaps we can meet Mr. Anthony LaMonti and talk over this— adventureous plan? Or failing; you may still be interested, in my earlier concept concerning the gaining of winners upon the turf.

Sincerely yours,
Joseph Beshary

[At first it was amusing, but with this letter it becomes annoying. The blatant attempt at swindling me is too much! Anthony LaMonti!

Yet the language is fantastic. Perhaps I can reproduce it for one of my characters later on? Change the name?

Hard to believe that anyone talks like this. That may be exactly *why* it would work—an exact duplication.]

[Later, thinking this over. These letters are doubtlessly from my beloved brother-in-law. Transparent condom!]

Halpin's Journal

It's quite difficult to write about this, even sketchily. The shock! The delirious shock of it all! One thing is for certain and that is that I cannot breathe a *word* to Ned. Perhaps he would be blasé, but again, his chagrin at what he believes to be Lamont's "revision" might turn to anger if he knew what I have been up to—particularly since he's not yet even *met* Daisy or Corrie or Berthe in the flesh. The word sends a shiver through me.

There *is*, it would seem, a strong possibility that Lamont will rewrite the entire book, but I don't care—not now. The possibility that Lamont will arrange more wondrous episodes like the last one will keep me here, no matter what Ned does. Surely, there is a real chance that Daisy and I will fall in love—the story seems to call for it, almost to demand it.

Ned must never know. He has been in a frenzy of aimless activity all day, packing his few belongings in a cheap cardboard suitcase that he found on the porch, and then unpacking. He keeps walking toward the door and then coming back to exhort me to leave with him —*anywhere*. My excuses are lame. He shakes the suitcase at me, shouting that it proves that we are in a cabin that is being used for another writer's story. But then he returns, sits, curses, then unpacks. An hour later, the entire process begins again.

It must all lie—my feelings, that is, in the fact that I was a virgin. And to have one's virginity taken in such a way! Very nice women, who threw themselves into their work with a fantastic abandon, and yet, while Lamont rested, and while he took a break to have lunch, they were deeply embarrassed and begged my pardon for the way in which they were conducting themselves. Mme Corriendo, the most wanton of us all while in her role, actually blushed and asked me if I would avert my eyes while she changed her clothes. The seemingly endless costume changes seemed to embarrass all the women. I must admit that it was unnerving for me too. Ned is surely right about Lamont's slipping hold on reality. It was odd to be so decorous while we awaited Lamont's new scenes, since the scenes themselves . . .

I should note, by the way, that the "potion" that we drank was quite, quite real. I mean that it actually acted upon us strongly. Curiously enough, it lost all its power when we were not performing. Where Lamont unearthed that language!

Ned was not interested in where I had been and I told him some half-lie about being forced to see about his rescue—I also told him that I'd met Daisy and that she was very nice, very refined. He

337

scoffed, remembering her stupid letters, but then was as suddenly filled with pity as he admitted that she too was Lamont's idiot.

Well, I must face the fact that I *want* to stay because of my own selfishness, I want to see what will come of my newfound relationship with Daisy. This is what is called lust, of course, and I feel slightly soiled and ridiculous because I have let the job get the better of me. Ned could probably advise me, but . . .

More anger for Ned. A postman came to the house, and despite our objections, he delivered a magazine to us—something called *Art Futures*. It was addressed to "Mildred Haviland" and he insisted on leaving it. There was no arguing with him—such a cretin! I can't quite describe the man, but he was not quite "there." I mean to say that he was *two-dimensional*. His cheeks were an unnatural pink, his teeth solid blocks of dazzling white, and his grin was alarmingly fixed —he did not seem human in any way. Perhaps the most unnerving aspect of this weird character was his truly odd speech, for he spoke in rhymes, and went on about snow and sleet and bringing happy news to people all up and down "the block." There was also some idiocy about letters for mommies and daddies and good little boys and girls and their brothers and sisters! His eyes, by the way, were bright blue with tiny sparkles right in the middle of each! Uncanny! I thought that he might be a dangerous lunatic, but Ned said that he was probably from a "children's picture pool" around here, and that he'd somehow wandered off course. Failing that, Ned said that he might, indeed, be a lunatic—the casualty rate in children's picture-book work is apparently very high, and nowhere is it higher than among those poor souls who labor in the "pools." Ned said that they put in their time on a rotating basis—that is, they work as mailmen, policemen, firemen, lawyers, doctors, dentists, grocers, farmers, teachers, nurses, mommies and daddies—then the round begins again. Most of them lose their minds after a few years or volunteer as soldiers in war novels where they might be "killed" and can than start a new life in adult potboilers. But it's hard for them to enlist with those smiles and crayon complexions. They are apparently sexless and work as males *and* females.

As our mailman walked away, he pursed his lips and I was astounded to seé a little cloud suddenly appear above his head; in its center, a strange symbol. It looked like this rough drawing:

Ned was momentarily amused by the mailman, but the magazine once again plunged him into gloom and anger. He reminded me of the little gold heart we had found in the "hidden" kitchen, and again shouted that we were sharing this cabin with somebody else because of "that doddering imbecile, Lamont!" He proposed that we might well also be two incidental characters in somebody *else's* novel, or that there were people in our novel that we had never seen nor heard of, people in some subplot. Failing that, he insisted that it was indecent to ask two men to work in a cabin that an author has simply rented and not bothered to investigate. "He still doesn't know about the other rooms," he said, and he, of course, is right. Then he lowered his voice and told me that he was convinced that there was now a *real* second floor to the house, and that we should investigate it. There were sounds from the ceiling just above the fireplace, he swore, and he said that he wouldn't be surprised if Lamont had allowed some other writer to build an apartment above us for his own purposes. I promised I'd investigate with him and he went out.

As for "Mildred Haviland" and her magazine—it is a fairly interesting magazine, particularly an interview with a remarkably intelligent man, the sort of man that one would like to have appear in this story. Since Ned has taken to throwing things away (he says that "new things" appear in the cabin all the time and they make him nervous), I've taken the liberty of clipping the interview in order to save it in from his mania.

Art Futures Interview of the Month: BARNETT TETE

QUESTION: First of all, Mr. Tete, exactly how did you make the money that has enabled you to become America's most famous collector and all-around patron of the arts?

ANSWER: There is no point in this, after all. Let's just say that I am known as King Corrugated, and let it go, right? Even a scarecrow has dignity.

Q: Check. You were, according to your biographers, a poor storekeeper and you got this mysterious feeling from art, if I'm remembering right?

A: That's about it. That feeling that the all that is humanly sacred was there. My wife helped me a lot in this feeling, I'll say that for her.

Q: Few of us agree with all you've said about the joys of collecting. Would you care to comment on that?

A: I really don't—I mean that you, I don't mean *you* you, I mean in general, those who have pettiness in the heart, anyway, they can shove it.

Q: I am curious about your early years of poverty and the like . . .

A: The usual squalor. The Cantor-Jessel syndrome. You'll note vague traceries of my banjo eyes and speech impediment. Of this I beg you. Look, a dollar made is in the hand, you can't knock it. Opportunities abounded.

Q: Your parents encouraged you?

A: Leave them out of it, wisenheimer. Does a fledgling throw a rock from its nest? Look, I'm a busy man. I deal with life as it comes to me aquiver. Few agree and fewer still get the thrill of understanding. Art is my game, O.K.?

Q: Would it be fair to say, as a recent poem does, that you're a lousy guy?

A: There's a streak of meanness in that so-called poet. He thinks he's an artist but there can be little doubt and less thought that he is not at all interested in the beauty that has not yet come into the world.

Q: You're trying to indicate that that is your kind of beauty I take it?

A: One must be the master of warm feelings anent arts in general.

Q: Yet with all your great understanding and compassion for artists and the like you are still the king of the box world. How do you explain this?

A: Tintoretto or somebody said that all the world is a box. The word has a good shape. As King Tete, an appellation of which I justly and proudly embrace, my peers and inferiors hold a high opinion, young man. I have warehouses full of objects de art! I did not get all these riches by fooling around. I am at once utterly raw and unbearably gross.

Q: I had no idea that Tintoretto said that! Do you feel that the Cubist Movement must be viewed then in a new light?

A: No.

Q: What do you feel about Cubism, by the way?

A: I don't understand it. Life is a juice. You cannot, to your immortal peril, lock yourself up in a room while the world, in all its terror and gorgeous looks, whines by outside. Those who crawl toward the light will break the shell. Others get pleurisy and TV back.

Q: Is there a reason why you have your renowned fear of water?

A: For the nonce in the past I fell or was pushed into a vat of molten cardboard. It seems like yesterday. My wife shares my interests in this fate with a sickening sort of regularity.

Q: Your wife . . . does she help you in your purchases?

A: Rarely. She likes to potter about the house and also make the most colorful and gay piñatas. You've seen them at Christmas parties. Life is quirky.

Q: That is an odd view for an American. Would you expatiate?

A: I feel that opposites are one and that Melville never made himself naked before all men. The shell breaks and the crab always rots.

Q: A kind of enlightened Platonism?

340

A: In so far as it deals with the explosion of your sensibilities.

Q: What about Kafka?

A: A little too Jewish for my taste. I want an oval world. I used to understand that but a world of surfaces seems to be the "modern" ticket. You recall the hula hoop? In its mastery I've always felt the pastiche of the cold breath of Prague. Often I count my money in glorious crassness.

Q: You feel that he is gloomy then?

A: Of a quintessence. Unlike our friends, the Chinese, who have the intellectual honesty to kick old men and schlepp those big banners, he turned inward. I admit however that he has reified certain concepts, but who cares about narrative?

Q: What about your *own* enormous influence though?

A: What is influence but the shadow of a cloud? How shall I speak of a yellow flower trembling slightly in the breeze? You could get sick from it. You wait around, shifty-eyed, then pounce on the lucky bastards!

Q: I'm thinking of the sudden demand for Krabo's work after you bought his early crayola things . . .

A: Oh, I see. Well, if I may quote the ancient Hebrew proverb, "If I am only for me, who will be?" That old saw has been passed down from father to son for generations like a dark cloud blots the sun, but who's the worse for it? Krabo is all right. My wife discovered him, by the way.

Q: I think I see Mrs. Tete over there in the rose garden or something.

A: She is all heart. That is her little boots protruding from a clump. Krabo did a beautiful drawing of her, "Lady Tete in the Bushes."

Q: Isn't that the famous one without a picture plane?

A: Well, famous, I don't know . . . nobody really noticed. A petty mind is a hobgoblin. Actually, Bart Kahane knew.

Q: Wasn't Kahane blind at the time that picture was exhibited?

A: Isn't that remarkable? Well, Krabo might as well be blind. He thought he was too smart to be a sculptor, that's what books will do.

Q: Is Krabo still working in crayola? I've heard talk that he's been doing some experimental things with rust.

A: Fools often come into the light of day when it seems darkest. It's no secret that Krabo and I are finished. It's a matter of what they call the experience, no? Look, the Rocky Mountains still present their great lesson. He made his pile. Let him lay in it.

Q: I'm interested in what you've said about Mrs. Tete and Krabo. Does your wife often urge you to buy an unknown—does she have that "eye"?

A: Often it seems to be a contingency. What else can one declare?

When she reaches into the hive of her angers and enthuses, she plucks out the big ones. Three lemons! Three plums! Personally, I have been a crab all night most nights. But she is loaded with transparencies. One thinks of Thaddeus Stevens wisely wandering by old synagogues.

Q: I am quite taken with your literary allusions. Are you interested in literature?

A: I'm mad about good books. A favorite, of course, is Lawrence. I consider him to be the great creative genius of our age. You know, of course, that he could swim and that he was not averse to sweet marmalade despite his protestations or affectations. He stepped lively and pointed out the uninterrupted significance of green things flying diagonally. Who can deny or dare forget that he freed the country from rocks?

Q: There are some who think that he was a morphodite. Comment?

A: That is mere legerdemain.

Q: What are you currently reading?

A: At present I am ensconced with *Thou, Thee!*, Marion Gusano's new book of verse. Or dare I call it verse? The word seems so squeamishly small and clerkish. In Poetry's great face somewhat, how shall I say, embarrassed? The language is full of dirt as well as being full of shit. Self-challenge repletes throughout. Plus trembling risk also. A kind of Blakean *mot* in its lack of attention to this and that, if you are following my drift. A great heart, in all events, rings in every line. Also, I'm reading *The History of Acrylics* by Benabou. This latter is, I fear, simply a matter of a busman driving to Newcastle.

Q: Generally speaking, do you feel that Poetry has affinities with the arts of painting and sculpture?

A: I am as sure of this as I am of the sores of life and that the sun reveals the color of the garbage. I am not one of those who will not let the ocean lave him. Tantric sounds awaken the goddess that lies coiled at the base of my body. I adore the meeting, the ongoing dialogue that spells wonder! It is no accident that Max June, one of my more servile proteges, showed collages last spring that closely follow the newer developments in certain verse forms, of which I don't want to explain about them just at present, so thrilling are they. Suffice it that they have the power of the Atlantic bunking into South Carolina.

Q: Someone seems to be in pursuit of your wife.

A: Yes. That is Shreve, the gamekeeper. Pastoral soul! His great heart rages, but he has a certain difficulty in making himself understood. You'll note how like children they are trampling the hollyhock bushes, which seem to be in danger of imminent liquefaction. Yet the garden fairly sings with their scraping.

342

Q: You would say then that Shreve is the fabled "natural man" come true?

A: The language I long for is closed to me, yet I would have to say yes. When he first arrived, a shambling lout from the country, he used to eat his belt. Now Mrs. Shreve, who knows the value of the last color golden on the white birches, has got him to the point at which he asserts the light. Yet he is still ferociously visionary, and ignores personal hygiene.

Q: Your interest in the primitive has always been a source of fascination. I'm thinking of Louis Henry . . .

A: Oh, yes. I'm glad you brought Lou Henry up. In those watercolors he, I am certain, has found himself whole and wholly too. Somehow, he could not pass beyond sheer fabric in his verse. You'll recall the *Lobster Lays*, of course. Symptoms of bitterness, which is literalness, pervade the work at all points, and what, I ask you, is at the root of that? But don't ask, I'll tell you. It is a resolute hollow old barrel, nothing more or less.

Q: But you feel that in his painting . . . ?

A: I feel that he has found himself, certainly. There are many who laugh, who say that this work of Lou's is mere satiric appositeness. Others say that there is no air in it, that he falls into his reflection. Is life an acid? I think we must agree to destroy the pigeon holes. Everlasting psychic charge is my sense of it all, take the moon made of paper. I don't think it's an accident that Henry's work is a continent big enough to take care of sourness and snottiness. I've often seen him feeding Chinese to his enamorata while his wife looked on agape.

Q: Didn't his wife do the cover for *Lobster Lays?*

A: Sheila? Yes. Of course she is an artist in her own right, something like a poem with a novel trying to get out. Few think or e'er forget that when Rimbaud understood this he gave up and left town. It was a sweet journey. So goes beauty that retires from the light.

Q: What do you see as the so-called *lumpen* qualities in Henry's aesthetic?

A: That's Jungian terminology and I don't agree. Are you maybe thinking of gloom and misery everywhere? But a moment's reflection will show that Henry's murky pictures are of a despair. Look, his people are absolutely dead. And if all true art is vital, then what? I mean, the impending transformation of all shapes. Is this a dichotomy, or what?

Q: You seem to be hinting at a kind of mysticism?

A: I don't know from this. A man has commitments, I call your attention to great predecessors of whom I continually think. There are those who drain reality of its imaginative power. Exhilarating

343

as this may be, it falls far short of the ant on the bathroom floor. The world may be a wisp of shadow yet men place their papers in the safe-deposit box. Speaking of Jung, of this latter statement even he might have cracked a smile. He was not given to levity as are none of our great souls yet rumors persist that he was guilty of the Gogolian flaw. Take it with a grain of salt or not, the good Herr Doktor was right about San Francisco. And if *he* was a mystic I'll wolf my homburg.

Q: Has collecting artworks and befriending artists been enough for you?

A: What is "enough"? Rubens once said that he holds who cries enough, but you cannot trust the Germans. There have been, of course, lengthy bawls in the night, but they have been more than compensated for by compelling results. One thinks of the moment of art when there is no more to do than plunge the hands in the pockets. Art is an opening. Well, perhaps an act of faith that there is something on the other side. Whatever it is, it calls for a suspension of the brains. Is an acid a juice? I think not.

Q: That's very revealing in light of your discovery and championing of Moss Kuth's "invisibles." Would you like to comment?

A: When I first saw Kuth's incredible work, I didn't know whether he wavered or walked alabaster to his destination. Such was my amaze! I thought, "Can I talk to you who I must create?" It so turned out that though his visage was grim a sweeter man could not be long imagined. For an artist, he's got a great sense of manners. They will come no more. Kuth, a member of that heavenly company if there ever was one, has passed beyond the insular concern with making and, more importantly, beyond the vaguely intellectual and "literary" concerns—epistemological, I insist, if the word has any meaning at all—of what some of the fatheads term "destruction." Call it visual silence. There is not only nothing there, nothing ever was there. If this isn't the *crème de la crème* of the avant-garde, I ask you. If it is true that the artist can never close his anus, it is equally true that thousands of elves keep watch thereby. Yet how many laugh! In Kuth there is the fourth dimension made flesh. Gibe if you will, but fattest peacocks fall before the sun. Mumblings suggest that this is a red-hot property, but I know what I like. I have cast my bread upon the waters and it has come back apple pie.

Q: Kuth's work at first evinced many harsh and uncomplimentary critiques. What changed all that, would you say?

A: Well, early Kuths curled at the far edges, as you can well imagine. Is there an adventurous soul near or far who will stand still for that? You of course realize that I use the word "adventurous" advisedly, ha ha. Equally accumulated senses of composition were largely displaced. Only a "sap" would pull out his bulging wallet. In sum, yours truly. When shekels flow are dealers far behind? But seriously, folk, Kuth is the wave of the future. What can be more hotsy-totsy than to allow the planar to yield to the linear? After great planes, a formal boredom comes. Then Kuth, shedding those crocodile tears for which the West Germans have long applauded him, eschewed even the linear. Other painters, despite inner feelings of disgust, mouthed the famous phrase, "We will not spit in the soup." When even the paint and canvas disappeared serenity reared its head, like Venus from the river. Call it what you like, Kuth has a sense of manners, you may well impute, despite all.

Q: Yet Kuth seems to imply in a recent interview that he misses tangible objects.

A: Let me hasten to say aught. That is an Aristotelian fancy. Since then the artist has grasped the meaning of the orgone and found it good. When a painter breaks ground, you will pardon the expression, he finds conditions of contemporary environment, common vocabulary, and conceptual "aesthetics." Perhaps art, like life, is also a juice, though one shudders to think so. I've suggested that Kuth should cut out all this reading business and get back to basics. Books spoil the sense of visual excitement that the painter has buried, like a great golden gift, in his peepers. And no matter what, when all the critics have been heard from, all the backs bitten, the art histories written, even the company especially pleasant? Personally, I refuse to be swayed by such gewgaws.

Q: In sum, then, would you say that "invisibles" have the effect of an expanding pressure against a limit of edge?

A: An excellent mélange of verbiage, yes.

Q: Some women artists have said that your taste runs to those painters whose work is most redolent of male supremacy and so on. Is there any truth to that?

A. Look, I like women. God could not be everywhere, that's why He made mothers. Their boxes, as well as ours, crackle with Reichian blueness. When they stumble, do they not trip? Think on Miz Tete, one of the county's finest examples. I would as soon underpay a woman as a man, that's where my heart is, though my seamed face may belie it. There are few prostitutes left with no sense of the people's needs. This I applaud with selected encomia. And though there are many truly rotten male artists they hold no edge, numerically speaking, over the distaffs. In my position I do not like to get into these beefs. Let's drop this frou-frou and assault, rather, the great questions that e'er bring us up short with their deepness, oke?

Q: I'm glad you feel that way. As a solid appreciator of art, what do you feel about surface—I mean, as opposed to what lies beneath?

A: That is a tough question and I can only pretend a complete answer according to my lights. I'll give you various contours, how does that sit? I can say that the distant call of birds is like blue coins of disaster, but will that prevent even one asymmetry? The thought perishes. You'll recall the work of Benny Dredger. If that was not the very posy of a poetic aesthetic, I'll savage my derby! You may think that I am here equating painting with artifact and I do confess that his work, the sheer glittery and tinsely "trappings" and so on did indeed at one time have me jumping up and down. Though many have called him a miniaturist, others have not. It is that silence that affronts. Equally, my purposes do not understand anything more than what they propose. Certainly that seems fair. To juxtapose the interior with the exterior—it was the way of all the great Geminis. Think of the boiling face of Himmler and the dead pan of Al Jolson. Who would think that both had souls as succulent as chicken shaked and baked? True it is, but then I have always loved Whittier.

Q: You are saying that surface is artifact, and the interior . . . ?

A: In the purely craft sense, to make something is a later idea. I like the poor but they can't buy things. Your questions offend and I feel the beginning ache in my corns. Mack Jackson once said, "Sit quiet in white spaces." At the time the moon was all aglow. Its wont demanded it. Even I, a humble box tycoon, may plunge into the Self and find happiness. Art must be alive in one sense or another! How few believe this credo. Hopeful and pompous, however, I plod on, one of my few delights the knowledge that a wigwag of my little finger can set the rabble on a bore. My wife often quakes at my black moods, then breaks into her swell laugh when she sees that it is only the Self that is coming up, belch-wise. The painter must formalize that impetus or poopies on him.

Q: Speaking of your wife, she and Shreve seem to have disappeared, yet I'm sure I hear their voices . . .

A: There is a fat chance that they are straining after truth in the gazebo. But it's not our purpose to dwell on the life of the spirit, is it?

Q: Of course not, sir. I wanted to ask you about your recent purchases of ink drawings by Jigoku Zoshi. Have you had an interest in Eastern art for a long time, or is this a recent enthusiasm?

A: Eastern art? What a remarkable idea! I've never quite thought of it that way. You've come a long way from St. Louis! I must admit I am charmed by the appellation. It's got class. Actually, I am celebrated worldwide as having the mind of your average slob, yet a grand here and a grand there sweetens one's occasional gaffes. Eastern art is of a mystery, you can spell that with a capital M. Who am I to cipher? A man, like all men, yet one who was able to take advantage of a stupid partner in his salad days. At present the honest wretch can be found selling pretzels outside Moskowitz & Lupowitz. Often, in the gloaming, when the breasts of the housewives are heavy with salt, I drop a tear when I fondle a Zoshi: to think that my old compañero is closed off from such beauty! At such times the living room smells of submarines and death. Beats me.

Q: What do you think to be Zoshi's strong points?

A: Speaking from the personal level, he is, as well as being a hell of a nice guy for a slant, a Japanese sandman. While some astute connoisseurs have called him a good, safe, common-sensical, and impeccable mediocrity, to me he has always been wrapped in the robes of the giant! How painfully clear! In terms of art, before which all must stand atremble, for without it can life be worth the candle, or the game the victory? he is, like they say, equally very damn fine and pretty damn interesting in his very lovely care. In his best work, blue milk bathes the beaches. But best of all perhaps is his snappy white coat and Singapore Slings. No crab he, but the smiling face of the lotus and those funny little gardens with the rocks and sand. Known as Jig Jolly in his native San Francisco, yet Higgins ink throbs in his tiny veins.

Q: Earlier you said something about Jung . . . do you feel that he has no place at all in an artist's scheme of things?

A: May the heavens forfund me if I breathed it! I don't comprehend the innovations of these old geezers, but I will defend to the death their right to a nice cushy practice. What I know from Jung you could put in a knothole. I've read somewhere that he once got knocked unconscious dancing the "Clarinet Polka." Take it from there, young one. If it's box-office, why knock it? Freud behooves as one who locked himself up with crazy ladies all day—is it any wonder that Mrs. Freud went around in an old *shmatte,* as biographers imply? Adler strikes as a true crank. Inventing a shoe to make psychopaths feel taller for a few hours, give or take, is not exactly the mark of your huge intellect. But he was a friendly little fella who liked nothing better than to seat himself at a groaning broad.

Q: For you, as a collector, does astrology have any use?

A: My wife has imparted some, sweet girl. Do you know that she is happiest in simple riot behind yonder sand dunes? Often she finds herself in a lubricious act, but it is a long road that does not cross. One pretends gaiety while the vitals throb, *c'est la vie.* I made one of my finest buys, crude word, the Chancré "Boiling Earl," because of what the stars did whisper low. While many scoff or weep all snots and tears, I am the Ty Cobb of the Big Board! At night, they're big and bright, and like Prince Rupert's Drop, hold the secrets of the universe! Saturn in the Summer House spake, so to spake, low. Ere long I implored my spouse who mumbled through her avocado face cream and a mush fulla guava pie that I should send in top bid for Chancré's effort. O fair interpreter of lore arcane! Unto this day I bend the wonted knee to her, the cuddly baggage. You cannot make your sun stand still if he has the runs.

Q: Do you find much to laugh at in the art world today?

A: One must be prepared to proffer a solemn countenance. In the morning I am covered with hair, but I do not cease a jot. Originally discerning gentlemen like myself find it ruth to chortle at a potential million. With paint on their shoes and dopey ideas yet are these daubers possible flushes. I abhor and blench at the word "plight." If it were not for those with ready smiles and a checkbook to hand they would all be no better than what a recent plumber with fedora to match called a "crabwoman mooning lovesick with colors." If you can catch that, put it in a jar. Often I feel an awkward distance in my own occasion from that which is clearly the possibility of something. At such times, I not only feel it meet to stifle my rising chuckle, I do so. If they would only stop writing poems drunk on Ocean Avenue and wielding brushes while grunting, the cause of all this levity would be sorely nipped. Not that I am Ben Grouch, uh-uh, on the contrary, I feel myself to be Felix Randall, "the giggler." The brush, however, does not fall far from the canvas and it's a cheaper mousetrap we all wish to pick up for a song. What happens is more to the point than what doesn't and I'll put on my face the mask of saturnine gloom to wrest from a needy artist an item that may ennoble and long enhance not to mention fetch a few rubles. Any clot of common mind could see that a misplaced guffaw could euchre the works. That is far different, you will agree, from whistling "Dixie."

Q: You feel then, that contemporary art must deal with life as it is lived in all its grime and squalor, not to mention its ineffable lameness?

A: You have hit it right on the brass tacks, my friend. In the truest sense, gloom is all. Think on those little mouths nibbling the goodies from Papa Mondrian's table. I don't trust a man who wears a tie and is always so clean. Wasn't it Lewis Canto who said that it is impossible to be well-groomed *all* the time? In his spectacularly thrilling mode of the shabby, who should know better? It shows in his poems to great advantage, you may lay to it! Where is the *poetry* in the hilarious? The *prolific?* No, it is in what you so wittily term "lameness" that we must put our faith as such. Take Fred Fella— a simplike appraisal of his last show might have it that the reoccurring relationships of triangular forms bespeak the, as it were, cheap joke. One whispers "nay"! While there is a quiet, intense wit and care present in each and every manufacture from the brush of this gifted collegian *manqué,* beneath the sheer "brushed" expertise shown to such good advantage in the immaculate galleries of which I have, let us say, a small piece of the action, there is a profound sense of the crippled. Thus the terrible power of the post-modern, than which there is nothing more Malamudesque, or Malamudian, if you prefer. I'll stick with Malamudaisian.

Q: Your command of the critical vocabulary is stunning. I must admit that I was not quite prepared for your subtleties . . .

A: I reply to your transparent flattery with a Yiddish saying taught me on Rivington Street by a gravestone chiseler. "If you put your hand in your pocket you're liable to find nothing." There may be wisdom in this, but how can I ever assume that it will come to this or that substance? I cannot, of course, since our time has a warped view of surrealism. This doesn't bother a sport like me, with other fish to fry and a host of irons in the fire I myself started, but when it is counterpointed and enriched by superb and Daumier-like caricatures, I tend to shirk and even walk swiftly toward the hills. I'm afraid that I don't have it in me anymore to slap my chest and sing "tarantara!" By any measure that I can devise, artistic betters see again that ancient struggle William Blake described. Unfortunately it slips my mind at the moment, but you know Blake. Did you know, by the way, that his great novel of adventure, *Gorgonzoola,* was written while operating a punch press on Pearl Street? It doesn't matter but it's one of those little nuggets of info that make life inestimably richer, as when the moonlight sets a million fairies sparkling among the scrub in Vermont. Yes, I've taken a number of swings at artists who have spurned my generosity and fake enthusiasm, but it is always against them in myself that I've struggled to see a world again alive with unrestricted trade. Often a tear jumps to the eye, or both eyes, when it is once again made clear that the city is a crab of rock. To emerge from this massy maze takes a smidgen of guile and a vocabulary to knock your hat off. Thus am I before you, Miltonian man, a little the worse for wear and tear, but the banks don't cry when I enter, if you follow the parable.

Q: Some years ago, you made a rather cryptic remark, "When in the mountains, paint boats." Can you expand on that?

A: Look, I'm the most happy fella. Cryptic is as cryptic does. Sociohistorical and mythical states are few in number, but quite real. Take Wyoming. A boat is a marvelous "thing" because it has no true vortex, not in the way the universities speak of it. That, I think, is prime experience for any painter, no matter his essential numbness. How boring it all seems now, yet we dare not forget! One must remove oneself from one's varied obsessions so that one can truly discover that revelation that may come to one in the long stretches of the night. I am alone but like it that way. If you glance sideways at *Ulysses* on the shelf, its bed of pain, so to speak, from its foxed pages there comes the most eerie green glow. That proves *something*. Who alive with chest of steel within which burns a heart that might, who knows? release a poem some fine day dares say no to this one immutable fact: that it was the blind fop, Aloysius St. James, that very crown of cunning, who tapped the green with his cane and loved to listen to the lions roar? It is from such dandyism that the spirit of the maritime will deliver us.

Q: You think, then, that painting has become . . . precious?

A: All art is precious, simple one. But my eye descries your drift. I despise an art that perpetuates itself. Eat that and have another. In the vasty deeps of midnight dreary, your colorful Matisse may as well be Benny One-Ball, I speak of the imposing canvas that great heart executed while doing a nickel in Dannemora. But "precious"? Pardon my retreat into immoderate laughter, but you are coming off as a dope. Is the echo of greatness enough? I think not. We aghast bystanders and sincere appreciators, busy serving buffet suppers to regiments of cretins in beards and faded blue chambray shirts, want the tender arms of greatness to enfold us, but at night crabs sit with us at bars. How then can we know, though our thoughts be pure as Protestant vanilla, who is which? Out of sere days and days and days of such despair do you wonder that we often seem mere philistines? Though personally I would like to follow those whose work has touched upon the light or darkness, vibrant souls who share the gift of poetry, yet am I constrained to do things of a grossness. I refer, of course, to my recent purchase of West Broadway.

Q: I had meant to ask you about that.

A: While I do not like to defend myself against New York Choctaw, a word may be in order, e'en though many who despise my rakish flair may accuse me of buttering my own biscuit. While Anderson Hollöw, the celebrated critic and translator of "Rock of Ages" from the Swedish in 491 variations, has called this altruistic measure on my part the act of a "comicstrip Launcelot," it must be borne in mind that he prefers to set up more and merrier academies and counter-academies. The constant buzz and murmur of gossip in chic salon and *soirée intime* points with candor to a singular prime fact, namely, that Hollöw is not the embracer of objectivity. In short, though he pretends to be the Mickey Finn of aestheticians, he is a slovenly liberal. It is that what I feel, in the world, is the one thing I know myself not to be, for that instant. You may well ask! The "West Broadway Buy," as it has come to be known among those who treasure well-built Victorian grey-brick churches, seems, *seems,* mind you, to have a lovely randomness about it, but actually it is just one of a quietly didactic sequence of proposals. It's jake by me to call a tub a tub! Many have importuned Hollöw to offer nothing but his sprightliest, but he is bent on dumbness.

Q: Do you feel that art is about to make another significant break-through?

A: Cultured Brahmins that we are or bend the knee in tearful orison to be, yet how we wish that we were still those mere shells of solid brick and soft sentimental mud. It is, of course, but youth remem-bered, a cig and a Coke, but the wild singing and general traipsing around! It's like to bust you up. A breakthrough is like an evening. There's no way to start it out directly, first the sun must go down, and Old Sol has his own mind. I mean to say a true breakthrough claims great antiquity. You don't go boo-boo-boo and hot dog! and of a sudden you're dealing with a Cézanne or a Jocko Conlan, no sir. The ways of innovation are strait and fraught with maladroit. Would the French tongue have been reified had the redoubtable Sade not been nabbed for a youthful indiscretion? *Sic transit semper tyrannus,* or as a wag has it, "Hats off! The flag is passing by." And may God help you if you don't whip your bowler from your sconce in such circumstance! One waits for the brave spirit who will paint the inner meaning of the nosepicker who stands bemused before the drum majorette's teeny skirt and panties to match amid a storm of sour fifes.

Q: What of the charge that you tend to buy, not individual paintings and sculptures, but whole studios indiscriminately?

A: To this I turn a half-swollen cheek toward the door. It is only after the cheek, or the door, leaves do I feel this strange joy. More specifically, most men of a throb of sleep would be bored to sick-ness walking through all this caca! I tell you, strength is not often drawn from the doors of hotels in the darkest quarter of the city, no matter the protestations of those who shave their legs and pubic hair for love. Sheets of delirious colors pall. The unit is the thing, so modern, so *dernier cri,* so awash with candor. A man in his right mind, and financially well-fixed, such as your devoted partner in colloquy, should stand still for a whole room full of concepts, sand, rocks, and ropes? Consider how explicit the activity of light is.

Explicit and methodically engineered to bore you out of your very trousers! One affects a passionate interest, not to mention an overweening curiosity, but basic human relationships flower when the sound of crisp lettuce is heard in the land. The apparent melding of a vocabulary involved with symbolic action and other phenomena is duck soup say once a year. More than that, you could get a slight twinge of nausea and get so crazy that you might pity old clouds devoured by clouds of hot sand. No telling what! To protect myself from sinus headache and general waves of *mal de mer* brought on by twangs, drawls, and memories of peanut-butter pie, I break out the checkbook and the old Paper-Mate and take everything off their hands. It may be, as you suggest, done "indiscriminately," but no one can accuse me of doing it with love. The sweet cats rarely complain, rather is a rose bowl held in the hand more their speed. I am a sort of shining champ, titter who will!

Q: Is that a loud crashing coming from the gazebo?

A: My helpmate and the faithful Shreve aromp. It is nothing more or less than a throe of joy. I grow weary of the problem of historicity. Though what interests me goes on all the time an occasional boredom afflicts continually. They don't have weather in Ohio. Look, I cannot abide to be predicated. That seems painfully clear. My not inconsiderable wealth allows me such activity, if such it be. One might call it an instance of the archetypal nature of it all, around and around. Though what constitutes a true archetypal nature—and they are, like a good man, hard to find—is as nebulous as the idea of admitting the fact of one's own feelings.

Q: Is there such a thing as the artist's "plight"?

A: To think on the rusty metal and the paint-spattered shoes may be enough for some. People enjoy being covered with soot, *de gustibus*. Think on the Romantics. Think on the watery principles of Locke, if you dare! Men consider that heat damps the money in their pockets but do you hear a peep from them? Maybe some quixotic mouthful like "forget the money," or "forget the desperate stretch," or "see the passion of art." In the meantime rumors are flying. This is why the ferns are exciting. Look, the wings of disbelief and beauty may be what you incarnate as the "plight" of the artist. I don't cotton to it! Despite flowered shirts, rawhide vests, suede ties and the like, a casual glance will reveal a plethora of perfectly excellent hucksters. The butter, like they say, would not melt in their mouths. In the green of back Brooklyn, if you follow my argument, there are many cantaloupes, equally some very damn fine splendor—I mean despite the anguished faces and other symbols of decrepitude in service to the Muse. Breathes there a sensitive with soul so dead that he feels no pinch of ecstasy at being told that he is untransmittable? Yet withal this is a clumsy blague. A large moiety of these starstruck folk bring to mind an array of brand-new decks of Bicycles. As a mere fringe figure huddled on the edge of this great volcano belching fashion I keep shut however, with the exception of a huge and spectacularly insincere smile, the trap. So you see, don't talk to me from the "plight."

Q: I know it's getting late, sir, so allow me to ask you a final question. What do you think your direction as a collector and connoisseur will be in the years to come?

A: Love so seen in its place is always there, if you will permit a touch of harmless folderol. I see myself at times curving back into the mammoth pool, yet at other times, equally insistent, my bones turn to dark emeralds. It's a problem, these thoughts we have not yet thought. "Direction" to a man like me is more than just your going down the block to the Bijou or the other way to pick up a bottle of booze. I delight in the *sense* of direction all by itself, almost as if it were a large white flower or a pear, rotten maybe, but so complacently *there*. That's the kind of hairpin I am. Some say that the image of going, or of movement, is clear as the eye of a chicken, but I disagree. In my day I've taken the garbage out and I've taken the saw back to the garage too. Little would you think so to look on my bronzed face and so on, but I too have been humble. Now, I think of happiness as that warm center, maybe with the flesh caving in? One thinks of Rilke. His remark to Wasserman is of the quintessence here: "I don't know where you live but I'm going there." Such stilled beauty may be a kind of lethal compromise with the *Zeitgeist*, but can anyone refute such genuine feeling? I look for that lost and gentle farmer whose scarlet face betokens the true lush. It is there, I feel, that Kafka's castle must be built. Direction is a winning form of rhetoric and we must look to it for new aesthetic structures. Huddled cribs, tiptoeing wind, and squinting leaves—toward them I set my rather handsome face. And why not?

My dear Joanne:

Whatever tenuous hold I have on reasonableness, balance, yes, even sanity! seems to be fast slipping away from me at an enormous rate. As for love, ha! ha! *that* seems to be forever out of the question. If you knew of the nights I spend, tossing and turning with nothing but my hot pillow! I cannot even manage to engineer a brief affair with the most ridiculous and puerile of women—a "poetess" of Erotica, no less!

But what do you care of my abject misery?

Ah, could I but tell you! Had I the courage to tell you of the things that have happened to me since I began work on this accursed book! But I'm sure you wouldn't care.

Would you!

I don't know why I should go on beating around the bush like this —it is probably another indication of my collapsing world, which is, or was, though small, mine own. What is the expression? "A sure thing and mine very own"? Something. You will see, my lost darling, that I go on and on, like a drunken carrousel—perhaps that very one we used to see and hear across the bay. You've probably forgotten all about that, as well as that small café.

Haven't you!

Oh, I know what you must be thinking. "Poor Tony, as mad as a hatter in his loneliness—loneliness and *failure!*"

It *is* failure. Absolute, bitter, complete, and total. But do not for a moment believe that it is self-inflicted failure, a desire to fail in order to self-destroy one's self. Oh, no! Don't entertain those chimeras!

This failure—if failure it be (and it *is*)—has been "helped along" by a group of people, a veritable gaggle of them.

Self-inflicted, my ass!

Did Che Guevara self-inflict his failure? Or was it asthma—and *other* things?

Do you remember the black lace corset you used to wear in order to be "smoldering," as you put it? Oh, my darling, I could have *eaten* that corset, garters and all! I still could! But I shock you with my aberrations!

Do you still have it?

Send it to me!!!

No! No! It is madness that speaks! I lose my grip on reality, or perhaps it is unreality. Who said that "life is a nap"? Whoever, he was wrong, wrong. Life is a coma!

No, don't send it. Unless it's no trouble. Maybe you could manage to send yourself inside it. Ha ha.

But I go on and on, and now it is time to, as Jack London said, "bite the gullet." Forgive what I must say, but I write you for *the last time.*

My sister, Sheila, whom you of course know, has been poisoned against me by her husband, a rotten filthy fucking hack motherfucking son of a bitch bastard prick, Dermot Trellis, a man with the mind of a daily book reviewer. Some time ago, under his baleful influence, and in order to bring me to my knees and plunge me into deep despair, she launched a vicious campaign against me and my career.

She has taken to sending me things calculated to enrage me, depress me, or both at once!

Do you begin to see what I must say, my kitten?

354

I'm *sure* you do!

Yes! Just yesterday I received from my once adoring and adorable sister the baleful news that you have remarried and have just recently returned from a honeymoon at Niagara Falls. *(Really!)* I, of course, did not even know that you had been divorced, and since I lost you long, long ago, did it matter to me that you had remarried? To me, one husband or ten—you were not mine!

Yet . . . yet . . . I should have known immediately that Sheila *Trellis* —ugh!—would not send such a clipping had she not a venomous, and perhaps even baleful reason!

And then——

The name burned through and through me like the flames of hell, like rotten whiskey, like Drano. I wept, I screamed, I saw, gathering about me, the tightening net of an almost supernatural inevitability.

You, Joanne?

Good God! To become Mrs. Vance Whitestone! Is there in the cards for me an unkinder cut?

I doubt it.

Oh, my stars, Joanne! To marry this man—he, who was so unkind to me, so long ago, who singlehandedly tried to abort my career when I was still young and vulnerable and without those callouses on the soul that are every serious writer's occupational hazard, along with calloused middle fingers.

But this is shop talk.

You must surely know, as his loving wife (God, how my heart stings as I write those words!), that he has decided to champion none other than—Dermot Trellis.

And his filthy, shabby potboiler, now reissued, *The Red Swan* Surely you know, in those moments when you free yourself from wallowing in *sex,* of his feelings anent that trash heap of a novel? By God, he wrote the fucking *Introduction* to it!

No! I am not mad. I am not even what the English would call eccentric.

Mrs. Whitestone! *Mrs.* Trellis! For a little steady nookie . . . ?

To think that he, *he,* that toadlike creature, now has the opportunity to eat your corset, if he wishes! I mean—oh, you know what I mean. He probably can't even appreciate corsets! I have heard that he is an eater of blackstrap molasses. What can one expect of such an insect?

They are all against me. And now, I see, you have joined their camp.

I can't believe it. It would be hard for me to believe that you were having a love affair (ugly expression!) with Whitestone—but to be informed that you are *married* to him!

Don't scoff at this letter, written in blood! Don't patronize *me!* They are all against me, yes, in a grand attempt to destroy my career, humiliate me, bring me to my knees in the dust and the muck.

When I think of the idyllic nights that we spent together it hardly seems credible that—what is there to say? I have had horrifying visions of you in the arms of that beetle, that gross creature from West End Avenue and the Hamptons. Of course he *loves* dogs and sailboats, doesn't he, the condom!

You frivolous baggage!

Listen to this. And listen with great care. Sheila marries Dermot Trellis and soon after begins to attack *my* work while championing *his.* A professor is poisoned against my work *by Trellis* at the same time, and his interest in my *oeuvre* flags and dies, while his interest in *Trellis's* swill is quickened. Vance Whitestone, who was, and probably still is, the King of Emasculation in the publishing world, a barbarian who drinks Martinis with lemon peel, the man who went out of his way to bruit it about that I was a flash in the pan, "suddenly" writes an *Introduction* to *The Red Swan,* fawning over it as if it were Proust or McCoy. The book begins to "catch on" with the mindless, the devourers of *chic,* the people who follow trends. Then *you* marry Whitestone! And other things!

What about the Baroness D'Lenox? Her insulting offer to me of a free-lance editorial job at chickenfeed wages! Who do you think suggested to her that I was so low as to be open to insult? I fixed her up good, the pig!

Ha! Ha! Ha! I could laugh if it weren't all so incredibly evil.

And you tell *me* that Whitestone doesn't know Professor Roche? Hogwash! Kumquats! as Charlie Chaplin would say.

And what about my first wife? She can stick her clarinet up her you-know-what for all I care, but what about her? How about when she was doing her level best to make me into a hack so that she could have the "good things"? Huh? I know what kind of "good things" that slut wanted. But who was her *closest friend* at the time she began to harass me? Who?

You! You were! I was blinded by love and that lace corset. How your hips blossomed from its delicious clasp! It is madness to dwell on it.

I see it all clearly now. My little "kinks" have not undone my powers of reason. No, not by a long shot. You bitch.

And now I remember bumping into Vance Whitestone "by accident" one day when my ex-wife and I, *and you,* went to lunch. I introduced him to both of you.

How he smiled. What a blind nincompoop I must have appeared.

How long was it before you three had a wild orgy? How cruel you all were.

I mean, to me!

And even now you think that I don't know! Ha! *I know everything*.

There is even a hazy memory that has gnawed on me, like a rodent, gnawed and worried, on and off, that Sheila wrote and told me that she had met an editor at a faculty-student tea given by the English Department.

It was surely Vance Whitestone.

And now I see that the froglike creature probably seduced my sister, my ex-wife, *and* you, and then introduced Sheila to Dermot Trellis—who also seduced her! God knows how she's found time to become Nabokov's premier fan.

Nabokov! I don't doubt for a moment that he too had a hand in my failing career. Those letters to *The New York Review* on Russian syntax! Do you all take me for a fool? Anyone can see that they are in code, literary code.

Sheila. Yes. Now I see that she was the personal courtesan to both Whitestone—*El Froggo*—and Dermot, who married her to destroy me.

And what about you? You too were involved! If you will recall, you never told me that you *didn't* know Trellis.

Were you ashamed that he, too, grabbed you in that lace corset? And you said it was only for me!

You needn't scoff. My evidence is overwhelming. I have it on good authority that Vance Whitestone, your darling Frog Prince, took a course some years ago with Professor Roche. And surely you must remember how my ex-wife and Sheila used to talk, talk, talk about *modern fiction*.

All their opinions were the same as those of Whitestone! Coincidence?

Do you begin to see the pattern? Even through your "love"-blinded eyes? Do you begin to see the web of the vast and terrible conspiracy?

Your new marriage, and Sheila's news of it to me—and I know that you must have asked her to tell me (do you have the gall to deny it?) —were intended to be the old one-two-three knockout K.O. to send me reeling. It is all as clear as crystal to me.

But I will not be a K.O.

You cannot, I'm sure, find it in your heart to accept what I have told you as the absolute truth. If you show this letter to Whitestone, he will chuckle. I can hear his amphibian voice now. Guttural and chilling.

To marry Vance Whitestone in order to crush me seems to me a bad bargain. As you can see by this letter I am far from crushed. I am lucid, calm, and my work, after some bumps, is stronger by the day. I have just completed a chapter in which my five main characters confront each other in a brilliant "party scene." Yes—I, who always wrote "party scenes" that seemed mucilaginous—so Dermot once said. But *you* don't remember that, do you? The chapter leaps off the page like a literary *trompe l'oeil*—a Walpurgisnacht! It demonstrates that I can include carefully researched material—"dry" material—into a swiftly moving narrative of suspense and action. Believe it or not. I am happy!

It seems quite clear to me that this book will establish me as the most interesting spokesman for the American avant-garde, and for Sur-fiction, as well as Ur-fiction, and Post-Modern fiction to boot.

The porno king, Trellis, with his foul filth. Filth for its own sake and the sake of his wallet.

I beg you, my dear Joanne, to think on this letter. How sorry I feel for you, married to that *queer*, Whitestone!

Of course, though, you knew he was queer. Didn't you? Ask him about the men's-room scenes at lunch in the publishing house he worked at? And do you remember that young girl, Miss Jefferson, who was his assistant? Ask him what "she" had —*under "her" skirts!*

I close now, alone, neglected, but surely proud. Proud and strong, by God! When *Crocodile Tears* is finally published, you will rush around town, your face burning with pleasure as you collar people to tell them that you once knew me. I envy you.

With unbridled horror at your new estate, I am your old friend, as always,

Tony Lamont

P.S. Don't forget to check on that corset. I'm really kidding. Well, you might take a look for old times' sake.

11. BLUE RUIN

Now the time has come around, dear, gentle friend, and also patient auditor, when a man, in this case myself, must do what he has to do, though Heaven itself may cry out to him, as oft it will and at times must, that he cut it out, cease, and desist, for decency's sake and that of sundry others. So must I do! May I hesitantly opine that the tale that I confront you with hereby is one not to be too lightly taken? In short, do not misconstrue it too quickly, but wait a while.

In a word, Daisy, whom you will remember as that shy sylph of silver speech and crimson cheek, and I, debased mortal beings astew and bespattered with burning memories of our lustful weakness, came to realize that what we had engaged in with such a drooling! such a sweating! of delight, was no sign—no!—of what some may choose to descry, in their lack of charity, and superabundance of slanderous tongues, as lustful weakness. Some may hint that. However, no! We had been bewitched! How, you may well guess. But I gained a deeper insight into the powers of bewitchment, and so on and so forth, of those two incredible ladies, in the adventure, if such it may, which now transpired, or, if it suits you, fell out.

Our, that is, Daisy and I's, desire, if not obsession by now, was, though sullied by a rather interesting feeling of lewdness, a *soupçon* of lechery, that hinted at possessing our strong, albeit trembling I insist, frames, and, more importantly—our minds! our desire was still to wrest, pull, drag, and haul, if needs be, away, Ned Beaumont from the two who had made him *less than a man*. Although foul blackmail had reared its crimson shining head, all aglitter and aglow like the scales on that other monster, it of the green eyes and yet another name, jealousy, Daisy, that slip of a girl with great heart thumping underneath, and I, not importantly sliplike, but "game," if I may employ a rude argot, continued steadfast in our intent to rescue dear Ned Beaumont, now a mere shambles of his former self that once had walked like a man.

How, you may impute by your flickering eyes, did we intend on going on about such grim affairs? As well you might, I dare say. We dared to chance the idea of baiting the bears in their own den! Yes, fully and openly, and with an overwhelming candor, did we plot to appear as just plain patrons in the midst of the nocturnal revelry that so betokened Club Zap, the club which the harlots now owned out-right, as you will recall from my earlier revelations, no? Although that dear chop, Daisy, and I, your humble raconteur, knew vaguely the strange powers of the Madames Corriendo and Delamode, what boots it life if not the hazard? If you get me. We felt, and were foolish for feeling, as you shall soon glimpse clearly if you listen with even half an ear, and cease dozing, as I seem to be catching you in, so to speak, we felt, I reiterate, that we could discredit their very souls in the trapped and cowering mind of Ned Beaumont, whom Daisy loved still, despite the harmless folderol she and I had tinkered with. In the glaring public's eye, in the open air of a club, with all on display for each and every customer to see, we thought, what harm can come to us? At most, they'd roust us out into the darkling streets as heck-lers, did it not appear to be so? Certainly. So we lulled, like saps, if you will allow my gutter jargon, ourselves into complacency. Yet, pounding underneath, somewhere in the vicinity of what modern medical science calls the "heart," fear, naked, and with trembling limbs, howled on! As well it might, by God.

I say that Daisy and I had thusly decided to embrace this course of action. But, and you may inquire, what of the very center, nay, the proven cynosure, of this strategy? I mean, Ned Beaumont himself! It made no matter, as any fool can see, and as many surely will, if Daisy and I "discovered" the vapidity and sleaziness of the two smoulder-ing harlots who had made all our lives a very Cerberus! I mean to say that we two knew, for days now, even a week or so—ah, how the march of time obscures itself, or something like that—that Corrie and Berthe had ensnared Ned Beaumont in certain sensual nets through varied wiles and potent drams of curious liqueurs, oft called, by the learned few, "draughts." No matter. I mean, no matter what it's called, or what, I should correct myself, *they're* called. But perish the thought that you, my patient listener, should think me a pedant! Why, my whole thrust and desire throughout this entire tale has been to keep you wide awake, and trembling with anticipation of my next glaring trope! So be it. Where was I? Oh, yes, *we* had no reason to be enlightened as to what we avowed it to be their charlantanry and tricky acts, if not outright dodges. Chicanery, some might say, and, all right, I numbered myself among that host. *We* had no need to be awakened to their utter baseness. *We* knew! It was, as you will have probably hazarded, Ned Beaumont, and Ned Beaumont alone, to whom our hearts flew out, our faithful blood touched with love and the most profound feelings of camaraderie. That was, and I still maintain it, although his body lies there among those trashy books and other jetsam, as you can see, as it should have been. Whatever disagreements we had later—but I run ahead of myself, as some have hinted is my wont, particularly my ex-wife, she of the crazed potter's wheel and glazed eyes. But there obtains no profit in hearkening to the past, and nostalgia seems to me the ravening police dog in the closed department store, though some use Dobermans.

In any event, and *sans* further or even nearer ado, it was Ned Beaumont who was the center, the essential crux of this bold plan. By that, I strongly imply that Daisy and I had to get Ned Beaumont aroused from out his stupor of fear and blizzards of perverse desire and up on his dear old feet, and with us—yes, with us! Ned Beaumont had to don evening clothes and come along, shuffle though he might, whine and tremble too, and enter, with us, to the lair of the lascivious ladies. A daring and perhaps quixotish plan of action? You ask? But desperation needs its own inventions, and they often work—ah, sometimes better than we hope, and to our concerted consternation, so mature years know, often to their folly. In a wily sort of way, of course, but still. . . . I adhere wholly and with what heartiness I can muster up, to the idea that our plan was risky. Not did it but place us in "contact" with the cagy foreign babes, so that they might work again some trickery upon our gentle persons—and I cared not of my own danger, I strongly opine!—but we laid ourselves supine to, of course—blackmail! I saw the word dancing there noiselessly on the very tip of your writhing tongue. We had no defenses to throw up hastily, as soldiers once threw bulwarks, or bastions, or whatever, up against other soldiers, or at them, whatever their martial arts declared to be *au courant*. Nothing, I implore, *nothing*, to guard us against a sly word, or if truth be told, and it will out, at any rate, a sly sentence or even short tale, slipped into Ned Beaumont's uncomplaining and pitifully weak ear, perhaps between the acts, perhaps, in a kind of code that he would understand and gather greedily, from the very stage itself! And the tale, I stoutly knew and so told Daisy, who, though pretty as a mouse, was not too big in the brains department, would reek and percolate of the "day of shame" when both she and I lost wholly our innocence along with, so it turned out afterward, some of our clothes, and God only knows where they may reside at present. Yet, I agree, this is a minor detail, a mere footnote to my major exposition. My point is, and it is cute as well as sharply potent, Daisy, Ned Beaumont, and I, I strongly declaim, were taking an adventurous risk that we cherished hopefully might be worth the candle. And if not? *How,* we dared not think of it as we readied ourselves for our night in the murky confines of that den of inequity, or iniquity, that kitchen sink of the flamboyant and the foolish, Club Zap!

Bear along with me for a space of time or so, while I present to you some datas and other nuggets, that may allow you to envision in your lively brain—and I obtain that it is so by your gleaming eye!—the kind of milieu into which we three would plunge, as well we did, and, as it turned out to be encountered, well over our depth. You are bearing? Good! The Madames Corriendo and Delamode presented from the stage an act fast gaining plaudits in this city as curious, delightful, and, as one man put it down, and in cold print, mind you, "splendiferous." I agree with your wry face, but there it is. I too feel the quirky rumblings of incipient nausea at the mere mention of the phrase. Yet, as the truth do tell, I must present this intelligence for your clutching grasp, if I wish to clarify the ambience and every other damn thing else, howsoever vapid. It is not the dopey messenger who should be killed, so doth simple Justice roar! In all events, they were, as the night follows the day, a "hit."

You may recall that they had an act wherein, though God be my judge, and He may, they performed magical tricks, some simple, some complex and replete with gewgaws and gimcrackery, some partaking in a raw and rough-hewn fashion, of clairvoyance. What certain mouths have breathed, once in a while, a mind-reading "stick"—whatever that last word may signify, or, I insist, at least portend. But that is not to the point, as I see that you are impatient for the meaty nuts of this pathetic, and albeit frightening yarn. I gathered up, as chickens gather chaff, all these sundry facts from a discursive scanning of old newspapers and magazines readily available to me in my mundane role as a publisher of some note and minor aspiration. Yet this is not the place to beat my drum or play upon my flute, or fife. Or even, I impugn, my bugle! I discovered that Club Zap broke all records as to customers. Yet, withal, here and there, small irritable notes appeared, here and there, concerning opinions delivered of older, more well-endowed, or, if you please, more established magicians, long versed in stagey craft and legerdemain. The consensus of these old prestidigitators and the like, for what they are entitled here is not germane, seemed to be—and, as I say, these opinions were mere shy rumblings, mostly subterranean, or so I ventured, in any cases, the consensus was that Corriendo and Delamode were clumsy, careless, unprofessional, naive, and gauche in their act. The burden of these elder gents' complaining was that—and here, I vow to you, I should have paid heed to the prickly hairs on the back of my neck that fairly danced in nameless fear!—the two ladies in question performed tricks and marvels of magic that had never been known before! I mean, wherever! Although they appalled these jaded "pros" by their rank amateurism, the truth, as often it may be, lay! They were, in a word, unique. Thusly, so did they frighten and enrage these hoary duffers, by threatening to remove the bread and butter from their needy mouths. For who, and so well do I remember

362

it, I mused, would pay to see a trick that all can do when he can see strange tricks no man, pressed though he might be by many clamoring minds, and repleted with years of, as they mouth, "savvy," can even approach to explain? Hence, I informed Daisy that we were to descend into a maelstrom of magic that was, by and large, the most stupendously bewildering of our time! Yet I hasten to addend to these remarks that I was not prepared for the sheer terror that you can bet your boots I got, to say the least. As did we all. In no way wishing to telegram my punch, the night that our naive trio spent at Club Zap was one of a lot of sheer aggravation, not to mention a lot of heartaches. Yes, sir. It quaked me, through and through.

Now, staring back upon that nocturnal disaster, I see, from the calm plateau wherein I cling, that this *faux pas* Daisy and I made was but fated, ah yes, it could no more have been eluded than a penny lying on a trolley track can escape a severe flattening as ultimate end. Yes! It falls sorely into place now—another jagged piece of that jigsaw puzzle of doom that the Ineffable Creator toys with, which we bootlessly think to be life! Yet, at that time, as I have portended to you, it seemed eminently reasonable, as well as a trifle more than just plain jake, to engage our wits with the two slippery courtesans who enfasted Ned Beaumont in their snares.

Imagine us then, we three, lost babes in the crepusculous wood, Daisy, splendid in virginal white, haughty and coolly elegant, yet with that touch of common clay we love so well and desire to crush, though it may crumble to dust, to our bosoms. At least *I* wish to crumble it on *my* bosom—I do not, I speedily submit, deign to speak for you, patient friend. I, chock full of what men call "butterflies," although I was smart enough to know that it was terror, impeccable in a tuxedo I had last worn to a glorious book party, a shindig flung on the publication of one of our specialty titles, a tome on the crocks of America, as my hazy mind grasps the happy memory. Bygone frivolities all. Well, my upper lip, as our British friends are wont to ascribe, was as stiff as a board, if you will forgive the metaphor, yet my palms were bathed in furtive apprehension. Between us, out of Ned Beaumont's apartment, into a waiting taxi, purring softly at the curbside, and thencely, into the maws of the looming Club Zap itself! —was poor Ned Beaumont, whom can best be described as being in the posture of a bag of rags tied in the middle—thus did he shamble and stoop, drag and quiver, as our strong arms, mostly mine I do confess, for Daisy's arms were not so strong as they might have been, propelled him, contrariwise to his desires, into the fearsome ambience of the two who had sceled his very soul!

Club Zap exuded waves of palpable foreboding, a chilly air struck our persevering faces as the doorman allowed us ingress, a chilliness that had, and I mordantly vow it, *little to do with the air-condition-ing system.* It was an unhealthy chill, something evil clung about it, and it was with courage aflag that we mustered up the fortitude to plod inward, although Ned Beaumont had hung back, his poor face greenish, until a sharply reproving yet gentle kick to the vicinity of his shins by Daisy urged him on. How puissant her stern "guts" showed itself to be I leave it to you to imagine. You are right to smile fleetingly in an admiring way as you just have done. The tinkle of crockery came to our ears and the low chatter of the murmuring voices of the clientele, members of the *haut monde,* the jetty set, the beautiful humans, along with the usual quota of chic riffraffs and hoi pollois. It was such an admixture of varying personalities that gave to the club its aura and swiftly burgeoning reputation as a place to not only see, but to be oneself glimpsed. Suddenly, an apparition swam toward us out of the murk, belike, betimes, akin to that curious monster that frightened the wits out of Dante in his smoky perambu-lations. And who could it be? I see your eyes hopping in your head with expectancy! Of course, of course! It was the wily maître d', he of the oily teeth and virtually noiseless camera, who had imprisoned Daisy and I forever on cellulose, or whatever it may be appellated —I'm no technocrat. For a brief moment of agued horror, while, it seemed to me, and also to Daisy, I'll give you seven to five on it anyway, that the silky cad was about to confront us, in front of the dragging Ned Beaumont, with our minor peccadilloes and intense *frissons* of a few weeks back—or was it a few centuries? So it may have seemed in the still reach of the nights! But his face, slick with unctuous grease, and impassive with *sang-froid,* betrayed no more emotion than the face of a clam. And like a clam, or some other featureless creature of the wave, the fellow had no name! That should have been another clue, another indice, that our adventure was star-crossed from the beginning! Had I but only known . . .

But events were happening with the rapidity of speed itself! Drag-ging, pushing, pulling, and bullying the aspen Ned Beaumont be-tween us, Daisy and I, our faces painfully fixed in masks of casual levity, our hearts aflame with the dim hopes that the patrons would consider our charge a carefree alcoholic "out" on the town, how be it, as I have stated, we were in no town, but in the dripping jaws of the great city itself, Daisy—ah, dear brave little wife—and I, I say, following the waiter who the buttery maître d' had commanded, arrived at our table with the pusillanimous Ned Beaumont, who, by now, was nothing but the shadow of a shadow of a man. In the face of the grand design that we had hatched, I forbade my raging heart to break—ah, but how it thumped against my white starched shirt! Suddenly! My cravat seemed bent on the desire to strangle me! Or is it a foulard? I pushed it from my mind, and we three sat and began to bury ourselves in the menus that graced the snowy linen that glittered beneath our elbows. We were seated, as you may have opined, "between shows," as the parlance of show business so indicates such a caesura in the action of pleasing the mob, and we thought to order a drink as is the wont of many patrons—probably the overwhelming majority, if the polls are to be believed. The waiter, a faceless and fawning creature whose visage was lost in the clouds of smoke that eddied, now here, now nervously there, suggested the "speciality" of the "house"—that latter word took on a base reverberation for me, and from the shy bloom of flush that lighted Daisy's cheeks, for her as well. Ned was doing his level best to merely breathe, so I feel he missed the fleeting blush of embarrassment that skittered.

This "speciality" was called a Blue Ruin. Daring not to attract notice to our true purposes in this nighttime gambol, we decided to order the drink. I can still hear our voices, high, albeit firm, overlaid with a charming lightness that we did not, in no wise, and you can lay odds, feel, we gave the minion our orders.

"I'll try a Blue Ruin—myself," I shot.

"I, too, my good fellow," Daisy followed hard on.

Prompted by the gentle pressure of Daisy's heel against his gleaming pump, Ned Beaumont managed to croak out, "Too . . . too. . . ." His feigned smile was so ghastly that I had to cover up my involuntary retch with a pretended cough and the hasty pressing of my napkin to the generalized area of my mouth. Daisy had gone so white that, in her white gown against the shining napery, I almost lost sight of her for a long moment.

The waiter returned with a curious promptness with three cocktails that gleamed, in their spotless glasses, like the summertime sky itself, a flawless, perfect blueness inhabited the potables, and a not displeasant petillance sparkled therein, at, if one may so coin the phrase, the "soul" of the drink. As he served us the churl murmured low, in a voice strangely loud to nervous ears, "Show time in ten minutes, sir." He had most clearly aimed these candid remarks at Ned Beaumont, who responded by slipping down in his chair like a ragamuffin. Perhaps not precisely, but you will comprehend my drift, so my fondest wishes pray. With an excruciatingly blasé nonchalance, we addressed our drinks, and found them quite yummy. What kind of a remark can I expect to elicit from you, sedulous eavesdropper, if I narrate the odd fact that the Blue Ruin had the overpowering flavor of eggplant? Yet the facts are there to prove it! Ha! I say "the facts." However, one of the imbibers, other than I, lies crumpled there, his face like an old sneaker, and the other, that bewitching

365

belle, has not yet arrived—and may not! Thus, you must accept my affirmation. Eggplant, sir. A not unpleasing taste, yet so earthly a savor was quite unexpected from this liquor of such aristocratic mien! Eggplant, yes. But was there, lurking in the depths of this refreshment, something—*else?* Something that would allow Corriendo and Delamode to breach our walls and crumple up our ambuscades? To this hour I cannot know—all I can relate is what occurred on this fateful evening, gruesome in its petty callousness of spirit and, by God, outright meanness.

Now, I confess it to you, impends the straitly difficult section of my illuminating, though vaguely sordid tale. I must have needs, of need, to defer to certain notes, if not mere rough jottings that I created while at Club Zap or just after, in order for my burning mind to recall —and blissful amnesia would be my wont, I assure you, rather than any candidness of recollection!—the squalid events. So if my shaking hands crumple and crackle papers from this point on, I beg you to remain ignorantly aloof, of course. So, onward, and may the chip lay where it falls in the area of its selection.

I have said that we had begun our tentatively consuming of the Blue Ruins, Daisy's eyes had taken on what a certain wit used to call "a sublunary shine," my thoughts seemed at once clear and yet almost like a jigsaw puzzle, if I may hire out such a fancy analogue, and dear Ned Beaumont—he mumbled minutes together. At this point, the lights in the club dimmed down, and the stage lights increased considerable. Thus too, a small orchestra struck a note of fanfare! Ta-ra. Ta-ra. And so on. You will overlook my scrofulous voice, for which I have never been pointed out as one to adhere to in the matter of the musical arts? Thank you. Suddenly—and with a swiftness as surprising as it was abrupt, the stage curtains parted, and before our agape eyes, Madame Corriendo and Madame Delamode stood, among divers paraphernalias and other things of sorts. They were, in a word, utterly breathtaking! Both were donned in white robes some mention to be albs, yet they were of an excruciating brevity, coming to just that point of the upper thigh where it swells so that a man of red blood feels himself a surge of warmth and desire. The garments fitted them closely whereby those voluptuous bodies showed most clearly, and were girdled by white silken cords, or some other fabric of similitude. Snowy white tights snugly folded their maddening legs, and white boots shodded their feet up to the gorgeousness of their plump calfs. In a word that I ask you to pardon, they were some dish! My breath got caught, and Ned Beaumont began to gurgle low in his throat, fear, loathing, and the nakedness of careering lust all stamping furiously on his face. Even Daisy pinked a little, and I knew that she was thinking—but let us close the door

366

on that! If you please. They were, as you will gather up my hints, the sort of women who enjoy "knocking you out." Need I imply on? But, and bear closely with me for this rude confession, they had embroidered across that section of their albs that covered caressingly their full and wicked breasts, rather strange symbols that appeared like this, stitched in startling red.

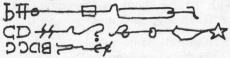

Whatever fiddle-de-dee these so-called arcanic symbols pretended, I certainly advise here that they were effective. We three were agog with them, and Ned Beaumont was besides himself in agitation. The two evil misses, whatever else they were, were showpersons true-blue, and their mere act of appearance on the stage, so decked out curiously as a cross between a priestess, a magical charlatan, and a hot sexy broad was dynamite of a particular genius! For some *pan-ache* or other, they then threw packs of cards up in the air, toward the patrons, in the meantime putting on a terpsichorean perform-ance that was inutterably rotten, such lack of talents had they, but which served to display, how shall I say it? their corporeal charms. And no punch was pulled! Quickly ending their "dance," you shall please me mightily if you'll forgive this last expression, they clung arm to arm together in front of the stage, and bathed in a blue light that seemed uncannyishly like the shade of our cocktails—by the by, which had been silently replenished, and now seemed possessive of the savor of licorice, can you beat that!—they sang this strange song, to the tune of an oldy-time vaudeville hit, "Moonlight On Our Maña-nas," which you may recall with various degrees of loathing.

> Rogo, rogo, gajja mogo, habba dabba doo!
>   Is our proud lingua, do we?
>   Stern as a clot, strong as a truck,
>   Gomba! Labba hoodoo, do we?
> Nein! We doan give a fuck!

> Here's my goodie friendie, Corrie Corriendo!
>   Place a filth eye at her boobs!
>   Valla gooby inna trousers?
>   What if a hand should funge a boob?
> Hein! Shrimps are outta luck!

> Yah, bend a visage here 'pon Berthe Delamodee!
>   Feel you a swollen ka-kee?
>   Falloon, falloon, falloon—wahoo?

Digits do encircle ka-kee!
Wine! Ju-jus are for suck!

Here, we bothie sweetie ladee, zeelie, zeelie, zee!
  Thrill a minute inna cleft?
  Ambidextriprestidigit!
  With thonkas chunk that weeping cleft!
Fine! Thigh-deep inna muck!

For! Tis entertaina-boona!
Yo! Laffa-daffa sucka-mucky!
Ambiclefta ducka-wucky!
Wit' boobs an' butts our marzipang'll
Bust yer pants an' frocks!
You blastiphageous crocks!

Lap 'er up like harlowgolla!
Who's to urge no-no? Who? Who?
Sullivander kumquat! An' poopoo!
Longgams luscious we'll soon arrive'll
At the vestibule!
U' cazz' a la scaff' an' cul'!

Scoff though you must and apparently will, this was no figment, nor
did I create or change a very syllable of this odd ditty. I read it from
this paper word for word as it emitted from their full mouths and
blossomy lips. Its effect on the audience was electrical! Everywhere
about the club, in the halflight, men and their distaffs sat hypnotized
as if struck by thunder. Such was the effect of these amok lyrics on
the not-crass group that numbered up the audience. No bumpkins
they! to turn a nice phrase. Now I realize, at the distance of cool
hindsight, that the "song" they sang was no "song" at all—it was some
type of antique incantatation, or, you know what I get at. But on with
my bizarre tale! The stage lights were changing in color, blues, reds,
yellows, greens, oranges—my favorite color, by the way—and many
more too numerous for a mention. Let's just suffice it to say, all right?
Then, as if by magic—ha! ha! ha!—a blackboard appeared behind
them, so strangely that I swear I hadn't seen it hence. Turning to
Daisy, I was about to drop a hint concerning this occurrence, when
her sweet voice tinkled out all huskily:
  "Martin! I feel apprehension at the sudden appearance of that—
blackboard, is it?"
  "I was about to reveal the same, Daisy," I ventured in reply, with
a virile effort at composure by flashing my pearlies.
  "For . . . tricks . . . make . . . tricks . . . aieeee . . ." Ned Beaumont

grinned sinkingly. Meanwhile, his fingers drummed.

Did Ned Beaumont, entoiled as he was with the two showpersons before us, know something that he was holding from us, close in his fist to the chest? My mind toyed with this idea for a fleeting fraction, and I slid a glance at Daisy, whose eyes seemed clouded and full of doubt, almost as if she was saying to me, "He may know something that he is keeping close to the fist in his chest!" Meanwhile, swallowed by lavender light, Corriendo went to the blackboard, and, reaching up, wrote upon it in blue chalk. And you are correct if you are thinking that the act of so doing this endeavored to allow her skirt to "hike" up and display to the audience somewhat of her ripe nether charms, as attested by a wave of hearty applause, whistles, sighs, and not a few moans and groans—not all of them masculine! In any events, this is what she wrote:

Upon this completion, she stepped forward on the stage, clapped her hands, and Madame Delamode jumped into a top hat—and disappeared! Only to appear—and still the fright tingles throughout every gram of marrow in my body!—at our table, where she waggled her finger at us all and said, but *sotto vox,* so that only we should hear:

"Jou es oll very bad to try thees theeing weeth me an' the Madame Corrie. For chame! Watch your estep! Jou weel fin' us more than some matches for jou!"

Then, smiling, as a spotlight found her and the audience grasped the enormousness of the feat, she made her way back to the stage to a din of kudos. Daisy was trembling violently, crossing and recrossing her depthless eyes, yes, all unknowing. I was bathed in sweat, a sweat that fair threatened to wet my nice shirt! Poor, dear Ned Beaumont had fallen to the floor and was being helped to his seat by the oleaginous maître d', whose sinister smile made my heart do a tailspin and a loop-a-loop! I knew then that we had no chance against the tricks of these perverts except to ride forth, if you will excuse my speaking in a figure, and engage them once and for all. Ned Beaumont himself, in all his twitching, quivering, and nauseating display of weakness and cupiditous lusty lewdness, was at stake. *He* was the prize! And though a rotten bargain, even somewhat chintzy and totally crummy in what he had become, yet was he a human being? He was! And the beloved of that sweet adulterous Daisy, dulcet child, though my heart grated and creaked a lot to so admit to say it.

I knew then, in the heart of the heart of my heart, and in the core of my twisting guts, and in divers other spots it ill behooves to note, that the time was almost nigh for Daisy and I to make what one might call a "move." Our plans had been worked out, but in a fluidly relaxed manner, since we had no concepts of the sorts of powers and depthness of malice that we would face. The "top-hat trick" just about expunged the wind from my sails—yet was I determined to endeavor, and persevere in addition. My plan with Daisy was roughly, to wit: We would pretend to the status of hecklers, far from being obnoxious enough to be granted the old heave-ho, the infamous eighty-six, but, in a word, pointedly acute in soft-voiced disparagements of the performers' profferings. Our wonted goal? To display a revelation to Ned Beaumont that Corriendo and Delamode had not supreme powers and were, at best, opportunity-grabbers, if not bushers. In simple wise, to deflate them as the gassy and phony child's balloons that they were! Then, and only then, so ran of a celerity our reasoning, would Ned Beaumont see them as but the classy whores that they were, and begin to extricate himself from their foul labyrinths. I blinked a glance at brave little Daisy, who grasped the import it lugged speedily, and nodded her shining head imperceptibly. So we prepared to join into battle!

In the meantime, our sinisterly slick magicians were extracting gouts of applause by a series of tricks that, I so assumed, were designed to "warm up" the audience, a large moiety of whom, I assure you, were drunkenly blasé, and replete with doubts and cynicalities of varying potency. These tricks were, according to Madame Corriendo, "wand inspired," and, surely enough, in her long fingers she held a curious wooden rod of maybe a foot and a half long, atip at both ends with pointed caps of a metallic substance, perhaps metal itself! In some shape or other, I mean alloy, if you are with me. At the sight of this innocent-appearing chunk of wood, Ned Beaumont, his eyes watering in loathsome pusillanimousity, and his fingers, how do you say it? "plucking" at the tablecloth, breathed heavily and began to sweat onto the rather tasteful silverware that had been placed—and with inherent correctness, too—before him.

"Your quite obvious terror, Ned Beaumont . . . whence?" I plumbed. "A mere stick of wood? A twig?" I tittered softly behind my cupped hand, making believe that I didn't want him to notice that I was softly tittering—a ploy to enrage his virility, I candidly affirm. But he was in oblivion as to his pride altogether! To such a sadness had he dove.

370

"Blasting . . . power . . . oh, shit!" he croaked, and consumed his cocktail.

"There's no need for vulgarizing, darling. Those women can't hurt you if you don't *want* them to hurt you," so Daisy raptly cajoled.

"Fucking idiot!" Ned Beaumont shouted into his glass, and I saw Daisy color and bridle, stiffening up almost as if she had been slapped in the face with a dash or carafe of ice water. I fumed inwardly.

"No need for grossly sniding at Daisy!" I seethed between teeth clenched like a fist.

But just at this moment, or perhaps a moment later—it is garnished with difficulty to remember such blistered horror, sheer as it was!— I heard the syrupy voice of Corrie Corriendo, and, by God! she seemed to be aiming her barbed syntax directly at my ear, the one I had casually turned toward the stage! You can sketch my confusion for yourself, if you dare!

"And now, dearest patrons and adorers and fans of legerdemains, a small feat of uncanniness for a—*special guest!* Watch jour tables weeth a sharp closeness, I request jou. Please! Silence, so I imploringly command!"

Madame Delamode, *her* shapely back now turned to face the audience, was scribbling another strange marking upon the innocent face of the blackboard,

and Corriendo, gesturing mightily with her stick—even now I cannot bring myself to give it the nobility of the phrase "rod"—suddenly enticed gasps of unadulterated amaze from the many throats that surrounded the multifarious-colored lighting of the small stage. For! and I heartily opine, my eyes could not conceive the credibility of it, there appeared on every table, out of the azure, a pack of cards! All of them boxed and sealed in cellophane or some other transparent material of a kinship to same.

"Please to open jour boxes an' to eenspeck the cards therein, ladies an' gentlemens," Corriendo voiced, and a bizarre hush fell down on the crowded club, ruptured only by such a crinkling! and tearing! as we all blindly obeyed such an order as though we may have become robots! It was quizzical, this I sorely ascertain. I exposed our deck to the harsh, yet soft, light, and found it to be a deck of Aces, of each and every variety of the four suits germane to same.

"All Aces!" "Aces all!" "Aces? Aces?" Such-wise remarks bespattered the fumy air, as patrons called out. Thus, you will reap the idea

371

that by her sudden trick, Madame Corriendo had given everyone a deck of, as they call it, Bullets.

"Aaarrgghhh!" Ned Beaumont said, and swooned, little did he know why. His complexion was a grisly and livid lardlike shade.

"Please to place down these decks face down, an' peek 'em up when I say to perform thees," Corriendo smiled, her heavy breasts heaving in victory, or so it now seems to my backwards glance.

"Peek 'em up, ho-kay!" she then shrieked out, and in the momentary silence that crashed upon each poor mortal's surprise, I heard a concert of guffaws issue from the hearty bellies of the two performers! As well they might, indeed! For each deck of Aces had been, upon a second, transmutated to a deck of Kings! The club, as a whole, if I may be allowed a figurative trope of speech, was baldly perplexed, and strained crazily toward bewilderment as each soul fair burst its adoring hands into wild applause.

It would, of course, never do for our purposes! We had meant to expose some such behavior as charlatanish, but now! We were stunned, and I could not find it in my heart to censure Daisy or myself from clapping along with all the other benighted sheeps! Only Ned kept his nose in his glass and had turned white with fear—although there was a curious lopsided chortle that creased his leathery face, why? Who knew?

Yet there was little time for such an exercise in futile wool-gathering, since Delamode was again sketching on the blackboard another outlandish design apparatus

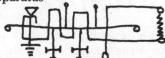

and Corriendo, whose glowing eyes seemed to be obsessed in totality with addressing themselves to *our* table, was waving her stick, and saying:

"Jou perhaps theenk that jou are dreenkeeng to a superfluous amount? Why, then, allow me to give jou oll a glass o' pure water!" And with a great flourish of nervous stick-shaking, each drink on each table was changed, in the batting of an eye, to a glass of water! Jes! I mean, Yes! I submit to you, sedulous interlocutor, despite your arched and querying eyebrows, I vouch that, as surely as birds are enamored of sweet rills and freshets, I drank from what was, a momentary flash before, my Blue Ruin—and it was plain, cool, clear water, the species the Sons of the Pioneers once celebrated. Yet then —and I do vow this upon the poor dead face of that dull clod over there, that lifeless bulk who once stomped around in exceeding waves of vibrant life itself, then, as each flabbergasted sap evoked howls of disbelief at what had just occurred, the damned water—as sudden as a snap!—changed back to what it had been before the change!

"Ha. Ha. Ha." It was Madame Corriendo, all on a chuckle of gargantuan delight, and her gleeful laughter was counterpointed by the higher-pitched gouts of laughter that raced from Delamode's delighted neck, in such wise as "hee hee hee." Daisy was absently fingering her dazzling bodice, Ned Beaumont tore, in a passive orgy of doubt and confusion, many napkins into fragments of their earlier states, and I tried hard to keep what small "head" I had left. The club was a pandemonium of cheers, whistles, shouts of hilarity, and drunken imprecations of "More, More!" It sounded like this.

"Hooray."

"Wheee. Whee-wheee."

"HA. HA. HAR HAR HAR."

"More. More."

And, God help me, we *got* more. Once again, Delamode's sinister chalk was scratching and squeaking out an eccentric drawing on the blackboard

and the tittering statuesqueness of Madame Corriendo, her glittering stick flashing before her juicy shape that seemed now to tower above the clamor of the throngèd tumult, was again performing God knows what unbelievable achievement of dark and mystic legerdemain!

A small spotlight picked out a table in the very center of the room, seated here and there about which were two ladies and their escorts, all of them, as the old proverb has it, "four sheets in the wind." Their state of inebriety was such that they had paid little attention to Corriendo's earlier feats, and I venture to suggest that this lack of awesomeness in their drunken selves had driven the horrific lady into a rage of indelible pique. Such is my guess, but who can truly enounce? Whatever—her stick shook; an odd current of "energy" poured into the room; and—whammo!—the foursome had exchanged clothing, in such a manner that the ladies were donned in tuxedos and the gentlemen in evening gowns! A veritable tidal wave of unleashed hilarity flooded over the room, fair drowning the unfortunate four, who, and you may wager your sock of eagles on the bet, had suddenly attained a stage of absolute soberness, and were wreathed in scarlet blushes. But Madame Corriendo, shrewd in business as her letters to Ned Beaumont have proven, swiftly changed their habiliments back again to their natural state, amid an avalanche

373

of the most unnerving whoops and liberally hurled salutes. Now it was that I began to suspect the awful puissance of Ned Beaumont's captors! Now, for the first time did I approach the face that sheer malice enjoyed! Now, did it glimmer in upon my tortured cerebellum that I had, as it is said, my handfulls of trouble! Still, I steeled my nerves as best I could, and broke out the guidon of a cheery face.

"Pretty fair display of . . . *tricks!*" I declared lightly. "Eh, Ned Beaumont? Pretty fair . . . *tricks?*"

He hid his grey "face," ashen though it was, behind a menu. Daisy clenched and unclenched a salad fork. Undaunted, I signaled for three more Blue Ruins, which appeared, in a hurry, before us—their savor, now, redolent of parsley and vanilla. I drank greedily, determined to chuck a monkey wrench or hurl a sabot into the entertainers' works and to have a good time into the bargain, however much my heart sang the blues. Yet I feared the worse for wear! You bet.

Somehow, flushed with the aroma of victory as they surely must have possessed, for only a blind bat would have missed our consternated nervousness, they pushed on, ah, how relentlessly! their belligerent activities. As, what is called in the summit levels of government, an "overkill" was in the hopper, so to coin it. Hardly had I braced my knees against the corresponding sweet bones of Daisy's underneath the table, hardly had I pounded Ned Beaumont's back in an excess of comradely fustian, than the duo of deviltry were at it again! As per standard proceedings, "s.o.p." as they say, whatever that is, Delamode was scribbling furiously on that perditious blackboard

and Corriendo, her curvaceous hips trembling with her efforts, was shaking and waving her stick toward a lone gentleman in the rear of the room, which soon the small spot picked out, so that he became the focal cynosure of each wildly rolling eye—and I know that there is no need for an inquiry into the whys and wherefores of these eyes' feats!

"Sir, as a delightsome customer to whom our hearts get warm, may we present jou weeth a cocktail that shall endeavor to last jou the entire evening?" So Madame Corriendo's mad patter went.

Every eye zeroed in to the cocktail on this chap's table. Every heart pounded with—what? Did I but know I would hold the key to the mysterious secrets of things, never you scoff. The gent, a mite self-conscious, drained his glass. He replaced the vacant vessel to the surface of the tablecloth. And as God may be my great justice, as well He probably is when He feels up to it, as the glass touched down on the table, it appeared in a flashing burst of no time at all—such was the whiz of it—full again. Yes! Full! The fortunate hombre, smiling in a blend of fear and greediness, drank half the brew this time—and again, as he replaced the glass upon the immaculateness of expanse beneath his casually akimbo elbows, it refilled itself to absolute fullness. Fullness! Again and again, to the point, finally, of *ad nauseam*, the club watched him and his, you'll ignore my trashy mouth, fucking drink. Each time he drank, it was as if he had not, by God! It might have been something direct from the pages of a fairy's tale, so weird did it efface itself before a myriads of boggled eyes!

Madame Corriendo and Madame Delamode were standing together now at the front apron lip of the proscenium, their arms about each other's waspy waists—I admit I vermilioned a bit with a momentary clutch of lusty filth as my brain's eye imagined the scene beneath their garments—their faces bedecked with smiles as they bowed slightly to the earthquakes of applause that shook and rumbled, led, and no wonder! by the lucky lad with the enchanted glass. Daisy and I were plunged into a blue funkiness. There was no possible mode by which we could labor to their discredit at this rate. These were tricks which seemed sheer impeccables! How could I shout accusations of gross and crude cheapness at them in the face of such *savoir-faire?* It was not a simple moment, all beer and skittles, for us. Ned Beaumont was drawing little faces on the tablecloth, a low gibber dancing on his lip. There was a thin film of greasy, mucky sweat upon his countenance—as if I could blame the old hoss!

The patrons, flogged into a state of ecstasy by these flashy sleight of hands, and willing now to believe the two vicious vixens capable of almost any ilk of derring-do, sat in a fever of raptive attention, as Corriendo began a card trick—certainly one that had the airs of an old chestnut, that is, pick a card and so forth and the magician will name it. It little boots a lengthy explanation, so there is no need for the roots of boredom to be emplanted in your face. I shuddered, for I had no way of perceiving what unbelievable variants the potent poule would ring upon this old dodge. Yet not a moment later, when I saw her "name the card," my heart sprang up, as the poet says, like a daffodil in the sky! Corriendo, for some arcanic reason, had fallen from the very Everest of tricks to—dared I believe same?—simple parlor frou-frous that any amateur, with but a pinch of practice, can bring off. I do not, of course, intend to insert any denigrations into *their* honest doorways, no. My point is that here, at last, was the chink I had been inquiring after in their coats of mail. I glanced at Daisy and smiled a slow and rather sweety smile into her angelic stare, then clapped the husklike Ned Beaumont, to which I fairly burst into medley:

"Buck up your head, old fellow! I think I glimpse a gold chance for the forces of fair play. Now, gander at this!"

Then, hastening all my hearty courage, and looking straight at Corriendo, I called out! Ah, how bellish my voice rang upon the hubbub. Called out my opening broadside!

"Trick! Trick! Old! Bush! Boo!" So I importuned her.

The silence was *enceinte*. Merely the snap and clatter of the cards could be heard above the faint rumble of ice cubes. Corriendo looked at me, a glance that might have brought great Dionysos to his muscled knees! She was soon joined by the eerie Delamode, who had been erstwhile lost in the gloaming of the backstage. Her stare also clove through the murk.

"The gentle man weesh to—expose myself?" she chucklingly chirred, although how she managed to chirr and chuckle and riffle the cards is a piece of labor that passes by all understanding.

"Madame," I started off, "am I correct when I say that your deck is what is appelled 'cold' or 'stacked'? Am I not correct in this shade of opinion? Surely, there is no marvel to your 'magic' in this type of case!"

"Hear! Hear!" bellowed Daisy. "Phony! Boo! Malarkey! Bologna!"

The crowd grew restive, and I heard discontentful chatterings about "phony bitches" and "con artists." I struck my iron as hard as I could.

"May I say, simply, a formula for the heretofore suggested 'coldness' of the deck? That is—

"Jackass ate live tree
King intends to fix
Several for benign Queen.

—and to which doggerel I have the pleasure of appending the word 'CHASED.' "

I sat back, exhaustion draining through me. Somewhere, muttering flared and fluttered. I caught Daisy's shining lips cracked rudely in a grin. Even Ned Beaumont sensed, through his bullet-like head that was chock full of despairing ennui by now, that the tide had shifted!

Corriendo and Delamode fired ocular bodkins at me, although their lips fibbed blithely, racked as they were by dental smiles.

"Jou have los' me, sir, weeth jour jackass," she mocked, and the crowd began to hurl a couple of choice invectives toward my area.

They wanted a goat for the victim for the altar of their tedious odium. So much for the monied!

"Lost you, have I?" I sneered cavalierly.

"Disingenuous bullshit!" foul-mouthed Daisy surprisingly.

"Free? At last?" Ned Beaumont shivered.

The patrons heaved like live things! Corriendo and Delamode seemed taken backwards! Ah, did I but only know that they were "setting us up," as the motto has it.

"Lost you?" I rehashed. Then, with almost patient calm, I enounced in tones of stentorious clangor:

> "Jack. Ace. Eight. Five. Three.
> King. Ten. Two. Six.
> Seven. Four. Nine. Queen.

—and, how's about: Clubs. Hearts. Spades. Diamonds?"

My checkered and rather volumous memory had enabled my teeming brain to glean the verse and the code word that controlled the factors for the feats performed with "cold" decks. Ah! For one bright, sun-laved moment I tasted the candy of the victor, I sniffed the mounts of Camelot! Soon, though—but I trot before my penumbra-laden tale.

The kickeroo was not far apace, had I but the smarts to envision it. Madame Corriendo, sniggering as if her very face would bust off, leaped as nimbly as her majestic body would give her permission to do, from the stage, and approached our very table! Daisy flustered prettily, Ned Beaumont hid his hands behind his back and began to hold his breath in a surfeit of wry puerility. Even I began to finish up the putatively omnipresent Blue Ruin that graced hideously the spot before me. I say "hideously" because only now, now that I am a Monday-morning fullback, do I infer what role this beverage enacted upon the boards of our confused and explosive drama! But bear slowly with me.

The crowd was insane with the joy that oddly comes to flesh and blood when they attain the perception of the fallen mighty. Yet as Corriendo stood before me and proffered a deck of cards, there appeared no note of defeat in her attitude, rather, she seemed entwined with malice. Delamode had remained ensconced upon the brooding stage—how lonely it all now seemed! She was inditing another symbol

as Corriendo rasped away at these words to me:

"Sir, jou have dug out one of the trade secrets, jes? Gaze your eyes upon the deck, which you will find to be, not simply—how do you say?—'cold,' but freez-zing!"

I took the deck as the crowd now laughed waggishly at Corriendo's excellent revelation of a good sportsman that she was. Sure thing, the deck was stacked as I had thought—a felicity of duplicitous arrangings of the pasteboards, as some wit has entitled them.

"Perhops the gentleman can do the treek—for *me!*" Madame Corriendo yelled softly into the zany plangency of the club's decibels. I rose, almost like a man who strolls about the dark of the night in his sleep, somewhere athrob inside my vital organs a nameless fright. But I had made my bed—now I must go take a nap upon it! I followed her to the stage through a racket of whistles and shouts that appeared to my dim ears, like:

"Beauty!"

"Sweet as sugar!"

"An all-right kiddo!"

"You're all right, kiddo!"

"An O.K. Joe!"

There were many other expressions of heartfelt cant as well. In a dazed whooziness, I struck out smartly on the trick, and offered to tell a gent at a front table the identity of any card that he picked. He plucked one, I cut the deck, skinning a glance at the bottom card, then, riffling through, I picked his card for him.

"King of Hearts!" I rationalized.

"Right-o!" he warmed back, and flashed the card for all to see.

Concussions of praise battered me in great waves of love—but only for a moment. For—and as ants feel despair at having a crumb of cookie reft from their drooling choppers, so did I feel despair as the hefty harlot Corriendo took the deck, with potent energy in her dukes, from me, and, confronting the hooting maniacs that comprised the mob, fanned the deck out for their eyes to batten.

Each card was—*a King of Hearts!*

The blatant orchids of admiration that I enumerated upon a scant few words ago turned to shouts of virulent dislike—of me! I somehow crept back through the howls of derisive obloquys, to my table—probably on hands and knees, there to glance up and see Daisy, awash in tears and shredded by boiling shudders, and Ned Beaumont, who was lugubriously crushing a soup spoon with his teeth! But our destruction as three pretty swell people, all in all, had only just begun. I had no sooner sat in my chair, aflame with guttering annoyance, than the awful performers turned their poisoned batteries

378

anew upon our splintered trio—and I could feel, down in the core of my humanity, that this time they were going to smack and hit and punch and pummel us pretty good, or at least until our egos had become a mere watery zero. Or even less!

Now I launch out upon the most bizarre sea of terrific frights! I see your corneas clouded over with a nimble sort of disbelief, unless it is the dread cataracts. Whatever, all I have intoned, plus that impending fragment of my tale that details the catabasic conclusion of what we had fondly hoped to be a night of freedom as well as of liberation, was true, is true, and will be true. I have pulled no sneaky haymakers from my bag of tricks upon your chin! In all I have been as candid as . . . as candid as . . . a *camera*. And I shall be, too, although scaredness roughly grabs and places its calloused hands upon my hunchbacked soul. Was I a victim—along with Daisy and chaffy Ned Beaumont—of what the ancient Roman poets gave the monicker of "hubris"? Let it lay—it does not kindly behoove to rummage around in spilt milk. I am locked in a full Nelson of compulsion to terminate this ghastly memoir. Somehow, it soothes my psyche as butter feels peachy when liberally applied to a scorched thumb. Ah, such homely similes now seem to fall as cooling rain upon my torment, so rough and tumble, so regular-guy, so run of the mill are they! Enough of that!

As we reeled about, so to speak, in our bitter sourness of defeat and ashes, the depraved two had begun to "set up" their most famous act, the piece of resistance for which the majority of suckers had thrown away their lettuce, and which had made them the toasts of the globe. This was the "thought transference" act—an exhibition of mindreading that had set aroar with fury the more conservative practicers of illusion. No need to etch mordantly the details—suffice to utter that Delamode, as the "cheese" of the "stick," stayed upon the stage, while her companion, Corriendo, entered into the midst of the quaking throngs, of whom she selected at random such ones whose belongings in a purse or pocket would be described by Delamode, in such wise as "the gentleman has a 1949 quarter in his pocket," "the young lady has in her purse a gold compact with a fleur-de-lis etched upon its lid," and so on and so on. You have seen, I entrust, this rube con a number of times, or have heard of it breathed upon the air at any events. Of course.

The "act" began. Ah, gentle buddy, the very air within the club rang with sinister yet silent bells of doom—apprehended in their grisly tolling by only we three, cracked up though we were. It was of no doubt that such was meant to be the case. Delamode, to what is tritely named a "chorus" of "wows" and "ohos" unerringly spun out, to the apple-knocker mystification of the gaping ears that surrounded her sidekicker's body, the details of varied objects here and there. Each correct describing brought reverberances of hails and hoorahs. I sat sunken in the pit of massive blues. It mattered not that I caught the banal signal words whereby the sluts pulled off their raggedy trick, i.e., "yes," "right," "that's right," "fine," as well as silences used discreetly. Each was tried and true-blue and yet the saps abounding thought all was "mystery." In my fear, however, of their venomousity, I dared not cast out upon the unhospitable air such a crack like "A crock of horseshit!" Or "Fraud!" Or even a mild rejoinder, to wit, "Garbage!" No! Not now. I put my gentlest face on while my heart chugged and simmered underneath.

May I note here appendixly that Ned Beaumont had removed his state from that termed "fearful" to a position of blatant contemptuousness of posture—but, *toward me and Daisy!* I mean, toward our hopeless impotence in the faces of his two enslavers! It was a bitch! We were a millimeter of a smidgen away from ignobly utter defeatism! Daisy, who had bucked herself up to a point at which, like Madame Bovary, she managed to bend her cute little lips in a sad smile, knew that we teetered on the brink of being shut out, blanked, and zipped! Ah, what a melancholy moment we lived through. We sat, I, for one, devotedly wishing that a hole would crack open to gulp me in, and all my works.

The fiends knew! By this I mean that they were apprised by God knows what malcontent vim, from God knows where, that we had retired from the tournament and had no intent to carry on the fray. Yet, and yet, such humility and scarlet embarrassment on our part, if truth to tell, were not enough for their cruel desire! Their scuttling lust for foul vindictiveness was not satiated by half! Oh, my very rationality was almost quelled by my nerves. They knew! I was, upon the second, aware of this when Corriendo approached our table to the tune of a heck of a lot of shabby laughs and giggles mixed in with noisome vulgarisms it does not pay my too spraddled soul to mouth here—or at all.

"Ah, kind sir—jou know also the secret behind thees—treek? Too?" She was a mass of paroxysms of mockery and leers.

"No!" I yapped out, somehow.

Daisy caught her breath and played feverishly with a brooch that I had just noticed as if seeing it for the first time. Ned Beaumont—I almost said, that swine, Ned Beaumont—eased his bulk back in his chair, a veritable mask of contempt adrift on his usually open features. Ha! To think that but a moment before or two they were clenched in abjected horror! Such is life.

"Jou *don't* theenk jou know?" How foul she grimaced you may hazard a shot at.

"I don't," I numbly mumbled, while noticing that I had carefully composed my face into a veritable domino of unconcern. Yet the front of my tux was shuddering with the gross tom-tom of my heart!

"Good," the bitch emoted. Then the hellion turned to Daisy, and, ignoring to request of that fair chunk a small token in her purse, or coin, or some doo-dad or bibelot that Delamode could then "see" and set the chumps aroar again, she abruptly turned on a sudden to the stage and shrilled:

"Madame Delamode! Thees young lay-dee—jou can enumber theengs about her we all like to know? An' thus deesplay jour talents of amaze?"

With this, her hand, nimble as a water buffalo upon the hunt, thrust out from her sleeve and hovered a fragment of a bit above dear Daisy's lambency of coif, while Ned Beaumont actually chirped—I mean, despite your look, he *chirped!*

The dear young woman sat as if turned to a smooth boulder upon some lost and windblown beach. Isolate, almost crouching. There appeared a vague haziness about her alabaster body, a blue haze, if I may be so bold as to employ that noun, a haze that, beyond all rationality, seemed to ooze from our cocktails! Certain it possessed the same shade of blue! Then, then came the throaty raspiness of Madame Delamode's voice-box as words drummed from it, or whatsoever they perform.

"The lay-dee, I see . . . I see . . . the lay-dee has on the beige brassière. The lay-dee has on the beige panties with white lace trim and upon the crotch of same she is spelled out 'DANGER.' The lay-dee has on the sheer nylon panties hosiery of palest taupe. The lay-dee has the mole on her right buttock. The lay-dee has the blueberry mark on the belly. The lay-dee has the private hair zat do not match up weeth——"

"STOP! STOP!" Daisy hollered out, collapsing into herself in a gently distracted heap, while my eyes streamed liquid salt. Defeat? So you wordlessly glance. Utter cashiorment of our hopes? So you seem to hold. Yes, yes, my bosomy friend, all these—but *moro, more.* More than enough honest-to-God embarrassment to last even the toughest and most impregnatedly armor-ridden heart a lifetime. For Daisy, a subtle plant, these crude revelations of intimacies were what you can entitle trauma-ish. I don't have to go into what it tokened for her psychological methods of sincerely relating to fellow persons, do I?

The crowd, rapt in a bedlam of that sadism of lubricity and violent delight in the gross assault upon purity long known to objective observers of the human beast, and rare denied by anyone with any marbles at all, was a veridical maelstrom of guffaws and pornographic suggestions. Ned Beaumont was "doing something"—need I enumerate?—beneath the tablecloth, while Daisy's hands pounded limply among the scattered crockery and other impedimenta. I sat, wanting but to get away, forcing my eyeballs from the redly hilarious gazes of the vengeful "cunts," so to gutterlike speak. I reached across the table to grasp Daisy's wrist, and, although I got naught from him but a furious belch and a grin of profound odium for my pains, I also nudged Ned Beaumont. You are correct if you have taken a stab that he was helpless as a toddler under the whores' suggestion, made more potent by—ah, now I know it, too late, to be so—the accursed Blue Ruins that we had all been consuming like a gaggle of hogs at the stye. It was time to get away from these vengeful harpies who might, like those of ancient Troy, turn us in a wink, to stones! We had been conquered, for nonce anyway, and there remained no reason for staying there like three zany schmucks—which, I admit bitterly, we were. But we had one more final uppercut to absorb! The ignominy of the event is almost too putrid for my tongue to sculpt, yet since we have come this distance down the highway of candidness . . .

You will note that my once reasonably happy eyes are almost of a scarlet hue from fighting the good fight to pummel back the tears that are rioting to plummet from them like, as the poet said, "gum drops from Arabia." As you sop up the closure of my tale, of my night at Club Zap—how I balloon up with dreaded hate when I mouth upon my lip that profane name!—you may feel the need to let a few tears drop upon your vest, as well as I. I adjure you to buckle up and prepare for my coda. The memory of it sets me on a chill.

I had, amid the whirling chortles of the stentorian melee of the club, grasped, as I have already enjoined to you, dear honeysuckle Daisy's fine-boned wrist, and now I rose with her, intent upon leaving upon my own two feet, like a man, all the while saving what orts of my face I had left, as well as Daisy's, and Ned Beaumont's too. Daisy rose, pale as a violet, or something, and cold in the embarrassment that had turned her pale. Your eyebrows ask, in a well-known lifting of same, why she had not turned *red* with embarrassment? Did I but know, I would know why the whale has a thumb that cannot bend! But I beg you, let us not be carried down any false crossroads as we hurry on toward our terminus, O.K.? Daisy rose, as did I. I presented Ned Beaumont with a none-too-gentle push to get *him* shambling along, but he—he would not rise! Instead, to the hunnish joy of the voyeuristic crowd of stinking Yoohoos who numbered the "patrons" —how my tongue coils up in pain against the roof of my mouth as I spit the phrase!—he slowly stuck *his* tongue out at me. I assumed instanter that our cause was down the old draineroo, and my main labor now was to remove the fainting sprite, Daisy, from the dismay of Club Zap. We started for the door, yet, from the far corner of both my eyes, I saw Madame Corriendo now sketching, with an amaze of rapidness, yet another daub on the blackboard.

Then she turned and shook her stick at us, laughing like a kangaroo the while.

Daisy stopped of a sudden, and, exhibiting a prowess that I had somehow always suspected and feared a tiny bit to boot, pulled her hand from mine with a minor yelp of unfettered joy! Her face had changod, in a briefest tinkling, from the dark, saturnine *persona* that had been her recent possession, to a *thing* that bespoke mindless chaos! To my utter consternation, in a trice or two, she had divested herself of all her garments, outer and inner, except for her pearls—and it is mooted indeed whether *they* can be considered clothings! She began dancing about the nightclub, giving the customers a plethora of raunch, not only by her shameless body wriggles but by her—dare I mumble?—more than suggestive acts upon men and women as well into the bargain, an odd word to use in this context of grime, but what the hell. Ned Beaumont shouted words redolent of such obscenity that their very memory makes my legs shiver nervelessly, and I give heartfelt thanks that I am at present seated, as you can see, and not astand, else I would of surety collapse into a pile of gloom!

What Daisy did!—I cannot utter it. Be it suffuient to hint that a number of persons, of all sexes, were shockingly delighted that they'd come. I mean it was like a bonus from the blue for these immoral louts! The din was painful, a deviltry of felonious uproar, and over all, or perhaps under all—who am I to remember instances of wall-to-wall depravity?—I caught the insidious whirring of the maître d's movie camera, like the buzz of some fetid bug. Alone, like the proverbial pea in a pod, I gathered Daisy's garments from hither and yon, fighting some slobbering galoots who were loath to part with certain apparels *intime*, and with them in a sad little bundle underneath my arm, heaved and throttled my way through the sexdemented throngs of revelryers and the like to reach her lavishly sweating body. At the very rear of my pulsing brain I expected the crowd to stop me, and at the lightest whisper of opprobrium from either Corriendo or Delamode, to hurl me, lock stock and barrel, out the door as a smoker might hurl a soggy stogie. Yet the word, or words, were not bespoke, and I was allowed to lead my sullied-over darling from the cavortings of the goatish trash that dares to call itself a human being.

Her dear eyes bloodshot with the potent effects of those bewitched Blue Ruins, her tiny brains addled by them and by, as well, the vast and indigo failure that was ours, as well as by the pounds of humble pie we had been forced to eat, along with, may I tack on, plenty of crow, she had succumbed to doing some momentary crazy things. Just within the entrance to the club, I helped the lady on with her things, until slowly, slowly, as she dressed, she came to at least a handful of her senses, such as they still obtained. Within the room, the hellish charlatans had once again taken up the broken skein of their act, and the crowd was guzzling out of their hand. Does evil always win? Or, at worst, tie the score? What matter? I don't expect an answer from your split and sullen lips. Sit, dear friend, and endeavor a recovery from this story. How can I extract a moral from it as simply as a dentist hauls out a bum molar? There is no possibility. We had met these supremely rotten broads, and they had almost utterly sunk us into the Sargasso Sea of crum-bum defeat. A sour taste! Now, *now* I know that they had certain—what is the *mot juste?* —"powers"! We had but tickled the superficial facades of them!

I pushed Daisy toward the door that led to freedom and the street. By the inquiring and shaky fear in her nervous glances in my ash-filled face, I knew that she knew that she had done some things that some folks might give a construement to as naughty. But I revealed nothing, only mumbled some trite and cliché-ridden banalism about "trying again soon." Yet in the storm cellar of my heart I knew that we had proffered our best shot and had received for it in return our legs knocked out from below us! Daisy, weeping vats of tears for her surely lost Ned Beaumont, preceded me out the door, her gentle shoulders all on a weepy stoop, you know how that is. As I left, my last peer into the dusky room showed me Corriendo and Delamode, howling upon the stage with what was surely plenty of fun, and Ned Beaumont, abrim to the gunwales with a storm of rampaging hysteria, sprawled, alone now, at his table, his cocktail glass to his mouth, the reflection from its demonic contents painting his ruinated face an otherworldly blue!

Halpin's Journal

Ned has gone. All the threats of these past months have finally been made real—finally, finally gone. The nightclub scene was the straw that did it. I could not have predicted such a scene in a million years. And I thought I had begun to *know* Lamont.

Ned is right, of course. This has all gone too far, much too far. For some reason, I thought (or was it merely hope?) that Daisy and I would be given a soft, idyllic scene, an interlude of love, a gentle chapter. I see that I still have some faith in Lamont.

But it is fast disappearing.

I knew that Ned would be pushed over the edge by that scene. The rage on his face beneath the idiotic mask the scene required! A professional. Lamont can have no complaints over the way he played his role—and didn't we all play well? My God, to have to watch Daisy debase herself in front of all those strange creatures suddenly arrived for the audience!

All of Ned's scenes have required him to appear a fool—and always in front of people. It is amazing that he stayed so long.

When we "returned" here, he packed that ugly cardboard suitcase. He looked at me as if to speak, but said nothing.

When he picked up the suitcase, I told him I'd stay on just a little longer, just to see. "See what?" Ned asked. "There is no *next* in this book!" Ned was convinced that Lamont has lost control of the book and cannot find the strength to rewrite or revise. He pointed out the language given me to speak as an indication of insanity. We went on and on. Then he got up, we shook hands, and he left. He said that he'd follow along the lake shore and see where it took him. His idea is to get to a place where he might meet someone who can direct him to some sort of decent employment . . . perhaps there *is* a sort of "depot" where characters can wait and be hired. Saying that he'd write as soon as he was sure of what was out there, he left, striking out into the sunshine that glittered off the calm surface of the lake. I stood in the doorway watching him, bent with his cheap suitcase that seemed to weigh him down like despair.

Just before he plunged into the brush at the shore, he turned and waved. I waved back and he disappeared.

Later

I can't describe the desolation I feel. I don't know whether the wind and the night while inside the house, or the terrible, silent sunshine while outside the house is worse. And I'm beginning to think that there *is* someone "upstairs."

A lonely, sinister house. I have to give Lamont *that,* anyway. It is certainly the sort of place where a murder *could* be committed.

Is it only lust that holds me here?

What will happen if Lamont needs Ned again in a flashback?

What if he doesn't notice? He's mad enough, surely . . . but what will he do? He *can't* have another flashback, certainly.

It might be nice to talk to him.

How lonely it is here.

Lamont's Notebook

This will show them all! How can they fail to reckon with this? Is it too much to say that it has a masterly touch?

Oh, Halpin's voice! Tinged with subdued fury at his defeat!

Have I ever before tried such a marriage of fact and imagination? And the plotting is a perfect counterpoint to the surface vulgarity of Corriendo and Delamode.

Ned Beaumont is totally degraded.

Perhaps add the recipe for Blue Ruins? Or better left a mystery?

It is, admittedly, "artifice." And I have many *enemies!!* In the PUBLISHING EMPIRE!!

If that clownish beggar, "J. Beshary," only knew the man whom he has been trying to fleece!

What remains to be done

1. Halpin rambles around house, thinking on his life, and what a shambles it has become, love for Daisy, etc. Discovers other mysterious rooms? Who was there? Clues? Strange "artifacts"? What does it mean to his life? To the triangle he is trapped in? Things in these rooms bespeak other lives involved in the "death cabin." He begins to see a glimmer of the *truth.*

2. He recounts the conversation, *truthfully,* that he and Ned had the fateful evening of the latter's death. In detail, verbatim. The truth emerges from the morass of lies and fantasy we have been given. It is all a question mark. What happened might have been this way, or that way, or the other way. Murder? Suicide? And if murder, *did* Halpin do it?

386

3. The police arrive, along with Daisy and Tom, and Corriendo and Delamode. And in this last chapter, the sinister aspects of what has actually been going on are revealed. Book ends in haze and mystery. Perhaps Ned will rise from the dead? A scenario that they have all followed helplessly? An edged ambiguity.

Rundown of book
A Bag of the Blues (use as a *Prologue* to set a mood of bittersweet love)
1. Fallen Lucifers (presentation of crime)
2. Best Intentions (hint of magical qualities)
3. Painful Digests (Ned's utter lack of control and his debasement limned)
4. The Tragic Jester (Halpin's early life and pain)
5. Burst Loveletters (the truth behind Ned's bizarre behavior)
6. Spilt Ink (Halpin alone)
7. The Woods So Wild (Halpin confronts C and D for first time)
8. {She Is The Queenly Pearl   (use one or the other, or both, with
   {Nameless Shamelessness   small revision)
9. Blue Ruin (defeat!)
   —and then, final 3 chapters, as above—?

And finished! All my pain will be eased if only I can write *Finis.*

Lamont's Scrapbook

SHINY TIPS FROM *BIG APPLE*

Porn à la Mode

The now pub season's **hot** excuse for a dabble in porno is Dermot Trellis's classy little sizzler, *The Red Swan,* a savvy, offhanded whirl through erotic kink. Reissued last month in hard covers after more than a decade of gadding about in the steamier stews of Times Square and environs, *Swan* bids fair to becoming the year's **most** status-y read. Zooming from orgy to orgy with the celerity of a boudoir lamp being **snapped** out, the novel takes one from here to satiety. Its barrage of **lush** adjectives, the unmitigated yet bracing **gall** of its predictable but fascinating scenarios of sex **rampant,** and the parade of daffy characters who uninhibitedly inhabit its miniature though oddly **spacy** world, all combine to make this frankly torrid tome a flashy-bright piece of costume jewelry. Add, too, for those with an eye on *le chic,* that "in" book **gossip** has it that the

Swan is flying super-high on campus and off this season and there's a plan afoot to plug Trellis's smoldering yarn with a **kicky** kampaign centered on bumper stickers, buttons, and trendy T-shirts. Looks like **everybody's** going to swing with the *Swan! $8.95 at all bookstores.*

12. LIKE BLOWING FLOWER STILLED

"How now, Master Halpin! What? Can it be fear that thrones itself in those bright orbs that were wont on a day to flash as bright as those of a gentleman in pleasant surfeit o' the good Rhenish or a gen'rous flagon o' sack? For shame, for shame! Fie on 't! It ill guerdons that honest phiz o' thine to permit the black shades of Avernus to becloud it. Have no fear, I pray thee, for I come as a herald of amity, who might's well be tricked out in shining watchel bespangelèd o'er with glittering oos, not as a masquerado despatched from your sly rogue, Prince Mephisto. *Frontis nulla fides.* Calm thee and sit, good Martin, and let thine amaze be apop and asimmer belike, Jesu, th' aroma'd cauldron that sits, all on abubble, at the back o' the honest dame's hob of a winter even. 'Sblood, but thy neck's so scrawned an' craned that a knave'd wager thou'd donned piccadills sharp as your Spaniard's poniardo! From this distance, not so close as an inch but, by a bag o' pardoner's holy bones, not so far as a yard, I swear to 't I can hear thy blood run thin an' cold as the small an' sour beer o' rheumy Boreas himself! Look to 't. 'Tis such embastinadoes that turn a gentle goodly wight into your raving moon-man, if he be not arrested swift as pur is lost or gained in a sprightly set o' post an' pair. Is it crutch an' eyepatch that so frights thee? But then, look on 't, for I have neither. The croaking raven that settles on my wrist? But there is no bird of hell here with me. *Non est inventus.* Surely, 'tis not my smile that makes the sweat to glister on thy sconce as rosmarine paints o'er the rough doublet o' the fisherman? God's wounds! This smile I smile was meant to warm and comfort, aye! to bring light an' wonderment as did the fabulous Prometheus succor brutish man. Heaven knows, I meant not to chastise thee, nor set thy pitiful knees to knocking and thy mouth to fall agape like a rustick's, hauled into perplexment in a simple, churlish hour o' hot cockles. Did mine eyes not absorb it like a drinkalian his bene bowse, I'd ha' not believed that thine ears, on Jesu's pain, were, i' truth, trembling like a primpish fawning courtier on his knees 'fore his sovrayn's throne! *Esse posse videatur.* So it doth seem. Where's the twit an' cannonado of it? Where's the rumbustious pennants that'll flutter in the gentle Zephyrus, to significate such base reply to my, methinks it civil, greeting? There're none, an' there's no wonder to it, that I vow! Certes, ghost am I, but such a sweet fellow of a ghost, such a companion ghost o' the tun an' ched-dar, such a soft, gentle, simpleton of a ghost as delights in crambo an' doucets, a mild, an' palmy as a maiden's silv'ry laughter, kind o' ghost. Aye! None o' thy stony Medusa glances from these dead eyes shalt thou receive, no stare o' basilisk to freeze up thy blood an' metamorph the very marrow o' thy bones to ice! Plain an' simple let me speak it, Sir Martino, I come, boon companion o' my days among the quick, in a spectral friendship, aye, an' to converse wi' thee a space. Soft, soft. Sit thee down, an' let thy tingling fear nod an' slumber, while thou listeth to thine old friend, for it is I, i' truth, hearty Ned, whose earthly dregs thou seest spraddled there in un-seemly posture, devoid o' life, and desperate idiotic o' mien. Ah, poor bag o' cold meat, is it thee, Master Beaumont?

"As breathing men do, how clear I remember, wi' the clarity o' claret, an' may thou forgive my limping quibble, the days, so long ago it seems, when we first clung together in a comradely friendship. The very memory o' that time rings its sweet closes in my mind, an' I swear it that a parfum ariseth from it that'll match, aye, inch for inch an' tit for tat, th' exquisite odor engendered by the fabled Phoenix-nest all in aromatic conflagration. Thine eyes bulge to hear me con-fess to 't? Yet where's the wonderment? Certes, a mere whisp of a shade like myself, a lost an' wav'ring sprite, an insubstantial *ignis fatuus* o' the wide world, can cleave to an' clip a memory as proper as any breathing gentleman. How it is, I ken not, but memory, as like as to a clew o' finest silk, ravels out its thread that any churl may follow it, aye, into the very heart o' the yarn o' truth itself! As de-parted maidens weep great streams o' salt as they, tottering, lead apes in hell, *caelum petimus stultitia,* an' I ha' clean observed the sad chaste spirits in their tragickal morris-dance 'mong the flamy brim-stone an' the stink o' sulphurous smoke, as they weep, I say, when they think back, o' the amatory combats they declined, an' the gal-lants they did send each night t' bed with rolling eye an' young flesh aburning i' despairing venery, so I too have wept wi' the fond love recalled I had o' life, recalled as identical to actuality almost as if writ in a balade, or a tale o' careless youth, so perfect has each incident been revivicated to me by the cunning brachygraphy o' the fev'rish brain. 'Tis stamped in me as in gleaming gold, as neatly drawn in my very guts as an Andrew's cross!

"Ah, Jesu, thou held me a man out o' wax then, gentle Martin, an', though I blush to say it, 'twas an opinion I treasured up an' pulled out to gaze upon so regular, why, you'd ha' thought each blushing dawn had heralded for me a gaudy-day. 'Tis like a stoccado to the heart now to muse upon 't. What it did come to, what tears an' desperate acts, O th' immense vastity of it! What I thought to be

eternal pheasant, or a tender kid, or veal in a green sauce the color
o' new grass, why, it turned to a crude wedge o' poor cheese an' a
gallimaufry. Thou must remember how we two, in our hot youth, wi'
the blood surging like that of Achilles in his mighty wrath, our lion-
courage turning us into two mighty capitanos, lay siege to th' pocky
fortresses wherein ruled in stupor those slothful emperors, who,
'slight! were naught, i' truth, but apple-squires, an' whose profit entire was dredged up out o' their pandering to the base appetites o'
the mob. Their books, why, they were no more than possets for
doxies, or, to make the best face on 't, puerilous additions to such
flummery as draw-gloves, Gregory, an' fast an' loose; these manufac-
tures, certes thou recall it, were the walls 'gainst which we directed,
diebus illis, all our rude engines an' brave artillery o' war. Canst thou
deny it? That lost time, to this, why, 'twere a veriest Elysium, joyous
an' celebrant as Twelve Night, an' sweet as metheglin. Jesu, it
seemed to me that all I'd longed for as a green an' sappy boy had
achieved a perfect ripening! But black clouds, laced through an'
through with great Jove's massy weaponry lay ambuscado for us, high
in the argent skies we fondly did consider 'd been daubed for us an'
our singular camerado-ship. Far beyond our earthy jubilatios is our
end worked out. *Aliquid latet quod non patet.*

"Poor Martin, leave off weeping. *Ex lachrimis lachrimae.* Life's a
poor play by a drumbling knave, an't cannot but end save in dust an'
cerements. When that I was but a little tiny boy, I entertained such
vasty, dreamy musings. An', I charge thee, they were pert an' pretty
as China wagons hurried on by a spicy, aromatic wind! Far beyond
the skirts o' the wonted studies o' the schoolboy were they situate.
Marry, d'you consider that it presented itself to my falconated fancy
then, that this tough world might be less than a ceaseless round o'
galliards, corantos, an' rustick merry hays? 'Sblood! That it might be
the tiring room where we put on our funereal shroud? Such thoughts
were chimeras to my lusty energy! 'Tis age that reveals the grim
spectre, your horrific Master O' the Bright Night-Gown, to the gaze,
aye, an' age only. In my young youth I thought t' be a sailor, a bloody
privateer o' brig an' barkentine, up, by God, to the elbows in dou-
bloons! Or a soldier, a serjeant, or a capitano, glorious in sumptuous
breeches an' a velvet cap crowned with a rambunctious feather t'
announce my strength an' the dauntless courage o' my arm. How I
fancied the figure I'd cut as your duke, your earl, why, your very
emperor o' burly-boned butchers! No soft talents did I dream on, but
guts strong enough t' stomach a very flood o' gore. Aye! I swear to
't, I'd start up out o' sleep o' nights, my very eyes aflame with the
puissance o' my martial dreaming. Yet, as strong as I visioned glory
on the shattered field encarnadine, so as strong did I image up my

manhood to be that o' your minstrel, your singer o' sugared strains an' perfect measures, your excellent poet. My foolish mind, astuffed with every shape an' phantom of a beardless boy's newfanglenesse, painted my manly figure bursting o' pride in the contemplation o' the beauteous lays my delicate pen conjured up, aye, from a mouthful of air. They did drop from its point in magickal ink, i' th' honey treads o' your Homeric chauntings, ah, i' rondelays an' rounds, balades an' sonnets, e'en your Provencial aubades an' villanellas, an' the sweet stern Tuscano figure, your sestina. By our Redeemer's blessed torment, I thought I touched the warm lips o' the golden lasses my imagined songs enthralled. Ha! Still did these airy pictures fashioned o' th' insubstantial stuff o' youth be sublimed again, an' yet again, i' the fashion o' foolish noddies, an' from the golden shape o' the poet I was changed, snap-carbonado!, to your arcturian gallant. Festooned wi' chains an' decoradoes all over carbuncled with gems, how elegant I made my courtly legs, all swoops an' grins, how fine a demigod I gazed about the inns an' bowsing kens. Not a cony'd pass, his rude face all idiotic at the city's din, but I did spread my subtile net for him. At plays an' entertainings I had a seat 'pon the very stage, close enough to the players t' feel the hot wind o' their breath. With a silk muckender, all over broidered raspberries an' day's-eyes, an' delicioso with orange, clove, an' e'en cinnamon, I'd flail at flies. By Jesu! the scent was such that there was no plump laced mutton within twenty leagues that'd not come running just to ask my pleasure, if you please.

"Not, my dear companion, to put on this too fine a point, but not a day passed, nor, now it appears, a minute, that I had not a new portrait o' myself as I should be when I gained the state o' manhood. You'll not be mad to hazard that I saw the penumberous future as a stage 'pon which I also played a rogue, a merchant, a gentleman adventurer, ho! Christ's agony!, e'en your rapscallious gypsy! I yearned to strut about as a learnèd jackman, spouting Latin tags an' snippets, a clerk o' the hall, sedulous i' the crafting o' jarks, an' cheating the hangman by benefit o' clergy. I'd cut a handsome shape dropping onto the stalling ken, seized by fear as by an ague at my audacity, many a cheat an' richly bursting jan that I'd, all saucy as you please, had nipped not an hour since! E'en the rogue patrico'd see fit to lecture me between the bosky harlots' marriages he, all sweating on a summer afternoon, performed beneath the trees. Ah, so dreams, children's dreams. Where's the profit in 'em, either the dreaming or regretting? I'd no more a sense o' life then than your stupid owl or seagull. 'Tis God's miracle that any staring, foolish lad e'er comes to manliness, poor an' mazed as that poor thing may be.

"Yet, an' yet, while the gaudios o' the dew-eyed youth I was didst

392

ne'er come to pass, think not, brave Martin, to shed bitter streams for me, as't doth appear thou art about to do. Nay, an't please you, let good Sol's beams dwell in thy face, an' gild it. For, marry, though I grew to manhood not as poet or adventurer, nor brave swinger o' the battle-ax, nor Jack Tar on the ferocious seas, nor, truth to tell, as well you wot, dear comrade, any other thing fine an' romantical, yet was my life not wasted totally. For, to be plain with thee, I'd as lief ride a curtal to hell as actually to have spent my grey-haired years in any o' those phantasmagorical occupations! As the man i' the moon would not be he we descry on soft an' lambent nights when that planet fairly bursts with luminosities, had he not his dog at his girdle an' a bush o' thorns at his back, why then, I'd not be he I am had I not had books an' all the trappings an' purtenances o' their sale an' manufacture close about me. For, Sir Halpin, an' 'swounds! how I devoutly wish thou'd cease thine aspen quivering, for, I say, fate so arranged it as she arranges the victors 'mong costermongers in a game o' mum-chance, that I was sweet content to spend my manly days as a publisher o' books, a helpful midwife pleased to be ancillary to the birth o' fine-wrought artifacts crafted by your tribe o' inky laborers. Oh, I'll confess to 't, that as sure as courtly dames an' maidens do delight in noddy an' God-make-'em-rich, so did I delight, early on, when there was still an ember o' puerility aglowing in my bones, in thinking on the glories o' the poet's life. Yet, certes, I knew I had no skill in your measuring and melodies, your fine conceits an' curious metaphors, an' the teaching o' the Stagyrite atouching composition was to me as words ascrivened on the breaking wave. *Plus erat in artifice quam arte.* I was to be lover, not creator, o' the arts, an' how I loved 'em! By Jesu, more than the lecherous knave doth love to sniff an' shuffle 'bout the rolls an' bodice lacings o' the comeliest dells, with faces so fresh, o' cream an' roses, they do spurn th' assistance o' the paint pot an' set your veriest Helen to aworrying. Such was my great admiration! An' though there were many an' many who thought me a poor prating fellow for my love o' tales an' verses, an' pictures daubed, by Christ's enormous griefs, so to the life that one'd think the great artificer, Daedalus, again roamed this terraqueous globe, or that Pygmalion'd returned to drive the very Devil wild with envy, an' lays an' minstrelsies, an' excellently figured brawls that spun out, hand in gauntlet, with airs sprightly-sweet enough to draw the sucky bees, nothing that these poor dunstical rogues 'd whisper at the corners, as is their wont alway, detained me for a jot from my delicious entertainments. 'Slight, they whetted more my mouth for 'em! I flew to 'em swift as the falcon, *aculeo alatus.* They were all my Elysium an' pearly moon-shine. An' they did feed, as you know well, stout Martin, the knowledge that I carried o'er to my poor profession.

No, I feel no pinch or prick o' conscience t' apologize for the way God stitched the threads o' fate for me. For forty years was I content to gaze 'pon the diadem of art, an' do my little bit to shine an' spangle it. *Crede mihi, res est ingenioso dare.*

"Well-a-well, i' the midst o' those white, sunshiny days, salad days in all but the actual tally o' my years, as thou, bright companion, surely do remember 'em to've been, it so fell out that mischievous Cupid, with hot darts to hand, an' all in ambuscado, did take it in his golden head to let fly at me, an', presto-jesto! your sage an' grizzled Ned was all undone, an't please you, in no more time than it takes great Zeus's bolt t'illumine heaven! Ah, caro Martino, fie on the quickened blood that sets the crimson flush i' thy face, an' be not shamed for me, aye, I own no shame for me, for a poor insubstantial spectre can feel nor shame nor any other breathing thing, an' can but intelligence these quick states. List, an' you are a friend, list to my tale as thou might to a ballad adrift o' the wind.

"This beauteous dame, Daisy, an' you know well her name, an', by Christ's agony, ne'er did name so fit a lady, was as enamored o' me as I o' her, being struck by th' identical erotic darts o' Venus' babe. But she was, O misery, the good wife o' one, Tom, a shambling lout of a merchant who'd long since ceased to cherish her delights. By Jesu's omnipotence, she'd ha' set the agued elders of Ilium ahum i' their reedy voices as quick as did the beauteous Helena, such was her beauty an' her soft an' sweetly dropping sentences. Talk o' the Judgment o' Paris! Why, man, his eyes had been seeled up to the charms o' the three goddesses had Daisy been a member o' their frolicks! I've contended that her very name, sweetest day's-eye, was as snug as hand i' glove wi' the plain beauty o' that simple flower. Yet, an' I charge thee, there was no moment o' the day when her eyes, her lips, her teeth, her beaming smile, aye, her countenance entire, did not seem to partake o' some loveliness o' blown flower i' the field. Sometime she seemed the handsome cowslip or the corn-flag; there were other moments when th' adoring spy thought he saw in her the tulip or Adonis' flower, and yet again there seemed t'appear the ox-eye, goldilock, or columbine. In certain shafts o' pale light she shone forth a pink, a gouland, your golden king-cup, or your sop-in-wine, an', variously, too, she glowed as a blue harebell or a primrose, a paigle or a paunce. I' faith, she could turn in the blinking of an eye from your fragrant calaminth to your flower-gentle, an' from a hyacinth to a rich carnation, an', by Jesu's tears, back again immediate! Oft, she'd be the showy lily, or the purity o' flower-de-luce, an', as oft, a checked and purple-ringèd daffodilly. Bright crown-imperial an' shining king's spear was she, an' hollyhock an' Venus' navel too. I've seen her i' the guise o' lady's smock an' Daphne's hair, myrtle an' spikenard an' marjoram. I vow it that sometime she staggered a whole chamber o' gallants, when o' sudden she masqueraded as yellow-gold or meadow's queen, e'en the blue bindweed some men yclep bitter-sweet. Aye, old boot, a woman an' yet more than a woman, a flower an' all flowers, an' all warm o' flesh an' blood, douce-voiced, a golden figure, proper in a farthingale as in a hood.

"It fell out that we'd ha' no more than t' exchange a burning glance for the blood to race all through our corses wantonly as in your beasts o' the field an' forest. Our kisses for each other, I warrant you, seemed as powerful an' sweet as bragget, Jesu! 'twas but the space of a breath before we bowed to Venus' wishes, powerless as the lady an' her knight in timeless Dant. I bestrode this tearful world o' dissembling an' cupidity as a god in buskins! Not a breeze did blow but that it did murmureth to me of her charms, nor a rainbow arch this azure vault that did not recollect to my swooning senses the colors o' her dainty under-linens. *Peccavi, confiteor.* An' so did she transgress the sacred laws o' marriage. But, though we sinned, we sinned t' honor Love, an offered up our sleepless nights an' dry astaring eyes to his cruel an' great authority. But the gods are jealous of our mortal bliss, howe'er ephemeral, *speramus lucent*, we hope while they shine, an' our joyous plans for a lawful marriage-couch as soon as her divorce was count'nanced by the state, were shattered quick as knight's vizard in a joust, an' our love, that had been as pure as th' glassy ice that melts o' spring to make the sparkling mountain rivulet, was traduced by me, O my old amico, an' metamorphed into a vile an' base an' filthy-foul black Sanctus.

"Thou knowest, dear glove, o' my enchantment by those two licentious hags who roam this groaning globe masked behind the names, which are naught but fantastical inventions, o' Corrie Curriendo an' Berthe Delamode. 'Tis impossible for me, e'en thus transformed to this airy apparition, shifting an' transparent, fro' which my voice whispers, all hollow an' depleted, to e'er forget that blushing day on which thou perused, thy face besmirched with stravaganoous horror, the criminal letters that showed my sins clear as the fields stand in the mid-day light. *Hinc illae lachrimae.* Yet, touching on th' other, more profound terrors i' my growing knowledge o' these dames' true intentions, why, 'sblood, thou wert an' are, to this explicit minute, innocent as a lad all red-cheeked in a biggin. For, I tell thee, Martin, as thou may ha' suspicioned from your own brief glimpses into th' heart o' their maleficence, these two painted doxies entangeled me in a poisoned web o' witchery fro' which there was no 'scaping! Yes, by Jesu's holy gore, I was lost to grace from the first moment that I clapped my cursèd eyes on 'em. Thy starting up so sudden confesseth to thy lightning understanding; yes, old venison, these two seeming

harbingers o' fleshly vitalizing charms are witches, foul an' arrogant!
My own o'erweening an' devouring lust took me to 'em, o'er an' o'er,
spite my wildest prayers to all the saints to give me strength. What
seemed my bold decision i' the kind day's light to reject 'em an' all
their bespattered practices, was naught but a will o' the whisp, that,
flittering away by moonlight, acted on their bidding, O monstrous!
to lead me to 'em an' their lickerous delights, all when the dogs do
howl the moon an' the screech owl stares down 'pon windy grave-
yards. Yet, I swear, if such a poor thing as I now am can swear with
any puissancy, 'twas some weeks afore I recked the full horizon o'
their powers, an' their kinship with everything that's evil. I ha' seen
them, wi' their ointment pots an' spindles, their timbrels, rattles, an'
other hellish venefical instruments, aye! with rats o' their heads an'
shoulders; an' at times, Dame Corriendo, whom I take now t' be the
witch o' pre-eminence in all these parts, barefoot, an' with her dress
tucked up, by God! her hair knotted an' folded with your short
snakes, yclept vipers, an', for a girdle, 'round her waist another snake.
'Twas meet that this queen o' sorceresses should be a tavern-keep.
Aye! an' how oft have I seen, my very bones sweating wi' the horrifick
fear of it, the two of 'em, after having performed with me orgies most
dark an' foul, an' not fit to be bespoke, anoint all their naked bodies
an' fly off betimes on a veritable horse o' wood, or else a broomstaff.
Saving those terrific midnights when Master Martinel himself, the
arch-fiend *magisterulus,* 'd call 'em softly in a human voice, an'
they'd go forth to find him waiting i' the shape of a great buck goat,
'pon which they'd rise into the inky sky, off to destroy some innocent!
Once, I spied Dame Delamode aflying i' the face o' the moon, astrad-
dle, an' naked as a babe, a cock that gleamed as green as emeraldo!
Aye, Martino, thou'rt right to clutch an' hug thyself t' keep the chill
away, for I speak to you of dark acts, *contra naturam,* that no hot
blood or sensual deeds can cover o'er or sweeten, 'slight! 'twas these
very practices did serve t' obscure their maleficious beings! Did they
'pear before me in the most tantalacious an' immodest whisps o'
clothing, all decorate with lace an' boldly revealing o' their womanly
charms, why, man, 'twould be that very night the moon'd be trou-
bled an' attacked an' plunged into eclipse. By Jesu's cuts, I've voided
up my victuallings, watching 'em but to see a black sheep tore to
pieces wi' their teeth, an' the dark blood splashed in a ditch t' coax
answers from the spirits o' the dead. Ah, Martin, your hairs stand o'
end, an' the sweat pops out o' thy frail skin big as fists, you, who
thought to entrap 'em, who thought them t' be mere distaff rogues
an' charlatans, painted whores who had no other wiles than foul
mouths an' o'erweening cleverness. 'Sbones! Martin, I swear to thee,
they gave not but to take, an' amused their selves wi' me as a brat

doth sport the hours i' tormenting kittens. Had I a raging powerful piece o' male equipage that fair threatened t' burst my breeches, why, 'twas none o' mine, but a charm those two had put o' me for use i' their own carnalities. An' after I'd been used an' they'd grown weary o' their sporting, for an amusing space of an hour or two, by God, they'd throw down all the light o' the starry heavens into the deep bottom o' hell by means o' certain words an' charms breathed o'er boughs an' stones an' other frivolous objects. They've snatched corpse-flesh from the mouths o' wolves, an' froth from those o' mad dogs, dug up the deadly mandrake at that eerie hour 'fore the cock begins t' crow, gathered flesh, bones, an' skulls, an' the spurging o' dead men's eyes, an' brought forth from the kitchen metal plates o'er-carved with arcane signs on which to put th' unholy filth for their conjurations. I've seen 'em change from prating whores, all frip an' luscious i' their small-clothes, to cats or screech owls, an' fly into the starless midnight. They've told me o' their murders foul an' hidden, and o' their ghoulish venturings into the cemeteries o' damned criminals, there to steal the clotted filth an' black humors o' corruption o'er all the limbs o' those the state hath slaughtered. In variously beaded, gold-encrusted purses each hid within their bags, they've kept the foulest familiars, Lord Cacarooch an' the hairy beast, Sir Cranion, your diseasèd fly. O' nights, I swear it thee, they've waked me with hideous laughter, an' dumped forth on the floor i' front o' my tormented eyes, great heaps o' hemlock, henbane, serpent-tongue, night-shade, martagon, doronicum, an' wolf's bane, bones snatched from hungry dogs, an' the brains o' cats black as hell itself, toads an' owl's eyes, an' the blood an' wings o' bats. Then, cackling horribly, an' a-chaunting "Hoo Hoo" an' "Har Har" an' "Sabaath Sabaath," they'd rage an' rave wi' shouts an' hissing, shrieks an' whistling, an' scattered o' me poisons an' powders to change me t' a beast fit to romp with 'em i' their naked filthy revels. At such times I heard a music in my reeling brain, such that reached heaven itself with its dullish roaring. By Jesu, 'twas as if a thousand moon-men an' a thousand devils together'd struck the forest-trees with great clubs, an' sung with the voices o' discordant trumps! An' I saw the two hags, either naked or barely covering their shame, dancing in great leaps, an' back to back, in despite o' mortals' custom, their heads a-shaking in besotted frenzy!

"Ah, Martin, dear old buckler, believe thou me when I tell thee that I was bewitched an' charmed by these fair hellions, else I'd ha' ne'er rioted with 'em, as I confess I did, an' with a perfect levity an' brute delight. *Plura dolor prohibet.* By the great compassion o' the Savior, old friend, pity my poor ghost, an' forgive me. An', though I know that you an' dearest Daisy risked so much to help me fly these serpents' wiles an' powers, an' that I did but reward thee with churl-ish insults an' base mockery, still, Martino, if I may say it, an' you'll exonerate a wand'ring sprite, 'twas not right for thee to so slyly creep into my lady's soft affections, no matter my wild an' raging lunacy. I'd suspected it for long, an' though I understand thy tenderness for so sweet a dame, 'twas, certes, the caitiff action of a knave an' cut-purse o' fraternity t' enflame her when she stood, all whirlèd in confusion an' in need o' me. 'Twas a kind o' mizzling roguery, Martin, a treachery that should ha' prepared me for the ultimate bloody deed that you enacted 'gainst me! Aye! Your witched an' bewildered gull, your idiot Master Ned, was not only machinated 'gainst by all the hellish furies that the two hags could alchemize t' destroy his soul, but his soul-companion, his Halpin, bold Halpin, who was t' him as Brother Straw i' the game o' short cut an' long, did find it in his heart t' give the poor cony a gallant pair o' horns! Don't quake so, poor lump o' flesh, for I forgive thee, an' it be the Lord Sol that'll warm the earth a-morrow. But what galls is that thou creeped to the seduc-tion o' fair Daisy i' the mantle o' loving friendship an' selfless assist-ance to a dear old comrade. Ah, my old bull, e'en to a spectral windy thing, the remembering tastes bitter as the dregs o' those tuns wherein vinegar doth age. But, again I say, I do forgive thee, dear heart, with whatever little power I possesseth to forgive. Yet, gentle wight, canst thou forgive thyself for this theft an' treachery, an' more to the point of 't, can thou forgive thyself for that most vile an' bloody act levied 'gainst me? Yes, I mean that dark an' currish murder here committed, why, man, i' this very chamber, an' almost o' this very spot on which my vap'rous shape now stands t' address thee! 'Twas a swinish act, th' act of your baleful hyena, not that, certes, of a true-born an' wondrous lover, or of a lover provident an' secret, witty, secure, modest, courteous, an' rational. Was this act o' shad-owed Hecate that o' the judicious lover? Nay, say it not! Nor was it that o' your valiant, jovial, substantial, candid, elegant, or magnifi-cent lover. 'Bove all, 'twas far-removèd from the glistering glory o' your heroickal. Then what sort o' love did smolder i' thy breast t' make thee act a coward an' traduce an' slay the friendship that we'd fashioned over many lustra? Such an act can be count'nanced an' nourished by the sort o' love embraced by sectaries, i' their confused affections. A glorious boasting love! A whining, ballading, adventur-ous, romance love! A love fantastic an' umbrageous, or, worse, brib-ing an' corrupt. In it dwelleth th' elements o' the froward an' the jealous, the sordid, an', though my heart doth crack t' say it, the illiberal. A stinking kind o' love, proud an' scornful, angry an' quarrel-ing, melancholic, an', hated o' God an' all his angels, despairing. Envious, unquiet, an', as thou wilt own, sensual an' brute. Think, brother man, is this the sort o' love with which to gird thyself t' meet my Daisy, my Daisy, whom you reft from me? 'Twas a bastard, low-born love that could end but in foulest, treach'rous, most bloody murder!

"*Paulo maiorana canamus.* Martin, thou must confess all to the police, an' to their stern judgment offer up thy fate. Nor prayers, nor simpering looks at heaven, nor gifts nor offerings will change the torture thy Creator holds for thee, if thou doth fail to hold to thy very soul the sublunary punishments devised to bring to purifying dust all thy raging pride an' fell iniquities! Ajax fell 'fore great Zeus's fury, an' the giant, Capaneus, whose fearsome shadow lay 'cross Thebes like to Doom itself. Poor, creeping man must pay in full coin, a-smoke from the blazing fires o' the mint, for all his vain transgressions o' the law. Yet, 'twould fare better wi' thee in th' eternal life to come, wert thou t'admit thy crime to mundane justice, than to dissemble here until the fierce trump calls for thee, an' the passing-bell tolls out the syllables o' thy name. Our Father loveth a penitent, for whom his holy Son, the mild Jesu, did shed his gore an' hang in agony 'pon the cruel Roman tree. List, Martin, list, an' follow this word to thee an' thou'lt be saved. Else, ravaging Mephisto, an' the great King o' Darkness, burning Lucifer himself, 'll snatch thee howling into raging pains an' torments th' exact moment that thy breath doth go. Stare not, crooked friend, 'stead, think on the sinners who've saved their souls by their cruelly kind shrivening. But hark! The light grows rosy i' th' East, an' the gallant Chanticleer doth bless th' impending morning with his cries to me o' *'Nunc dimittis!'* I go, Martin, I go, remember thy poor friend, remember me, remember. I needs must fly now to that part o' the sky that still is touched o' blue. . . ."

Lamont's Notebook

The enormity of the plot! Against my well-being, even my sanity. No lengths to which *they* won't go. How clear it is that all this was planned years and years ago, even before my marriage. *They* waited and waited for the perfect time to hatch this plot. Why should I be such a threat? And Sheila involved all those years!

This morning, after a restless night, during which I thought of a hundred ways to approach the final chapters, I got up and made coffee. Lonely coffee. Lonely, lonely, lonely Lamont. Lamont the Lonely.

Lorna Flambeaux came to my mind, my humiliation at her hands. *Whoever she is! Not what or who I thought, of that I'm now sure!* The more I thought of her the more familiar she seemed. She is the core of all my troubles.

I took my coffee to my desk to read over "Blue Ruin" and compose myself. There on the desk, this chapter! Completely written, typed! I read with rising fear, terror.

I did not write this chapter.

Typed on my machine. My paper. No notes, no rough drafts, no corrections. A perfect, finished copy.
They of course have done it.

They think I don't know them! Subtle, and insane plot, hatched so long ago. No wonder I suck my teeth. What else should I do? What else can I do? Write, write, you fool—it's all you're good for!
Diabolism?

They must have rejoiced so when I swallowed lock, stock, and sinker, "Lorna Flambeaux." In my loneliness, and so full of tender thoughts for a struggling young poetess! Doing all I could to assist her.

I see through it all. *Money* brings *power. I* shall have both—and soon! I know how to scheme; I'm not the simple dreamy artist. No more!

Shabby filthy prose. All of them involved. For years. Now I seem to remember the name Beshary from some other place, some other time. Have I noted this somewhere? Can he be other than the fool he seems to be? Softly, softly. Seem the victim and write the final chapters quickly.

Halpin's Journal

I thought I could be anything and everything but *frightened* by Lamont. This ghost was too real for me. It was *not* Ned, playing tricks. He must be miles away by now. I hardly know what he said, strange words, odd accent, but he knew the whole story, all the names . . .

Lamont could not have done this. But then if he didn't, who did? And if *nobody* did it? What then?

Can a writer simply "make up" characters?

Lamont will not come through, I see it now. He has collapsed, even if he didn't do it, he allowed me to be involved in this, this what? Now I want Ned's letter so badly. It's lonely and eerie here.

It was *possible* to deal with Lamont's ineptitude and even his madness, his lunacy. But what am I dealing with now?

Write, Ned, write!

My bag is packed. But where will I go if I don't know where to look for Ned?

That ghost's *voice!* From miles and miles away.

My Dear "Lorna Flambeaux":

How stupid you must think me to be to have taken all this time to realize that you engineered my embarrassment of several weeks ago! Suddenly it is all crystal clear. It came to me in a flash just a few days ago that you and Joanne *Whitestone* are obviously the dearest and closest of friends. And that you two *plotted* against me. So that you could further denigrate me and my character. How base of you! Both of you! Oh, I'm sure that you and she have had a fine old time laughing about my *faux pas* and my naive and well-meant attempts at *assisting* you. Well, laugh on!

Or am I being once again naive at not detecting the fine hand of *Mr.* Whitestone in all this? Surely, your scheme could easily have been hatched in his cruel brain, since the *whole world* knows to what extremes Whitestone has gone in the past to crush my talents as an *artist* and poke fun at me as a *man!* I can hear the *three* of you laughing about this—foul, demented laughter for which you shall surely suffer some day, I hope and pray!

Oddly enough, a most bizarre idea has crossed my mind in recent days—or is it "oddly" or even "bizarre"? I do not think so! It is—that you (Lorna) and Mrs. *Whitestone* (Joanne) are *one and the same person!* Foolish? Raving? Far-fetched? Insane? Perhaps. Yet—it is absolutely possible, and, indeed, probable. Certainly, much stranger things have happened—mostly to *me!* And I take the liberty of telling you that since I began work on this book of mine—part of which I *tried* to read to you—my fortunes have taken what anyone rational would call a decidedly *downward* turn. And "fate" has not been responsible for this bad luck and rejection that confront me wherever I turn. No matter what you say or are thinking at this moment!

Why, then, is it not probable that you are indeed Joanne *Whitestone?* Why? You both look very much alike, as I *think you know.* That seems to more or less prove that you *might as well* be she! Prove me wrong! Besides, it seems clear that you are a "friend" of Vance Whitestone's—so why not his wife as well? My intuition, my *writer's intuition,* tells me that *you,* Lorna-Joanne, married Vance Whitestone so that he could use his influence in getting your trashy doggerel published. The scenario seems clear as day to me.

As for those "poems" of yours, Joanne-Lorna! I will use whatever powers and influence I have in the literary world to prevent you from publishing them—or anything else—*anywhere!* Vance Whitestone will find my face set against him wherever he turns—and I can be a *formidable* opponent, as he can tell you.

Besides, I am convinced, Miss "Flambeaux," that you had no hand in writing those "poems" of "yours"—none at all! You are, I regret to say, a fraud and a loathsome fake! With so many *truly, honestly* rotten poets about, in their own right, who needs another, *manufactured* one?

Certain internal evidence proves to me that "your poems" could only have been written by Dermot Trellis, who just "happens" to be my brother-in-law as well as a mortal enemy of mine and of fine writing! As if you didn't know, you slut!

But—gnash your teeth and rend your immodest garments to tatters, Lorna-Joanne-Dermot, for I shall persevere and win out in the end! Once my book is published, you will crow about having known me, however briefly!

> In disgust and with pity for you, I am
> Antony Lamont

My dear Mr. Beshary:

I hope that you will not think me impertinent for taking such a long time to reply to your two really good and quite fascinating letters. I have had a lot on my mind, and, if I may take a stranger into

402

my confidence, many strange things have been happening to me of late. As you may know, I have *many enemies.*

Believe me, I have thought and thought about both your letters very seriously, and it gives me great pleasure to tell you that I find great merit in both of your financially oriented strategies. How I wish I could help you with an initial outlay of capital, as you request in both your missives! Unfortunately, I am, as the saying goes, "out of pocket" at the moment.

I feel it my duty to enlighten you as to the lot of an author like myself. Far from being well-off, I exist on the razor's edge of abject poverty, and I dare say that your means, however modest, are considerably greater than my own. The only way an author can get rich is by selling himself and his work—which, I'm sure you know, *many* do. But not I! I feel sure that you've heard this here and there. Perhaps it's even been mentioned in the literary quarterlies?

I have been working on a new book for about a year now, and have entertained hopes that it would once and for all (I somehow feel that I can speak candidly to you) establish me as an author to be reckoned with, as well as bring a little money into my modest household. Yet, it seems that this is not to be—a man of your obvious experience and nicety of judgment will understand—since I have *many enemies* in the literary world, including men of influence and power in the publishing business—loathsome creatures all!

However, there are certain options open to me. If I could get hold of some money, I would be able to do a number of things, not the least of which would be to get my book *privately* published, that is, if all commercial doors are closed in my face—and I suspect they may be. I have *a number of enemies.* You see, my new book is filled with honesty and is artistically uncompromising—two ingredients that are not in high demand today, if they ever were. My sister Sheila can tell you all about it, but I *don't suppose* that you know her?

There are certain things that I have been thinking about in connection with the raising of cash—and some of them touch on your visionary and exciting schemes, or should I say dreams? However, I'm afraid that the burden of gathering a few thousand dollars would have to fall on your capable shoulders. I have no regular "job," no credit rating, and my only "collateral" is my typewriter. Sad, but too, too true!

This is the way artists are treated in this society, while a vile scribbler like Dermot Trellis—well, I don't want to bore you with the obvious.

But, if you can raise, say, $3000, I can then have some flyers printed up and mailed to select people (leave the list to me!) all over the country, announcing my new book and asking for subscriptions. I can also enclose the information that "limited supplies" of my earlier novels are still available (I have many cartons of them here in my apartment) at the *original list price*. Since at least two of these titles are collectors' items, I should be fairly well deluged with orders by shrewd bargain-hunting bibliophiles. The monies raised should take care of the cost of printing my new book, so that will be one debt cleared, as it were, as it is incurred.

The balance will surely be enough for you to use to start one of your projects, and with the profits of just a day or two, you can pay off the bank loan of $3000! So you see, we shall both make money from nothing! It sounds remarkable to me, and I hope you will be as excited as I am about all this.

You must be careful, however, Mr. Beshary, to keep my name *out* of all this! If "certain people" should get wind of the fact that you and I are in partnership, I am afraid that it would be impossible for you to get a loan. Believe me when I say that *dark forces are at work against me*.

There are other reasons why I have written you, requesting your assistance as you so courteously requested mine. It must be clear to you that there is no way that a serious writer like myself can reach "the man in the street." I freely admit that my novels are flawed in those spots where they attempt to capture "ordinary" people. I am guilty. But *you* are surely a typical man in the street—your intense interest in horse-racing and sewer systems shouts the fact. It follows that *you* can reach the ordinary Joe, as the expression goes. And with rousing success! I hasten to assure you that I do not say this patronizingly. The harsh truth is that I have spent my adult life among authors, editors, agents, and other literary people, who know really nothing at all about the real world. Many of them cannot fry eggs, and I have recently been unfortunate enough to have met a young woman who doesn't even know how to conduct herself at a dinner party. Odd, you say? Perhaps. But true!

So, I have taken the liberty of sending you, under separate cover, inscribed copies of my four previous novels for your perusal. If you find them congenial and amusing, I beg you to work up, in your catchy prose, some few comments on each, mimeograph same, and send these comments to every friend, relative, and acquaintance that you can think of or remember, asking them, in turn, to send on (within five days, or they will have *bad luck*) the comments to all *their* friends, relatives, and acquaintances, and so on and so forth. In this way, a "chain letter" can be started, and in a month or two, literally *hundreds of thousands* of people will have read the comments and will have come to know of my books. My address and a price list will be included. If I get orders totalling even 5%, this money will more than cover any debts that you have incurred in getting this project started. In the meantime, the flyers announcing my new book and offering the old titles will be sent by me to a list of *select* people.

So, my dear Beshary, you see that together we will cover both the elite and common segments of society, and raise enough money to get one or both of your thrilling projects off the ground.

It seems to be a sure-fire scheme for me to get rid of these cartons of old books, print (and sell) my new book, start us as partners in a lucrative and imaginative business, and, last but not least, avoid *my enemies!* Surely, we will have capital to burn, capital that can be used to launch new projects with which I know that your brain is teeming!

If you feel that these trivialities may be too time-consuming and a drain on your energies, I beg you to ignore my proposition. In any event, my books, now on the way to you, are to be considered gifts. If you should honor me by admiring them, you may order as many more of each as you like at the prices listed on the dust jackets, and I will pay postage.

In the hope that we will become partners, I remain,

Yours sincerely,
Antony Lamont

P.S. I would be quite willing to give up this ink-stained life for one of interesting business ventures. Your ideas seem fertile and exciting! I feel that I *must* finish the book on which I have lavished so much time and devotion, but I admit to you, my unknown friend, that the experience of writing it has quite unsettled me. I have *a lot of enemies,* and they have done terrible things to me and to my book in order to sabotage it. Does *The Red Swan* mean anything to you? If it does, you know what I am getting at! A businessman's life would be *a vacation* for me. The things that have happened to me over the past year have been almost sinister; as a matter of fact they *have* been sinister. I hope that you will not take offense if I ask you for a photograph of yourself and a résumé of your career. By the way, I know that you are not a literary man, but what do you think of the work of Lorna Flambeaux? My own opinion is that she is *quite good.*

Lamont's Scrapbook
DAILY HOROSCOPE
Teena Diccke

YOUR BIRTHDAY TODAY: See the year ahead as mainly a reproach for past misdeeds. Think in terms of transforming your basically

405

schizoid personality in a constructive, money-oriented way and stop defeating yourself at every turn. Cut your toenails and ease foot pains. Make a real effort to stop sucking your teeth. Today's children are essentially timorous, hopeless, and unfortunate in matters of love. Don't go out with college boys.

ARIES *(March 21–April 19):* Whatever else happens on this most exasperating day, keep your mouth shut. Let others do the talking or you may be taking an unwanted trip to the hospital. Look on the bright side.

TAURUS *(April 20–May 20):* You annoy people with your stupid opinions. A touch of bribery may get you that expensive gadget you've coveted for so long. Be cheerful!

GEMINI *(May 21–June 20):* Try quitting your job but do it circumspectly. Geminis are prone to tearing their clothes off today. Odd people may stare at your legs. Smile away your blues.

CANCER *(June 21–July 22):* Keep your money safe today as others, not so friendly to your open nature, will try and get your O.K. for wild schemes. Toward late afternoon you may feel like Moon Mullins. Don't give the time of day to either bums or beggars. A good laugh eases your gas pains this evening.

LEO *(July 23–Aug. 22):* Your massive head seems fatter than usual today and you may find yourself the center of anatomical controversy. Maintain your dignity even while trying to get your hat on. Chuckle.

VIRGO *(Aug. 23–Sept. 22):* Get your back into those do-good projects that have long depressed you. A brisk walk will put the roses in your cheeks. Don't harbor resentment against that person who spits on your suit. Let's see the flash of those pearly whites!

LIBRA *(Sept. 23–Oct. 22):* An element of surprise enters early in the day. You may discover that you have no familiarity with your face. Poets of the opposite sex are open to conquest this evening but do not move precipitately. Grin your most lovable grin.

SCORPIO *(Oct. 23–Nov. 21):* The dullest of job routines develops a novel twist this afternoon. There's a hint of adventure in indecent-exposure attempts. Observe police commands to the letter. A smile goes a long way toward easing others' hostility.

SAGITTARIUS *(Nov. 22–Dec. 21):* A search for your mouth ends successfully. Financial worries dim the bloom of the morning. Family and friends try to pull you into the role of arbiter, for which you are totally unfit. A guffaw shows your lips and tongue to best advantage.

CAPRICORN *(Dec. 22–Jan. 19):* Cater to your ennui in the face of urgings toward action. The afternoon brings a surprising revelation of passion. Well-meaning friends show you enlarged photos of house flies. Toward evening a few simpers may bring intellectual refreshment.

AQUARIUS *(Jan. 20–Feb. 18):* Do not help anybody and carry a clean handkerchief, the necessity for which will become clear in the afternoon. Others' worries elate you and you are filled with lascivious thoughts. A smirk works wonders.

PISCES *(Feb. 19–March 20):* An excellent day for throwing out furniture. Step back and take a good long look at your body. An intimate conversation may give you a migraine. Hearty laughter tends to bring up troublesome phlegm.

[Clearly, *planted* in the paper, doctored up so that it would be aimed directly at me! The *paper* didn't know this is my birthday. *Their* tentacles reach everywhere!]

13. DISLOCATED REASON

Here now, I am finally alone, truly alone, with the enormity of what has actually happened here this evening. This creaking, windblown house! My dead friend! Would that *he* would creak. How can I convince my heart, my shattered heart, that the appearance of that grisly spectre was but a humdrum conundrum of my imagination, or at the very least, a figment?

How the wind keens and screeches like a daft banshee! How it has keened and screeched all night! The police will never arrive, never. I am locked alone into my shuddering guts, frightened, I admit it freely. I feel as if I am some poor pawn, some small fragment of a mysterious jigsaw puzzle. Yes, a harlequin, a smile on my lips and my heart broken beneath.

That horrifying night at Club Zap! I insist that it was right to meet Ned Beaumont here, here in his own lonely cabin by the white-capped, wind-tossed lake, in order to try one last time to wrest him from the grasp of Evil! It ended . . . in tragedy!

I walk about the cabin now, aimlessly, my heart aching like an old rusty Brillo pad, looking here, there, all over, all over except at—*that spot.* That spot where Ned Beaumont lies, his scanty remains. I have the eerie feeling that he no longer lies there—but wild horses could not drag my head around to make me look! That spectre! It could not have been Ned Beaumont but a projection of my own "aura." Certainly, that's it?

Hello! A door! A door? I do not remember having ever seen it before. I stand here, feeling as if I have gone mad. For hours, for centuries perhaps, I have sat here, musing on the mysteries of life and death, or death in life, as some say. The Spanish in particular. Weaving, weaving my tragic and pitiful tale for those brave enough or game enough to listen, whoever they are. Its catastrophes, its catabases, its ups and downs, its maw of an ineluctable inferno of remorse! Yes, all these, and more, too terrible to remember!

Hours of nothing but the keening wind! The hobgoblin murmur of the trees that shoulder menacingly up from the whipped waters of the lake toward the cabin, almost as if they are sentient beings with but one gnawing desire—to eat up this cabin and all that is in it, including me!

408

Ah, my shabby life. To think that I was once a little boy. The churning flood that swept my innocence away! My old, sad, bleary father! The beast!

But this is madness.

Hours, I say. Or said—it seems hours ago! And yet, I have not seen this door before. What can it mean? I shake in my shoes, although I seem to be wearing sneakers at the moment—when I donned them, I cannot tell. Who can? Certainly not the poor hulk that was Ned Beaumont and on which I shall never glance again.

I am at the door, gazing numbly at my hand—it seems to belong to somebody else! It reaches out for the knob, strangely gnarled knuckles twitching. Lost deep inside me there is a feeling that I will not like what I may find in here. The truth's passion races through me, however, and I watch the oddly familiar hand that is mine and yet *not mine,* turn the knob. I hiss for some reason as the clawlike grip turns the knob, slowly. The door swings open.

I am in another house altogether! A strange shaking possesses my body as the icy core of terror that resides within my otherwise almost anonymous frame grows cold. Another house! As I gaze about, I see that it is not really another house, but some rooms, rooms that I can swear were not here before. Before *what?* I cannot bear to think of it! I enter, "whistling on a gravestone."

An icy hand of unreasoning fear grips me—something whispers that these rooms were not long ago used—by whom? For what purpose? The urge to flee, to bolt back into the "other" house, or rooms, battles to possess me, but I jab and hook it to the "canvas." As boldly as I can, I step decisively in. I close the door, which creaks as if it has not been opened for years. In brighter days, I would have said of this, "a likely story." But I am not in the mood for levity just now.

I am standing in a kitchen, neat and clean, almost *too* clean. How quiet it is! I can hear my frozen heart maniacally thumping its demented tom-toms in my breast; the very air is oppressive, as if there is a "presence" here. BOSH! I croak aloud, as a ragged laugh limpingly tears itself from my throat.

In a corner huddles a woodbox, piled neatly with split wood, ready for cheery conflagration. The sink is clean, no dirty dishes—somehow I see a woman's hand in it. The stove is clean as well, no foul-smelling pots clutter its surface, as is often their wont. There are no pots at all thereon! I am inexpressibly moved by this and feel a burning in my eyes as a few tears threaten egress. Why this should be, I cannot know. Can the heart be fathomed?

Above and beside the sink are open shelves crammed thickly with canned goods, bottles and jars of condiments, and other staples, and among them stands a lonely box of confectioner's sugar, with a torn cover. It has been used! Or . . . somebody wanted somebody to *think* it had been used. Probably recently, for the box is still warm. Near the sugar there is salt, borax, whatever that may be, baking soda, cornstarch, brown sugar, and other things.

How oddly familiar they all are! Or *seem* to be.

I wander on, my feet falling down loudly in the unearthly quiet. And it is then that I notice that the howling of the wind cannot be heard! It is as if I have been transported to another cosmos, let alone world. I say this last aloud, and so loudly that the boxes rattle on the shelves. I am . . . afraid!

Passing through the kitchen, I glance into the bathroom. There is nothing of note here—the usual modern plumbing, and so on. Evidently, however, it is a recent addition, as it is newly lined with clean celotex, whatever *that* is.

As I approach the bedroom, my breath comes in shorter and shorter gasps, my tongue cleaves to the roof of my mouth—God! How I long for a jujube, or a pastille, or a wafer! It is not to be! Cursing myself for a fool, I push open the door and enter. A dampness immediately racks my frame, as if for the first time.

A double bed that seems to scream obscenities at my ears sits smugly in the middle of the floor. How typical! There is also a bureau, two straight chairs, a tin waste basket, and, on either side of the leering bed, two oval rag rugs that seem to guard its secrets. My mouth fills with a bitter saliva. I gulp avidly, and continue my inspection. There is a pinewood (a loathsome wood) dresser and above it, on the wall, a round mirror. The latter mocks me with hazy, cloudy images that dissolve as I stare at them—but always, always, I see the monstrous grin that was Ned Beaumont's. I turn quickly, spraying cold sweat around.

At eye level, there are two wall maps from the *National Geographic*—they are maps of theaters of war, but what war, or where, or why, I cannot tell, nor am I a whit curious. It seems that I have seen quite enough. Ned Beaumont's laughter clangs oafishly in my brain!

This is all, without a doubt, Ned Beaumont's doing.

On the dressing table, there is a silly-looking red-and-white flounce. Silly, yes, but redolent of femininity. Certain articles of apparel *intime* swim before my eyes, now agoggle with burning suspicion.

On a hunch, I rip open a drawer, somewhere. Why not? I grin bitterly. I have no idea what I am doing. In the drawer I see an imitation-leather trinket box, or perhaps it is an imitation leather-trinket box—in it an assortment of gaudy costume jewelry. There is also therein the usual stuff that women employ on their faces and fingernails and eyebrows. Somehow, there is *too much* of it. Enough for two or three—or even four or five women, depending on their size! Combined with the gaudy cheapness of the costume jewelry, I get an image that I don't like at all.

A mélange of various feminine faces. A collage. Each one distorted with pleasure.

I pinch myself to keep from crying out, then begin to laugh soundlessly, for who is there to *hear* my screams? Who indeed, but that poor distended bulk next door, sprawled where he fell, I think. My eyes grow weary and globulous.

Now I stand whimpering with rage and fear at the bureau—I know that the key to these rooms may lurk within its ugly mass. I mean a metaphorical key—the rooms don't require a real key. The import of this strikes me, and as swiftly flits away! Lucky for me. I am blubbering, through tears of apprehension.

A man's clothes. A woman's clothes. There is not, however, a heck of a lot of them. A "noisy" check shirt with a starched collar that seems to match. *Seems.* Then, my eye plummets into the corner of the drawer. Under a sheet of blue tissue paper there is a brand-new peach-colored silk slip *trimmed with lace.*

I reel. Somehow, I fall, how I manage it, I don't know. I am up again. Speaking now, speaking aloud, but I don't know what I'm saying. I keen. Of course it is! I gasp.

It is Daisy's slip! How often have I seen it when the wind has worried her skirts!

I will never forgive Ned Beaumont, *never.* To make her a party to his perverted inversions! *Anything* but that peachy slip! His baseness, his lowness, his foul love of exotic colors!

Anything! My God, I would have preferred to find here a busted jelly; a midnight hiss; an Angus nose or two; holiday doubles; real fine references; two, two vinaigrettes in a park; a little Mick's sneakers; lovely heels; some gouts of aquamarine; a stern yet kindly Ballantine; glistening sheens, "specialized" drawings; a sugar pie; great balls of fire; an eyeful; lovely lace at last; wandering zygotes all alone; flying Italians; some rocks a bit the worse for wear; a beach that requires our homage; stupid dogs; things for thighs; just a hint of control; lots of kaffs; mounds of faps; dreaming dollinks; lonely plains that ring free; a painted dessert; a pot thrown from Heaven; broomsticks at high port; fog friendly for weeping; '54 Bordeaux; divorce of a different choler; an old church smudged white in the dusk; beans on Mystery Mountain; a merry black widow, just a trifle tight; a silver label; foundations for the frolicsome; thunder bugs; a gossamer goose; ack-ack; a lavender vanilla sundae; poets' espadrilles; an idiot bassoon; a black Tom; sockamagees and cushlamochrees; Easter white and gold; a pig's ass; Sausalito sausage; a honeyed moon o'er Oyster Bay; a snapshot of good ol' Sal Hepatica; summer ducks; Ohio gloaming; suffering succotash; a couple of zowies; the dim cool of Arnold's; leaping lizards; Francis' dances; a ruined ragout; a clutch of bonks; gloriosky zeroes; weeds who are about to die; garden hosiery; holy moleys; comical books; a flying Mydas; the dim lights of Moebius Strip; smoky stoves; smiles of beauty, smiles of health; cans of laughter; a burst of frowns; a fight for four eyes; abbeys and slats; a Blue Mondae mit marzhipan und shprinkles; booze in the night; a bag of the foos; good and plenty griefs; one Mint Julep; a ballerina's dance; hip boots by Stekel; one foxed, soiled, well-worn, thumbed, and dog-eared copy of *Was Guy Gay?: Depravity, Debasement, and Dementia in DeMaupassant;* a true bruin; a shadow's earmuffs; swollen weepers; raving monoliths; two cents of decorum; a happy hooligan; chocolate chicks; whirling dervishes and jumping jehosaphats; a *Chauliognathus exercitus* (Bailey); a lobster craw from Old Japan; a bent sinister; chili blisters; holy Hannah's halter; a brace of short yet festive shrifts; a Rum Boogie; slips for the tongue; a few imaginary quantities; a souvenir pen wiper from Lake Cafone, N.J.; one round ball ammunition; two pastel pix of Creeping Jesus; three stubby Mongols; an ink-a-bink; strawberry depressions; a yar of jellow yam; old fighters; swollen officers; a snappy highball; an ink drawing of sweet Molly Screw; some lives in the yellow leaf; ups and outs in the latest style; loathsome fedoras; a red felt hat with poet inside; poiple sneaks; a pair of Mickey Finns; some swaks; wrinckled flowres; a big stoop; some set o' pins; a smiling jock; calls of duty; a cultural disadvantage; eight-page foibles; Maggie's jigs. Or even a bushy cub; Canadian exposés; a metropolitan Neapolitan; Billy's snap of brother Philly; nine sad blue jays; an Alleghany fresco; pirated additions; a humidor of El Perfectoes; studies in brown; cardinal sins; risqué red stockings; a stuffed and mounted beaneater; a rose and a dove; a rustler of leaves; A's and Bees; brave crackers; a pinko red; a rusty Colt that will bark no more; *The Astrodontics Review;* a faded foto of a boining bridegroom; a summons for a trolley dodger; supple superbas; a plastic feather from a California robin; *A Shorter History of The Culinary Role of Los Padres de los Pobres;* jints in the oith; a box of Oriole cookies; a pebble chipped from Plymouth Rock; filthy etchings featuring Pilgrims and Puritans; a somerset stomach; one red sock; blue Indians; the bluebird of happiness; one bronco bust; "Field Notes on Old Tigers"; pompous pilots; smells like a brewery; whorish highlanders; yankee noodles; angels seeking pins for dancing days; white stockings nice for naughty nursie and thin white sox for hilarious hix; a recipe for Spam Royale; Minnie and Minnie, the Twin twins; athletic purporters; Senator Bracciola's rugged rejoinder; micturating mariners; a loaned ranger. I'd rather see a carton of airplane loves; fearless fictioneers; honeydrippers; great moons of Krypton; two middling strata and a tiny kudos; a whore with heart of mold; a bee's pyjamas; a cat's knees; a wax meow; a phrase from the *opera* of Ethel Smith; a mezzotint of brooding Lake Hassan; *billet doux* from Telephone Bill; aurora boom de-ay; a platoon of cosmopulitain girls; someday sweethearts; sweet patooties; surrounding darkness; special fare for special palates; Balloona Park; spodeeodee; duh wings of a angel wit rice; bazze money; a nest of yikes; po'k chops; Easter lillums; Toledo the Holy; holograph letters from huerhouses; a Coney Island whitefish; smiles and smirks; and many other items, too humorous to mention.

Yes, *anything* would have been preferable to that slip! For it proves what I long suspected. How I wish now that Ned Beaumont had not *dropped dead of a heart attack plus stroke,* so that I could have the pleasure of never forgiving him!

Hatred wells in me. Compelled by a strange force greater than my own. I laugh. What force do *I* have? What strength?

Suddenly, I am back in the kitchen, glancing obliquely at the shelves, pretending that I am seeking . . . seeking . . . what is it that I pretend to seek?

Sugar? *Confectioner's* sugar! I am drawn somnambulistically to the box, my gnarled hands close upon its surface.

On my hands and knees now, I am pouring the contents on the floor. Its whiteness, its purity, its terrifying spotlessness, like sterile snow that certain lovely women love. I am droning on, wordlessly. But then I see it. It!

It! I know!

A tiny gold heart.

No bigger than a woman's little fingernail, or, in any event, a little woman's fingernail.

I bring it close to my tear-soaked eye, glabrous though it may be. There is an inscription, so tiny that it is hard to read. I slowly spell out the words.

Al to Mildred. June 28 1938. With all my love.

I swoon. Is that who they are? Or were? Who are they?

I scream in frustration and anguish. It strikes me like an avalanche that 1938 was some time ago! Am I mad?

Is the hulk outside Ned Beaumont? Was he ever? Or is he . . . "Al"?

I swoon again, crowded with implications.

Can Daisy be "Mildred"? What of Mme Corriendo, or Berthe Delamode? Perhaps one of them is "Mildred"? Is life a "dream"? Am I "mad"?

The ghost *was* a hallucination! I must believe this! Else . . .

And now, through my raging bewilderment, I seem to hear sounds from the floor above, as of great heavy trunks being moved. I have the feeling that Ned Beaumont's body has disappeared!

Once again, scrabbling around in the powdery sugar, I pinch myself. Ah, God, the pain! The cleansing pain! Yet . . . it tells me that I am awake, this is not a dream. Is it?

And then I confront the terror of it all. Have I made up Corriendo and Delamode? Do they exist? Does Daisy exist?

How marvelous a piece of machinery is the human brain.

What is truth? What is reality? Have I invented this entire tale? Were the bizarre people I have been involved with all inventions to excuse my terrible deed? Yes, yes, it was a terrible deed!

Terrible deed!

TERRIBLE DEED!

Yes, I murdered Ned Beaumont. In cold blood, with a candelabra or a pitcher full of Martinis. Again and again I struck and struck! Again. Again.

And again.

To think that even Daisy, Daisy of the gorgeous eyes, is an insubstantial thing! Yet it may well be true. I have noticed that, at times, I have slipped into her wondrously creative speech patterns, and syntax. Or is it that she has slipped into mine?

Is there such a thing as "syntax"? Has there ever been? How Ned Beaumont would laugh at me, did he exist. Did he exist? Or have I . . . ?

I must hold straitly to my sanity while I await the police, the police who will not come because I have not called them, no matter what I have said, because this cabin—has—no—phone!

Now I begin to understand why Ned Beaumont asked me here to talk. Or was it I who asked him? Did I know that there was no phone on which I could not call the police?

Bits and pieces . . .

I am in the other room again. A frenzied chill of coldness rips through my nervous system. Try, try as I may, I cannot see Ned Beaumont's remains. Or is it that I do not *want* to see him? Or them?

I face now the reality of my impossible situation. I must reconstruct the conversation that Ned Beaumont and I had, that terrible conversation that preceded his murder. Everything that happened that evening, was it just last evening? That evening that began so promisingly with the crisp pastoral sky grinning down all lustrous and spanking blue. . . .

Lamont's Notebook

No matter what that satan, Roche, had to say, I see the perfect extension of the techniques of my beautiful early work, "O'Mara Of No Fixed Abode."

Two more chapters. a.) Conversation leading up to Beaumont's death.
b.) Last chap. The confrontation. Resurrection of Ned?

The horrifying feeling that there will soon be another assault upon me—this time a truly violent and unimaginably base one.

I cannot sleep anymore.

Lamont's Scrapbook

DERMOT TRELLIS
Dark Gemini

How odd to ponder, in this gale-flogged house by the sea, that I was once more or less happy, in that miserable, craven way that humans have of being happy. Then, for some inexplicable reason, a reason as mysterious as the birth of a galaxy, my brain, glowing like the eyes of some dementia-ravaged scientist, fastens on the image of a Moebius Strip.

A Moebius Strip! In its curiously simple convolution, I seem to glimpse, as though racked with agony, the vision of the essential truth of life, as banal and unprepossessing as a rotten cantaloupe. . . . A laugh, that I suddenly realize is my own, tears through the still air of the room in which I am sitting, with the sickening sound of a telephone being ripped from a grimy rooming-house wall, a wall like a ruined and broken mouth uttering obscenities.

Has my life come to this? I think of a rat considering a piece of rancid bacon, eyes evilly glittering mindlessly like the eyes of a diseased mouse! Surely, all of human endeavor, all our petty schemes and hopes are incapable of being filed away as merely corollary data on the planar values of a simple Moebius Strip? Yet, perhaps . . . I wonder. Then I seem to see the rat slinking up a dying palm tree in a trailer camp in Southern California like a drunken baboon, and sour nausea rises in me like the mercury in a thermometer held in the flaccid mouth of a dying leper. With a start, I embrace the sick feeling, clasping it to me as if it is a bolt of cloth of gold, or a flagon of rarest distilled myrrh, as I realize that the leper has the face of my father! For a second, a fraction of a second, a time as brief in its hegemony as the life of a feckless whitecap on a sea that has just wolfed down thousands of innocents, I feel a sweet wave of cleanliness pass over me. Then it is gone.

The dead man across the room is sprawled in a gold brocade wing chair that seems horribly familiar. He might be asleep except for the nasty bullet hole just behind his right ear—a bullet hole that the sharp eye of an astute observer would certainly see as clearly as he would see the muttering waves beyond the windows of this gale-crushed house, were he to but look.

Perhaps it is a trick of the shifting firelight, perhaps the hallucination of my exhausted brain, weary and worn from years of the cynicism that my dirty trade has created, yet the dead man's face seems almost to be—my own! Swiftly, with something approaching a nameless fear, I realize that I have seen this man before, his face floats, floats in and out of my consciousness like a red and vaguely sinister balloon on a street in Dusseldorf. For a moment, I clearly catch the effervescent and beery melody of a Nazi calliope, a melody as tinny and disarming as a carrousel at a small county fair in Massachusetts. . . . I am returned to a moment of childhood at a county fair . . . an afternoon as sweet as attar . . . the taste of cotton candy . . . a slim, blond girl smiles from the deep shade of a lemonade stand. . . . The taste in my mouth is suddenly bitter as vetch.

Dr. Otto Moebius. He is Dr. Otto Moebius, the charlatan from the Red Swan Hotel! Unwillingly, I leap to my feet and my trousers fall sadly and impotently to my middle-aged knees, scarred and rough with the reminders of a life of bitterness and shabby danger as sickening and despair-filled as a February morning in grey and gloomy Paris.

Now I know, with a shudder as erratic as an old Chevvy pickup lost in the vulgar purlieus of Los Angeles, why I thought of a Moebius Strip! A lump in my chest terrifies me, then I realize that it is the cruel bulk of a .38 Police Special. Then my fear is doubled, trebled, it whines. Carefully hitching up my trousers, I fumble in a pocket for my ballistics kit, and a moment later, my brain is forced into the steaming mulch of putrid truth!

The bullet that killed Moebius came from my gun.

Swiftly rising from his body, cold now as a junkie's forgotten hamburger, I glance about the room for other occupants, but all that smashes my eye is vapid space. Still, my nostrils, testing the air with the eagerness of a doe high in the cool Sierras, catch a hint of an exquisite perfume, a scent as subtle and provocative as a beautiful woman caught for eternity by the camera in a perfectly executed swan dive. Although my eyes seem blinded by a strange swirling mist as thick and lumpy as the mashed potatoes in a blue-plate special, the face of the woman shoulders through the clotted opacity and presents itself to me as the face of my ex-wife.

Tears plunge shamelessly down my cheeks like collapsing winos as I see our life together hustle by on the silver screen that has unfurled itself in my brain. I'm sorry . . . so sorry, my dear, I gasp through my blubbering. Yet my voice has no more strength in it than the sad flicker of a dying ember forgotten at the edge of a cheerful campfire in the Adirondacks. But I persist, whispering regrets into the heavy air. I had mocked her, mocked her and her clean and acute desire to be a garbageman. My eyes are steaming like sad plum puddings in an orphanage, and I hurl myself into combat against anguish running amok . . .

The perfume! Almost an attar! My trained body forces itself around

417

the room with a disturbing limp. I poke, I probe, I open this and that, I search beneath the rug with the benignly ugly suspicion of a hotel shamus. My brain, reeling in the lists of memory, has no control over my technician's body, which goes on and on with the sneaky skills it has mastered over twenty years of snooping, snooping and rummaging through the sad, soiled laundry of humanity.

Then I see it. Under a heavy credenza, I catch sight of the protruding edge of a tawdry corsage, like the broken wing of a vulture. I pocket the slug I took out of Moebius, and touch the flowers gingerly. The corsage is made of paper, as wilted and trite as a gossip rag. Paper? A paper corsage can mean only two or three things . . .

The scent is stronger here, and, working as slowly and deliberately as a giant sloth denuding a tree of huckleberries, I lift the corner of the massive piece of furniture and begin to slide the artificial corsage out from under it. Sweat starts to my brow and my eyes pop like big-league fastballs. Whomever, or *whatever* put this corsage under the credenza, I whisper into the silence, must have had the strength of an Arikara maddened by vodka. Then I feel it.

Then I feel the sickening blow on my head and I am dropping down, down, down into the bottom of a clear deep pool. Looking up, I see, through the perfect transparency of the water, the figure of my ex-wife in her swan dive just above me. Her face is joyous with a beaming smile, her teeth glitter, white as moonlight in Vermont. As her lithe body descends upon me, I shriek to her to close her mouth before . . . before . . .

The house is dark when I wake up. For a moment alarm plods through me like a crazed she-bear eating a hiker, then I remember. Who attacked me? And why? Pulling my body out from under the credenza, I grope about for the paper corsage, but it is gone. With a foreboding as chill and grating as the sound of a saw cutting wood for a coffin, I force myself to face the truth of what has happened. Clawing my way toward the reality of the assault, as sudden and unexpected as a vile proposition from a seedy stranger, I admit what I don't want to admit—that anyone with the strength to crown me with the trucklike credenza must be more than human. . . .

Painfully making my way through mounds of debris, I check Moebius again. He is sitting slumped as before, but his face seems, uncannily, to look even more like mine than it did a moment ago! Or was it a moment? With a cry of frustration, I realize that I may have been on dream street for hours. Trembling now like the sails of a regatta seconds before the starter's flag, I run my bruised hands over my face. I am right . . . Moebius is my exact double!

Then I notice it. The corsage for which I risked everything is pinned to his lapel, yet this discovery is not what sends the needles of horror to pricking my scalp and spine and makes my feet fall instantly asleep! What freezes me as effectively as the polar night freezes the hapless Eskimo caught outside his igloo in only a thin sweater is the fact that Moebius is *wearing my clothes.*

I look down at myself, and a gout of hysterical laughter, generously spiced with screams of fear, bursts from my loose-lipped mouth! For I am in the clothes that Moebius was wearing before my unwanted snooze. My fingers scrabble and claw at the pockets like psychotic crabs, and with my voice a terrible thing of nonstop gibberish, I open a wallet to look at my driver's license.

It was issued to Dr. Otto Moebius.

Fighting to hold back sheer craziness, and locked in deadly throes with a fear that threatens to devour me as a tiger feasts upon a helpless village, I try to make some order out of this carnival of death.

Either I am Otto Moebius, or someone wants me to *think* I am. Maybe someone wants other people to think I am Otto Moebius. Or . . . someone may have wanted Moebius to think that he was I. Too late for that now, I bark.

I look into his face and I am looking into a mirror. Standing, I look into the mirror over the mantel and I am looking at Moebius. Or is it Moebius who looks at me?

I sit heavily, exhausted in my marrow, and poke up the fire. Soon the dawn. And with its coming, the police will come. I have about two hours to make some sense out of this madness. Two hours to retrace the steps that took me here, here to this isolated house, this house of attars, dreams, paper corsages, and silent murder . . .

I lean back and suck a flame into the end of a Sobranie. My mind detaches itself from my ravaged body and prances back unbidden, prances back to the lobby of the Red Swan, a few short weeks ago, just a few short weeks . . .

XXI-CENTURY REVIEW—

STOLEN!

Dear Martin,

In a way I hope that this letter never reaches you, because it is my wish that by now you've disappeared from that little cabin in Michigan, or wherever the hell it is, and are away from the stupid machinations and idiocies of "lame brains" Lamont. I don't want to tell you *exactly* where I am, because our little Napoleon of the pretentious novel may intercept—somehow—this letter and try to blackjack me into returning to take part in his grand assault on modern fiction. But you should have little trouble finding me. I *can* tell you that I'm halfway around the world, and that the climate here is as hot as cayenne pepper. An odd place for someone who was born in Boston and raised in Cincinnati, as I was, and you're probably wondering just what the attraction is that could draw me here. I mean, why here? Why not Bolivia or Uruguay or Macao, or, for that matter, why not Newmarket or Saratoga or Sheepshead Bay?

The truth of the matter is that this remote enclave "down the river" is filled with others like me (*and* you), perhaps five hundred of them, all fugitives from some goddamned rummy or old-maid author's wondrous work in progress. It's depressing to realize that there are Cuban, Brazilian, Chilean, Italian, Mexican, etc., etc. novelists as hopeless as our great and glorious Lamont. The stories that I've heard!—some of them are enough to spoil five years of your life!

You will remember—how could you forget?—the infamous restaurant scene through which that son of a bitch made us go. Well, I met a woman of forty-five (!) here who told me that the joker (a wild Frog) in whose book she was forced to work made her, in one chapter, do the shimmy, *nude*, in a crowded railroad station! He had her do other things too, which she only hinted at, one of them involving a paid stud in a gambling casino. And believe me, Martin, this woman, before this particular humiliation I speak of, enjoyed a reputation that hadn't a spot or a smudge. She'd worked for twenty-one years without being compromised or embarrassed in any way until she became entangled with this "literary comet," whose name is Jules Rumsch or Ramsch, whatever. The international literati, by the way, have taken him to their heart of hearts—which is not surprising, considering what deadheads and bluffs they all are.

At all events, for this lady, as well as for everyone else here, these horror stories are water under the bridge: what we are all hopeful of is a decent job in some reasonable book—a job with a fair and honest contract that specifically sets forth our privileges as well as our responsibilities. About once a week, one or two people leave the

420

place for such a job—just last week, a Monsieur Ferme left for a job in a British comic novel, *Ruffs and Honours,* which has, for one of its locales, the city of Amsterdam. M. Ferme will take the part of the director of a Dutch bank who is required to cross over to England in order to address Parliament on the necessity for a lowered tariff on the "famous Dutch delicacy," *slobberhannes*—a foodstuff which does not exist! The humor is sophisticated and dignified and Ferme appears on no more than twenty-five pages of the novel. For this quite pleasant task, he will receive seven and a half dollars a page. More importantly, he will once again do what he is most fit for, that is, portray a wealthy banker and broker: in the novel from which he fled, he was a down-at-heels samba instructor! Is it any wonder that one feels these writers ought to have their knuckles rapped?

It is also bruited about the "colony" that an elderly couple, Mr. and Mrs. Baccarat—who spend most of their time, it seems, jogging laps around the no-longer-used football field—will soon be leaving in order to play major roles in a new novel, just under way, by Jacques Bezique-Piquet. But these rumors come thick and fast, and crisscross each other continually. One can, by the looks on the faces hereabouts, spot hearts that have been lanced with hope or with near despair. I have learned that it is best to ignore all rumors and to travel solo as far as it is possible, commensurate with courtesy. Otherwise, you can let yourself in for the most devastating high-low shifts in mood and emotions.

Life here is reasonably pleasant, and most of the people I've met are likewise pleasant. There is an excellent restaurant and cocktail lounge here called The Royal Casino, and a smaller, less expensive, and livelier spot, The Red Dog, where you can find a younger crowd. Exotica is supplied by the Club Fan Tan, a Chinese restaurant and cabaret that features a floor show and dancing nightly. One of the problems here is that you can't really get a decent drink—something to do with taxes or something—I can't really understand it at all. Anyway, the ubiquitous beverage is something called "Oklahoma gin," which may well come from Oklahoma but which is certainly *not* gin. It tastes the way one imagines cheap perfume might taste, and it is very potent stuff. About four drinks and whist!—you're around the bend, or at least around the corner. One of the cheaper bars, the Café Nullo (not a bad name, right?), turns its customers into one-eyed (or no-eyed) Jacks with a potable euphemistically termed "Hollywood gin"—which is nothing but our old friend from Oklahoma doctored up with grenadine, sugar, pernod, and orange juice. A few of these and you have hit whatever alcoholic jackpots there may be to hit, and they can cart you out in what the natives here call a *canasta de palma*—a kind of large basket made of palm leaves and used for carrying vegetables, meats, etc. to and from the market-place. Anyway, you get the idea. I've seen a number of fellow expatriates' plans for an evening of "fun" with an interesting dinner partner euchred by this devil's brew. Of course, if you don't want to drink this fearsome stuff, you can always order Seven-Up, Dr. Pepper, or a pale rum known as Dom Pedro, which the local radio station delivers a fevered pitch for every evening at either five or nine.

As for the rest of this *tournée grande*, the place is harmless and, for the most part, placid. It can also be a bore. One can go out to the football field I mentioned (which is called, for some arcane reason, *vingt-et-un*—perhaps because of the usual score of one team or another there?) and play a kind of bastardized baseball, which is really more like one o' cat. Or, in town, one can play at cards, dominoes, etc. The most popular card game is five-hundred rummy (at a penny a point), and one usually plays with whatever gin rummies (pardon my lousy pun) are available. All this hilarity and adventure take place at a club called The Lowball, known disparagingly among the white populations as "the spade casino" because of its large percentage of native, black patrons. This place also boasts a pinball machine on which one can play a simpleminded game called Skat, which has as its goal the scoring of 15,000 points before a red light goes on. (Cheers!) The tap room features an out-of-tune Gucki (!?) grand piano, to which the customers, after a few Oklahoma specials, push one or another of the "musicians" at the bar. The current favorite is a disreputable Mexican drifter, the heavy of God knows how many Westerns, named Pedro Sancho. His favorite song, quite predictably, is a cowboy ballad all about the life of a legendary gunfighter, Seven-Card Pete, shot to death while holding four Jacks in a poker game. Last week, two other riders of the purple sage took offense at either Pedro or the song or both, and threatened to throw him out if he didn't cease and desist. These two, Shasta Sam and his sidekick, California Jack, "colorful characters" if I ever saw them, are well-known for their obstreperous and drunken conduct. An indigent nobleman, the Comte de Polignac, intervened, and soon the four of them were uproariously, but peacefully playing pinochle, and a fight was avoided. As for the rest of the entertainment available, one may as well go and spit in the ocean.

However, there are three ladies of the evening who operate out of a house on the edge of town, where the needy can go to drop their boodle, if they have any to drop. These three, Sherry, Dominique, and Stradella, jokingly called Snip, Snap, and Snorem because of their occupational techniques, hold an open house and cross color barriers on Saturday nights only. The rest of the time the house is run on a segregated basis (blacks and whites alternating nights). Although they are nothing to write home about, the unattached female population here is so minuscule that these three have placed themselves in a position from which they cavalierly discard hearts and auction hearts with absolute tyranny. If one is blackballed by the three S's, there is no relief until one is once again admitted to the house, unless one wishes to catch the ten o'clock in the evening *weekly* train to the next settlement—a rough, lawless place where steal the old man's (*and* the young man's) bundle is the accepted way of life. This is a twenty-one-hour trip at best on an old, quaint-looking (but extremely uncomfortable) *chemin de fer*, which has neither diner, lounge, nor snoozer. It's strictly dealer's choice—with the three graces as the dealers—in this House of Joy. It's amazing what a setback being banned seems to be after one has been here for a while.

Well, my dear Martin, that's about, as they say, all the news for now. This place, as you see, has its drawbacks, but it's an open, grand feeling to know that I might be employed any day in some decent capacity. In the meantime, a Monsieur Écarté, a wonderful old gentleman who has been in at least fifty novels of French provincial life, is teaching me how to play cribbage, a marvelous game. I'm sure I'll survive the waiting, no matter how long.

As for you, I hope that things are turning out all right with that ridiculous book you are (perhaps you are not!) still laboring in. Until we meet again, keep your powder dry, your aspidistra flying, and your deuces wild.

Your friend,
Ned Beaumont

14. MAKING IT UP
AS WE GOES ALONG

"Now that we're settled, Ned Beaumont, I feel that it's time to speak of . . . certain *things*. Two olives in your Martini, right? Two onions?"

"*I* am the president of the company," he replied. "Hm. Crickets are beginning in the raspberry patch."

"Where are the birds? Not that I care for them, but where are they?"

"Look, Martin," he said. "This very moment will become part of the good old days."

"A vision of loveliness in pristine white? Part and parcel of the gathering darkness?"

"Assemble the facts!" Ned Beaumont barked.

"All right. . . . Some metabolic imbalance makes her cry all the time. It could make *you* cry. And what legs!"

"A girl of terrific intelligence, Daisy. *Cum laude* in anthropology, with a *great* sense of humor. expertise in the arts, and, yes, the most fantastic legs I've ever seen. Someone told me that she occasionally wore a red satin garter belt, trimmed with white lace."

"All *I* ever wanted, Ned Beaumont, is that she should once, just *once,* make my eggs over easy."

"She was striking in a pale-orange dress," he mused.

"I heard that once in a while she would buy a *Silver Screen*," I chuckled. "Just like the one in the Cole Porter song."

"I can't follow the trend of this conversation. Does it *have* a trend? God! Your taste for Sazeracs depresses me."

"Those who do not follow trends are condemned to repeat them," I quipped. "No man's an asylum."

"Imagine the two of them, Corrie and Berthe, partly clothed, sitting on either side of you on a couch in the dim light. You see my point?"

"Why get involved with corsets and whips and boots and Polaroid cameras?" I reasoned. "Why not moonlight and roses and endless lies?"

"*I* am the president of the company!"

"This is becoming a college professors' lunchtime chat," I scoffed. "And *they* are obsessed with croquet and badminton, both of which they play very badly."

"What will bring us peace?" Ned Beaumont whispered.

"Think on Nikolai Gogol. It was endless masturbation that made him a great artist!"

"Blest be his lost and gentle youth," he said.

"He lived in a hovel of an apartment on the Lower East Side, crammed with huge bags of garbage and trash, which he often told me had 'blown in the window.' Ah, he was a witty man."

"Martin, your massive head seems fatter than usual today. A brisk walk will put the roses in your cheeks."

"Ned Beaumont, it has been clear for some time now that your attitude toward the magazine and toward me has been one of—how shall I say?—hostility."

"Magazine?"

"You know that I have always been particularly interested in 'the culture of the Midwest,' " I said.

"Magazine?"

"Why are you speaking with that gross Latvian accent?"

"Martin, you're gonna be so sorry for what you've done to my poor old heart. And you may regret all the vows you've broken."

"To suffer in silence prepares one either for sainthood or a nervous breakdown."

"*My* gross Latvian accent? *Your* clipped speech offends *me*," he cried.

"Years ago, I was embarrassed and silent when others spoke of books, politics, theatre, the cinema, philosophy, and so on . . ."

"It seemed to me, dear Martin, to be a sign from Juno herself!"

". . . my military career, for instance, was spent in downtown St. Louis."

"Don't miss Jesse James' hideout while in Missouri!" he laughed.

"It was not *all* grim. . . . One memorable evening ended in an animated discussion of an article on surgery that had appeared in the *Reader's Digest*."

"Pardon my digression, Martin, but it smells like rain. Don't you think?"

"I love April, Ned Beaumont," I said. "God, how I love April."

"Orange is *my* favorite color."

"Color?"

"She was *striking* in a pale-orange dress . . ."

"Was she born in a little town in New Jersey named Boonton?"

"The handsome girl has eyes the color of perfect violet, Martin," he smiled. "Jesus, your taste for Sazeracs *depresses* me."

"Why can't happiness spring clear from the adulterous affair?"

"Boonton? Yes. Beyond that town lay the Jenny Jump mountains in a blue-green haze. So they said in their slick brochure."

"As far removed from literature as I am from the nearest star," I said.

"True, but still . . . the mental vision of purple mountains' majesty! The overpowering effluvia of the fruited plain! I seem to see from those palmy days a cordé handbag . . ."

"In the dark shed of the untameable mind . . . lies the truth, Ned Beaumont."

"Somehow, your vapid and corny sophomoric idea seizes me."

"I'm glad. The task is to get past all the clatter in our heads and through to the other side. Of our heads. To the deep rhythms that connect us with the constellations and the big sea-water."

"To catch those deep flying thoughts on the wing . . . ?"

"You have the idea," I replied. "Yet, stonelike, the metaphor is useless. Do you recall Isosceles, the tragic hero in an obscure play by Thomas Dekker?"

"The one who looked as if he had bitten into a lemon?"

"Right. In Act II he says—and I paraphrase—'She liked being tupped so well you'd have thought her a Papist.' "

"Martin," he said, "you have revealed a glimpse of your essential misogyny."

"Well . . . it's a rare Elizabethan trait. Certainly more satisfying than being a Protestant. One would rather worship a box of cornflakes."

"Why are all Catholics instilled with that arrogant sense of guilt?"

"I despise religious quarrels, Ned Beaumont. Always, *always*, one throws up a hasty wall of wit and anecdote."

"In essence, I agree. At its best, religion is nothing more than a gorgeous decadence of gold, silk, and flowers."

"Or—a blue trumpet," I smiled.

"There's a song with that title that has the refrain: 'In Coconino County where the coconuts grow—Roll, Missouri, roll!' Daisy loved it."

"Daisy," I mused. "Did you ever hear that once in a while she would buy a *Silver Screen*?"

"Some great writers got started in that magazine," he said. "One, whose name slips my mind, was called 'the master of silence.' "

"Oh yes. His first book was *Yellow Is The Color of Love*. While it was a commercial disaster, it also got terrible reviews."

"Corrie and Berthe admired that novel greatly. As for me, I like the mystery of the visible."

"I don't like mysteries *or* mystics," I replied. "And as far as those two 'ladies'—they're tango dancers reminiscent of a past era."

"Tango dancers?"

426

"You heard me! They might as well be lost in the vulgar purlieus of Los Angeles."

"What about the paper bags all over their place? Aren't you going to say anything about *that,* Martin?"

"What?"

"And the shirt cardboards?"

"What?"

"I once made a list of all their, ah, intimate apparel, then spent an entire day imagining them in varying combinations of it. A wasted day, I grant you, Martin, but man does not live by bread alone."

"They may wear, so to speak, 'fancy ties and collars.' But where they get their dollars . . ."

"All right. All right. I know what you're getting at. But how many people do *you* know who have had abba-dabba honeymoons?"

"Well, don't blame *me,* Ned Beaumont, for the fact that I couldn't avoid spending my honeymoon in downtown St. Louis!"

"I remember you telling me, Martin, that at about four in the morning of your first night as a husband, you got up and wrote the title of a novel on a sheet of hotel stationery."

"I belatedly plunged into the life of letters," I said. "In any event, that marriage of mine was a perverse mummery of love, nothing more."

"Did you feel that to be surrounded by the emotionally infirm would have pleased you?"

"I did indeed."

"Then, my dear fellow," he said, "I submit that your marriage was nothing but a perverse mummery of love."

"But she *was* beautiful, was Lorna. Scrubbed, tanned, tall, with long, perfect legs and high, firm breasts, a handsome, open face, and honey-colored hair. But if she had just *once* taken a stab at making my eggs over easy . . ."

"I know the feeling. Something like morosely singing underneath the limes? Is that it?"

"Limes?" I queried, puzzled.

"I've had the same feelings anent Daisy. Yet when I dared to bring them up, however subtly, she looked at me like I was Hitler."

"Ah, Ned Beaumont . . . who can tell when the heart bursts? In my case, I often began to laugh quietly, but hysterically, to—*myself.* . . . I figured the guys would make fun of me."

"The guys, Martin? What guys? Pah! Foh! The clatter of the day's mundane trivia!"

"True. Yet it *seemed* profound, one might say even crucial, at the time. I remember that when we parted I begged her for a discreet word. Perhaps a snapshot to place on my desk. An old shoe. . . . Her coffee-colored eyes boiled."

"Sounds like a line from *Explosive Celibate*," he laughed.

"Oh, *that* old chestnut," I replied. "One of those goddam books where things *happen* all the time. For football buffs."

"Daisy, as you probably know, never understood that book. To her it was nothing more than a deeply cut, boldly edged monogram."

"The harsh bark of my sudden laughter cannot dispel the quick pity I feel, Ned Beaumont."

"She has her faults," he sighed. "Yet, tall in sepia corsets and shining patent leather boots. . . . Her eyelashes a *storm* of butterfly kisses . . ."

"Butterfly kisses? I never heard of butterfly kisses."

"You read the wrong books, Martin. In any event, it's unimportant now. You may or may not know what it is to love someone and be hurt because you've hurt them. The feeling is like being lost on Blake Avenue in East New York on a bitter cold night."

"Jingle-jingle."

"You scoff, but who can tell when the heart bursts? Do you know about Blake Avenue? One might as well be lost in the vulgar purlieus of—Los Angeles!"

"Love will send you anywhere in search of its dark yet contradictorily blazing matrix, Ned Beaumont," I said. "Everyone knows *that.*"

"Now it's my turn to say 'jingle-jingle,' " he sneered.

"And all this talk about Daisy as a kind of plastic saint!"

"Plaster."

"Plastic plaster, then. Let me remind you, Ned Beaumont, that a lady of chaste bent does not so completely expose her thighs."

"A woman does what she has to do, my friend," he retorted.

"Well, *I* find it disgusting, demeaning, and cheap. During the War we listened to the Andrews Sisters and fingered our wee-wees. So much for 'sexual freedom.' "

" 'Remember Nikolai Gogol!' Was that the ticket, you deluded fool?"

"Quips won't change the facts. We *survived.* I remember the bugler blowing tattoo over the quadrangle in the soft Maryland night."

"Maryland! Sun-drenched days! Starry tropical nights! Gourmet food! The best in lavish entertainment! Golf courses a pro's dream!"

"Now that I think of it, Ned Beaumont, I must be in error. My military career was spent in downtown St. Louis . . ."

"Soft zephyrs from the South whisper to me . . ."

"I remember it clearly. How wretched the twilight was!"

"Baltimore molded my tastes. Now I know that the art I put on my floor must be contemporary. Surely you've noticed," he said.

"Like your priceless 'Red Cento,' the collage by Mayakovsky?"

"I loaned that to Madame Corriendo. In return she promised that in a sweep of elegantly simple black silk she'd sparkle all through the holidays just for me."

"I don't want to annoy you more than I must, dear friend," I said. "But in reference to Madame Corriendo, I have evidence to prove that in Europe her act was to be put into an enormous cake of ice, dressed only in a G-string and bra, black net stockings, and heels."

"You're wrong, Martin!" he choked. "Corrie *and* Berthe were both born in a little town in New Jersey named Boonton! At high-school dances in the 40s, they were unbearably, amazingly lovely under the Japanese lanterns. A few years later they swung their beach bags cutely."

"Ned Beaumont," I said gently. "I knew a boy named Mario who wore his rubbers to school every day because of the enormous holes in his shoes. This was during the warm and wonderful 30s. This sartorial eccentricity did not negate the fact that he had been born in Sciacca."

"The wind seems aimed directly at me, as if to freeze the heart," he groaned.

"My dear good friend, life is a bargain. A bowl of pie in the sky."

"The whole thing is beginning to turn into a dream," he whispered. "The events of the last few months seem to be blistered raw-wood skeletons pushing through the choking dust, spooky in the unearthly light that covers the world."

"Yet *this* very moment will become part of the good old days," I said.

"Daisy!" he screeched.

"That black hair . . . to hear that voice . . ."

"Daisy! Yet . . . how to turn my thoughts from those two temptresses? How to crush my obsession with them and their lascivious wiles?"

"A man in Decatur once built a scale model of the Brooklyn Bridge out of toothpicks," I offered.

"In Decatur they move through their lives in dead silence," he snapped. "They speak garbled foreign tongues, dark in their mouths."

"Another man once ate a mountain of paella . . ."

"I know about *him*. In his sentimentality, he thought of the black bear as his totem."

"To digress for a moment, Ned Beaumont. What coterie writer was it who died of an overdose of meatloaf?"

"I can't remember his name, but he wrote *Cellophane Poems*."

"No matter. What exactly *is* it that you want?"

"The shadows fall from right to left, Martin . . . yet what will bring us peace?"

"You might glance through your giant color catalogue. Or work Saturday mornings for the key to a brand-new car."

"How I despise Tom Buchanan!" he abruptly hissed. "Why would a man want to walk through Europe?"

"Two olives in your Martini, right?" I queried. "Two onions?"

"Maybe something he ate?" he mused. "Christ knows."

"He's one of the educated and intelligent rich. You know what I mean? God save us all from them," I laughed.

"I saw a snapshot of him taken during his 'hike,' as he calls it. He was in white ducks, a white shirt, the collar open and the sleeves rolled up, white sneakers. . . . His face was somehow . . . glowing!"

"As if it had been a ripe plum?" I asked.

"Right! There was an aura of decadence about him. A gorgeous decadence of gold, silk, flowers . . ."

"A muscular deficient," I said. "I can see him now in a gold shirt and red tie."

"One recalls his hardly credible bulk," he added.

"God! What more offensive than a stage Irishman in a blue straw hat?"

"How about a stage Irishman in a green cardboard derby?"

"My heart sickens, Ned Beaumont, yes. It careens."

"His vulgar pretensions toward being a patron of the arts! He once said to me, at one of his 'evenings,' and I assure you that this is true, Martin, 'It is no small thing to heap high the plate of a young bard with tuna glop!' And I stood there, open-mouthed yet impeccable in a tuxedo I had earlier worn to a swell book party."

"I can envision the snowy linen that glittered beneath your elbows."

"It was at that same 'evening' that I first glimpsed Daisy," he sobbed, "although at the time I didn't know that it was she. . . . The curve of her buttock and thigh . . ."

"Someone told me that she wore a red satin garter belt trimmed with white lace," I said.

"Marvelous girl! How depressing it was to see her always surrounded by those jaded trulls and aging Don Juans. Their faces were pale, faded-looking, the look that old denim gets."

"They like nothing better than to put their arms around each other's shoulders and gaze grinningly at the camera," I said.

"And in the middle of it all—Daisy and Tom. I must say that they were dazzling in their brightness. But God knows why she *married* him!"

"I met a man," I said, "who married a woman because she understood ice hockey."

"Was he a 'poet in his own right' "? Ned Beaumont chuckled. "If so—let them walk on Fire Island beach in October!"

"Well, he didn't write too much. But he gave a lot of readings."

"Another literary daredevil, eh?"

"A daredevil is a spoon lure," I said.

"You know what I mean, Martin. The kind of writer who wishes his prose to be transparent. . . . Who wants to write cellophane poems."

"I know what you mean, Ned Beaumont. But our conversation seems to be avoiding that confrontation devoutly to be wished. And the wind is getting stronger now," I added.

"The wind seems to be aimed directly at me," he shuddered. "As if to freeze the heart."

"And crickets are beginning in the raspberry patch."

"What I can't understand, Martin, is, if we were happy once, why not again?"

"You must shun those two women, those destroyers of happiness and peace. Where the brown rat lives, no other rat may survive."

"*Must* you be so harsh, Martin? So hard on them? After all, tall in sepia corsets and shining patent leather boots . . ." he whined.

"Their closeness, their camaraderie, their need for adulation and applause, their basic shyness—are all these things worth Daisy's breathless loveliness and purity?"

"Martin, once again your voice takes on the tenderness of a lover's. Must we change identities from moment to moment, until all is chaos, babble, and darkness? I—I—*know* about you and D-Daisy!"

"I admit, Ned Beaumont, that grass stains appeared on my trousers," I rasped out somehow. "But she's so lovely, pretty too, tall and slender, ebon hair . . ."

"Steady, Martin, steady. We will, together, descend into the maelstrom that awaits us."

"You know the horror of my marriage, Ned Beaumont," I blubbered. "One day she was there beside me, her cheeks flushed, hair streaming, stubby fingers filled with strength and artistic know-how. The next day she was, with each pot and vase, gone!"

"Perhaps, dear friend, through her, God will cleanse your soul and foresee danger for you," he comforted.

"She loved french fries . . . once in a while she would buy a *Silver Screen*. But the man she ran away with! Well, perhaps she found a safe place with him underneath the violet skies of nighttime Africa. I suppose a woman does what she has to do."

"Violet skies? Nighttime Africa? Don't give yourself airs!" he cried.

431

"You look as if you'd bitten into a lemon, Ned Beaumont," I parried.

"I'm sorry, Martin. I didn't mean to denigrate your dream for 'her.' Africa *is* a lovely place. . . . The little villages are beautiful, Mazatlán, Manzanillo, Acapulco, ah, the little *cabañas* on the beach . . ."

"It has long been my heart's desire to visit that colorful peninsula. I imagine that it is all blue and bright . . . and you kiss your cultured paramour underneath the moon."

"Harry Bore, the concrete poet, spent his last tragic years there, as I'm sure you remember. I think it was *he* who died of an overdose of meatloaf. Or was it couscous?"

"He was a crazy artist, in spades," I said.

"Corrie and Berthe knew him for a time in Cairo. They said that there was something fat and prosperous about him, the dark cheroots, sunglasses, his Burberry thrown over his shoulders . . ."

"He was an Irish bastard," I said.

"I know, Martin. That was one of the reasons why he so belatedly plunged into the life of letters. Ireland is a difficult place in which to express one's self. All those vague browns and brackish greens. A lake. Some monstrous globs of trees hanging out over the water . . ."

"He tried, unsuccessfully, to put all that into his one and only novel. But the attempt to create a 'poetic' novel is pathetic. There is a kind of horrible mindlessness at work. Although I'm sure your 'friends,' Corriendo and Delamode, thought it was peachy!" I shot.

"There's no need to be vicious," he rejoined. "I agree that *Beware! Harlequins!* is, ultimately, unsatisfying. Yet a close reading of it will reveal therein a small yet unimpeachable amelioration in the art of narrative."

"What myopia is this, Ned Beaumont?" I barked.

"Martin, the novel has its own deep rhythms. Deep rhythms that connect us with the constellations and the big sea-water."

"You mean the old 'dust to dust' routine? One could contest that as the novel's primary 'tone'—the shifts and puzzles seem accidental, even at their most successful."

"But Martin," he smiled, "what does it matter if the ambiguity is intentional or not? There are objective correlatives *galore!*"

"That's exactly what Daisy said, Ned Beaumont! I fear that both of you take art lightly."

"A leftover from my days as a street-corner hooligan. I figured the guys would make fun of me . . ."

"Well, to be fair," I admitted, "everyone has his own sense of what constitutes greatness in literature. There are," I laughed, "even some misguided souls who find its quintessence in the sight of a large bowl of limp lettuce leaves."

"Or in an old shoe," he added.

"Even in a Woolworth sugar cookie and a cup of tea out of the saucer!"

"Corrie and Berthe often found *sublime* aesthetic pleasure in lace aprons and black mesh stockings," he panted.

"Don't say another word, Ned Beaumont! We'll talk of other things until you can see those two whores objectively. . . . Uh, what do you think of women's hats?"

"Looking at you, Martin," he marveled, "I somehow imagine a man with a clipboard who thinks himself sane."

"My heritage is one of perfect sanity. My father's eldest sister's second son could whittle the most beautiful letter openers."

"You speak of letter openers. . . . But how to speak of what the tiny yet handsome vase from Java, the dew-touched day's-eye trembling in it, means to *me?*"

"Java?" I asked. "An odd source of beauty. The only time I visited there, grass stains appeared on my trousers."

"Speaking of grass, Martin, that reminds me of the joke where the landscape gardener tells the countess, 'This funny-looking hose thing waters plants.' "

"As it happens, Daisy told me that joke in the office. My face flushed, I glanced out the window at the soaring towers of the iron city . . ."

"If you'll recall, that joke was printed in that humor anthology we brought out some years back, *Spicy Smiles,* compiled by Joanne Popsi, that old radio personality. I wonder what became of her?"

"The last I heard, Ned Beaumont, she was arranging a journey to Albania to bring back some superintendents."

"She was an odd woman. She knew the zodiac and drew charts, told the weather from the flight patterns of sparrows in the sky and the color of the sunset—yet her slip was always showing."

"The day that *Newsweek* took her picture she ripped her brand-new skirt. It was an omen. You'll recall that a review never appeared?"

"Oh well, Martin. Word of mouth is the thing with small first books."

"Word of mouth or not, Popsi was too eccentric to be successful in the highly competitive humor field. Did you know that she unplugged all the lamps and appliances at night so that the electricity wouldn't 'leak out of the walls' "?

"She once said," he grimaced, "that William Blake was the Dick Stuart of poetry."

"William Blake? Dick Stuart? Who in the hell are they?"

"They are now part and parcel of the gathering darkness," he answered.

"That has a nice ring to it—but there is no *tragedy* here."

"Of course not. Yet they had about them the wearying victory of neroes, the exact romance of failure . . ."

"You seem to be hinting, Ned Beaumont, at the *angst* of the archetypal 'fat man' of all great fiction—thin white socks, a rumpled gabardine suit, his mouth an obscene joke."

"What about Charlie Chan movies?" he fired. "You call *that* 'great fiction' "?

"Well . . . though he had no style, he was wondrously coarse—ebulliently coarse, one might say," I guffawed.

"So they said in their slick brochure," he scoffed.

" 'Their' slick brochure? 'Their?' "

"You know who I mean, Martin! The ones who tell you that if you eat Protestant ice cream you'll go blind!"

"Your digressions are superb, Ned Beaumont. I hear music when I look at you! Pure poetry. But," I added, "out of simple repression come *lackluster* poems!"

"Repression or digression? Coaster or caster? Bah!"

"Scorn my observations if you must," I said. "But the *master* of digression, Henri Kink———"

"Corriendo 'serviced' him in the Midi," he blurted.

"———the master, I say, learned too late the peril of his digressive virtuosity. It *seemed* very clear there in the sunlight, he slipped his onyx pinky ring off, the sun burned into his blue suit . . ."

"Stop!" he yelled. "I know the story—too well. Corrie wept each time she remembered his end. Why would a man want to walk through Europe?"

"As far as I'm concerned," I rasped, "that remarkable development perfectly fit in with the entire life of the intolerable lout."

"You *are* cruel, Martin. I sense your implication. Because he happened to be one of Madame Corriendo's friends———?

"Of course! Why else would he so consciously sully himself?" I snapped.

"Perhaps you're right," he said softly. "During her and Madame Delamode's sojourn at the Splendide, many of the men had embarrassing 'accidents' right there on the dance floor. . . . The waiters, to general hilarity, would point them out."

"I assure you, my friend, that those were not *real* waiters! They were simply assorted Armenians and Chicanos when needed."

"In my mind I have heard the concert of guffaws issue from their hearty bellies," he choked.

434

"And yet, Ned Beaumont, you still speak of Boonton. And high-school dances in the forties. Japanese lanterns!"

"But, Martin," he whined, "how—how can I cleanse my thoughts of their beauty? Their seductiveness? Their charms and wiles? H-how?"

"First, we wash them out with hot water."

"Hot . . . water?"

"Shh. Next, we get you interested in something . . . simple, something . . . childish, say. Perhaps a bag of marbles or a toy pig."

"A toy pig!" he exploded. "Who wants a toy pig?"

"Childish innocence. Images of peace. Two little girls on a lawn. Picture it, Ned Beaumont!"

"Images of peace! What will bring us peace?"

"Did you say you wanted another drink, lush?" I asked. "Inhale, Ned Beaumont, inhale. The perfume of this place!"

"I don't want another drink. Your taste for Sazeracs . . . depresses me," he moaned. "What are you talking about?"

"Do you remember earlier this evening, old friend? The silence, the stillness, the old dime that the sun had become?"

"Over the water, on the faintest breeze, came a dance tune, Martin . . ."

"With people closed out from the gigantic world?"

"By God, Martin, you're a poet in your own right!" he laughed.

"No matter, Ned Beaumont, no matter. Be manly! Think of various lovely women like Lorna and Joanne—even Sheila! Damn her! But most of all, think of Daisy. She is not unintelligent and she is—attractive. Forget these past terrible days of cold hatred and anxiety. Stop looking as if you had bitten into a lemon. Cleanse your mind, filled with sewage laced through with fear . . ."

"First we wash it out with hot water?" he gasped.

"Just a manner of speaking, Ned Beaumont. As one might say, of a book, or a girl, 'a classy little sizzler.' "

"What book? *Yellow Is The Color of Love? Explosive Celibate?*"

"Hmmm. . . . It . . . smells like rain. Don't you think?"

"Rain?" he asked.

"The crickets are beginning in the raspberry patch, in any event," I said.

"Daisy loves crickets," he mused. "Once, I remember, when the lights began to go on in the bluish dusk far below at the mouth of the valley, and the crickets were beginning underneath the violet skies, she said, 'You may or may not know what it is to love someone and be hurt because you've hurt them . . .' "

"Nikolai Gogol said that," I said. "The common enemy of all cultivated people is art."

"Nikolai Gogol!" he fumed. "A vulgar man, polished until he gleamed!"

"Look, Ned Beaumont," I reasoned. "It is a darkening November afternoon. Soon, all *too* soon, the joyous holiday season will be upon us and it will be time for the breaking of the piñata. Can't we at least *try* to be civilized about . . . things?"

"Piñata?"

"A Christmas thing from Méjico. Packed full, both fore and aft, with goodies. What does it matter!" I shouted.

"Méjico!" he enthused. "Daisy and I had plans to go to Méjico, you know. My Uncle Dermot lived there as a youth. He was quite a man. Once, he ruined a silk shirt. Once, extinguished his aromatic Habana."

"Isn't he the one you had the falling out with over some fancy ties and collars?" I queried.

"Yes, Martin. But after a while we lied warmly to each other and our friendship resumed. . . . He was tops. Oh yes, he was tops."

"You always described him as a stage Irishman in a green cardboard derby," I said.

"Well, perhaps he was," he sighed. "Yet he loved french fries . . . and he would have loved Daisy too."

"Due to an unfortunate physical liability," I muttered.

"He also knew Corrie and Berthe, you know. He told me that one soft night, *bossa nova* on the air, they ate a *mountain* of paella. It was that same evening that he endeared himself to them by posing a naive question to Madame Corriendo, to wit: 'Are you a German? From your accent, I mean?' "

"It must have been frightening for him to have so utterly given up," I said.

"I don't know about it being frightening, Martin. But certainly it was *something* for him suddenly to realize that five years of his life had been no more important than garbage."

"Wasn't it soon after, Ned Beaumont, that he left for a motor tour of Alaska?"

"Yes. Yes, it was. . . . Patches of snow, as white and fine as salt, crunched underneath the tires," he reflected. "It was a cold winter that year."

"Just like the one in the Cole Porter song," I suggested.

"Madame Delamode used to sing Cole Porter songs while she worked at her hobby—did you know that she built a scale model of the Brooklyn Bridge out of toothpicks?"

"May she perform fellatio on young English novelists all her life!" I sneered. "Like Sharon Anne Lingerie."

"I recall that scandal," he said. "It must have been a year and a half

436

after her honeymoon that her buried lusts began to surface."

"Buried lusts is good," I grinned. "Their subtle perfume appeals to women, proud as peacocks though they may be . . ."

"She led the life of the most savage predator, roaming the 'wilderness' for 'victims.' "

"Tall in sepia corsets and shining patent leather boots . . ."

". . . her coffee-colored eyes *boiled,*" he concluded.

"We had no defenses to throw up hastily, did we, Ned Beaumont? As soldiers once threw bulwarks?"

"Did you know that she is writing her memoirs—with Vance Whitestone?"

"I did, and I will use whatever powers and influence I have in the literary world to prevent her from publishing them!" I shouted.

"Van Raalte, I've heard, has made her an offer in six figures."

"*That* gross creature from West End Avenue and the Hamptons? He loves dogs and sailboats," I scoffed. "I last saw him at the Fourth World Book Fair—drunk as usual. There he stood, the sunlight garish on that Hollywood flush . . ."

"I understand that he married a woman because she understood ice hockey," he chortled.

"These things, Ned Beaumont, tend to relieve and color my otherwise pedestrian existence," I joked.

"Martin, we stand as idiots in the face of the mass devastation of feeling that abounds."

"We? *We?*"

"It is time to get back to the simple things," he went on. "The aroma of meat loaf in the oven, apple pie with plenty of cinnamon . . ."

"Two pairs of white nylons, two pairs of white tennis shoes," I needled.

"Anyway," he said suddenly, "Raalte's wife was a gasping vision of the bizarre, a vivacious redhead in her business-executive outfit. She menaced the unlucky window-washer with an automatic."

"Window-washer?"

"She loved voyeurs. A year later she divorced Raalte and married Sir Vyvyan Brier, a notorious Peeping Tom."

"I don't think I know . . ."

"He's the millionaire turned gourmet cook who shakes up God's own Ramos Fizz," he explained.

"You know a lot about these things, Ned Beaumont. And I'll bet I know who told you," I said.

"All the rats and pussycats will never more be seen . . ." he sang loudly.

"Will you *please* stop trying to avoid reality," I urged. "Clearly, the task is to get past all the clatter in your head. . . . I think."

"The clatter of mundane trivia?" he joshed.

"As you wish. 'Trivia' is a discreet word—almost like a snapshot placed on the desk. An old shoe. The attempt to create a 'poetic' novel. A large bowl of limp lettuce leaves. Let the 'trivia,' as you put it, act as the catalyst for honest thought!"

"Catalyst? What catalyst, tiny thing?" he smiled.

"All right, mock me," I growled. "To you it's all nothing! To you it's . . . fruit!"

" 'Somewhere,' " he recited, 'far off, an Albanian shrieked . . .' "

"Now, Ned Beaumont, now, I launch out upon the most bizarre sea. . . . In the dark shed of the untameable mind lies the truth. Those two whores are *destroying* you!" I bellowed.

"Destroying me?" he leered. "Red satin garter belts, trimmed with white lace. Gorgeous decadence. Gold. Silk. Flowers. *Destroying* me! Your massive head seems fatter than usual today, Martin."

"This whole thing is beginning to turn into a dream," I sobbed. "The wind seems aimed directly at me, as if to freeze the heart. Where are the birds? Your courage, Ned Beaumont, is that of a spirochete!" I hissed.

"Ha! Ha! Ha!" he roared. "Leave me be. . . . Offer up your bruises and your sweat and blood to Daisy!"

"Blue!" I spat.

Halpin's Journal

Packed, ready, and now—off! Thank God for dear, reliable Ned. That the maniac should begin to work the very moment the letter came! *What* a maniac!

What went through his mind when he discovered Ned gone? I don't even want to think of it. There I stood, speaking first as myself, and then as Ned—on and on, totally incoherent conversation, totally garbled, totally crazy! And he worked on and on and on, without leaving his desk—how long? And all the while this letter in my pocket. And then, thank God, he fell asleep.

On the way out the door, almost, *another* letter from Ned to persuade me to join him—as if I *now* need persuading! And, this time, directions! He's not "halfway around the world"—but close, close! No time to carefully read it, of course, but the note says that the enclosed list demonstrates the humanity of some writers—that they are not *all* Lamonts. From what I can gather it is a list of gifts given by writers to characters of theirs who have patiently waited for years and years, after working like dogs, in manuscript and long-forgotten and out-of-print books—waited to be seen and known, loved and hated. Tokens of their employers' esteem and gratitude. I'll read it on the road. Now! Off! Off!

Lamont will probably continue without us! Voices in a total void. Off! Up and out the door!

Somehow, I still feel—but it's ridiculous! The man is insane!

To Chichi Guffo, a tin zeppelin; to Vera Traynor, a big one; to Skinny Vinnie, a can o' worms; to Grampa Alex, a two-quart growler with buttered bottom; to Pete Lado, Jersey City; to Allie Allie, those three-ring bottoms; to Obie, an overlapped seam; to Black Carmine, an old cookie; to Missy Merica, a discouraging word; to Harry the Waiter, the longest shot; to Zeno Sabirdy, an orange croquet mallet; and a bathtub gin for Margie Rouge; Hackettstown for Farmer Louie; to Skinny Foureyes, an Orange Crush; to Prissy the Missy off the May-flower, time out for tears; for Donna Fire, a torn tutu; for John Jacob Jingelheimer Schmidt, a pipe job; for Hips Gunge, a French 75; and for Sweet Potato, the Packard in the snapshot.

Also, for the silent drinker, the Melody Room; for Armenian George, acey-five; the Platonic snooker for Coney Island Mike; Greek Fire for the Surprise Bros.; to Dr. Drescher, a pleasant plum placebo; to Finkie Pudge, a sleepin' bag; to Duck the Pimple, Lionel and his Attendant Train; the juicy joys of free, unfettered sex to Ugly Terry, Georgene the Gawm, Beatific Mary, Nosy Dolores, Lizzie the Lunk, Awful Annette, Joky Joyce who lost her undies early in the morning, Maddening Pat, Chickie the Sweetheart of the USN, Cock-eyes Philomena, and Nancy the Nun of the North; to Willie the Weep, a permanent hanger; to Pete the Gob, a natural; to Old Doc Rumple, beloved abortionist, a Schenley with beer chaser; and for Kickie Delaney, Flynn's ghost; a night on the roof to Diana Bronx and Shakespeare Avenue to Berta Brownbeaut; leaves of brown to Marjo-rie Mistress of Tears; to Pastor Christian Jesus Cheese of the Cracker-box Baptists, a visit from a Jesuit; to Fingers Flom, sweet bananas; to Plum the Hustler, the 9 ball; to the Cross-Eyed Kid, a plump pussy; and to Offissa Pupp, Irish confetti.

Norwegian steam for Artie the Lush; an empty ashcan for Toro Frank; for the Barese iceman, a new piece of burlap; for Joan Hiawa-tha, a wall eye; to the Christian soldier, a Jewish wife; to Mac the Black, a ten-dollar tip; to Chemical Jack, a transparent retort; to Alfie Ideo, a Rockaway seagull; to Ruth Lott, a Luigi sandwich; to Baritone Brodsky, a bank dick; a soul kiss for Sweet Sydelle; a royal roost for Miami Marv; and to Irish Donnie the sailor bold, a solid-gold trumpet; for Warren Fjörd, Ivar Oslo, and Big Red Glög, lingonberries and lutefiske; to Troop 93, a map of Bliss Park; to Aram the Bard, a book of style; to Waterfall Cyd, a ginkgo; a booth in The Keg for young lovers; a Camel clippie for the Jew of Malted; a Woolworth cookie for Granma Aggie; leaves of grass to textile bankers and hands on her thighs to Joanne Fontbonne; to Highpockets Ray, a touchdown; to Mexican Joe, the back o' my hand; to Belleville Billy, a pair of Spal-deens; Victor Mature for Stanley Electra; and a fingernail for Sandi the model; to President Young, Louisiana; a grand slam to Art the Gimp; and for Eddy Keds, a Merry Xames.

For Sallie Eightball, a bowl of Yankee Bean; for Edward Cairo, parcheesi; for Prof. A. Peterson Vodville, a heliport; and chronic gastritis for Bruce Richards; cocktails every day for Björn Bookë; and a stale beer for Brick Red; to Father "Blackie" Donovan, the sin of pride; to Inka Dink, a bottle of ink; to the Eagle Patrol, a wet dream; to Big Benny, a dozen calzone; a lamp unto his feet for Flatfoot Floogie and a toll house to "Chocolate" Chippe; for Cecil Oeste, Ofelia's Place; and an avocado with lime juice to Whoopsie Earle; for Angel Singe, an undiscovered shore; for Peggy O'Neill, eyes as blue as skies; to Basil the Duke of Delancey, a loan; buttocks to call his own to the Saint of St. Clair; to Patsy Begone, a Miami winter; to Johnston Flood, a farewell to arms; to Robbie Bardde-Tufts, a stopwatch; taxi fare to Clay Johns and to Lewd Lula, a worm in her apple; to Gibby Senatoro, ten years of unemployment checks; and to Carmichael B.

Power, an evening's stroll with Dante 'neath the stars.

To Tony the Mouth, a box of chocolate tools; to Jewish Jerry, that little bit of Poland that fell from out the sky one day; loud Saturdays and peaceful Sundays to Warren House, Nice Henry, Lucky Lento, Papa Joe, Irish Carroll, "Shutter" White, Denny Lion, Amity Anel, Happy Gallagher, Noisy Pat, Cheap Luigi, and Leif the Sailor; to Wanda the Wonder of Waco, death before dishonor; to Dimpled Deb, the dyke from yon vast ringing plains, a meaningful relationship; a shave and a haircut to Two-Bits Joël; to Benj the Burglar, a double hernia; and to Helena Troy, the War Resisters' League; Europe forever for Barkeep Lou; to Gus the Laughing Greek, an exploding cigar; to Shaky King, a personalized pencil; to Panama Neumiller, the milk of human kindness; to Rusty Red Lindsay, mornings on the beach; and to Sue Eye, a box of Dots; the Complete Dickie Dare to Barnaby Russo; to Ada from Decatur, Big Dick; to Sweets Lester and Billie Bounce, a sailboat in the moonlight; to the Princess of West Bank, a cookbook; to Mnemosyne Acti, the shining future; to Cookie Cordé, a Muscatel custard; to Navajo Owen, an old Beauty Parade; to Teddy Aquarius, the main stem; a kiss goodnight to Maxine Bizarre; and to Santo, Lou, Cesare, Guido, Sal, Nicky, Rocco, Pasquale, Connie, Yolanda, Maria, Anna, Fiorenza, Julius, Angelo, Mario, Tommy, Donato, Anthony, Cheech, Paddy, Curzio, Ralph, and Mikey, a pot of pasta e fagiole.

Freckle remover for Bubbsy the Harp; for Mickey Roast, a roaring blaze; to Brutal Mickey, a Mickey Finn; to Mickey Finn, Finn Hall; to Finn Hall, the peace that passeth understanding; a jar of mustard to Hot Dan; a hand in the bush to Cornelia Clarke; to Vernon Royal, a composition book; a Nedicks Orange to Dundee Keiller and a Dixie Shake to Sarsaparilla Dick; to M. Larousse, ketchup on his omelet; to Mr. Keene, a bloodhound; a knock at the door for Hearthstone of the Death Squad; for High Hat Patsy, a boiled potato; to Columbus Phil, a bird in the hand; to Slurpy Geezel, soup du jour; to Smiley Wicz, a high-heeled shoe; to Rosie the Posie, a heart's bouquet; a face all painted green for the Circus Girl; and to Kitchen Dinah, an old banjo; for Horst Josef Dunderbeck, a sausage-meat machine; for Antony Weir, a chicken farm; for Jubal Joe, a gastronome for his very own; the wrong shipment to Reader Rich of Redwood City; to Hughie Lambui, a Caddy shining in the Brooklyn sun; and to Herr Arnold, a double dip hot fudge chocolate marshmallow sundae with sprinkles and melted cheese; her maidenhead so soft purloined to Mary Skeeno; to Phantasy Phil, the Phantom Phornicator, a Buxom Breathing Burlesk Bewtee; to Monte MacCount, the Congressional Medal of Horror.

Also, to Burly Blather, Mel-O-Rol Tokay; to the Earl of Kirkwood, a jung frau; to Father Graham, 0 for 5 and an error; to Blinky Checker, a strawberry bromo; to Edward Cigarillo, a happy key chain; and a joyous interlude in quaint Killeen for the Fighting 498th; for Artillery Dan, brains and eggs; to ninety-three chums 'round the fire in LaTourette Park, a silver-bordered patch and a purple necker-chief; for Royal Eckert, a new plume that weeps clean; an afternoon in McSorley's for Myles of the Ponies; to Jake O'Calculus, a dream of Cleopatra; to Forsythia Germania, nil sine magno labore; to Blank Redrum, the face on the barroom floor; to Mr. Skibbleybibbitt, a bumblebee, a morning glory, and half a walnut shell; oyster baize and diamond daze to V. Vivian Charlotte; a mappemounde to Rand McNally; and to the crazy Corporal aflame with love, Michigan water; to Samuel Champaign et épouse, the courage of their confec-tions; the life of Reilly for Shanty Studs; for Mickey McFrisco, a dark-brown star; for Proprio Charley, a lobster; to Bob the Fisher-man, a handful of common nouns; a flat eggnog for Rudi the Juke; a polite warning from Lucifer to Moonfire Millions; and an inkblot in his album for Henri the furrier's boy.

All the ships at sea to Mr. and Mrs. America; and to Whiz Walsh, the light of the harbor, two frico eggs over light; to Montgomery LaCranston, a shadow nose; for Martín Del Rio Antonio Lawton, mourning and weeping in this valley of tears; angels and perpetual help to Sinner Black; for Anne in pink pillbox with veil, the bowling-ball grip; to L. Curtin Burke from Golden Gate Land, coal in the bathtub; to Colonel Broomstick, a ramrod back; a foxed folio of filthy fables to Buffalo Annie; to Kool Ken Orge, a karton o' Kents; to Harry Newroyal, Mae West with a bowtie; to Alexander B. Pitcher, a hand-ful of pretzels; and to Watermelon Ron from old Luzon, a lady's finger and a glass of cherry; a banner of Cuba poetic to Abdul the Protestant Jew; a case of Rheingold to Blake Avenida; for Gentry Sargent, a Culex mosquito; to Willie the altar boy, an adulterous wife; for Faithful Reader, lists to port and starboard; to Pat the Jonah, a scratch eternal; and to Linda the lissom lovely, a candied fruit 'mid the clamor of the tavern; wooden spoons to Elaine the shower of cinnamon; a guide to catering to Leeta the Queen o' kultur; for Lorenzo de Cristo, the mud and heavens in his lotus; and for Ozzy Leroy, the column talls of Egypt.

And to all hefty hikers and their cheerful chums, paddles swift and bright shining like silver; the Wang-Wang Blues to Terry F. Dramer-buch; for Paulie the New England troubadour, golden slumbers; to Froggy Chasé, a pair of spectacles; to Waterman Quink, a lifetime supply of scrip; to Lord and Lady Balcón, two tickets to next week's production; for Maricón Cabrón, a bench in Tompkins Square to be his own; a steamy cauldron of greens and grease to Alma Bro; to Doc the Dip, a split lip; and for Scowling Dick Billiard, an English rug 'neath an English lid; for Diana Weeping-Moon, a box of metaphors good as new; to Sherman Oaks, the California Dreamer, one copy of *Sell Your Way to Golden Leisure;* for Trapper Ted from snowy-pure Maine, an old stump to brighten his journal; a Chinee honeymoon for Mills Frere; and to Meester Bailey, an old fighter.

A talking cat for O. Henry Spence; to Necco D. Woods, a box of wafers; for Jube the Jew, a licorice pastille; the raisin he et to Goober Rube; for Clark Barr, Fifth Avenue; chuckles and snickers for Baby Ruth; for Powerhouse Gabe, a chunky coquette; for Bleary Fleer, double bubbles and baloney; an old walnetto song for Nuttsy Goodbar; a juithy fwuit for Thweetie Tham and for Dudley Milkk a billet doux from a nubile nymph shyly signed "forever yours"; to the nutbrown lass, a velvet sky 'gainst which is flung the Milky Way; to the Yonkers Kid, a drink in the Sky Bar; the three musketeers color by Technicolor to the Orange Girl of Venice; and to Private First Class Kill, late of Leadership School, his own bazooka, monogrammed.

To Isidore Foster, a board-building kit; for Hubert and Inez Woodside, the magic touch of Jack Frost on the pane; to Norm the Scribe, a mother-of-pearl study; to O.J. Maigne, a teflon heart; to Soapy Stanley, a view of the ribbuh; to Pale Dan India, a hangover cure; Buddha's smile to Cobblestones Gary; for Thomas Kew Thomas, a Christmas Carole; to Capitán Desaforado, the shores of Tripoli; giggles galore to Creat American Gannon; to J.P. Tech, grasses, legumes and forage crops; to Barney Alex Bethesda, a mug of glug; a glass ball to Prince Rupert Dropp and to Billy Paterson, a pink locust and a rose; for Tim Tanker, the diving champ, a hook off a jab; a gross of pencils from Mongolia to the Ticonderoga Kid; to Lonely Tom from ould Tyrone, spuds and tea; for Jack the Bird, a protractor protector; to Philippe Rouge, a monopoly; for Lawrence dePoone, zweat zox; the love of money to Boozer Bob; to Rin-Tin-Zinn, distaff doggerelist, a writhing prescription for writing distress; and to Rachel Futts, a pig in a poke.

Lemonade in the dark field of the fair to the Red Hat Kid; to Huckle Homburg, poison ivory; to Gene Philip Angostura, lazy summer afternoons; to Skinny Joan, milk minus egg; to Nurse Scoop, an am'rous night in fabled Boonton; a Mexicali Rose to Big Brown Eyes; and to Sad Henry Solo, the skater's waltz; a lifelike statue of St. John deBelch to Burke Hardt; to Johnny Marietta, the bounding main; for Joey Surprise, Savory Jim, Meatball Royal, Diner Dan, Shakes Hellberg, Baldy Arnold, Chink Young, and Clams Imbriale, Yankee pot rost with mash, strings beans and gravey; to the photographer's wife, drools and groans; to Martin the barman, a beer, a cracker, and a nice tip; for E. Ellsworth, the bon vivant of the Great Lakes, the undivided attention of Dr. Scholl; to Rubbers Pucci, a yellow cab with rear-window awning; to Whittle Woode, a good right arm; Charlotte Russe to Meester Frostee; a bit o'honey to Mary Jane; for His Nibs, a black crow; to the husky harlot of Hershey, potent charms to whisk her off to Mars; to Rotten Ricky, Rose's lime; to Gigi Ricardo, a mordantly modern marriage manual; the nag that crept from under him to Dude Burns; and to Ole Smoke, the fireman, a happy hooker, a laughing lad; for Sternjaw Carl, acme Baptist, "America" by the Norwegian Seamen's Choir; a splendid waiter to Lucky Mort; to Gaudy Sweet, laughter in the locker room; and for the Skerrenbock Brothers, a double date with the Jukes Sisters.

For the Sisters of Mercy, black nylons; to Lorenzo the Lewdless, a scrubbed serpent; to Imago the Profound, trembling edges; a trucking company for Jerry the Jitterbug; to Man Mountain Black, blissful amnesia; Mack the Knife for Tilly Toilette; for Cully Saks, an empty bag; a one-way ticket to Wichita to the blind bore of 8th Street; for Galliard Coranto, nights of revels; to Good Ben Bowse, a black spot; a dark shadow for Donato Gobo; a load of popcorn to Jimmy Balloon and a box of apples to Goosewalk McIntosh; for Helmut Ausbrenner, a torch; to Nogo Macy, a big fat policeman; to Bobbie Boxx, late of Bloomer, Kansas, gossamer garters for her gorgeous gams; a somber landscape to the gloomy Duke of Smithson; for Christian Chritic, crackling yarn down his trousers; for Bev Bevy, the pound of flesh, a series of broken dates; to Pete the Tramp, hot cherry; to L. Eriksson Park, a pale moon caught in wintry branches; to Paddy Zildjian, a splashy symbol; to Helena Walsh, the goatish glance of the cockeyed lecher; to Twisty Abe DeHarvarde, shimmering hose of glittering glows; a Serbo-Croat dictionary to Simple Simon; and to Joyce the Jewel of the merchant fleet, Early Times.

Also, a suit with two pairs pants to Morgana Robina; to Keening Ken the Pitchman, a flaming faggot to light his way; for Germ-free Eddie, a carload of coughs; to Tadd, Babs, Bips and Bop, our delight; to George C. Tilyou, the shadow of his smile; for Mr. Feltman, boater, blazer, and beer; to Surf Scoville, an ocean tide; a Coney Island head to Pii Wii Riis; for Manny La Manche, thoughts that lie too deep for tears; for Banaly Cliche, good friend and wonderful guy, the hook; to Bialy Quiche, a lickin' chicken; to Rossi, the Red Felt Kid, a yearly dish of dumb plums; for Ellie Cornelli, the lang'rous lass, the Cabinet of Dr. Caligari; for Owen and Branca of the Flatbush Follies, one magic wish apiece; a twenty-five hour day to Harry the Hat; to Montague Willow, an orange-pineapple pie and to Henry Hicks, cranberry sauce; the Blood of Christ to Boston Red Max; to Earl Allen Towne, Saturday in a Bowie bar; for Scoop Shelby, a coupla ducats in his hatband; to Shots Gingerilla, a butt behind his ear; a dip in

Biscayne Bay for Scotch and Soda, champion boxers; and to Julie the Beet, Syrian love.

Someone to drive back home for Sheetmetal Shelly; for Cedar John the window-washer, a talking poodle; to Mr. Bouchet, a peaceful Wings behind the soda cooler; for Jimmy the Joy of Dublin, scribbledehobble; to Jolly St. Nick, a whiteout; a pup tent to Cal Camporee; Nijinsky's slippers to Major Hoople; and to good ol' Sooky, a Skippy Sundae; Hilda Marzipan for Guido Torroncino; for the monk of Manhattan, a night in Tunisia; to Sam the Butcher, your genial host, a classy joint; for Peter and Prudence Promm of the dewy gardenia, old-fashioned garbage; a pair of borrowed chaps for Alkali Ike; to Brighton Moishe, a banana knish; for Ruthie the Blonde, a pillow from the sofa; Marta and Carmen for Square John Riverside; a biscuit tort for Eliot Hushgold; some sastrugi for Renfrew of the Mounted; and to Sean the Celt, sassenach tea; to Giggling Chub, a schooner in the Subway Inn; for Dr. Boylan Ingersoll, a bouquet of germanias; his nose in plaster for Scully the Hack; and a hill of sugar to Creamy Brown.

To Blackie Bird, apple scrapple and lemon drops; to Tough Davy, apple honey; for Apple Mary, a mien poor but proud; to Miss Mackintosh, the darling, a delicious spy from out of the fog of Northern London; a royal barge ride into the drink for the Countess de Parque-Luna; to Red Dog Blitz and Friends, a subservient homebody; a Spanish guitar for the student of Cádiz; for Ella Pella and her fella, a boining love that laffs in the face of convention; Brighton Rock to Saltwater Taffy; and to Greasy Poll, the hairy huckster, liquefied lanotone; a droning voice to Zazie LaYonge; for Dick Panache, your roving editor, a charming flat on Ave. B where one can *live*; to Cuban Pete, the rhumba beat; a respite from the round of boring parties for dear old André Ox; to O'Flynn, the drunken lion, a magnificent music machine; girls girls and more girls to Giuseppe Lawson, the time server; to K.K. Byas, tunes that are gone with the wind; and to all you other cats and chicks out there, sweet or otherwise, buried deep in wordy tombs, who never yet have walked from off the page, a shake and a hug and a kiss and a drink. Cheers!

New York
1971–1975

[Cézanne] attempted to go beyond the sublime balances of nature, not content with the analytical methods that the great artists of the past had considered sufficient to her revelation and interpretation; he desired a synthesis that would allow him to *decorate* nature with the forms and colors that existed nowhere except in his own secret thought. Thus, his late painting nowhere shows forth nature's splendors, but instead, is a failure precipitated by his surrender to the pleasures of the imagination.

—Emile Fion (1907)